The Cook of Castamar

THE COOK OF CASTAMAR

FERNANDO J. MÚÑEZ

Translated by Rahul Bery and Tim Gutteridge

An Apollo Book

First published in Spain in 2019 by Editorial Planeta

This edition first published in the UK in 2024 by Head of Zeus Ltd,
part of Bloomsbury Publishing Plc

The Cook of Castamar by Fernando J. Múñez, translated by Rahul Bery and Tim
Gutteridge. The translation of this work has received aid from the Ministry of
Culture and Sports of Spain.

MINISTERIO
DE CULTURA
Y DEPORTE

Translation rights arranged by IMC Literary Agency

9 7 5 3 1 2 4 6 8

A catalogue record for this book is available from the British Library.

ISBN (HB): 9781803285603
ISBN (E): 9781803285580

Printed and bound in Great Britain by
CPI Group (UK) Ltd, Croydon CRO 4YY

MIX
Paper | Supporting
responsible forestry
FSC
www.fsc.org   FSC® C171272

Head of Zeus Ltd
First Floor East
5–8 Hardwick Street
London ECIR 4RG

WWW.HEADOFZEUS.COM

THE
COOK
OF
CASTAMAR

PART ONE

10 OCTOBER TO 19 OCTOBER 1720

1

'No pain lasts forever,' she said, in an effort to convince herself that her suffering was temporary. 'No joy is everlasting,' she added. Perhaps the phrase had lost its power from so much repetition and now only expressed the disappointment she had experienced over the last few years. She felt like a rag doll coming apart at the seams, trying to mend her spirits at the end of each day. It was only thanks to a courage born of necessity and her own determined character that she had found the strength to survive. 'Nobody can call me a coward,' Clara told herself.

Completely hidden beneath a thick layer of hay, she avoided looking at the milky light that filtered through, concentrating instead on individual raindrops sliding down the stalks. Despite this, she occasionally glimpsed the immensity that lay beyond the cart that was taking her to Castamar. When this happened, she had to take deep breaths, because the mere idea of not being enclosed by the walls of a house set her heart pounding. On more than one occasion, such an attack had caused her to faint. How she hated her weakness! She felt vulnerable, as if all the ills of the world were about to fall upon her, and she was overcome by lethargy. This fear reminded her how torn she had felt when Señora Moncada had told her there was a position at Castamar. The burly supervisor of the hospital staff had approached her to inform her that Don Melquíades Elquiza, a good friend of hers and head butler at Castamar, was in need of an assistant cook.

'This could be an opportunity for you,' she had said.

Clara had felt compelled to accept but she was terrified at the same time, as it would mean stepping outside of the hospital where she both lived and worked. Just imagining herself on the streets of Madrid, crossing the Plaza Mayor as she used to do with her father, had brought her out in a cold sweat and left her feeling weak. Despite this, she had tried to find her own way to the Alcázar, but was overcome by panic almost as soon as she set foot outside the hospital and had to turn back.

Señora Moncada had been kind enough to speak to Señor Elquiza on Clara's behalf and to vouch for her culinary prowess. Their friendship went back a long way, to a time when Moncada had been in the service of the Count of Benavente and Señor Elquiza was already part of the Duke of Castamar's household. Thanks to her, Señor Elquiza had learned that Clara's love of cooking came from her family, and that her mother had been head cook for Cardinal Giulio Alberoni, a minister of King Felipe V.

Unfortunately, the prelate had fallen into disgrace and had returned to the Republic of Genoa, taking Clara's mother with him. Clara, who had risen to become her assistant, had been obliged to leave the service of the cardinal, who had only allowed the head cook to travel with him. Clara had lowered her expectations in the hope of finding a less exalted position and, in the meantime, had earned her living looking after the poor unfortunates at the Hospital of the Annunciation of Our Lady.

She felt profoundly sorry that her father, Doctor Armando Belmonte, had gone to such lengths to provide her and her sister with an education, only for it to come to this. But she could not blame him. Her father had behaved like the enlightened gentleman he was, until his tragic death on 14 December 1710. *All that education for nothing*, she lamented. Their governess, Francisca Barroso, had maintained an iron discipline over the girls' education from an early age. As a result, the two sisters had knowledge of such diverse subjects as needlework and embroidery, etiquette, history and geography, Latin, Greek, mathematics, rhetoric and grammar, and modern languages such as French and English. They also received piano, singing and dancing lessons, which had cost their poor parents a pretty penny, and on top of it all, they were both compulsive readers. However, after the death of their father, their education had been of no use at all, and they had slid inexorably down the social scale. Instead, it was the mother's and the daughter's shared passion for cooking – a passion the father had always complained about – that became the pillar of the family's survival.

'My darling Cristina, it is not for nothing that we have a cook,' Clara's father used to remonstrate. 'What would our friends say if they knew that you spend all day in front of the stove with your eldest daughter when we have servants to spare?'

During the good years, Clara had read all manner of recipes, including translations of some Arabic and Sephardi volumes, many of which were censored in Spain. Among them were *A Book of Soups and Stews* by Ruperto de Nola and *A Treatise on the Art of Confectionery* by Miguel de Baeza. She had been in the habit of accompanying their cook, Señora Cano, to the market, where she learned to select the best cabbages and lettuces, chickpeas and lentils, tomatoes, fruit and rice. How she had enjoyed sorting through the chickpeas while they were soaking, picking out any bad ones. What pleasure she had taken when she was allowed to taste the broth, or the bitter chocolate obtained by her father, thanks to his connections at court. Once again, she wished she was at her mother's side, making sponges, biscuits, jams and preserves. She remembered how they had convinced her father to build a clay oven so they could expand their repertoire. At first he had refused, but eventually he had given way on the grounds that it would help make the servants' lives easier.

After receiving Clara's credentials from Señora Moncada, Señor Elquiza had accepted her for the position. For Clara,

Castamar represented the first rung on the ladder of her aspirations, a return to a real kitchen. Working in the household of the Duke of Castamar – who had been one of King Felipe V's most distinguished followers in the War of the Spanish Succession – represented a secure life in service. She had been informed the house was an unusual one in that, despite being one of the grandest in Spain, it employed only a third of the staff one might expect to find in such an establishment. Apparently, the master of the house, Don Diego, had shut himself away following the death of his wife, and his appearances at court were few and far between.

Before setting out for Castamar, Clara had written to her sister and mother. After sending her letters, Clara had had to wait while Pedro Ochando, who was in charge of the stables at Castamar, finished his tasks for the evening. He had loaded the cart with bales of hay at first light next day and was kind enough to collect her from the hospital coachyard so that she had no need to hide her fear of open spaces. Fortunately for her, it was raining.

'I prefer to travel at the back, if you don't mind,' she had told him. 'That way I can shelter under the hay.'

They travelled along the Móstoles road towards Boadilla in the pouring rain for more than three hours. Occasionally the cart hit a pothole, terrifying her with the possibility that the hay load would shift and expose her to the elements. But she was lucky. Before too long, and with her muscles aching from the ordeal, the cart rumbled to a halt and Señor Ochando, a man of few words, announced their arrival.

She thanked him and climbed down from the cart with her eyes closed. She shivered as the cold rain trickled down the embroidered collar of her dress. Then, waiting until the sound of the creaking wheels had faded into the distance, and with her heart in her mouth, she tied her scarf over her eyes. Peering through a slit so narrow she could barely see the ground beneath her feet and using a crook to guide her like a blind man, she walked towards a small walled courtyard abutting the rear of the mansion. She kept her eyes on her own shoes and prayed the scarf would continue to conceal the rest of Castamar from view. She walked as quickly as she could, her pulse racing and her breath coming too fast as she felt her hands and feet start to tingle. As she passed through an archway into the courtyard, she barely registered that she had crossed paths with a serving girl who was stifling her laughter as she gathered some laundry from the line.

All of a sudden, she felt lost in the open space, unable to orient herself by dint of what little she could glimpse from beneath the scarf. She looked up, and on the other side of the courtyard, beneath an overhanging wooden roof, she spied a door. She didn't care that it appeared to be firmly shut. With her body shaking and her strength waning, she ran towards the door, begging the Lord to save her from falling headlong or fainting. Upon reaching the safety of the doorway, she removed the cloth from her eyes, rested her forehead against the solid wood, no longer thinking about the wide-open space she had just crossed, and knocked with all her might.

'What's up with you, girl?'

The voice came from somewhere behind her and had a tone of dry authority that made Clara's heart miss a beat. She turned around, struggling to maintain her composure. Her eyes met the severe countenance of a woman in her early fifties. Clara held the woman's gaze for no more than a second, just long enough to register her stony expression.

'I'm Clara Belmonte, the new assistant cook,' she stammered, holding out the reference signed by Señora Moncada and her own mother.

The woman slowly looked her up and down, and somewhat reluctantly accepted the piece of paper. To Clara, the moment seemed to last a lifetime; she was almost fainting from vertigo and was forced to lean surreptitiously against the wall. The other woman, seeing that Clara was on the verge of passing out, raised her eyebrows and inspected her. It was as if she was peering into the very depths of her soul.

'Why are you so pale? You're not ill, are you?' she asked, before returning to her reading.

Clara shook her head. Her legs threatened to give way and she knew she could no longer sustain the illusion of normality. However, she also knew that if she revealed her inability to tolerate open spaces then she would lose the job before she had even started, so she clenched her teeth and took deep breaths.

'Señor Elquiza told me he'd be sending someone with experience. Aren't you rather young for all this?'

With a curtsy, Clara replied that she had learned from her mother, in the household of his eminence, Cardinal Alberoni. With a gesture of indifference, the woman returned the document to her. Then, with an economical movement, she took out her keys and opened the door.

'Come with me,' she ordered, and with a feeling of relief, Clara went inside.

As she walked along the bare white corridor, following in the woman's brisk footsteps, Clara began to regain her calm. The woman imperiously informed her that the door they had just passed through was always closed and the proper entrance was on the other side of the courtyard, opening directly into the kitchen. This was a relief, as Clara had no intention of venturing outside the house.

They came across three servants with loud voices; several maids who, at the mere sight of the woman, adjusted their uniforms and hurried away; two tired-looking boot boys; and the man who was responsible for supervising the kitchen supplies, Jacinto Suárez. At his side was Luís Fernández, who oversaw the pantry, the vegetable store, and the supplies of coal, firewood and candles. The woman haughtily greeted both men by their first names. A little further along the passageway, they met two lamplighters, who bowed their heads so low that their chins rested upon their chests.

'You'll be on probation until I decide otherwise, and if your work or your application are not to my liking, you'll be sent straight back to Madrid. You'll receive six reals a day, you'll be given breakfast, lunch and dinner, and you'll have one day's rest a week, which will usually be a Sunday. You will be free to attend mass. You'll sleep in the kitchen, in a small alcove with its own door,' she clarified, as two laundry maids passed by. She paid them no attention.

Clara nodded. If she'd been at court – and if she'd been a man – her salary would have been eleven reals a day, but although Castamar might be one of the grandest houses in Spain, it was not the royal palace. And she was not a man. Even so, she felt lucky; there were girls who scrubbed stairs for less than two reals a day. At least she'd be able to set a little aside for if her fortunes took a turn for the worse.

'I don't tolerate idleness or secret relationships among the staff, and absolutely no male visitors,' the housekeeper continued.

They continued down the corridor, with its elegant, coffered ceiling, until they arrived at a pair of cherrywood doors, beyond which lay the kitchen. Suddenly, another chambermaid appeared, carrying a silver tray. On it was a breakfast consisting of chicken consommé, milk and chocolate in separate jugs, buttered toast sprinkled with sugar and cinnamon, poached eggs, soft rolls and some bacon. Clara noticed the consommé had been over-seasoned, the eggs had been cooked for too long, and the rolls were not properly fired. She noted the absence of a footman to accompany the place setting, bread and food from the kitchen to the master's table. Only the bacon appeared to have been prepared correctly, finely sliced and fried in its own fat. But what drew her attention most was the presentation. Despite the refined porcelain and the elegant silver cutlery, which included an unusual four-pronged fork, she could see that it had not received the care one would expect in the household of a Spanish grandee. The separation between the different items of cutlery was haphazard, and worst of all, there was a scandalous absence of even the slightest floral decoration; the white embroidered cloth hung over the edges of the tray; the baked goods, consommé, bacon and eggs – which should have been concealed under their respective silver domes to keep them warm – were, instead, in plain sight. One look from the housekeeper was enough to stop the maid in her tracks. She approached, carefully placed the coffee spoon at the correct distance from the breakfast set and rearranged the silver jugs.

'And don't let anything move, Elisa,' she ordered. 'You can go now.'

Clara understood that the housekeeper had a strong sense of etiquette and protocol, even if she was unaware of the sophisticated culinary presentation associated with the haute cuisine King Felipe had introduced to court circles.

'Of course, Doña Ursula,' Elisa replied, performing a curtsy with the heavy tray and waiting for them to enter the kitchen.

Everyone stopped what they were doing and bowed or curtseyed. It was clear the housekeeper was in charge of preparing the duke's food. At a gesture from her, the activity resumed, and Clara watched as two scullery maids continued to pluck capons for that day's lunch. Somewhat distractedly, another maid seasoned two pullets, while in the background, a fat woman supervised them out of the corner of her eye while she prepared a mushroom sauce to accompany the meat.

Clara could not help concluding that the staff was small indeed for so prestigious a household as Castamar. It could do with at least three more kitchen maids, several additional footmen and boot boys, and another scullery maid or two to sweep and scrub, and to pluck poultry. However, according to Señora Moncada, the master lived alone on the estate with his brother, and while it was true that some of the finer details were lacking, four people were more than sufficient to cater for his personal needs.

Clara wondered how it was that a housekeeper had achieved such dominance. It was normal, in an aristocratic household, for this person to have all the female staff under her supervision, from the chambermaids and housemaids to the scullery maids, laundry maids and seamstresses. However, this woman appeared to exercise the same degree of control over the male staff. It was more as if she were some kind of steward, charged with inspecting the premises, establishing prices and payments and managing the estate. The royal bureau – the body presided over by the head butler, which administered and managed the court – consisted of several high-ranking nobles in the service of the king and queen. At Castamar, of course, the bureau would consist only of people of humble birth. For the moment, its two visible members were Don Melquíades Elquiza, the head butler, and this imposing woman who stood before her and who she would soon learn was called Ursula Berenguer. She wondered at the nature of the relationship between the butler and the housekeeper.

'There is only one week until the annual commemoration of our beloved Doña Alba, the master's deceased wife,' Doña Ursula told her, solemnly. 'It's very important for the duke. The event is attended by every aristocrat in Madrid, and by Their Majesties the King and Queen. We must do the occasion justice.'

Clara nodded and the housekeeper looked over to the far side of the kitchen.

'Señora Escrivá,' she said, sharply, 'let me introduce your new assistant: Señorita Clara Belmonte. Inform her of her duties.'

The fat cook came over and Clara felt that she was scrutinizing her with her piggy eyes, as if she were a piece of meat. The housekeeper departed, leaving a tense silence in her wake. While the other women didn't take their eyes off her, Clara took the opportunity to observe the kitchen more closely. Her mother had always told her that a kitchen's appearance spoke volumes about the cook. After seeing the breakfast that was on its way to the master, she wasn't surprised to observe that the stove was black with soot, the oven had not yet been cleaned, the utensils were all muddled up, the drain was blocked, and the well cover was open. On the shelves, the spice caddies were smeared with grease, and it was impossible to tell on what basis they were organized. Next to them were the flour chests, from the bottom of which hung yellowish threads of lard. The high double windows overlooking the north courtyard were dirty, and on the work surface were remains of blood, wine, spices and entrails from earlier preparations, concealing the colour of the wood and telling her that, although it might have been cleaned daily, it had not been scrubbed with the necessary vigour.

'What a scrawny pigeon they've sent me,' said the head cook, casting her a pitying glance.

Clara started and took a step back. When she placed her foot on the slippery tiled floor, she felt something crunch beneath her boot. Señora Escrivá smiled as she observed Clara lifting her foot to reveal a squashed cockroach.

'You've already started to muck in, that's one less to worry about. It's impossible to get rid of them, however much we try. They're like a plague,' she said, and everyone present laughed. 'I'm Asunción Escrivá, the cook here at Castamar, and these two are María and Emilia, the scullery maids. Over there, preparing the poultry, is my help, Carmen del Castillo. And down there is Rosalía. She's as mad as a goose. The master took pity on her. She carries and fetches things.'

Clara looked down and discovered a fifth person beneath the table. Rosalía looked at her and greeted her with a sad smile. Then she held up her hand and showed her another cockroach.

'I like how they crunch,' she said, with some effort. Clara was smiling back when Señora Escrivá took the girl roughly by the arm.

'Start peeling those onions,' she ordered. 'Hurry up! You're here to work, not to daydream!'

The cook reminded Clara of a fat old sow, squealing in her sty. Any illusions she might have had of working under the orders of a great chef vanished in that instant. It was enough for her to look at Señora Escrivá's fingernails, grimy with food and soot, to understand that there would be little to learn from her. It was clear the master of Castamar had given himself up to a routine of food presented without decorum and prepared without the necessary hygiene. No self-respecting noble household would have tolerated such neglect.

10 October 1720, midday

Men liked to be in charge of situations, but Ursula had learned the painful lesson that she must never again allow anyone to bend her to their will. And so the arrival of the new assistant cook, without her approval – indeed, without any warning before the appointment was made – had unleashed her fury. From time to time, Don Melquíades challenged Doña Ursula's dominion over the household but hers was the louder voice, as the butler was only too aware. If he were to confront her, he stood to lose far more than his job. It would have been better for everyone if he had departed some time ago, taking his dark secret with him. That would have left everything at Castamar under her careful supervision, running as smoothly as a meticulously adjusted pendulum clock.

Lost in these thoughts, Ursula made her way along the corridor, passing the stairs to the upper floors on her right, and coming to the door of the butler's office. She gave two light knocks, trying to hide the turmoil inside her. From the other side of the door, the deep voice of Don Melquíades invited her to enter. Ursula closed the door behind her. The butler was writing in one of his scarlet notebooks, a book that nobody would ever read. She was sure his prose was deplorable, sprinkled with learned words and phrases designed to give the impression that he was a highly educated man. He filled his diaries with all manner of details, striving to convey on the page the dedication he brought to his life as a butler. A dedication which, in Ursula's opinion, had gradually been diluted over the years until he had become a servant to routine, lacking any ambition to improve. She waited until he raised his head from the book. A weighty silence followed, one of those that she found deeply irritating. Don Melquíades glanced up briefly, then continued to write as he spoke.

'Ah, it's you,' he said, laconically.

She ignored the disrespect and waited like a hunter in the dark, before humiliating him for his failed attempt to impose his authority.

'I have come to inform you that the new kitchen assistant has arrived,' she said. 'I hope she is suitably qualified and—'

'You only have to read her references, Doña Ursula,' he interrupted drily, without raising his head.

She fell silent again, and he raised one of his bushy eyebrows and looked her up and down, as if trying to make her feel uncomfortable. Ursula waited. She knew the game would end in her victory.

'Perhaps we should prepare one of the rooms in the east wing for the commemoration dinner,' she said, changing the subject.

He didn't reply, continuing to write instead. She told herself that the silence no doubt made him feel powerful, as if it was up to him to grant permission for such an action. Even so, she did not allow a sound to pass her lips, while he remained mute for a few more seconds.

'As you see fit, Doña Ursula,' Don Melquíades finally replied.

She allowed a moment to pass before striking the fatal blow. She approached the desk and scrutinized him as if he were an insect.

'Don Melquíades, would you do me the favour of putting down your pen for a moment and actually listening to me?' she asked, in a courteous tone.

'I apologize, Doña Ursula,' he replied immediately, as if he hadn't realized she was still there.

With a faint smile, Ursula came a little closer, making him seem smaller and more hunched. Then, smoothly, she let drop the hurtful words, the words she knew would inflict most damage on his pride, as a man and as a servant.

'Don Melquíades, you are the head butler of Castamar, please behave accordingly.'

The man blushed and stood up angrily.

'Especially in my presence,' she concluded.

Don Melquíades wobbled like a jelly that had just been turned onto a serving dish. She deliberately delayed saying anything more until he was about to speak.

'Or I will be forced to speak to his lordship about your little secret,' she cut in.

Don Melquíades, knowing he had no choice but to capitulate in the face of such a threat, assumed an air of dejection, while glaring at her with an offended expression in an attempt to maintain what was left of his dignity.

The corners of her lips turned up in a smile. It was the usual victory – one she had first inflicted on him many years ago and one which he needed to be reminded of from time to time, a victory over male power and over the repressive society that had once done her so much harm. Don Melquíades's little shows of insubordination had become less and less frequent, until one day, he had finally accepted that the big decisions at Castamar were not taken in his office but instead were delivered to him there as *faits accomplis*. Ursula turned to leave, as usual. However, when she reached the door, she decided the butler needed to show greater capitulation.

'There's no need to be so annoyed,' she added. 'We both know who really runs this house. We're like an unhappily married couple, keeping up appearances.'

Don Melquíades stroked his moustache. His face bore the expression of a defeated soul. Ursula turned again to leave, observing as she did how the head butler slumped back onto his pathetic throne.

2

11 October 1720, morning

Clara rose early and spent more than four hours washing pots and pans and scrubbing chopping boards. She sanded down the worktable and scoured the soot-stained walls and floor tiles until they regained some of their original colour. The cockroaches fled to the courtyard. Then she arranged the spice caddies in alphabetical order. She tidied the flour chests, the honeypot and the earthenware jugs. Finally, she drew four tubs of water from the kitchen well, washed the cloths and sluiced out the pails, all before anyone appeared. She knew she could be making trouble for herself, but she couldn't work somewhere so filthy. Any day now, someone could fall ill from eating food cooked there.

To her surprise, Doña Ursula was the first to enter. Clara did a small upright curtsy and lowered her head. From the corner of her eye, she detected a hint of surprise in the housekeeper's impassive face as she breathed in the scent of lye. She sauntered around, admiring the fruits of Clara's labour, before fixing her eyes on her, as if trying to decipher the motives behind all the cleaning. She ran her hand over the braziers, the knife handle, the saucepans and even the stove. Then she directed her gaze towards the spice racks, scrutinizing them without saying a word. At last, radiating authority, she looked at Clara with the trace of a smile.

The door opened and the rotund Señora Escrivá stopped in her tracks. Clara greeted her politely, but the cook didn't even respond. From her expression, Clara could tell she barely recognized the kitchen. When her eyes met Doña Ursula's, her face was a mask of terror.

'I see, Señora Escrivá, that you've fulfilled your duty of cleaning and tidying the kitchen,' Doña Ursula said as she walked out. 'I want it to always be like this.'

The housekeeper's voice faded in the corridor. The head cook surveyed the scene with a frozen smile on her face, trying to locate her familiar smells, her pots and pans, her soot-covered stove. She observed it all as if some conjurer had completely transformed the kitchen. Her indignant, boar-like stare came to rest on Clara. She took two steps and slapped her across the face. Clara's lip burst open and a few drops of blood trickled down her chin. She had to make a huge effort not to return the blow. She looked at the cook in a rage and reached for the rolling pin. Señora Escrivá came no closer, but held up her index finger.

'Now we're all going to have to work harder, thanks to you. You can make cleaning the kitchen one of your daily chores!' she roared. 'Leave it like this every day or I'll beat you to a pulp.'

When the head cook had turned away, Clara also turned her back and, without uttering a word, focused on basting the lamb with lard. From the corner of her eye, she noticed something through the crack in the door. On the other side, Doña Ursula was watching over everything. She remained there for a few moments before walking off, no doubt satisfied. Clara directed her gaze outside, her face still throbbing from the blow. Drizzle was already falling from the heavy clouds, presaging a storm. If things continued this way, she feared her time at Castamar would be brief.

She finished greasing the lamb, then washed her hands over the sink and began covering some tarts with a reduction of honey and almonds for the master's breakfast. Her mind wandered to more pleasant memories, when life had been simple and her father had provided them with everything they needed.

Whenever she pictured her father's round face, with his neat moustache, she felt as if no time had passed. Ironically, those days, when a bloody war was being waged for the Spanish throne and European hegemony, and men of all nations killed without mercy in the name of King Felipe V or Archduke Carlos, had been the happiest of her life. Her father was a cultivated man, who had travelled in his youth and loved books, and his only wish had been for that savage war to end as soon as possible. As a doctor, the Hippocratic oath was sacrosanct, specifically the principle of 'do no harm' or *primum non nocere*, which obliged him to safeguard human life. And as an educated man, war went against all reason, not to mention against God.

However, it was not his ideas on the subject of war that had made him one of the most renowned doctors in Madrid, but rather his constant studying and love for the profession. This had allowed him to rub shoulders both with the Spanish aristocracy and with those who had arrived from France with King Felipe. The poor man had always hoped his daughters would marry into houses of nobility or, if that was not possible, at least ones of good repute. This goal had not been shared by Clara, but her sister, Elvira, who was more naive, had always dreamed of being introduced into society and finding a good husband – one who was rich and handsome and who loved her at least as much as her parents loved each other. However, the war had cut this short when every potential suitor had been recruited into the army, and Elvira became a lost soul, walking around the house with a glazed expression in her eyes.

'At this rate, once the war is over, there won't be any marriageable young men left,' she had often said.

Clara was cut from a different cloth. She preferred being around books and the charcoal-fired heat of the kitchen to spending her time searching for a husband. If she wished for anything in life it was not merely to find a husband but, rather, to find a suitable one. She had believed that King Felipe's victory would present them with an endless supply of illustrious

Habsburgs who, having fallen into disgrace after the war, might view with great favour the prospect of marrying the highly respectable Belmonte family's two heiresses. And yet, their father had also striven to give them an appropriate education.

'You know I always wanted to have a male child to follow in my footsteps in the field of medicine,' he had told her one afternoon as the two of them ate freshly baked pastries, 'but the Lord blessed me with two girls. Although you cannot be doctors, my dear, your being women does not mean you cannot employ reason the way men do.'

As a man of science, her father had based his life around the precepts of experimentation and reason. Thus, he affirmed that, scientifically speaking, there was no conclusive evidence that feminine reason was incapable of study and understanding. In fact, he believed that a suitable education would make them excellent mothers and better spouses and not, as some claimed, drive them mad. Of course, this would not equip them for other tasks which, in every sense, belonged to the orbit of men, such as finance, the military or matters of State. In such matters, especially in politics, Clara's father always maintained that women had a diminished capacity for theoretical reasoning because of their sensitive nature and were only capable of finding solutions to practical problems. This was quite apart from the purely physical professions, where, obviously, women could not compete with a man's skills and strength.

Clara had responded to such claims with ideas from other authors who argued for the equality of the male and female intellects.

'They come from an English author called Mary Astell. She concludes that women should be educated in the same way as men, with the goal of doing the same things.'

'The same things, poor woman! Her theory lacks common sense,' Clara's father had answered incredulously.

Still, he acknowledged that, where study and comprehension were concerned, he had no doubt whatsoever that the differences between men and women were minimal. He had considered the question from every possible perspective.

'That God created Adam in his image and likeness and that Eve was born from the rib of the former does not in any sense imply that the latter had less of a head for study or understanding,' he had stated.

A few days before his unexpected death, he had tenderly confessed that he did not regret having no male heir, that God had blessed him with a good life, since he saw in Elvira an extension of himself, and in Clara an extension of his wife. This was certainly true. Her younger sister had inherited her father's calmer, more level-headed soul, while Clara had been touched by her mother's resolute, decisive spirit. Now, with each sister living a very different life, it was clear that the paths they had taken were simply the outcome of their different characters.

As Clara ground the almonds for the master's pastries, she wondered how Elvira's life in Vienna was going, in those cold and distant lands. What deep longing she felt towards those memories, which chimed away like the hours on a clock: uncontainable, incessant, fleeting. And yet, they brought her such comfort! She smiled as she recalled those beloved days before Don José de Grimaldo had enlisted her father for King Felipe's war, when all Madrid was preparing for King Felipe's arrival from Valladolid, and the three women were waiting for the master of the house. They had imagined he'd be tired from doing the rounds of his patients – wealthy aristocrats who had remained in the capital.

That day, she and her mother had served a slow-cooked stew of pig's trotters and tail, beef shank, capon thighs and breasts, chorizo, morcilla sausage, ham bones, tender chickpeas, cabbage, turnips, carrots, a good stuffing made with breadcrumbs, garlic, minced pork, a sprig of parsley and finally their special touch: a handful of new potatoes. When he had arrived, her father only had to inhale the aromas to know they'd spent all day at the hob. How he wished they would spend more time tasting food than making it! But his protests had fallen on deaf ears, and despite knowing it was unconventional for women of their social position to spend the day cooking, he had not been a man to deny them anything. He had enjoyed their stews, and with the passing years had become so accustomed to them that if they didn't cook he would feel the loss. Even so, he had often feigned objection.

After twenty-six years of marriage, her father, who had lacked a refined sense of smell, was nonetheless able to distinguish the aromas from the drawing room: mutton hotpot, duck with quince, braised pig's trotters, roast bream, stewed chickpeas, and their signature stew. Whenever he inhaled that fragrance, a smile would spread across his face, and he had to make a real effort to feign seriousness. The poor man had only just finished uttering his reproach when he had been subjected to his wife's piercing gaze.

'The eyes have defeated you, Father,' Clara had said to him, as she often did.

Even so, Armando Belmonte had tried again and again. Clara always assumed it had more to do with finding a way to soothe his own fears, since clearly, deep down, he did not want his wife to abandon the stove.

That meal was the last happy memory Clara had. Moments later, Venancio, the butler, had come to announce the arrival of a letter from Don José de Grimaldo. The War Secretary had requested that her father join the Bourbon troops. This memory was followed by others, all of them painful. Clara treasured that scene in her mind, summoning it whenever she was in need, recalling its smallest details with a faint melancholy that dispelled her tears and made her feel safe. Most nights, when sorrow came in search of her soul, she resisted and pulled it up by the roots. Some nights, however, when her spirits were down, she found herself defenceless and took refuge in that image, dwelling on every tiny detail. Then she would inhale sharply, trying to remember the essential oils of rose and lavender her father had been buried with.

11 October 1720, midday

Diego had been riding since first thing that morning. He often did this to refresh his tired mind, and even more frequently at present, with him feeling so out of sorts. He was always miserable about everything. To avoid falling into an even greater state of apathy, he had fetched that morning's mail from Madrid himself. He had discarded the letters of engagement, and picked out the one from his mother, Doña Mercedes. After tucking it into the cuff of his jacket, he had left the estate to avoid seeing his brother or any servants. Ever since his wife's tragic death, Castamar had reflected his spirits. Although the passing of time had mitigated that pain and turned it into a monotonous litany, the chant had become louder in recent days as he prepared to mark nine years since her death, making him highly irascible. He had enough self-awareness to know he could easily succumb to one of his outbursts of rage and do something unjust.

He reached high ground and admired the boundaries of his land, demarcated to the east by the hills of Boadilla and to the north by the estate of Alarcón and the town of Pozuelo. On the horizon lay the blurry Sierra de Guadarrama. He filled his lungs with the clean mountain air.

'Winter is approaching,' he said to himself. 'Another one without her, Diego.'

He turned around, causing his chestnut horse's head to shake, and made out the palace of Castamar, with Madrid further in the distance, and the Alcázar clinging to the edge of the river Manzanares. Beyond that there was only the horizon, leading the way to Guadalajara, Brihuega and Villaviciosa de Tajuña.

Many good men on both sides died out there, he thought.

The victory of Felipe's troops, commanded by the Duke of Vendôme, at Villaviciosa on 10 December 1710 had complicated the enemy Habsburg alliance's objectives, and it was there it became clear that the Bourbons could actually win the war. Images of exhausted faces with sunken eyes came to him, the wounded lying bleeding on stretchers, fighting for their lives. He remembered the cries of pain, some of which had lodged themselves in his heart forever. Again, he saw himself behind the battery of cannons thundering in the face of the enemy troops, and the cavalry charge which destroyed the Habsburg left flank while Felipe watched from the rearguard. With the Marquess of Valdecañas at the helm, they had forced the majority of the enemy to retreat and disperse. And then they had encircled the rest of the contingent.

He felt no sense of soldierly pride. War was a monster capable of snatching everything away, including honour and dignity, if one was not careful. That day, like many others, he had killed without mercy, sowing rancour among the enemy troops who had fought with just as much bravery and fearlessness. It was said that he had been the shield of God, sent to the world to protect the Bourbons, and the king's French grandfather, Louis XIV, had wanted to bring Diego to Versailles for his own security. After the battle, the archduke's troops, under the command of the Austrian Guido Von Starhemberg, had been forced to retreat. The Habsburg alliance's return to Catalonia had not been easy, hampered as they were by their own people.

Finally, after the siege and capture of Girona, Barcelona had surrendered in 1714. But Diego's wife had died three years earlier, on 2 October 1711, trampled by her own horse, and he had not been there to enjoy the victory of Barcelona's surrender because the king had kindly granted his request to retire from active service.

'My dear cousin, going into combat in your current state would simply result in your death,' he had said.

The days when he had been King Felipe's bastion, frustrating the various attacks against him, were now long gone. He could still remember the time he had discovered a small phial of poison in His Majesty's breakfast. Don Diego and his guards had hunted down the would-be assassins, who were disguised as footmen, and dealt them a swift death. Such feats had earned Diego a reputation for being 'the mightiest sword in Spain'. He had never given much credence to it, believing that, with duels, as with war, one bad day could take any man to his tomb. Days later, it had been revealed that the men had bribed one of his lieutenants, Beltrán Burgaleta, to let them in.

Yes, His Majesty had been wise to allow Diego to retire from service after Alba's passing. He had not been the same after the death of his beloved wife. His spirit had wandered, dyeing the galleries of Castamar the ashen colour of grief. He had become a shadow of his former self – once full of laughter and optimism, he was now a shattered silhouette who, over nine years, had dragged himself through that vale of tears, gluing the pieces of himself back together like broken Meissen porcelain.

The first days following her death had been unbearable. Every time he had looked in the mirror to see his growing beard, time had felt like a heavy tombstone, and he its poorly written epitaph. He had told himself his sorrow could only be lessened by the passing of time, always whispering in his ear: *The only way to survive is to forget her*. And then there was the voice of his spirit, which rebelled against this and told him he would never forget her, that he must bear the pain without complaint.

After the tragedy, he had withdrawn from life, spurning visits from his closest friends such as Francisco Marlango and Alfredo Carrión. He had also denied entry to his dear chaplain, Father Antonio Aldecoa, and to this day he had not attended mass despite the pleas of his priest and his brother. He had let go of more than half his servants; he had closed entire rooms in the palace, including his lady's bedchambers; he had shut up his farmhouses in Andalusia and his houses in Madrid, Valladolid and the other towns. He had retired from royal service, and permitted his mother and brother to disturb him only because they refused to entirely respect his desire for solitude. Since the fateful day of his wife's death, he had done nothing but ask himself why God had been so cruel. He had continued to celebrate Alba's birthday as a matter of necessity – it was the only way for that shattered porcelain to remain intact.

Alba had established a tradition of inviting the entire Spanish court to Castamar, because she was addicted to soirees and social gatherings. No sooner did she get a new idea in her head than she would put it into practice. Everything was a game to her, and there wasn't a single lady or gentleman in the Madrid court who did not want to make her acquaintance, for she was the epitome of eloquence, style and beauty, someone who made everyday moments into something special. She had loved to see the breakfast room filled with flowers in the morning, to ride daily, to wear two or three different costumes each day and to change her hairstyle a few times more, depending on the occasion. Other activities had followed, such as playing the piano, speaking French in the mornings and, of course, singing. The moment she got distracted, some ditty or other would escape her lips. And yet, this image of Alba was only a tiny part of the woman he had known, a profound and sincere woman who, at the same time, had been capable of enjoying the superficial and frivolous. She was a devoted wife who possessed unparalleled strength of character, capable of doing anything for the sake of those she loved. This had meant that, at times of mutual anger, a deafening storm would erupt, until at last – he driven by a need to be with her, she by the desire to forget an ultimately pointless argument – they would return to a state of absolute devotion to one another. He smiled as he remembered how her brow used to wrinkle when something went against her wishes.

It was so difficult for him to bid farewell to that world... Even so, after the first years of mourning, his mother had tried to get him to forget his pain, and his refusal had been the cause of furious arguments. She viewed his stubbornness as selfish and irresponsible. Perhaps it was. For wider society, the duties that came with his surname were more important than his mourning and even Alba's memory. His mother seemed less agitated now, though. Perhaps his mother viewed his attendance at some informal meals in the Alcázar and small gatherings at friends' houses or the theatre as a ray of hope. As the years had passed, he had learned to push away the desolation he felt towards these most mundane tasks, until night fell, and he again found himself alone. Time had tempered the pain of his loss.

He remembered he was carrying his mother's wax-sealed letter in the cuff of his juste-au-corps and slowed the horse until it came to a halt. He took out the document, broke open the seal and read it carefully.

My dear son,

By the time this letter reaches you I will be on my way to Castamar. I write to inform you that I have taken the liberty of inviting Don Enrique de Arcona, of whom I have spoken to you on other occasions, to the festivities. I hope that you will become great friends, for I am convinced that his good influence will benefit you – he is a man full of life and possessed of a generous spirit, as my friend, Doña Emilia de Arcas, whom you know well, can confirm.

A fine example of this spirit is the good deed I have recently discovered he did for her. Seeing her carriage stranded in a ditch in the middle of a storm, he kindly rescued her from her predicament and accompanied her to her destination. Naturally, Doña Emilia reciprocated by inviting him in for a bite to eat until the storm cleared. When she discovered that Don Enrique was making his way to Valladolid to collect and escort me to Castamar, she wasted no time in informing him of our mutual friendship. As you will have guessed, she wrote to me almost immediately to tell me about this deed. In short, Enrique has good judgement and exquisite

manners. I say no more. I hope to see you in a few days. Send my
love to Gabriel, whom I also greatly look forward to seeing.
  From your mother who loves you,
    Doña Mercedes de Castamar, Duchess of Rioseco and Medina.

He smiled when he finished reading. His mother had the virtue of making him forget his sorrows. He looked up and continued to trot towards the Castamar family pantheon. He crossed one of the bridges over the Cabeceras stream, which ran through his estate, and approached the ancient chestnut grove sheltering the mausoleum. On the other side of the trees was the chapel of Father Antonio Aldecoa, celebrated for his dedication to the weak, the old and those who had fallen on hard times. He had even established a small parish where, despite their parents' indifference, he taught the servants' children to read.

Diego reined back his horse to quieten the noise of its hoofbeats, as he was not in the mood for talking to Father Antonio, and dismounted in front of the high railings that protected a mausoleum marked by four big columns. He opened the gate and walked down the narrow, black-tiled path until his hands came to rest on the marble door, pushing it open. He did not pass through but instead remained outside. There were too many painful memories inside that islet of granite and jasper. Not only of Alba but also of his father. He leaned against one of the columns and struck up an internal dialogue with his wife, telling her that in five days' time her birthday celebrations would commence, and for two nights and one day Castamar would glow with that blinding intensity which used to delight her. He remained like this for a few moments, content to simply caress the stone as if it were Alba herself. While he did this, he told her about the visits he was receiving, the latest goings-on with the servants, the news from the court. Wistfully, he said goodbye and closed the door behind him.

'I wondered how long it would be before his lordship showed his face here.'

He turned to find himself looking into the cleric's doughy face. The man had served the family since the days of his father, Abel de Castamar. Diego guessed that the priest had been waiting for him to finish speaking to his beloved before intervening.

'I presume you entered from the other side to avoid meeting me,' the priest continued.

'You're right,' Diego said, 'but you know full well it's not because of you.'

Diego looked him in the eye. The priest came a little closer, with that air of his that made Diego feel uncomfortable and slightly vulnerable. The presence of the clergyman reminded him of his indifference towards the Lord. The priest embodied God's patience, understanding and infinite love, the precise things Diego found unbearable. He didn't need God or His understanding; he didn't need His forgiveness and he certainly didn't need His love. God had snatched his heart away, only for the priest to take pity on his suffering and praise the strength he had found to endure the death of his wife. He knew well that Father Antonio was not to blame for this association, but he still felt that way. Every Sunday that he had not attended mass or confessed or taken communion was a day on which he had committed the sin of pride against the Almighty, and the worst thing of all – he didn't care.

'You're aware, Father, that God and I have a very distant relationship,' he said.

'And you know that I will not give up trying to reconcile you to each other,' the priest replied, crossing his hands. 'You can't be angry with God forever.'

'Perhaps I can, Father,' he replied, placing his hand on the man's shoulder. 'Perhaps I can.'

Father Antonio weighed up his words for a few moments.

'You know, your grace, one day you will discover the true meaning of your dear wife's death,' he said at last, 'and when you do, you'll see that all the pain, all the rage that Doña Alba's unjust passing provoked in you will stop making sense. God understands why you blame Him, even though He bears no blame.'

'You know the way I think,' Diego said calmly, 'and though I thank you for your words, it was He who tore her away from me. He should not have done it if He did not seek my enmity.'

He hoisted himself up onto his horse and, after a polite goodbye, started his return to Castamar. As he rode away, the cleric called out to him that God's persistence was greater than his resentment. Diego smiled at him in thanks. Then, without looking back, he galloped to the estate. His friend Francisco Marlango, the Count of Armiño, would have arrived by now and he did not want to make him wait.

3

Clara observed how Ursula ran her eye over the kitchen. The mere presence of the housekeeper left no doubt that any change, however minor, must be approved by her. She checked the cleanliness and shot a quick glance at Clara, who felt she was being judged. The housekeeper scrutinized the spice caddies on the shelves, just as she had done the morning before, and Clara noticed that Señora Escrivá kept her head bowed as if she were in the presence of the duke himself. Clara copied her. Only poor Rosalía looked up from her corner, smiling vacantly.

Doña Ursula gave the head cook a scornful glance. 'Please come to my office at some point during the course of the morning, Señora Escrivá,' she said.

The dumpy little cook swallowed and turned pale, and they both curtseyed as the housekeeper left. After Doña Ursula had swept out, Clara felt the kitchen recover some of its charm, as if a black curtain had been lifted, allowing the light to enter. Even the unfortunate Rosalía laughed, as if joy had suddenly returned. Clara was about to start blending a mixture of egg yolk, starch and half a pound of sugar when the head cook approached, glancing nervously at the door as she did so, to guard against the possibility of an unexpected return by Doña Ursula.

'You'd better not have messed things up again,' the cook threatened, jutting her jaw at her.

Clara looked at her in silence. The head cook turned and kicked the pail.

'Do something useful and unblock the drain in the courtyard,' she ordered.

Clara shuddered slightly and stopped what she was doing. Not at the prospect of clearing the drain, even though it wasn't her job, but because she knew that, as soon as she stepped outside, she would reveal her weakness. And that would be the perfect excuse for the head cook to throw her out, with no references.

'I told you to get outside!' grunted Señora Escrivá, like an angry boar.

In a cold sweat, Clara picked up the wooden pail, her head suddenly filling with images of the void that awaited her. She cursed her bad luck at being left on her own with the head cook. The two scullery maids and the help, Carmen del Castillo, had gone to market in Madrid to assist Jacinto Suárez in his purchases. She dodged Rosalía, who was winding circles of hair around her finger, and approached the door to the courtyard. Her pulse was racing and she felt sick to the pit of her stomach. She walked with a heavy step as the dirty water swilled around inside the pail like a restless sea. Clara looked at the door, her heart beating wildly. She grasped the handle and sighed. Just as she was trying to summon up all her willpower to go out, the door opened, knocking the pail and spilling some of its contents on the floor.

'Watch what you're doing!' the cook scolded, clicking her tongue.

Rosalía pointed at her, laughing grotesquely like a character in a Lope de Vega play. Clara stepped back, and a well-built if elderly man appeared on the threshold. Clara made a small curtsy, and the man removed his hat, revealing his grey hair. He had a weather-beaten appearance, but it was clear he preserved much of the strength of his youth. From the rake in his hand and the wooden wheelbarrow behind him, she guessed he was the gardener. He had large, sinewy arms which ended in huge, bony hands, with long calloused fingers and nails blackened with soil. Clara, still a little out of breath, looked into the stranger's face. He gave her a warm smile, revealing the gaps in his teeth, and her anxiety subsided a little, as if the old man's gaze had temporarily reassured her.

'I'm so clumsy,' he said, and then looked at the pail of water. 'Let me help you. Is the drain still blocked? They need to get it fixed, Señora Escrivá. Put an end to the bad smells.'

'There's nothing I can do about that.'

The old man sighed, picked up the pail of dirty water and went outside. Clara stepped carefully over the threshold and thanked the Lord for her good fortune, and when the man returned, she smiled at him.

'Clara Belmonte,' she said, making a small curtsy from force of habit. 'Thanks for your trouble.'

'Simón Casona, head gardener. It was no bother at all,' he answered, a little disconcerted.

'Pleased to make your acquaintance,' she said, eager to get back inside.

She couldn't help noticing Señora Escrivá's disdain at the way she had introduced herself, but it was still a relief to pick up the pail and enter the safety of the kitchen again.

'What's up with you, Simón?' snapped Señora Escrivá.

He smiled calmly, as if inured to the untidiness surrounding the head cook, then glanced sideways at Clara, who was mopping up the spilled water as her pulse returned to normal.

'I came to see if you could give me some of the ash from the tray, if you haven't emptied it yet,' the gardener explained. 'I use it as fertilizer.'

Clara raised her head and he looked at her for a moment, smiling at her again. She timidly returned the gesture.

'You can take as much as you want,' Señora Escrivá replied, as if he were her subordinate, before turning to Clara. 'Fill up the bucket and help Señor Casona take it out to the garden. I can't keep Doña Ursula waiting.'

Clara felt her pulse accelerate again. Rosalía shrieked a greeting to Señor Casona, as if she had just noticed his presence. The gardener nodded politely, and wheeled the barrow to the ash store, a cupboard next to the courtyard door, far from the stove.

'The gardens of Castamar are the envy of the duke's friends,' the old man said, as he loaded the barrow.

Clara couldn't help noticing that the gardener's words sounded flat. As she looked out to the yard, she felt her legs weaken. She clenched her jaw and focused on shovelling ash into the barrow. The old man sighed, muttered something about his lost youth, and set off towards the door. Trying not to look, she followed behind, keeping as close as she could to the shelter of his broad back. Even so, as soon as Señor Casona crossed the threshold and she was bathed in the grey light of day, she stopped short. She had to force herself to keep going, gripped by fear, ignoring the danger signs. She was breathing irregularly, her heart was racing, and she realized she would have to turn back before she fainted.

The old man had stopped to look at her, and Clara, held by the invisible chains that tied her to the threshold, returned his gaze for a second before closing her eyes again, barely able to control herself.

'Very sensible, Señorita Belmonte. Better not to go outside today – the ground is very slippery. I'll take the ash to the gardens,' he said quietly, as he took her by the shoulders and guided her back into the kitchen, to a wooden bench. 'Before I came to the city, I lived in Robregordo, up near Buitrago. I remember a good friend of mine, Melchor, who never liked being alone in the dark.'

Clara finally opened her eyes, trying to regain her composure and focus her attention on the gardener. He was crouching next to her, talking softly, and stroking her hands to calm her. She didn't care at all how rough or dirty they were; their warmth was a great source of comfort.

'When Melchor opened his eyes in the middle of the night, he would start screaming and shouting, and he woke up half the village,' the old man continued. 'A lot of people thought he was crazy, until one day my grandmother, may she rest in peace, came up with the answer to his problem.' The gardener paused, waiting for her to participate in the conversation and distract herself from her fears.

Still trembling, Clara gave him a faint smile. 'And… what was it?' she asked finally.

'She advised him to leave a candle stump burning when he went to sleep,' he concluded as he stood up. 'It's best to take these things slowly, señorita. And now that I can see you're feeling better, if you will excuse me, I should continue with my duties.'

Clara nodded and wiped the sweat from her forehead, while still clutching the gardener's hand, preventing him from leaving. Then, very gently, she clasped Señor Casona's huge hand with both of her own and whispered, 'Thank you.' He gave her a warm smile, revealing the gaps in his teeth.

Clara remained seated as she regained her breath and, as soon as she felt strong enough, got up and set to work separating out egg yolks for the duke's custard. Suddenly, she realized Señora Escrivá had been away for a long time. She went over to the stove, opened the iron door with the poker, and found that the bread that was baking underneath the lamb had been spattered with the fat spilling over from the meat above. She remained there for a moment, feeling the heat of the oven on her cheeks, and as she watched the grease bubble over the sides of the clay dish, the thought struck her that the grey day was a reflection of her own mood, and she had the premonition that nothing good would come of Señora Escrivá's delay.

12 October 1720, evening

Enrique sensed that the weather was cooling, announcing the approach of winter. Even so, they had been lucky enough to avoid any rain since leaving Valladolid the day before, and it had held until they had reached Segovia. They had stopped for the night before tackling the pass of Fuenfría, where the slightest carelessness could send the carriages tumbling down the mountainside. They had had to unharness the horses and yoke the mules to the carriages to make the ascent. He had heard that King Felipe wanted to build a proper road to replace this terrible goat track, some sections of which were so narrow that the Berlins had to pass with their outside wheels jutting out over the void. For that very reason, he had ordered Doña Mercedes de Castamar's coachmen to stop the carriage, whereupon he had mounted the lady on his own powerful chestnut horse. The Duchess of Rioseco and Medina had climbed in and out of the carriage with no difficulty, and walked over the stony ground without need of a stick.

'You are a very intrepid woman,' Enrique had complimented her. 'That's why it's such a pleasure to accompany you on this journey.'

'When I was young, and my husband, Don Abel de Castamar, was still alive, we both liked to go for long walks on the estate, and to journey on foot through the Sierra de Guadarrama,' she had replied.

Enrique was pleased by her answer, which was undoubtedly true as the lady feared neither heights nor old age. For his part, he was not lying when he had praised her fearlessness, although his decision to accompany her to Castamar was motivated not by pleasure but by his interest in her son, Don Diego, a man whom he detested with every fibre of his being.

His animosity towards the duke stemmed partly from their opposing political interests. Since the death of his father, Enrique's greatest ambition had been to see his surname elevated with the added title of Grandee of Spain and for his family to become one of the country's leading noble houses. For this reason, during the War of the Spanish Succession he had secretly served the Habsburg side, reporting all manner of details about the court of King Felipe. Don Diego, on the contrary, had been Felipe's most loyal supporter. However, this political rivalry and the success of the Duke of Castamar had only provoked a mild animosity; many nobles had supported the Bourbons and had never been anything more than temporary adversaries. It was only years later that Enrique's animosity had hardened into hostility, when Don Diego had robbed him of the only woman Enrique had ever loved: Doña Alba de Montepardo. And that hostility had turned to implacable hatred on 2 October 1711, when his beloved Alba had lost her life in a riding accident. *It was her husband's fault that she died, and he must be punished for it,* he told himself.

Since that moment, he had been obsessed with the idea of vengeance and had plotted his course with great care. A couple of years ago he had forged a friendship with the duke's mother, Doña Mercedes, engineering apparently chance encounters at social gatherings in the capital. On their first encounter, he had paid court to her, inviting her to a private dinner party that he had organized, and which she had graced with her presence. Subsequently, they had run into each other at plays in the Buen Retiro and picnics at the Alcázar, and had shared hot chocolate and sweetmeats. He had to admit he couldn't help feeling a certain liking for this elegant lady, whose looks belied her age, although his affection was not strong enough to outweigh his hatred for her son. The duchess was, ultimately, nothing more than a means by which to achieve his revenge, and it was for this reason he had travelled to Valladolid so that they could arrive at Castamar together.

'You are the perfect gentleman, Marquess,' she would say. 'If I had a daughter, I would be delighted to see her marry you. Have you found a wife yet?'

'My dear, I wouldn't choose anyone who did not meet with your approval,' Enrique would answer. 'I am counting on your advice in this matter. Who better than you to recommend a good match?'

'That's very true,' she would concur. 'If only my son were of the same disposition.'

'Don't you worry. I'm sure your son will marry again. He's a Castamar and he knows his duty,' he would say with an encouraging smile, as he courteously offered her his arm.

After leaving the narrow pass behind them, they had finally reached El Escorial late in the evening and had stopped for the night at La Granjilla de La Fresneda. Thanks to the duchess's close friendship with Queen Isabel de Farnesio, and her status as a grandee since the time of Emperor Carlos I, she was permitted to stay at this establishment on her travels; they would undoubtedly have a better night's sleep here than at a traveller's inn.

A courier had been sent ahead to warn the steward, who had received them satisfactorily. Enrique had said goodnight to the duchess and, now alone, informed his manservant that he was going out for a walk. He actually planned to meet his trusted accomplice, Hernaldo de la Marca, who should be waiting for him nearby, as instructed.

Leaving the building behind him, he walked towards the bushes, where Hernaldo was waiting in the shadows.

'My lord.' After the whispered greeting, a small lamp appeared, illuminating the man's weather-beaten face.

Enrique approached and asked if his orders had been executed. Hernaldo, a veteran soldier now in his forties, nodded curtly.

'They have, your grace. Just as you ordered, your agent has acquired all the young lady's debts. She is already on her way to Madrid.'

'You told me there was someone who didn't want to sell.'

'He sold up too, after I paid him a visit,' the man answered, with the casual air of one who is quite accustomed to dealing out death.

Although he had no gift for politics, Hernaldo had a simple view of the world which allowed him to see things clearly. His right cheek was decorated with a scar that gave him a menacing air, although the impression was misleading. If there was one thing Enrique had a talent for, it was understanding people's motives, and although Hernaldo had sent many to their graves, he was not moved by hatred. He was a pragmatist and a survivor who felt eternal gratitude and unquestioning loyalty for Enrique. But the mere sight of his huge, knotted hands, the knuckles rough and scarred, the arms as hard as granite, inured anyone who met him with an urge to flee.

'And the other business?'

Hernaldo nodded. 'Soon, I think. I'll bring it to you as soon as I get hold of it.'

Enrique prepared to take his leave.

'One last thing – we finally have a name,' he said. 'You'll have to pay a visit to the Marchioness Doña Sol Montijos soon.'

'Just tell me when.'

Hernaldo vanished as silently as he had appeared, and Enrique made his way back to the building, his mind now at rest. He instructed one of the servants to bring some cheese and pickles to his bedroom for a late supper. He removed his gloves and his jacket and, before calling one of his attendants to help him undress, looked down onto the courtyard below. When he turned, his gaze alighted on a painting of His Majesty the King, when he was younger and the War of the Spanish Succession was at its height. He was wearing a red hunting jacket and had that distracted air so beloved by portrait artists.

'Damn that Bourbon dog!' he muttered. 'If it wasn't for him, I would now be the most prominent member of the court of Emperor Carlos.' He reproached himself, yet again, for not having realized that the Bourbon faction would emerge victorious from the war. What's more, following their victory, the Bourbons had packed the Council of Castile with nobles drawn from more humble lineages, people who were more inclined to study the law or economy at universities like the one in Salamanca. Instead of wasting his efforts spying for the archduke all those years, he should have focused on making progress at the court of Felipe, but Enrique understood little of jurisprudence and less still of systems of government. He was a born politician but not a patriot. His enthusiastic and unwavering support for the archduke had been motivated solely by practicalities.

Personally, he was utterly indifferent to both Felipe and Carlos – for all he cared, they could both die at dawn and he wouldn't waste so much as a prayer on them. *They are kings, and all you can do is follow them – until they became a problem, at which point it is best to overthrow them.* He laughed wryly as he recalled his younger self, waiting at his house in Guadalajara for news of the battle of Villaviciosa de Tajuña. How unpleasant it had been when his morning was interrupted with news of the Habsburg cause's defeat. If only he had received the news in the library, reading Xenophon's *Anabasis*, or upon returning from his morning horse-ride – anywhere but at the breakfast table. He had always felt at ease on that little estate, and he was particularly fond of the cosy parlour where, since childhood, he had been accustomed to take his breakfast.

He still remembered how he had sighed with exasperation when Hernaldo ushered in one of his men with news of the battle. The emissary had ridden through the night to reach Guadalajara by dawn on 11 October 1710, and Hernaldo's expression had told him everything before the man even opened his mouth.

'Felipe's troops have driven back the Habsburg forces, Don Enrique. When they reach Barcelona, there won't be much left of the eastern army.'

Enrique had tutted and looked at the sweaty forehead of the messenger standing before him.

'Hernaldo…' He had sighed with irritation.

For Enrique, it was essential that the different art forms around him flowed together to create a harmonious whole. It was not a question of simply covering spaces with the baroque trends of the past century but rather that the lines of each piece of furniture, each ornament, even the scents in a room, should complement the colour of their vestments. He himself was part of the scene: the slush outside; the overcast, melancholic skies; the fireplace with its slender columns supporting a jasper mantelpiece; the walls, hung with Gobelin tapestries of *The Rape of the Sabine Women*; even the screen that stood behind him, carved by skilled cabinetmakers. They all came together to complete the harmony of that moment, which Hernaldo had just destroyed with his disheartening news.

'I fear the time has come for us to accept that we will continue to be ruled by Don Felipe of Anjou,' Enrique had said, dabbing his lips with the linen napkin and taking another sip of hot chocolate mixed with sugar and vanilla.

Nobody would have guessed, just a few months earlier, when the Habsburgs had taken Madrid, that they had been on the brink of defeat. But political life – not just in Spain but throughout Europe – was like the wind, the prevailing influences changing from one day to the next.

Hernaldo had looked at him nervously and dismissed the messenger.

'My lord, we could try to arrange for the king to suffer an accident.'

It was a desperate proposal, and Enrique had shaken his head.

'Committing regicide is beyond our boundaries, Hernaldo: murdering the king is like taking the life of one who is protected by God. That sacred shield is guaranteed by the captains of the royal bodyguard and, in particular, Don Diego, Duke of Castamar. Don't you remember the previous attempt?' On that occasion, the assassins had got no further than the corridor when they had encountered Don Diego, unleashing a search for conspirators all over Madrid and endangering Enrique's own safety.

'My lord, in that case we must get rid of the duke,' his henchman had replied, throwing back the Alicante wine that he had poured for himself. Enrique had not been surprised by this second proposal. Any plan would necessarily involve the removal of Don Diego from the board – although this was a complicated matter if Enrique were to avoid arousing suspicions. Until that moment, he had shrunk from attacking the Duke of Castamar for practical reasons, as it would have risked, yet again, exposing his situation as a spy at court – murdering Don Diego, the king's favourite, would lead to an investigation that might well conclude with their heads on a spike. However, the outcome of the battle of Villaviciosa changed everything. Only the death of King Felipe could have delivered the continuity of the House of Habsburg to Spain, allowed Enrique to get his hands on political power and, most important of all, enabled him to obtain his beloved Alba. Until that moment, all his hopes had rested on his side winning the war. If that had come to pass, he would have used his position to rescue her from the death sentence to which she would have been condemned alongside her husband for their support of the Bourbon faction. But the defeat of the Habsburgs had rendered his strategy futile.

'It could be our only chance,' his man had insisted.

His henchman had no idea that Enrique had long yearned to send Don Diego to meet his Maker. Needless to say, he had never allowed himself to display this animosity to anyone, not even to Hernaldo. Discretion was the most important principle of all when it came to survival at court.

'Perhaps…' he had said, as if weighing up the proposal, 'if the death could be made to appear an accident – nothing that would lead to an investigation.'

Lost in his memories, he scarcely heard the knocking on the door. It was his manservant. While the servant helped Enrique to undress and made his bed, Enrique recalled how, in his desperation following Alba's death, his first impulse had been to ensure that Don Diego met his death at the first possible opportunity. He would have stopped at nothing, throwing caution to the wind. However, once the pain had subsided and he had come to his senses, he had reached the conclusion that he needed to draw up a new plan, one that involved Don Diego losing everything before he died.

A decade had passed and only now were the conditions ripe for him to carry out his revenge. The intrigues, the war, the failed strategies and frustrated aspirations were all far behind. He had spent ten long years like a cat stalking his prey, planning how best to exact compensation for all the pain Don Diego de Castamar had inflicted on him, and there was nothing in this world that could prevent him.

4

Following her meeting with Doña Ursula, the head cook burst angrily into the kitchen.

'Write up the menus!' she growled at Clara, slamming ink, paper and a quill down on the table. 'Get a move on!' And she began to dictate, wrinkling her nose as she tried to make out whether Clara was taking down her words accurately or using the opportunity to expose her to ridicule.

Apparently, the housekeeper had given her less than an hour to present the menus for the annual celebration so they could be submitted to the master for his approval. Clara now understood Doña Ursula's enigmatic expression upon seeing the kitchen so clean and tidy.

'Ever since you arrived, you've brought nothing but trouble! You won't last long around here.'

Clara didn't answer. As she took down the details for breakfast, lunch, afternoon tea and dinner for two nights and one day of celebrations, Clara tried to imagine the conversation that had taken place in Doña Ursula's office. Not without some pleasure, she pictured Señora Escrivá, rigid with fear under the housekeeper's basilisk stare, as Doña Ursula said, 'Above all, I was surprised you managed to arrange the spices like that. But as you have suddenly learned to read, then no doubt you can write as well. I'll come for the menus in an hour's time. You may leave now.'

Clara told herself she shouldn't take pleasure in the suffering of others, and offered up a short prayer to God, asking him to forgive her this small sin. After all, she hadn't cleaned the kitchen with the intention of creating problems for Señora Escrivá. *How could I have known the cook of Castamar didn't know how to read?*

Asunción Escrivá was an efficient and resourceful woman, who knew how to make the most of a limited number of dishes and their variations, principally game and poultry. This efficiency and the fact that the duke did not have a particularly refined palate had allowed her to remain in her position for several years, but in Clara's opinion, she was not up to the standards one would expect of a house such as Castamar. And to cap it all, Clara had now discovered Señora Escrivá was illiterate.

Although Marisa Cano, the cook who had been in their service back when Clara's father was still alive, had struggled to write correctly, she had been quite capable of jotting down a shopping list. But Señora Escrivá, despite her lack of education, was a survivor. She had no doubt resolved the problem by having recourse to Carmen del Castillo, an assistant who could write well enough to compile the menus but could scarcely compete with Señora Escrivá when it came to practical knowledge. Clara suspected the housekeeper had chosen her moment quite deliberately, in the knowledge that Carmen was away.

She sighed. She would soon have the opportunity to help Castamar prepare for one of the most important events in the Madrid social calendar. Carmen had told her that, for the festivities, the resident chapel-master, Don Álvaro Luna, had hired additional musicians to perform various pieces by the king's official composer, Joseph Draghi. There would also be a performance by a troupe of actors, who would present two plays by José de Cañizares.

The house would be teeming with people: butlers, footmen and boot boys; servants to assist in the bedchambers and the kitchens; pages, seamstresses and scullery maids; cooks and their assistants; waiters, washerwomen and perfumers; apothecaries to prepare remedies; grooms and stable lads to look after the horses and to help the ladies to mount; beaters for the hunt; doctors and surgeons; decorators and florists; painters to record the banquet; and a continuous flow of carts and coaches from Madrid, bringing all manner of victuals. To this must be added the servants each noble or member of the court would bring along to bolster their own standing. Almost all the rooms had been opened up, and that very morning, Clara had heard Doña Ursula order that Castamar should shine as it had done when Doña Alba was still alive. Apparently, the tradition had been started by the duchess herself, and the passing of each year was considered more than sufficient motive to organize a reception for the nobility of Madrid, including the king.

Clara finished writing the menus, and Señora Escrivá set her to peeling garlic and onions and to cleaning, as if she was a mere scullery maid. She didn't protest. When supper was over, she was left to tidy up alone, as a punishment.

'When I arrive, I want this kitchen to be as clean as a mirror, girl!'

'Yes, ma'am.'

'Less of the politeness and more work – that's what you're being paid for.' Clara was well aware the head cook would have her sacked given half the chance. But Escrivá was smart enough to know that, if Clara was dismissed, Doña Ursula would come down on her like a ton of bricks the moment the kitchen slipped back into its former state, and the housekeeper was quite capable of refusing to hire a replacement assistant for the simple satisfaction of watching Escrivá work herself into the ground.

Clara spent the final hours of daylight tidying the kitchen and scrubbing the floor until her bones ached. When she had finished, she retired to her alcove. She didn't mind sleeping there, on a small cot behind a low screen against the back wall. She felt safe and warm. She pulled the blankets over herself and blew out the candle. The only light came from the embers in the stove, and the room was tinged crimson and black. Lying in the stillness, as she drifted off to sleep, she imagined she was the head cook. She rolled over beneath the heavy blanket and allowed her muscles to relax. She slept fitfully as she dreamed that her dead father was smiling at her from a distance, and saw her mother standing over a huge copper pot. She felt terribly far from them and from the life that was no longer hers.

She was rudely awoken by a loud crash and realized the sound must have come from the palace entrance hall, directly above. The kitchen, the wine cellar, the pantry and the other stores were all on the lowest floor, the domain of the servants, whose only direct entrance was from the rear courtyard. She heard another thud, a little further away, and then a third, right above her head. She pushed back the screen. The embers barely gave off any light at all, and she imagined it must be very late. She felt slightly afraid at the thought that thieves or vagabonds from Madrid might have entered the palace. She told herself the duke would protect them – not for nothing had he been captain of King Felipe's bodyguard during the war, and was reputed to be one of the finest swordsmen in Spain. Even so, if they were robbers then she ought to sound the alarm.

She emerged from the shelter of her alcove and threw a shawl over her nightgown. She made her way barefoot across the kitchen to the passageway, her feet quickly becoming cold. Suddenly she heard the sound of heavy chairs being dragged across the floor of the salon above, and she stopped in case her own movements had been noticed. Satisfied they had not, she ascended the wooden staircase, supporting herself on the wrought-iron banister so that the treads would not creak. When she reached the hallway, she heard whispering. She wondered if perhaps it was the master and some friends talking late into the night, but she told herself that if there were intruders in the house then they would undoubtedly keep their voices down too. She had to confirm or dispel her fears, for everyone's sake.

She crossed the hall by the light that filtered through the

panes of glass at either side of the main door. She reached the corridor, which was in almost total darkness, and the wooden floor threatened to betray her presence. She stopped and observed that the door to one of the salons, next to the right-hand wall, was ajar. Through the crack, a shaft of light from the lamps inside fell on the corridor. She approached stealthily, and when she reached the doorway, she could hear two male voices.

Holding her breath as she crouched in the darkness, she peered inside. The first figure she saw could hardly have looked less like a bandit. He was an attractive young man, with brown hair and a self-assured air, no more than thirty years old. He wore a perfectly tailored blue frock coat over an unbuttoned shirt.

'My friend,' he said, as he poured himself a glass of brandy liqueur, 'my father always said you tended towards bluntness.'

Clara couldn't see his interlocutor. However, she could hear him quite clearly, his voice expressing the very directness of which his friend accused him.

'I can't stand those clucking hens cooing over my life as soon as a lady approaches me,' he said from the other side of the wall.

The young man sat down and swung one of his legs over the arm of his chair, the shoe with its fashionably high heel dangling from his foot.

'Come, come,' he replied, taking another sip of the liqueur. 'You can't deny you're the most eligible bachelor in all Madrid.'

'Widower,' said the hidden voice.

Clara guessed it must be the duke who was speaking to the young man, who crossed his legs and shook his head, as if to say that such a fine distinction was of no importance.

'Okay, widower.' He smiled. 'But you won't deny that, today, at the Corrala del Príncipe, Inés de Rojas didn't take her eyes off you during the entire performance. You tell him, Don Gabriel – you were brought up together, after all. Perhaps he'll take more notice of you.'

Suddenly, a third voice spoke up, so close by that Clara was worried she would be caught eavesdropping. Just to her right was a tall, burly man in a satin shirt, over which he wore a vanilla-coloured frock coat. She couldn't see his face, but she told herself she had already heard enough to confirm they were not robbers. She had decided to leave, feeling guilty at listening in on a private conversation, when the third man took a step sideways and his face came into view. She raised her hand to her mouth and blinked several times: he was black.

'You already know my opinion,' he said. 'You asked me some time ago and I don't want to talk about it anymore. He knows he should marry for the sake of Castamar; Mother has been telling him for years. The future of the name is at stake.'

'And what about Señorita Amelia de Castro?' the younger man interrupted. 'A very beautiful young woman.'

'Nothing came of it,' Gabriel answered. 'The ways of the heart are mysterious.'

A negro, dressed in the finest of clothes, with a silk neckerchief and the manners of a gentleman! Clara thought. Her head was spinning. And apparently, he had been brought up with the duke! Perhaps that was why he had received an education. No doubt he was a slave whom the duke held in great esteem, enough to explain the way he addressed him with such familiarity.

'She was, and I'm sure she still is,' said the third voice, from the other side of the room. 'My heart is not made of stone, Gabriel. You will have observed that I have resumed something resembling a social life. Even Felipe has congratulated me.'

'And you should push yourself further, my friend. Come back to court – the ladies will be attentive and the king will be glad to see you,' argued the young man, flourishing his glass as he spoke. 'You need to try—'

'No,' came the reply, in a tone that made it clear the topic was not to his liking.

There was an awkward silence, and the young man with the liqueur tutted as if in disapproval. Clara once again reproached herself for intruding and was about to leave when she realized the duke was now standing with his back to her, looking out through the windows onto the garden. She couldn't help being captivated by his appearance. He cut an elegant figure, with his hands behind his back, his broad shoulders, his long hair tied in a ponytail with a ribbon of black silk. The black man took a couple of steps forward and spoke once again with a familiarity that seemed to belie the status of a slave or a servant.

'Diego, Francisco only wants what is best for you.'

The name confirmed that the other man was the duke. Clara saw the duke was about to turn so waited a little longer, and when he did, she saw his calm expression, his large amber eyes full of determination. Don Diego sighed slightly. His face bore the sweetness and sensitivity of a portrait by Murillo, and Clara waited for his response, curious to see if this grandee was capable of overcoming his pride.

'I'm sorry, my friend. I shouldn't have spoken to you like that. I know you said it for my good, and I am grateful. However, my heart still needs more time to mend. In the meantime, gentlemen, I believe I must take refuge in my solitude again.'

The young man, Don Francisco, gave an ironic smile, as if he were accustomed to witnessing the duke's bad temper. He got up and stood in front of him, drank the last of the liqueur, put the glass down on a small side table, and placed his hand on the duke's shoulder.

'Diego, your loneliness won't bring Alba back,' he remonstrated. 'Remember her as much as you want, organize the anniversary dinner and anything else but... put the past behind you and live your life while you still can.'

The duke gave his friend a sad look, as if he were listening to an uncomfortable truth for which he had no reply. Then he nodded. Don Francisco, after a short silence, turned and picked up his stick, his gloves and his hat, and walked over to the doors that gave onto the garden.

'While you enjoy your solitude,' he said as he left, 'I am going to visit those two ladies we were going to meet at Santo

Domingo. I will have to satisfy both of them, my dear friend, to protect your good name.'

Clara blushed – Don Francisco appeared to be a libertine. Don Diego smiled faintly at his friend's audacity and stood watching as Don Francisco departed. Now they were alone, he turned to the black man.

'I know you agree with Francisco's advice. I can hear your thoughts from here,' he said. 'Won't you at least tell me I'm on the right path?'

This struck Clara as even more remarkable. The duke, Don Diego of Castamar, asking a negro for advice as if he were his equal. She had always heard that Africans lacked intellect, that they were an inferior race best suited to physical labour. She had occasionally come across them, mainly slaves, along with the occasional freedman who continued to serve his former owner. Her father had told her many of them did not wish to cease being slaves because serving their masters was an intrinsic part of their nature, even when they had obtained their letters of freedom.

'You know I do, brother,' the other man answered, calmly. 'But I also think you are very headstrong, and that's why you need so long to recover. And now, with your permission, I am going to bed.'

Clara took a step back, afraid she was about to be discovered, but the man left through the same door as Don Francisco and disappeared from view. She heard the door close and then the duke's measured breathing. She wondered what type of noble would permit a negro to address him as 'brother', even in private. It was beyond any explanation and, no doubt, had she witnessed such a scene before she came down in the world, she would have been censorious. However, now she had experienced the vicissitudes of life, she was more forgiving and tried to avoid preconceptions. Her old world – of courtesy, etiquette and modesty, of social gatherings where one took chocolate, tea and cakes while gossiping about the indiscretions of others – had been replaced by one in which a terrible anonymity was the rule, where protocol had given way to pitiless criticism, a place where survival was the only goal. She had had many surprises during recent years. She had met ladies and gentlemen who possessed very little nobility, despite their illustrious genealogies, and whose good manners were merely a screen for their rotten souls. And she had also encountered men and women who, despite having no lineage whatsoever, had hearts that were full of goodness. She had suffered so much from the indolence, brutality and lack of decorum of others that she now preferred to reserve her own judgement when encountering something new or strange.

She was shaken from her reverie when the duke poured himself some red wine and looked in her direction. For a second, she had the sensation that he had seen her face through the opening in the door, and she drew back into the shadows. She felt like a busybody, sticking her nose into other people's business, but she couldn't help taking one last glimpse to reassure herself that she had not been discovered. The door flew open and the duke rushed out, towering over her, his eyes smouldering with rage.

'Who are you? What are you doing here?' he shouted. 'Why are you spying from behind the door?'

Clara retreated in terror, overwhelmed by a sense of shame and foolishness at having been discovered and unable to give a coherent reply. She made a huge effort to speak but could only utter two words.

'Sir... I...'

'Has nobody told you it is rude to listen to other people's conversations?' he yelled, making her feel like a small animal that was about to be devoured. 'Who gave you the right to do such a thing? Answer me!'

His order echoed down the corridors of Castamar. Clara knew that the next day the whole household would know about her misdemeanour and she would be dismissed without further ado.

'Nobody, sir. I heard voices… I'm truly sorry, I…'

She wrapped the shawl around her, suddenly realizing she was standing in front of her master wearing only a nightgown, and she stared at the floor and blushed. She held back her tears and took a couple of steps away from the lion that stood panting before her.

The duke approached her, put his index finger beneath her chin and tilted her head back, trying to work out what position she held among the servants. She continued to look down, until she sensed that the fury in his eyes had abated. Then Don Diego turned and swept back into the salon as quickly as he had burst forth from it.

'Go back to bed,' he ordered in a surly tone, without looking at her. The door slammed behind him, and she felt as if she had emerged unscathed from the battlefield. She was momentarily rooted to the spot, unable to make her way back to her alcove, but as soon as she got moving, she was overcome by a sense of urgency and ran to the hallway and down the stairs, no longer worrying that the creaking treads might betray her. When she finally reached the safety of her spot behind the screen, she breathed deeply and felt like a complete fool. She rubbed her cold feet and told herself that next morning the duke would doubtless demand an explanation as to why one of the servants had been spying on a private conversation. She felt bad about how this would reflect on the references that Señora Moncada had given her, and she was appalled at what Don Melquíades would think, having given her the opportunity to serve in this house.

She pressed her face into the pillow to stifle the sobs that came from the very depth of her soul, but the tears trickled forth, nonetheless. She wept in silence, tormenting herself for having been so foolish. She reproached herself over and over again for not having left when she had the chance, and in her anger, she squeezed the blanket so hard her knuckles throbbed. She lay like that for a moment, then pounded her fists against the thin woollen mattress to relieve her stress, continuing until her strength was exhausted. She turned and stared into the darkness that filled the tiny space that was barely seven cubits long and four wide.

She had lost the job through her own stupidity, and the prospect of her whole world collapsing yet again made her recall everything she had been through in recent years. Her suffering had destroyed fond memories of her childhood, transforming them into painful ghosts of the past that caused more pain than pleasure when they appeared. The phantoms whispered that she would never return to that lost paradise, and they made her feel exhausted, worn out more by the monotonous struggle of life since her father's death than by the misfortunes that had befallen her. At the beginning, she had believed that it was just a passing phase and that eventually everything would return to the way it had been before. *How I miss you, Father!* she said to herself, yet again. But the words were hollow. Even the lines and wrinkles of her father's face, which she once had been able to recall merely by closing her eyes, had now become blurred, as if covered by a veil.

Since then, only the strength of her spirit and her love of cooking had enabled her to survive. She tried to slow her breathing and, as on all those other occasions when she had been mistreated by life, she called upon her courage. She told herself she would take things one step at a time, that she would find a way to be taken into service in another kitchen, even if it was in a more modest household. Although she was crestfallen at the thought of finding herself once again without employment, she refused to be beaten. There was no point worrying about tomorrow; right now, she had to sleep. 'The only good thing about adversity is that it teaches you to cope with each problem as it comes,' her mother had always said. 'Each day has enough trouble of its own.'

She fell into an agitated sleep, convinced that tomorrow she would have to leave Castamar.

5

13 October 1720, morning

Don Melquíades informed Diego of the imminent arrival of his mother and her companion, and Diego ordered him to make the necessary preparations. Gabriel, who was sitting in an armchair reading Calderón's *The Constant Prince*, barely looked up. Diego observed the gardens from the library window, his soul still as ashen grey as the weather outside. He had been trying to keep his spirits up and had suggested to his brother that they play a game of chess after breakfast. As they played, Diego had recalled the previous night's encounter with the prying servant and felt a sudden burning curiosity about her, perhaps precisely because she had dared to spy on him. Had he felt her to be uncouth or gossipy, he would have punished her boldness, but her reaction had made it clear that she harboured no ill intentions. Since the chess game, his thoughts had alternated between curiosity about the young woman and his own gloomy spirits.

He was still distracted by such thoughts when he saw a pair of four-horse carriages and a rider mounted on a powerful black steed coming up the avenue towards the house.

'Mother's here,' he said, still looking outside.

Don Melquíades had assembled a small troop of servants to receive them: the housekeeper, the lodging master Don Gerardo Martínez, four assistants, the two porters and a few extra lads to help with the carrying, two stable boys to take care of the horses, and a groom to help the guest dismount. As soon as the coachmen had stopped the carriages, the head butler and the lodging master walked over to the main coach to assist Diego's mother. The porters went to the second coach, where the luggage was stored, and the stable hands went over to help the coachmen. Finally, the groom assisted the guest.

Diego watched his mother getting down from the coach, her foot on the step and her hand supported by Don Melquíades. He smiled to see how splendidly she carried herself in this world, the one she had built for Gabriel and him. He suddenly recalled that childhood night when muffled voices in the house had woken him and he had sneaked into his mother's bedroom to find his father sitting on the bed, holding his mother's hands and crying. He had just returned from Cadiz with a two-year-old black boy he had bought at a slave auction. She could hardly believe it.

'I couldn't bear to see that poor child in that state, Mercedes, sitting beside his dead mother, the flies eating him alive,' he had told his wife. 'You know how I detest slavery. I just had to do something, I had to...'

Diego had been four years old and didn't understand any of it, but it had shocked him to see his father cry while his mother shook her head: 'Abel, Abel...' That night, his mother had accepted Gabriel, unaware of just how far his father would break with custom by educating the black child and bringing him up as a member of the family. At first, the poor woman took it very badly, but ultimately her heart overcame her head and she doted on Gabriel as much as she did her firstborn. The two boys had grown up together, sharing everything: adventures in the attic, fights to the death against English pirates, races through the kitchen garden, and all the usual trials and tribulations of childhood. Their father had never treated Gabriel differently and neither did Diego, who lacked any prejudice regarding skin colour. Gabriel was simply his brother.

He looked over at Gabriel, still absorbed in his reading, and when he looked back at his mother, he smiled to see that a gust of wind had blown her hat right up to the gates. Her manservant, Rafael, ran to fetch it. Diego chuckled and Gabriel looked up for a moment.

'Has Mother dropped something already?'

Diego nodded, still observing the scene.

'My hat, Rafael!' he heard her cry. 'I can't enter my son's house without my hat on. Quick, for the love of God!'

She was always dressed for the occasion, as if ready to have her portrait taken. That was why he found it so amusing to see his mother flustered in any way: spilling custard on her dress, tripping on her petticoat... She always attempted to remain dignified in such situations, acting as if nothing had happened. This was her way of avoiding any unseemly fuss, accustomed as she was to the art of putting on a show. She was constantly adding details from her imagination to sweeten reality, as if composing a perfect picture of good manners. That was how she lived, like she was always performing.

Diego looked over at his mother's guest – a tall, handsome man, dressed in the French style, his frame richly decorated with blue silks, with gold embroidery on the sleeves. Wigless, his hair was elegantly gathered into a small ponytail, and he carried a riding crop. From the way he rode, barely leaning off the saddle, Diego took him to be an experienced horseman. Then he focused in on his angular, well-formed face; he had seen him at court occasionally, made-up, though not excessively so. He was said to be a perfect gentleman who had still not found a suitable wife. Diego imagined that, like him, he must be feeling the pressure to fulfil the duties that came with his title.

'Mother's guest has also arrived,' he commented to his brother, still watching the rider's movements.

'Do you know him?' Gabriel said, without taking his eyes away from his book.

'I know of him. He's the Marquess of Soto. Mother holds him in high esteem. They say he's very agreeable. She's mentioned him more than once, but I hadn't put a face to the name.'

He waited until they had all entered the house, looking out at the gardens a little longer as he recalled Alba running from tree to tree while he pretended not to be able to find her. How could he ever forget her gift of a smile, her tempestuous moods, the way she'd wake up excited by whatever whimsical thought was passing through her head, her large blue eyes and that soft brown hair that mesmerized his soul? How could he forget her girlish expressions, or the soft fluttering of those long eyelashes that could entrance a king, or the voice which flowed as smoothly as water? He felt a tightness in his chest and a knot in his throat as he remembered that fateful day when the horse had fallen on Alba and crushed her. He had remained by her side, powerless, not yet understanding that he had lost everything in a fraction of a second.

Banishing these thoughts, he turned round as he heard the library door open. The head butler announced Diego's mother's arrival, and Diego smiled, realizing how much he had missed her. He watched her enter the room, and once she had kissed them both on the cheeks, he asked how her journey had been. She took off her hat in a perfectly rehearsed movement. Diego and Gabriel gave each other a cheeky, knowing look, aware that this elaborate gesture was the reason she had not wanted to enter the house bare-headed.

'A little sore from the bumps on the road from Valladolid. Thank goodness Don Enrique accompanied me,' she replied, wiping imaginary sweat from her brow with a handkerchief while Gabriel attentively arranged her hoop skirt to make sure it covered her ankles.

Gabriel sat down next to her, and at that moment the head butler announced the arrival of Don Enrique de Arcona, Marquess of Soto and Campomedina.

'Don Enrique, it is a pleasure for us to welcome you to

Castamar as our mother's guest,' Diego said, holding out his hand.

'It's a pleasure for me to visit your estate and receive your hospitality.'

'I'll give you a tour tomorrow, should you so wish,' Diego said, inviting Enrique to sit. 'Would you like a liqueur, or a glass of wine perhaps?'

His guest nodded and was just settling on the sofa when he noticed Gabriel and his face froze. Diego watched his mother unfold her fan and reluctantly signal to his brother to leave the room. Straightaway he knew that, true to form, his mother had not mentioned Gabriel to Don Enrique. His father had been in the habit of giving guests prior warning, so they did not feel forced to greet a black man or share space with him as if he were an equal, an idea many found insulting. Even so, Diego hated the notion that anyone, even his mother, could decide where his brother could or could not be, and he gestured to Gabriel to stay where he was.

'I see, Don Enrique, that my mother has had one of her lapses in concentration and not told you who this is,' Diego said, shooting her a glance intended to make her uncomfortable. 'I ask that you forgive her forgetful nature.'

The duchess shuffled uncomfortably in her seat, wishing for this unpleasant moment to pass quickly. Diego knew she hated telling Gabriel's story. Now she would have to suffer the consequences of her silence, as would his poor brother, who would be forced to endure being talked about as if he were not there.

'I will not deny that I am surprised by the presence of a slave dressed up like a gentleman,' Don Enrique said smoothly.

'That's only natural,' Diego said, serving him his liqueur. 'Gabriel is a free man. My father never believed in slavery and granted him his freedom. He was raised as a member of this family.'

'One of my dear Abel's extravagances, may his soul rest in

peace,' his mother intervened, fanning herself even faster, trying to make up for her awkward silence and Gabriel's presence in the room.

'I understand,' the marquess mumbled.

'Guests are usually given advance warning to avoid any misunderstandings, since Gabriel is a member of our family and will be sitting at the table during the dinner that precedes the festivities. Nothing could be further from my intentions than to cause you offence. I understand completely if this poses a problem for you, and I will be sorry if you would prefer not to attend.'

A tense silence settled, during which the marquess looked at Gabriel and then held Diego's gaze for a moment before attempting a smile.

'My dear Don Diego, Doña Mercedes's slip is entirely understandable, and as for me, I have no objection to sharing a dinner table with a member of the Castamar family. None of which should be taken to imply that I accept him as my equal.'

Diego smiled back.

'Nobody in this house would assume any such thing, Marquess, you may rest assured.'

'Problem solved.'

'Don Enrique, you're an angel,' Doña Mercedes said. 'I'm sorry for my omission, my head is not what it was, and I certainly should have warned you. Gabriel has been with us for so long that we've grown used to it.'

'My dear Doña Mercedes, you should never apologize for such things. Not to me.'

Diego walked over to one of the armchairs, an uneasy smile on his face. He watched Gabriel sigh and take his leave, sending Diego a wordless glance before leaving the room. He knew Gabriel had felt no more marginalized on this occasion than on any other. Although it pained him to see his brother like this, their father had left them with no illusions: the rest of society would never view Gabriel as a Castamar. And yet, for an instant,

Diego had detected a subtle hint of artifice in the marquess's voice, as if he had already known Gabriel was part of the family and had simply wanted to make them feel uncomfortable. He immediately dismissed this idea, reminding himself that Don Enrique could not have been more understanding. Most guests refused to share a table with a black man and, in fact, those who accepted his presence tended only to do so to gain the trust and favour of a duke.

'You see, Don Enrique, my dear Abel was always very charitable,' his mother commented, more relaxed now. 'He never allowed a servant to be mistreated. Diego has followed his example – once, he even reprimanded a guest for abusing our gardener.'

'I'll toast to that,' the marquess replied, raising his glass. 'Your husband acted like a good Christian.'

'Personally, I don't believe in ill treatment for ill treatment's sake, but servants are idle and petulant, and at times they need a firm hand,' his mother said breezily.

'I agree,' Don Enrique said.

They all made a toast, the two men maintaining eye contact the whole time.

Diego reflected that the marquess was one of those intelligent men whose thoughts were not easy to divine. Perhaps that explained his good repute at court. He knew when to speak and when to keep quiet, a tricky balance few were able to master.

'It's easy to confuse ill treatment with firmness, my friend. At Castamar, I prefer the latter to prevail,' Diego replied, raising his glass once more.

They made another toast, finishing off the liqueur.

'I believe this year's celebration is going to be even more spectacular than previous occasions, if such a thing is possible. Isn't that so, Diego?' his mother commented.

'The parties at Castamar are famed for being celebrations of the highest order,' Don Enrique said.

Diego nodded in agreement and headed over to the windows.

His mother's error had worsened his bad mood and he would rather stay quiet than engage in small talk. Most likely aware of this, she had taken over. They both laughed behind him at one of the marquess's quips. He felt worn out simply from being there. If he had desired his mother's company just a few minutes ago, now he loathed it. He had sufficient self-awareness to know he would spend the celebration hating the entire cursed court, and that this was just one more way of punishing himself for having failed to save Alba. He felt out of sorts and needed to soothe his spirits in solitude. That was when he remembered the kitchen girl again.

'If you will excuse me, I have an unresolved issue to discuss with the head butler.'

'Must it be now?'

'Yes, Mother. It won't take long,' he answered.

With a forced smile, he left the room, and as the marquess's voice faded, he felt comforted by the growing distance between them.

Clara woke disoriented, her heart thumping. Once she had found her bearings, she began to feel an enormous emptiness in the pit of her stomach; she would be expelled from Castamar that very morning. She got up and gathered her things in a bundle. After getting ready, she began her routine by firing up the stoves. It was Sunday and many of the servants had the day off to attend mass and see to their own chores. She preferred to pray in private and avoid mass before leaving Castamar. Driven by her anguish, she tried to find out if any of the master's foremen were headed for Madrid that morning. That way she could return to the capital, beneath the hay bales, protected by the cart's side and back boards. A footman informed her that a cart would be setting off later that very day.

Señora Escrivá returned from church after eleven o'clock

and ordered Clara to pluck and gut a pigeon for the duke's consommé. The morning unfurled slowly for Clara, her head fizzing and her eyes focused on every one of her fellow workers' movements, on Señora Escrivá, on every unexpected noise. Sooner or later, the master would wake up and demand that she be expelled. *How could you be so stupid?* she berated herself. *Spying on the Duke of Castamar! It's beneath you.*

After finishing the bird, she began preparing some mackerel for pickling. Despite Clara's fears, Doña Ursula did not make an appearance. In fact, no one came looking for her. And the master had risen some time ago. Perhaps he'd forgotten last night's incident, in which case the best thing to do was to keep a low profile. Every now and then, Señora Escrivá looked at her in disbelief, incapable of understanding why she cleaned so much. She didn't hesitate to reproach Clara for wasting so much time on such tasks: if she wanted to clean, she should do it after. How could Clara explain that the best way was to do it while you were working? So she continued whenever she wasn't being watched. Then she helped Carmen del Castillo to finish making the consommé of cabbage, kale, hard-boiled eggs and chickpeas for the servants. As in any noble estate worth its salt, just as in the court itself, the kitchen staff had to prepare two different menus: the fine food for the masters, and more basic fare for the servants. Once the masters' food had been served, she finally turned her full attention to this second phase.

After a short break following lunch, the kitchen team returned to prepare the afternoon tea. That was when Elisa, the maid she had crossed paths with several times over recent days, came in to ask for some soup. Along with the other chambermaids, she had been preparing the bedrooms – airing, warming and tidying them for the guests – and she had barely had a moment to eat.

'Come on now,' Señora Escrivá replied. 'It won't be the first time you've worked on an empty stomach.'

Carmen del Castillo shook her head in silence. Señora Escrivá snorted and Carmen turned away as if it wasn't her problem. Clara told herself she could not be complicit in Señora Escrivá's cruelty and the other woman's silence. If she was going to be dismissed, then at least she would give the girl a happy memory. She waited for Señora Escrivá and her assistant to take their customary break after preparing a tea of freshly baked buns, slices of fruit, and porcelain cups filled with chocolate for the master and his guests. While María and Emilia, the two scullery maids, scrubbed the floor, cleared away the embers and prepared the stoves for dinner, Clara discreetly poured some of the leftover soup into a bowl. Then, when the girls went out to the courtyard to dispose of the dirty water, she hid the bowl behind the screen that separated her alcove from the kitchen, took Elisa by the arm, and quickly handed it to her.

'Thank you so much,' the poor thing replied as she handed back the empty bowl. 'I was feeling faint.'

Moments later, the head cook and her helper returned, and they began threading pigeon meat onto skewers and skinning two hares and some young rabbits. Clara was about to take down one of the knife sharpeners when suddenly Doña Ursula entered the kitchen with the sommelier, Andrés Moguer, and the storekeeper, Luís Fernández, whom Clara recognized from the day of her arrival. The sommelier, a thin man with bags under his eyes and a neck that was too skinny for such a big head, gave her a warm smile. In contrast, the storekeeper, squatly built and with a low forehead, leered at her. She felt it was best to keep that one at arm's length.

Unwittingly, she gave them a full curtsy, as if she were a lady, and the scullery maids laughed at her. Poor Señor Moguer, taken aback, sluggishly tipped his chin forward while Señor Fernández joined the chorus of laughter, doubling over until he almost dropped the two notebooks, inkwell and quill he was holding. Señora Escrivá snorted and shook her head. She was about to say something, but a look from Doña Ursula was enough to instantly silence all the laughter and the huffing and puffing. *She inspires such fear*, Clara thought, admiringly. *No one dares defy her, and I'm not surprised.* The housekeeper signalled her to follow. Clara looked at Señora Escrivá for some acknowledgement of permission.

'Get a move on, can't you see you're wanted,' the head cook yelled, gesturing forcefully.

Doña Ursula walked off, and Clara, her heart in her mouth, cleaned her hands and followed the basilisk, the two men following behind her. She told herself she had been naive to think the duke would forget the incident. The only thing she didn't understand was what the sommelier and the storekeeper were doing there. She was puzzled when the housekeeper turned off before they reached her office, instead heading down the corridor to the pantry.

'With your unexpected arrival, I did not have time to properly inspect your credentials. However, after studying them and watching the way you write the menus, I see you are an educated young woman,' she said.

Clara just nodded. Then they walked around the corner and along the corridor until they reached the double doors of the pantry, where an older man, tall and pot-bellied and with smallpox scars on his face, was keeping guard. His half-shut eyelids opened as soon as he noticed the housekeeper. She looked him up and down with her predatory gaze and the man stood up straight immediately, as upright as the towers of the Alcázar.

'Señor Sales,' the housekeeper said, unfazed. 'If I find you like this one more time, you can pack your things and leave.'

The man nodded in terror. Clara followed the housekeeper and found herself in a high-ceilinged corridor, with three closed doors along the wall and the door to some stairs at the far end. She walked slowly, reading the signs on the doors. The first was the pantry, the store where all the meat, eggs and fish were kept; the second was the larder where the pulses and vegetables were kept, and the third was the fuel store, which held coal, wood, oil and tallow. Clara looked down the corridor, towards the stairwell, and Doña Ursula explained that this was the back entrance to the wine cellar.

'Can you handle numbers and mathematical calculations?' she asked.

Clara nodded. The inscrutable housekeeper pointed at a double door.

'From now on you will have an additional duty. I want you to help the overseer. Do you understand what I'm referring to?'

'Yes,' Clara said.

In the royal court, one of the head chefs would act as an inspector of victuals, a duty which carried the greatest responsibility in the royal kitchen. Every morning, the overseer and the storekeeper had to go into the pantry and take from it whatever was needed to prepare that day's menus.

'Every time something is taken to the kitchen, it must be noted down in the inventory. It will be done in parallel to the inventories made by the storekeeper here and the master of the wine and bread stores, Don Gervasio García,' she explained, while the storekeeper showed Clara the two notebooks. 'You will be paid extra for this work.'

Clara nodded again, and Señor Fernández, who was staring shamelessly at her, started to explain how she was to record the quantities of barrels of cider, marinated meat, jars of pickled fish, bottles of red and white wine – including their provenance – the cheeses and lunchmeats, the sausages, the bags of sugar, the spices, which ones and in what quantities – each item on a specific line of each notebook, one for the pantry and another for the larder.

'The inventory must not only keep exhaustive stock of the master's supplies, but also take note of any changes, especially with the huge amounts of victuals that will arrive from Madrid to supply Castamar's annual celebration,' Doña Ursula explained. 'After finishing this work each day, you will hand over both notebooks to Señor Fernández and Señor García, so they know what the kitchen has consumed. Early the following morning you will collect them from each of their respective offices to carry out the task again.'

'Yes, ma'am, thank you for trusting me,' she answered, disguising her surprise.

It was now clear that the master, for some incomprehensible reason, had still not given the order to dismiss her. She had just sighed in relief when the door to the wine cellar opened and the master appeared, clutching a bottle of Valdepeñas. Clara lowered her head immediately and curtseyed as she had several times before. The duke, who had not noticed her or the two men, addressed the housekeeper in a polite, respectful tone.

'Ah, Señora Berenguer, you're here,' he said. 'I assume you and Señor Elquiza have supervised everything with respect to my mother and her guest's needs.'

'The bedrooms are fully prepared, your grace. The guests' luggage has been taken to their rooms. And chambermaids and manservants have been put in the service of the duchess and her guest, the marquess, to assist them in any way they require,' Doña Ursula explained.

'Perfect.'

Clara wished with all her soul that the duke would not recognize her, that this fateful encounter would not herald the end of her time at Castamar. However, just as she was about to continue on her way, the duke shot her a quick glance and stopped. To Doña Ursula's astonishment, Don Diego approached Clara and gently placed his index finger beneath her chin, tilting her head back, while the sommelier and storekeeper watched from the corners of their eyes. She felt herself tremble as his eyes fixed on hers.

She resisted the temptation to stare back at him, instead looking down at the floor, but he waited.

'Your grace…' Doña Ursula said, visibly uncomfortable.

The duke continued to wait until, unable to avoid it any longer, Clara looked back at him. She was met with a plain, direct expression, containing none of the fury of the night before. Clara presumed he was trying to understand the motives behind her eavesdropping on his private conversation. Andrés Moguer and Luís Fernández stared at the ground and shuffled their feet, while the housekeeper cleared her throat nervously.

'Would you like anything else done, your grace?' Doña Ursula asked.

'No,' he answered, without looking at her.

Clara wished she would stop trembling like a leaf, and eventually he turned and left without uttering another word. Doña Ursula and Clara curtseyed, and the sommelier and the storekeeper bowed in unison. Now they were alone, the housekeeper gave her a meaningful look, entreating her to explain what had just happened. She remained silent, simply lowering her head in the hope that Doña Ursula would order her to leave, but she did not.

'We'll deal with the small problem of the master's chamber later,' she said drily to the sommelier. 'Off you go now, both of you.'

They both nodded and left. Clara curtseyed this time in a way that was more appropriate to her status. Doña Ursula approached her.

'Had you seen the duke before this morning?' she asked.

Clara stayed quiet for a moment, unsure what to do, aware that lying would not get her off the hook but that the truth could condemn her. She went for the second option, trying to minimize the damage, for lying was unchristian, and perhaps Doña Ursula would not expel her if the duke had not mentioned the incident.

'Yes, ma'am,' she replied. 'I heard him arriving late last night with two other gentlemen. The noise woke me, and I saw them when I went to investigate, ma'am. I thought they might be vagrants or thieves. That's all.'

The housekeeper fixed her with a stare. She loomed threateningly over Clara.

'I understand,' the housekeeper said serenely. 'From now on, there must be no contact with Don Diego, unless he expressly declares such a desire, is that clear?'

Clara nodded and the housekeeper abruptly dismissed her. Clara turned and sighed, hoping that her encounter with the duke would have no further repercussions. As she quickly made her way to the kitchen, she could feel the housekeeper's eyes boring into her. She crossed the threshold and returned to the welcoming aroma of roasting meat, but something inside her stirred, telling her this relief would only be temporary. She only had to see the look on the face of Señora Escrivá, who was waiting for her, to be reminded that she was still among strangers.

6

Ursula had never believed in goodwill – to her it was something human beings had invented in order to get along. Beneath outward displays of cordiality, there were only individuals bearing the weight of existence alone, in a bitter fight for survival. Life had taught her that it was far better to look out for your own interests than to go around doing good deeds for which no one would thank you. There were some honourable exceptions to this general principle, like the duchess, Doña Alba. No servant had wept for her loss so much as Ursula had. She had done so alone, of course. Crying was a luxury which could only be afforded to noblewomen; others should avoid displaying this weakness. She had been devastated by the loss of her saviour, and would forever be devoted to her, yet during the long period of mourning that had followed Doña Alba's death, Ursula had hidden her sadness away. Many years later, she still sometimes thought she saw Doña Alba passing through the galleries or contemplating the flowerbeds from the upstairs drawing room. Once Ursula had absorbed the tragedy, she learned a lesson: no matter how secure things seemed, everything could change in an instant. *Surviving is the profession in which I have the most experience*, she always told herself. And she swore to God that she would look after Don Diego as best she could, so that his wife, up in heaven, could observe how she continued to show her loyalty and gratitude.

Beyond those feelings, what mattered was staying in the place on which you had made a mark. That's why she would never let the power she had amassed at Castamar, through sheer determination, slip through her fingers. Thanks to the duke's fondness for her and the efficiency of her work, she had positioned herself as a kind of steward. She supervised everything, even, behind the scenes, the head butler. The only matters she kept out of were the purely financial affairs and expenses. She left those to Don Melquíades, who had more of a head for numbers, and the registrar, Don Alfonso Corbo, who kept her up to speed. Even the temporary butlers, who were not part of the permanent staff, knew from the outset that it was she who made their jobs possible. That's why she had made a show of her power over Señora Escrivá in front of the new assistant cook: to make it clear who led the servants at Castamar.

What had struck her about the new girl was how well she concealed her feelings. If it hadn't been for the duke recognizing her in the storerooms, Ursula wouldn't have realized they'd seen each other before. For a moment, she had believed the girl was a gold-digger, hoping to seduce a noble, but she had quickly dispelled that idea. Rather, the girl appeared to have fallen on hard times and was wise enough to know that anyone who entered into such an arrangement with those intentions would leave with a swelling belly, ending up abandoned to God's mercy with a bastard tied to their back. Besides, any attempt at seducing a man like Don Diego de Castamar was destined to fail. *That man reserves all his love for his wife's ghost*, she told herself.

Everything about Clara Belmonte intrigued her, which was why she had sent one of her trusted men in secret to Puerta de Vallecas, where the Hospital of the Annunciation of Our Lady was located. The girl's most recent job had been there, and it was there that her man had gathered references and information about the girl's past. One Doña Moncada, thinking she was doing the girl a favour, had talked a great deal about her wonderfully diligent work. She had also revealed that Clara's father, a renowned doctor, had died in the war.

Ursula planned to share these details with Don Diego. Once her master knew that the girl was just one more victim of men's cruelty, his curiosity would be sated. The occasion arose that very afternoon, when she received an order to present herself to the duke. After returning from a ride with the Marquess of Soto to show him the outskirts of the estate, the duke had retired to his office to attend to some matters, leaving the guest with Doña Mercedes.

Doña Ursula headed to the upper floor and crossed the passageway to the oak doors of the duke's office. She knocked softly and waited for Don Diego to call her in. When she entered, she found the duke sitting behind his desk.

'Your grace,' Doña Ursula greeted him.

'Señora Berenguer,' he replied, getting up and walking over to the bookcase. 'Who is the girl I saw with you yesterday?'

Ursula kept silent for a moment to avoid giving the impression she had prepared her answer.

'Clara Belmonte, your grace,' she said, adding no further detail, wishing to gauge the level of the duke's interest.

He stopped searching the shelves and looked at her in surprise.

'That's it?' he asked.

'Oh, pardon me, your grace,' she answered, feigning innocence. 'She works in the kitchens. She comes highly recommended. Her credentials say she was the senior assistant cook, though this is according to her mother, with whom she worked for the last few years. She can read and write English, French and some Greek, and she plays the piano and the harp.'

The duke listened in silence. Having found the volume he was looking for, he removed it from the shelf and walked back to his desk. He pondered something for a moment, lost in thoughts the housekeeper would have paid to hear, looking down at the book and pursing his lips. Ursula said nothing, observing each movement to try and understand what had struck him about the young woman.

'It seems her father was Doctor Armando Belmonte.'

Don Diego's gaze rested on her, and he nodded. Maybe that was what had struck him: a familiar face he had not been able to place. The duke, still pensive, turned round and took a seat.

'I believe I've heard that name before,' he said. 'What became of him?'

'He died in the war. As far as I know, her mother earns a living in the service of his eminence, Señor Alberoni. She went to him when she fell on hard times. It seems that Señorita Belmonte wished to work near Madrid. Don Melquíades hired her.'

Don Diego took a deep breath and focused on the book.

'Thank you. You are excused, Señora Berenguer.'

She left promptly and, once outside, waited a few moments, making sure the corridor was empty. Then she rested her hand on the doorknob and gently opened the door again. She watched Don Diego sitting at his desk. She could barely make out his expression, but from the way he was absorbed in his book she convinced herself that all his curiosity regarding Clara Belmonte had disappeared.

15 October 1720, dawn

Clara was woken by a thud that penetrated the kitchen walls. As on the other night, she thought it might be thieves or soldiers and promised herself she wouldn't leave her den. The good thing about sleeping in the alcove, at least, was that it was hidden behind a screen, which might save her from being spotted. She heard another noise and remembered hearing Elisa Costa say that the master and his guests had retired to rest in their rooms once supper had ended. Perhaps one of them had been unable to sleep and was walking over to the library. However, she could clearly make out laughter in the kitchen's outer courtyard. Driven by a sense of responsibility, Clara left her sleeping place and crept over to the door.

Peering through the panes into the darkness beyond, she saw two figures approach the storeroom. One of them took out a key and unlocked the door. She told herself it was not her business and she returned to the security of her cave and got back under her blankets, listening to the laughter and murmurs of the two shadows until they could no longer be heard. Silence extended once more throughout that part of the house, until she heard a soft gasp. She thought she must be mistaken but it was followed by another. She got up again and scurried across to the other corner of the kitchen. The double door leading into the pantry was half open. She could clearly hear a woman's muffled, staccato moans together with a man's heavy breathing.

The light from a candle shone out from the bottom of the stairs that led down to the small cellar. She headed towards the stairwell as the woman's gasps of pleasure reached a peak of ecstasy before suddenly stopping and then unravelling into deep breaths. She waited until she was certain the secret encounter was over. Passing over the first few cobbles, she reached the open doorway to the cellar. Inside, lit by several lanterns, she saw Señora Escrivá with her breasts hanging obscenely out of her bodice and her skirts hitched up. A tall, lean man, ill-kempt and with several days' stubble on his face, still had his hand on her thigh. Acutely embarrassed, Clara covered her mouth to muffle a scandalized cry and looked away.

'You must go, Santiago,' the head cook whispered to her partner. 'Hurry, Señor Casona is sleeping nearby.'

'That deaf old fool won't hear a thing,' he replied scornfully.

Clara looked again. Now Señora Escrivá was adjusting her bodice and underskirt. The man was inspecting the wine collection.

'I said go. Now.'

'I'm going to borrow a couple of the duke's bottles. The bastard's got far too many of them.'

Señora Escrivá angrily whispered at him not to speak ill of the duke. They both climbed the stairs – she with her cheeks bright red and he clutching two bottles of Valdepeñas, before stopping at the entrance.

'Until next week, my darling,' he said, smothering her with kisses.

Clara predicted the head cook would not return by the courtyard, but rather down the corridor that led to the kitchen, so she ran off on tiptoes as she listened to the cellar door closing shut. She crossed the threshold of the larder without touching the door, ran down the passageway, turned the corner and entered the kitchen and the safety of her den. Once inside, she lay completely still, listening to Señora Escrivá's heavy and still slightly uneven breathing as she crossed the kitchen. Praise God, she hadn't been caught this time. She turned over and closed her eyes. Castamar was no less full of secrets than the king's court, all intrigue and traded favours, she thought as she drifted off to sleep for what was left of the night.

Clara woke with a start, her pupils burning as Doña Ursula prodded her shoulder with the blunt end of her stick.

'You can gather your belongings and get ready to leave.'

Still drowsy, Clara babbled uncomprehendingly. First, she thought she was still asleep, but looking through the window she realized she had just over half an hour to go before she needed to be up. She looked again in dismay at the housekeeper's terrible eyes, with no idea what she could have done to incur her wrath.

'Don't deny it,' Doña Ursula exclaimed. 'The cellar supervisor has informed me that two demijohns of wine which were in the inventory yesterday are now missing. And Señora Escrivá has told us you receive nocturnal visits from a man who is clearly not a gentleman, winning his favour with bottles of his lordship's red wine.'

Clara looked at Señora Escrivá, who was standing behind

Doña Ursula with a defiant glimmer in her eyes. Letting her lover pilfer two bottles could be part of Escrivá's plan to get Clara expelled from the estate, but after analysing the head cook's expression in more detail, it dawned on her that the woman was illiterate, stupid and scared witless. Señora Escrivá didn't even understand why it was necessary to catalogue the meat, wine and other produce.

'I haven't. Why are you accusing me?' Clara said to Doña Ursula, standing up straight and looking at Señora Escrivá.

The head cook's lips formed a slender line. Clara clenched her fists, enraged.

'You're a thief and a whore!' Señora Escrivá shrieked.

Rage welled up inside Clara, preventing her from saying anything. Her own manners prohibited her from countering the head cook's accusation, and to make things worse her word was her only defence. She looked to Doña Ursula but was met with her frosty glare.

'I admit I would not have expected this from you. Gather your things, that's my final word,' the housekeeper declared, then turned to leave the kitchen.

The anguish settled into Clara's stomach, and she pictured herself off the estate, with no references and completely defenceless, out in the open where she would surely end up in an asylum because of her nervous disorder. She looked at Doña Ursula with determination.

'I have not stolen anything, nor received any visits, and certainly not from a man.'

Señora Escrivá stepped forward and grabbed her arm.

'But I saw you with your skirts hitched up, howling like a bitch on heat,' she said, so close that Clara could smell her acrid breath.

Clara shook her off, and when Doña Ursula tried to walk past, she blocked her way.

'Doña Ursula, I come from an honourable family which has never had to steal, far less defend its honour. I care nothing for whatever Señora Escrivá may have told you. Her reasons for lying will be immediately clear if you look her in the eye,' she said, anguished and furious in equal measure.

If the housekeeper accepted Clara's word, she would have to cast doubt on Señora Escrivá's, which would lead to the expulsion of the head cook just one day before the celebration. Her departure would be traumatic for Castamar, given the sheer number of servants joining them that same day for the feast, whereas Clara was a simple kitchen hand. And the thieving was the least of it: the fact that she had been fornicating in secret and at an ungodly hour, under the duke's own roof, was a stain on the respectable image a great house in Spain must maintain. Clara understood that Doña Ursula was considering all these factors as she narrowed her eyes. She even felt that the housekeeper believed in Clara's innocence, though ever since her arrival, it had been clear that for some mysterious reason the housekeeper found her to be a nuisance.

'I want you to leave the grounds immediately,' she ordered.

Señora Escrivá smiled in satisfaction. In her ignorance, Clara considered, she didn't realize that after the celebration she too would be thrown out: the basilisk had decided to exile both women from her domain. She lowered her head in silence. Doña Ursula pushed her away with her stick and had begun walking when a voice suddenly stopped her in her tracks.

'I fear, Doña Ursula, that this is most unjust.'

The voice was calm and serious. There, framed by the doorway, stood Simón Casona, who had, discreetly as ever, entered the kitchen in search of more ashes for his plants.

'I don't think this is any of your business, Simón,' the housekeeper spat. 'You tell your gardeners what to do, and I'll concern myself with this matter.'

The man removed his straw hat and dangled it from his wrinkled, veiny hand. He walked to the main table, put down his rake, and rested on a footstool.

'It is my business, my dear Doña Ursula. It's always my

business when an injustice is being done. You cannot dismiss her on these grounds when the only one receiving an undesirable visitor is Señora Escrivá,' he said, bluntly.

Doña Ursula's eyes glowed, and she frowned at the cook.

'Is that right?' she asked.

Judging by her expression, she had not even considered that Señora Escrivá would use her own sins to accuse a kitchen hand. The head cook began issuing nervous denials. Clara understood that Señor Casona's age lent his words more weight, especially since it was so extraordinary for the head gardener to involve himself in a dispute like this.

'Come, Doña Ursula, you know it is,' he said calmly. 'Señora Escrivá is accusing this young woman because she knows it's the best way to be rid of her competition.'

The housekeeper shot him a quick look.

'I wasn't talking to you, Señor Casona,' she snapped, glaring at the cook, who suddenly seemed shrunken and cowed. 'Is that right, Señora Escrivá? Have you put Castamar's reputation in jeopardy?'

Wearily, the gardener walked towards Doña Ursula, who looked at him, incapable of understanding why this humble old man was rising up like a giant in front of her.

'But I am talking to you, madam,' he stated calmly, 'and I must tell you, with all due respect, that the only outcome I will allow is the truth. I shall go to the duke if necessary.'

Clara gulped, feeling immense gratitude towards him. The man, so tall he almost had to hunch over, had become her shining light, a Titan defying the powers that be. He had made it clear that he had direct access to the duke, a claim few other serving staff could match. The housekeeper looked at him and winced before directing one last icy look at Señora Escrivá, who burst into tears.

'That won't be necessary. The truth is plain to see, Señor Casona,' Doña Ursula stated. 'Señora Escrivá, you are dismissed. I want you out of Castamar right now.' Then she turned towards the gardener and gave him a cold stare. 'I hope, Señor Casona, that in future you will speak only of matters concerning the garden, as is your duty.'

The gardener nodded and shrugged, ignoring her words, satisfied that justice had been done. Clara sighed with relief as Doña Ursula left the room, then returned silently to her alcove to get ready for the day. The only person left in the kitchen was Señora Escrivá, wiping away her tears and shouting that there would be no one to make the supper, as if she did not understand that, in an instant, she had lost all the security the kitchen at Castamar had afforded her.

15 October 1720, morning

Don Melquíades smoothed his moustache as he lectured his nephew on the duties and obligations that came with being a valet. The boy had to know he would be positioned within a hierarchy, above the boot boys but below the manservants, just as they were beneath the footmen, who in turn answered to Señor Moguer, the duke's sommelier, who was himself answerable to Doña Ursula and Don Melquíades. He gave a dramatic pause to see if the boy had understood.

As skinny as an asparagus spear, the boy had inherited more of his mother's bearing than his father's. The butler's sister, Angeles, had written to Don Melquíades asking him to take her son onto the house's staff as a latrine cleaner. The butler had felt that if the boy could tolerate that job, then with luck, he would make progress.

The boy had soon been promoted to porter, then to boot boy, eventually taking the leap to valet. He now had a respectable income, part of which he had been sending to his mother every week since his father's death in the war. Don Melquíades, too, had been supplementing the lad's payments with a generous stipend for the boy's mother. He had taken on the responsibility of keeping his sister and her son from falling into the deepest poverty. And he had to acknowledge that seeing his nephew standing in livery before him filled him with a profound sense of family pride.

'Naturally, female visitors are not permitted, and if, by some chance, you start a sentimental relationship with another servant, you must make it known immediately. Come to me or, in my absence, to Doña Ursula,' he clarified.

'Thank you for this opportunity, Uncle. I won't let you down,' the boy said, as if standing to attention before a military commander.

Don Melquíades stood up and walked towards him. He noted that the boy was somewhat uncomfortable in his presence, but it did not bother him because it showed the boy was getting off on the right foot.

'One more thing, Roberto,' he said, stroking his moustache once again. 'Don't forget what I've told you: look, listen but remain silent. There's nothing worse than a gossiping servant.'

The boy nodded enthusiastically. The butler knew his nephew would give his best. He expected no less of an Elquiza.

'Yes, sir,' the boy answered.

Someone knocked softly at the door.

'Come in.'

Don Melquíades watched Doña Ursula enter and, anticipating potential problems, told Roberto to return to his allotted tasks. The boy nodded, then left the room. Don Melquíades sighed as Doña Ursula awaited her greeting. *That is all I will ever get from this woman*, he told himself. *Good manners covering up the fact that I do not govern the servants at Castamar.* He could not understand what went on inside that woman's soul to make her turn everything into a conflict. From his perspective, the war between them could have ended long ago, but he only had to glance at her to know she would never change.

'Good morning, Doña Ursula,' he said, finally.

As predicted, she returned his greeting, feigning the weary cordiality they had established with each other, and announced that she had come to discuss a matter of the utmost urgency. Don Melquíades once more felt the sword on his neck, the constant threat that had been there ever since she had discovered his secret. She remained silent. He wondered what had got her goat this time.

Polite as ever, he said, 'Take a seat, Doña Ursula, and tell me.'

They both sat and looked at each other. This time they stayed silent, the butler restraining his spirits in the expectation that she had decided to make the sensitive information she had on him public and that his whole world was about to come crashing down.

'I've been forced to dismiss Señora Escrivá with immediate effect. It appears she has been receiving nocturnal visits from a man, with whom she has been having licentious relations under this very roof,' Doña Ursula said. 'Besides that, she thought it proper to give her visitor demijohns of his lordship's wine.'

Melquíades put on his best surprised look, but underneath it he felt enormous relief that Doña Ursula had not decided to tell Don Diego about his past. Compared to this, any news seemed trivial. Even so, this was extremely serious; he had to acknowledge that the housekeeper had saved him from the disagreeable task of having to expel the head cook himself.

'I am certainly most surprised to hear of Señora Escrivá's behaviour,' he answered, breathing out sharply. 'You have acted correctly. I will speak to those concerned and inform the duke.'

Doña Ursula once again wielded her power over him.

'I will inform his grace myself, once I've found a new head chef.'

He gave Doña Ursula a cold look.

'I will leave for Madrid immediately to find a competent replacement among my acquaintances,' she concluded.

He stood up, trying to summon all his authority, and raised

his hand for silence. She obeyed, mainly out of decorum, but just as he was about to explain that informing the master was his duty, she mercilessly cut him off.

'I would be grateful if you would limit yourself to informing the rest of the servants of the events and warning them to stay silent regarding the matter, Don Melquíades.'

He clenched his fists until his knuckles were white. Once again, he had to admit defeat, despite being a man and occupying a higher position in the household. He felt a burning urge to go to Don Diego and reveal his secret himself, though that would entail her definitive victory over him. The consequences of such an impulse would, undoubtedly, lead him to a life of wretched poverty – although he would return to his beloved Catalonia with his savings, he would do so with no clear profession, since no one would ever consider him for a similar post.

'As you wish, Doña Ursula,' he answered.

With a curt 'thank you' she exited the room, leaving him with the feeling that he was only half a man, a pusillanimous being. He collapsed onto the chair, his soul reeling from yet another defeat. He stroked his moustache again and walked to the door, putting on an air of dignity. He stopped for a few moments, gathered up the shattered pieces of his pride, and crossed the threshold with a rehearsed smile to walk among the serving staff again, like a king without a crown.

7

Diego observed Francisco. He was a picture of elegance as he sat there, one hand resting on the carved head of his stick, the other cradling a brandy glass. Then Diego glanced over at Alfredo, who was warming himself by the fireplace. They had both travelled from the capital without encountering anything more dramatic than a little mud along the way, and had arrived at Castamar shortly after noon, in time to have lunch with the duke and attend the celebrations the next day.

Alfredo Carrión, Baron of Aguasdulces, had always been a close friend, of both the family and Diego. He was nearly fifty, and this age difference meant he had been something of an elder brother to the duke. Their fathers had been friends since the time of the Habsburgs, and both men had been among the leading lights at court, despite their very different temperaments: Don Bernardo, Alfredo's father, had had a propensity for drinking and was given to excessive punishment, so his son had often sought the protection of Diego's father when he was young. Alfredo took after his mother, a gentle person who enjoyed conversation and sharing advice. He was passionately interested in politics, and just now he was criticizing Spain's lack of initiative in Europe.

Francisco and Diego had been listening attentively but were starting to show signs of boredom. Alfredo, as always, was blissfully unaware.

'Defeat by the European coalition is a clear sign of a shift in the balance of powers on the Continent and of Spanish weakness,' he remarked. 'One need only observe the disastrous Treaty of The Hague, which has granted all Europe licence to plunder the rights of King Felipe.'

Diego simply nodded.

'My dear Alfredo, I don't think that's something we can resolve from Castamar,' Francisco commented wryly. 'Anyway, I'm hungry. Let's eat.' He put his arm around Diego's shoulder and the three of them made their way to the dining room. 'Won't your mother and the Marquess of Soto be joining us?'

'No. They have gone into town. There's a performance at the Corrala del Príncipe at five. *The Man Bewitched by Force* by Antonio de Zamora,' Diego replied.

'And what is the marquess like?' Alfredo suddenly asked.

Diego shrugged, and the three of them entered the dining room, over which presided a painting in blue and gold tones, a gift from King Felipe of which Alba had been so fond.

'I've barely exchanged more than a few words with him, but he doesn't seem to be the usual type who wants to worm his way into my confidence so he can ask me for favours,' Diego answered. 'He's been a friend of my mother's for two years, but this is the first time he has visited Castamar.'

They seated themselves around the table, which had already been laid with the cutlery that the duke himself had commissioned from Paul de Lamerie, goldsmith to King George I, on one of his rare visits to London. The pieces, set out in perfect order, complemented the Meissen porcelain, manufactured in Saxony and incorporating the crest of Castamar in its design. The butler, accompanied by the sommelier, Señor Moguer, and the footmen and assistants, awaited the duke's signal to begin serving. Once the three men had settled, Diego picked up his napkin to indicate the soup could be served. Alfredo tucked his napkin into his collar to avoid splashing his shirt with the broth. Then, resuming his conversation about the marquess, he mentioned that he had heard at court that the marquess was close to the king's eldest son, Luís.

'All I know,' said Francisco, spreading his napkin on his lap, 'is that he doesn't have many lovers and…'

He was silenced by the deliciously fragrant aroma rising from the tureen. He inhaled and identified a whole multitude of smells which came together to form a harmonious, perfectly blended whole. He discerned cloves and fresh parsley adorning small portions of freshly baked bread, cut into delicate strips and toasted in lard. He leaned over his bowl and observed that his two friends were doing likewise, relishing the vapour rising from the consommé. Even the butler, the sommelier and the footmen seemed to be making an effort to restrain themselves from falling ravenously upon the food.

In silence, Diego dipped his spoon in his bowl, blew on it a couple of times, and tasted the soup without waiting for Alfredo to bless the table, as was his custom. The elixir released one delicious flavour after another: cinnamon and hard-boiled egg, farmyard chicken, the perfect quantity of salt, and almond sauce. He even detected a faint hint of mature sheep's cheese. None of the diners uttered a word. Instead, they savoured the chicken soup, spoonful by spoonful, as if it were a secret essence that had been stolen from the gods of Olympus. When they had finished, Alfredo dedicated a few words to the Almighty, thanking him for the exquisite food. As had been his custom since Alba's death, Diego did not share this moment with the Lord, although his stomach was grateful for the best consommé he had ever eaten.

The soup was followed by spit-roast pigeons, cooked to perfection and encased in a golden crust of breadcrumbs, paprika and egg yolk. The meat was as soft as warm butter, with a sumptuous, delicate flavour. As he bit into another piece of pigeon, he saw that his friends were sighing with pleasure, a mixture of satisfaction and surprise on their faces. Although he did not have a particularly discerning palate, he was amazed by the flavours his cook had conjured up. The next course was roast duck, drizzled with quince sauce. He waited expectantly, thinking to himself that it would be difficult to improve on what had gone before. But he experienced such intense pleasure that he let out a small sigh. How could anything taste so delicious? He tried to define it, and the word that came to him was *aristocratic*. The succulent duck meat was flavoured with spices, sugar, vinegar, wine, cinnamon... and those quinces – how they elevated the sauce to celestial heights. He inhaled the sweet aroma as he observed his companions, who had abandoned all pretence of conversation and were dedicating all their senses to the food before them.

Diego watched in amusement as Don Melquíades, standing at the far end of the room, surreptitiously inhaled the aromas, imagining for himself the taste of the meat that was giving off such a delicious smell. Next to him, Señor Moguer flared his nostrils as he, too, sought to partake of the olfactory delights.

The footmen glanced sideways at each other, their cheeks tense and their appetites suddenly aroused. There was no conversation, just small, happy sighs as the diners tasted the duck, and quiet gasps of admiration at the quince sauce.

When the main course was finished, the sommelier and the rest of the servants replaced the Meissen porcelain with some fine Milanese tableware and a clean set of linen napkins. They presented bowls of creamy custard, accompanied by wafers and freshly baked cinnamon tarts. Diego observed his two friends, each of whom was licking his lips as they wordlessly awaited the latest delicacy. Before serving the desserts, the head butler explained that the cook had prepared two versions of the dish, one with goat's milk, the other with almonds. When Diego tried them, he had to confess that he had never tasted such custard before, so light, so smooth, flavoured with fresh egg yolk, neither too thick nor too sweet, just simple perfection, like every other element of the meal. Unable to contain his curiosity, he beckoned the butler over.

'Señor Elquiza,' he whispered in the butler's ear, 'did Señora Escrivá prepare this meal?'

Don Melquíades raised an eyebrow while he searched for an answer.

'If you'll forgive me, I'm afraid you'll have to ask Doña Ursula. She was quite insistent on that point,' he eventually replied, 'and... out of courtesy, I agreed to her request.'

Diego nodded, not quite understanding why his butler preferred the housekeeper to explain matters rather than doing so himself, although if that was what they had agreed, then who was he to argue?

'Call Señora Berenguer, I'd like to speak to her,' he ordered, while his companions dabbed their lips with their napkins and declared themselves full to bursting. Don Melquíades made a face, as if struggling to work out what to say, and then leaned forward and said quietly, 'I'm afraid Doña Ursula is not in the house at the moment. She has been out all day for reasons relating to this very issue.'

Diego instructed the butler to send Señora Berenguer to see him as soon as she returned. Then he smiled to himself with satisfaction as Francisco sang the cook's praises. He invited his friends to repair to the library, to drink a glass of sherry and smoke some Havana tobacco. As they walked down the corridor, however, he couldn't help wondering who from among his staff could have prepared such a celebration for the senses.

15 October 1720, late afternoon

Luck had finally smiled upon her, Amelia told herself, as she looked down from the ladies' gallery in the Corrala del Príncipe, dressed in her finest clothes and with a spyglass pressed to her eye. Among the guests in the Duchess of Rioseco's box, she had spotted Doña Mercedes. Sitting next to her was the Marquess of Soto and Campomedina, Don Enrique of Arcona, a very discreet gentleman to whom Amelia was immensely grateful. Without his assistance, her current aspirations would have been out of the question.

Amelia amused herself as she imagined what it would be like to seduce a man who was so intimately involved in the intrigues of the court, although the true focus of her interest lay not with him but with Don Diego of Castamar. Rumour had it that the duke had not forgotten his wife, even though more than nine years had passed since her death. *I need a wealthy, powerful husband*, she told herself, *just as he needs a new spouse.*

Many years earlier, her father and Doña Mercedes of Castamar, old acquaintances from court, had spoken of marriage. The duchess, desperate to find someone capable of making her son forget his grief, had looked among the daughters of the best families but all to no avail. At that point, some six years ago, Doña Mercedes had turned to her friendship with Amelia's father and invited the daughter to spend the summer at Castamar. Amelia had struck up a good relationship with both mother and son, and although she had not managed to find her way to the duke's heart, she believed she had at least made him forget his sorrows. For a few months, he had smiled from time to time.

'I am sure, my dear, that were it not for the sorrow that afflicts his heart, he would have chosen you,' Doña Mercedes had told her at the end of that summer. 'I don't know what more I can do. We will have to wait for a better opportunity.'

But that opportunity had not arisen, either for her or for Don Diego. Amelia's life was no longer what it had once been. And in light of her difficult situation in Cadiz, her only remaining friend, Verónica Salazar, had reminded her of that brief foray in the past and of the opportunity it represented.

'My good friend Don Enrique of Arcona tells me that the duke has appeared at several social occasions,' her friend had informed her, 'and he has assured me it is quite possible that Don

Diego is ready to marry again. And he should know, because he is a close friend of Doña Mercedes, the duke's mother.'

'I would love to visit Castamar again,' Amelia had replied, 'but I can hardly show up without an invitation.'

'If you wish, I can ask the marquess to help. Perhaps he could arrange a meeting in Madrid that would appear fortuitous, and then lead to your being invited to the annual festivities,' Doña Salazar had suggested. 'Your appearance could come at just the right time. After all, you were the only one who managed to thaw his heart even a little.'

Desperation makes the impossible seem possible, she had told herself, and she had begged her friend to speak to the marquess on her behalf, but without saying anything of her tribulations in Cadiz. Don Diego was her best and only hope. She knew perfectly well that, in the court of King Felipe, there was stiff competition for marriageable nobles, and too much political strategy was required for her to obtain a desirable husband in that arena, but the duke had ceased to be accessible to the ladies of Madrid. It was many years now since he had been among the influential members of the court, despite being one of the king's favourites.

The marquess's response had been swift. She was to meet Doña Mercedes at the evening performance at the Corrala del Príncipe on 15 October. The marquess had reserved and paid for a seat in her name. Not only was the marquess prepared to help her but he had also declared that, should he be unable to secure her invitation to Castamar, then both she and her mother would be welcome to stay at his estate for as long as they required. And so, she found herself sitting there, looking over at the box. Nervously, she glanced away and prayed that news of her misfortunes in Cadiz had not yet reached the capital, otherwise her future would be fatally compromised.

As soon as the performance was over, Amelia left the gallery with the intention of bumping into Doña Mercedes, as had been arranged. She awaited the right moment on the left-hand side of Calle del Príncipe, just as night was falling. She was on tiptoe, straining to pick them out among the crowd, when from behind she heard a man's voice calling her name. She imagined it would be the marquess who, having known where she was seated, would already have identified her. As she turned around, the smile on her face transformed into a grimace of horror. Standing before her was one of her father's acquaintances, Don Horacio del Valle, a spice merchant whose stomach was only matched in size by his self-regard.

'What a delight to find you here,' he said.

'The pleasure is all mine, Don Horacio,' she replied curtly, hoping against all hope that he was not aware of her misfortunes.

'It's a pity we've only met now, my dear,' he said. 'I'm about to leave for Cadiz.'

'A pity indeed,' she replied, smiling bravely, as she searched among the crowd for the marquess or Doña Mercedes, terrified they would appear at just this instant. 'We could have spoken at leisure.'

'We certainly could, my dear,' he said, taking a step towards her, a lascivious smile hovering beneath his moustache. 'I'm sure we would have had plenty to talk about.'

She was overcome by panic when the toadlike man placed his hand over hers. *He knows*, she told herself. *I'm done for.* Amelia instinctively retreated, unable to take her eyes off the glistening fleshy lips sitting in the middle of that hairy face. The contact revolted her, and she tried to withdraw her hand, but he prevented her. She was a prisoner, and she was just starting to struggle when a stick came down smartly on the toad's forearm. Don Horacio took a step back, and a gentleman came forward and placed himself between Amelia and her assailant.

'Can't you tell when a lady has rejected your attentions, sir?' he asked, with a chilling calm.

'How dare you!' Don Horacio blurted out, angrily. 'May I know to whom I am speaking so that I may demand satisfaction?'

'I am Don Enrique of Arcona, Marquess of Soto,' the other man said, advancing until he was just a few inches away, 'and this lady, whom you are importuning, is under my protection.'

Don Horacio's expression suddenly changed, and the fury in his eyes turned to abject cowardice. 'It seems... it seems... there has been a misunderstanding, sir.'

Don Enrique didn't reply but simply stared implacably, and Don Horacio said a swift farewell before disappearing into the crowd. Doña Mercedes, who had been contemplating the scene surrounded by her entourage, hugged Amelia, complained about how difficult it was to find a decent gentleman nowadays, and asked after her health.

'I'm very well,' Amelia answered. 'I'm so pleased to see you. And in such good company,' she added, directing a glance of gratitude at the marquess.

'My darling, you can't imagine how much I have spoken of you, how I have missed your presence.'

The duchess introduced Don Enrique as one of the most delightful gentlemen in all Madrid, and Amelia allowed him to take her hand and place a delicate kiss upon her fingers.

'It's a pleasure to meet you,' she said, making a small curtsy and bowing her head, as she smiled seductively.

'The pleasure is all mine.'

The duchess was delighted and, true to form, took no time at all in inviting Amelia to stay at Castamar for as long as she wished, at the very least until the annual festivities were over. As decorum required, Amelia refused, under the indulgent gaze of Enrique of Arcona.

'I simply cannot permit you to stay at an inn,' Doña Mercedes insisted. 'And it is high time there were more ladies at my son's gloomy mansion.'

The journey to Castamar passed quickly, primarily due to the presence of the marquess and his veiled glances. She responded only fleetingly, and with feigned modesty. Perhaps, if her original plan failed to bear fruit, the marquess would make a good alternative. However, this was not the moment, and so she tried to avoid his gaze for the rest of the trip. Instead, she struck up an agreeable conversation with Doña Mercedes about that evening's performance. The duchess recommended Molière, in particular his play *The Affected Young Ladies*, and another more scandalous piece, *Tartuffe*, which had been banned in France.

'I understand that your mother is still the same, the poor thing,' she added. 'As soon as we heard about the tragedy, I wrote to your father.'

'We were very grateful. Ever since she had the stroke that affected her mind, she's scarcely been herself,' Amelia replied. 'That's why Father decided to stay away from court.'

'The court can be so troublesome at times,' Doña Mercedes replied wearily.

'But also so necessary, my dear Doña Mercedes,' the marquess commented.

Finally, the carriage passed through a gateway and onto a paved road lined with chestnut trees. They left behind them the gatehouse with its small detachment of armed guards, the coach houses, stables and estate workers' quarters. As they passed, Doña Mercedes related how her son had had them renovated out of concern for the comfort of their inhabitants. They also crossed a bridge, with stone pilasters at either side supporting spheres of granite, just as Amelia remembered. This took them over a stream, and they continued up a pine-covered slope until they came to a small plateau. When they reached the top, they saw the great house of Castamar, its lights glowing in the darkness. Amelia was overcome with the same sensation as when she had seen it for the first time.

The building was simple and majestic, more in accordance with the Bourbons than with the Habsburgs of the previous century. It was surrounded by high railings with gilded tips, and on either side of the straight paths, neat flowerbeds were laid out. Amelia thought the gardens a match for those of France, burnished by the reds, yellows and oranges of the setting sun. The carriage came to a halt in front of the main door, a grand affair with a heavy lintel resting on fluted columns, where the servants were waiting to assist them. As she stepped onto the footboard, Amelia admired the four-storey palace and had the sensation of returning to a safe haven.

She descended, assisted by one of the footmen, with Don Enrique following behind. Doña Mercedes, removing her hat, asked the butler for news of her son. When they reached the top of the flight of stairs that led up to the entrance, a footman appeared, bowed, and took their coats. The duchess smiled and invited the marquess and Amelia to wait in one of the small rooms off the enormous, marbled hallway. Meanwhile, she instructed the head butler to provide them with whatever they might need, and then disappeared down a corridor.

Amelia looked out of one of the room's high windows. 'What a wonderful view,' she said, to fill the silence.

The marquess placed his cocked hat on an armchair and poured himself a glass of liqueur. Amelia, her back to him, pretended to admire the view. The butler, seeing that nothing more was required of him, pulled the doors closed behind, leaving two ushers on duty outside the room.

'Señorita Castro, I have a confession. Our friend has told me your secret,' the marquess whispered.

On hearing these words, Amelia froze inside, but she forced herself to hide her feelings. She didn't even turn around.

'I know your father died two years ago,' the marquess continued, 'that he sold the Cadiz estate in an attempt to pay off his gambling debts, and that all you inherited from him was his poverty. And Doña Mercedes has told me of your father's previous attempt to marry you off to Castamar, and I am sure that, driven by desperation, you are going to make a second attempt. You need to be very careful – if people at court find out about your situation, you will be a pariah. Nobody will receive you in their home.'

Could he have brought her here just to take advantage of her misfortune, as others had done in Cadiz? She turned towards him, her head bowed, scarcely able to look at him for shame.

'Verónica shouldn't have told you any of that,' she said. 'All she needed to say was that I wanted to attend the party.'

'A true friend never lies,' he replied discreetly. He took a sip from his glass and approached slowly, until he stood just a few yards away. 'But don't worry, you have nothing to fear,' he added calmly. 'I'm here to help you and to keep your secret safe. My friendship with Verónica Salazar goes back many years, and my dedication to you is a tribute to that, but I could hardly have abandoned a damsel in distress.'

Amelia gulped. She was desperate to believe him but was unsure what to say. This man had brought her to Madrid, had saved her from the clutches of the odious Don Horacio a mere two hours ago, had gained her entry to Castamar, and all this in full knowledge of her past. She felt torn between immense gratitude and deep concern at the harm he might do her.

'If they find out about my situation at Castamar, if they find that – despite knowing about it – you brought me here, you could have...'

She was overcome by the memories of the last four years, and her voice trailed off. Her father had made his fortune as a young man by importing tobacco from the Americas and had made a name for himself as a merchant in Seville, Cartagena and Cadiz. He had built up his connections with the aristocracy, who had been among his best customers. She could still remember what he'd said once as they took a ride through Seville in their carriage. 'You're going to marry into nobility, my darling.' And so, she had turned down proposals from wealthy Andalusian families while her father continued to search for the perfect match that would bring her a title. And finally, they thought they had found it at Castamar. But the plans came to nothing and while their search continued without any sign of striking gold, her marriageable years were passing. A year after the setback with Don Diego, she had celebrated her twenty-fifth birthday, a day she would never forget.

Don Luís Verdejo y Casón, Baron of Zahara, was invited to attend the festivities by her father. He had already spoken to her and, despite the age difference, he was set on making her his wife. But everything had changed with her mother's stroke. The poor woman had been struck down during the party. Driven to madness by the loss of his wife, Amelia's father had taken to drink and gambling, and neglected his duties to his daughter. In just two years, he had frittered away his fortune, his wife's dowry, and the money that had been set aside for his daughter's marriage. Don Luís, the baron, had disappeared as soon as he had heard the rumours of his future father-in-law's derangement and the situation of the mother-in-law.

Amelia, who had had plenty of suitors from among the highest echelons of Andalusian society, was now rejected by them all for being too poor. The family had scarcely been able to keep up appearances while their creditors came knocking at the door. It had come as no surprise when, one January morning, she had found her father dead. And she was left alone with her mother, a woman who could barely speak. Amelia had inherited a pittance, and they had scraped by on this for the last two years, seeking protection wherever they could find it. Eventually, one of their sponsors had converted their misery into a commercial exchange in which Amelia had been obliged to give in to his requests in order to keep starvation at bay.

She forced herself to abandon her gloomy reverie as Don Enrique approached her again.

'Señorita Castro,' he said gently. 'Look at me.' She obeyed slowly. 'Don't you worry – it's our little secret,' he whispered to her. 'If you don't want any more help from me, I'll respect your decision. I'm only offering.'

'What do you want from me?' she asked. 'I know that nobody gives something for nothing and—'

'Don't offend me, Señorita Castro. I have never asked for anything.'

'I'm at your mercy. I...'

Amelia's cheeks were burning, and she was struggling to hold back her tears. She felt powerless and frustrated. She had already lived with the humiliating shame of watching her father fall into the abyss, and she now saw herself facing the same scenario in Madrid.

'Don't be silly. I assure you nothing will happen if you allow me to protect you. Nobody will be permitted to slander you,' he concluded. 'I will be your shield and I will crush anyone who dares to try such a thing.'

She didn't know why, but together with her desperation, she felt a powerful, silent attraction snaking in circles in her belly. Perhaps it was the way Don Enrique had uttered the words she had so longed to hear, his innate elegance or the seductive manner in which he had taken her hand.

Just then, there were two knocks at the door. Don Enrique moved away, and as the door opened, Amelia looked out of the window and tried to master her feelings. Reflected in the glass, she saw a negro dressed like a gentleman, whom she immediately remembered. Before her previous visit to Castamar, her father had told her to behave correctly in his presence but to maintain a certain distance. All of Spain mocked Don Abel's eccentricity, although nobody ever said anything to his face.

'Please forgive my interruption. My mother has asked me to accompany you to the salon, where Don Diego is waiting for you,' the man said, with exquisite manners.

'Good evening, Don Gabriel,' Amelia said, turning to face him.

'It's a pleasure to see you again, Señorita Castro,' Don Gabriel replied, bowing slightly.

'I don't think anyone gave you permission to enter,' said Don Enrique, visibly annoyed.

Gabriel looked at Enrique, who was standing before him. Amelia felt the awkwardness of the situation. Don Gabriel was a full head taller than the marquess and more heavily built, and he held the marquess's gaze as if they were equals. She half expected Don Enrique to take offence and leave, much to his host's embarrassment.

'The door was ajar, I did not intend to intrude,' Don Gabriel replied, not lowering his gaze.

The marquess came yet nearer until they were barely a hand's breadth apart. 'Don't enter again without asking permission,' he said curtly. 'It is a question of manners.'

'I am afraid I must inform you that I have no need for your permission,' replied Don Gabriel. 'I am a Castamar, this is my home, and you will speak to me as an equal.'

Amelia took a step back and raised a hand to her mouth in shock. Don Gabriel had defied the marquess as if he were Prometheus challenging the gods of Olympus to give fire to humankind. For a black man to speak to a white man in such a way was unthinkable, particularly when the white man was a member of the nobility, regardless of the status accorded to Don Gabriel within the household of Castamar. The marquess would have been well within his rights to demand that his host apologize for this lack of respect, but instead he simply smiled.

'I will do no such thing, but as Doña Mercedes considers you to be her son and I have great respect for her, I will say no more on the matter,' he answered calmly.

'That will be sufficient,' the other replied, with a blunt finality. 'And now, if you will follow me, I will show you through to the salon where your fellow guests are waiting.'

Amelia nodded without knowing quite what to think about the scene she had witnessed. She smiled politely at Don Gabriel, just as she had done in the past. She still did not know how to behave in his presence. She followed him along the corridor, her emotions in turmoil. As she entered the cloistered courtyard, with its Doric columns and Gothic arches, she sensed that the decision to come to Castamar would have some unforeseen consequences.

8

Clara stoked up the fires and began preparing the birds for the soups and the main dishes: fillet steak marinated in onion with apple compote, chicken rissoles and spit-roasted pigeon. This would be followed by a roast goose. As well as the salads, she had prepared a blackberry fool for dessert that was sure to delight the duke. According to Elisa Costa – the only friend she had made so far – Don Diego liked to pick them during his walks around the estate.

She was conscious that the joy she gained from making the dinner would only last a few more hours, until the dreaded housekeeper returned from Madrid. Still, she could not remember being this happy at any point over the past ten years. She looked to one side, expecting Carmen del Castillo to enter at any moment with the two scullery maids, who, like a pair of lost cats, only ever seemed to be in the kitchen because they had nowhere better to go. She smiled to herself, dipped the ladle into the warm porridge and gave poor Rosalía something to eat. Clara remained lost in thought, sitting on a small footstool. Surviving these first six days at Castamar had been nothing short of miraculous. She had not expected to do anything beyond peel garlic, grind spices and gut chickens, and yet she had already taken over the planning and cooking of meals for the master and his guests. Strangest of all, she had the housekeeper to thank for this.

Before setting out for Madrid, Doña Ursula had told Carmen del Castillo it was her responsibility to make sure Señora Escrivá's absence was not noticed until that evening. Carmen was made to understand from Doña Ursula's expression that, if she let the housekeeper down, she'd be out on the street. As it happened, though, Carmen had a solid grasp of no more than twenty dishes, and of these, only two or three were fashionable and practised sufficiently to be presented to the standards expected. After Doña Ursula had left, she had been so nervous she began to shake so much she was incapable of even beating the eggs. The scullery maids had not even looked up from the table as they plucked the pigeons and sliced the bread. Half an hour had passed this way until Carmen had slipped out to the passageway. Clara had found her crying behind the door. She had gently placed her hand on the other woman's shoulder. Carmen had turned round, wiping away tears, and had given her that world-weary look which Clara recognized all too well.

'They're going to kick me out,' she said. 'I'm not a good enough to cook for the duke.'

'But I am,' Clara replied boldly. 'If you permit me, I assure you that Don Diego and his companions will eat the best food they've had in a long time.'

Once she realized her position was safe, Carmen had looked at Clara as if she were an angel. Clara had smiled as she watched Carmen's face visibly relax, while her own face in turn lit up with the joy of knowing she would be running the Castamar kitchen for the day. Together they had returned to their positions, where, under Clara's direction, they began preparing the food for the duke and his friends. Now, as night began to fall, there was no denying things were going marvellously. The whole day had been like a dream come true.

Clara had just given the last spoonful of porridge to Rosalía, and the affection-starved girl hugged her impulsively. Clara laughed and then wiped the girl's face and hands with a clean cloth. It was a miracle she had survived in Señora Escrivá's care.

Clara got up to stoke the fires again, just as Carmen and the two scullery maids returned from their brief rest. After giving them some instructions, she headed to the pantry to tell the porters to bring the loin for the fillets. Then she went to fetch some ripe apples to be cored and seeded and cooked into a compote. She took her two notebooks and used her quill to note down what she would be taking, but when she tried to open the door, she found it barred from the inside. Her hand slipped from the handle, and she hit her knuckles against the wood. She cried out in pain, and when the door swung open and she entered the room, she found herself standing face to face with the duke.

'Forgive me, your grace, I didn't know—'

'It's alright, Señorita Belmonte,' he interrupted. 'My clumsiness is to blame.'

She lowered her head as she realized he had addressed her using her surname, making it obvious Don Diego now knew about her.

'Your grace.'

'Let me see that hand,' said Don Diego.

Clara felt his firm grip and couldn't help looking up. She scrutinized his features, which looked as if they'd been painted by an artist, and his amber eyes examining her hand. She watched his fingertips unconsciously stroking her palm, causing the hairs on the back of her neck to stand up. She remembered how Don Diego had caught her spying on him and felt the need to apologize, but the duke looked up, and for a moment they gazed at each other in silence. After another second, he smiled, tilted his head to one side, gracefully withdrew his hand and took a step back.

'It doesn't look too serious. My apologies once again,' he said, rather awkwardly, and turned to go.

Clara took a breath and was about to curtsy once more when the duke stopped and walked back to her as if he had only just remembered why he had come down to the kitchens. This time, she kept her eyes fixed on the floor and waited for the duke to speak.

'I came to inform Señora Escrivá that I will be dining alone tonight. The others have already eaten, and Don Francisco and Don Alfredo will only require a light supper. They're very tired from hunting this afternoon,' he told her.

A silence settled on them, forcing her to look at him. His amber eyes rested on her once more. She felt she could detect an excuse in his words. It wasn't normal for the master of the house to come down to these quarters and it certainly wasn't his personal responsibility to inform Señora Escrivá about the number of diners, since any servant could have delivered that message. She couldn't imagine what had brought him here. Clara nodded while keeping a prudent silence, reasoning that, if he hadn't heard already, it would be unwise to inform him of Señora Escrivá's expulsion. Perhaps Doña Ursula didn't want him to know until she had everything under control.

He cleared his throat to break the silence. 'As well as the marquess and my mother, we will have a new guest in the house. Señorita Amelia Castro, who will dine in her room,' the duke added. 'I hope it will not be a problem to inform Señora Escrivá at such short notice.'

They looked at one another for a third time, and Clara gulped, not quite knowing what to say.

'Absolutely, your grace,' she answered finally.

Without another word, the duke turned to leave. She stood still as he disappeared around the corner. Then, as she thought about how she ought to send one of the scullery maids to find out what Señorita Castro wished to eat, she unconsciously lifted her hand to her nose and breathed in the sweet fragrance of rose and lavender that Don Diego had left on her skin.

15 October 1720, night

Diego left his encounter with Señorita Belmonte as intrigued as he had begun it. From the girl's discomfort while talking to him about Señora Escrivá, it was clear something had happened in the kitchen. However, he had preferred not to ask her, knowing all too well what her response would be. None of the servants had revealed who had cooked that divine lunch, all of them deferring to Señora Berenguer as the only one who could reveal the information. Had he insisted, they would have been obliged to tell him, but he felt that if Señora Berenguer preferred to tell him herself upon her return from Madrid, then it must be to save him from needless worry. So, he had preferred to wait, respecting the wishes of his cherished housekeeper. He had not failed to recognize that she was indispensable to Castamar, the functioning of the entire estate relying on her capable presence. Don Melquíades must hold her in very high esteem, since more than a housekeeper, he had elevated her to a kind of steward, always trusting her to solve problems on his behalf.

Diego not only allowed this situation, he encouraged it. *Had she been a man, she would have been the best of all butlers*, he told himself. He felt a genuine affection towards her, especially because of Alba, who had helped her with some personal problems. When Alba had passed away, he had given the housekeeper a piece of jewellery from his wife's trousseau, a wrought pendant with a small sapphire encrusted in the middle. Señora Berenguer had been speechless upon receiving it and had polished it every week since. Alba had also bequeathed some money to the cherished housekeeper, alongside a few of the other long-standing servants.

If Señora Berenguer had been the apple of Alba's eye, his own favourite, like his father's before him, was without doubt Simón Casona. The two men were kindred spirits, united by a shared passion for horticulture. His respect and admiration for the old man knew no bounds. While many others had used his friendship to gain favours, the head gardener had never asked for anything, not even when he had needed it. Diego remembered the time there had been a terrible leak in the gardener's bedroom ceiling, and how, almost two months later, Don Melquíades had discovered him climbing up on the roof to fix it, in freezing conditions, having used his own salary to pay for the materials. When Diego had intervened, he discovered that not only was the roof leaking, but one of the poor man's braziers was broken and his mattress was completely threadbare.

'Good God, Simón,' Diego had scolded him. 'It isn't right for you to be in such dire straits and for me to find out only because Don Melquíades spotted you on the roof.'

The good man insisted he could do the repairs himself. Of course, Diego had not consented to it. Not only did he get the roof repaired, he also had the whole room remodelled, making it bigger and installing a fireplace, a small larder, a good wardrobe and a wall clock. In addition, he had had the mattress and bedframe burned and commissioned a small canopy bed and a feathered mattress to be made. The poor man had wept with emotion and said he was not worthy of such lavish treatment.

Things like this were what made Diego feel such a deep affection towards the old man who had been a constant presence since childhood. There was a whole library of good memories involving the gardener inside his head: Simón finding simple solutions for the most complex problems; his pearls of ancient wisdom on the subject of trees; the great comfort he had been after Alba's death, when he had made Diego reflect on the life and death of everything on this earth; the unwavering way he managed his inferiors, firm yet affable. Simón was highly cherished at Castamar, not to mention indispensable.

The duke walked among the flowerbeds. It was dark now, and he would not have seen the old man without the lamplight. He found Simón by the tool shed.

'Isn't it a bit late for you to be working, Simón?' he asked, as a breeze came down from the mountains, foreshadowing the changing season.

The man continued gathering his tools and smiled. Diego felt that Simón, illuminated only by the lamps, was like the ancient, primitive force of nature itself.

'Your grace, the fertilizer must be delivered to the plants at the correct moment. You know that better than anyone,' Simón replied, hanging the spade on its hook.

'Leave that and come over here,' Diego ordered gently, indicating that it was time to stop working.

'Wait, your grace. Just a moment,' Simón answered, knowing his friend would indulge him.

Diego sighed and waited for the old man to put away the last of the tools, knowing how important it was for this tireless spirit to finish things properly. He remembered being a child and Simón always telling him, while teaching him to care for the plants in the greenhouse, that if a job was worth doing it was worth doing well.

'I would like to ask you something,' Diego said.

The man nodded and Diego waited a moment before formulating his question, not wanting his curiosity to be misinterpreted.

'The new kitchen girl,' he said.

The old man smiled, making it clear he knew exactly what this was about.

'She's an angel, your grace,' he answered.

'Señora Berenguer has told me that she is educated. In fact, the name of her father, Doctor Belmonte, is not unknown to me. I'm told he was a respectable man.'

'The girl's education is abundantly clear,' Simón said.

'What I don't understand is why a girl with her education would rather work in a kitchen than marry or be a governess,' he speculated.

Señor Casona shrugged. 'It's certainly strange. A girl of her beauty and diligence could conquer the heart of any man.'

Diego nodded. The girl was very beautiful, and although she might well be over thirty, she was still young enough to be fertile and find a good husband. Her misfortune had been not doing so when her father was alive and able to give her a good dowry and a respected name within Madrid society.

Diego enquired no further about Señorita Belmonte. Aside from confirming what he had already suspected just from being in her presence, the old man had also revealed his special fondness for her. Simón took his leave and walked away with his slightly hunched gait. He had barely gone a few yards before Diego addressed him again.

'By the way, Simón, do you know who cooked lunch today?' he asked, trying to downplay the importance of the question.

The old man, wiser and more astute than his friend, smiled. He knew the duke's way of trying to make important questions sound insignificant.

'Without wishing to offend you, that is a matter you should take up with Doña Ursula. Your grace knows what will happen if I tell you.'

'Very well,' Diego said. 'I'll wait for her to return.'

He did just that, and after Alfredo and Francisco had retired to their chambers, he revelled in a solitary dinner fit for a king. He enjoyed a delicious soup, savouring the flavours of basil and mint, the soft centre of the bread, the egg threads and the capon meat that had been cooked to perfection. Next, the sommelier uncovered the porcelain dish to reveal a beef fillet stew, cooked over a low flame in onions, garlic and fresh peeled tomatoes. He breathed in its aroma, detecting the smell of woodsmoke and the rich blend of spices: cumin, coriander, saffron, pepper and a hint of ginger. It was elegantly accompanied by a floral-patterned dessert dish containing an incomparable apple compote, crowned with white tulip leaves. As at lunchtime, Don Melquíades had to swallow hard to restrain himself from commenting on the sumptuous aroma. To finish, there was a light blackberry fool accompanied by freshly baked puff pastries, sprinkled with cinnamon and finely sieved sugar. After Diego had eaten, he was genuinely tempted to ask for another helping out of pure gluttony, but he resisted the impulse and told Don Melquíades that, until Señora Berenguer arrived, he was not to remove the leftovers from the table. He waited there until around eleven o'clock, reading Flavius Josephus's *The Jewish War* and nursing a glass of anis.

It was late when Doña Ursula finally presented herself. She walked over to the armchair by the fireplace, where he was sitting, and curtseyed.

'Your grace, I came to see you the moment I got here.'

Diego nodded and pointed at the plates that were still on the table.

She got straight to the point. 'With your permission, sir, I must inform you that I've been forced to dismiss Señora Escrivá.'

This surprised him. He had assumed the head cook had merely been indisposed and that a substitute had prepared those meals in light of the following day's celebration. Señora Escrivá had worked in the house for years, having started as an assistant when the duke's father was still alive. Though such jobs tended to be carried out by men, when the head cook had died, Señora Escrivá had taken over running the kitchens. This had not been of any concern to him, perhaps because of the sorrow that had taken hold of him in recent years. He could not imagine what problem could have led to such a sudden dismissal, especially on the eve of the annual celebration. He asked for clarification, which the housekeeper dutifully provided.

'It appears she was receiving clandestine nocturnal visits in the cellar from a certain man, with whom she was having... carnal relations.'

'Good grief!' the duke exclaimed. 'Under my roof?'

'And in addition to that crime, the man was helping himself to your grace's wine, with Señora Escrivá's consent.'

Diego's eyes opened wide. He couldn't even imagine that woman inviting a man to fornicate with her in his own cellar.

Luckily, his housekeeper was discretion personified and had doubtless gone to every length to avoid Castamar's reputation being harmed. It wasn't much fun to discover that your servants were having illicit lustful encounters in your house.

'Señora Escrivá. Who would have thought it?' he muttered. 'I imagine Señor Elquiza has been kept abreast of this situation.'

'Yes, but I didn't want to worry your grace and I asked him not to mention anything until I had solved the problem.'

'Hence your absence, I assume,' he ventured.

'My intention was simply to find an urgent replacement for the celebration,' she explained. 'I am sorry that today's lunch and dinner have not been up to standard. For this, your grace, I beg your forgiveness, especially since your friends were—'

Diego got up from his armchair, raising his hand to interrupt her. He sipped his anis and put the glass down on the table.

'Don't apologize, Señora Berenguer. You've acted with the greatest diligence and courtesy, as always.'

'I thank you for your faith in me, your grace,' she said, curtseying briefly.

'You've more than earned it,' he told her.

He understood Señora Berenguer's absence and the discretion they had all maintained, but he still did not know who was behind all those culinary delights. So, somewhat delicately and with a small hand gesture, he got his housekeeper to confirm to him what he had already begun to suspect.

'Who did the cooking today, then?'

'Oh, yes: I've been told it was Señorita Belmonte, your grace, but I assure you there are no grounds for concern. I have a new cook, and his credentials—'

'Forget about him,' the duke interrupted.

He noticed Señora Berenguer's concerned look. Diego sat down on one of the dining chairs.

'You see, Señora Berenguer, lunch and dinner today were quite possibly the two best meals I've ever tasted. I'd venture to say that you would not eat so well at the king's finest banquets.'

The housekeeper's face puffed up as he said this, and she almost shook her head in incomprehension.

'From now on, I want Señorita Belmonte to be our head cook,' he said, a half-smile hovering on his lips. 'You can rest easy – you no longer need worry about the celebration. It's clear that not only is Señorita Belmonte highly talented, she is also extremely diligent and possesses a splendid knowledge of how to run a duke's kitchen.'

Diego, who had never given too much importance to culinary matters, had now experienced for himself the difference between a mediocre kitchen and a superb one. He was certain that both the private dinner before the main dance and the subsequent light supper would surprise all the diners. *Perhaps there will be more eating and drinking than dancing*, he thought, smiling to himself. In defiance of French custom, he had always preferred to avoid unnecessary pomp. He felt that too much food on a table signified not prestige but a lack of reason. But Señorita Belmonte's skill had made him conscious that an extraordinary kitchen could indeed bestow prestige upon him. And his was now beyond compare. He was sure that even Pedro Benoist and Pedro Chatelain, the king's own head cooks, would do whatever they could to employ that girl as soon as they sampled her offerings. Obviously, he would not allow it.

'You may go, Señora Berenguer,' he said.

The housekeeper excused herself with a brief curtsy, confirming that she would do as he wished, before leaving the room in a state of shock. Diego was sympathetic. The poor woman had wasted the whole day travelling to Madrid and conducting interviews there. But the problem, he now realized, was not new but long-standing, and it was his fault for agreeing to let Señora Escrivá take over after Macario Moreno's death. His wife had always worried about the small details: the decorations, clothes, jewels, what food to serve depending on the season – employing her exquisite taste for little things. At one point, she had actually suggested a change of just this kind, but he had not paid much attention, embroiled as he had been in King Felipe's war. Now, the need to have a worthy cook was clear to him – not just because of the prestige it would bring him in the eyes of other noble houses and guests, but also because food would cease to be a simple act of sustenance and become a daily delight.

'Ah, my dear Alba,' he said to himself. 'How right you were to look after the small things.' Then he opened Flavius Josephus's book and continued reading about the Roman siege of Masada.

9

Ursula sat down on the chair, which creaked in complaint like an old woman. She took a sip of hot milk and honey to soothe herself at the end of what had been a long and trying day while she waited in her office for the sommelier, Señor Moguer. In all her many years in service, nothing like this had ever occurred. Having awoken this morning as a mere assistant cook, Clara Belmonte had gone to bed as the new inspector of victuals and personal chef to the duke.

Although a whole host of additional servants had been hired for the occasion, this was no guarantee that the kitchen would be able to cope with the demands of the occasion, and Ursula would keep the details of the experienced cook she had found in Madrid, just in case. She struggled to believe that a woman as young as Clara Belmonte could have impressed Don Diego so much with her artistry that she had been given responsibility for the whole kitchen. But she deemed it even less likely the master had taken a fancy to the girl – something that, were it true, could prove very inconvenient. Although she told herself that the duke would never do such a thing – he was a man of honour and would not bed the girl to make her his concubine – if the girl had caught the duke's eye then he might be tempted to curry favour with her in all sorts of ways, even if this meant undermining his housekeeper's authority. If his sentiments had indeed led him to single her out for special treatment, then the situation would be more serious than Ursula had supposed: the girl had only arrived six days ago and was already in charge of the kitchen. And so, for the moment, she preferred to think that this rapid promotion really was due to the young woman's culinary excellence.

After speaking to the duke, Ursula had roused Elisa Costa from her bed to accompany her to the men's corridor, where she instructed Señor Moguer to get dressed and come down to her office – the other woman's presence vouchsafing the housekeeper's reputation. The two women had then returned to the kitchen, and Ursula had asked Elisa to heat up some milk and honey on the embers of the fire and bring it to her office.

And so, as Ursula sat sipping her drink, Señor Moguer knocked on the half-open door and craned his long neck around it, a hangdog look on his face. She instructed him to enter and to leave the door open behind him. The maid was standing guard outside, at a sufficient distance that she would not be able to overhear their conversation. Ursula gestured to the sommelier to come closer. The latter, trembling slightly, had fear etched upon his face. Perhaps the housekeeper was displeased with his service. Technically, he was not under her direct authority, but he was clever enough to know she was the de facto ruler of the servants' realm and that her word would be enough to have him expelled from it. He approached as instructed and Ursula told him, in a quiet voice, to treat the matter they were about to discuss with discretion.

'Of course, Doña Ursula,' he replied.

'Señor Moguer, I have to confess I am surprised. Tell me, has Señorita Belmonte had any contact with his lordship?'

The man's expression relaxed now he knew the housekeeper only wanted information about what had happened in her absence.

'No. She spent the whole day in the kitchen, as far as I am aware,' he answered.

'Are you sure?' she pressed him, attentive to any sign that he might be covering up for the girl.

'Absolutely,' he said, without a moment's hesitation. 'I attended to the duke personally for almost the entire day... apart from the evening when I was asked to help his lordship's guests, Don Francisco and Don Alfredo, when they returned from hunting. I guess they could have had contact then, but only if the duke came downstairs, because Señorita Belmonte didn't leave the kitchen all day.'

It was clear he was telling the truth, and it was also obvious that any contact between Señorita Belmonte and his lordship had been initiated by the duke and not by the cook.

'The master has told me that, from tomorrow, Señorita Belmonte is to be the new inspector of victuals and the duke's personal chef,' Ursula replied.

'If I may be so bold, I am not in the least surprised. Both the lunch and the dinner that Señorita Belmonte prepared for the servants were simply delicious.'

'I see,' she replied.

She would have to accept the evidence: the girl was clearly highly talented and full of surprises. She thanked Señor Moguer and gave both him and Señorita Costa permission to return to their beds. She leaned back, took another sip of the milk and made a mental note to keep a close eye on the situation.

Every single member of the staff had their secrets, minor vices that she had ferreted out over the years. It was her knowledge of these misdemeanours that enabled her to rule Castamar with a rod of iron: Señor Moguer's mid-morning break for a glass of aniseed liqueur; the furtive glances Elisa Costa directed at the duke's friends, dreaming of an impossible romance with the handsome Marquess of Soto and his like; the shortcomings of the kitchen assistant, Carmen del Castillo; the furtive family visits of the two scullery maids on market trips to Madrid; the tendency of the duke's coachman, Señor Galindo, to drink too much brandy on Sundays; the theft of soap by the laundry maids, and so on, in a long list – at the top of which was the secret belonging to Don Melquíades. She needed to discover the young cook's shortcomings, if she was to keep the girl under her thumb.

Ursula played her own cards very close to her chest. The other members of staff knew little of her life, and none of her secrets, beyond the fact that she was the duke's housekeeper. In the past, she had been oppressed, and she was all too familiar with the terror of not knowing when to speak, sit, eat or give her consent, and so she had sworn that under no condition would she allow herself to be ruled over by another man or woman of her station.

And yet, in just six days, Señorita Belmonte had evaded her control, and the housekeeper scarcely even knew how it had happened. The cook's independent character, her training, the determination with which she overcame problems, her talent in the kitchen and a faint air of intellectual superiority, combined with her undeniable beauty, made Ursula suspect that any weaknesses she had must be well hidden. She finished off her hot milk and told herself that, if she was not careful, Clara Belmonte could become her rival.

16 October 1720, morning

Ursula appeared in the kitchen just as Clara was washing Rosalía's hands with water she had heated on the stove. Clara's first thought was that the housekeeper had come to upbraid her about something. However, Ursula instructed Clara to follow her, and the cook felt a sense of nervous anticipation as they made their way up the stairs to the wing of rooms where the duke's personal servants lived.

'His lordship has informed me of his wish that you should be head cook at Castamar,' the housekeeper informed her.

She spoke the words without even turning to look at her, and Clara was so surprised that she kept her head bowed so Doña Ursula would not see her flushed cheeks and her smiling face.

Before they reached the corridor where the chambermaids' bedrooms were located, Ursula stopped in front of an oak door. On it was a small wooden sign indicating that the kitchen servants' quarters lay beyond. On the other side was a long corridor, interrupted at regular intervals by doors which stood to attention like obedient soldiers. Most of the kitchen staff brought in to cater for the celebrations had been installed in these simple rooms. As Clara walked down the passageway, she deduced, from the way they acknowledged her, that everyone else had already been informed of her elevation. They ascended a staircase that led to the senior servants' rooms. Five doorways gave off one side of the corridor, with a sixth at the far end.

When they reached it, Doña Ursula opened the door. From the impassive expression on her face, Clara understood that she was not best pleased by the situation. The housekeeper was undoubtedly surprised by the turn of events and perhaps suspected that Clara lacked the ability to supervise an event such as the one that was about to take place. In fact, Clara's whole life had been a preparation for this. As assistant cook in the Alberoni household, she had often been in charge of a team of staff, cooking for the many visitors who were entertained by his eminence. At the same time, it was also true that she was a bundle of nerves, worried by the prospect of failing to deliver and all too aware that producing a meal for five or ten was not the same as providing for the huge number of guests expected at Castamar. She assumed that, in such cases, Señora Escrivá gave the menus to the other cooks who had been hired for the occasion, and supervised their work to ensure it was performed satisfactorily. And that was the approach Clara also planned to take – rather than doing any cooking herself, she would supervise to ensure that everything was correctly seasoned and cooked to perfection, and that each dish was presented appropriately.

'I would be grateful if you could tell his lordship just how honoured I am by his decision to place his trust in me,' she said to the housekeeper before entering the bedroom.

'These will be your quarters from now on,' was Doña Ursula's only reply as she handed her the key. 'Your salary will be increased to twenty-five reals a day, with another four reals for your duties as inspector of victuals.'

Clara opened her eyes wide in surprise. It was almost as much as a head cook at the royal court would have been paid. She would even be able to save some money to put towards the purchase of a house!

The room was furnished only with the bare essentials, but to Clara, it was as if she had been assigned one of the bedrooms reserved for the duke's own visitors. In the right-hand corner stood a wide bed with a wool-stuffed mattress, fine linen sheets and a pair of pillows. On top of it sat a pile of neatly folded blankets and a bedspread. There was also a narrow wardrobe to the left, a shelf, a brazier and two oil lamps. On the wall hung a small mirror, its reflective surface somewhat blemished, the gold paint peeling from the frame. Two fresh candles stood on the small table beneath the room's only window. Fortunately, thick curtains obscured the view of the world outside.

'I assume you will take care of Rosalía, just as Señora Escrivá did. Otherwise, she will have to be taken to the poorhouse,' Doña Ursula said, in what sounded like a severe warning voice.

Clara, who had crossed the threshold, turned around and was silent for a moment as she tried to imagine the feelings this woman harboured in her soul.

'There's no need to have her taken anywhere, Doña Ursula,' she replied calmly. 'I'm sure it won't be hard to take better care of her than Señora Escrivá did.'

She sensed that the housekeeper was annoyed, and when Doña Ursula took a step towards her, Clara had to make an effort to hold her gaze.

'Don't forget, Señorita Belmonte, that I am in charge here,

and that as far as I am concerned, you are still on probation. Now that you have seen your new room, you can return to the kitchen.'

Clara curtseyed, put the key in her apron pocket and, sensing Doña Ursula's eyes boring into her back, made her way down the corridor. She looked forward to the days ahead, relishing the thought of taking charge of the kitchen, even though she knew it would be hard work. By the time the sun had risen, she had already prepared breakfast. She asked Emilia Quijano, one of the scullery maids, to feed Rosalía and take the girl out to play in the back courtyard.

Not long after, an army of scullery maids, boot boys, kitchen porters, cooks and ushers reported to her. To accommodate the expanded staff, the three side kitchens were opened up, and the cooks and other servants were assigned to them. That night, there would be a private supper for the family's closest friends, and after that, the celebrations would start, and the guests would continuously consume food and drink in abundance. A fireworks display in the gardens would light up the sky above Castamar. And the party would continue throughout the following day and the one after.

During the course of the day, Clara drew up the menus for lunch, for the private supper and for the food to be served at the banquet. There would be soups and consommés, with rich stock made from chicken, pigeon and beef, some to be prepared *au chaudeau*, thickened with egg yolk and flavoured with wine, cinnamon and sugar. These she assigned to Martín Garrido, a cook whose references praised him as an expert poultry chef. She sampled one of the stock pots and added some spices and a pinch of salt. Garrido accepted her instructions without complaint. Garrido would also cook some of the starters, including braised pigs' trotters, stuffed eggs, pheasants in mushroom sauce on a bed of celery, and platters of cold meat and pickles.

The second kitchen, under the supervision of Jean-Pierre de Champfleury, would be responsible for cooking the larger cuts of meat and the game pies. Accustomed to having free rein under Señora Escrivá, Champfleury was far from amused when Clara instructed him to serve the fillets of duck breast on a bed of orange sauce, to make a more elaborate garnish for the goose and to flavour the partridges with truffle. After receiving her suggestions, the Frenchman had turned away and muttered to himself in his own language, in the belief that she would not understand him. 'I won't permit a woman to question my palate. The seasoning is perfect.'

Clara had smiled politely and replied, 'Of course you will permit it. That's why you are here.' The cook didn't say another word and Clara, after drizzling a little stock over the goose and sprinkling a touch of grated truffle onto the partridge fillets, declared herself satisfied. When it came to the large cuts of meat – fricandeau of beef loin, leg of pork, braised kid – she barely made any adjustments, and congratulated him warmly.

In her own kitchen, she had a third cook under her instruction, Alfonsina Serrano, a dependable woman who was not exactly an inspired chef but was humble and hard-working. Unlike the Frenchman, she didn't mind being corrected. She was put in charge of preparing platters of roast quail, woodcock, capons and chickens. Later, she would prepare poultry that had been grilled slowly while being basted with a mixture of breadcrumbs, lard, egg yolk and pepper. The desserts would be prepared by a team of confectioners whom Clara had instructed to make puff pastries, sponges filled with cream and chocolate, milk buns, cherry tarts, custard, crème brûlée and fruit stewed in syrup.

Clara drank some water and dried the sweat from her forehead with a clean cloth as she checked the menus for that evening and the following day. As she reviewed her instructions, she looked up for a moment and glanced out at the courtyard. At first, she didn't give a second thought to the figure she saw on the other side of the glass, instead concentrating on the stews. *They must be cooked slowly, until the garlic softens and the onion is golden, then seasoned with some good wine, vinegar, cloves, pepper,*

*saffron and a little water. The meat is to be cooked over a low flame
on a bed of lardons, spiced and with a little ginger.*

Next, she reviewed the fish dishes for those with a lighter
stomach. She glanced out of the window again and saw the
silhouette of a person climbing one of the pillars, towards the
roof of the coachyard. No doubt somebody had been instructed
by the estate office to carry out repairs. She returned her attention
to the list of sea bass, plaice, eel, grouper, turbot, lobster, clams,
and shrimp fritters.

Finally came the drinks. She had decided to serve a selection
of refreshing beverages throughout the day: lemon water,
iced milk, tiger nut *horchata* with lemon and orange zest,
and cinnamon water. And, of course, there would be aniseed
and brandy liqueurs, and the very finest red and white wines
from Valdepeñas, Jerez, Alicante and Malaga. Needless to say,
chocolate would be consumed in every form, and ice would be
required to keep the drinks cool.

She moistened her fingertips and turned the page to check
the final sections of her notes, when her eyes once again alighted
on the blurred form outside. The individual was climbing the
pillar with their own hands, without using a ladder. Clara slowly
approached the kitchen door, curious to know who the climber
was. As she made her way across the room, she continued to
scrutinize her notebook, running through the instructions for
the preparation of tomorrow's stews, with chickpeas, cabbage,
sausage, black pudding, pork stuffed with egg and breadcrumbs,
chicken and potatoes. Each department was to follow her
instructions to the letter, including in matters of decoration,
with floral motifs, pastry shapes, chocolate moulds, carved fruit,
pheasants' feathers arrayed to represent a peacock, and a whole
world of shapes and colours. *Every garnish on every dish must be
presented...* Her train of thought was suddenly interrupted as she
realized who the climber was. Taking a deep breath and trying
not to think about the wide-open space of the courtyard, she
looked out. There, almost at the ridge of the roof, was Rosalía,

more than five yards above the ground. Clara's first instinct was to rush outside but it was as if her body was chained to the threshold. She forced herself to take a step forward, feeling herself trembling and cold sweat beading on her forehead.

'Don't climb any higher, Rosalía!' she shouted impotently from the doorway.

The girl looked down, holding on with one hand as she waved at Clara with the other.

'I want to fly!' she answered.

Clara clenched her teeth and took another step forward. Behind her, the whole kitchen was suddenly thrown into turmoil.

'Rosalía! Come down now!' she cried hoarsely. The girl, seeing the servants below, hesitated. Clara could feel her strength draining and pressed herself against the courtyard wall. Rosalía took another step.

'But I can fly…'

Clara tried to shout again, but her strength failed her, and it was all she could do to stop herself from falling to the ground in a faint. Rosalía carried on climbing. The scullery maids and Carmen del Castillo were screaming at her. Suddenly, the service door flew open. Elisa Costa ran across the yard and stood in front of Rosalía.

'Come down immediately!' she shouted, pointing at the ground.

Rosalía began to descend and, when she reached the bottom, burst into floods of tears.

'You've been told a thousand times not to climb up there,' Elisa scolded her.

Clara felt as if she was going to be sick. She needed to make her way back inside and pretend she was okay, but she was rooted to the spot. Elisa turned towards her and hesitated for a moment as she saw the look of panic in her eyes. Then she took Rosalía by the hand and led her towards the kitchen. Clara bit her lip but she was trembling as wave after wave of nausea hit her. Everyone would discover her secret. She looked away and saw that Elisa had stopped and was waiting for her. Closing her eyes and stretching out her hands in front of her like a blind person, she allowed Elisa to guide her. Clara couldn't bear to look at the courtyard, afraid it would swallow her up, as she made her way back to the kitchen with Elisa's help. When they were inside, Elisa hugged her and told her Rosalía was safe and that she should not worry. Clara leaned on her shoulder, grateful for the opportunity to regain her composure. Eventually, she was able to stand on her own two feet. Work in the kitchen had already resumed, as if nothing had happened. Having recovered her strength, Clara went over to Rosalía, who was curled up in a ball in the corner, and scolded her.

'But I can fly,' the girl replied, sucking her thumb.

'No, you can't! Don't you understand? You can't!' Clara yelled. 'So don't try it again. Ever!'

'Every now and then she climbs up there,' Elisa explained. 'It isn't the first time.'

Clara nodded. 'Thank you,' she said, taking Elisa's hand again.

Elisa shook her head, as if it was nothing to worry about, and marched off with a carefree air. Clara returned to her menus, still keeping a close eye on Rosalía, who was soon fast asleep. She would have to be watched more closely. If something happened to the poor thing while she was in Clara's care, she would never forgive herself, and Doña Ursula would no doubt use it as a pretext to have her expelled from Castamar for negligence.

10

16 October 1720, before breakfast

Diego had gone out with Señorita Castro to show her around the estate. It had been his mother's idea, and they were joined by the duchess and Don Gabriel but not by the marquess, who was a late riser. While Gabriel and the duchess showed Señorita Castro the fishponds, Diego, pulled along by his memories, decided to head straight for the wooded spot he used to ride to with Alba on mornings like this. He stroked the neck of the steed that had belonged to his wife and galloped until he reached the location, where the solitude brought him a certain joy. He went straight through the oak grove, passing the chapel and the family pantheon on his right, until he reached the stream. Every time he set foot in this remote spot, he remembered the day when everything had changed.

That morning, nine years ago, he had risen early because Queen María Luisa had organized a gathering with hot chocolate and sweet pastries. He had been sitting in one of the Buen Retiro Palace's sunlit courtyards, discussing the politics of the day and the ongoing war with Alfredo and Francisco when Alba had burst onto the scene, her exuberant figure clad in that charming sky-blue dress of hers. Her hair was tied up in a bun which left her slender neck on display, and she had removed the hat that had been partly obscuring her face and her immense blue eyes. She had walked among the guests, stopping to greet them, unconsciously cultivating a climate of expectation, as if the queen herself had just entered.

Francisco and Alfredo had greeted her, and she had coquettishly allowed them to help her sit down as she took out a pearl-lined fan. Then, with that smile of hers that could bring down an empire, she had drawn Diego's attention to her displeasure, publicly announcing that he had completely forgotten their morning horse-ride. Alfredo had smiled and predicted that Diego's armada would be defeated before the battle had even started.

After taking leave of his friends, Diego had returned to Castamar with Alba, who had chided him for his insolence and described how he would be punished in the most horrific ways possible. He laughed now as he recalled it. Life for Alba was pure pleasure. She had loved riding, dancing, reading, music, laughing and, above all, travelling. She had already toured Europe before marrying him. However, the war had got in the way of her desires, and she had spent her last years feeling hemmed in.

'When will it all end?' she had said to him once. 'Those Catalans will never give in.'

'They certainly have no intention of doing so, and I am sure they will fight until they can fight no longer,' he had answered.

And so they had. The town of Cardona, unsuccessfully besieged by the Bourbons, bore testament to that. The stronghold had laid down arms only at the very end of the war, after the fall of Barcelona. He had to acknowledge the courage of the Catalan people and the respect due to them. For Alba, though, the war was simply a nuisance. She hated the violence, which she felt was more befitting of animals than men.

Diego entered the wood, down the path they used to ride along together. He ascended the gentle incline along the riverbank, and once he'd reached the top, he stood up in his stirrups to admire the landscape. Under that immense canopy, as he listened to the Cabeceras flowing rapidly into the Manzanares, he travelled back to the moment when he had lost his wife. They'd come there after a race, which, as always, she had won. They had bet her birthday celebration on it, although it would have gone ahead no matter who won. *It was an annual fixture, no matter what*, he thought, smiling sadly. He remembered how she had laughed and kissed him, knowing she would be the winner regardless of the outcome.

'You miss her, I suppose.' A woman's voice cut short his painful reverie.

His horse tossed its head and he turned to be faced with Señorita Castro. He looked at her delicate skin and her pleasing features, her slender lips and straight nose. She came closer, mounted on one of the Castamar horses. He tipped his head to one side to greet her, aware from the voices in the distance that his mother and brother must be close by.

'A great deal. Alba and I were very close; we had known each other since we were children. She died after being trampled by this horse,' Diego explained, stroking the animal's golden mane.

Señorita Castro fell silent for a moment and gazed at him intensely, as if she were trying to convey she understood and was sorry for his loss. Diego returned her look with a more straightforward one, intended to convey he did not need her consolation. Señorita Castro broke the silence by directing her gaze towards Diego's mount.

'Many would have had him put down.'

He smiled and sighed at the same time.

'It was not the horse's fault. Something scared him and I couldn't stop him,' he said brusquely.

Amelia slipped her hand over his. Diego observed her touch and looked her in the eye. The contact with feminine skin was pleasing. It had been so long that he'd almost forgotten that delicate pleasure.

'I imagine you must have suffered a great deal,' she whispered.

'That doesn't matter,' he answered somewhat bitterly, withdrawing his hand.

'Of course it does, Don Diego,' she said, taking his hand again.

He looked at her, trying to gauge whether her pity towards him was real or if it was motivated by some other cause. Perhaps it was a mixture of both. Something about her expression told him she was no longer the sweet and innocent damsel he had met some years ago. The woman before him seemed more serious, weighed down by the suffering that comes with experiencing the sorrows of life. They remained silent for a few moments until they heard the voices of his mother and Gabriel looking for them.

'Ah, there you are. Come, dear Amelia. I'm about to show you one of the most beautiful views of Castamar,' his mother said, sitting elegantly atop her horse like an Amazon.

Amelia gave Diego one last look.

'Excuse me,' she said, innocently caressing his hand as she withdrew it.

She rode over to Doña Mercedes, and Diego gestured politely while Gabriel slowly approached him. His brother stopped and looked over his shoulder to make sure his mother and Señorita Castro were out of earshot.

'Be careful,' Gabriel said, looking distrustful. 'She's not the tender young thing we once knew. Yesterday I saw her whispering to Don Enrique de Arcona.'

Diego nodded, wondering if the pair could be plotting something. From what he'd been told, they'd met by chance at the theatre. She did not, however, seem like the kind of girl who would try her hand at intrigue. Neither could he understand what could link her to a man like the marquess.

'Thank you, brother,' he answered, before spurring the horse to catch up with his mother and her guest.

Diego still did not understand what had happened that fateful day. After the race, Alba and he had ridden side by side as she talked about the urgent need to refurbish the entire east wing of the palace and he had remarked that it had not been a month since work on that part of the house had been concluded.

'I know. But it needs to be different.'

'Why?' he'd asked.

She'd fallen silent, making it clear she had a secret. A smile had lit up her face, before it was distilled into a sentence that had filled him with immense joy.

'Because it's too gloomy for a child.'

He had stopped the horses, looked at her searchingly, needing only the glimmer in her eyes to grasp her meaning. He had told her he loved her, drew her close and kissed her.

His eyes still shut, he felt his wife's face brutally tugged away from his. When he opened his eyes, his own horse was already rearing up on its hind legs. He'd managed to control it, and when he looked to the right, he had watched his wife's horse, also in a frenzied panic, fall backwards. Experienced rider that she was, Alba had tried to tug the reins and settle the horse like he had done, but it was impossible. Her horse had jumped backwards and fallen to the ground. Realizing she was about to be trapped under the horse, she had tried to leap to one side as it fell, but it had been too late, and she had crashed down onto the ground beneath her mount. The animal's hindquarters had fallen on her chest in a movement like a rocking chair, breaking her delicate bones with a sickening crunch. The horse had got up immediately, fracturing more bones as it did so. Alba didn't even make a sound. By the time Diego could react, her chest was already crushed and the last traces of life were ebbing out of her with each futile attempt to draw breath.

No one could understand why the horses had reacted like that. The senior groom, Belisario Coral, couldn't explain it. He had conjectured that the horse might have been frightened by a snake, one of the vipers that were so common in the hills around there, or perhaps an insect bite. Not that it mattered to Diego. Burying her had been the worst pain his soul had ever experienced. In those dark days, he did nothing but weep for the dead bodies of Alba and his unborn child, and since that fateful day, he had needed to believe that Alba was still, in some incomprehensible way, present at Castamar – there in spirit, watching over him and those he loved.

He halted his horse, overcome by a thought that filled him with terror. Something had inexplicably stirred within him, and for the first time in nine years, he felt that Alba had been gone from Castamar for a long time. He knew he was the only one still clinging to the past.

They all returned by the long path, Diego avoiding Señorita Castro's furtive glances, his mother describing the estate's many superlative qualities to her, and Gabriel, as always, in silence, trying not to attract attention. When they reached the stables, the head groom and some of the stable boys held the reins for them to dismount. Then Señorita Castro grasped his forearm as they headed down the paved walkway towards the main building.

'I'm not sure you've ever been to my homeland,' she said. 'It's so beautiful.'

'I have properties in Seville, Malaga and Huelva, but not in Cadiz,' he replied. 'Perhaps I should acquire some land near your father's estate. Its beauty is famed even here in Madrid.'

A fleeting smile crossed her face and she fell silent. Diego felt that his politeness had put the young woman at ease.

They entered through the main door and, led by Don Melquíades, reached the drawing room, where the table was already laid with fine Talavera china on a cloth of La Coruña lace. They were greeted by the aroma of toasted bread, chicken consommé, fresh eggs, freshly baked pastries, sweet and savoury *tortas de aceite*, hot chocolate and wonderfully light madeleines, as well as some cold cuts of mountain ham and other cured meats. The marquess, impatient to sit down for breakfast, was waiting for them.

'Finally, you're here!' he said, briefly gesturing to greet the duchess, Señorita Castro and the duke, while pointedly ignoring Gabriel. 'I don't think I could have put up with the delicious fragrance of this food any longer without sinking my teeth into it.'

They sat down at the table and Diego gestured to the head butler for the footmen, led by the sommelier, to serve the consommé. When the porcelain lid was lifted from the tureen, Diego waited a few seconds as the conversation gradually faded to silence. He shared a complicit look with his brother, who laughed noiselessly at the other end of the table. After sampling the consommé, his mother closed her eyes, trying to hold on to that majestic flavour; Señorita Castro, praising the food to the heavens, had to taste several consecutive spoonfuls to keep that intense sensation on her palate; the marquess frowned, unable to comprehend how a simple soup could possess such character.

'I envy you, my friend,' Don Enrique said. 'These dishes have been assembled by a cook of the very highest standards.'

'Don't let him go, my child,' Diego's mother commented as she savoured another spoonful of the soup. 'That man is one of a kind.'

Diego nodded, enjoying the breakfast as much as the others.

'The cook is a woman. And yes, she certainly is unique,' he answered.

A new silence settled, peppered with further sighs, and when the madeleines arrived, Diego repeated that his new cook was a real treasure.

'A truly gifted woman,' his mother said. 'I assume she's not married?'

'Indeed not,' Diego responded. 'According to Señora Berenguer, she's educated too.'

'So she can read and write?' the marquess enquired, sceptically.

The duke just nodded. He savoured the chocolate, as smooth as cream, a perfect blend of initial sweetness and bitter aftertaste. The marquess raised his cup of chocolate as he finished off his pastry, declaring that it was quite extraordinary to have an educated cook.

'I've been told she knows English and French, not to mention the dead languages,' Diego replied.

'Good God!' Don Enrique commented. 'With such gifts I'm not surprised she hasn't married. A woman like that would be unbearable as a wife.'

They all nodded in agreement with the marquess. He had, however, stirred something inside the duke. Perhaps the image of that sweet girl cut too sharp a contrast with Don Enrique's speedy dismissal. The marquess's assessment was surely correct. It would have been easy for an educated young woman like her to find a husband if her father was alive and able to provide a good dowry. But now he was dead, her education had become a disadvantage, because such a cultured woman, capable of reading the English empiricists or the French rationalists in the original, would leave any husband feeling like a simpleton. Even some nobles might fear such a woman, let alone common men who could barely read a royal proclamation.

Don Enrique was right, and yet, despite this, Diego shot an annoyed look in his direction. The marquess did not catch it. The duke felt that this throwaway comment had been charged with a subtle impertinence. He noticed that he was being taken by one of his fits of anger, accompanied by a strong urge to make his feelings known. He restrained himself and concentrated on the delicate flavour of the madeleine.

His mother said she was surprised a woman like that had not found a husband while her father was alive. 'Does she not want children?' she asked.

'Perhaps she's not attractive enough, or too old,' Don Enrique said.

'Quite the opposite,' Diego said.

His brother, who had noticed his impatience with the marquess's tone, gave him a look from the other side of the table to remind him not to act impulsively. But his thoughts were no longer on Don Enrique. Rather, he was once again taken by the curiosity regarding Clara Belmonte that had been boiling up inside him for days now. It suddenly struck him that her coming from a respectable family and his seeing her at work in the kitchen was what had set his thoughts off-kilter. He still did not know whether working in the kitchen was a consequence of her misfortune or if it was motivated by her excess of learning. Unannounced, Diego got up from the table. The others had no time to react and scrabbled to stand as a sign of respect.

'Forgive me,' he said hurriedly as he walked towards the kitchen, to the astonishment of all his guests.

16 October 1720, during breakfast

Clara tutted discreetly. Doña Ursula had appeared just as a large number of servants had gathered behind the door, drawn by the aromas coming from the kitchen. In that brusque tone of hers, she had asked what they were doing there, salivating over food they would never taste. They had all tried to disperse but the housekeeper stopped them and ordered them to enter the kitchen.

'As you know, Castamar's annual celebration begins tonight and I trust that everything will be quite perfect, just as Doña Alba would wish it to be, for though she is no longer with us, she is still the spirit of this house. If I witness any further idle behaviour in any of you, there will be instant consequences. I hope that's clear. Now be off with you,' the housekeeper ordered.

Doña Ursula waited for them all to leave and gave Clara a look, indicating that the warning had also been aimed at her. Yet Clara could see that the housekeeper was still unconsciously inhaling the vapours which filled the whole room and the adjacent corridors with delicious fragrances, even as she stepped out of the kitchen. Just then, the duke appeared. Doña Ursula curtseyed, her face colouring with surprise.

'Does your grace need something?' the housekeeper asked.

Seeing him in person before her, Clara had immediately curtseyed along with the rest of the team. Don Diego completely ignored Doña Ursula's question and walked past her and into the kitchen without even answering.

'Is your hand alright, Señorita Belmonte?' the duke asked.

Bewildered, Clara nodded. From the corner of her eye, she confirmed that the door was still half open and the housekeeper was watching them.

'Yes, your grace, thanks for your concern,' she answered.

The duke looked at her. Clara gulped, not knowing what to do or say. Don Diego did not seem to mind that the entire kitchen staff was standing right there, contemplating this unusual scene. Rosalía, who had just woken up, pointed at his lordship from her hiding place.

'Don't worry, sir,' Clara said, expecting the duke to get angry. 'She doesn't really know what she's doing.'

Don Diego walked over to Rosalía and gently stroked her face.

'How are you, Rosalía?' he asked. 'Don't worry,' he said, turning to Clara. 'She's the daughter of my late wetnurse, someone for whom I had a great deal of affection.'

'I didn't know, your grace,' Clara answered, trying to control her nerves.

'I've come down personally to see you,' he said.

The kitchen staff, heads lowered and frozen stiff in the duke's presence, dug their chins into their chests and gave each other furtive looks. Clara blushed and noticed Doña Ursula taking a step into the kitchen. Don Diego came closer to Clara, and once again she smelled that fragrance which reminded her of her father.

'I wish to ask you a question,' he continued.

Clara forced herself to keep her composure, but her burning cheeks gave away how she felt inside.

'Your grace,' she said, resting her gaze on the duke's beige dress coat.

'Look at me,' he ordered.

She obeyed him, discerning in his amber eyes a deep sadness living alongside a fearless strength.

'An interesting conversation arose as we were enjoying your exquisite cooking. It was suggested that it is strange for a woman of your education to not be married but, rather, be earning a living in the kitchen. It has even been proposed that you lack any aspirations to do so,' he explained plainly.

Clara gulped before answering, weighing up her words so there would be no misunderstandings.

'Nothing could be further from the truth, your grace. A suitable marriage is one of my aspirations, but I must confess that I love cooking as much as life itself. That's why I told Doña Ursula how honoured I am that your grace has placed his trust in me. I feel very lucky.'

'More than if you were married to a good husband?' he asked.

'Yes.'

'How is that possible? Isn't a woman's natural aspiration marriage and delivering a new generation?'

More than simply discovering her opinion on the matter, he seemed to be putting her to the test.

'It certainly is. My father always taught me to think that things should be so, your grace,' she answered, more calmly now. 'But my mother also taught me that I could have other aspirations beyond marriage.'

A quiet sigh, one which didn't go unnoticed by her or Don Diego, was heard among the servants. Clara saw that the servants were wide-eyed with amazement, and although they said nothing, they were awkwardly glancing at each other.

'So must I conclude that you do not wish to marry?' he said, still looking at her.

She lowered her head for a few moments before looking at the duke again.

'I don't know if I'll ever find a man willing to put up with such thoughts, judged, as they are, to be inappropriate for members of my gender. When I'm cooking I feel completely satisfied,' she explained. 'And I am convinced that marriage with any man would take me away from that happiness.'

Then the duke did something that caught her by surprise – he came closer to her and, his mind made up, inclined his head towards her as he would do with a lady.

'Not all men have the same character. I'm sure that in the future you will find someone who not only puts up with your thoughts but feels proud to have a wife who thinks that way, Señorita Belmonte,' he said.

She couldn't even answer him, simply curtseying along with the rest of the room as he left, and when she looked up, she met Doña Ursula's astonished gaze. Clara turned to find her bearings in the kitchen, her legs trembling. Out of the corner of her eye, she noted the housekeeper's continued presence, trying to understand what was going on – a question Clara herself could not answer.

16 October 1720, after breakfast

By the time Diego returned to the room, the marquess had already finished breakfast, the duchess was resting in one of the armchairs, and in another corner, Don Gabriel was chatting to someone about some trivial matter. Diego sat down as if just a few seconds had passed and the conversation that had caused him to leave had not finished.

'She won't marry because she loves cooking,' he explained succinctly to the marquess.

Don Enrique raised his eyebrows quizzically, making it clear that he considered the duke's behaviour inappropriate, and the duchess exchanged a rapid glance with the marquess.

'My dear friend,' he said, smiling, 'it was not my intention to upset you. I didn't know you took these light-hearted conversations so seriously.'

Again, Diego detected that condescending tone and felt forced to back down, putting on a false smile. His mother's guest seemed to have a special skill for using social conventions to disguise cutting remarks aimed solely at him. Perhaps his first impressions had been right, after all. He steadied himself and looked at the man without blinking. The marquess returned his gaze, and that was when he detected a dangerous glint behind that perfectly framed smile.

His mother smiled at him. 'What Don Enrique means, my child, is that it doesn't matter what the cook thinks,' his mother clarified.

'Of course,' Enrique answered.

The marquess held Diego's gaze for a few moments more before going over to Doña Mercedes, who smiled and suggested a game of draughts. Diego grabbed his cup of chocolate as he considered that perhaps Don Enrique's subtle barbs had a purpose and were not merely his natural way of being. The man's smile had sent a subtle message that he did not fear the duke at all. But the marquess seemed unaware of the beast within Don Diego that he was provoking. If he continued to do so, that monster would make an appearance, and Don Enrique would almost certainly come to regret his behaviour.

11

16 October 1720, mid-morning

Hernaldo heard someone knocking at the door and opened his eyes. He assumed his daughter, Adela, had gone out to the market while he was still asleep. He sat up on his miserable straw mattress and saw that the fire was barely smouldering from the night before. Dust floated in the shafts of light that filtered through the gaps in the shutters. There was another knock and Hernaldo put on his worn leather trousers and his boots, unsheathed his épée – a gift from his master – and grabbed a sharp knife. Madrid was not a safe place, and even less so for him, who had arranged for many unfortunate souls to meet their Maker. It was quite possible that a brother or other relative of one of his victims might come seeking vengeance, and he accepted the prospect of such a death as one of the risks of his trade. He shouted to warn whoever was out there that, if they knocked again, he would gladly slit their throat.

'Who's there?' he asked, approaching the door.

'A delivery,' a boy's voice replied.

Hernaldo half opened the door. A boy, no more than twelve years old, was standing outside.

'Here you are, sir,' he said, handing over a small package wrapped in cloth.

Hernaldo accepted the object and dismissed the boy. He slammed the door shut and undid the package. Inside was a key. This was good news for his master, Don Enrique of Arcona.

The marquess would now have complete freedom of movement within Castamar. Obtaining the key had been the first of the tasks Enrique had entrusted to him. The second would have to be performed today, and it involved Doña Sol Montijos, a woman whom it was wise to treat with caution. The Marchioness Sol Montijos was a useful ally of the marquess. However, Hernaldo was unaware of the precise terms of the marquess's request for her assistance. All he knew for certain was that Doña Sol was to attend the private supper that night at Castamar with her husband, and that her presence played a part in Don Enrique's plans. She had requested a few days to consider what price to ask in exchange for her services. Hernaldo couldn't imagine what it would be. Doña Sol Montijos was a formidable woman, married to a man twenty years her senior; she was as cunning as a snake, with fire in her belly. Finally, last night, he had received a note from the marquess stating that Doña Sol had *established her recompense*. Hernaldo, who had only barely been taught to read and write by the village priest, always struggled to unravel the marquess's elaborate language and had on occasion asked him to simplify his style. Only after puzzling over the lines for some time had he understood the order. He was to visit her to gather the information.

He put his sword back in its scabbard, threw a leather jerkin over his shirt and strapped a dagger to his back. If his years in the tercios and the battles they had fought across Europe had taught him anything, it was that there was no such thing as honour in a duel, only a sordid fight to the death won by whatever means possible, including the tricks he had picked up both in the army and the back alleys late at night. In such situations, the only thing to do was to kill as quickly and cleanly as possible, and that went double if one's adversary was a fellow soldier. The alternative was to risk one's own demise.

Hernaldo had an infallible ability to sense the fear beating inside the breast of others, fear that reflected what had happened to Spain. The country had been reduced to a façade; the greatest empire in Europe was now little more than a French puppet. *Jesus Christ! Half a lifetime fighting those bastards and now they're in charge.* And so, when the new king had ordered that the tercios be disbanded some fifteen years ago, Hernaldo had known his military career was over. His only option had been to sell his sword to whoever was willing to pay him a few reals to do their dirty work. He had soon ended up in prison in Seville, condemned to the gallows for spilling the guts of two porters and a nightwatchman in an unfortunate encounter at the inn in Tresaguas.

Hernaldo downed the contents of his brandy glass, and as he relished the way the burning sensation in his throat reminded him he was still alive, his memory took him back to that filthy hole where he had suffered a year of beatings and humiliation from his jailers. He had finally come to accept that he would draw his dying breath at the end of a rope, soaked in his own piss, when a man had come striding down the passageway as if he were in the royal palace in Madrid. The scent of his perfume had mingled with the stench of shit that permeated the prison. The man had stopped in front of him, a jailer by his side.

'This is the one,' the jailer had said. 'He's due for the gibbet tomorrow.'

Hernaldo had looked up for a moment, and the aristocrat, holding a handkerchief to his nose, had scrutinized him.

'He might be just the man I need.'

The jailer had struck Hernaldo to make sure he was listening, but he had barely felt the blow, inured as he was to such treatment by a year of beatings. The jailer was swearing at him when the aristocrat raised a hand, gave the man a few reals and told him to retire. Then he had turned slowly. With his stick, he had lifted the hair from Hernaldo's face and tilted his head back as he pronounced his name. Hernaldo had looked at him with apprehension, convinced that the visit of a nobleman could only bring him more pain before he was finally allowed to quit this life.

'Don't worry, I'm not here to harm you,' Don Enrique had said, upon seeing the man's terrified face.

'What do you want from me?' Hernaldo had asked, shrinking back.

Then the marquess had uttered the words he would never forget for as long as he remained on God's earth.

'You are about to die, Hernaldo de la Marca, but if you listen to me, you could still have plenty of years ahead of you,' Enrique had said, crouching down next to him.

Hernaldo had shaken his head in bewilderment. Don Enrique had spread his hands and smiled as if talking to a child.

'Do you want to die on the gallows tomorrow?'

Hernaldo had squirmed, realizing that an answer was expected of him.

'No, sir.'

'Listen to me,' Don Enrique had said, as he brought his face closer, still covering his mouth and nose with his handkerchief, and rested his stick on the man's shoulder. 'We are at war. A war that will decide the fate of Europe, Spain and the king. You have served the house of Habsburg for your whole life and I'm afraid you will no longer be able to do so, but you *can* serve the house of Arcona.'

Hernaldo recalled now how that proposal, which had fallen into his lap, as if from the sky, had garnered in him immense gratitude towards this man, his guardian angel – even if it was clear the marquess had not gone to the prison in search of Hernaldo de la Marca in particular, but rather in the hope of finding any man who matched his requirements. Hernaldo remembered how he had grabbed the marquess's hands and kissed them, and how Don Enrique had withdrawn a little.

'Get me out of here and I swear I will serve you as faithfully as I served Archduke Carlos. The very last drop of my blood will be yours, sir,' he had said.

Don Enrique had raised a finger. 'You can start by not touching me unless I tell you,' he had said with a faint smile as Hernaldo begged his forgiveness. 'Before we seal our pact, I want you to understand something. You will be released into my safekeeping. If you betray my trust, you will be returned to this place, and I will personally ensure that your jailers make what is left of your life a living hell. Do you understand?'

Hernaldo had nodded, and swore he would have no other master, that he would die by his master's side.

'I will become the instrument of your wishes. I will not fail you,' he had said. 'You have my word.'

The marquess had stood up and touched the head of his stick to the prisoner's lips, instructing him to keep silent.

'There will come a time, Hernaldo, when you will have to choose between loyalty and betrayal. Remember today's words. Loyalty is only tested when the storm is at its fiercest,' he had said, before disappearing down the passageway.

That had been fifteen long years ago. Since then, he had served the marquess through good times and bad and, just as he had sworn, was prepared to die for him if the need arose. Serving the Habsburgs had brought him nothing but misfortune, and the Bourbons had cast him aside after his many years of service. Don Enrique, by contrast, had shown himself to be noble, cunning, brave and cautious all at once, not to mention highly capable and influential. Some time ago, when the marquess had ordered him to arrange the unusual death of Castamar, he had almost been successful. Very few were familiar with the details, and had they been revealed, everyone involved would have ended up on the gallows, but Doña Alba's tragic accident had been one of the occasions on which he had demonstrated his loyalty. Nobody could explain why her horse had crushed her like that.

For Hernaldo, however, there was no mystery at all. He had arranged the whole sorry business: he knew an apothecary, one of those who specialized in the kind of knowledge others preferred to steer clear of. He had walked halfway across Madrid to the apothecary's shop on Calle de los Reyes, at the very edge of the city. There, Vicente Hermosilla had given him the solution he was looking for. The old man had found a weapon that had at first struck Hernaldo as witchcraft, something that would leave no trace: a simple wooden whistle. When Hernaldo saw it, he had stared in blank disbelief. But then the apothecary had showed him how he could use it to commit murder without leaving a trace. He had put the whistle to his lips and blown, but no sound had come out. Suddenly, the apothecary's mastiff appeared from the backroom and sat down at his side.

'People can't hear the whistle, but animals can,' Hermosilla had informed him.

'It's like magic,' Hernaldo had said.

'Not at all. It's just nature. With one whistle, the dog comes, and with two...' He had blown again, and the hound returned to where it had come from. 'You see.'

'And what exactly am I supposed to do with this?' Hernaldo had asked.

'Ah, Hernaldo, I'm sure you are highly skilled in the use of arms, but in this case, you must use the whistle to train whatever animal you wish. Associate the sound with pain, with rage, with whatever you want, so that the animal itself becomes the cause of the death you wish to bring about. You could, for example, train a dog to attack upon hearing the whistle. Nobody would know you were involved – it would seem like an accident.'

The man had come up with the perfect solution to the question of how to send Don Diego to his death without anyone suspecting foul play. It was said the duke had proved his valour on the battlefield, and Hernaldo respected him for that. However, his own personal feelings towards the Duke of Castamar were neither here nor there. The target of his plot had been Don Diego and not his wife, but that day, the couple had swapped their mounts. If fate had taken a different course, it would be the duke rather than his wife whose body was rotting beneath the soil. *All that effort for nothing*, he had told himself, time and time again. Luck had not been on his side, but it was only a question of time.

He armed himself with a flintlock pistol and headed for the house of Doña Sol Montijos, intent on performing the task his master had charged him with. If there was one thing of which he was sure, it was that, one way or another, Don Enrique would assure his own position as a Spanish grandee – and the downfall of Castamar.

The kitchen was a hive of activity: pots sat steaming on the hotplates, wood and charcoal blazed in the stove, servants were gutting fish and boning meat, cooks were preparing almond sauce, basting roasts with lard, covering poultry with strips of bacon, and candying fruit in sugar. The hubbub had distracted her from thinking about the incident with Rosalía, which had almost cost the poor girl her life, and about Don Diego's unexpected visit to the kitchen. Clara recalled Doña Ursula's astonished face. An appearance of that kind by Don Diego was unusual enough in itself, but it was the way he had taken his leave of the head cook, as if she were a lady, that had made the scene so remarkable. Clara smiled at the memory, feeling a tiny thrill at the thought that she had escaped the housekeeper's control.

The racket had prevented her from speaking to the new assistant who had taken Clara's old place in the hierarchy when she had been promoted: Beatriz Ulloa, a clumsy girl who lacked any real skill. Clara assumed that Doña Ursula had taken her on in order to prevent Clara from choosing a protégée of her own from among the temporary staff. Clara had set her to supervise the scullery maids, keen to ensure she would not hinder the more experienced assistants.

Clara stirred the stew and tasted it to check the seasoning. She added a little red wine, incorporating it slowly. Then she left it in the hands of Alfonsina Serrano and looked again at her new assistant, who would be sleeping in the same alcove in which she herself had awoken that very morning. The girl's work was shoddy, and the batonnet cut she was using to slice the potatoes was uneven. However, Clara recognized in those brown eyes the look of the survivor, the steely glimmer of someone who, like her, had suffered and had overcome adversity.

As she made her way to the other kitchens, the melody of a harpsichord being played with great virtuosity floated down from upstairs. She remembered the day when she had been sitting practising at the keyboard with her sister, waiting for her father to arrive for lunch. Hearing a knock on the door, she had rushed to welcome her father and give him a hug. But instead of her father, it had been a courier bearing a letter from the War Secretary, Don José de Grimaldo. Upon reading it, she had had to sit down as her mother and sister stared at her and asked her what had happened. Clara, her eyes brimming with tears, had taken some time to answer.

'Nothing. Nothing's happened,' she had said.

And then she had fainted. When she regained consciousness, everything had changed: her father was dead, and she had become afflicted by a nervous condition that gave her a paralysing fear of open spaces. Some days later, the secretary himself had informed them of the true circumstances of her father's death.

'He died like a hero and a patriot,' Don José de Grimaldo had declared.

Apparently, a Habsburg detachment had found a way through the Bourbon lines and planned to attack her father's hospital camp, in search of food and opium. Upon being warned of the assault, her father had organized the defence, setting a small squadron of the least seriously wounded soldiers to guard the bridge over the Tajuña River. While they defended the camp, he had ordered the reserves of food and opium to be hidden, and sent the other patients and the womenfolk to safety across the river. Later, it was discovered that one of the king's nephews had been among those patients.

'Your father held out for almost an hour, but when he saw

that the bridge was about to fall and he realized the Habsburgs would massacre the wounded if they crossed the river, he blew the bridge up beneath him,' the secretary had recounted in grave tones. 'I mourn his loss. Your father was a brave man. He saved many lives that night. I know that the king, upon hearing the news, said he should be granted a posthumous award.'

But the award had never arrived. The war swept many people's good intentions aside, though Clara was never able to understand why His Majesty had failed to honour his word. Ever since then, she had known nothing but poverty and suffering.

Her thoughts came to a halt as she turned the corner and found herself face to face with Doña Ursula, who was descending a wide staircase. Next to her were two girls who, to judge by their aprons, appeared to be kitchen assistants. The housekeeper gestured at Clara to stop, as if she were conducting an orchestra. Clara could tell she was still disconcerted by Don Diego's unexpected visit, and she struggled to suppress a smile.

'Their Excellencies Don Diego and Doña Mercedes, together with Don Enrique and Señorita Castro, are to have a picnic in the gardens of Villacor,' Ursula informed her, without any preamble.

'One of the ushers has already notified me. I understand that Don Gabriel will also accompany them,' Clara replied.

'That is correct,' the housekeeper responded, raising her eyebrows slightly.

Clara perceived a certain awkwardness in Doña Ursula's demeanour, perhaps because she resented having to serve a negro. She supposed it was understandable, and yet, if Don Gabriel was a free man, he had the same right to enjoy his liberty as any other, and if the duke had been brought up with him as if they were brothers, then it was to be expected that he would love him as one. Clara herself felt no discomfort at the prospect of cooking for him. After all, she prepared the meals for the servants, many of whom were beneath her in rank. And if the master had asked her to cook for his livestock, she would have done so without complaint.

'These are your two new assistants for the celebrations,' Doña Ursula said, changing topic.

Dolores Carvajal and Benita González, both at least ten years her senior, greeted her politely but with a hint of scepticism in their eyes.

'Delighted to meet you,' Clara said, unthinkingly greeting them as if she were a lady.

She immediately realized she had once again been betrayed by her upbringing and couldn't help but feel irritated at herself. The two women looked at her, unsure what to say, and curtseyed clumsily. Doña Ursula frowned, and Clara sensed that she would use this slip to strengthen her grip.

'You are both to follow the instructions of the head cook. Señorita Belmonte, can I have a word?' the housekeeper asked.

Clara nodded and gave instructions to her two assistants to start preparing some fruit compote. Grimacing slightly, Doña Ursula remained silent until the two assistants had left. Clara patiently waited for her attack.

'Señorita Belmonte, please take care not to mistake the kitchen for his lordship's ballroom. These maids have no use for your courtesy – they are here to work,' she said, in a tone that brooked no dissent.

Clara waited a moment before replying.

'With all due respect, Doña Ursula, I speak to people with the courtesy that my mother instilled in me. I don't see how my good manners can do these girls any harm.'

It must have been the first time anyone had spoken to her in such a way, because Doña Ursula opened her eyes wide and cut in.

'I am sorry, Señorita Belmonte,' she said coldly. 'It is clear that your mother taught you excellent manners, just not the right ones for handling the staff of a kitchen. And it appears that your mother didn't spend much time in such places, other than for her own amusement.'

Clara clenched her fists and was about to respond, but Doña Ursula denied her the opportunity.

'It is also clear that she failed to teach you when to remain silent and follow an order,' she concluded. 'Treat the servants appropriately; we can't have everyone getting ideas above their station. Now get back to work.'

Clara did as she was told and walked in the direction of the kitchen. She was aware that this display had been more of a reaction to the scene the housekeeper had witnessed that morning than to her own excessive politeness towards her new assistants. Even if her courtesy was unusual, it could hardly be the source of such annoyance. She could feel Doña Ursula's eyes boring into her back as she walked down the corridor. She turned to check whether the housekeeper was still there and, just as she passed the stairs to the floors above, noticed a figure who must have been listening in on the exchange. It was Elisa, who, pressed up against the wall, gestured to her to say nothing and continue walking. Clara remained silent. At the other end of the corridor, the housekeeper was still ruminating on something.

It was not until later, when she entered the main kitchen after having supervised the activities in the other two, that she found Elisa Costa waiting for her in the courtyard, carrying a basket of neatly folded and pressed linen. Upon seeing Clara, Elisa gave her a sign and made straight for the service door at the other side of the yard. Clara nodded discreetly and headed for the corridor. She waited there until Elisa appeared at the far end.

'I heard the old witch. Don't worry, she's like that with everyone,' Elisa whispered.

'I noticed. Even Don Gabriel,' said Clara.

'She can't stand serving a negro,' Elisa replied. 'She's got such a high opinion of herself...! I mean, it's understandable. They say they're not like us, that they're not very clever. But Don Abel, the duke's late father, raised him like a son.'

Clara realized that Elisa was a simple sort, very fond of talking. She knew that the manners of the humble classes, to which she herself now belonged, were very different to those she had learned from her parents. It was a world in which people were blunt and to the point, where everyone belonged to the same group, where they all knew each other and nobody minced their words – perhaps because they all experienced the vicissitudes of life as one.

'That old witch could never stand having to treat a negro like a master,' Elisa went on. 'She hated it so much, apparently, that she was on the verge of leaving. Don Diego even told her she should quit if she didn't like the idea.'

'But she stayed,' Clara said quietly. 'She loves having power over the servants.'

'That's right. But she's a sour old hag. Even her husband couldn't bear to stick around her,' Elisa said, raising her voice without realizing it. 'Years without a man will make you like that!'

Clara looked around, aware that somebody could appear at any moment.

'Keep your voice down,' Clara implored, laughing.

'The old witch can't hear me – I saw her go upstairs,' Elisa answered.

They were laughing when, from the other end of the passageway, they heard Rosalía cackling. She had appeared like a ghost and suddenly started to shout, 'Old witch! Old witch!' giggling without the slightest hint of malice. Clara and Elisa ran to quieten her. Just when Clara was explaining that she shouldn't say such things, she sensed the kitchen door move slightly as if someone, on the other side, had been listening to their conversation the whole time.

12

16 October 1720, midday

Melquíades was writing in his notebook. Ever since being named head butler at Castamar after the death of his father, Don Ricardo Elquiza, he had been filling these ledgers with the most important events of each day. Once a notebook was full, he'd file it in numerical order on a shelf in his office. He fancied himself as a chronicler, describing each day in great detail, even adding illustrations. Of course, he had no intention of publishing them; it was just a form of personal entertainment, as well as a way of making sense of life on the estate.

Now, as he waited for his nephew, he was describing the attempt to dismiss Clara Belmonte, as told to him by his good friend Simón Casona. It seemed that the promotion of the young woman, until then, just one servant among many, had taken everyone by surprise. As soon as they heard that a humble servant girl had taken Señora Escrivá's place, rumours had spread among the staff like wildfire. Malicious tongues even went so far as to say that the girl had won the duke's heart. Of course, Melquíades had used his authority to quash this rumour as soon as he'd heard it. But it hadn't been until mealtime the following day that the chattering tongues had fallen silent.

The taste of Clara Belmonte's chickpea and spinach stew had left everyone perplexed. Used to Señora Escrivá's plain cooking – bread soup, stuffed aubergines and an oversweet pudding – that meal had tasted like manna from heaven. Some asked her, as they ate, just how she had obtained such a flavour. Somewhat timidly, the girl had explained how the spinach, chickpeas and potatoes should be cooked on a low flame in an earthenware pot, with the boiled egg added at the end.

After that first meal, there had been no further discussion about the motive behind her promotion. The housekeeper, however, had not yet tasted the young woman's cooking, having spent the previous day in Madrid looking for a cook. She had merely tasted that morning's breakfast, and Don Melquíades could tell from the way her eyebrows had shot up that it had surprised her. He knew her too well: Doña Ursula had said nothing because her pride had forbidden it. He had to admit that this brief loosening of the housekeeper's iron grip over Castamar felt like a gust of fresh breeze in high summer.

The first time he had set eyes on Doña Ursula, he had judged her to be the perfect housekeeper, and despite being hounded by the woman for all these years, there was no doubting it was still true. Before Doña Ursula had discovered his secret, Melquíades had felt deeply drawn to her. Perhaps it was her diligent way of going about things, her perfectionism and the dedication she put into her work. He never failed to acknowledge that, behind her surly expression, she was a very good-looking woman. He had once secretly held on to the hope that, somewhere inside that desolate wilderness, there might flourish a trace of pity, and perhaps, by watering it with his affection, he might discover the more human side of that woman of steel. This had turned out to be a futile dream, and as time had passed, his hopes had faded. And now, he cursed his stupidity every time he recalled how she had abused his trust and discovered his secret.

It had happened some months after she first entered Castamar as housekeeper, by which time he was already stealing discreet glances in her direction. Just as Melquíades had been on the verge of revealing his tender feelings, she had destroyed any possibility for affection of that kind. He remembered in precise detail how Doña Ursula had entered his office to inform him that Doña Alba, that angel of a woman, required his presence. Don Melquíades, who had been writing in his diary at the crucial moment, had rushed off with the housekeeper, leaving his notebook open upon the table. He had been halfway there when he had realized his mistake and, as meticulous as always, he had sought to correct it immediately. Doña Ursula had offered to put the diary away for him so that he could get to Doña Alba without delay. His naivety had turned him into her puppet.

'I'm counting on your discretion,' he had told her.

'Of course, Don Melquíades,' Doña Ursula had replied without blinking.

So, he had asked her to put the notebook he'd left on the table in his small cupboard, handing her the key. The gullible butler had headed to the room where Doña Alba was waiting. While the lady of the house revealed that she was with child and that she wished to surprise the duke that very afternoon, Doña Ursula had discovered the letter, accidentally or otherwise, as she was putting the notebook in the cupboard. That accursed letter had compromised his entire future. He had placed it inside the notebook two days earlier, when someone had interrupted him just as he was weighing up whether to destroy it or not. Then he'd forgotten about it. That lapse of concentration and his naivety had condemned him to play the part of the fool in a ridiculous tragicomedy. He scolded himself harshly for lacking sufficient courage to reveal the nature of the letter, and the impious acts described within, to the duke. Until he did, he was putty in Doña Ursula's hands.

He despised himself for his cowardice and for the feelings he had felt towards her. He told himself he was less than a whole man, a broken puppet bearing fake medals of authority. Several times he had been on the verge of confessing to the duke, but he had always ended up retiring to his quarters, trembling and drenched in sweat. He had often considered leaving the estate, but at fifty-five he would struggle to find another job as head butler. Besides, Doña Ursula could still use the letter to destroy his reputation wherever he went. That's why he was a prisoner at Castamar, just like Don Gabriel – both of them prisoners in gilded cages.

Two knocks at the door interrupted his writing. His nephew, Roberto Velázquez, dressed impeccably in livery, stood before him.

'You called for me, Don Melquíades?' he said.

'I did, Roberto. As you know, today, his lordship will take lunch in the gardens at Villacor,' he said. 'Tell the head groom to prepare two carriages to accompany them.'

As he'd expected, the boy found this strange, since the master and his guests wished to walk to the gardens. It didn't make sense to take carriages. He waited patiently for his nephew to question him. He wanted to get it across to him that a good manservant should always anticipate any situation and stay one step ahead.

'I beg your pardon, Don Melquíades. Don Diego himself has said that their excellencies will go on foot.'

'I'm guessing you're not familiar with the gardens at Villacor.'

The boy shook his head and lowered his chin slightly.

'They're less than half a league to the west,' Melquíades said. 'My intention is that you do not make mistakes others have already made.'

The boy nodded nervously, unclear as to where his uncle was going with all this. Melquíades waited a few moments. The advice his nephew was about to receive had been imparted to him by his own father.

To serve is to anticipate your master's wishes, he'd said. *Anticipation is an essential quality for any good servant.*

Now it was his nephew's turn to be taught.

'It's far enough away that, were it to rain, their excellencies would be completely soaked by the time they arrived,' he explained. 'Make sure the carriages are available just in case.'

'Thank you, Don Melquíades,' said the boy.

You must always plan to prevent such inconveniences from occurring. If it comes up, it was your idea all along. Is that clear?'

After straightening his collar, the butler put his hand on his nephew's shoulder and told him he was doing well. The boy left the room almost on tiptoe.

Melquíades detected the intoxicating aroma of game casserole. That fragrance stayed in the air even after his nephew had closed the door, giving him a taster of the food they'd be eating today. It reminded him that there was someone new in the kitchen – someone very different who might unknowingly ring in great changes. He would have to get to know Clara Belmonte personally, he thought, since at the end of the day, he was still the head butler on the estate – even if in name only. Swayed by the delicious aromas, he let himself believe that one day Castamar would be his again.

With each hour spent at Castamar, Enrique felt more at ease. Don Diego had shown himself to be a rather surly man – not as distinguished, he thought, as one would expect of a Spanish grandee. The statesman that dwelled within Don Diego was educated and well-read, trained since childhood to govern Castamar and be one of the chosen few at court. And yet beneath that skin was hidden a wild beast which would, it seemed, given free rein, destroy everything in its wake.

The dart thrown at breakfast had been followed by other comments on topics such as servants and slavery, opinions which, though commonly accepted among noblemen, he knew would meet with Don Diego's disapproval. He noticed that his comments had begun to irritate the duke without the others even realizing what he was doing. Soon he would ramp his comments up a notch to rile the duke even further.

Enrique had known about the duke's weakness in dealing

with his servants since before arriving at the estate, but over the past few days, he had seen it with his own eyes – that way he had of addressing the head butler, the clear respect he displayed towards the housekeeper, and the anecdote Doña Mercedes had told on the day of his arrival about scolding a guest for mistreating the gardener. To Enrique, as to most noblemen, that was all a waste of time. Machiavelli had said in *The Prince* that he who builds on the people, builds on mud, and if forced to choose between them loving you or fearing you, the latter was preferable. Enrique was indifferent to his servants' love for him, and he had none whatsoever for them. Servants were meant to serve from the mud from which they came. Besides, a master should ration his servants' liberty, since most of them did not know what to do with it. In general, the humble classes were dim-witted simpletons, and they would never be his equals.

Now, as he walked towards the Villacor gardens with Señorita Castro and Don Diego, he ruminated upon his plan's progress thus far. Finding a candidate to seduce Don Diego hadn't been easy. She had to fulfil certain requirements: give the appearance of respectability while still having known men, be trained in the ways of seduction and, most of all, be manipulable, caught in a difficult situation which he could take advantage of. After waiting and waiting, watching all the noble and rich families who had fallen upon misfortune, she had appeared by chance. Doña Mercedes had revealed her existence to him in a throwaway comment.

Believe me, Marquess, the only young woman to have received any attention from my son at all is Señorita Amelia Castro. A delicious creature, from a respectable Andalusian family, though they lack titles. Furthermore, had my son fallen in love with her, I would not have opposed the marriage, despite her lineage, for the simple reason that it might have shaken him out of his sorrow. But nothing came of it.

So, he had focused all his attention on Señorita Castro's

misfortune. And now she was walking guilelessly ahead of him, completely at ease, employing her arts of seduction on Don Diego, just as Enrique wanted. Don Gabriel followed behind, not taking his eyes off him. That fool had no idea what lay in store for him.

'Actually, Don Diego, I didn't see Villacor on my last visit,' Señorita Castro was saying.

'Well, that was an unforgivable oversight, and one we shall rectify today,' Don Diego replied.

Enrique, who could not stand this type of conversation, distracted himself by thinking about how he had added to Señorita Castro's misfortune. He had bought her estate and the debts left by her father before meeting all her outstanding payments; he was largely responsible for spreading the rumour around Cadiz that she was a certain gentleman's kept woman, and finally, after nudging her into misfortune and despair, he had discovered through a female acquaintance of his, Verónica Salazar, that Don Diego's defences were beginning to weaken.

'Doña Mercedes says this is one of your favourite places,' Señorita Castro was adding.

'We all adore it, especially in spring, when it's at its greenest,' Don Diego said, smiling.

Poor Señorita Castro, Enrique thought. She had no idea that his intrigues had provoked her flight towards Madrid. Enrique had simply waited for her to come begging for help. Finally, they had met at the Corrala del Príncipe.

'What about your mother, Don Diego? Won't she walk with us?' Enrique said, entering the conversation.

'She left early. She loves to walk to Villacor in the morning,' the duke answered.

Amelia Castro gave Don Diego a coquettish smile.

'If I had known, I might have gone with her. A lone woman with two men… what will people think?' she said.

Careless, Enrique said to himself. If she wished to gain Castamar's hand, she should not leave out Don Gabriel. With her comment, she had made it clear that she did not see the African as a true member of the family, but rather a domesticated beast of burden, while for Don Diego, he was a brother. Even so, he knew the duke would not dwell on it, accustomed as he must be to such lapses.

'I give you my word that you will be in no danger. You are in the presence of three gentlemen,' the duke replied.

She realized her slip and smiled sweetly at him.

'I am satisfied, Don Diego. No one could feel safer, protected by two Castamars and the Marquess of Soto.'

Enrique smiled in response to such praise, though deep down he did it more because he saw she had realized her mistake. They heard the clunking sound of a wheelbarrow, and to their left, there appeared the enormous, slightly hunched figure of the gardener. The man stopped, took off his cap and greeted them.

'Good morning to you, your grace, and to all of your honourable companions.'

'Good morning, Simón. We were just on our way to Villacor,' the duke replied affably.

'It's wonderful at this time of year,' the man responded wistfully.

Don Diego and his brother stopped for a few moments to pass the time with the gardener. Meanwhile, Enrique strode over to where the young woman was standing.

'Señorita Castro, we were interrupted yesterday,' he began, 'and I was not able to tell you that I do not wish you to feel uncomfortable in my presence.'

'Quite the contrary, Don Enrique, you cannot imagine how grateful I am,' she answered serenely.

'I don't wish for you to thank me at all,' he said, walking with his hands behind his back. 'You know my motivations. Just let me act as a benefactor to you.'

'More than you have already? To accept that would be discourteous.'

He noted how agitated she had become. He could sense that little head spinning, trying to work out if those words were true. He reached out a gloved hand to touch hers.

'I understand.' He nodded. 'You're right, we've only known each other for a few days. To make you understand my noble intentions, this very morning I have ordered my administrator to pay off all of your debts in my name… yours and your father's. That includes buying back the family house. You are no longer in debt.'

'But Don Enrique!' she whispered, her eyes wide in amazement.

He was amused by Señorita Castro's trembling lips, which reflected her fear, her bewilderment, her incredulity. She had run away from Cadiz, from her creditors and her tattered reputation, only to find herself in the hands of a single creditor. In a flash, the poor woman had realized that, despite his altruism, he was now the master of her entire life.

'I… will never be able to repay you,' she said.

'Hush, don't worry. I couldn't bear the idea of watching you suffer while it was within my means to help you. A fine lady such as yourself cannot be put in such a lowly position.' He smiled attentively. 'Besides, you will struggle to win Don Diego's hand without a dowry. You know well that it would be seen as an unequal marriage.'

In a way it already was, in that she had no title, while Don Diego was from an ancient, noble lineage. In her favour, it was widely accepted at court that the duke would die a bachelor.

'I don't wish to offend you,' Señorita Castro said hesitantly, looking at him in astonishment, 'but tell me the truth. What do you want from me?'

Don Enrique did not answer and smiled serenely when he noticed that the duke and Don Gabriel were approaching from behind.

Unobtrusively, he walked away from Señorita Castro, giving

the impression of an understanding between the two of them, while Don Diego positioned himself to the other side of her and, further away, Don Gabriel flanked Enrique, still watching him closely.

'Your servants are highly competent: the kitchen, the gardens. I'm most impressed, Don Diego,' Señorita Castro said flatteringly.

'The servants are one of the best things about Castamar,' said Don Gabriel, unexpectedly taking part in the conversation. 'My brother has always had a reputation for taking great care of them.'

Enrique felt the African looking at him. His meddling was a real hindrance. He appeared at the least convenient times and places, as on the first day, and would not take his eyes off him. He reminded himself that he was still a long way from being able to give that insolent man the punishment he deserved. He had to rein in his impatience.

'The gardener seems a little old to be in sole charge of so much land,' he commented, without so much as glancing at Don Gabriel.

They'd reached the end of a path that ran between dry reeds and rocky sand. The landscape was peppered with oaks and voluminous grey granite rocks from the local mountains.

'He is, Don Enrique, and though he has more than enough help, he's as stubborn as a mule,' Don Diego answered. 'Our head butler, Señor Elquiza, has provided seven gardeners for him, but he always ends up doing the work himself instead of delegating.'

'It's a common flaw in a servant's nature that they are unable to govern others,' said Don Enrique.

'I've read somewhere that a servant's bad behaviour is usually caused by a master who cannot govern well,' Señorita Castro commented with a sweet, candid smile.

'I can only agree with Señorita Castro,' the duke answered. 'A master's poor orders will be carried out by their servants just as diligently as good orders. I'd say that there is as great a variety of characters among servants as there is among those of high birth.'

'I disagree, my friend,' Don Enrique countered. 'It's commonly acknowledged that, in general, servants don't possess the strength of character necessary for governing others, and it's only in exceptional cases that one of them shows any inclination towards command, for example the best butlers and stewards.'

Don Diego did not answer, simply shrugging his shoulders to put an end to the argument. Don Enrique remained silent, telling himself that the duke was showing the same weakness of character that his father had demonstrated by bestowing freedom upon a negro. As he walked, he felt that, despite his manoeuvre with Señorita Castro, he would have to take the initiative there and then, if he wanted his strategy to pay off. They walked for half an hour longer, and this time, Señorita Castro, having learned from her errors, included Don Gabriel in the conversation.

Beneath a great oak at the top of the hill, they found Doña Mercedes, ensconced in a seat and surrounded by a small group of servants. A little way off was a small farmhouse. The duke told them it had not been opened for a long time but was in perfectly good condition. As he came nearer, Enrique saw that, from the hill, you could make out the Alcázar and the river Manzanares in the distance. After greeting Doña Mercedes, he reclined on a small velvet-upholstered divan which must have been taken from the house. He stayed there contemplating the views, captivated by the beauty of the moment, and asked to be brought some grapes and a glass of sweet wine.

'Don Diego, this divan is incredibly comfortable. I'll have to commission an identical one of my own,' Enrique said.

The duke smiled and remarked that it had been his wife's favourite. Enrique felt his smile freeze, and for a few seconds he could make out Alba's angelic face right before his eyes, whispering the wonderful words she used to say to him every time they saw each other at gatherings, dances and spectacles at the Buen Retiro Palace: *You are the handsomest man in the whole court.*

13

16 October 1720, before lunch

Sitting in her office, half an hour after the masters had set off
for Villacor, Ursula repeated to herself that if she wanted to
rule over the kitchens as she ruled over the rest of the household,
then she needed to know more about Clara Belmonte. *Everyone
has their secrets*, she thought to herself. *Everybody has a past.*

Her own past had not been without its fair share of trouble.
She had married Elías Pereda at the age of twenty-eight, fleeing
from her father's insults and blows. In her innocence, Ursula had
thought him a good match, with his position as head groom for
the Baron of Robles. She had convinced herself that he offered
an escape from the hard life she led with her father. She had
never loved her husband. He, however, had been besotted with
her, at least to start with, but once they were married, she had
soon become little more than someone on whom to take out
his frustrations when he lost at cards. He would come home
from the tavern drunk and angry and force himself upon her.
And she never knew whether to resist him and risk a beating
or simply resign herself to the inevitable. Once, she had taken
a knife from the kitchen with the aim of defending herself, but
he had smiled, as if her small act of defiance only increased his
pleasure, before savagely beating her with his belt.

Less frequently, he would come home at night, euphoric at
having won a few reals, and throw himself down beside her,
reeking of sweat and wine, stroking her hair and telling her he

loved her and couldn't live without her. On those occasions, Elías told her that she was to blame for his ill humour, that he didn't want to hurt her, that he only did it because she was so stubborn. But the worst had still been to come.

Thanks to Father Aurelio and the nuns of the convent of Our Lady of Miracles, where she had learned reading and writing along with some arithmetic and geography, Ursula had risen from a position as maid to the post of housekeeper. Her father, an idle slob, had only allowed her to work so that she would be able to support him, but she had managed to squirrel away enough coins to permit herself a degree of independence. Elías, by contrast, had demanded that she give up work immediately, saying he couldn't permit his wife to work when his wages were more than enough for both of them.

Her neighbours had congratulated her on her good fortune, for finding a man like Elías who was willing to look after her. They had had no idea. Her marriage degenerated into a farce. All Elías had wanted was for Ursula to dedicate herself to his needs while he went out whoring. *I've married a monster*, Ursula had thought to herself. *If I leave him, he'll kill me.* Once, Ursula had been watching through the window as he reeled home drunk, and one of the neighbours had asked him if he was going to beat his wife. Elías had replied, with a smile, that Ursula was good for nothing else.

'You'll kill her one of these days,' the man had replied.

'Don't worry,' Elías had replied, exhaling a cloud of wine fumes. 'Somebody has to keep my bed warm for me.'

That night he had tried to force himself upon her several times, but his manhood had failed him. Each time, he had hit her and accused her of being frigid.

Ursula had brought the marriage to an end one night in 1704. In the cramped kitchen of their small dwelling, Elías had looked at her in disbelief when she had told him she was leaving.

'What are you talking about, woman? You're out of your mind,' he had said as he slurped his soup directly from the bowl.

She repeated what she had said, summoned up her courage, looked him in the eye and told him she had never loved him and had only married him to slight her father. He had merely looked at her with contempt.

'Ursula, you can't leave me. I'm your husband. Bring me some more soup before I lose my temper,' he had ordered, dismissively.

'Get your own soup,' she had replied, and with a lifetime's worth of anger that had accumulated inside her, she hurled the bowl at him.

He had hesitated for a moment. Then he took two steps towards her, but she had stood firm, her eyes blazing. Elías slapped her so hard that her eardrums had vibrated. Her jawbone had crunched; she had lost her footing and fell to the floor with a split lip.

'Don't play with fire, Ursula.'

She had got up slowly, her mouth smeared with blood, and faced up to him.

'Your power over me ends tonight,' she had spat defiantly.

Elías had raised his fist, his face contorted with rage. But she had stood her ground, her chin jutting out defiantly. Just as Elías was about to strike, there had been a loud knock at the door followed by the cry, 'Open up, in the name of the king!'

Elías had frozen. Then he had turned to look at Ursula.

'What the hell is this?' he had asked, as he moved towards her, pulling a knife from his waistband. 'What have you done?'

Anticipating his response, she had already taken shelter behind the table, from where she shouted that the traitor was trying to kill her. Elías had overturned the table and chairs, but the front door had burst open, and he had found himself staring at a squadron of soldiers, all training their muskets on him. He had been accused by his own wife of collaborating with the Habsburgs.

Many suspected that Ursula had made up the accusation to rid herself of a violent husband, yet nobody said a word. Elías had a few friends in the neighbourhood, but none who were prepared to speak out to defend his innocence. With the war at its height, taking the side of someone found guilty of treachery carried too many risks. Some of the women had exchanged a silent and sympathetic gaze with her on the day she left Calle de la Palma. But the majority had been less understanding, accusing her of provoking him into losing his temper or of worse things still.

Ursula hadn't looked back. With the money she had set aside, she had headed for Castamar, where she had secured a position without her husband's knowledge. The estate was some way from the city, and by the time he regained his freedom, if he ever did, he would be unable to find her. Little had she imagined that her past would not relinquish its grip on her so willingly.

A knock on the door of her little office called her back from her reminiscences. Ursula instructed the person to enter, and the new assistant cook, Beatriz Ulloa, timidly stepped over the threshold. Ursula knew that, despite her naive appearance, Ulloa would not miss a chance to capitalize on any situation.

'Excuse me, Señora Berenguer, I don't want to seem nosy but—' she said, feigning reticence.

'I hired you to be nosy, girl. Otherwise, it would be best if you packed your bags,' Ursula interrupted emphatically, to make her requirements quite clear and avoid wasting any time beating around the bush.

'Yes, Señora Berenguer, that's why I'm here. Señorita Costa and Señorita Belmonte were talking...'

She stopped, perhaps wondering about the consequences if her role as informer were subsequently discovered.

'I don't have all day,' Ursula said.

The girl nodded and resumed her account.

'They spoke about your bad temper, and Señorita Costa said that you're bitter because you haven't... had a man for a long time,' the young woman concluded as she lowered her head and blushed. 'She even dared to say that... your husband... left you because you're... an old witch.'

Ursula was well aware of what the servants said and cared little about it. She had heard all manner of rumours and tittle-tattle, some of which she had even found amusing. A girl, who hadn't lasted long, had believed she made secret pacts with the devil and fornicated with him at night. *God Almighty*, she had thought, *some people allow their imaginations to run away with them when they're afraid.* And so, she was unaffected by Elisa Costa's opinion of her. Her skin was as thick as armour, forged by pain and suffering, and she scarcely cared about the opinion of a low-ranking servant.

'Anything else?' she enquired.

'According to Elisa, you can't stand the idea of serving the duke's brother because he's a negro. And Señorita Belmonte said you enjoy being in charge of the household.'

There was a silence. Ursula suspected that Beatriz Ulloa enjoyed being able to repeat these insults to her face with impunity. She didn't care. The young woman was just a pawn who served her interests, and if she failed to do so, she would be out of here before her feet could touch the ground. Anyway, Elisa Costa was right. She loathed the idea of serving some house-trained African who had had the good fortune to encounter the charitable soul of Don Abel de Castamar. But that was how things were: she had to entertain her master's flights of fancy, for better or for worse. She gave the girl an inquisitive glance, in case she had anything further to add.

'That's all,' she said, with a bowed head and frightened eyes. 'I hope I've done the right thing, Señora Berenguer. You know that what I want most is to work my way up—'

'You have acted correctly,' the housekeeper interrupted her. 'That's why I hired you, so you would tell me everything that goes on in the kitchen. Thankfully, you have a prodigious memory for such matters, just as your mother said.'

The girl nodded.

'Did they discuss his lordship?' Ursula asked. Beatriz shook her head. The housekeeper suspected that the girl was more concerned with promoting her own interests than keeping Ursula informed.

'I particularly want to know about Señorita Belmonte, is that clear?' she reminded the girl. 'Keep a close eye on her. That's all for now.' The girl disappeared, and Ursula once again found herself alone in her office. She felt tired, exhausted by the constant demands of wielding power which left her no time for happiness, for those little moments, for that romantic love which seemed to be reserved for the masters. There wasn't a single moment when she wasn't engaged in either bolstering or retaining her power. But she accepted that. Otherwise, she would soon lose her grip on it and then she would be no different from any other woman who had been mistreated by life, just like all those others who bore their burden of pain and suffering with little joy.

16 October 1720, lunchtime

Amelia had concluded many years ago that women were nothing more than fragile beings, ruled by the laws of men, that marriage and life in society were designed to procure male freedom, and that whatever charms she might possess now would inevitably fade with the passage of time. That was why making a good match was so important for a lady. And she, with her debts in Don Enrique's hands, didn't know where she stood. Just thinking about it made her sob with shame and frustration. But she had to maintain a cool head – and keep the marquess at bay. In just two days he had awoken in her such contradictory and uncontrollable feelings. On the one hand, she couldn't help being attracted to him: he symbolized her ideals of success, elegance and status; he was a paragon of the kind of husband to whom she would naturally have aspired. The way he

expressed himself, his intelligence, his boldness in dealing with
Don Horacio and the sensual way he looked at her... All these
things excited her, stirring her basest passions and inflaming her
imagination with thoughts that had surprised her in the middle
of the night, invoking a mixture of shame and desire. On the
other hand, a voice of caution warned her to be on her guard.
*Nobody buys up the debts of a poor girl with a blemished reputation
from the goodness of their heart,* she told herself. *He's after something.*
The proof of it was that at no time had the marquess spoken of
a possible marriage between the two of them. Instead, he had
encouraged her to marry Don Diego. 'Benefactor' was how he
had defined himself. A slippery term which could conceal a far
darker purpose.

Whatever she did, she was in his hands; she could only pray
he would treat her with honesty and kindness. Don Enrique was
aware of the scandal that had attached itself to her in Cadiz, and
he was also her only guarantor. One word from him would be
enough for rumours of her damaged reputation to spread like a
plague through high society. Her desperation gave her no choice
but to believe his words.

And then there was Don Diego, who, unlike the marquess,
was above the intrigues of the court. He was the perfect
gentleman, elegant and restrained, so self-assured that his mere
presence comforted her, as if nothing bad could happen while
he was close by. Although he was weighed down by sorrow,
there was in his gaze a reassuring tranquillity and she felt that,
if only she could win his affections, he would never leave her.
She was fascinated by the duke and by the magnificence of
Castamar, just as she had been on her first visit that summer
several years earlier. He possessed one of the greatest fortunes
in Spain. He owned land all over the Peninsula, plantations in
the Americas, villas in the Low Countries and in the Duchy of
Parma, properties in London and Paris, and even a small fleet
of ships in Cartagena and Malaga. It was said that his was one
of the few noble houses that could compete with the wealth of

the Duke of Medinaceli, who had been accused of conspiring against the king and had died in the castle of Pamplona nine years earlier. Castamar was close to the king's heart. Doña Mercedes had confided in her that the king had recently urged Don Diego to follow his example and find a new wife.

'One cannot simply wish the ills of the heart away; only time can heal them,' the duke had responded.

Now, all Amelia wanted was to seduce Don Diego and ease the terrible anxiety that the marquess had caused with the purchase of her debts.

They had started upon their picnic at an earlier hour than was usual because, with the warm weather and the walking, they had worked up an appetite. Two servants poured out glasses of lemon and cinnamon water. The footmen had laid out slices of cheese, some drizzled with olive oil, and there were grapes, candied egg yolks, pancakes with honey, and loaves of freshly baked bread. The guests also tucked into a venison pie. Accompanied by the Valdepeñas wine, it reduced the diners to sighs of pleasure.

'I have to say, Don Diego, that it has been a long time since I enjoyed such delightful scenery and such delicious food,' Amelia declared.

The duke turned towards her, and she struggled to hold his gaze.

'I am glad, Señorita Castro,' Don Diego finally declared. 'I often come to this spot to ease my mind with views of the landscape and a good book.'

'Darling Amelia, as you know, Diego is an avid reader,' Doña Mercedes said.

Don Diego responded to his mother's praise with a self-deprecating smile, and Don Gabriel urged him to read to their guests. He refused, explaining that he was sure nobody wanted to spend their afternoon in so dull a manner. Amelia waited for the right moment and, glancing surreptitiously at the marquess, who hadn't taken his eye off her, declared that she would love to hear some poetry.

'Please,' she said eagerly. 'The last time I was your guest you read to me twice, and I always hoped you would read to me a third time.'

She hoped her request did not reveal the turmoil she felt inside.

'Don't be so modest,' the duchess scolded him. Don Diego smiled and stood up.

'Okay, okay,' he said. 'But don't say I didn't warn you. I won't be blamed for ruining the afternoon.'

'Don Diego, take care when giving in to a woman's demands,' Don Enrique remarked, sipping his cinnamon water. 'You never know where it will end.'

Amelia forced herself to smile. Don Diego seemed not to catch the marquess's meaning, but Don Gabriel gave her a quizzical look, as if aware that she and the marquess were plotting something.

'I think it might already be too late, Don Enrique. Luckily, whenever I come to Villacor, I bring a few books, and I'm sure I'll find something to please the ladies,' the duke replied.

He took a few paces towards the large oak tree, under which the servants had deposited the baggage. Amelia immediately realized that this would be an excellent opportunity to be alone with the duke.

'Please allow me to choose,' she said.

'I warn you that Señorita Castro is a great lover of reading,' the marquess commented.

This time, she didn't look at Don Enrique – whose words appeared to support her plan – but simply waited for the duke's invitation. The latter smiled at her and extended his arm. She stood up with his help, and they headed towards the tree. As she walked away, she overheard Doña Mercedes remark that she was adorable, to which the marquess replied that he was certain she would soon find a husband. That was all she heard as they reached the tree and Don Diego unlocked the small chest containing his books. She knelt next to him and began by ruling out Lope de Vega and Garcilaso, saying they should look for something more intense. The duke offered her another volume and she rushed to accept it, taking the opportunity to brush his fingers.

'The sonnets of Quevedo strike me as an excellent choice.' She smiled, as their hands touched.

Don Diego paused and looked down. He turned slowly towards her, in silence. She struggled to meet his gaze, and she found herself hoping he would rescue her from the enigmatic marquess and all the trials and tribulations that beset her. He came closer and her hopes rose when he took her other hand in his. She trembled because he was taking the initiative for the first time.

'Señorita Castro, will you permit me to address you by your first name?' he asked, gently.

She nodded instinctively, as if he were about to reveal something that had previously been concealed.

'Amelia, I recognize in you that powerful force that is capable of overcoming the most adverse of circumstances, and whatever it is that you are going through...'

Don Diego halted, and she felt suddenly vulnerable, sensing that this man was capable of intuiting the hidden secrets of her soul.

'I don't understand—' she began, before he gently placed a finger on her lips.

'Sssh,' he said, looking directly into her eyes. 'Allow me to take the liberty of offering you a suggestion, out of the friendship that once united us. Whatever it is that is happening, don't allow yourself to be led astray by following the wrong advice.'

She swallowed nervously.

'What are you trying to say?' she asked, struggling to master her emotions.

'I know that, in order to survive in this world, we sometimes do things which we regret for the rest of our lives.'

Her distress was impossible to hide, and she swallowed again.

It was as if Don Diego was peering into the dry well of her soul, as if, with a single gesture of his hand, he could fill it with cool water. She recalled how she had been rejected by the man who was to be her future husband, the Baron of Zahara. He had vanished from her life the moment he had heard about her parents' misfortune. She remembered how she had been abandoned by her friends, who shunned her, withdrawing social invitations and even crossing the street to avoid her as if she were carrying the plague. Her words caught in her throat, like a chain around her neck. Finally, she recalled the Count of Guadalmin, Don Arturo de Orca y Nardiel, a friend of her father and fifteen years her senior, who had appeared at just the right moment to rescue her from her predicament, apparently offering her protection.

Tears welled up in her eyes as Don Diego came a little closer. She tried to speak but the words refused to come. He was still holding her hand. She couldn't sustain his gaze any longer as she remembered with shame how Don Arturo had rented a house for her and taken on her debts, saying that he was only repaying her father's friendship. By the time she had finally realized what was going on, half of Cadiz was convinced he was keeping her as his concubine. That night she had confronted Don Arturo and he had confessed that all he wanted was to bed her. He had put a small fortune on the table and told her to choose between accepting his proposition or being thrown out on the street. As poor as a church mouse, her only possessions what was left of her mother's trousseau and a few showy clothes, she had undressed and gone into the bedchamber.

The next day, she had said farewell to Verónica Salazar, the only friend who had remained loyal to her, meeting her in secret in order to avoid contaminating Verónica with her own dishonour. Verónica had kindly provided a small house for her mother in El Escorial, with four servants to look after her, while Amelia tried to find a husband who would solve her problems. After that terrible night, she had taken the money acquired in exchange for her virginity and set off for Madrid with her mother in a coach on the advice of her friend. She had left her reputation, her dead father and a trail of debts in Cadiz.

She lowered her head, appalled by her own dishonesty.

'Look at me. You can count on my support, Amelia,' Don Diego told her, plainly.

She looked into his eyes and once again observed that expression of frank sincerity. She felt both intimidated and comforted at the same time, as if this man could make all her problems disappear at a stroke. And then Don Diego placed the palm of his hand upon his chest.

'You won't find love or passion in this heart, but I want you to know that, if you wish it, you can count upon my sincere friendship and, of course, my assistance,' he said.

Amelia tried to suppress her memories, but she couldn't. The images of that night crowded in upon her: the baron on top of her, penetrating her, lacerating her body and her soul. She took a deep breath and forced herself to speak.

'If… if I might speak candidly… I…' she stuttered, her eyes watering. 'I… would tell you that…'

'Are you okay?' It was the marquess. 'Doña Mercedes is keen to hear you read.'

Amelia turned and dried her tears while Don Diego stepped forward to conceal her disarray.

'We have made our choice, Don Enrique,' the duke said cordially, showing the book to the marquess. 'I hope it meets your approval.'

'I am sure you will have made an excellent selection,' the marquess replied, waiting for them to return together.

Don Diego paused for a moment, then turned to help Amelia stand. She composed herself and walked by his side, glancing at him surreptitiously. For a moment, it had been as if this man had reached into her soul, granting her such a sense of security that she had almost surrendered to the impulse to tell him the truth about her situation, even though the most likely outcome was that his reaction would be the same as everyone else's. She shouldn't deceive herself; she was no longer an innocent girl. But that step was one she could only take when she was absolutely certain her future was assured.

For now, she had to be cautious. The reality was that she was suffocated by debt, her invalid mother was living in a borrowed house in El Escorial, and she was here in search of her fortune. Suddenly, she saw the beautiful villa of Castamar as a battlefield, one on which she could be a trophy or a damsel whose honour had been lost.

She had an inkling that she was caught up in a game of chess, a game that went far beyond her own simple desire to find a husband. She cursed her stupidity for not realizing that attempting to ally herself to one of the greatest fortunes in Spain would not be without its dangers. She felt a rising sense of panic, unable to trust anybody or anything: not the kindness of Doña Mercedes, which could be a pretence; or the frankness of Don Diego, which could be false; or the African, Don Gabriel, who never took his eye off her; and certainly not Don Enrique of Arcona, whom she suspected of having hidden motives. She knew that, if she allowed her emotions to get carried away, as she had come so close to doing beneath the oak tree, she could imperil her reputation even further and expose herself to the possibility of exile from polite society. She might just be a pawn in their game, but even a pawn had the right to struggle for its future.

14

16 October 1720, midday

If Francisco knew one thing about Alfredo it was that he was one of the most skilful wielders of the épée, although he could not match Diego, whose mastery was the stuff of legend. He had been trained in the French and Tuscan styles and was able to switch effortlessly from one to the other. Although he was nearing fifty now, he was still quite capable of outwitting his younger opponent.

After several brief bouts, the majority of which Francisco lost, the two men had decided to head to Their Majesties' mid-morning refreshment at the Buen Retiro Palace. They rested beneath a sunshade, where they were served glasses of *horchata* with too much lemon and cinnamon. They talked about politics, about the war which had raged between all of Europe, including France and Spain, for the possession of Sicily and Sardinia. In the end, Spain had had to sign a letter of surrender at The Hague, ceding control of the two islands. Eventually, Francisco grew bored of this topic and moved on to a topic he found far more interesting.

'Will you be bringing anyone to the celebration tonight at Castamar?'

'No, I couldn't find anyone suitable,' Alfredo answered. 'I fear that, at my age, falling in love is neither pertinent nor prudent and pretending to fall in love even less so.'

'As I have always said, you will have to marry eventually,'

Francisco responded. 'There is no one else to continue your line for you.'

While Francisco knew that, when the right moment came, he would have no problems marrying any woman worthy of his position, title and riches, with the goal of continuing his line and distributing the family's possessions, Alfredo had no desire to feign happiness in an ill-advised marriage. While Alfredo had rejected every possibility of marriage, Francisco had always evaded the possibility by hopping from one scandal to another. In the end, his father had decided to send him to the Collège de Louis-le-Grand to see if they could set him on the right path. When war broke out, Francisco had found himself enlisted, at eighteen years of age, into a dragoon regiment financed by his father. After three years of war, and before dying from two lead pellets between the ribs at the battle of Almansa, his father had told him for the first and last time that he had always loved him and that he hoped Francisco would always show enough valour to exalt the surname he bore.

'Francisco, my son, you must take a wife and beget male heirs,' he had told him from his deathbed.

Thirteen years had passed since Francisco had sworn he would do everything possible to perpetuate the Marlango dynasty. As fortune had it, his father had not forced him to settle on a date for the promised nuptials. Obviously, Francisco would honour his word, but only when the time was right.

Noticing his continued silence, Alfredo glanced sideways at him and made an attempt to renew their conversation.

'Shall I take it that you have invited someone?'

Francisco took a sip from his drink, mischievously ignoring his friend's question. Like Diego, he saw Alfredo as an older brother. He had still been a boy when his father had arranged for him to attend classes from the same renowned tutor who used to teach the future Baron of Aguasdulces, Don Alfredo de Carrión. Francisco must have been ten years old, Alfredo over twenty, and he had soon become the young boy's inspiration.

Francisco had never had one before, because his mother had died giving birth to him and he had learned early on that solitude is a constant state which is only occasionally alleviated. He had soon realized that his father could not help but blame him for his mother's death, and so the young Francisco had never expected any affection whatsoever from him. In Alfredo and Diego, he had found his only true friends.

Alfredo smiled and asked again, 'Should I take it from your asking me that you have invited someone?'

'Maybe...' Francisco replied cheekily, with the hint of a smile. He took another sip.

'I know you too well, and I hope the rumours I've heard are false,' his friend said, fearing that the celebration might end with a dawn duel.

Francisco chuckled.

'Am I so predictable?'

'I can read you like a book.'

His friend knew the kind of woman he fell for, all too well, for save on certain occasions when the temptation of the flesh overwhelmed him, Francisco generally preferred those who had married young to older husbands, those for whom the years had passed without them having enjoyed the art of love. This art required cunning and surprise, giving his lover everything she desired but could not ask for. He enjoyed taking such women to the heights of ecstasy, watching as all their education, poise and good manners vanished and transformed into violent spasms, uncontrollable panting and filthy language. As was to be expected, this habit had caused a few small scandals, resolved at dawn in swift duels against ageing, cuckolded husbands.

Pure, virginal girls, on the other hand, were rather tedious: they required uninterrupted devotion. Besides, his reputation as a seducer was common knowledge, and their parents had already warned them against him. 'Steer clear of the Count of Armiño,' they said. 'Behind his fine manners there lies a lustful beast.' And they were right.

'You think I haven't heard the rumours linking you to Doña Sol Montijos?' said Alfredo, arching one eyebrow. 'I know she's been invited to the celebration, and I imagine the invite came from you.'

'My dear Alfredo, I have no idea what you're talking about.'

'Of course you do,' Alfredo answered. 'You must be careful with her; you could be biting off more than you can chew this time.'

Francisco laughed, unable to contain himself any longer. It was clear that rumours about his two previous encounters with Doña Sol had spread around the court. Both encounters had been too chaste for his liking, with her husband close by. He loved being involved in such skirmishes – intentions discussed via glances and whispers and in the coded flick of a fan. For him, the act of fornication was nothing other than the culmination of a play staged for a court audience but only performed in the intervals, behind the scenes, hidden by the curtain.

To this end, he underwent a thorough routine every day: first, his manservants would perfume him with lavender and rosemary, and soften his hands with essential oils of grapefruit and bergamot; then he was shaved by his barber, who would tidy his wig or gather his hair in a ponytail; finally, he was dressed in a different outfit each morning. The silk taffeta jacket and matching morning suit had to be immaculate, with gold and silver buttons over starched shirts, and great attention paid to the details: heels, white stockings, velvet gloves, a cane with a handle of gold, silver or mother of pearl, perfumed lace handkerchiefs.

He had had many victories and some defeats. He liked to approach slowly at first, be introduced as a respectable man, only then to begin the process of stolen caresses, pointed looks, precise gestures, all of it seemingly by accident. Women, for him, had a hidden allure, a mystery beyond the individual words and actions of any single one. It was an essence they all shared, making them the most delicious creatures. The best thing about it was, however much you delved into their breasts, swam in the ocean of their voluptuousness, you could only take it in for a few moments, like a vague idea that then escapes through your fingers like a sea breeze. Those who thought of them as celestial beings would never taste this elixir.

This meant that, whenever he heard of a man having carnal relationships and unnatural contact with another man, he would shudder, believing such wretches to be suffering from a perverse sickness. The unnatural predilections of some noblemen were well known. The only thing that could be said in their favour was that their existence meant less competition for female attention.

'It is said she loves to seduce young men and then spurn them,' Alfredo said, before draining his cup.

'In that case I don't see why she should interest me.'

He knew all too well that Doña Sol was exactly the kind of woman he would seek to woo. Just past forty and on her second marriage, age had bestowed upon her an enigmatic aura which only accentuated her beauty. He had only had to exchange a couple of glances with her during a morning walk in the grounds of Buen Retiro, veiled by the fan, for her to smile back at him from behind her fan as she walked arm in arm with her husband, the Marquess of Villamar.

'Please tell me you don't plan to seduce her at Castamar.'

'Are we leaving now?' Francisco answered, with a careless smile.

Alfredo stood up and nodded. Francisco knew that as soon as they'd finished saying goodbye to the others, Alfredo would want to know everything. Deep down, Alfredo followed Francisco's amorous adventures as if he were observing a performance of *The Trickster of Seville*, which was why Francisco preferred not to tell him all the details in advance and instead allowed him to enjoy the show, which would be a veritable bonfire of the vanities.

As soon as they had left the Retiro and begun making their way along the Carrera de San Jerónimo, Alfredo put his hand on Francisco's shoulder to slow him down.

'You're a libertine.'

'And you've become a prying old hen.'

'Tell me something, at least.' Alfredo smiled. 'I'm older than you and could offer some advice.'

'Ha!'

Francisco gave nothing away. They rode in silence until they crossed the Puente de Segovia, in the direction of Castamar. He didn't want Alfredo to coax any part of his plans for that night out of him. Still, he felt the voice of lust bubbling away inside him. It was a whisper he knew very well, which impelled him again and again to recall Doña Sol's breasts heaving away inside her corset, her slender, elegant ankles beneath her underskirt and that defiant expression on her lips.

16 October 1720, afternoon

Clara rapped on the door with her knuckles, waiting for the head butler to call her in. She guessed that he had called for her that morning, just before lunch, with the intention of getting to know her in person. The butler's gruff voice called out from the other side of his office door. Don Melquíades, with his neat moustache and his immaculate livery, rose the moment she entered. She greeted him and he, unable to disguise a smile, welcomed her in as if she were a relative he had not seen for a long time. He placed a numbered notebook on the shelf and turned towards her.

'I called for you because you've been in the house for several days and we haven't had a chance to talk yet.'

'Thank you, Señor Elquiza,' Clara replied. 'I'm very happy here, adapting to the change in circumstances.' She still had to remind herself that she was now the head cook. Yet, despite Doña Ursula's constant vigilance, she was beginning to feel that

Castamar was the place she'd been waiting for since her mother had left and her sister had migrated to Habsburg territory. 'I hope to live up to the trust you have placed in me.'

'Don't be silly, Señorita Belmonte. You earn your right to be here with every meal you cook. Even his lordship has mentioned your wonderful talent,' he said, beaming at her.

'I appreciate your kind words,' Clara replied, wondering if there was a hidden motive behind this extraordinary show of friendliness.

However, the head butler's bright, gleaming eyes soon convinced her that Don Melquíades had no hidden intentions – rather, this was a spontaneous, heartfelt act. For some reason her promotion gave him cause to rejoice.

'Personally, I haven't been as happy at mealtimes since my mother was cooking them, God rest her soul. In fact, after yesterday, everyone is wondering what you will surprise us with today.'

'Well, today there will be game stew for the celebration. I hope it will meet such lofty expectations, Señor Elquiza,' Clara said, slightly overwhelmed. 'I fear tonight's dinner has consumed all my efforts.'

'Don't be so modest. I smelled it as I walked by and the aroma made me wish I was sitting at the table right now,' he answered.

She smiled, trying not to blush. She was moved by Don Melquíades's show of respect and warmth towards her.

'The best way of discovering if the stew's aroma matches its taste is to try it,' she suggested, attempting to replicate his friendliness.

He nodded and, smiling beneath his moustache, raised his hand to point the way, though before leaving, he took her arm and stopped her for a moment, somewhat solemnly.

'Señorita Belmonte, may I tell you something?'

'Of course, Señor Elquiza,' said Clara.

'We are all delighted to have you with us, and those who aren't… will just have to put up with you.'

Clara's eyes opened wide as she heard this, and she felt comforted by his words. After thanking him, they left the office together, walking towards one of the servant dining rooms on the ground floor. She assumed that Don Melquíades had been alluding to Doña Ursula, since she did not know of anyone else who might be uncomfortable with her presence. His statement highlighted not only the fact that the housekeeper was unhappy with her promotion, but also that Don Melquíades and the housekeeper did not share the same view regarding her presence at Castamar. She had always assumed that the butler had no particular opinion and she had taken it for granted that he was only concerned with her good credentials and the excellent references given by his friend, the esteemed Señora Moncada. Generally, a head butler, especially in a great house such as this one, did not give too much importance to the hiring of a kitchen assistant. But if the duke and he were so happy with her work, then Doña Ursula's opinion and her constant vigilance were of little significance. Even so, a little voice inside was saying that it was not good to be caught in the middle of someone else's battlefield, if indeed such a thing really was going on among the senior staff at Castamar.

They reached the dining room, where the servants were already waiting for Don Melquíades. They all rose when they saw him, until he casually gestured at them to sit back down. The elongated room, its whitewashed walls clad to waist-height with varnished pine, made a deep impression on her. She felt like she was entering foreign territory, governed by the iron hand of Doña Ursula, who was sitting to the right of the head of the table. The housekeeper watched her the whole time with an icy gaze. From the inscrutable look on the housekeeper's face, Clara could tell it had not escaped the housekeeper's attention that Clara and Don Melquíades had arrived together.

Don Melquíades sat down and ordered the stew to be served. As on the previous day, all the diners fell silent, enchanted by the aromas which rose from their plates. The silence delighted

Clara. For a few moments, all that could be heard was the sound of the stew being sipped.

'To be frank, Señorita Belmonte, the servants at Castamar have never eaten so splendidly,' Don Melquíades pronounced.

In a flash, the sommelier, Señor Moguer, and Señor Ibáñez, his lordship's manservant, added their congratulations. Others nodded as they wolfed down the stew. She thanked them.

'Credit is also due to the rest of the kitchen staff,' she added, glancing sideways at Doña Ursula to gauge her reaction.

The housekeeper's face – her cheeks lit up by the flavours and her eyes gleaming with the vapours – gave her away. Despite this, her pride stopped her from expressing her feelings. Clara felt her to be an insufferable woman, since all Clara had done was try to gain her respect and make her understand that she posed no threat at Castamar, quite the opposite in fact. All she wanted was for Doña Ursula to be pleased with her work and for their relationship to be placed on a firm footing after the change wrought by Clara's promotion. However, Doña Ursula's silence demonstrated that admitting how the stew delighted both the servants' and her own palate would mean watching her power wane. For the housekeeper, uttering such words would not simply be a matter of giving sincere praise but would be an admission of defeat, accepting that Clara's culinary know-how had defeated her authority. *I really don't know what to do with this woman*, Clara thought.

'You are an extraordinary cook,' Simón Casona intervened from the other end of the table, interrupting her thoughts.

'You haven't tried the warm buns made with honey and butter that she makes for his lordship,' Elisa said. 'The other morning she let me try one that was left over, and I've never tasted anything so delicious.'

Smiling with exhilaration, the sommelier, the coachmen, the manservants and the footmen all exchanged opinions about the wonderful flavours of her cooking. When she had finished her stew, Clara dabbed her lips and smiled timidly.

'You're making me blush,' she told them.

'Your skill in the kitchen is undeniable, so you might as well just accept it,' Don Melquíades said, making the other servants laugh.

Out of the corner of her eye, she saw Doña Ursula, her lips pursed, gripping the spoon between her fingers and finishing off her stew in silence. Her silence was so pronounced that it spoke volumes, but after the housekeeper's comments about Clara's dear mother in the gallery, insinuating that she only spent time in kitchens to entertain herself, this bath of humility was just what was deserved. Clara saw Don Melquíades, covering his mouth as he laughed, shoot an inquisitive look at Doña Ursula. That vindictive glint revealed to Clara that there was something far deeper than a simple disagreement between these two.

'What do you think, Doña Ursula? Isn't it just delicious?' the butler asked. 'You haven't said a word.'

The laughter stopped almost at once, and everyone looked over at the housekeeper, who was now glaring at Don Melquíades. Clara guessed that she was plotting a devastating revenge for such impertinence. The entire room waited, while Clara wondered how Doña Ursula could allow such an act of defiance from the head butler at Castamar, who, with his smile camouflaged by his moustache, arched his eyebrows slightly as he waited for an answer. The housekeeper scanned all the diners, who automatically lowered their heads. Then she gave Clara another glacial stare. Holding her head high, the cook glimpsed something in that stare that made her shudder.

Clara realized Doña Ursula had remained silent during those eternal seconds, not only because of any private duel she might have with Don Melquíades, but because she somehow believed Clara had something to do with the affront. Suddenly, she imagined the picture the housekeeper had formed when Clara and Don Melquíades had entered the dining room together.

'Yes, quite delicious. Congratulations, Señorita Belmonte,' she said solemnly.

'Thank you, Doña Ursula,' Clara answered, only now lowering her head.

She took a breath and, as they served the rest of the food, told herself that the butler's victory over Doña Ursula had been interpreted as a challenge to her authority made by Clara. If previously she had simply made the housekeeper feel uncomfortable, Clara had now become a direct adversary. Even so, with each spoonful, her will grew firmer, and she told herself that under no circumstances would she allow the housekeeper to unfairly expel her from the kitchen.

15

16 October 1720, after lunch

Enrique had no knowledge of the despair that was born of
poverty, and no real concept of the devastation it caused
in those poor souls into whom it sank its claws. However, he
sensed that it was a kind of terror that suffused everything, a
storm which forced its victims to trade their dignity for survival.
And it was this insight that he exploited as a tool with which to
achieve his objectives. It was said that hunger, misery and debt
were the true agents of death, shortening people's lives, stealing
their best years, robbing them of joy. Few could withstand such
an onslaught without either capitulating to adversity or losing
their principles along the way – facts he used to his advantage,
playing upon them as if they were instruments.

Poor Amelia Castro thought he hadn't registered her fear, that
she had succeeded in hiding her true desperation beneath her
elegant manners. After listening to Don Diego recite Quevedo's
sonnets of past glories, she had cheerfully suggested they take
turns to read other authors. Don Gabriel had surprised them by
selecting a book and dedicating the reading to Don Enrique.

'*The Valiant Negro in Flanders*,' he had announced, 'by Andrés
de Claramonte.'

The text was about a freed slave who had risen to become
a commander of the tercios. *What nonsense!* Enrique thought.
*Nobody in their right mind would allow a negro to command a
tercio.* He lay back without saying anything, although he smiled

to keep up an appearance of civility. He knew that Don Gabriel was eager to demonstrate that he was as cultivated as any gentleman, that he was not some slave recently brought from Africa who could neither speak nor read Spanish.

Next, Señorita Castro entertained them with a *seguidilla* that she sang delightfully. Enchanted as he was, Enrique could not stop thinking about whether Hernaldo had obtained the skeleton key that would allow him to move freely around Castamar. He hoped to take delivery of the key when he went riding before supper – having it in his possession would make his task far simpler. He was just reminding himself of the need for patience when it began to rain. The party took cover beneath the parasols while the servants scrambled to tidy away the picnic.

'I'm afraid the sunshades won't keep us dry for long,' he said grumpily.

Don Diego announced that they could take shelter in the farmhouse until the rain stopped, but one of the servants approached and informed them this would not be necessary.

'I took the precaution of warning Señor Cebrián to bring the carriages, in the event of such a situation,' he explained. 'They are on the other side of the hill.'

'Good thinking...' Don Diego said, waiting for the servant to give his name.

'Roberto Velázquez, your grace.'

'Señor Elquiza's nephew?' Don Diego asked, in a friendly tone. The lad nodded, and Don Diego told him to bring the carriages round as quickly as possible. Enrique thought to himself that the setback could be an opportunity to find himself alone with Señorita Castro. He assumed that the duke and his brother would opt for the second carriage, to protect their mother from the rain. He would follow Señorita Castro, who, anxious to be safe from the downpour and perhaps from him, would no doubt hurry to the first carriage. And so, before the carriages arrived, he took up position next to Don Diego, well away from her so that she would not suspect his intentions and, in an attempt to strike up a casual conversation, commented to the duke that they had been unlucky with the weather. As soon as the carriages arrived, the duke said farewell and took his mother by the hand to assist her.

As he had foreseen, Señorita Castro, thinking that Don Diego was following close behind, made for the first carriage. Enrique hurried after Señorita Castro, who quickly climbed the steps and got inside. She turned and flashed a smile, expecting to see Don Diego, but her smile froze when instead she came face to face with Don Enrique. Giving her no time to react, he entered the carriage, blocked her exit, and drew the curtains. A tense silence reigned as the carriage set off: she avoiding his gaze, he waiting patiently. Finally, she looked at him.

'Marquess,' Señorita Castro said. 'Please tell me the truth. What is it you want from me?'

He tutted, pretending once again to resent the question.

'Señorita Castro, I assure you I have no ulterior motive. As I told you, I cannot bear to see you suffering such injustice. All I desire is your friendship.'

She clenched her jaws in frustration as she tried to think of a way out of this labyrinth. He admired this survival instinct of hers, this rebellion in the face of misfortune, armed with nothing but her wits.

'You know I have no wish to insult you, Don Enrique. I am very grateful to you.'

'Then you should also trust me. I have nothing but good intentions. With my help, I am sure you will persuade Don Diego to marry you.'

'Please don't be offended if I find it hard to trust you,' she replied in discomfort. 'As you know, I was deceived by someone who claimed to have my best interests at heart, only to have him take my virtue. I cannot let that happen again.'

'Of course not,' he answered calmly. 'You are a fighter and that is what I most admire about you.'

'Marquess, please understand that I am' – her voice cracked a little as she spoke – 'terrified.'

He took her gently by the hand to console her. He looked into her eyes and she returned his gaze, her eyes brimming with tears, at once desperate to believe his words and frightened that she would regret it. But she had no alternative, and her desperation gave her no option but to place her trust in him. She was trapped in a web of invisible codes and unspoken rules, and he was there to offer her salvation. Don Enrique had simply waited for all those rules to gradually wear her down and break her spirit. He drew close, preparing for the moment when he would free her from her chains.

'Allow me to be your benefactor and you will have no more problems of any kind,' he said, his face close to hers.

She imagined herself free of debt, of pressure, of pretence, while simultaneously distrusting the sensation. Poverty had sunk its claws into her and was beginning to erode her spirit.

'I only want what's good for you.'

Her eyes no longer glimmered, as if she had finally been defeated by the exhaustion of living on the edge of the abyss, desperately trying to maintain the pretence of social respectability and financial security while she searched for a solution to her misfortunes.

'I don't see what can be done, Don Enrique,' Señorita Castro said. 'My past weighs so heavily on me.'

Enrique sat next to her so that he could spill his poison into her ear.

'Tomorrow you will have sufficient money that you will never need anybody again, not even me,' he said, taking the liberty of brushing her earlobe with his lips, as if it were merely the accidental result of whispering to her to avoid being overheard by the coachmen.

She looked at him sceptically.

'A fortune that will provide you with a fixed income for

life, allowing you to maintain servants, properties and status,' Enrique told her, as he inhaled the perfume on her neck.

Señorita Castro opened her eyes and, almost without realizing it, surrendered. Enrique whispered to her again, his lips grazing her ear with each syllable. She felt her hair prickle and pulled back slightly.

'Please don't lie to me,' she said weakly.

Enrique continued with his promises, describing the riches that would come into her possession. 'The mansion in Cadiz will be yours for life and I will renounce any claim to it for so long as you are alive. You will be the owner of the house in Madrid that once belonged to your father.'

Seeing safety within her grasp, the remainder of her resistance crumbled. She was no longer able to contain her desperate desire to escape this precipice.

'How can I be sure of what you say?' she asked, so overcome by agitation and desire that she was scarcely able to speak.

Enrique smiled as he looked upon his work.

'If this is not enough, tell me what more I can do to gain your trust,' he replied, turning her face towards his.

'I can't trust you,' she gasped, as she felt Enrique's gloveless fingers caressing her chin.

'I'm sure you can find a way, Señorita Castro,' he replied, brushing his lips against her cheek.

As she sighed, sensing independence was within her grasp, her breasts heaved beneath her bodice. The voice of caution that had warned her against him fell silent, and overwhelmed by the debts and the misery of recent years, she capitulated in return for a promise of security.

'You'll put it in writing before a notary,' Amelia said breathlessly, looking him in the eye.

He smiled, savouring his victory, and stroked her face like a devoted lover.

'As God is my witness,' Enrique replied, his fingers sliding towards the nape of her neck.

She groaned, then trembled uncontrollably. The marquess kissed her softly on the lips, bringing a flush to her cheeks, then brushed her tongue with his. She surrendered to him. Enrique sensed she had never been kissed like this before, that her desire had lain dormant.

He traced a sensuous line down her elegant neck towards her breasts, and she felt the needs of the flesh awaken. Inflamed by passion, she grasped his hair and pulled his head back.

'Tell me what it is you want from me,' she gasped again.

He didn't answer. He lifted her skirts and caressed her thighs. Then, as she shuddered, his head disappeared between her legs, and she experienced a pleasure she had never known before. She raised her hand to her mouth so that her groans would not be heard outside the carriage. She was overcome both by ecstasy and by the hope that she had avoided the precipice. And yet Enrique, who understood the suspicious disposition of those who have survived misfortune, knew that even now a tiny voice inside Amelia's head was whispering that she had made a pact with the devil. A voice she herself had silenced out of necessity. All that remained for him was to take delight in the knowledge that Amelia Castro was now his.

16 October 1720, evening

Hernaldo rode unhurriedly, as was his custom, his hat pulled down over his head and his cloak wrapped tightly around him. His lantern was unlit on account of the full moon. He had come to meet Don Enrique to give him the key. Hernaldo knew that his master would be delighted to receive it, and he in turn was happy to be of use to Don Enrique once again. He looked up and saw ahead of him the stone wall that surrounded the estate of Castamar.

Whenever he came here, he felt as if he was approaching a burial ground in which he was the gravedigger. He had spent half his life surrounded by death, dealing it out for the flimsiest of reasons simply to keep hunger at bay, without pausing to ask whether his victims deserved their fate. It was simply part of a trade at which he excelled. However, the death of Doña Alba de Montepardo had not been one of those jobs that was quickly forgotten. It was a constant wound to his pride, a reminder of failure whenever he approached the estate.

We plotted to assassinate her husband, but we caused the duchess's death instead, he told himself. He had said as much to Don Enrique once, and his master, with a murderous look in his eyes, had replied that the sole responsibility lay with Don Diego, whose idea it had been to swap the horses that morning. 'Don't ever suggest otherwise again,' he had said, 'if you want to remain in my service… and keep your head on your shoulders.'

Hernaldo had obeyed. *That's the bad thing about conspiracies. They always involve death, sometimes accidental and sometimes not.* His master and he had left a fair few corpses in their wake, making sure to cover their tracks so as not to arouse suspicions. And in connection to the death of Doña Alba, he recalled one of the rare occasions when administering death had afforded him a certain pleasure. The victim had been a ruffian who went by the nickname of Tuerto, on account of the fact that he was missing an eye.

At the time, Hernaldo had been looking for a groom to train Don Diego's horse. He had needed to be sure that whoever he found for the task was not some inexperienced novice, as it was no easy matter. The steed would be trained, at the sound of the whistle, to rear up on its hind legs and then fall upon its rider with all its weight. Finally, after much searching, Tuerto had mentioned El Zurdo, a dangerous, violent sort, the kind whom it was best not to cross. From the moment Hernaldo first met the ruffian, he had sensed that they might come to blows at any moment.

'He knows what he's doing,' Tuerto had assured him. 'He's trained horses for some of the most powerful men in Spain. You should be able to find him at the Zaguán; he's taken a shine to one of the whores there.'

The Zaguán was a brothel in Lavapiés frequented by gamblers, swindlers, prostitutes, soldiers of fortune and thieves. Hernaldo had sent Tuerto off with a few reals and continued on his way.

It was only much later, after the death of Doña Alba, that Tuerto had reappeared, with two henchmen by his side, demanding payment for his silence. Hernaldo hadn't hesitated. He ran his sword through Tuerto's chest, and one of the dead man's sidekicks, seeing how things were shaping up, had turned on his companion in an attempt to curry favour with his assailant. But it was too late. He already knew too much to be spared. Hernaldo's victims didn't tend to be honourable men, and neither was he. They were drinkers, degenerates, mercenaries... Anyone who might be an inconvenience to Don Enrique had to be removed. *That's why you can't remember their names*, he thought as he skirted the wall.

He continued at a trot until he came to the grove that concealed a breach in the boundary. His men had made it two nights ago so that he could enter the estate without being seen. He passed through the gap and made for the appointed place – a thicket of bushes that was not far away. His master was already there waiting and, seeing him, gestured to him to make haste. Hernaldo broke into a gallop that soon brought him to Don Enrique's side.

'I have to return before I am missed,' Don Enrique told him. 'Have you got it?'

Hernaldo produced the key and allowed himself a satisfied smirk. Don Enrique put the key in his pocket and gave him a grateful look. For Hernaldo, his master's recognition was the best payment.

'Am I right in thinking that you have Amelia Castro in your clutches?' Hernaldo asked.

Don Enrique merely smiled.

'I am delighted, your grace.'

'Did you visit Doña Sol? Did she tell what she wishes in return for her help?'

'To do away with her husband, the Marquess of Villamar, in a chance accident. Apparently, he has always been a weight around her neck and he has now become too heavy. She suggests poison, as he is an incurable glutton.'

Don Enrique, who appeared unsurprised at Doña Sol's request, smiled at the comment.

'Make the preparations but not too hastily. Such a payment cannot be made in instalments, so she will have to keep her side of the bargain first,' he said, and turned his horse to leave.

'I will have everything ready for when the time comes, your grace.'

Don Enrique nodded, and Hernaldo waited until his master had disappeared. Then he set off back towards Madrid, imagining El Zurdo's expression when he received his part of the payment for providing the key. He chuckled softly to himself. Everything seemed to be going exactly as his master had planned: Amelia Castro was already at Castamar, Doña Sol had agreed her price, and all that remained was to wait for the fruit to ripen. Poor Don Diego – he could not begin to suspect the terrible misfortune that hung over him, his family and his loved ones.

16

16 October 1720, evening

Diego was keen to resume his conversation with Señorita Castro, so as soon as his mother and Gabriel entered the house, he gently took Amelia by the arm.

'Will you honour me with your company a little longer?' he requested. 'We can talk at ease in one of these rooms.'

'Only on the condition that you call me by my name,' she answered.

From her expression he guessed that she was embarrassed at having displayed her emotions in front of him. Diego let her past and closed the door behind him.

'Amelia,' he said, after a few moments. 'Are you well? I felt you were just about to confess something when we spoke earlier.'

She smiled to feign normality, then looked away.

'Pay me no notice, Don Diego. Sometimes the loss of my father overwhelms me and I act like a fool.'

He understood that Señorita Castro's urge to speak honestly had vanished. Don Enrique had probably already worked his influence on her, and since Diego and Amelia barely knew each other, he assumed she also held a level of distrust towards him. Even so, he suspected that Señorita Castro's reasons for keeping silent had more to do with the first cause than the second. He indicated he was taking his leave of her with a slight bow, but Señorita Castro stopped him, saying his name as if she wanted to give some explanation for her change of heart. He did not let her continue, since he was sure she was only going to lie to him, and he could not tolerate hypocrisy.

'There is no need to pretend, Señorita Castro,' he said. 'It's clear that you lost your desire to be sincere with me on the journey from Villacor to the house.'

On hearing this, she fell silent and he left her alone.

Alfredo and Francisco were waiting for him in the drawing room. The three of them, together with Gabriel, enjoyed each other's company until dinner time, discussing King Felipe's possible designs on the French throne.

As the sun was setting, a manservant notified him of the first guest's arrival, and Diego went out to greet her. It was Doña Almudena, the Baroness of Belizón, with whom he maintained a close friendship. She had married very young and had lost her husband, twenty years her senior, after he had overindulged in crayfish one evening. She was a regular guest at Castamar, mainly because Alba had been her mentor at the court. Since she had no living relatives after the war, she confided almost all her important affairs in him.

Not much later, he was informed of the arrival of the Marquess and Marchioness of Villamar, Don Esteban and Doña Sol. It was the first time they had attended the private dinner, and it had been to Diego's surprise that Francisco had invited them. Every guest had the privilege of bringing a companion, provided they were happy to share the table with Don Gabriel on equal terms. From the smile on his friend's face when Don Diego had told him they were coming, he assumed the invitation had more to do with the presence of Doña Sol than that of her husband, whom Francisco barely knew. Alfredo had scolded him like an older brother for taking the liberty of inviting a woman who had a reputation for having affairs with young men behind her husband's back. Diego acknowledged the hilarity of the situation and, downplaying the matter, welcomed them cheerfully.

Diego stood waiting for everyone else to settle in their seats. When Gabriel sat down, an awkward silence spread across the table. Diego looked over at the Marquess and Marchioness of Villamar. Don Esteban was sweating, sneaking glances at Gabriel, and Doña Sol was ignoring him as if he were nothing more than a servant in the wrong place. Most of the nobles who agreed to come did so because it was impossible to reject an invitation from a duke who was so close to the Crown. They sought his friendship and favour and accepted willingly despite being warned about his brother. The problem arose later, when they confronted the reality of actually sharing a table with a black man.

Seeking to break the silence, Diego gave a short welcome speech. When he finished and took his seat, his brother stood and announced that he also wished to make a toast. Diego found this strange, since Gabriel was not one to draw attention to himself. In fact, once the private dinner was over, he would usually shut himself away in his chambers and not reappear until the celebrations had finished.

Gabriel, you must never appear among them; don't try to make them accept you; do not confuse your privileges at Castamar with the ones you lack in the outside world, his father had often told him. *It will only result in misfortune.*

Lamentably, his father had been right.

'I wanted to say a few words this year, to wish you all good fortune and many years of friendship,' Gabriel said, holding up his glass. 'Brother, you know that I admire and love you and that I will always be by your side, ensuring no ill befalls you. To Castamar.'

Diego understood the motive behind the toast as he sipped his wine. That final sentence was aimed at Don Enrique de Arcona. Gabriel did not like him, suspecting he had hidden intentions, and he had suggested they investigate as a matter of precaution, since the marquess could have designs on their mother. The duke, however, did not agree. The marquess's hurtful and unfortunate comments had irritated him, but he did not see in them any intention to harm their mother. Only occasionally did the man's displays of warmth towards the duchess, revealing their close friendship, make Diego uncomfortable.

'My dear friend,' Don Enrique said. 'I beg you – please, lend me your cook for my celebrations.'

Gladly, if you can wait until Judgement Day, Diego thought. Before long, everyone at Castamar, nobles and servants included, would have become so used to eating well that any other food would simply be a disappointment.

After the first two courses and the roast, amid trivial chitchat, knowing looks between Francisco and Doña Sol and further comments from the marquess, the conversation largely focused on the exquisite food. The dinner had been a delight for the senses, and it was only towards the end that the conversation took an unpleasant turn, when some began to gossip about the court and its scandals.

Diego always tried to avoid such conversations, where one was imprisoned in the shackles of courtesy, forced to listen to and make statements about others' lives. The conversation turned to Doña Leonor, the Countess of Bazán, a good friend of his and Francisco's. After a few critical comments about her reputation at court, they looked at each other, aware of where this conversation would lead. Doña Leonor had been married twice, and both of her husbands had died. The last one, Diego's friend Roberto de Bazán, had perished heroically at the battle of Almansa, like Francisco's father and so many other men during those years. Leonor had been left alone, only twenty-five years old and with no offspring. Her age and wealth had granted her an independence she no longer wished to squander on another marriage.

'I won't confirm the claims of flightiness attributed to Doña Leonor, but nor will I deny her inclination towards bedding both gentlemen and vassals,' Don Enrique had said, to general laughter.

Doña Sol mentioned Doña Leonor's need to go looking for boys in the back alleys of Madrid in the small hours; the duchess noted her inability to conceive a child despite the fact she was also rumoured to have a bastard; Alfredo opined that this was owing to her extreme case of repressed concupiscence; Señora Belizón claimed to have heard that she had lost her virtue before marriage; and many accused her of having an insidious, dissolute nature.

Diego could see Francisco was squirming uncomfortably in his seat before the circus of slander in which all were participating: the duchess, Señorita Castro, Señora Belizón, Doña Sol, Alfredo and, naturally, Don Enrique, who told the story of how one of Doña Leonor's supposed lovers had bumped into her husband, the Count of Bazán, wearing a juste-au-corps taken from that man's wardrobe. To get out of this tight spot, and to avoid the count discovering that he was a cuckold and his wife an adulteress, the lover had expressed surprise at them both using the same tailor. Only Don Esteban, the Marquess of Villamar, did not participate, absorbed as he was in the desserts. The poor man did not notice that Francisco, having drifted away from the conversation, had lowered his hand beneath the table to gently stroke Don Esteban's wife's leg before she pushed his hand away.

Diego looked at Francisco to intervene. He did this a couple of times in the hope that the conversation would flow elsewhere. His patience finally wore out when Don Enrique asked him if he knew of any of the lady's recent adventures.

'Enough!' said Don Diego, striking the table with his open palm.

'I'm sorry?' the marquess responded.

'No more talking of Doña Leonor. She's a friend of mine and I don't like it. If anyone has anything to say about her life or character, I ask them not to do it under my roof and certainly not in my presence.'

After this incident, the conversation returned to its previous course and everyone talked about the excellent food. Once the meal was over, Diego decided to communicate the diners' praise to Señorita Belmonte in person. Without any further explanation, he made his apologies and left the room, smiling to himself.

Clara finished checking the roasted fowls and brushed each one again with the reduction she'd prepared from a base of butter, ground pepper, breadcrumbs and egg yolk. Next, she attended to the loin steaks. She breathed in the aroma of roasted meat. The sumptuous odour stirred her memories, and she suddenly recalled her mother's recipe book, its handwritten pages full of her mother's own recipes along with others from many different sources. Such moments blended into others in a cascade, until a melancholy smile formed on her lips. She felt a longing to hear her mother singing again, to feel her stroking her neck and combing her hair. The poor woman had continued to do this even after her husband's death had turned Clara into a living ghost. When Clara had developed her deep horror of being in open spaces, she had been almost bedbound for many weeks, barely eating or drinking. One night, tired of the sheets and her constant cold sweats, she had got to her feet, fought back the nausea and headed towards the drawing room, guided by the lamplight that filtered through the doorjamb. She had been about to enter when her mother and her sister's voices stopped her.

'She still hasn't eaten anything?' her mother asked.

'Every time she gets up, she's sick. She doesn't want to go out,' her sister replied.

How Clara deplored that weakness, the worry she had caused them just when they needed her most. She would never forgive herself. Her father so recently dead and she just creating more pain and worry for the family. That night, her mother and sister had whispered to each other so as not to wake her, about their approaching calvary. Their home was part of the hereditary estate which their great-grandfather, Santiago Belmonte, had established during his life as a high-ranking official in the court of King Felipe III. He had entailed the estate, stipulating that it should pass in its entirety to the firstborn son or, in his absence, the closest male relative. It had been thus ever since, and so, Clara's uncle Julián, envious and obsequious by nature, had seen their father's death as an opportunity. Hiding his covetousness behind good manners, he had written a letter to Clara's mother to make his involvement known and take charge of the inheritance, which he would administer for their benefit.

Unlike her father, her uncle had never viewed study as a way of attaining greater knowledge and understanding, seeing it merely as a means to achieving his own goals, and while he was being supported by her grandfather, he had made use of all the opportunities his position had granted him to graduate in law. He had become a skilled jurist and worked as a copyist for the Marquess of Valdetorres. Clara's uncle and her father had not been on good terms since before her birth, when it had come to light that Julián had seduced a girl of only fifteen, a friend of the family, leaving her pregnant and promising a marriage, a promise he had no intention of fulfilling. Clara's grandfather, Don Pedro Belmonte, who had walked straight and upright through life like a candle at mass, had intervened before his son was accused of rape and the matter was put in the hands of the law. He had assured the young girl's family that Don Julián would take her hand in marriage and he contributed a generous dowry. They were married in the shadow of the scandal, but both the girl and the baby had died in childbirth. Uncle Julián emerged from the affair free of charges and with his pockets full, and still had the nerve to state that his wife had been bad business.

Clara was very small when her grandfather had died, and her father had inherited the estate and booted her uncle out of all the properties, leaving him with only a small house in Salamanca and some cash. Clara and her sister had only met him on occasional visits, when he came to their father with his good manners and hypocritical propositions, hoping for an introduction to the court. That's why that night, when she overheard her mother say that Clara's uncle was going to take their whole world away from them, she had blanched, having to prop herself up against the wall in the corridor.

'Don't worry, my child,' her mother had told Clara's sister, Elvira, trying to protect her from the fear. 'We have some savings to get by on. I'll think of something. For now, don't say anything to your sister. We need her to get better.'

The echo of those words still tore at Clara's heart. She frowned as she cooked and thought about how she had to rid herself of those unhappy memories. Her father had always told her that although the past is directly connected with what is to come, you cannot live in it, for doing so will turn you into a ghost. And the same was true of the future. Happiness was to be found on a narrow pathway, on which one neither thought too much about the future nor dwelled excessively on the past.

A footman entered the kitchen, bringing her back to the present. She concentrated on her work again, amid the sounds of knives being sharpened, meat being minced, and the deafening hum of voices and thuds and clatters. The kitchen was like a chaotic stampede. The host of servants seemed to Clara an endless tide of people coming to the stoves like waves to the shore, only to disappear through the doors, bearing the food away on silver and porcelain plates. She enjoyed the hustle and bustle: the mortars, which went from hand to hand among the kitchen boys as they ground and mashed spices and garlic, the bubbling pots, slotted spoons and skewers clashing, the ladles, the carving forks and the constant movement of the steel trivets used to heat the pots and pans. Together they became a harmonious concerto from which she drew inspiration.

'Since the desserts have been served, the only noises you can hear are "mmm" and "aaah",' Elisa whispered in her ear.

Clara sighed with relief to discover that the duke and his friends were satisfied. Now the private dinner had been served, she could breathe more easily. Out of the corner of her eye, she watched her assistant, Beatriz Ulloa. Elisa took Clara by the arm and led her out into the passageway, away from the kitchens.

'I tell you, the witch and Beatriz are up to something,' she said. 'Whenever we're together, that girl tries to listen. I wouldn't be surprised if she goes and tells her everything we say. With that face on her, as if butter wouldn't melt…'

'Even if that is the case, it doesn't matter. That's Doña Ursula and Señorita Ulloa's problem,' Clara answered. 'Worrying about these things too much only makes them worse.'

Elisa dried her sweat with a linen rag.

'You're too smart by half,' she said.

Clara laughed a little as they once again heard music drifting down from upstairs. Throughout the day she had recognized the sounds of gavottes and galliards, even the French dances that were more to the king's taste, such as minuets and passepieds. She remembered her first introduction into society, in front of Queen María Luisa of Savoy, at one of the dances held by her father's friend, the Count of Montemar.

'I would love to attend one of these balls and dance with a nobleman,' Elisa mused.

'I attended a few when my father was alive,' Clara said. 'If it hadn't been for the war I'd have danced at more.'

'You must miss them.'

'Not so much. What I miss most is reading. My father had a library as big as the kitchen here, and a new book every week.'

Carried away by the music, Elisa gave a little hop and began to imagine her intervention into high society.

'Señorita Elisa, may I have this dance?' she said before positioning herself on the opposite side and adding, 'Of course, Don Enrique.'

Clara laughed and applauded. Elisa continued, pretending to move in unison with her imaginary gentleman.

Clara was touched to see the simple and unattainable dreams of her friend, who was spinning clumsily in imitation of the steps of the ballroom dances. Elisa, who smiled at her with every twist, confessed that her greatest wish was to find a husband.

'If only the marquess would propose to me... or his lordship himself,' she said, chuckling at the impossibility of this scenario. 'I have always considered the duke to be a very attractive man.'

'To me, he comes across as somewhat surly, but I believe that behind that initial gruffness hides a beautiful soul,' said Clara.

'Señorita Belmonte.'

The voice had come from the other end of the corridor. Clara looked over and there, like an apparition, illuminated by the candles, appeared the figure of Don Diego. Elisa and Clara greeted him and could barely contain their surprise. They didn't know how long he'd been there and how much of their conversation he had heard. Clara didn't even want to countenance his having heard their comments about him, and her cheeks turned scarlet. She lowered her head to disguise her turmoil. That same morning, before leaving for the gardens at Villacor, he had appeared in the kitchen and interrogated her. And now here he was again, walking towards her in that self-assured way, his eyes fixed on her the whole time.

Clara looked up until her eyes met his, and a silence settled, an absence of sound that swallowed up the chorus of dull, metallic clangs coming from the stoves. Even the sounds of the minuet from the upper floors vanished. She was suddenly overcome with a sweet sense of stillness, and she was certain, for some inexplicable reason, that she no longer felt any discomfort looking at him, that her burning cheeks had cooled off and that Don Diego's bright eyes were like a peaceful sky in which she was reflected.

Diego saw in those eyes a determination which reminded him of Alba. Perhaps Clara's determination was harder, more sober and direct than his late wife's, because she had suffered hardships which had forced her to survive in an environment she had not been brought up for. Despite her demureness, there was something fearless in her expression. Diego was taken aback, captivated by those cinnamon-coloured eyes, contemplating her as if she were a work of art.

'I have come to relay to you the effusive congratulations I have received on your behalf for the extraordinary dinner you have prepared this evening,' he said, somewhat stiffly.

'I am honoured by your guests' kind words and very grateful to you for coming to communicate them to me in person,' Señorita Belmonte answered, displaying the exquisite manners that contrasted so sharply with her role as cook.

'It goes without saying that those include my own,' he said.

'You honour me, your grace,' she said, after a few moments.

Diego did not reply. Realizing that he was standing before a cook and not the educated daughter of a doctor, he suddenly felt uncomfortable. He politely took his leave of her, ignoring the maid's presence, and walked away, but once he'd turned the corner, and without knowing why, he slowed his pace to listen to the nervous laughter of the two young women.

For a moment, it was as if the war and Alba's loss had left no mark on him; he did not feel guilty about his wife's death, or about the drop of happiness brought to him by listening to that conversation.

17

A voice inside Amelia's head urged caution. She told herself she should persist with her initial plan to win over Don Diego. What had taken place that afternoon in the carriage could not be allowed to occur again, not until the marquess had delivered everything he had promised. Once that had happened, she would be free to decide how she wished to live her life. Despite the voice, she could not supress her body's scandalous desire to be possessed by the marquess. At the private supper that night, despite trying to avoid him, as soon as their eyes had met, her passions had been inflamed once again. She couldn't help recalling the tenderness with which he had awakened her desire. It could not have been less like the crude and unrestrained approaches of the Count of Guadalmin in Cadiz.

However, to her surprise, throughout the firework display, the dancing and the toasting, Don Enrique had kept his distance. Rather, the marquess had popped up here and there, propitiating her encounters with Don Diego. He engaged other guests in conversation, brought Amelia and Don Diego together with the pretext of a toast, and even created the odd diversion so that the two of them would be alone. As a result, she had been able to relax a little and enjoy the ball with Don Diego, Don Alfredo and the other gentlemen. At the end, tired of flirting with the duke for little reward, she had decided to withdraw to her chamber. *That's enough for the first night of the celebrations*, she told herself.

Now, as the chambermaid undid her bodice and her skirts, the mere touch of the servant's fingers on her neck was enough to recall the marquess. After dismissing her, Amelia slid between the starched sheets and snuffed out the candle. She soon fell asleep, and it was not long before the marquess entered her dreams. She was floating on a calm sea, the waves gently lapping at her hair and caressing her body. Her senses were gradually aroused, her cheeks burning and her lips moist. A pair of hands were caressing her breasts and stroking her thighs, and there was the intoxicating scent of peach. A tongue brushed her neck, and she awoke to the realization that Don Enrique was in her bed, naked by her side. If only she had locked the door when the maid had left.

'Don't resist, Señorita Castro,' he whispered, as if he were the devil himself. 'Don't worry. Tomorrow you will receive the papers from the notary for your approval.'

She sighed and tried to slip out of his grasp, but he held her tightly against his chest so that she could feel his heart pounding as he continued to caress her. He smelled so good, his body was so lithe, his words so seductive that, both angry and confused, aroused by the words this man was whispering in her ear, she soon found she was struggling not against him but rather against herself.

'Give in. I know that you desire me as much as I desire you,' he challenged her. 'I will be a slave to your body until dawn breaks. I will kiss every inch of your skin, until you are in an ecstasy of desire. I will uncover secret pleasures and we will explore them together until you can take no more. And when we have finished, you will be utterly changed, unable to forget the night on which a man truly possessed you.'

Against all her wishes, her body was aflame with desire. She was becoming wet, and he prepared to enter her. Then she realized that he was wearing upon his manhood a smooth sheath of oiled intestine. She had heard of such things being used by men who frequented prostitutes, to protect themselves from the pox, and she felt both insulted and overwhelmed. Only once had she been with a man, and that had been under duress, and yet here she was being treated like a whore. But all she could do was groan. Don Enrique's whispered words resonated in her ears, and she crossed herself in a futile effort to suppress the heat that was rising from her loins. Then she surrendered. She was so tired of living on the edge of the precipice. She gave in to his honeyed words, which had unleashed her own savage desire. Abandoning herself to the urgings of her flesh, she arched her back and pushed against him, lost to reason.

'You are the devil in person,' she murmured.

'I only wish to give you the pleasure you deserve, Señorita Castro,' he replied.

'What will become of me?'

The marquess pleasured her three times before the sun rose, whispering words that both scandalized and inflamed her.

When she awoke, he was no longer in the bedchamber, but true to his word, before breakfast a leather portfolio arrived, containing the papers granting her a comfortable income for life, the house in Madrid and permanent usufruct of the villa in Cadiz. She read them carefully. Everything seemed to be in order, but she decided to send the papers to a lawyer in Madrid, a former confidant of her father, to confirm their validity before signing them. Although she did not understand Don Enrique's true purpose, she was determined to escape from poverty. Her original plan had been to seduce Don Diego and become his wife. But if Don Enrique was going to provide her with a fortune, she saw no reason to lose her independence. However, she would continue with her strategy of pursuing the duke until she received a reply from the lawyer within a few weeks. Don Enrique was not to be trusted: he seduced her by night while helping her to win Don Diego's hand by day – behaviour that hardly suggested he was driven by good intentions.

After breakfast and a solitary walk around the gardens, she contrived to ensure that her path crossed with that of the duke, but they scarcely had time to exchange more than a few words before he hurried back inside on hearing that Their Majesties were awake. He then spent the whole day playing host, attending to the king and queen and other illustrious visitors, so that even Don Enrique's subtle efforts to make their paths coincide were in vain.

And so, Amelia spent her time with Doña Mercedes and Doña Sol Montijos and other acquaintances from better days, listening to cutting remarks about those who were not present. Occasionally she recalled the night before, with the marquess, and she shivered with desire.

Later that afternoon, she tried to approach the duke again, but he always seemed to be surrounded by a phalanx of people. She wondered whether it would be seemly to strike up a conversation with his brother, but there was neither sight nor sound of him all day long. It was clear that he kept his distance from the court. After the siesta, the theatrical performances, the chamber music and various readings, as she was walking down the corridor, Don Enrique found an opportunity to whisper in her ear.

'I will try to bring you together with Don Diego.'

He continued on his way, and Amelia – who was still turning everything over in her mind – didn't even have time to ask him why he was so interested in making possible her marriage to the duke. Finally, thanks to the intervention of Doña Mercedes, no doubt egged on by the marquess, she had the opportunity to dance with Don Diego. However, just when she seemed to have got him on his own, King Felipe called for Don Diego and didn't allow the duke to leave his side for the rest of the night. Amelia resigned herself and, after the fireworks and the operetta, returned to the peace of her chambers. This time, she locked the door, despite her wish that Don Enrique might return and once again rob her of her reason. She left the key on the bedside table, slipped between the covers and could feel herself grow wet when she thought of him. She knew that her body desired what her reason rejected. And yet it was not long before she was shaken from her dreams. Once again, he was in her bed, making her very soul shudder.

'Follow your desires...' he whispered, awakening the demons inside her.

She was soon groaning and trembling uncontrollably. And then he took her, unleashing waves of pleasure until, carried away, she begged him for more. *What has this wicked man done, to make me sin against decorum and against God Himself?* she wondered. This was now the second night on which she had succumbed to him. She was torn between her desire to preserve her social reputation and the arousal of her own carnal desires when she felt him inside her. Finally, their passion exhausted, they slept until the first rays of dawn. When they awoke, Don Enrique prepared to take her once more, but she resisted his advances.

'Once the papers have been signed, we can sail together again, but not before,' she told him.

He smiled and said nothing. He gathered up his clothes and, half dressed, vanished like a ghost.

She slept until late and heard the guests, including the king and queen, leaving Castamar. After a delicious breakfast, she ordered the servants to pack up her belongings. While her luggage was being loaded onto the carriage, Don Enrique approached and suggested that she should prolong her visit to the estate.

'I still don't understand why you want me to marry the duke,' she said, unable to contain herself.

'Do you not wish it for yourself?' he replied, enigmatically.

'Of course,' she answered, almost whispering and with a smile flickering on her lips. 'Even so, extending my visit would be completely impossible. It's clear that he will question my intentions if I ask to stay on for no apparent reason.'

The marquess appeared to be satisfied with her answer, but something inside Amelia told her he was not pleased to see her leave Castamar.

'We will find another occasion, my dear,' he assured her. 'And do tell me when we can sign the papers.'

'If possible, and if you have no objection, this very week,' she replied. 'I will never forget what you have done for me.'

After saying goodbye to everyone, guests and hosts alike, Don Enrique mounted his horse and galloped off. Amelia prepared to climb into the carriage that would take her back to Madrid. She reflected on the fact that she had arrived at Castamar almost a virgin, chaste and pure, inexperienced in the game of love, appearing to possess a certain social standing but, in reality, poor, in debt and on the brink of the precipice. But now, leaving the estate, she was on the verge of becoming a rich young woman... one who was well versed in the ways of the bedchamber.

'Your time here must have cheered your heart, my dear girl, and I'm glad for you,' Doña Mercedes told her, as she bade farewell. 'You look more carefree and less serious.'

'At Castamar I have found much of the peace my poor heart yearned for following my father's death,' Amelia replied, with a smile.

She finished saying goodbye to Doña Mercedes, who was departing for Valladolid, and then, alone, she took her leave of Don Diego. The duke bowed to her.

'You are welcome to return whenever you so desire, Señorita Castro.'

'I will take you at your word,' she replied.

In the carriage, as she took her last look at the gardens with their autumnal tones of red and yellow, she told herself she didn't give a fig for Don Enrique's schemes. As soon as the papers were signed and she had achieved her independence, she didn't intend to follow any of the marquess's plans. And when it came to her marriage, she would seek in Don Diego a loyal friend, rather than a husband, with the aim of winning his heart that way. She had seen that a man like him, if he truly loved her, would never permit anything bad to happen to her, and if Don Enrique was not the man he appeared to be and tried to play a trick on her, all the marquess's wealth would offer him no protection at all against the wrath of the Duke of Castamar.

18 October 1720

Ursula nodded when the servant brought her the message informing her that his lordship wished to see her. She ordered the maids and the boot boys to finish preparing the rooms before closing up the east wing of the house. Many of the guests had been accommodated there, and it had to be left in perfect order until next year. The page informed her that his lordship was with the registrar, Don Alfonso Corbo, who acted as administrator and secretary of the estate. As she walked from the other end of the building towards the estate office, Ursula thought about how this year's events had been a success. The servants had acquitted themselves well, and she had to admit that Señorita Belmonte had performed her duties with aplomb. The fireworks, the theatre performances, the music, the games and, above all, the food had delighted the royal party and the other guests. The head cook of Castamar had won the respect of his lordship and had conquered the palates of the king and queen. No sooner had they tasted the delights on offer than they had asked whether Don Diego's head cook was a Frenchman. Their surprise had been even greater when they had discovered that the cook was neither French nor a man.

Throughout the festivities, the food had garnered constant praise from the guests. And with each compliment Don Diego received, Clara Belmonte's position had become more firmly established and Ursula's own power had correspondingly weakened. There was nothing she could hold over Clara other than her own authority, and it was generally accepted that in noble households the head cook was answerable only to the butler. As Ursula was not a man and could never aspire to become a butler, it was inevitable that, sooner or later, Clara would fall under the sway of Don Melquíades.

Now, just as on other occasions, she pondered how this girl, with her unusual background, had become the duke's personal chef. *It was all so fast, I didn't see it coming*, she thought as she made her way along the corridor, her eyes peeled. *Don't be too hard on yourself, Ursula. Nobody could have foreseen this.* In just eight days, the girl had risen to the top of the pile, while Ursula had had to spend her best years as a cleaner in the household of the Duke of Villares to support her father. She still remembered that old fool, Doña Perfila, the housekeeper. Ursula had been only twenty years old, and her face was bruised from the beating her father had given her the night before. Doña Perfila had entered the music room and was issuing instructions with her steely voice. Standing in front of Ursula, she had inspected her face contemptuously and, without realizing it, delivered a lesson on the life that awaited Ursula if she didn't keep her wits about her.

'I see that drunkard of a father has beaten you again,' the housekeeper had said. 'I hope this kind of thing isn't going to interfere with your work.'

Terrified, Ursula had vehemently denied that it would and, before the other woman left, had foolishly tried to make a good impression on her.

'Doña Perfila,' she had ventured, 'I know how to read and write, and some arithmetic too.'

The housekeeper had looked at her as if she were a worm and had tutted.

'And why should I care what you know?' she had asked.

'Perhaps I could be of more use to you,' Ursula had answered, her hands crossed in front of her and her head bowed.

'In another position, you mean?' the housekeeper had enquired, raising one eyebrow.

Ursula had nodded, as if to say that she would be happy with whatever position the other woman assigned her to. The housekeeper had remained silent before letting out a short laugh. Then she had turned and, as she headed for the door, had issued a final, cutting remark.

'The best thing you can do is work hard, unless you want your father to beat you to death for being a sloven,' she had declared.

From that day, Ursula understood that there were no good people in this world, save for a few exceptions such as Doña Alba. She ascended the final steps that led to a broad gallery, lined with portraits of the scions of the House of Castamar, from the first duke, back in the time of Queen Isabella and King Ferdinand. She walked along at a rapid pace – despite her age she was still physically fit – until she came to two panelled oak doors. She knocked and waited for the duke to invite her to enter. He took a while, as was his custom. When she entered, her path crossed with that of the registrar, Don Alfonso Corbo, who greeted her courteously. Ursula bowed slightly in reply while Don Diego continued to write with a quill fashioned from a swan's feather.

'Your grace, Doña Mercedes's and Don Enrique's baggage has been prepared,' she reported, assuming that this was why she had been called to see him.

'Excellent,' said the duke as he continued to write.

She waited for a few more moments, until Don Diego signed the letter. With an air of ritual, he picked up the pounce pot, sprinkled a few grains of powder over the paper to dry the ink, folded the paper and stamped it with his seal. Then he offered it to her, a smile on his face. She approached and took it from him, the wax still warm.

'Do you know the bookshop on Calle Mayor?' he asked.

She nodded. 'I have never visited it myself, but I know that your grace orders many of his books from there, particularly those concerned with botany.'

'This note doesn't contain my usual order for botany books, but a special request,' he declared.

Ursula suspected that the missive had something to do with Señorita Belmonte, and she involuntarily stiffened.

'Tell the new boy, Roberto, to take one of the mares and deliver the order to the bookseller, Señor Bernabé,' Don Diego instructed her, oblivious to her discomfort.

Ursula, concealing her agitation and making a small curtsy, took her leave, assuring the duke that his instructions would be implemented. As soon as she was out of the door, she strode towards her small office. On her way, she passed a group of boot boys and ordered them to go and find Roberto Velázquez, Don Melquíades's nephew, and send him to see her. She pursed her lips until she reached the servants' floor and entered her office.

There, protected by the solid door and with her nerves jangling, she picked up a paper knife, carefully broke the seal, and read the contents. After the usual preamble, the duke asked the bookseller to procure whatever collection of recipes he might have, if possible by a famous chef and written in Spanish, Latin or, as a last resort, some foreign tongue. Ursula quickly lit a candle stub on one of the lamps and, taking a bar of wax, applied a couple of drops to the seal to hide her interference. She was waiting for the wax to set when Roberto Velázquez knocked at the door. She gave him the note and sent him away again, eager to be left alone to ponder her discovery.

Once he had left, she closed the door and leaned against it, trying to calm her nerves and think about what steps to take now. It was clear that Clara Belmonte had won the affections of Don Diego. Once the book had been procured, a bond would be established between them that Ursula would no longer be able to influence, and this link would grant Señorita Belmonte direct access to Don Diego, a privilege that was at present reserved to her and to the head gardener. Following the success of the festivities, the girl had become a serious threat to her authority.

She locked the door and made her way upstairs, nursing fond memories of the days when Doña Alba had been in charge of the house, and she had felt secure under her mistress's protection. She continued to feel gratitude towards her, and to miss that tranquil world. Ursula would never forget that day, among the rose bushes and the statues of the flowerbeds, when she had been on her way to the arbour. She had made preparations to serve almond cake and hot chocolate to the duchess and her cousin, Don Rodrigo, Duke of Castañeda and Villalonga, who had recently arrived from Cartagena. All of a sudden, Ursula's husband had appeared, out of nowhere, and had grabbed her by the throat. Elías, missing an eye and showing every sign of having been subjected to torture, was thirsting for revenge.

'It hasn't been easy to track you down, you filthy whore,' he said, his mouth quivering with rage. 'You're going to pay for what they did to me.'

He had tightened his grip around her neck, and she had felt the lifeblood draining from her. But just as she was preparing to breathe her last, the steely point of an épée had pressed against her husband's throat.

'Let her go or I'll sever your jugular,' ordered an imposing voice.

The anger in Elías's eyes immediately transformed into a look of terror so profound that he released her immediately, and Ursula fell to the floor like a rag doll. Surrounding them were a captain of the guard of Castamar, two manservants, Doña Alba and her cousin Don Rodrigo, still holding his sword to Ursula's husband's throat. She had begun to cough and gasp, as if trying to trap the life that only a few moments earlier had been escaping her body. Don Rodrigo's épée had grazed the skin on Elías's throat, and he ordered the man to kneel, with his hands on the ground. One of the guardsmen helped Ursula to her feet, and Doña Alba, with her characteristic consideration, came over to make sure she was alright.

'Are you okay, Señora Berenguer?' she asked, and Ursula could only nod, overcome with shame.

The duchess turned to the odious Elías.

'Who are you and what are you doing in my gardens?' she demanded.

Her contemptuous tone had made it clear to Elías that, if he failed to give a convincing explanation, he could end up swinging from the gallows.

'I'm her husband, your grace. This woman falsely accused me of betraying the king and I was tortured as a result,' he replied, his voice faltering. 'I was released yesterday because there was no evidence against me.'

Don Rodrigo put away his sword and turned to his cousin.

'This is a private matter between man and wife. The best we can do is not become involved.'

Ursula threw herself at the duchess's feet in desperation.

'Don't abandon me, my lady, please,' she begged, her hands trembling and the panic rising within her.

'If her husband beats her, he must have a reason,' Don Rodrigo said to Doña Alba.

At this, the duchess had turned and, looking at her cousin, uttered the words that Ursula had never forgotten. Words that had ensured her freedom, a guarantee that nobody would ever be able to hurt her again and, of course, had won her unconditional love for Doña Alba.

'Cousin, your words are not those of a gentleman, and this is certainly not a private matter. This woman is in my service, and I cannot allow her to come to any harm', she had said.

Then she had approached Elías and, with the tip of her parasol, had raised his chin and forced him to look her in the eye.

'Listen carefully, you pathetic wretch – if you haven't disappeared from the capital within two days, I will ensure that you are garrotted as a traitor to the Crown. If you value your life, you'll come no closer to Madrid than Finisterre.'

Elías had nodded, his body trembling with fear at the thought of being tortured again. Only when Doña Alba had satisfied herself that Elías had truly understood the seriousness of her threat did she allow him to stand up. She had dismissed him with a warning that she would ensure that he kept his word. And that had been the last time Ursula saw her husband. He never wrote to her again or appeared at Castamar, not even after Doña Alba's death. Perhaps because he knew the duke would afford her the same protection and would be less forgiving than his wife had been. After it was all over, Doña Alba had told her she would never have to worry about the problem again. And she, her eyes brimming with tears, had kissed the duchess's hand in gratitude. The duchess, with her usual serenity, had instructed Ursula to return to the house and take the rest of the day off. As Ursula had walked away, she heard Doña Alba tell her cousin not to express opinions more suited to people who lacked an education and a good upbringing.

'The weaker sex must be defended from men like that. A gentleman cannot permit such mistreatment of a woman, and even less so if the perpetrator is her husband.'

Don Rodrigo had blanched at his cousin's diatribe, apologized profusely and begged to be forgiven. Doña Alba, feigning anger, had told him he would only be forgiven when he had truly made amends. *That's what she was like*, Ursula thought. *No housekeeper in the world could have been prouder of their mistress than I was of her*. At that moment, a relationship had grown up between them which transcended the difference in rank. Doña Alba had protected her in every sense: she had raised her salary, assigned her more responsibilities and trusted her more than any other member of the household.

Upon reaching the wing of the house that was about to be closed up, Ursula entered one of the rooms and came face to face with a life-size portrait of her old mistress above the fireplace, radiant, sheathed in satin and silk, seated, a fan in her hand, her aristocratic bearing clear to see. Ursula stopped to admire her.

'If only you were here now, my mistress,' she said to herself. 'How little I would care about Señorita Clara Belmonte and her arrival in the kitchen.'

18

After attending to that morning's business with his clerk and bidding farewell to all the guests, Diego decided to play the harpsichord. The night before, at the queen's bidding, he had performed some pieces by François Couperin, and on recalling this he had an urge do it again. He'd felt different over the last few days. There was something new in the way he was sensing Alba's distance, as if his sorrow was now closer to a lament than extreme pain. Alba would always occupy a place in his heart, but perhaps he was tired of saying that he did not want to forget his wife when, in reality, he had wearied of her death surrounding everything. Previously, when his thoughts had turned away from Alba, he had always returned to embracing the empty sheets and his old companion, frustration. But it had not been so this time, and despite the barren landscape that still lay within him, a new stream was flowing, one with the potential to irrigate his drought-stricken soul.

Perhaps this was why he had got carried away by the juvenile impulse to buy the book for Clara Belmonte. That strange fluttering he felt in the pit of his stomach was the same sensation that had told him the previous night that it was better to wander down the passageways of Castamar in silence, ruminating on the change happening inside him, than to return to his bedroom and ask no questions of himself. So, when the final guest had gone to bed, he'd chosen to reflect further among the golden frames which embellished the portraits of the many members of the Castamar dynasty.

He had not imagined that his ruminations would be cut short by a casual encounter with his friend Francisco. That rascal, wishing to prolong the celebrations by taking them to Doña Sol's bedchambers, had been crossing the corridor ahead of him, holding a candelabra. Taken by surprise, Diego had kept walking and, in order not to interrupt the *affaire* that was surely about to happen, had hid in the shadows. Francisco had knocked gently at the door of the marchioness's room.

Doña Sol had feigned resistance, complaining that her husband was sleeping only yards away, in the next-door bedroom.

'That only makes it more exciting,' Francisco had answered.

'One more step and my cries will be heard all around the house,' she had threatened.

'Believe me, Doña Sol, I hope to elicit a few myself,' he had replied.

They had closed the door in absolute silence, making Don Esteban a cuckold, Doña Sol an adulteress and Francisco a libertine. Of course, this was nothing new. Each one had been fulfilling their respective roles for a long time. Diego did not mind Francisco seducing a woman under his roof, provided it was done discreetly.

At sunrise the duke had ordered breakfast, wondering what his new cook would prepare for him. As expected, she had not let him down, and a perfectly seasoned pigeon consommé, sweet lemon pastries, poached eggs, buns sweetened with honey and almonds and, of course, hot chocolate had appeared. It was all beautifully presented, as if each plate were a canvas.

After finishing, and motivated only by gluttony, he had been tempted to ask for some other delicacy but Don Melquíades had informed him that his guests were about to depart. The last of them had been Señorita Castro, who had not opened up to him again since their conversation in Villacor. They had shared a few dances during the celebration. Although he hardly knew her, he felt some affection for her – or perhaps it was pity – deducing that, behind that veil, there dwelled a wounded soul in need of comfort and warmth. He told himself that something about Señorita Castro and her erratic relationship with Don Enrique didn't quite fit. The naturally suspicious Gabriel had not taken his eyes off them. In fact, his brother had decided to do some research as a precaution. To that end, he had recruited the services of a trusted acquaintance, a former slave called Daniel Forrado.

The duke continued to slide his fingers over the keys of the harpsichord. His resuming of this old habit of playing on Friday mornings must have taken all the servants by surprise. How Alba would have loved to hear him.

'Future events are illusions, my love, they do not exist,' she would say, trying to soothe his anguish over the war. 'It is foolish to be governed by ill omens when we cannot know if they will come to pass. If we are going to summon illusions, it is far more enjoyable to imagine the best possible outcomes.'

'I'm worried, Alba. This is the second time Felipe has had to leave Madrid and the second time the archduke has entered the capital,' he'd said to her once, as the Habsburgs took the city again. 'And I know there are traitors in our midst, apparent allies who secretly wish the king harm.'

Alba, resolute, had responded that though it was indeed the second time Archduke Charles had entered the city, it was also the second time no one had proclaimed him as their new king. He had smiled at her and kissed her on the lips, nuzzling into her bosom and then, still in the grip of fear, he had told her that if Felipe was defeated, they would lose everything. Everyone at the court dealt with the fear in their own way – some recognizing it and wagering everything they had, as was the case with Diego; others not staking anything at all, while giving the appearance of loyalty and honour, planning to side with whoever was the victor; and then there was a third party, hedging their bets by supporting both sides equally and thus adopting betrayal as a survival strategy. Alba, with her blind faith in destiny, was content to know that lady luck was protecting King Felipe, and so, nothing bad could happen.

'Who put him out of harm's way that fateful night in Almenar?' she had asked Diego, referring to the time they had been surrounded and forced to flee, and Diego had whisked the king away from enemy lines.

Time, thank God, had proven Alba right.

Diego was just finishing another toccata when he heard someone knocking at the door. He gave them permission to enter and young Roberto, Don Melquíades's nephew, came in holding a parcel. Diego smiled as he took it in his hands and dismissed the boy. He then opened the parcel and contemplated the fine binding and the inscription in Latin with the author's name and the title of the work: Apicci Coelii: *The Art of Cooking*. It was accompanied by a note from Señor Bernabé, the bookseller.

> *Your grace,*
>
> *A few years ago, the book I am sending to you fell into my hands on one of my visits to the printing houses of the United Provinces of the Netherlands. This is a second edition, printed in Amsterdam in 1709, and is one of the first books about Roman cooking, and perhaps cooking in general, written in Latin by Marcus Gavius Apicius. I hope that the book is to your liking.*
>
> *Your faithful servant,*
>
> *Don Manuel Bernabé*

Diego sat down and, with childish glee, wondered how to deliver the gift to Señorita Belmonte. Under no circumstance could he offer it to her personally, since that would send the wrong message regarding his intentions, as if he were the kind of noble who took advantage of his status and established relationships with his servants just for amusement. Nor could he deliver it through another servant, since that would only generate rumours and put Señorita Belmonte in an uncomfortable situation. Besides, it was only a gift for her work in the kitchen and he didn't want it to take on any other meaning. The best thing would be for the book to appear spontaneously in her room and for her to decide whether to accept it. His mind made up, he took a sheet of paper from his bureau, picked up the swan's quill and began writing her a note.

El Zurdo swallowed his bean and rice soup, noting the onion and garlic mashed together with saffron. He looked up and saw Hernaldo de la Marca walk in through the door. As he strode, you could see the ugly scar which split the right side of his face in two, from the top of his jaw to the corner of his lips. There would never be any camaraderie between them. Firstly, because neither were the kind to have friends, and secondly, because they knew that each could kill the other in the blink of an eye.

'You look hungry, Zurdo,' Hernaldo said.

'Order something for yourself,' El Zurdo answered as the soldier took a seat.

Lately he'd been visiting the Zaguán brothel more often because the food had improved greatly. Sebastián, the owner, had been convinced by one of his whores to allow her to cook. And there was no doubting she made good stews. La Zalamera, as she was known among the regulars, had been a great discovery. Since Sebastián had stopped cooking and she had started, the Zaguán had begun to fill up with customers, and its owner could not have been happier.

'She's a damned good cook,' Sebastián had told him discreetly, so that La Zalamera would not overhear and ask him for more money.

El Zurdo had smiled and replied that Sebastián must not raise the prices because the Zaguán was not a respectable house but a brothel. Sebastián, whom he had known for years, was famed for the many cheap whores who constituted the bulk of his business. Court officials did not bother him too much, since some of them availed themselves of his services. El Zurdo was himself a regular. To start with, he had frequented the place in order to enjoy Jacinta, a gap-toothed harlot who for a few coins was prepared to do anything. Subsequently, he continued to go because, apart from it being cheap to eat there – in spite of the watered-down wine – it was a good source of work.

Sometimes a servant from a wealthy house would appear in search of someone to tame their colts, or a discharged soldier would come seeking to employ him as an assassin, to help them dispose of some disgruntled so-and-so. Such offers were fairly regular, mostly because he knew all the senior grooms at the noble estates. Thanks to their recommendations and his own skill, he had been able to work at the stables of these gentlemen. By these means, he had earned a living as a groom, while also carrying out the dirty work for many of these nobles. He'd been dedicated to both occupations for many years now, and his skill with the blade was known throughout the alleyways and cul-de-sacs of Lavapiés.

Scaring some fop or stabbing some drunken soldier who owed someone money left him indifferent, whereas he adored spending time with horses. It was one of the few things in life that made him happy. No horse had ever judged him or betrayed him or reared up against him for no reason. When he was in their company, he felt he had no sins before the Lord, as if he were absolved of all the crimes he had committed. 'The most beautiful animal on earth,' he'd always said. That's why he looked after them so well, washing their coats, combing their manes and sweeping away their dung without feeling any sense of obligation. He liked to stroke them, to whisper sweet words into their ears, to break them in gently. His dream was to save up enough to have his own herd of horses near Madrid, a reserve of pedigrees, ideally Carthusians from the region of Jerez, and with input from some acquaintances, he would rear studs and sell good specimens to nobles at the court. But buying the land, building the stables and selecting the fillies and stallions would not be cheap, and even if he started off in a modest fashion, he would need a fortune. After fifteen years, he was still a long way from achieving it – he only had eight thousand reals for something that would cost hundreds of thousands.

Even so, his love of horses and his dream kept some balance in his life. In fact, his protectiveness of these animals had even led him to spend time in prison, after he had slashed the face of a man who was savagely beating his ancient nag with a crop because it refused to walk. The poor horse had been badly shod, meaning it found walking even more painful than its master's blows.

Prison hadn't changed him much. When he got out, he'd gone back to training horses, marking the rhythms of all the different strides, from a simple trot to a full gallop. And precisely because of this, an acquaintance had introduced him ten years ago to Hernaldo de la Marca, for a delicate job. Since then, they had only ever met in passing in the Zaguán and other places of ill repute, exchanging curt glances and greetings, knowing they shared secrets that could cost them their heads. That had been the case until recently, when Hernaldo had come to him to ask for the Castamar skeleton key, which he had had since working there.

'Did the key work?' El Zurdo asked, as he licked his spoon.

By way of an answer, Hernaldo dropped the pouch of coins onto the table and sat down facing him.

'That's not the only reason I'm here,' he said, pointing at the bag. 'It's a simple job.'

El Zurdo nodded, took a sip of wine and smiled ironically. The most difficult assignment he had ever undertaken had come from Hernaldo de la Marca ten years ago. On that occasion he had been asked to train Don Diego of Castamar's horse, so that, when the steed heard the high frequency sound produced by a silent whistle, it would rear up and collapse onto the rider with all its force and weight. The true difficulty of this assignment, for him, had not been training the animal, but knowing that, to succeed, he must break the horse's pure spirit through pain, terror and anguish until it became a killer of men. He had considered refusing the assignment, but he couldn't. Hernaldo had given him a sum of money which made the dream of his stable a little more real – and he had made it clear that if El Zurdo did not do it there would be consequences.

The head groom at Castamar had been the victim of a convenient nocturnal assault. And El Zurdo had appeared two days later to stand in for him, after being recommended by the Baron of Noblevilla's head groom, who had days earlier received a succulent incentive in exchange for the tip. After Don Melquíades, the head butler at Castamar, had accepted, El Zurdo had gained access to Don Diego's horse, a purebred Carthusian with a golden coat, muscular neck and abundant tail and mane. *An animal like this would break anyone's heart*, he had thought as he trained it in secret. Every crack of the whip had been like a stab in the guts. Two weeks later, entering the head butler's office in the dead of night, he had made a copy of the skeleton key using clay moulds.

What Hernaldo did not know was that El Zurdo had been informed of a change to his instructions by a new client, who had offered him a princely sum to train Doña Alba's mount instead of the duke's. On the day Don Diego was meant to die, nobody understood why his horse had merely reared up while his wife's had crushed her. Hours after the incident, Hernaldo had appeared in the Zaguán with a murderous look in his eyes. As soon as they went out into the courtyard, Hernaldo had grabbed El Zurdo by the throat and smashed him against the door.

'Whoreson! Tell me what happened, or I'll slit your throat! It was Doña Alba's horse that fell,' he said.

El Zurdo had calmly alerted his assailant to the fact that the point of his own blade was pressed against the man's leather doublet, directly over his stomach.

'You'll have to slit my throat very quickly if you want to do it before I slash open your guts and watch you bleed out like a pig,' he answered.

The soldier had considered this for a moment and let him go, cursing him and demanding an explanation. His story already prepared, he had looked at Hernaldo, still holding the knife in his left hand.

'The horses are twins. They swapped them,' he said.

Hernaldo looked at him, trying to gauge if he was telling the truth.

'I hope you haven't stabbed me in the back,' he warned, one hand on his short sword.

'What reason would I have for killing the lady? You paid me to train the horse and that's what I did.'

That was how they had left it. Hernaldo departed, convinced by El Zurdo's explanation. And the marquess must have accepted it too, because there was no reprisal.

El Zurdo finished eating and wiped his snout with his sleeve. He looked at Hernaldo and, before continuing the conversation, told Jacinta to wait for him in her room. Hernaldo lowered his voice.

'It's to do with Don Diego's negro,' he murmured. 'You must watch him from now on.'

'Why?' El Zurdo asked.

'Because the scoundrel is watching us,' he answered. Then, taking out another pouch of coins, he added menacingly, 'And because I'm paying you to keep your mouth shut and do your damn job.'

19

Clara felt her position at Castamar had become more secure, particularly with regards to Doña Ursula, who appeared to have accepted her as head cook. She hoped this apparent tranquillity would last until winter and that her presence would no longer be seen as a threat by the insufferable woman.

The cold of the previous night had brought Rosalía knocking on the door of her room, complaining that her feet were freezing. As soon as Clara had opened the door, the poor thing had hugged her tight. Rosalía would start each night in the bedroom where her mother, Don Diego's wetnurse, had slept, but just after midnight, she would wake up and let out cries that disturbed the other servants. She would always be found curled up on the kitchen floor, in front of the stove.

For a long time, according to Elisa, nobody had been able to work out what was causing her to scream with terror. Don Diego even called Doctor Evaristo, who had concluded that it was the result of a nervous disorder, caused by the loss of her mother, and that it would be remedied by infusions of camomile. When this had had no effect, the doctor suggested she be confined in a madhouse, but the duke had flatly refused, having sworn to the girl's mother to look after her. He even told the doctor that, if no solution were found, he would not hesitate to call him out every night of the year to attend to her in person. Despite this threat, the doctor had been unable to come up with a remedy.

It was Señor Casona who managed to get to the bottom of
the problem. One night, he decided to keep vigil in the room
next door. Rosalía, as usual, woke up in a terrible screaming fit
but calmed down as soon as Señor Casona lit a candle. It turned
out that Rosalía was terrified of the dark, and when she awoke
to the pitch-black, she would be possessed by panic and flee
towards the only place where there was some light. Henceforth
it was agreed that she would sleep with a candle burning, but
sometimes this went out, and Rosalía would return to her old
ways. Moreover, there was the risk that the girl might end up
starting a fire. Once again, Señor Casona found a solution,
constructing a shed with a window for the girl's exclusive use,
so that the glow from the garden lamps, and often the rays of
the moon, shone into her room. Since then, Rosalía had ceased
to be a nuisance.

Even so, Clara suspected that, as the winter drew in, the
girl preferred to slip into Clara's bed in search of warmth. She
knew Rosalía had taken a liking to her, as if she were an older
sister. Before dawn, Clara got up and heated some water on
the kitchen stove, then decanted it into a tub in her bedroom.
Using soap she had made herself from olive oil, salt and lye, she
bathed herself before attending to Rosalía. She was aware that
if anyone saw her, they would think her mad, but her father
had accustomed her to bathe regularly from an early age, and
gradually, it had become a pleasure, both in winter, in a large tub
close to the hearth, and in summer, when the heat of Madrid
was oppressive and bathing was a good way to cool down.

Rosalía, who knew nothing of all this, had simply enjoyed
the warm water, splashing the floor and the walls while Clara
washed her. Afterwards, Clara had rinsed her with water from
the washbasin. Once they had finished bathing, Clara donned
her cap and her apron, and left Rosalía to sleep some more. She
opened the door carefully and saw a package on the threshold,
with no sign of whoever might have left it there. She picked it
up. From the weight and size, she knew that it contained a book.

She undid the parcel to reveal a volume bound in soft leather. It was accompanied by a small note, sealed with the duke's coat of arms. Furrowing her brow, she retreated into the room and closed the door to avoid prying eyes. She read the title, the name of the Roman author and a few pages written in Latin. 'A recipe book from the Roman era,' she said to herself. She ran her hand over the binding, caressing its texture, then held it to her nose and inhaled its scent. She gently put it down on the bed and opened the sealed envelope.

Dear Señorita Belmonte,

It would be a great shame were a talent such as yours not to be developed fully due to a lack of access to information. For this reason, I have taken the liberty of presenting you with this small gift. If you think this inappropriate, you need only leave the book at your door, where you found it. In that case, I beg your forgiveness, as nothing could be further from my intentions than to offend you. If, on the other hand, you are happy to receive it, then allow me to say that it will not be the last and that other volumes may come your way as I acquire them. I will leave them in the small cellar, in the niche at the back. This will allow us to avoid any unpleasant talk that might be harmful to your reputation.

According to the bookseller on Calle Mayor, this volume is highly informative on the subject of cuisine from Roman times. And, in the event that you have already read it, I hope you will enjoy any passages or recipes that you may have forgotten. I hope that you see in this gesture nothing but a sincere desire to satisfy your needs as a reader, for I conceal no other intentions.

Don Diego de Castamar, Duke of Castamar

Clara felt her heart race as she read the note. She took a few moments for herself, rereading the lines and inhaling the scent of rose and lavender from the paper. If she accepted this gift, and as a book lover she dearly wanted to, then it would establish a link whose nature would be somewhat unclear, for she would still remain the duke's servant and not a lady of standing. Moreover, he appeared to intend to present her with a small collection, a prospect that excited her. If she accepted the first volume, then it would be logical to accept the rest. She guessed that this text, given its rarity and its condition, must have cost in the region of three hundred reals, a sum that would be difficult for a head cook to afford. At the same time, the letter clearly stated the duke's desire to *satisfy your needs as a reader*, an entirely legitimate goal for a master with respect to one of his servants.

She decided to keep it, delighted at the prospect of being able to read again and, trusting in Don Diego's word, placed the volume on the empty shelf. Her spirit somewhat agitated, she left the bedroom and headed for the kitchen. She walked quickly and in silence, trying not to awaken the other servants, who had another hour of sleep ahead of them.

It had been too long since so many good things had happened to her all at once, perhaps since the day her uncle, Julián Belmonte, had arrived to claim his inheritance. She recalled his pompous gait and his ceaseless chatter, adorned with fine words, the day her mother, her sister and she had welcomed him into what had ceased to be their home. After greeting him, she had withdrawn, accompanied by her sister, Elvira. The two had, however, listened in on the conversation. Uncle Julián had broken the silence by commenting on Clara's health. Her mother had told him that Clara had been suffering from a nervous condition ever since her father's unexpected death.

'The poor girl. The loss of one's father must be devastating,' he said, with his feigned good manners.

'Just like losing a brother,' Clara's mother commented wryly.

'My father's house has been well looked after. Everything is in its place, just as I remember,' he said, changing the topic as he walked about the room, inspecting its contents.

'From this moment on, you may do as you wish. The estate was entailed on you and is now yours,' her mother replied, bitterly.

He remained silent for a moment, rubbing his thumb against his fingers.

'Dearest sister-in-law, I cannot allow you to say that. I have not come here with the intention of depriving you of your home, quite the contrary. It is my wish that all of you should continue to live here with me.'

Clara's mother had been shocked when she realized that he wanted to reduce her to the condition of a guest in what had been her own house. Finally, he explained what he had in mind.

'Marriage would provide you with an honourable solution, my darling. I would gain two daughters instead of two nieces, and you would all be saved from calamity.'

'Sir, I fear that it is impossible—'

'Moreover, if I were your husband,' he had continued, 'you would benefit from my legal expertise and I could safely administer my brother's inheritance, which you would doubtless squander due to your condition as a woman.'

'As I was saying, your proposal is unacceptable. Marrying you, whatever financial advantages it might bring, would not only be the greatest of misfortunes for my daughters and me but would also be a complete betrayal of the memory of my deceased husband.'

With this sentence, Clara's mother had not only ruled out any possibility of a future with Clara's uncle but had also brought to an end the way of life they had known up to that point. Expelled from the house and reduced to penury, they had moved to rented rooms.

This had been enough to ensure that any friendships that had survived their original change in fortune would no longer endure, and they were no longer welcome in polite circles. There was no sign of the posthumous honours the king had mentioned, and when they had tried to speak to Don José de Grimaldo in person, his assistant had explained that he was unavailable, too busy dealing with the war. Their meagre savings were soon exhausted, and Clara's mother was forced to seek employment as a cook. Their situation had gradually worsened. Their former high standing now worked to their disadvantage, as nobody wanted to hire a lady. They had clung to the hope of finding a position in an aristocratic household, reasoning that such an establishment would be less reluctant to employ a widow who had fallen upon hard times. Meanwhile, they were forced to peel garlic to sell in the market for a few reals in an attempt to get by. Time had passed slowly, bringing disappointment and ruin in its wake.

One day, on the edge of despair after noticing the lines of defeat and failure etched on her mother's face after so much fruitless effort, Clara had taken out her frustration on her sister, who still naively believed that they could support themselves by selling garlic. *Poor thing... how innocent she was*, she had often thought, since those days. She tried not to think too much about what had come next, because whenever she did so, she felt her spirit becoming overwhelmed by sadness.

Thankfully, those difficult early days had also been left behind, and now they were no more than memories. Her past had become a contradiction, a dilemma she was forced to resolve each and every day. Brought up to become a lady, educated like a man, she found herself working as a cook. And every day she told herself that the fine lady now only existed inside her. However, a quiet, tired voice whispered back that, despite everything, she could not forget who she really was. And now that the Duke of Castamar had gifted her a Roman recipe book, she struggled to find the appropriate response. Clara Belmonte, a well-educated young lady, would have immediately replied with a note thanking him for his courtesy and kindness, admitting herself to be flattered and delighted by the attention he had shown her. She would once again have expressed her gratitude and let him know that she wished to repay his gesture in some way. However, in her current situation, such behaviour might be considered to constitute an attempt to secure promotion within the household or even to indicate that she harboured amorous intentions towards the duke. She was thus unable to write a single word, despite the fact that her upbringing required her to do so. She was the cook and he was the lord of Castamar.

When she entered the kitchen, she told herself her only option was to send him a simple message through the medium of her work. And so, she set out to prepare a menu which would include some of the duke's favourite dishes. She would surprise him with an unusual opening course, including giblets in pepitoria, sautéed calves' brains, of which he was very fond, and chicken rissoles. She would also prepare some black pudding with aniseed and oregano, and some roast beef with ginger, caraway seed, parsley and pepper. Next, she would serve her *pièce de résistance*, the calf's tongue, which would be cooked to perfection and filleted so that it would melt in the duke's mouth. She would finish with a morello cherry tart and a fruit salad of apples from the orchards of Castamar, pomegranate seeds, mint, lettuce hearts and lemon.

She knew that the servings would not be particularly abundant, but she had noticed that large meals were not to the duke's liking, however much they might be favoured among the nobles of the court. After checking that the kitchen was perfectly clean, she headed for the pantry to collect what she needed. She smiled to herself, certain that nobody would notice her subtle correspondence with the duke, while he would know that the food was a token of her gratitude for the gift she had received.

Diego took his seat at the table and Señor Moguer, the sommelier, admitted the footmen. The duke was joined by his brother, Gabriel, who had just returned from Madrid, having investigated the affairs of Don Enrique and Señorita Castro, and wished to speak with him. From the grave expression on his brother's face, Diego suspected that his concerns had grown.

The sommelier whispered to him that the cook had prepared a special menu, which would not begin with the usual chicken consommé but rather with a series of entrées, almost as if they were eating a picnic. He was surprised by the change but nodded to indicate that the food should be served. Diego asked them to serve a little of everything, and started with the sautéed brains, which were delicious. For a moment, he and Gabriel sat in silence, savouring the rissoles, the black pudding and the roast beef.

Señorita Belmonte had prepared the meal with great attention, putting one of his favourite dishes at its centre. Diego took a small sip of Alicante wine and guessed that this display of flavours was no coincidence. It was, rather, an indirect thank you note from Señorita Belmonte for the gift. He thought to himself that his cook was both cultured and discreet. None of the servants would realize, far less gossip about it – he alone had received the message. He suspected that they were sharing a secret language of flavours and aromas, a suspicion that was confirmed when the sommelier informed him that the cook had prepared a dish of wild mushrooms to bring out the flavour of the calf's tongue.

How much his father would have enjoyed this meal, he thought, and when he looked up and his eyes met those of Gabriel, he had the strange sensation that Abel de Castamar was there with them. Where everyone else saw slaves, members of an inferior race, his father saw people who bled when they were cut, who suffered pain, who laughed if they were happy. And yet, for a long time, his father had blamed himself for rescuing Gabriel, reasoning that by so doing he had inadvertently fed the insatiable mercantile monster that rules men's spirits. Gabriel had cost almost four thousand reals, because he was a child and had a whole life of service ahead of him. Normally, once they had reached the age of forty, slaves were given away for nothing, while the more magnanimous owners granted them their freedom.

'If there is one thing man must struggle against more than anything else, it is his own character,' his father had told Diego on numerous occasions. 'Anyone who wishes to be a freethinker must first rid himself of the ideas with which he has been imbued on the basis of mere custom rather than the exhaustive analysis of reason.'

His father had shown him the path of rational thought as the most secure and reliable, and it was precisely through the use of this analytical capacity that he had come to the conclusion that the purchase and release of Gabriel, regardless of how he might inadvertently have profited the traffic in human beings, had had a beneficial effect for Don Abel's firstborn son. Diego had grown up free from the preconceived ideas that were so widely held in society as a whole.

Although they were both keen to exchange their impressions of Daniel Forrado's findings – he to hear about them and Gabriel to recount them – the conversation had not yet begun. If the entrées had been exquisite, the fillets of calf's tongue were so delicious that they forgot their concerns and exchanged glances of pleasure, subtle gestures and expressions which confirmed the excellence of the food. It was only when the salad was served that Gabriel addressed the matter that concerned them both.

'Daniel came to see me at home,' he began, referring to the townhouse they kept on Calle Leganitos. 'Don Enrique has had no contact whatsoever with Señorita Castro, or at least none that I have been able to observe while I followed him. However, my man has told me that she inherited nothing but trouble from her father. That is why she left Cadiz.'

Diego paused for a moment, dabbing at his lips with a fine linen napkin. He understood that, for a young woman like Señorita Castro, the pressure of her father's creditors must have been a difficult burden to bear.

'Perhaps that explains her erratic behaviour,' he remarked.

'Not entirely, Diego,' his brother replied. 'She no longer has any debts. Daniel visited some of her father's creditors and they have all been repaid in full by Señorita Castro herself.'

He immediately thought of Don Enrique. Would he be capable of seducing a girl in a desperate situation, whispering words of salvation into her ears, when in truth he was only interested in himself? His brother guessed at his train of thought.

'Think about it. A girl with no prospects, besieged by debt but who suddenly repays everything. That money isn't hers, Diego. I can't help fearing she has been seduced by the wealth and desires of a powerful man,' Gabriel went on.

Diego shook his head and said that wasn't exactly what he was thinking. He knew what he had seen at Villacor, and he had the feeling that Señorita Castro had not been pretending when her eyes had filled with tears.

'Perhaps she has been carried away in her desperation and has accepted help from the wrong quarters, but I don't think she is ill-intentioned. It may be that her consternation that day at Villacor sprang from the situation in which she had become embroiled. I can't help thinking that the girl was about to open her heart to me.'

'Brother, something tells me that Don Enrique has some unhealthy interest in you and in Castamar. What if it was he who provided Señorita Castro with backing as part of a scheme against us?'

'And what interest might that be? What could be his motive?' Diego asked.

'I don't know, but that's what I want to find out. Didn't you notice how he was trying to goad you at every step? And the conversation I interrupted between him and Señorita Castro in one of the salons...'

'Gabriel, Don Enrique has only behaved like any other man of his station. The opinions he has expressed are no more disagreeable or extreme than those expressed by anyone else. Indeed, they are opinions shared by society at large, including our own mother. They only seem out of place to us because of the education we received from our father. To find hidden intention in such gibes is mere speculation.'

'Not when you are the Duke of Castamar.'

'For the time being, we should remain vigilant and not do anything that might compromise us.'

Gabriel shifted in his seat.

'Let me see if I can extract some information from Don Enrique's servant, Hernaldo de la Marca,' he insisted.

'No,' Don Diego replied. 'It may be that Don Enrique has ill intentions towards us, but we have no proof, not even a clear indication that such intentions exist. We don't know if it was he who paid Señorita Castro's debts and, if so, what his motive might have been. We do not even have any certainty that it is part of a scheme against us. Such suspicions are not enough to take action against a noble.'

No more was said on the subject for the moment, and they talked instead of Francisco and his conquests, and of the praise for the food that had been served during the festivities. Gabriel told Diego he would leave again, as soon as his baggage was ready. Don Diego did not prevent him. He knew that when Gabriel got an idea into his head, nothing could stop him and now, after the duke's refusal to act, Gabriel wanted to be in Madrid, where he could keep his ear to the ground.

Two hours later, his brother set off for the capital, and Diego was left alone, pondering the conversation. As he watched Gabriel's horse gallop down the avenue, he recalled the taste of the calf's tongue and its delicate texture. He smiled as he thought about how Señorita Belmonte's cooking had the virtue of distracting him from his problems. However, he was suddenly hit by a disturbing notion. Was it the cook's food that distracted him from his tribulations, or was it, rather, the memory of her eyes and their gentle but determined expression?

PART TWO

20 JANUARY TO 28 JANUARY 1721

20

Enrique looked out into the darkness. Winter had draped its veil over Madrid, mirroring his own gloomy spirits. As he waited for Hernaldo in the first-floor drawing room, his thoughts wandered to Señorita Castro as he observed her from the window, waiting to be collected by Don Enrique's carriage after one of their encounters.

She had confirmed her independence to Don Enrique in writing three months earlier, shortly after leaving Castamar, and almost immediately, as he had expected, she had begun to think marrying Don Diego was no longer necessary.

He had waited another week before putting the second part of his plan into action. Clumsily, he had tried to convince her of his reasons for wanting her to become engaged to Don Diego, while always emphasizing that he wanted to fulfil her wishes. They met in secret at each other's houses where, driven by lust, she would perform the most depraved acts before being overcome with shame, as if she did not recognize herself and was scandalized at having committed such sins against herself and God. How he had enjoyed watching Señorita Castro's fine manners turn on her like a jackal.

He had brought their games of seduction to a brutal end the night she coquettishly remarked that she suspected his insistence on always addressing her as señorita, and never simply by her name, was nothing but a ruse to further excite her desires.

'That's not the only reason,' he had confessed. 'It's a matter of trust, my dear Señorita Castro, and it's clear that you have not gained mine.'

She was taken aback.

'I thought that our intimacy, at the very least—'

'You thought wrong,' he had interrupted. 'You must return to Castamar. It's been a week now and it is essential that you become engaged to the duke.'

'I fear I am in no position to do such a thing,' she retorted. 'Don Diego is a—'

He cut her off again. 'I understand that your mother is in good health, and that you wish for her to stay that way.'

Her jaw had clenched as she asked him what he meant by such a comment.

'Provided you do what I ask of you, I can assure you that your mother will continue to receive the best care possible.'

She had been overwhelmed by panic.

'Poor Señorita Castro,' Enrique had said. 'Once again, helpless before the predator.'

She had stood up, shaking like a fledgling that had fallen from its nest, and with all the courage she could summon, she had told him that the house where her mother was resting belonged to her friend Verónica Salazar and that she would not let him lay a finger on her.

'That's where you're wrong. Your friend's house actually belongs to me.'

'I'll go to the duke,' she said, her eyes welling up with tears as she backed away from him, her hand covering her mouth. 'And I'll tell him—'

He got up and followed her.

'Don't be ridiculous, Señorita Castro,' he scoffed. 'How will you explain to Don Diego that you came to Madrid with the intention of seducing him and securing his hand when you had already lost your honour? I have proof, and all of Cadiz knows it. Or perhaps I will tell him personally how you tricked me, promising marriage when really you only sought to improve your social standing. I have proof of that too, since I've paid all your debts and am accommodating your mother in my house in El Escorial.'

Horrified, she had turned and run off, but he soon caught up with her, took her by the hair and tugged it brutally. Her slender neck had curved back and she cried in pain. Without giving her the chance to react, he punched her in the stomach, causing her to keel over, spluttering and moaning as she collapsed onto the floor. He pressed down on her with his body and covered her nose and mouth with his hands as she waved her arms in a final attempt to resist. Contemplating her face for a moment as she collapsed, he felt there was something beautiful about Señorita Castro, like a work of art: that great desire to survive flowing through the swollen veins of her temples. He had always admired her courage. She convulsed a little before beginning to lose consciousness. Then he had let go, allowing her to breathe. She began coughing uncontrollably, gulping in big mouthfuls of air, and he slid closer until his lips brushed against her earlobe.

'Listen carefully, my dear Señorita Castro,' he said, very slowly. 'Your life is in my hands, your mother breathes because I permit it, you breathe because I permit it. If for whatever reason you blab to Don Diego or anyone else, I will find out straightaway, and mark my words, you will never see your mother again, except in small pieces which my men will be glad to send to you.'

'You monster,' she said, still coughing.

'That I am,' he replied. 'And so, if your mother's life isn't enough to make you hold your tongue, perhaps yours is. You can nod if you've understood.'

Unable to control her coughing fit, she had given him a petrified look. Finally, she had nodded.

'I see we understand one another, my dear,' he said, rising to his feet. 'I want you to return to Castamar as soon as possible. While you come up with an excuse for the visit, I propose, as an incentive, that you come to see me three nights a week, to satisfy my appetite for you. I hope I won't have to come looking for you.'

Smoothing out his suit, he had begun to walk away.

'So that's what you wanted,' she said from the floor after catching her breath, the tears sliding silently down her cheeks. 'For me to be your concubine.'

He had stopped and glanced back at her.

'Oh, no, my dear,' he answered. 'That's only what I want from now on. Before, I just wanted to seduce you so that you would be my lover by choice, for you are an exquisite creature. You can go now, Señorita Castro. I have things to do.'

As he'd hoped, Señorita Castro had tried to return to Castamar as soon as possible so that she would not be forced to satisfy his sexual urges. However, all her attempts during those months had been frustrated. First, they had tried to arrange for her to bump into Don Diego at various gatherings, none of which he attended. Before winter had set in, they made several trips to Madrid and invited him to join them, but again and again, he had amiably declined their offers. Enrique had even made Señorita Castro ride close by Castamar, hoping they'd meet by chance. None of these plans had been successful. He regretted not forcing her to stay after the October celebration, but it was too late now. After the last thwarted attempt at the Countess of Arcos's house, when Diego had failed to show up at a poetry reading, Enrique was beginning to feel the duke would never leave his estate again.

In the end, Enrique realized he was leaving too much to chance. He had to expedite things. His opportunity had finally come by way of Don Gabriel, who seemed intent on spying on every step he took. Enrique would use him to arrange for Señorita Castro to return to Castamar, exploiting the brother's chivalry to his advantage. He was sure he could stir his enemy's protective instinct, something that came naturally to such generous souls.

Hernaldo appeared punctually to tell him that everything was in place. He just needed to give the order.

'Remember, I don't want her dead, just frightened. And it must look like a random attack.'

He dismissed him, stating that he would not rest easy until the man returned. Hernaldo turned around and headed for the exit. Recalling something, Enrique smiled, cursing himself for almost forgetting a detail crucial to the success of his strategy, one that would teach Señorita Castro that women who exchanged riches for carnal favours must learn what men really think of them.

'Slash her face,' he ordered.

'It will make her less attractive,' Hernaldo answered.

'Certainly, but it will inspire more pity,' he said, draining his glass. 'And Don Diego has a weakness for defenceless beings. Once he's in love, the physical aspect will no longer be a problem.'

Hernaldo nodded and disappeared down the passageway. Enrique watched the black clouds casting off their watery load onto the streets of Madrid. That night would herald a significant leap forward. His political interests had also stagnated and would only gain traction if the court gave him the opportunity. Since the Habsburg emperor was no longer an option, it would have to be the Bourbon king. For now, there was little else to be done: Spain had given in to an alliance of other European countries, which only served to prove its weakness. For his part, he had carried out a few trifling diplomatic missions, aiming for a bilateral agreement that would extend the links between France and Spain. José de Grimaldo, secretary of state and a close acquaintance, was preparing such a treaty, and had asked for his advice and intervention at certain moments. That would open the way to achieving the greatness he so desired for Spain as he brought the Castamar chapter to an end. It had gone on long enough.

★ ★ ★

Gabriel galloped towards the grove, his spirits perturbed. Some months ago, he had agreed upon a simple system for seeing his man, Daniel Forrado, in secret. Every time they needed to meet, he or his informer would send the other a calling card. Thus, they would silently inform the other that it was necessary to meet at a beech grove off the Móstoles road. To stay on the safe side, Daniel always sent these missives to the house at Leganitos using an errand boy, so that nobody would make the connection. Once it had been delivered, Gabriel would make his way to the rendezvous on horseback. Most of the time, to throw off any potential spies sent by the marquess, he would head to the Puente de Segovia; on other occasions, such as this morning, he would go north, only then to take the Camino del Río or the Prado Nuevo down to the banks of the Manzanares. He was certain that Daniel must have made an important discovery, perhaps one important enough to incite his brother to act.

Daniel was able to gather information from all the black servants across Madrid, since he was widely known and respected as a benefactor among his own kind. Gabriel had known him for a long time, since Daniel's days as the slave of a family friend who had visited Castamar. At sixty, his back was already hunched over from carrying too much weight as a luggage porter for his master since childhood. On that visit, Gabriel had convinced Diego to buy Daniel's freedom, aware that an offer from himself would not be taken seriously. He had wanted to do for Daniel what his father had done for him. Once free, Gabriel had taught his protégé to read and write, and he was now able to earn a living.

Gabriel reached the beech grove to find Daniel waiting by a pack mule. He seemed somewhat nervous as he walked over to greet him with a hollow smile on his face.

'Good day to you, sir,' he said.

'Good day, Daniel.'

'I have some news to report,' he said, looking about him to ensure there was no one listening. 'Señorita Castro has completely changed her habits over the past few months. As I told you, she visited the notary's office several times to sign certain documents and, following this, hired a dressmaker, a lady-in-waiting and a small Berlin carriage with her own driver. But the most interesting thing is that she recently moved into her new house in Madrid, together with servants.'

'She has her own income, then,' Gabriel concluded.

It was clear that this change was not coincidental, and his intuition continued to tell him that the marquess had something to do with it.

'So it seems,' Daniel replied. 'The visits are still taking place: Don Enrique sends his carriage every few days, and she goes willingly.

'There's another thing,' Daniel continued. 'The marquess's man, Hernaldo de la Marca, has on two occasions visited a house of ill repute in Lavapiés called the Zaguán, where he meets other cutthroats like himself. I suspect they might be up to something.'

'Good work, Daniel. Stay vigilant. I may need you to take me there tomorrow.'

'It's no place for a gentleman,' Daniel warned him.

'Don't worry about that.'

Gabriel mounted his horse and rode back to the capital.

Despite all this information, he doubted that Diego would take the risk of acting on it. He didn't want to make a false move and Gabriel recognized the prudence in that, but he also thought it was necessary to take the initiative. If his brother had let him, by now they'd know what that snake, Don Enrique, was plotting. Gabriel would have grabbed Hernaldo de la Marca and made him sing like a canary. He knew that doing so would be risky, for if Don Enrique did turn out to have no hidden intentions, they would be the ones committing the crime. However, he intuited that the longer they waited to act, the more chance there would be of the marquess's plot being successful. So, as soon as he arrived at his mansion in the capital, he sent invitations to Don

Alfredo and Don Francisco, inviting them to dine with him that night. He knew all too well how angry his brother would be if he knew Gabriel was getting his friends involved. But he was so sure the marquess had some hidden agenda that he needed help to get to where he could not go. He suspected that Don Enrique had gained his mother's affection in order to be present at the estate before the celebration. He had guessed this when he saw Enrique next to Amelia in the drawing room: from their wordless looks, loaded with a meaning that escaped him. And then there had been the marquess's rude, cutting comments, aimed at constantly provoking Diego, as if he were putting him to the test.

After eating and sleeping for a while, Gabriel received two cards, confirming that Don Francisco and Don Alfredo would dine with him.

Gabriel waited until after dinner, when they had moved into one of the drawing rooms, to tell them about his suspicions. Once he had finished, neither of them said a word. Don Francisco, sitting with his legs crossed and one hand on his stick, had just drained his glass of anis. At the other end of the room, Don Alfredo was watching the storm through the window. Gabriel glanced at the fireplace and once again felt estranged from the reality surrounding him. He couldn't say if this was a rational conclusion or just a feeling he had. Sometimes, the whole world around him lost any objective meaning and he could not discern why he was there or why this white person's life had been bestowed upon him.

'I understand why you called for us.' Don Alfredo's voice brought him back to the present. 'And you were right to do so, even though your brother won't like it. It is necessary for us to intervene, not in a direct way, but cautiously. We must make sure the marquess is definitely plotting something before we take any steps.'

Don Francisco raised his glass in agreement.

'I can certainly ask questions at court about ladies who've

shared a bed with Don Enrique,' Don Francisco said. 'Perhaps we'll dig up some information about his character.'

'That's exactly what I need,' said Gabriel from his chair. 'The court is no place for a man of my skin colour.'

They laughed a little at his way of putting it.

'Don Gabriel,' Don Alfredo said, 'I am convinced that, in the future, slavery will be seen as an abomination, but until that time comes, your position within high society is truly extraordinary.'

Gabriel nodded and was about to add something when there was a knock at the door. One of his manservants entered bearing a calling card on a small silver tray. He looked at it in amazement. Either Daniel Forrado had made a new, highly important discovery, or something so serious had happened that he had needed to send the card for the second time in less than ten hours, even in spite of the late hour and the downpour lashing the whole of Madrid.

'It's from my man. There must be a problem. I have to go,' he told them.

'Please, let us come with you,' said Don Francisco, rising to his feet.

The three men descended the stairs in silence, towards the inner courtyard. As he donned his heavy leather overcoat and cocked hat, Gabriel had the feeling that something really bad had happened. After ordering the servants to bring them a lamp, Gabriel considered the possibility that Don Francisco and Don Alfredo were walking into a trap prepared only for him. He stopped for a moment as he was mounting his horse.

'You are under no obligation to accompany me, and I would understand completely if you didn't,' he told them.

'Don't be silly,' answered Alfredo, spurring his horse.

'I have nothing to add, dear Don Gabriel,' Don Francisco commented, riding off behind Don Alfredo and smiling as if it were all a game.

Gabriel moved off, and the three men travelled north, the water coming down on them in torrents. They took the shortest route through open countryside, riding to the banks of the Manzanares and from there towards the south. It was so dark they could barely see two feet in front of them, and as soon as they crossed the Puente de Segovia they slowed to a trot. Quickening their pace when they reached the other side, they took the Móstoles road to the meeting point.

After more than an hour riding in the rain, they followed the stream until they reached the meeting place, their senses on high alert. They dismounted at Alfredo's signal and, with only the meagre light from their lamps, plunged into the thicket on foot. With a firm step and one hand on their swords, they had only advanced a few yards when they were confronted with a dead body.

'Daniel,' Gabriel stammered, overcome with grief.

He had been stabbed several times in the stomach, and there was another wound, clean and precise, between his lungs. Gabriel knelt and gently closed the dead man's eyelids. He dedicated a few words to him while Don Alfredo asked if this was his man. As Gabriel nodded, a lightning flash split the sky in two, illuminating the landscape for a moment.

That was when he noticed a second figure, a little way off. He rose quickly, and Don Francisco and Don Alfredo drew their swords, alert to any movement. Gabriel approached, lifting up his lamp. It was a woman's body. There, her clothes in tatters, a deep cut on her cheek, her face bruised black and blue, and her lips swollen and crimson, lay Señorita Castro, frozen stiff and caked in mud.

'Good God!' Gabriel shouted.

'Her pulse is weak,' said Don Alfredo, assessing her state. 'She must have been out in the rain for quite a while. We need to give her as much warmth as possible.'

Unhesitating, Gabriel took her in his arms and carried her to his horse. He thought about heading immediately for the Leganitos house, but he stopped. It would take at least two hours to get home, settle her, and find a proper doctor. Doctor

Evaristo, however, lived close to Castamar, and was a man of repute. They'd be there in less than an hour.

'We must take her to Castamar,' he said. 'Don Francisco, would you be so kind as to go ahead and warn Doctor Evaristo?'

Don Alfredo told him he would stay behind to help. Once Gabriel had mounted the horse, they placed the young woman on it and covered her with a saddlecloth.

In grim silence, they rode their steeds as fast as they could until they made out the walls of the Castamar estate. Gabriel remembered poor Daniel, tossed into a swamp and soaked in his own blood, and clenched his fists. He would make sure, at a later point, to give him a proper Christian burial. Such villainy was no random incident. Now he was certain that his instincts regarding the threat posed by Don Enrique had been correct. Despite the lack of proof, he knew that the marquess's henchmen had sent a clear message with his calling card, marking a red line that could not be crossed without causing even bigger problems: 'No one spies on Don Enrique de Arcona.'

21

Same day, 20 January 1721

Clara looked out through the kitchen window. The heavy sky was threatening to unleash a downpour on Madrid, and the servants were in a commotion, as if lightning was about to strike Castamar. Clara, however, enjoyed these winter days, which provided the perfect excuse for curling up by the fire to read. She had closed the door that led out to the courtyard, both to help keep in the warmth and to stop Rosalía from wandering.

As usual, she had prepared the master's breakfast, including a jug of hot chocolate, and some eggs poached with a little vinegar. During recent weeks she had not had to prepare food for Don Gabriel, who was in Madrid and only came to Castamar occasionally. And so, with more free time, she had written to her sister and her mother to tell them about the new home she had made for herself at Castamar. After sending the letters, she had tried out some recipes from the books the duke had given her, as a way of thanking him for the gifts.

Every time she found a new volume waiting for her, she felt like a young girl collecting a secret note from an admirer. She knew it was not the same, that Don Diego was not a besotted youth, nor she a nervous young girl, but that did not detract from the fact that the master took the time to feed her passion for reading, so neglected since her father's death.

She had arranged the books in chronological order on her shelf. Only that day, she had received a volume on the art of making pastry, cakes and conserves. As soon as she had found it in its niche, she had tucked it into her skirts and brought it back to her room to add it to her library. However, instead of placing it on the shelf, she had removed all the books from their place, wrapped them in a blanket, and left them under the bed, intending to carefully dust them one by one that evening.

After she had finished making breakfast, carried away by her emotions, she was unable to resist the temptation to write a few lines to his lordship for the first time, leaving them in the niche in the cellar.

I lack the words to adequately thank you for your generous attentiveness towards me, so please allow me to continue to repay your kindness in the best manner I know. If it is to your liking, I will prepare recipes from the volumes you have so kindly bestowed upon me.

Yours,

Señorita Clara Belmonte

Since then, she had not stopped thinking about her latest acquisition. Suddenly, she was brought back to reality by a cold draught on the back of her neck. Seeing that the door was open, she turned in annoyance to Carmen del Castillo.

'Did you leave the door open? It's cold.'

Carmen shrugged, and Clara suddenly felt a pressing urgency that defied all logic. Something was missing and she wasn't sure exactly what it was. She moved cautiously towards the door, checking everything, and her eyes met those of Beatriz Ulloa. That was when she realized what was wrong. She moved Rosalía's now empty stool out of the way and saw the girl perched on the roof beneath which the carts were unloaded. Without thinking about the consequences, she rushed out into the yard, shrieking at the girl to come down. Rosalía looked down and, spreading her arms, replied that she could fly. Clara had scarcely taken two steps when the heavens opened. She came to a sudden halt and broke into a cold sweat, weighed down by her fear as if it were an anchor.

'Rosa-lía, Rosalía,' she stammered, unable to breathe. 'Beatriz... Get her down from there.'

As she sank to her knees, she heard the other members of the kitchen staff shouting wildly to the girl to come down. One of the grooms had started to climb up when Rosalía looked at Clara and launched herself into the void. There was a sickening crunch of breaking bone as her skull hit the ground. The impact was followed by a scream that cut to the very core of Clara's soul. Gasping for air, her heart pounding, she saw Rosalía's vacant eyes and the twisted smile on her face. Then, as the servants gathered the unfortunate child up from the cold ground, Clara's last ounce of strength abandoned her, and she fainted.

She came round when she felt somebody slapping her on the cheeks. She was lying on her bed, with no shoes on. She couldn't think clearly and her vision was blurred. She closed her eyes again, not knowing whether what she recalled was a nightmare or reality. Another slap brought her back to her senses. A bony hand gently raised her head and brought a glass of cool water to her lips. When she finally managed to focus on the person who was attending to her, she found herself looking at Doña Ursula. That was when she understood that Rosalía was dead, and she couldn't rid herself of the memory of the girl's lifeless eyes, her hideously twisted neck, her broken skull, her lolling mouth, the blood running into the cracks between the courtyard cobbles.

Her eyes welled up as she recalled the fall, and she could hardly hold the housekeeper's gaze. Suddenly, she panicked at the thought that Doña Ursula would see all the books his lordship had given her, and she glanced over at her shelf. Then she remembered she had put the books away under her bed that morning and, despite the deep sadness that enveloped her, she also felt a sense of relief in the knowledge that the housekeeper would not discover her in the possession of all those volumes she could not have purchased with her meagre salary. She tried to speak but the words stuck in her throat and all that came out was a low moan. Doña Ursula told her that Doctor Evaristo had inspected her a while ago and had given instructions to awaken her within half an hour.

'You neglected your duties to that poor girl,' the housekeeper went on, wagging a finger at her. 'You and you alone are responsible for her death.'

Clara lifted her tear-stained face and tried to speak again, although her voice was hoarse and her spirit was broken. Doña Ursula was right and there was no denying it; unlike on other occasions, she could not draw on her moral strength to confront this woman, who appeared to have been born to fight. Rosalía was dead because of Clara's negligence, because of her stupid, proud belief that she could care for the girl better than Señora Escrivá, because of her incompetence and secretiveness. If she had explained that she was unable to withstand being in open spaces, if she had not kept her silence, the girl might still be alive.

'I hadn't realized she was up there, I—'

'Silence. I still remember when you promised that Rosalía would be safe in your keeping,' the housekeeper remonstrated. 'And then there is your silence regarding the serious nervous condition from which you suffer. Don't dare deny it! What exactly are your symptoms?'

It was clear that Doña Ursula had looked into matters as soon as the kitchen servants had informed her of Clara's strange behaviour and of how she had fainted when in the yard. No doubt she would have interrogated Doctor Evaristo to discover why a person in excellent health might collapse, break into a cold sweat and be rendered speechless simply upon going outside. If she had found Rosalía dead, she might argue that her behaviour had been a reaction to the shock of seeing her like that, but Clara had fallen to her knees long before Rosalía had jumped. She shook her head and apologized for her negligence.

'I can't… As soon as I find myself in the open, I sweat and all my strength deserts me,' she blurted out.

Doña Ursula gave her a cold, disapproving stare.

'Your excuses won't bring that poor girl back to life,' she observed.

Clara slowly sat up and looked at the housekeeper through sorrowful eyes, her cheeks burning with shame and on her lips a thousand unvoiced reproaches towards herself. She was about to speak when the housekeeper raised a hand, commanding her to remain silent.

'It is incredible that you accepted responsibility for the care of that girl, knowing that you suffered from such a condition. I want you to leave Castamar by dawn tomorrow. From this moment, your services are no longer required. You may stay here until tomorrow. Carmen del Castillo will perform your duties in the kitchen,' she went on. 'You may collect what wages you are owed from my office before you leave.'

When the door closed, Clara lay curled on the bed, sobbing inconsolably. She felt so alone, as she had on so many occasions during recent years, but now it weighed heavier with the knowledge that tomorrow an exile awaited her that would sink her yet further into poverty. Rosalía's death would feature in any reference she might be given. Doña Ursula would make sure that was the case, and despite her success at the festivities of Castamar, the likelihood was that her reputation would precede her at every noble house where she might seek employment. As a result, she would be forced to take work that was below her status, and even if she did manage to secure a position as a cook, her salary would be lower.

But right now, that was of no concern to her: the only thing on her mind was the body of the unfortunate girl and the duke's disappointment upon discovering that she had concealed a secret about her nervous condition. She didn't even want to think about the horrible impression Don Diego would form of her. Her secrecy had led to the death of his wetnurse's daughter.

She felt so remorseful, so upset at having disappointed the duke, at having created expectations about her flawless behaviour, when in reality, she was nothing but a liar... He had behaved like a gentleman towards her, had presented her with her beloved treatises on cookery, and she had repaid his kindness with deceit.

She felt dirty for failing to have the courage to overcome her embarrassment and tell him about her problem, for not having made him aware of her illness. If she had, the misfortune could have been avoided. She took out the books from under the bed and, her spirit broken, began to clean them and put them back into their place as if they were pieces of her shattered soul. She felt no desire to read them, however. Instead, she lay down and fell asleep, still thinking about the duke's disappointment and the sad fate that awaited her the next day.

She didn't wake up until Elisa brought her some porridge with bread. She didn't have much appetite, but her friend insisted that she at least try some, and that she drink some water. After drying Clara's lips with a cloth, Elisa urged her not to blame herself for the death. She told her how Rosalía had been trying to jump from the coachyard roof ever since she had been old enough to climb, and that she had never been so happy as when she had been in Clara's care. Clara nodded, but the words washed over her without lessening her pain.

'I must leave Castamar, Elisa, as soon as dawn breaks,' she told her sorrowfully. 'I don't know what will become of me.'

Elisa shook her head.

'From what I've heard, the duke has informed Doña Ursula that on no account are you to leave Castamar.'

Clara opened her eyes in astonishment. The duke had refused to expel her, despite her having hidden her illness, despite her being responsible for the death of his wetnurse's daughter! Elisa took her leave and warned Clara that the housekeeper might appear at any moment and that it would be better not to provoke her. Clara was left alone again, pondering the tragedy, and soon fell asleep.

After some time had passed, Doña Ursula woke her up with a knock on the door. By the light outside, Clara could tell that it was already evening. Clara patted down her hair and opened the door, greeting the housekeeper with a respectful curtsy. Doña Ursula looked her up and down, as if keen to assess how much she had suffered during the intervening hours.

'Señorita Belmonte, I have reconsidered my decision with regard to your presence at Castamar – you will report for duty tomorrow morning,' she ordered.

Pride would not allow the housekeeper to admit the truth: that she was only complying with Don Diego's wishes. Clara nodded and was about to thank her, but the housekeeper turned and left Clara with the words still upon her lips. Clara closed the door and sat down on the bed. Without thinking, she looked at the books and picked up the volume by Martínez Montiño. She turned the pages, stroked the binding, and lost herself inside it for hours, inhaling the smell of the paper and imagining she could detect Don Diego's scent.

When night fell, she recognized the duke's silent footsteps outside her bedroom door. She had heard them before, when the master had visited the cellar to leave his gifts in the secret niche. On those occasions, she had pressed her ear to the cellar door, imagining a chance meeting and the resultant conversation, as if she were a lady who had been presented to society and he was a gentleman who had come to pay her a visit. Of course, he never came to the kitchen. Instead, he would deposit the latest volume and leave, as silently as he had come, through the main door. She would wait an appropriate amount of time and sneak into the cellar to inspect the contents of the hiding place. She would remove one of the bottles of Valdepeñas and slide her hand into the empty space behind. As soon as she had collected the new book, she hid it in her skirts, hoping it would be accompanied by one of his notes.

She had to admit that, whenever she opened the cellar door, she did so in expectation. However, on this occasion, Don Diego was not in the cellar but outside her bedroom, and it was unlikely that he had come down to present her with a book when he had given her one that very morning. And so, she waited, holding her breath and drying her tears, and listened to the footsteps pause for a few seconds at her door. There was silence. She listened out for any noise that might indicate what he was doing but heard nothing, not even the sound of his breathing. *He is wondering whether to knock*, Clara told herself. She got up very slowly, careful not to make any noise that might betray her presence, walked over to the mirror on the wall, and pinched her cheeks. Just then, she heard a gentle knock on the door. *It's him.* She waited for a moment, so as not to give an impression of haste, and opened the door.

Don Diego was waiting, impeccably dressed in a cream-coloured suit, his jacket over a tightly buttoned waistcoat, his hands clasped behind his back, exuding a perfume of lavender and roses. She greeted him as if she were a lady and he responded with a gentlemanly gesture.

'My dearest Señorita Belmonte, I don't wish to inconvenience you,' he said. 'I took the liberty of calling upon you with the intention of offering you some words of consolation.'

She smiled awkwardly.

'It is a great honour that you have come to my door,' she replied, her voice wavering.

'I want to tell you how sorry I am about Rosalía's death. It has been a tragedy for all of us,' he said.

Clara wanted to reply but she could barely speak. The need to express her guilt at Rosalía's death, her regret at not having informed him of her condition, his pain at what she imagined to be his disappointment, and the bitterness and frustration at her inability to alter the course of events had deprived her of the power of speech. She tried to control the rush of emotions.

'I am sorry... so sorry for having hidden my... condition,' she declared, haltingly, feeling all the time that her eyelids were like dams that would not withhold the flow of her tears for long.

'Your condition, Señorita Belmonte, was not the cause of Rosalía's death. It was she who climbed up there and leaped from the roof, and I fear that, even if you had been in full command of your faculties, you could not have prevented it,' he said, his hands still behind his back. 'I know you did everything possible to help her. You mustn't punish yourself.'

Clara looked at him, still trembling. Her brown eyes were filled with remorse, desperate to obtain the forgiveness she could not grant herself. Accompanying the remorse were grief and a profound sadness. She felt a cascade of emotions building inside her. But the harder she tried to control them, the more they struggled to emerge, as tears welled up in her eyes and her body began to tremble. She lowered her eyes in embarrassment and squeezed her lips tight.

'Señorita Belmonte...' the duke said, with a note of concern.

Clara burst into tears, and felt even worse than she had before as she reproached herself for playing the part of the victim in need of succour when she herself had caused the tragedy.

'I'm sorry, your grace, I'm so sorry,' she repeated. 'Forgive me, I beg you, please... I... shouldn't have hidden... I should have been...'

Don Diego gently raised her head and looked into her eyes. She was unable to staunch the flow of words and tears. The duke wrapped his arms around her. She leaned her head against his chest.

'It's okay, it's okay. You should be kinder to yourself,' he whispered. 'I know from my own experience how guilt, contrition and pain can overwhelm you at times like this.'

She wished his protection would last for all eternity, that Don Diego would never leave, and that all her years of sorrow would disappear, dispelled by his fearless gaze. Just then, he brought his lips closer to hers and they kissed. They remained like that for a few moments, frozen like a sculpture by Bernini, until he

– still looking into her eyes – withdrew slightly. They were silent for a moment, until the duke spoke.

'Here,' he said, offering her a handkerchief.

She thanked him and took a step back as she dried her eyes.

'Your grace, please forgive my tears. I was overcome, I feel so ashamed…'

'You have nothing to apologize for, Señorita Belmonte.' He paused and then said, 'This is for you.' Clara had not noticed that he had been holding a package wrapped in the same brown paper that had contained every volume he had given her. She tried to restrain her tears as she told him how grateful she was.

'Take it,' he insisted. 'I would have left it for you with the other one this morning, as I ordered them both at the same time, but it only arrived from Madrid this afternoon.'

'Your grace, I don't know…' she said, her feelings plain for him to see. 'I…'

'There is no need to thank me.'

'Of course, your grace,' she replied, blushing.

'I will inform Señor Elquiza that you will be resting for a few days.'

She was about to acquiesce but then she changed her mind.

'If it isn't too much trouble, I would prefer to get back to work tomorrow. I think that would be best for me.'

Although he advised her to rest, Don Diego raised no objection to her plan. He took his leave and walked along the corridor. When he reached the door at the end, he turned and looked at her, silhouetted against the light. She looked back as he waved a final farewell and disappeared.

Clara closed the door, her head a whirl of thoughts and impressions, memories of Rosalía, Doña Ursula's icy stare, the kind words of Señor Casona, the sounds and smells of the kitchen and, of course, Don Diego, his smile, and the unexpected touch of his lips.

She could scarcely believe that he had kissed her, that she had yearned for him to do so. She couldn't answer the questions that arose in her mind: why had she so desperately – so suddenly – wanted him to kiss her? And why, then, had he stopped and why had she withdrawn? She had to lean against her bedroom door and close her eyes to calm the hurricane inside her. Then she remembered that she was still holding the parcel. When she opened it, she found it contained a book that she adored, one she had read many times in her father's library. It was a French edition, the cover proudly engraved with its title: *Le Viandier*. This gem was one of the most influential books on medieval cuisine, written by Guillaume Tirel. Tucked inside the cover was a small note. She unfolded it, wary of the possibility that this new gesture might once again open up the gates of her sadness, gratitude and contrition.

> *I am told that this volume belongs to the highest traditions of French cuisine. I imagine that you will appreciate it more than I could. I hope this gift serves both as an encouragement and a consolation, so that you may not feel so alone in your suffering.*
> *Yours,*
>
> *Don Diego de Castamar*

She clutched the book to her chest and fell onto the bed. She pulled the covers over her and cried until she fell asleep, and soon she was lost in a tragic dream in which she was surrounded by the ghosts, memories and images of the past. She was visited by her father and by Rosalía, who looked at her without blinking and told her that, thanks to Clara's oversight, she could finally fly. She saw herself in the great rooms of the Buen Retiro Palace, where she had once been, many years ago, dancing with gallant gentlemen, without realizing that death, too, danced among them, demanding the lives of those who had gone to war. Almost without stopping, she danced a pavane, a minuet, and several *gallardos* with the corpses of innocent young men who smiled at her as they left, while in the distance, the roar of cannons could be heard, announcing the progress of battle. She felt out of place among the courtiers, until as she passed from one hand to the next, Don Diego appeared and held her before she collapsed in a faint. Suddenly, she heard the artillery much closer, shaking the windows, and she pressed her body against his, seeking protection.

'Don't fear, Señorita Belmonte, I'm here,' he told her.

The bombs began to fall on the roof, and dust and rubble rained down on the ballroom. However, despite the death and destruction, she remained unharmed. The huge figure of Don Diego continued to hold her tight, like a guardian angel holding a divine shield above her.

'Señorita Belmonte, wake up,' he was saying. 'You are needed.' The voice of Don Diego mixed with another, more feminine and harsher. It echoed through her mind as she opened her eyes, trying to locate its source. The voice of the duke transformed into the voice of Doña Ursula, and the cannons spitting fire became the knocking on her bedroom door. She got up, sleepily, and opened the door as quickly as she could. Doña Ursula ordered her to get dressed immediately as her services were urgently required.

The nervous look in the housekeeper's eyes and her clenched jaw seemed a bad omen, making Clara's thoughts jump to the possibility that some misfortune had befallen Don Diego. She closed the door and listened as the housekeeper retreated with short, rapid steps. As she dressed, the sense of foreboding grew inside her. The innocent exchange of cooking books had established a silent bond between the duke and Clara, and she was now appalled at the thought that Don Diego might have suffered some kind of mishap.

She entered the kitchen, adjusting her cap, and found Beatriz Ulloa heating a pot of water on the stove.

'Do you know what's happening?' Clara asked immediately.

Beatriz shook her head.

'I was asked to heat up some water, on the orders of Doctor Evaristo,' she said.

Clara's sense of foreboding grew.

'Doctor Evaristo? Is his lordship very ill?'

'I don't know,' her assistant replied, 'but judging by the looks on people's faces, it's a bad business.'

This reply unsettled Clara further, but just as she was about to speak again, Doña Ursula appeared in the kitchen, carrying a candlestick. She handed Clara a piece of paper and ordered her to prepare what was written on it. As soon as Clara read it, she understood what the matter was and, unable to stop herself, looked up.

'Señora Berenguer, has his lordship suffered some misfortune?' she blurted out.

The housekeeper looked at her like she was vermin.

'What is the reason for your question?'

'I know perfectly well that this preparation is a poultice for a knife wound and not a remedy for a sore stomach,' she explained, holding out the piece of paper. 'My father was a doctor.'

The housekeeper raised an eyebrow, as if such questions were an unnecessary impertinence.

'Do as you are told and don't create problems,' she said.

'Problems?' Clara replied, aware that her anxiety was causing her to lose her self-control. 'Señora Berenguer, I only want to know whether his lordship has come to any harm.'

The housekeeper turned and, as she left, told Clara to stop wasting her time. Clara, indignant at such rudeness, caught between anxiety and anger, took a step forward.

'I won't do it.'

Doña Ursula stopped and turned, her gaze flashing anger, her face barely controlling her emotions. Beatriz looked on, astonished.

'What did you say?' the housekeeper asked, incredulously.

'I won't make this preparation until you tell me whether his lordship has come to any harm.'

'Señorita Belmonte, I am under no obligation to tell you anything. If you don't get to work immediately, I will find someone who will. And I swear on all that is dearest to me that from tomorrow you won't find any house in the country where you can engage in your beloved cookery,' she answered haughtily. 'And you can get to work too, instead of standing there gawping,' she barked at Beatriz, who replied with a terrified curtsy.

She turned and disappeared from the kitchen, leaving Clara angrily clutching the piece of paper in her trembling hand. Then Clara also turned and, leaning on the table, took a deep breath and tried to steady her nerves. As the colour slowly returned to her face, she realized she had directly challenged the housekeeper's authority and, by so doing, had provided the woman with another pretext to expel her from Castamar. The most remarkable thing about it all was that Doña Ursula had not done so.

22

Same day, 20 January 1721

The day Ursula had always feared had now arrived: her power over the servants at Castamar had begun to wane. She had always believed that knowing people's secrets granted you power over them, but this only worked with the weak of spirit. Those with stronger characters faced the consequences head-on, despite their inner fears, with their heads held high and refusing to give in to blackmail. Clara Belmonte belonged to this category, and worst of all, her presence made others remember the courage they'd forgotten they had.

Ursula reached the top of the stairs and clicked her heels to announce her arrival. She had collected the poultice from the kitchen and was now taking it to Doctor Evaristo as quickly as possible. That same night, Señorita Castro had been brought to the house, covered in blood and with her face slashed. It seemed that some scoundrels had attacked her carriage and, after robbing her, had beaten her and left her lying in a field close to the Móstoles road. *My goodness, who would do this to such a poor, defenceless creature?* Ursula asked herself. *Men are such savages; I'd happily skin them alive.* She sensed the weight of all the hatred and rage she carried on her back and felt that her load had grown even heavier with the cook's defiance.

Nobody, in all her years at Castamar, had challenged her authority like that; nobody had dared to contradict her, except for Don Melquíades, who as head butler felt obliged to do so from time to time. But now this cook from a good family, whose status lay somewhere between that of the servants and the nobles, had become a widely admired figure of defiance. Even the duke himself had seemed rather taken with her when he gave her that book a few months back. *It was just the one, thank God*, Ursula reminded herself. Ever since the girl had entered the house, Ursula's world – which she'd worked so hard to build – had begun to collapse. Proof of this was that, despite the confrontation that had just taken place in the kitchen, his lordship had made it abundantly clear that she did not have the authority to expel Señorita Belmonte. Just as she had suspected, the cook's connection to the master had become inexplicably stronger. Ursula had now discovered just how far she was from governing Clara Belmonte.

When Doctor Evaristo had informed her that Señorita Belmonte had fainted from some nervous affliction, she'd been overjoyed at the thought that she would be rid of her forever.

Don Diego had taken the news of Rosalía's death as expected – he had had a great deal of affection for his wetnurse and had always wanted her daughter to be well looked after.

'Take care of the funeral arrangements, make sure mass is said and see that she is buried in the Castamar cemetery,' he had ordered Ursula.

'There's something else,' she had told him. Diego frowned. 'Rosalía's death was caused by a serious error on Señorita Belmonte's part.'

'In what sense?'

'When she came here, she deliberately hid from me the fact that she suffers from a serious nervous condition. Of course, had Señorita Belmonte informed me of her affliction, I would never have put her in charge of the poor girl.'

Don Diego had walked over to the fireplace to warm up and waited a moment before answering.

'Don't blame yourself for something you didn't know, Señora Berenguer.'

Ursula had nodded as Don Diego reverted to silence. She waited a few moments more to let him meditate on the whole affair, before uttering the sentence she had wanted to say for so long.

'If you will allow me, I shall look for a new cook straightaway.'

The duke's eyes had suddenly narrowed, as if her proposal went against all decorum.

'No,' he had answered immediately.

Having thought that success was assured, she had been rocked by his refusal. She knew how the duke reacted when something went against his wishes, and she knew there was nothing she could say to change his mind. Still, she had tried as hard as she could to convince him.

'Your grace, it was completely irresponsible of her to look after that child given her illness.'

'I said no,' he had repeated.

'As you wish.'

She had curtseyed and was just leaving when Don Diego asked her to stop. Calmly, he had walked over to Ursula and admitted he'd been short with her. Ursula had paid it no mind, since she knew he had the spirit of a tame lion, only remembering its animal nature occasionally. If anyone was able to inspire forgiveness in her it was Don Diego. For some reason she couldn't quite grasp, Don Diego had developed a soft spot for the cook, doubtless because he had been moved by her story. *As if the lives of everyone at Castamar aren't in some way tragic,* Ursula had thought.

'Señora Berenguer, you're right when you say it was remiss of Señorita Belmonte to hide her condition. But we mustn't judge her so harshly. I don't think anyone feels worse than she does about this tragic loss. Believe me when I say that the greatest punishment one can endure is to suffer one's own remorse.'

Choking with indignation, Ursula had had to return to Clara Belmonte's bedroom and inform her that she'd changed her mind and that the cook's services were not dispensable after all.

She was annoyed with herself for being so impulsive, for not having had the wisdom to wait and use the cook's secret as a way of controlling her. But her battle with the cook was not the only one she'd lost. A few hours later, at lunchtime, Don Melquíades had joined the affray. Just as she had arrived, Señor Moguer, the sommelier, was asking the butler about the young woman's condition.

'The duke has informed me that Señorita Belmonte wishes to return to work,' the head butler had replied. 'Of course, I have forbidden her.'

This was too much. If his lordship had informed Don Melquíades of the cook's wishes, that meant he had visited her in person. Ursula, her anger now bubbling over, cracked her knuckles and raised her index finger.

'Next time, Don Melquíades, I expect to be informed of the decision beforehand,' she had said in front of everyone.

'Doña Ursula,' he had answered, throwing the napkin onto the table, 'I am quite capable of taking such decisions on my own.'

'If you don't mind, in the future I'd appreciate being informed if any of the servants are to be temporarily replaced,' she had persisted.

'I shall do so only when I consider it appropriate.'

'I do hope you will find it appropriate.'

'Doña Ursula, will you shut your mouth once and for all,' said Don Melquíades, striking the table with his open palm. 'I was the head butler of this house long before you arrived, and I will inform you when I find it appropriate to do so.'

The servants, who had never before witnessed such disagreement between the head butler and the housekeeper, looked on in shocked silence. Ursula understood that open warfare was futile, since it was obvious that all the staff, who saw Don Melquíades as the highest authority, would support him. Instead, she had politely asked him for a word in her study.

Alone in her office, she had ordered him to duly inform her of everything, for the sake of his own future. But Melquíades was no longer the defeated man of yesteryear. A change had come over him during the three months since the cook had arrived, as if he had rediscovered the courage that had once dwelled in his heart.

Shouting angrily, he had said he would inform her just as promptly as she had informed him when she had dismissed and then rehired Clara Belmonte. She had huffed and puffed. Of course she had not informed him, knowing that his opportunism would have prevented him from doing what was required. Clara Belmonte was guilty of lying to her superiors and it had been best that she left the house as soon as possible, despite the fact that the good-hearted Don Diego had pardoned her and Don Melquíades protected her to bolster his own power.

'I am the head butler of Castamar, and never again will I allow you to coerce me,' he had shouted furiously, rising up over her like some mythological monster.

Quivering with rage, Ursula had moved even closer, wagging her finger in his face.

'I run this house, and I will not cede one inch of territory, far less to a man like you, one who betrayed his master's confidence,' she had spat.

It was then that, behind the sparks of anger flying from Don Melquíades's eyes, she had glimpsed a look that unsettled her, as if behind all that display of unleashed strength, his soul wished to end this war between them. Even so, they had said nothing more. He had made it clear that he would no longer give in to her threats while she had hinted that she would be sharing the letter she'd found in his notebook with the duke.

As she reached the top of the stairs, she knew that the iron rule she had established over Castamar had begun to slip through her fingers. Of course, she had some excellent hands still to play, starting with Don Melquíades and those self-incriminating lines written in the letter that was in her possession. Perhaps a clue to how the situation might be resolved could be found in the intensity of feeling Clara Belmonte had shown towards his lordship.

At last, she reached the guest bedroom where they had put poor Señorita Castro. She handed the poultice to Doctor Evaristo and took leave of Don Diego and his brother, who, it seemed, was the one who had brought her there on horseback. She hoped for her master's sake that Don Gabriel was not to blame for what had happened to the girl.

As she was leaving the room, she came across Elisa Costa, carrying several white towels and a basin full of hot water, as ordered by the doctor. She walked along the tiled floor and went to check on the bedchambers she had ordered to be prepared for the duke's guests, Don Francisco and Don Alfredo, who had arrived with the doctor and Don Gabriel, respectively. Ursula sighed and clenched her teeth.

Diego had barely finished giving his orders when his brother and Alfredo, breathless and soaked to the skin, had entered carrying poor Señorita Castro in their arms. After getting some chambermaids to undress her and wrap her in one of Alba's nightgowns, they'd put her to bed, with several blankets to warm her up. Doctor Evaristo had instructed Doña Ursula to order a poultice to be prepared for the wound on Señorita Castro's face. Alfredo, Francisco and Gabriel had taken off their wet clothes and gone to the drawing room, where they sat by the fireplace. Minutes later, Don Melquíades came to tell them that Señorita Castro was in bed and Doctor Evaristo was examining her. Only the duke and his brother had gone up to her bedroom.

Don Gabriel was furious about Daniel's death, mumbling that it was obvious Don Enrique was behind it, even if he lacked proof.

Gabriel was pacing nervously while Doctor Evaristo applied the poultice to Señorita Castro's wounds. He lowered his voice as he stated again that Don Enrique's lackeys had murdered Daniel. Diego walked over to him, took his arm to move him away from the doctor, and tried to convince him that he needed irrefutable evidence that the marquess was behind everything. He guessed that this would soon turn into the same well-rehearsed argument: Gabriel wanting to act, and he avoiding doing so until he had some proof with which to confront Don Enrique.

'What more proof do you need?' Gabriel spluttered, pointing at Señorita Castro.

'Proof! Gabriel, proof!' he said, raising his voice and startling Doctor Evaristo. He clenched his fists and whispered again. 'Don't you think this situation disturbs me? But I can't stand before the king and accuse Don Enrique de Arcona, Marquess of Soto and Campomedina, of involvement in such acts when I have no proof… And let me remind you that he has, as yet, done nothing against us. Nothing we can prove, at any rate!'

'Let me find that henchman of his, Hernaldo de la Marca,' Gabriel suggested.

'No,' Diego stopped him. 'If we do that, the marquess will find out and we'll be putty in his hands.'

Gabriel frowned in frustration. 'You're the most stubborn man I know!' he shouted.

Diego was well aware of it. But he would not allow the devious Don Enrique to make Castamar take a false step and lose its standing and renown.

'I must tell you that I am not at all happy you've got Alfredo and Francisco involved,' Diego said. 'I didn't need their protection, and now they're downstairs, waiting to be informed about a problem that was not theirs until you made it so.'

'I don't care. They're your friends,' Gabriel replied. 'And just so you know, ever since Alba's death, all you've done is whine like an old nag.'

Diego looked at his brother with fire in his eyes. 'Since it was you who brought her here, make sure Señorita Castro wants for nothing,' he said, making his exit and closing the door behind him.

Gabriel did not respond, and Diego went downstairs to thank Francisco and Alfredo for their concern. As soon as he entered the room, he informed them that the patient's prognosis was still uncertain, as she had a fever and was in a lot of pain. Before he could attempt to alleviate his friends' unease, Alfredo interrupted him.

'There's no longer anything you can do to stop us being involved. We're here now, and we're going to help you.'

'It may simply be a quarrel among servants... but that's very unlikely,' Francisco said. 'That calling card came to your house in Leganitos, addressed to Gabriel, and I honestly don't believe that the only intention was for us to find a dead black servant in the grove. I fear that somebody wanted us to find Señorita Castro. If not, why leave her alive and, what's more, next to a man she had no connection with?'

Diego didn't want to argue any further and, after thanking them, took his leave. It was clear that Daniel Forrado's spying had been discovered and that the poor wretch had paid the price. Don Enrique was dangerous, a brilliant courtier, a schemer, capable of all kinds of plots if they worked to his own advantage – a man who was best kept at a distance and considered an enemy. He was also renowned at court for having survived several duels in France and in the Kingdom of Naples thanks to his skill as a marksman. Luckily for him, these duels had been resolved with pistols rather than rapiers for, according to Francisco, the marquess was a mediocre swordsman and actively avoided any confrontations using the blade. Despite his manipulative character, Diego could not surmise what interest Don Enrique might have in Castamar, Diego's family or himself, beyond being a friend of his mother. Personally, he hadn't had more than a couple of conversations with the marquess since he'd appeared at Castamar. Even so, he knew that the key to deciphering the marquess's intentions regarding Castamar involved unveiling his motives. He had to admit he could see the delivery of the calling card to the Leganitos mansion as an intentional plan for the three men to discover both poor, lifeless Daniel and Señorita Castro in her pitiful state. However, they could have unwittingly provoked this by watching Don Enrique and his associates. He knew that, save a few exceptions, the court was a hornets' nest in which everyone sought royal favour. And Don Enrique was precisely the kind of man who would look for an alternative way of achieving his aspirations, whatever they were. Perhaps his being watched had interfered with other unrelated plans.

This was precisely what Don Gabriel did not understand, having spent his life cut off from the court, not knowing its ins and outs and internal politics. You had to know how to exist among courtiers, learn their alliances and their tricks so as not to fall for them yourself. Nevertheless, if Don Enrique was behind this attack, if Señorita Castro was just a tool in that scheme, and if his wish had been for Gabriel and not someone else to find her, Diego's intuition warned him that he himself was probably the ultimate target of the marquess's plans.

What Don Enrique did not know was who his adversary really was. If Don Enrique was guilty of Daniel Forrado's death and what had happened to Señorita Castro, or if he was plotting something against Castamar, then he would be unwittingly awakening a beast that would gladly put a bullet in his head – or a sword through his chest. Diego would not be acting in some attempt to gain royal favour – his own sense of justice would suffice.

As he walked, trying to relax, his thoughts wandered back to Señorita Belmonte. That girl and her ochre eyes had become lodged in his thoughts, and at every meal he felt the need to converse with her. He knew that he had only ever felt that kind of attraction once in his life – with Alba. To begin with, he had tried to pay no heed to the tingling sensation inside him. He'd chosen to deny it with different excuses: because of Alba and her memory, because he was her master and she his servant. It was true that they had established a silent connection, through the books he gave her and the meals she prepared for him, but he had felt that it was nothing more than a special relationship between servant and master. However, the relationship had gradually grown until that afternoon, when, like a helpless animal, she had asked him to bestow upon her the forgiveness she could not grant herself for Rosalía's death. Something inside him had gushed forth, opening a channel that had been sealed shut for nine years, and all he had wanted to do was kiss her and make her his own. He had contained himself for the sake of decorum and out of the respect he had for her. She was his servant, and he would never cross that line, for to do so would be to dishonour her. He was not like Francisco, with lovers all over the place, and he prized her virtue above all else.

He turned the corner and approached his bedroom. Señor Moguer was waiting there in case his master needed anything. Diego bade the servant goodnight and dismissed him. He got into bed and listened to the storm raging outside, reclaiming its dominion over the earth. As he lay there, he remembered the heat of Alba's body, but felt somehow that his wife was further away than usual. And with this distance came the sense that Alba was in a better place, a place from which she offered her blessing on the happiness he was experiencing now.

He closed his eyes, and as he sank into sleep, he had a fleeting premonition, warning him that if his inner voice, the one which was causing his stomach to flutter, became louder still, then sooner or later he would have to listen to it. And he knew that following this voice's commands would mean fighting against a world that could not tolerate seeing a duke in love with his cook. The problem was, if that moment came, there would be no one capable of making him change his mind.

23

Francisco stretched, rolled over and hugged Sol Montijos. Only gradually did he realize that his face was resting not on the soft bosoms of his lover but on the pillow in his room at Castamar. He sighed as he recalled the tragic events of the previous night and felt pity for poor Señorita Castro.

Those barbarians, he thought. *They have never learned to respect the weaker sex. I hope they all swing for it.* Nobody deserved to be treated like that, let alone a respectable lady like Señorita Castro. He hoped she would make a speedy recovery and reminded himself that he should tell Alfredo to pay her a visit as soon as the doctor allowed it. After bathing, he perfumed himself with essential oils and then called for the barber. Finally, he put on one of the suits that he left at Castamar for such emergencies. He preferred to do this rather than wear one of Diego's, which would be too large for him and would make him look like a puppet.

As he read the gazette, Francisco recalled Sol's naked body and smiled to himself. Since the celebrations back in October, they had maintained a relationship that was less secret than it was licentious. Their midnight encounters, his furtive forays into the bedroom in her house in Madrid while her husband slept in the room next door, their tumbles in the forgotten salon of some villa to which they had been invited. Despite this, his enjoyment had placed him in a difficult situation, and at their last encounter, their leave-taking had been far from pleasant. After a night of pleasure, she had got up and told him to leave. Her anger had taken him by surprise, as he had thought they would take advantage of the fact that her husband was out of town for at least two days to spend some time together.

'The fact that my husband is absent does not necessarily mean we must spend all of this time together,' she had said, turning away from him.

'Of course, my darling, my presence should never become an obligation,' he had replied, surprised by her reaction. Then he'd added, 'I had already been warned of your erratic behaviour.'

As she sat at the dressing table brushing her hair, she had given him a superior smile and observed that talk of her erratic behaviour was nothing more than a sign that he felt afraid of rejection. More confused than ever, Francisco had furrowed his brow as he buttoned up his shirt.

'I don't understand what you mean.'

'I mean that men can't bear it when a woman dares to reject them, while we – more exposed and supposedly weaker – learn to handle scorn, humiliation and neglect from an early age,' she had concluded.

He couldn't help laughing. In her words he had detected a certain bitterness, and he understood that his abrupt dismissal was part of that game in which some women of a certain age engaged to maintain their status and power. She was assuming that his involvement with her was not just sensual but emotional.

'My darling, I don't know what is on your mind, but I assure you our clandestine visits are no more than that. If you wish me to leave, I shall,' he had said.

'Go, then,' she had replied with indifference.

'You could at least feign a little courtesy at our parting,' he had reproached her.

She had approached playfully, treating him as if he were an angry child and, kissing him on the neck, told him that was more than he deserved. Sol was one of those who practised the art of seduction as a form of power, something he found far more tedious than their secret meetings, their flirting, their complicity. That dangerous pastime – which usually ended with a broken heart – was something Francisco had already seen far too much of. He had looked at her before leaving and asked her if she really wanted to play this game.

'It's the most amusing entertainment I know, and what's more, I never fail to hit the mark,' she had replied, scarcely turning her head.

He had opened the bedroom door and, just before crossing the threshold, had said, without turning, 'There's a first time for everything.'

He had closed the door and had not seen her since. It was not that he particularly minded that the relationship had ended in this way, or that the decision had been hers. He understood that any liaison required the involvement of both parties, and he respected her right to put an end to it, if that was her wish. What he could not accept was for this decision to be mingled with discourtesy and rudeness. It was beyond all comprehension to lose one's sense of decorum, even in the face of an angry cuckold. In such cases, one must act with circumspection, and if the husband demanded satisfaction, then one should oblige, with seconds and witnesses at dawn, far from Madrid, so as not to call the attention of the authorities, since King Felipe had issued a decree prohibiting duels, on pain of death and the confiscation of one's property. In reality, the new law had had little impact, and less still among the Madrid aristocracy; the duel would always be a matter of shame and honour, of offence given and received, principally between nobles, who saw it as a direct solution to every problem.

He had fought three of them in his time – two with swords and one with pistols – and he had survived them all to see another day, although not without a touch of fortune. The aggrieved husbands, by contrast, had suffered a double humiliation – physical defeat adding to the pain of their wounded pride. However, he had not killed any of them, inflicting a few superficial cuts on the first two and grazing the ear of the third with a bullet. He always behaved in accordance with the rules of etiquette, and it was for this reason that he could make no sense of his lover's display.

Francisco, after putting on a short wig with three plaits fixed by metal hoops and tied with light-blue ribbons, went down to the drawing room, where his friends would be having breakfast. Alfredo, Diego and Don Gabriel were discussing the girl's situation over some rather mediocre food. Alfredo, leaning against the mantelpiece, raised his cup in greeting. Diego invited Francisco to join them, even if the breakfast was not up to the usual standards. Apparently, the cook was absent, with Diego's permission, due to the tragic event that had occurred in the household. After sitting down and asking for some poached eggs, Francisco learned that Señorita Castro was out of danger, although she was still in a great deal of pain. Don Gabriel had taken charge of her care and had also ordered that his confidant's body be collected. He would personally make preparations for the funeral, and word had been put out to alert the night watchmen, bailiffs and warders to pursue those guilty of the dreadful deed.

'They'll struggle to catch them,' Don Gabriel warned, spreading out his napkin.

Diego gave him a sideways glance, his lips pursed. It was clear Gabriel was upset by the situation, and Francisco waited for him to explain his thinking.

'They would only make the effort to find the assailants if the victim had been a rich woman. What's more, if Don Enrique was behind it, then the perpetrators will already be far away – if they aren't already dead themselves,' he continued.

'According to Don Gabriel, the Marquess of Soto and Señorita Castro have frequented one another over recent months,' Francisco said.

'Even so, we do not know if it is a mere friendship or

something more serious,' Alfredo replied. 'Let us imagine they were engaged. That he had paid off all her debts in return for becoming betrothed, and she, seeing herself free, decided to break it off. And the marquess, driven by jealousy, punished her as an act of revenge.'

'That wouldn't explain why he left her next to a dead negro and notified us with a calling card,' Alfredo said.

'Perhaps he discovered that you were following him and decided to kill two birds with one stone,' Francisco said. 'All I can say is that he maintains an excellent reputation at court.'

'The only thing I can say with certainty is that I do not believe Señorita Castro to be guilty of such premeditation,' Don Gabriel added. 'Perhaps when she wakes up, she will be able to clarify matters.'

Francisco smiled at the remark and looked at Alfredo, who had turned towards them. After taking a small sip from his cup, he settled into an armchair.

Diego got up and walked around the room.

'Gentlemen,' Diego said. 'It is clear to me that Señorita Castro cannot have become involved in this situation through her own volition, though she might have been the victim of some dangerous individual who has been toying with her. Perhaps Don Enrique took advantage of her desperate situation and exploited her for his own ends.'

He said nothing more, but Francisco sensed he was uneasy. If the marquess was behind all this, then he was a skilled player, a man who would stop at nothing to achieve his objectives.

Francisco suggested a game of pontoon to ease the tension, but Diego didn't even answer. It was Gabriel who, seeing that his brother was gazing out of the window, came over to Francisco and offered to continue the game of chess they had begun the last time Francisco had been at Castamar. He agreed and they sat down at the board, taking a moment to agree whose turn it was to move. They left Alfredo and Diego deep in their thoughts. As he focused on the board, Francisco had the premonition that they, too, were in some way pawns in a game of chess, one in which their friendship would be put to the test.

Once more, Sol inhaled the fragrance of mint that Francisco had left on her pillow the last time he had visited, some days ago. 'Go, then,' had effectively been the last words she had spoken to him. However, Sol had sensed that this was not like those previous occasions when her younger lovers had taken offence and reacted with tantrums and anger. With surprising indifference, Francisco had simply disappeared from her life. Their paths had not crossed at social events, he had left no visiting cards, sent her no gifts, as his predecessors had done. Instead, he had vanished as if she had been a mere pastime, and the only memory he had left was the smell of mint on her pillow.

Perhaps she should have taken care to draw him further into the relationship. She had been deceived by his delicate manners, his praise, his little presents, his constant attention. His ardour between the sheets during his nocturnal visits, while her husband slept just a few yards away, had seemed to her sufficient proof that he was besotted with her. But she had clearly been wrong. She was worried by his distance. Not because she missed him but because there was far more at stake in her seduction of him than mere entertainment.

A month before the party at Castamar, Don Enrique of Arcona, one of the most dangerous men she knew, had approached her after she had signalled her consent with a flick of her fan. The meeting had taken place in her box during a performance at the Coliseum Theatre, and he had remarked that the time had come for them to renew their partnership, an idea to which she had been receptive. It was clear that the marquess wanted her help, and she already knew what she would request in return. And so, in a conversation in which nothing was said but everything was understood, he had communicated his wishes.

Sol was to describe her friendship with Francisco in correspondence with the Marquess of Soto. The final letter would place Francisco's reputation in the hands of Don Enrique. The request was hardly free of risk, and she was particularly exposed. Francisco was a close friend of Don Diego of Castamar, a man whom she had more than enough reason to keep at arm's length.

'May I ask what your motives are?' she had enquired.

'You know full well that is out of the question,' the marquess had replied.

Sol had smiled, expecting the marquess to ask her price. However, he had allowed the rest of the evening to pass without asking what it was she wanted. And precisely because Don Enrique had not asked and because it was never wise to seem too eager, she had told him she would need some time to decide upon what payment she would require in return. Some weeks later, worn down by the man's inexhaustible patience, she had sent him a simple note: *You may visit me when you wish*. It had not been long before Hernaldo de la Marca, a sinister-looking man, had made an appearance to hear her answer.

'I want to be free again,' she had told him. 'Free like I was before I married my husband. The Marquess of Villamar is a weight around my neck and he has now become too heavy.'

No more words were needed for Hernaldo to understand the only way in which she could attain such independence. Since then, she had kept her side of the bargain with the marquess and had handed him all her correspondence with Don Francisco up until the day of their rupture. She had only withheld the final letter, the one which jeopardized her young lover's reputation. This was, of course, the very letter that Don Enrique most desired, but she had no intention of giving it to him until she had received payment of her own. *Always keep one card*, her father had counselled her. *Just remember, Sol, that your beauty is a powerful weapon – but it is not eternal.* And that was why she had been eager to make a rapid ascent.

Her father, a wealthy merchant from Valladolid, had left her no title, just a large dowry, which she had used to marry Demetrio Velarde, a man almost thirty years her senior who was a secretary at the Treasury and whose position had provided Sol with a connection to the court.

When her first husband had died, she had decided to obtain a title. She had her eyes on Don Rodrigo, Duke of Castañeda and Villalonga, who had come to Madrid in search of a wife and with the intention of establishing himself in the capital. She had met him at one of the gatherings organized by Queen María Luisa, in the absence of King Felipe, who was still embroiled in his war against the Habsburgs. Oh, these men and their wars! She had spent the whole evening subtly flirting with Don Rodrigo, ensuring their fingers made contact as they both reached for the same pastry. Don Rodrigo had made her the centre of his attention. During the weeks that followed, they had exchanged notes in which the duke made his interest clear. It had been at another encounter, in the house of the Countess of Arcos, that he had appeared with an elegant woman, younger than her, who threatened to upset her whole plan. Rodrigo had introduced them to each other.

'My dear Sol, this is my cousin, Doña Alba de Montepardo.'

'Any friend of Don Rodrigo is always welcome in our little group of friends. We must admit you without delay, my dear,' Sol had said, slighting the newcomer by implying that she had no circle of friends of her own and she was in need of their charity.

The woman's expression of surprise had led Sol to assume that she attributed this discourtesy to clumsiness rather than evil intentions. The problems came later when Don Rodrigo innocently praised Doña Alba's social gifts.

'Really, Don Rodrigo, you are too—' Doña Alba had replied.

'Well, of course, my dear,' Doña Sol had interrupted, 'you have a special innocence.'

Doña Sol had smiled and reminded Rodrigo that he should present himself to the queen. Once the two women were alone, Sol had smiled at Doña Alba.

'Forgive me for being so direct. I see that you have a particular interest in Don Rodrigo, but I fear you are wasting your time. He would never settle for a woman like you, and what's more, I happen to know there is another who occupies a place in his heart,' Sol had said, but Doña Alba had merely laughed and given her a somewhat condescending look. 'Even so,' Sol had continued in a whisper, like it was a secret, 'I have heard so much about you that I hope we will become lifelong friends.'

'I hope you have heard nothing but praise,' Alba had replied.

'Of course,' Sol had said, continuing with her pretence.

At that moment, Alba's expression had changed slightly, and a dangerous glint appeared in her eyes.

'In contrast, I have not had the pleasure of hearing anything whatsoever about you. Indeed, I did not even know of your existence until my cousin invited me to come along to this gathering so that he could introduce us,' she had said.

It was at that moment that Sol had understood that this woman had no marital designs on Rodrigo. She had smiled, seeking to avoid the confrontation she herself had initiated, and said she didn't understand.

'My dear Doña Sol, of course you understand,' Doña Alba had interrupted. 'I don't know why you thought I could be a threat to you as regards my cousin. It is true that he is well disposed to you, but he also has certain reservations, on account of some disturbing rumours about you. Perhaps that is why he sought my advice.'

Sol had known then that nothing she could say would make things better.

'Doña Alba, I must have committed some terrible error. All I wish is to be his loyal friend...'

'You are not the first to wish such a thing; there have been others before you. But, honestly, my dear, after this evening, I very much doubt that my cousin will flatter you with his attentions again.'

'Doña Alba, I had no intention—' she had tried to say.

'My darling, of course you had an intention, and that's what makes it so amusing,' Alba had replied cruelly. 'Because, my dear, I am Doña Alba of Castamar, Spanish grandee: my circle is the only circle that matters; any other is of no consequence.'

The next day, the entire Madrid aristocracy had abandoned Sol. Doors that had always been open to her had become blocks of stone. Desperate, she had turned to a man she had met at the burial of her first husband: Don Enrique of Arcona. Trying to conceal her anguish and bitterness, she had begged the marquess to intercede on her behalf with Doña Alba, whom she had heard was a long-standing friend of his. He had told her they had drifted apart some years ago but that, as chance would have it, he happened to possess some information regarding goings-on at Castamar. As a result, he could advise her when Doña Alba left the estate and arrange what would look like a casual meeting, where Sol might be able to resolve their differences. She had thanked him profusely, and as soon as she was in her carriage, she had ordered her servant to find out who the marquess's confidant was. That was the first occasion on which she had collaborated with the marquess.

Despite acting on Don Enrique's advice, however, her attempts to engineer an encounter had been frustrated by Doña Alba's determination to ignore her. After some weeks had passed, and resigned to her ostracism, to her surprise she had received a visiting card from Don Rodrigo inviting her to meet. She had agreed immediately and had even dared to believe that Don Rodrigo might be about to ask for her hand, despite his cousin's advice. He did indeed propose, and she had accepted until he informed her that it was his intention to leave

Madrid and return to Cartagena, as his fortunes had declined, and although he would give her a comfortable life, he could not sustain their presence at court. At that moment, she had decided to reject his title and the meagre fortune that accompanied it in favour of a more ambitious target.

From an early age, her father had encouraged her to be ambitious, and she was sure he would not have been disappointed by the progress she had made thus far. And so, she had declined Don Rodrigo's proposal, caring little that this made it clear she had more interest in his wealth and status than in his person. Hours later, the duchess, surrounded by friends among the flowerbeds of the Buen Retiro Palace, had laughed at her in public, making it known that her cousin was still in possession of a huge fortune, and that her little manoeuvre had simply revealed Sol's true intentions.

At that moment, as their laughter tore at her pride and she saw that all her work had been for nothing, she had sworn to avenge herself upon Doña Alba, even if it cost her her life. And she had done exactly that, she told herself, recalling how she had moved heaven and earth to achieve her objective: she and no other had been the author of Doña Alba's death.

She had found the opportunity for revenge when she remembered that Don Enrique had someone inside the household of Castamar, and she had become obsessed with finding out who it was. It was not long before her clerk, who had been in her service since her father's day, discovered that it was a groom called Emilio, better known as El Zurdo, who had been assigned the mission of training Don Diego's horse so that it would become a lethal weapon. It had not been easy to convince the man to train the duchess's mount instead of the duke's. El Zurdo, her clerk and she had become players in a dangerous game. If they lost, Don Diego would become their implacable enemy, bent on destroying her, and Don Enrique would no doubt have them killed even more quickly.

After Doña Alba's death, Doña Sol had gradually been able

to recover her reputation until that old fool Don Esteban, Marquess of Villamar, had appeared some years later. Persuaded by her charms, he had married her, finally providing Sol with the position and the fortune she so desired. Her persistence had paid off.

As she stretched lazily and inhaled Francisco's scent on the pillow, her butler appeared to inform her that there was someone waiting for her downstairs: Hernaldo de la Marca. *The payment*, she thought to herself. *Perhaps I will finally obtain my independence.* She had been hoping he would appear, but she did not want to seem too eager, so she kept him waiting while she made her preparations. Finally, she entered the room. The marquess's sinister henchman looked at her and muttered a clumsy greeting that she did not return.

'Tell Don Enrique I have kept my part of the bargain and am waiting for my payment,' she said haughtily. 'It's been several months now.'

Hernaldo hesitated for a moment before taking a step forward. Sol fixed him with a hostile gaze, as if to warn him that he would pay for his insolence with his life if he crossed the invisible line that separated the aristocracy from the rest. It would be enough for her to give her clerk an order, for him to end up on the gallows in a public square.

'You don't have much faith,' he said.

'The only things I have faith in are money and the power of my position.'

'You shouldn't be so distrusting,' he said as he held out a cloth that was stained crimson. 'You can put on your mourning clothes. An accident in the carriage. The horses bolted.'

Sol accepted the news with satisfaction, took the handkerchief and checked that it bore the initials of her now deceased husband.

'Here is the weapon that will destroy the reputation of that conceited fool. My relationship with him is over,' she said, holding out a sealed letter. 'You may leave, and tell the marquess that I hope not to see him for a long time. He only calls me when it is in his interest.'

The man withdrew, and Sol smiled to herself at the thought that her father would be proud of her. Her hand squeezed the handkerchief as if she were grasping a noble title, so tightly that her fingers showed white against the red stains.

24

Clara rose early, with the intention of getting back to work as soon as possible and not dwelling too much on Rosalía's death. Her heart had been tied in a knot since the previous night, as she still did not know who the poultice had been for.

After getting everything ready for the day ahead, she sent a message to Elisa, asking her to come down to the kitchens at the earliest opportunity. From time to time, she had retreated to the larder so that she wouldn't be seen crying in front of her subordinates. Returning from one such trip, she was horrified to see the terrible job Beatriz Ulloa was making of cutting the veal. The girl irritated her. Ignorant and dim-witted, she was squandering the chance to learn a simple trade because she felt secure under Doña Ursula's protection. Clara walked over and, employing all her patience, took the knife and showed the girl how to cut the meat into even chunks. Beatriz sighed, as if she were being punished rather than taught something.

The kitchen servants were beginning to prepare the masters' breakfast when a smiling Elisa appeared on the other side of the door. Clara walked over, her heart beating rapidly, and closed the door behind her. She wanted to allay any doubts as soon as possible.

'Don Diego is well,' Elisa told her immediately. 'It was Señorita Castro. Some wrongdoers attacked her, and she was brought here in a terrible state. You don't need to worry about your lordship,' she finished, somewhat cheekily.

Clara felt relieved, though deeply sorrowed by what had happened to Señorita Castro.

'He's not *my* lordship. I'm just concerned about him. As we all are,' she whispered. 'And keep your voice down.'

Elisa laughed.

'Well, your concerns have brought you into direct confrontation with Doña Ursula, and now all the servants know it,' she said, taking Clara's hand.

Clara tensed up when she heard this, but relaxed upon discovering that she was not the only one who had had a run-in with the housekeeper. Don Melquíades himself had launched his own offensive during the servants' dinner. He'd even struck the table. Housekeeper and head butler had retreated to his office to continue their argument. That was confirmation for Clara that a war, hidden from the servants for all these years, was being waged between Don Melquíades and Doña Ursula. All of a sudden, she understood she had been the catalyst that had brought their poisonous relationship into plain view.

'You can't imagine how Doña Ursula's face changed when Don Melquíades banged the table. She was—'

The maid interrupted herself and half closed her eyes. Without saying a word, she walked to the door and opened it gently, revealing the figure of Beatriz. Elisa turned pale.

'What are you listening to, you busybody? Go and sniff around somewhere else!' she spat, causing half of the kitchen staff to look over at them.

Startled, Beatriz jumped back, jutting her chin defiantly.

'I work in this kitchen. You're the one who shouldn't be here,' she replied.

Clara intervened, sending Beatriz to peel garlic and telling Elisa that it would be better if she left before the situation escalated.

'Don't trust that one. Idle hands are the devil's playthings,' Elisa told her, still glaring at Beatriz.

As soon as Clara entered the kitchen, she went over to Beatriz and whispered to her to come with her. She could not tolerate such indolent spirits, destined to fail at a task before even starting it because they didn't put in sufficient effort. Her mother had taught her that if she was going to do something she should do it well.

The young girl followed her as the other servants shot furtive glances at them. As soon as they came out into the corridor, Clara turned and looked at Beatriz, hoping to see a more diligent attitude, but all she saw was the shameless face of an ignorant girl who bore the standard of a power that was not hers.

'Beatriz, you've been here for months now, and you still can't properly cut in the julienne style,' she told her. 'You're clearly not built to be a kitchen hand; you only got the position by agreeing to be Doña Ursula's eyes and ears.'

The girl shrugged her shoulders as if those words, which should have made anyone blush, had been addressed to someone else. Clara understood then that apathy came naturally to the girl, that she must have always hopped from one job to another, never sticking to any trade. She assumed this was the reason she had appealed to Doña Ursula, since this was exactly what the housekeeper had been looking for: a spirit lacking in all dignity, who carried out orders without questioning their morality, someone who would be a devoted follower of her cause in exchange for maintaining a salary and a position beyond her abilities.

'I'm doing my best. What do you want from me?'

'I want you to do better.'

'If you don't like it, talk to Doña Ursula.'

Clara wondered how Beatriz could not see that she was a puppet in Doña Ursula's hands.

'We both know she's not going to dismiss you, but if you think you will have better references from Doña Ursula than when you arrived, you're very much mistaken. Nor can you expect one from me if you keep up this attitude.'

The girl tried to answer back, but Clara immediately cut her off.

'Shut up and listen,' she said. 'Perhaps Doña Ursula will grow tired of you one day, or I might become sick of your attitude and have a word with Don Melquíades. Or maybe I'll leave, and a new head cook will come along, and then what? You'd doubtless be got rid of for being useless, and Doña Ursula would have no hesitation in allowing it because she would no longer need a spy. What will happen once you find yourself outside of Castamar? It will be you, not Doña Ursula, who ends up dying of hunger. You'll leave here as useless as when you arrived, having wasted the opportunity to learn a profession that would have put food in your belly.'

Beatriz winced and her haughty look vanished. The very idea of leaving the estate terrified her.

'I won't teach you anymore. Let me know when you decide you want to learn something,' Clara finished. 'Stop what you're doing and mop the floor, since that's all you aspire to do.'

She turned without giving the girl the chance to reply and disappeared down the corridor. Behind her remained the sad, pale figure of Beatriz, bearing the weight of fear on her trembling chin, with no remaining trace of her swagger.

With the master and the head butler's permission to take all the recovery time she needed, Clara informed her deputy that she couldn't continue and returned to her room, feeling shaken. Her spirit was carrying too much weight, and the argument with the kitchen assistant had awoken a feeling of deep sadness in her. Nor did she feel safe in her room when she closed the curtains and fell face first onto the mattress. She sensed how far away her mother was, and missed her words of wisdom. Then she remembered her sister, Elvira, who, in the period of greatest hunger, had gone out of her way to help Clara, guiding her like a dog, bearing her frustration in silence. Behind her, the ghost of

Rosalía rose up, with her haggard face and her hollow eyes, her neck broken, looking at her from the cold courtyard.

Amelia woke as she felt a lash of pain between her ribs, so acute it took her breath away. She felt disoriented and a sense of terror took hold of her soul. She moved a little until she understood that she was resting between soft linen sheets, and from the sound of it, someone was attending to her. She struggled to open her eyes, feeling trapped in her aching body. She made out two blurry figures who had walked over to her upon seeing that she was awake. As they approached, the terrible image of what had happened to her returned – that moment when the driver, in pitch darkness on the way back to her house after seeing the marquess, had stopped the horses and run off. She had not had enough time to understand what was happening before a hooded man, who stank of sweat, had punched her in the face and she'd lost consciousness. When she had woken up, they were dragging her out of the coach, pulling her by the hair as if she were livestock. They had thrown her into the mud, in the torrential rain. In terror she had tried to escape, slipping in the mud, until she had tripped, falling onto the stiff, lifeless body of a black man. She had shrieked in horror, thinking they would rape her before abandoning her lifeless body alongside that of the servant. She had tried to get up again but tripped on her own dress and fell face down. She had then felt a boot kick her in the ribs. Lying curled up on the ground, screaming in panic, she had been beaten for what seemed like an eternity, until her cries had been drowned in her own pain. Finally, the strongest of the men, who appeared to be the leader, had walked over to her, unsheathing a knife, and had announced that the hour of her death had arrived. Then, pulling her up by the hair, he had slashed her right cheek.

As she recalled this, she made a huge effort to lift her hand to touch her cheek. One of the blurry figures stopped her and told her not to touch it, since the wound could get infected.

'I'm Doctor Evaristo,' he said. 'You're in capable hands.'

She began to weep uncontrollably as she took in the fact that she had lost her beauty, that she would be a social pariah whom everyone would pity. Her father's fall from grace had left her victim to the cruelty of Don Enrique, who had forced her to have relations with him all these months. She lacked the strength even to insult him.

She deduced that she was now back at Castamar, in one of the guest rooms. She had no proof that her assault had been carried out on Don Enrique's orders, but knowing she was on Don Diego's estate was sufficient grounds for suspicion. She deduced that Don Enrique's obsession with her marrying the duke could only lead to the duke's fall from grace. He doubtless wished to use her tarnished honour against Don Diego after they were engaged. Even so, the motive that compelled the marquess to do all this remained a mystery to her.

She opened her mouth and asked for water. The aged doctor, who wore a short, powdered wig, helped her to drink as he told the second figure, a servant girl, to tell Don Gabriel to come.

'I don't want anyone to see me in this state,' she managed to say.

'I hate to disappoint you, Señorita Castro, but you were brought here in a far worse condition than you are in now. It will be no shock to him,' he told her. 'You've been in this fitful sleep for close to two days and, thank God, today the fever has subsided completely.'

'Who... brought me here? Was it... Don Diego?'

'No, Señorita, it was Don Gabriel, and had it not been for him, I doubt you would be alive.'

While he took her pulse and temperature, the figure of the doctor began to come into focus. The man placed her arm back on the bed, gathered up his small briefcase and headed towards the door, informing her that she must rest now and let nature do its work. As he crossed the threshold, she could hear Don Gabriel enquiring after her condition. She remained silent, holding back the tears, unable to understand how it was that she owed her life to a black man, a pariah in polite society, the stepbrother of a Spanish grandee, who bore a name he could only retain within the boundaries of Castamar. She felt that life was darkly ironic, since she was now as much of a pariah as he was. She would be invited to gatherings as a charitable act, but at the end of the day, no man of any standing would be willing to marry her.

'You must rest as much as possible,' Don Gabriel said gently. 'You're safe. The authorities have been notified of the events and will find the criminals responsible.'

She tried to smile but, with her swollen face, she only managed a grimace. She whispered a thank you, trying to convey the feelings that had overwhelmed her since she'd found out that he was the one who had saved her life.

'You must rest,' he told her. 'It's still morning and a nap before lunch would do you good.'

It was then that Amelia remembered she was part of the marquess's malicious plot against Castamar.

'I…' she stammered.

'Please, don't strain yourself.'

Don Gabriel assured her that she would want for nothing and that she was in very capable hands with Doctor Evaristo.

He was about to leave when Amelia blurted out, 'Would you mind staying by my side and holding my hand?'

'Of course,' he answered immediately. 'With your permission, I'll take the liberty of bringing my chair over to the bed.'

'I must confess… I am terrified.'

'Sleep easy, nothing will happen to you. Not while I'm here.'

She continued to hold Gabriel's hand, like a shipwrecked sailor clinging to a buoy, while he smiled warmly at her, hoping to bring some comfort.

It was midday when she awoke. Don Gabriel had dozed

off by her side and was still clasping her hand tight. Amelia took advantage of the situation to contemplate Don Gabriel: his strong chin, his high cheekbones, his short curly hair. Just then, someone knocked on the door and Don Gabriel opened his eyes. She blushed and abruptly withdrew her hand from his.

'Excuse me, I must have drifted off,' he said as he got up.

She felt foolish for having provoked the situation. She had been absorbed in looking at his face, which had suddenly seemed beautiful to her, and when she pulled her hand away, he had noticed her rejection.

She hoped Don Gabriel would stay but she wanted to avoid the rumour that Amelia Castro had asked a black man to sit by her side from spreading through the household, so she said nothing, and he took his leave like a gentleman. She ate and rested again, hoping that, before the day was over, Don Gabriel would come back so that she could make a proper apology, but, unfortunately, he did not.

25

After his most recent confrontation with Doña Ursula, Melquíades took a couple of days to make up his mind. The housekeeper had been watching him like a hawk to see whether his display of defiance in front of the other servants would go no further or if it was to be the start of a change at Castamar. After much soul-searching, and with his past weighing heavily upon him, he had eventually resolved that he could no longer continue to lead such a humiliating existence. The strangest thing about the whole affair was that, once he had taken this decision, a change occurred inside him, one that led him to hold his head high as he made his way to the drawing room, where the duke had resumed his old habit of playing the harpsichord.

He had long regretted what he had done, betraying an honourable man like Don Diego. He had tried to justify his actions to himself, arguing that it had been a time of war. However, as the years had passed, in addition to exposing him to Doña Ursula's blackmail, his behaviour had weighed on his conscience like a slab of marble. He had no regrets about having fought for the interests of Catalonia, but he could not bear that the cost had been the deception of his master. He should have left Castamar and joined the struggle. But he had never had a warlike spirit, and anyway, his loyalty to the man who was now emperor did not begin to compare to that which he felt towards Don Diego.

And so, having decided to reveal his secret to the duke, he felt a sense of relief, as if by restoring the dignity of the Elquiza name, he was also regaining control over his own life. He didn't care that one of Doña Ursula's spies had rushed to inform her. Her days were also numbered, as once he was expelled, there would be a new head butler whom she would not be able to blackmail.

He waited outside the door until the duke had finished his piece, and only then did he ask permission to enter.

'Good morning, your grace. I wonder if I could speak to you in private for a moment when it is convenient,' he asked.

Smiling, Don Diego got up and told him now was as good a time as any. The butler entered the room, bowing slightly, but just as he was about to speak there was a knock on the door. Doña Ursula appeared on the threshold, slightly out of breath.

'Your grace,' the housekeeper said immediately, 'I would like to have a conversation with you alone at some point this morning.'

Don Diego raised his eyebrows slightly, suspecting that something must be going on for the two most senior members of his staff to both have private matters to discuss. Melquíades smoothed his moustache and straightened his cuffs. He had not come so far just to allow Doña Ursula to orchestrate matters behind his back, so before she left, he said, 'If your grace doesn't mind, I would prefer to discuss my matter in the presence of Doña Ursula, as it also concerns her.'

Don Diego was even more surprised. Melquíades raised his head, trying to calm his breathing, and looked at the duke.

'I know that what I am about to say will come as a grave disappointment to your grace and I understand if you do not wish me to remain at Castamar.'

'Heavens above, Señor Elquiza, I cannot imagine what could possibly be so serious.'

The butler swallowed nervously and glanced at Doña Ursula,

who had fixed him with an icy stare. He looked back to Don Diego, who was waiting expectantly. What he said next would determine his future.

'Your grace, during the war I took advantage of my position at Castamar to steal secrets for the Habsburgs and their supporters. Some years ago, Señora Berenguer found the notes I had kept regarding this matter. She is here now with the intention of showing them to you,' he continued breathlessly.

Don Diego was furious to hear of this betrayal by someone whom he considered to be a faithful servant. He glared at the butler angrily, pursed his lips and clenched his fists until his knuckles turned white. Melquíades bowed his head until his chin was almost touching his chest.

'What did you say?' the duke asked as he approached, his voice heavy with disappointment.

'I was a supporter of Emperor Charles, your grace. Although, obviously, after he had abandoned the Catalan people, I no longer—'

'Silence!' the duke roared, like a wounded animal, so that even Doña Ursula took a step back. 'You betrayed me?' he continued, his eyes red and watery, as if it were only his rage that prevented the tears of disappointment from flowing. 'My family's loyalty towards you has been unstinting and... this is how you repay me?'

Despite his burly frame, Melquíades seemed to shrink, as if the shame had turned him into a despicable being, one who lacked honour. There was nothing he could say. He could not contest Don Diego's accusations; all he could do was await his expulsion, or an even worse fate. It was true that he had been the repository of the family's trust and now he was struck dumb, as if the words inside his head were a noose, preventing him from swallowing his betrayal.

Don Diego hurled the breakfast tray at the wall and then pointed at the butler, a wild look in his eye.

'Shame on you! I don't recognize you! I don't know who you

are! I don't know why you are in my house! If you were my equal, I would challenge you to a duel right here. Get out!'

The duke glared at the butler, and a heavy silence fell upon the room. Melquíades's eyes brimmed with tears, each one tearing at his soul as he tried to beg for a pardon that he knew he did not deserve. Don Diego suddenly began to walk in circles, rendered speechless with rage.

'Yes, your grace. I will leave Casta—'

'You will do nothing!' the duke shouted. 'You are nothing! You cannot even breathe unless I order you to do so! You cannot think! You cannot leave until I order it! Now, get out of my sight!'

He slammed his hand down on the table, making Doña Ursula jump. Melquíades scarcely looked at him as he left, knowing that he was leaving behind a part of his dignity, something he would never be able to recover. He knew the housekeeper would feign dismay when the duke asked her to explain why she had taken so long to inform him. Melquíades stayed outside just long enough to hear the cunning old vixen explain to their master that she had been motivated only by the desire to spare him further suffering. However, over the years the knowledge had become too much for her to bear.

Melquíades took a few steps away from the door, unsure where to go, like a rudderless vessel. Meanwhile, from the other side of the wall came the furious voice of Don Diego, who was now offloading all of his disappointment onto Doña Ursula.

'That was not for you to decide! That was my prerogative!' he roared.

'Yes, your grace. I beg your forgiveness for my misjudgement.'

'Out!' he shouted, just as Melquíades was reaching the end of the corridor.

He turned to see Doña Ursula leave the drawing room, and from the threshold, she shot him a look, one which said that, whatever the butler might think, her reign had now truly begun. Melquíades knew she would rule with a rod of iron, delaying the appointment of a new butler for as long as possible, preventing the under butler from being appointed to a position she deemed to be above his status. She would stall for as long as possible, until one day, Don Diego himself, upon seeing that everything continued to run smoothly, would decide that a head butler was not needed, hoping perhaps to avoid further disappointment.

Melquíades accepted his defeat, like a governor handing over the keys to a city he could no longer defend. The siege had lasted too long, and perhaps the time had now come to forget this unfortunate stage of his life. He couldn't help feeling a certain admiration for his adversary's strength and efficiency, but he told himself that she would never know either love or true human companionship. Sometimes, he wondered what these last ten years at Castamar would have been like if her temperament had been different. Even now, in the depths of defeat, he could not help imagining another Doña Ursula, one who was not bitter about life, one who was kinder and more easy-going. *Don't be a fool*, he reprimanded himself. *Better to forget everything about that woman.* He should go as far as away as possible, all the way back to his beloved Catalonia if he could.

He had spent his childhood there, in the care of his uncle and the company of his cousins. When Melquíades had been only a year old, his father and his pregnant mother had set out for Madrid. Twelve years later, his father had risen to become head butler and he had brought his son to join Melquíades's mother and his younger sister, Angeles, at Castamar. Melquíades had not returned to his homeland since, but perhaps now the time had come. With his savings he could establish a small business, a bakery, for example. But he knew this was just a dream, for if his reputation as a traitor got out, he would be condemned to poverty. And so, as he glared back at his enemy, he hoped with all his heart that a new head butler would restore the household to its natural hierarchy and teach that woman a lesson. With victory in her eyes, she turned and disappeared down the corridor, leaving him standing there as if he were nothing more than another portrait hanging on the wall.

He retreated to his bedroom like a prisoner, conscious that his days would be long and his nights would be lonely while he waited for his master to reach a decision. Now the war was over, he did not risk ending up in front of a firing squad, but perhaps the duke might decree that he be exiled from Spain for treason, or an even worse punishment. Whatever happened, his fate was now in the hands of God and the duke, and despite the fear gripping his stomach, he felt as if the weight of his past had been lifted from his shoulders. He made his preparations to leave Castamar, gathering up his belongings and his savings, though he did not have space for his greatest treasure – the hard-backed exercise books in which he had recorded the day-to-day events of the household. He would have to collect them when Don Diego permitted it or, with luck, ask his nephew to keep them safe. He knew the lad would soon hear of his uncle's treachery and reject him, never wishing to see his uncle again.

He was sure Doña Ursula would be eager to spread the news of his betrayal as soon as the servants sat down to eat together. However, the day passed and nobody came, either to bring him lunch or to bring him supper. Not wishing to starve to death, he went to one of the taverns near Castamar. It was not until the following day, at lunchtime, that Clara Belmonte appeared carrying a tray. She apologized for not having come the day before, explaining that Doña Ursula had only informed those she considered the senior servants, deliberately shunning Clara and keeping her in the dark, but Señor Casona, the head gardener, had told her everything.

'Don't worry,' he replied. 'I had supper in the little tavern by the Boadilla road.'

Clara insisted that, as long as she was head cook, he would have his daily meals and whatever else he needed, regardless of Doña Ursula. He had been naive to assume that the housekeeper would make public the reason for his fall from grace. She had been far more insidious, allowing the rumour to spread by itself, so that nobody could express their solidarity with the butler's predicament. She had already made it clear that nobody was to visit him, an order Señorita Belmonte had defied. Melquíades imagined the housekeeper's cheeks burning with fury. Clara Belmonte had no idea just how completely she had won his heart with this act of defiance and kindness. She told him she was greatly saddened by his situation, and even more so by the prospect of his ceasing to be the head butler at Castamar. He clumsily tried to explain the reason for his betrayal of the duke, as it had been weighing on his conscience, and since the end of the war, he had felt nothing but profound regret.

She listened patiently and replied with one of her mother's sayings. 'These things are always a good opportunity for forgiveness.'

After Señorita Belmonte had left, he ate the delicious chicken soup she had prepared for him, accompanied by fried chicken livers mashed with hard-boiled egg. Spread on freshly baked wheat bread, the chopped liver tasted divine. Just as he had finished eating, the door flew open. Roberto entered in a fury and walked in circles, agitated, his eyes wide, raising his hands to his head and running them through his hair.

'Is it true, Uncle?' he asked repeatedly.

Melquíades tried to make him understand that there had been a war. But his nephew only wanted to know if the rumours put about by Doña Ursula were true. The butler stopped trying to explain and confirmed that they were. The lad looked at him incredulously, in shock.

'Jesus Christ!' he said, his fists clenched. 'All that teaching, all the etiquette and the manners, and for what? What have you been preparing me for?'

'You're my nephew, I was preparing you for—'

'No. Don't dare say that. You've kept the secret... until now. My mother and I knew nothing.'

'We're Catalans—'

'I don't care. You don't understand, do you? Neither of us will be able to find work; we'll be treated like lepers. Nobody in Spain will hire the nephew of the man who betrayed Castamar. If the master expels us, we'll be condemned to a life of poverty.'

His nephew was devastated, the truth about his uncle's past having covered his somewhat idealized image with a layer of thick, black mud. Roberto stared at him uncomprehendingly. Melquíades placed a hand on the lad's shoulder.

'His lordship won't blame you…' he said, finally.

'He will. And even if he doesn't, Uncle, everyone else will.'

'Don Diego will never blame you for my errors,' Melquíades said, trying to reassure the lad, 'only for your own. I've known him since—'

'You've brought shame on the whole family. I have to talk to the duke. I have to tell him that I feel as badly betrayed as he does.'

The butler tried to dissuade him, to make him understand that it was better not to speak to Don Diego at a time such as this. But his nephew would hear no more and stormed out, slamming the door behind him. And Melquíades felt that the loneliness that now floated over him, like a dense, invisible mist, would pervade his life for many years to come.

Enrique woke up in an excellent mood and decided to celebrate his return to his estate by having breakfast in bed. He ate two poached eggs, drank a cup of hot chocolate and dealt with his correspondence. It consisted mostly of invitations to social gatherings, dinners and the occasional tedious reading. Only one, a poorly written missive from Hernaldo, merited any attention. Apparently, one of the tradesmen who supplied the duke's estate had, in exchange for a few reals, informed him that Señorita Castro was confined to bed and receiving the constant care of the doctor and, more surprisingly, the African. Enrique had not even contemplated the possibility that she would end up seducing Don Gabriel, but if she did, then it would be just as good for his plans as the seduction of Don Diego himself.

He dressed and went for a ride along the banks of the Valdeurraca, and then practised his marksmanship, something which he tried to do two or three times a week. He was considered one of the best shots in Madrid. With a duelling pistol, properly loaded and accurately calibrated, he could hit a target at twenty paces without any trouble. And this was precisely the fate that awaited the valiant Don Diego, although not before he had lost his prestige and his honour. The duke had deprived Enrique of his greatest treasure, possibly the only person he had loved in his life, and losing her had turned the marquess into a ruthless man. He well remembered those long summer hours on his estate, when the outcome of the war had still been uncertain, when he would receive his darling Alba with his warmest smile. He had met her at the house of the Duke of Medina Sidonia, and from the very first moment they had been drawn to one another. She had loved to talk about court affairs, and was a born hedonist, a lover of music, poetry and art who was always keen to display her exquisite education. He was enchanted by her elegance and by her attention to every detail. Not a day went by when he didn't miss her scent of lavender with a touch of mint. How could he forget that smile, those eyes that looked into his very soul?

He tutted while his armourer loaded his pistol, and he checked the wind and considered how it would affect the course of the projectile. Although he was skilled at understanding and anticipating human nature, he had not foreseen how Alba would slip through his fingers like a fresh morning breeze. As he took aim at the target on the chestnut tree, he remembered how naive he had been, and he told himself he should not have been so patient.

One summer afternoon, as was her custom, she had invited him to drink hot chocolate with her, to inform him of the latest social events, which she always knew about long before they appeared in the gazette. She had jokingly alluded to the fact that, whenever he appeared at court, he set all the ladies' hearts fluttering. He had subtly hinted that he might be particularly inclined towards one of them in particular, and she, almost immediately, had responded that she too might have an inclination towards a particular gentleman. At that moment, as he contemplated her brilliant blue eyes, he had felt very fortunate. He had always suspected that he had a place in her heart. She had laughed when he asked her to whisper the name in his ear.

'It's your turn,' she had replied, wafting her fan.

'I know, but I started. It's only fair that you be the first to take the next step,' he had answered.

Then, with her impeccable smile, she had brought her lips close to his ear.

'Will you keep my secret?' she had asked, her lips grazing his earlobe.

At that moment, the hair on the back of his neck prickling, he had felt an urge to take her right there, on the Turkish rug in the drawing room. He had smiled, expecting her to say, *You, my dear marquess, are the one who has stolen my heart.*

Instead, she said, 'Don Diego de Castamar. The nuptials will be announced tomorrow, and the celebrations will be held within a few months. And you are the first to know.'

He had feigned a smile, so far as his skills as an actor would allow, while he asked himself how he could have been so wrong in his assessment. Each time the blue eyes of Alba de Montepardo had looked at him, each time she had rested her delicate wrist on his forearm, each time she had ruffled his hair, each time she had laughed, each time they had danced, each time they had fallen silent, barely breathing, he had been mistaken. And so, he had refused to reveal the name of his beloved and, after saying goodbye, spent a sleepless night thinking about blowing Don Diego's brains out with his pistol.

But he knew himself, and he was not an impulsive man. Anyway, she had already made her choice. So, after the wedding – which he did not attend, despite being invited – he had his final meeting with Alba. In the evening light, he had wanted to find out whether he had been a complete fool, or if, on the contrary, he had caught a glimpse of something real. When Alba entered the drawing room with the smile of newlywedded bliss upon her lips, something died inside him, something that would never return. Another piece of humanity, one of the last, among the many that had gradually fallen by the wayside over the course of his life. He apologized for having been unable to attend the wedding, alluding to the duties of war. Not bothering to conceal her displeasure at his absence, she had detected that he was lying.

'You are very dear to my heart, and I deserve to know the true reason for your absence,' she had said. 'Tell me. Do you no longer value our friendship? Have I displeased you in some way?'

'Not at all, my dear Alba. Nothing you do could displease me.'

'Then tell me what is wrong. You no longer call upon me or answer my letters. I am distraught... You are one of my closest friends and you didn't even come to my wedding or present your regards to my husband.'

He had to admit that the imperious manner in which she had made her accusations merely caused him to love her more. He had hesitated for a moment and then, without directly saying that he loved her, had tried to explain why he had called her there that day.

'I don't think I can see you anymore, Doña Alba.'

'I don't understand,' she said, coming closer and taking his hand. 'Don Enrique, tell me the truth. How have I offended you? I must know the truth, so that I can understand.'

'I'm afraid I find it too painful to see you...'

He didn't know whether Alba's reaction was feigned or

not. She had responded with surprise, and he knew that her expression would be forever engraved upon his soul. Even now, sixteen years later, he could not forget the gleam of her blue eyes, lent a slightly turquoise hue by the evening light. He had remained silent while she, with her customary tenderness, had placed a hand on his cheek. He had prayed that she would never lift her hand from his face.

'Why is it painful now if it wasn't painful before?' she had whispered.

'You weren't married before,' he had confessed.

Alba had understood that his soul belonged to her, that his blood, his vital organs, his will, every breath of air in his body were hers and that, if she wanted them to be together, then nothing on earth would separate them.

'Don Enrique...' she had said.

Then, as on other occasions, she had stared into his eyes. He had drawn a little closer and she, her eyes shining, had turned her face towards him. His lips had gently brushed against hers. Alba had parted hers just enough to allow their tongues to touch. Then, carried away by the months of waiting, he had put his arm around her waist and kissed her passionately. She had sighed and responded, as if she too had been holding in her passion. But those fleeting moments of delight were rudely interrupted when she pulled away from him, when he heard her voice saying no, that this kiss was all he would ever receive from Alba de Castamar. She had turned and made for the door, but he had cut her off.

'Don't go. You feel something for me.'

'Don Enrique, please don't.'

'If you told me to, I would move heaven and earth to make you mine. There would be nothing—'

'Don Enrique...' she had interrupted. 'Any favour I might show would simply bring shame upon us both.'

'I don't care as long as I have you by my side.'

'But I do.'

There had been a tense silence while they looked at each other again. She took his hand tenderly.

'Were we to embark upon the relationship you say you desire, the only result would be to bring dishonour both to your own name and that of my husband. I love you enough not to wish you to suffer, but I love Diego with all my heart, and nothing could make me betray him. Not for you or for anybody. Ever.'

The hope that had been kindled by her fleeting kiss was extinguished by her words. He could not compete with her conviction and her sincerity. Accepting defeat, he had nodded and kissed her hand in farewell. She had looked into his eyes, which were brimming with tears.

'Now do you understand why we can't see each other?' he had asked, his voice breaking with emotion.

'I will miss our conversations,' she had replied, a tear running down her cheek.

'I will miss everything about you,' he had answered, moving aside.

She had reached the door without looking back, and he hadn't stood in her way.

'Alba,' he had said, as she opened the door, 'I will always remember our kiss as the sweetest of memories.'

'Of course, Don Enrique... But understand that I must forget it forever,' she had replied, closing the door behind her.

After that, they had occasionally met at social gatherings, at the queen's lunches at the Buen Retiro Palace, or at the theatre. In those moments, Doña Alba always responded with a friendly smile, making it clear that there would forever be a small place in her heart for him. His gaze, meanwhile, told her she would always occupy all of his heart. And so, he had made do, tortured by the passing of time as it whispered to him every day that she was not his. Gradually, however, his resignation had turned to cold fury.

That occasion, when Alba had left the drawing room of his house, was the first of two on which he had felt utterly defeated.

The second had occurred several years later, when Hernaldo de la Marca informed him of her accidental death. He had hoped that the death of Don Diego would bring Alba back to his arms, in search of the only man who had never disappointed her, but his plan was in tatters. And so, when he was told that Don Diego had ridden his wife's horse instead of his own, his hatred had welled up and he had felt like beating Hernaldo to death right there and then. His lackey had thought that his master's rage was due to the failure of his political ambitions. It was only some time later that Hernaldo had realized the true cause of his master's sadness, when Don Enrique's grief had persisted for longer than could be explained by political motives.

It was a pain so profound that for a long time he had tried to drown it in alcohol. Eventually, the last scrap of human empathy had disappeared from his soul. He felt only disdain for this duke who had foiled his plans for the Bourbons, prevented him from becoming a Grandee of Spain, and robbed him of that which he loved most in this life. And so, whenever he practised his marksmanship and took aim at the bark of the chestnut tree, he imagined that the target was Don Diego's head and felt great satisfaction when he hit his mark.

26

It was long past midnight when Hernaldo arrived home, his hands stained with blood. Adela was sleeping behind the shabby curtain. He attempted to enter silently without disturbing her, but her eyes were open the moment he shut the door.

Adela had appeared in his life in a rather unusual way – by the time he discovered her existence, she was already nine years old. Her mother had not even informed him of her birth. Then one day, Adela had turned up on his doorstep. The mother, dying of fever and despairing at the thought of leaving her vulnerable daughter behind, had told her to travel to Madrid to find her father. So the little girl, carrying a ring, a knife and a loaf of lentil bread, had undertaken the dangerous journey to his door... which he had slammed in her face the first time he saw her, telling her to go and find some other relatives. A daughter was the last thing he needed, and she was old enough to look out for herself. Refusing to give up, she had spent two days in his doorway. When he had finally decided to let her in, accepting that she was his daughter and it was his duty to look after her, she was no longer there. He had put on his shoes and descended the wooden steps onto the street. His attempts at locating her were fruitless. Thinking she had gone for good, he had turned to see her walking alongside a pimp. He was leading her by the hand into some godforsaken, stinking alleyway. Hernaldo had known this man well – he worked for a local criminal who ran whorehouses throughout the neighbourhood. Hernaldo's stomach had tied in a knot and he had been considering letting her go, when, suddenly, the girl turned her head and something had stirred inside him. He had told himself that nothing he had done in his life was worthy in God's eyes, and he was not going to let some whoreson rogue lay a finger on the girl.

By the time he had caught up with them, the pimp's trousers were round his ankles and Adela was desperately telling him her father would show up any minute. And so he did. He spilled the man's guts, cut off his member and slit his gullet without even giving him time to pull up his trousers.

'If you want, you can stay,' he said to Adela afterwards, 'but you must know that this is what I do.'

The girl had hugged him, and at that moment he knew that God Himself had sent him this precious gift. That night, as she slept, he had gone to settle up with the whorehouse owner, since he had done away with one of the man's lackeys. To begin with, the man had huffed and puffed, insisting he was owed money. Hernaldo had responded by saying that, if he wanted money, he should take it up with Hernaldo's master, Don Enrique de Arcona, who would be only too happy to shut down all of the man's whorehouses. The debt was settled on the spot. From that day on, his daughter had become Heraldo's only treasure, and he could not be separated from her.

When Adela sat up and saw his bloodied hands, she said nothing. She was used to him showing up like this, in the worst cases bearing an ugly wound, which she would tend to.

'I'll get you some stew from yesterday,' she said, helping him remove his boots. 'How was your night?'

She already knew the answer. Even so, he replied.

'Tough,' he said hoarsely.

'Why?' Adela asked.

Hernaldo knew what she was about to say. A recurring topic,

where she asked if they could leave Madrid for the coast and leave behind this den of hoodlums and harlots.

'You know why… I've had a lot of work.'

She served him the stew, with more vegetables than meat. His little dove was an unremarkable cook but that didn't bother him. All he wished was to ensure she would never have to work in the house of some unscrupulous rich man. That's why he'd told her she had to learn to read and write, some arithmetic and, if possible, some other subjects, whatever she could, so that if she didn't find a good husband, she could become a governess, teaching and looking after wealthy children.

'I went down to the Plaza de la Cebada early this morning. I heard they've found dead bodies near the Manzanares,' she said. 'The porters and bailiffs say it was the same people who thrashed that poor girl to within an inch of her life.'

'Yes,' he replied blankly.

He had spent half the night spilling the guts of the ruffians who'd assisted him in the Señorita Castro affair. Some, upon hearing that Castamar was pressing the authorities to find those responsible, had come to ask for more money in exchange for not running their mouths off. Over the course of the night, he had tracked them down and silenced them once and for all. Only one of them had reacted in time, managing to draw his sword when he realized he was about to have his stomach slashed, but Hernaldo had seen him coming and made the first strike, splitting the man's sternum in two.

'Was it you?' Alba asked.

He said nothing and ate another spoonful of stew. She looked at him as if urging him to answer, and he shook his head. Adela tutted in anger and resignation. It was her opinion that Don Enrique was simply using him. But he didn't agree – the marquess was many things, but he wasn't disloyal towards his own men, far less ungrateful. He had already had several opportunities to sacrifice Hernaldo to further his own plans and had not taken them. Had he handed him over to the justiciary, for example, as

Doña Alba's murderer, he would have gained the confidence of Don Diego and the king and perhaps even become a grandee. Besides, the marquess had shown many other signs of gratitude: he'd been generous with money, so that they wanted for nothing, and every time Adela got sick or Hernaldo was wounded, Don Enrique had paid for medicines and doctors. The marquess had also confided in him, shown concern and paid for his daughter's education, and given them the house they lived in, signing it over to Hernaldo. No Habsburg or Bourbon had ever given him so much. For this, he owed the marquess unwavering loyalty.

'It's too late to change my life,' he said at last.

'What about me?' she replied.

'That's different, my dove. You have your whole life ahead of you.'

His daughter dreamed of another life, a more peaceful one for him to spend his old age, after so much war, death and desolation. He knew all too well that this dream was unachievable, but he also knew the glimmer in those jet-black eyes, asking him to change his life, leave the marquess, travel to the coast and live by the sea.

'There's no point dreaming about the impossible,' he said.

'Father, I don't want to spend my life not knowing if something's happened to you, if you'll come home for dinner, if...'

Hernaldo got up and hugged her tight, overcome by the thought of losing his daughter, whispering in an attempt to soothe her, letting her know that his alliance with the marquess was unquestionable, a vow he was honour-bound to uphold. When he closed the door, he recognized that old feeling, sensing that their disagreement was just the beginning of an inevitable change. Then he remembered the marquess and consoled himself with the thought that his master could find the solution to any problem he might encounter.

24 January 1721

Ursula had waited less than a day before swapping her cramped housekeeper's quarters for Don Melquíades's office. She had ordered that his belongings should be gathered up and kept under lock and key in one of the storerooms, including, of course, the collection of worthless logbooks the head butler had amassed over the years. If he wished to get them back, he'd have to come and ask for them, another hard blow to his pride. In doing this, she sought to show him she had always had the power and that, now he had decided to break their tattered agreement by confessing his betrayal to the duke, it was time for him to vanish once and for all from Castamar. That defiant act during the servants' meal and the rebellious airs he had put on had cost him his position and the comfortable life he had been living up until now.

For her part, she had allowed two days to pass to allow Don Diego to calm down before presenting herself before him and expressing her repentance for not having revealed the truth sooner. Don Diego, although he was still roused to fury whenever the topic was raised, forgave her, understanding that, though she had been mistaken, she had only sought his well-being.

'I'll take over the running of Castamar until we find a new head butler,' Ursula told him, putting on the most downcast face she could muster.

Don Diego nodded in acceptance, since he trusted her more than anyone to control the under butlers. They had already been put in place, to perform Don Melquíades's duties, but none of them possessed the seniority and access to the duke which she had. That was why, after Don Diego's order that she take charge of everything – since really she had been de facto comptroller for years – she had installed herself in the head butler's office. Her intention was to exercise her authority in a clear display of her power. She listened to the murmurings of all the servants at Castamar. From her origins as a simple maidservant, she had risen beyond even the confines of her gender. She felt that Doña Alba would be proud of what she had achieved – stopping a Habsburg upstart, who had betrayed her house, from running Castamar. If her mistress had been alive, she would have demanded far more than mere destitution, Ursula told herself.

So, on the morning of Don Melquíades's fall, she had summoned the senior servants to inform them of his betrayal. Of course, she had avoided calling Clara Belmonte, making it clear that she did not consider her the true head cook. With the others, she had made it clear that from that moment on she would run the house. Everything must function perfectly during the period of transition, she expected maximum cooperation, and visiting Don Melquíades was prohibited. They had all nodded solemnly, except for the gardener, who, as always, had to say something.

'When are you planning to hire a new head butler?'

She had looked him up and down.

'Return to your duties,' she had replied curtly.

The old man had given her a penetrating stare, as if he knew there would not be a new head butler in the corridors of Castamar so long as she was in charge. She had been about to turn and leave when Simón stopped her, speaking in a tranquil voice.

'You should know that I will visit Don Melquíades when I consider it appropriate, and if you have a problem with that, you can speak to his lordship.'

'We'll see about that,' Ursula had warned him, adding to herself, *rebellious old fool.*

A veiled threat, which both knew would lead nowhere. Despite the bothersome gardener, Castamar was now hers.

Now, her spirits more resolved, she awaited the arrival of her kitchen spy, who apparently possessed some information of interest to her. After the fall of Don Melquíades, it was the turn of the cook, who had questioned her power with her rebellious airs and graces. As expected, Beatriz Ulloa knocked at the door and was called in.

'Señorita Belmonte and Don Diego are having a secret relationship through notes and the books the duke keeps giving her,' Beatriz announced.

Ursula raised an eyebrow. She had assumed his lordship's first order from the bookseller had been an isolated incident – seemingly she had not been vigilant enough. It was clear the duke had taken sufficient precautions to avoid being discovered and had tasked someone he trusted completely to bring the volumes onto the estate without being discovered. She felt a small pang of terror upon realizing that a direct and profound relationship had been established between his lordship and the cook – no wonder the duke's refusal to dismiss Clara Belmonte had been so categorical. It was now a matter of the utmost urgency to discover the true nature of that relationship. She gave Beatriz one of the master keys to the servants' wing and told her to slip into Clara Belmonte's room, taking the utmost caution, and find the books.

'There must be written notes,' she said. 'Bring me one as soon as possible.'

The girl took the key and headed towards the door.

'Wait! If you're discovered, I'll expel you immediately, and if you reveal that you acted on my orders, I will ensure that you never again find work in a respectable house,' Ursula warned before Beatriz left. The girl disappeared, knowing that her job and her very future were at stake.

Convincing the cook that she had to leave Castamar would be rather more difficult than getting rid of the head butler, even more so if she really did have an epistolary relationship with the duke. If this were the case, Señorita Belmonte would soon request autonomy for herself and her kitchen. Ursula knew her master's character all too well, and if he wanted the cook to stay, there was nothing he wouldn't do to see his wishes fulfilled. Regardless, it was clear Señorita Belmonte would not slip up in her job badly enough to provoke her dismissal. Even King Felipe himself had written after the dinner at Castamar to express his congratulations on the fantastic food. In any case, you only had to look at the case of Rosalía to know she would never be dismissed. In a personal sense, Rosalía's death had been a tragedy, but also – one might as well say it – an act of divine beneficence, for she had been a burden to all. *May she rest in God's glory*, Ursula thought.

She walked over to the dressing table, took out the bottle of rosoli that Don Melquíades kept there and poured herself a glass. She downed it in one, hoping the spirit would soothe the fear that had taken root in the pit of her stomach. The longer it took Beatriz to reappear, the more her sense of unease grew. She walked again to the desk and sat down, ruminating on how she could make Clara Belmonte wish to leave Castamar. Personally, she would happily write the most impeccable references if it meant the young woman could work as a cook in another noble house and leave them in peace. A line had been crossed, beyond which the housekeeper and the cook could not be together under the same roof for much longer.

There was a knock at the door. 'Come in,' she said, her body tense, not knowing whether Beatriz Ulloa would appear alone or accompanied by Clara Belmonte, having found the thief in her living quarters. She sighed in relief, feigning calm, when she saw the former enter alone, her hands in her apron pocket. She closed the door and produced the note. It carried the Castamar seal, and Ursula could see the elegant scrawl of his lordship's hand on it.

'Clara Belmonte has a whole heap of books on her shelves,' Beatriz said. 'This was tucked into the last one. It seems there is a note in each one and—'

'Give it to me,' Ursula said, snatching the note from the servant's hands.

There was no doubt that Señorita Belmonte was keeping a private correspondence with Don Diego. Ursula did not get the feeling they had crossed the boundaries of decency, but there was something clandestine about the whole business. The worst thing was, the duke seemed to believe he was writing to some well-to-do maiden, someone who, if not quite his equal, he certainly addressed as a fellow member of respectable society.

'I couldn't understand what it says, because I can't read or write,' Beatriz added. 'If you wish, I can look for more.'

'No. You've done enough. Take the note and put it back where you found it, using the greatest discretion, then bring me the key immediately.'

The girl nodded and made as if to leave while the housekeeper stood there, dazed by so many contradictory thoughts. She didn't realize that Beatriz had stopped in the doorway until she looked up and saw her still standing there, her face like a sad puppy.

'What is it, girl?' she asked, frowning.

'I had thought that... perhaps you could teach me to read and write.'

Doña Ursula looked at her in surprise. If she had shown some aptitude this might have made some sense, but Beatriz Ulloa was a rather dim girl, whose only aspiration in life was to pass through it doing a job that would feed her and little else. Wasting time on her would be like fertilizing a field that was better off left fallow.

'You don't need to read and write. You're not really a kitchen hand. You're barely even a scullery maid,' she said disdainfully. 'Remember, I only gave you the job in order to perform this function.'

'Yes, but I thought that someday I might...'

Ursula chuckled as she shook her head. How could people be so mistaken, to the point where they believed they could change their own nature? That poor unfortunate girl had seen a possible role model in Clara Belmonte and had truly felt herself capable of achieving some level of learning. She laughed openly, and the girl looked down at the floor, clearly humiliated.

'Someday what? You think now you're going to become

respectable? You are what you are, and you will never change that,' Ursula said, damningly. 'Such is life. Now, out.'

The girl nodded and left to carry out her duties. Ursula sat on her throne behind the desk, carefully weighing up her actions. Now the relationship between the duke and the cook was no longer in doubt, it was clear she had no option other than to be patient. Perhaps matters would take a different turn at some point or become complicated by some unforeseeable event. If that happened, she would expel Clara Belmonte as quickly as possible. On the other hand, if those circumstances did not arise, she would have to be prepared to deal with the cook for much longer, keeping her under her command while trying to interrupt the pernicious alliance. She knew that interfering in her master's desires was a dangerous game, so she would have to tread lightly, allowing things to happen by omission rather than action, until it was safe to take a step in the right direction. At least this way, even though she could not throw the cook out immediately, she could keep her under control while she awaited more favourable conditions.

She waited for Beatriz to return with the key before leaving the room for the upper floors. As she walked through the galleries, past the bowing butlers and manservants, she felt invested with an almost divine power, as if she could strike down or protect all of them.

27

Betrayal leaves a bitter taste, Diego thought to himself. *One swings between incredulity and self-reproach, like the pendulum of a grandfather clock.* He could scarcely believe that the son of Ricardo Elquiza, his father's butler, had brought shame to his own name and to his oath of service to the Castamars. *If his father knew that his son had used his position to pass information to his enemies, he would be spinning in his grave.*

He heard a door slam in the distance and felt a chilly breeze. A cold wind was blowing along the corridors and down the chimneys of the palace, and the duke found himself affected by it. He had felt torn ever since his butler had made his confession. On the one hand, there was the knowledge that a Habsburg supporter had been living among them all that time, a spy who had stolen secrets and given them to the enemy. On the other hand, when he remembered Don Melquíades, with his head bowed and a pained expression of guilt and repentance on his face, he felt that he had more than paid for his errors. He also knew that, in times of war, a man must follow his conscience, and that was exactly what the butler had done. The decision must have caused him great suffering, as he tried to balance his loyalty to Castamar against his love of the Catalan people.

Now Diego found himself facing the same dilemma as King Felipe, at the end of the war. For a long time, the duke had argued against the repression of the Catalans, and had even dissented from the decision to disband their council and parliament. Later, when Felipe had written to him informing him that work was to begin on the fortification of Barcelona, he had replied warning the king that these defences would be seen as a symbol of oppression. Fearful of renewed insurrection, Felipe had ignored his advice, and others had exploited the situation to repay old grudges against the Catalan people. The duke wrote again, arguing that one showed more greatness by forgiving the defeated than by punishing them, but his letter had no effect.

And the choice he faced now was the same: to forgive or to punish. But the problem was that his rational voice was drowned out by his disappointment and his rage. As a result, he had preferred to postpone the decision until his anger subsided, ordering the butler to remain on the estate until he had reached a fair and balanced judgement. He was grateful that Alba had not had to witness this situation as, after Doña Ursula, the butler had been one of her favourites. However, there was no avoiding the fact that his brother would need to be informed of the bad news upon his arrival.

Gabriel, after confirming that Señorita Castro's condition was now improved and having taken his leave of Francisco and Alfredo, had left for Valladolid two days earlier with the intention of warning his mother about Don Enrique. While his horse was being saddled, Diego had approached him. The two men had not exchanged a word since their argument in the presence of Doctor Evaristo.

'I'm sorry I shouted at you,' Diego had said.

'And I'm sorry I accused you of whining like an old nag,' his brother had replied.

It was not the first time they had fallen out, but the two had enough strength of character to both maintain their own opinion and set aside their differences once sufficient time had passed. Diego knew that Gabriel would not act without clear proof against Don Enrique, and also that he would do everything he could to obtain such proof. He also knew that Gabriel was outgrowing Castamar. A world that was reduced to the boundaries of an estate, however large it might be, was not enough for him. His brother had a restless spirit, and the duke was aware that one day he would seek a place where the colour of his skin was of no consequence. They had never spoken of the matter, and indeed, Diego knew they would only do so on the day when Gabriel informed him of his decision to leave. He loved his brother with all his heart and seeing him go without knowing if he would return would pain him, but he would not oppose it.

He returned to his office and sat down at the desk. He inspected the wax seals on the letters that had been delivered that morning and thought about how he should visit Señorita Castro to check on her progress. Since Gabriel's departure, Don Diego had not wanted to spend more time than was absolutely necessary in her company. It was obvious she felt uncomfortable in his presence, and she continually tried to cover the scar on her cheek.

Among the letters was a missive from King Felipe. He was just about to break the seal when someone knocked softly on the door. He instructed them to enter and looked up to see Don Melquíades's nephew standing in the doorway. He didn't remember the lad's name, although he recalled that he had had the foresight to prepare the carriages the day they had visited Villacor. The servant asked somewhat formally if he might be allowed to speak, and that was when the duke remembered his name: Roberto. The lad smoothed out his footman's livery, as if keen to ensure his appearance was impeccable. The duke guessed that the boy had come to argue his uncle's case while also wishing to maintain his own dignity; perhaps, should the duke decide to banish the butler from Castamar, the nephew would also leave. On the one hand, the duke did not see the need for the lad to speak to him in person. On the other, if the boy was brave enough to defend his uncle's actions, then he could hardly refuse to give him a hearing. Don Diego's father had taught him that the problems of the servants were also the problems of the master, and that it was his duty to resolve them. He would respect the family's decision and in no event would he blame the nephew for the actions of his uncle.

'Your grace, I only wanted you to know that neither my mother nor I knew of my uncle's low and treacherous behaviour. If we had, we would have come to you at once. We are not renegades like my uncle; we would never betray—'

The duke raised his hand. The young man's declarations had taken him by surprise.

'You have not come to argue your uncle's cause?' he asked.

The lad shook his head, referred to Don Melquíades as a filthy traitor and, had the duke not interrupted him, would have said far worse things.

'Silence!' the duke thundered. The lad blanched and took a couple of steps back. 'Before you say another word against your uncle, remember that he has cared for Castamar, for my wife, for my father, my mother, my brother and, of course, for me. I will not hear him spoken of in this way. Do you have anything more to say?'

'No, your grace,' the lad answered, his head bowed.

'You may go, then,' the duke said, and the lad made a hasty exit. 'Dear God, what a family!' Diego muttered angrily, after he had gone.

In an effort to calm himself, he turned once again to the letter from the king. As before, the king told him that he wished to abdicate, that the crown weighed too heavily upon him, that he was beset by fits of melancholy, and that he wished the duke was still the captain of his personal guard. He asked after the duke's own spirits and urged him to be strong. *I know you have never lost your strength of will or that determination that was a bulwark in the war against the Habsburg pretender*. Diego smiled upon reading this and was about to pen his reply when he spotted another letter in the pile. It was from his brother, sent from their mother's house. He must have written it the day he had arrived in Valladolid. He opened the seal and read attentively.

Dear brother,

I am writing to let you know that I will spend some days with Mother, as this is her wish. You know how stubborn she can be, and I lack sufficient strength to deny her. I should also say that I have spoken to her about Don Enrique and she insists that we are talking nonsense, that she is well acquainted with this gentleman, who, according to her, wouldn't harm a fly, let alone Señorita Castro, with whom he was on excellent terms at Castamar.

I made it clear that I completely disagreed, and I asked her to promise to show the utmost caution in his regard and not to mention our suspicions. She reluctantly consented, while complaining that she is quite capable of managing such issues with discretion. She also confirmed that she had no intention of seeing Don Enrique for some time, as her diary was already very full of engagements. However, she told me she would not cease to treat him as a friend of the family, unless I could demonstrate otherwise, and I do not therefore believe we can prevent her from inviting him to the celebrations later this year.

Please also find enclosed a letter for Señorita Castro, as I do not wish her to believe that I have neglected my obligations as a host, and I want to explain in my own words the motive for my departure and assure her of my impending return. I ask you to ensure in my absence that she lacks for nothing. I believe that she is in need of our help, and if previously I was inclined to think she might be conspiring against us, I now suspect you were right, that in the light of the tragic events she has experienced, she is more a victim of Don Enrique than anyone. I know you well enough to imagine that you will be smiling to yourself at this acknowledgement of mine. Did Alba not always say that your favourite sport was to be in the right whenever you argued?

Other than this, I hope all is well. In a few days I will return

to Castamar, and expect to arrive on Saturday night unless I am
delayed.
   Your loving brother,

                        Don Gabriel de Castamar

   Postscriptum: Now that mother has been warned as to the
   possible danger of Don Enrique, upon my return, and while our
   friends pursue their enquiries at court, I intend to investigate that
   house of ill repute, the Zaguán. According to information received
   from my man before his death, Don Enrique's lackey is a regular
   visitor. I must find out if someone can tell me more about the
   identity of the marquess's men.

As his brother had predicted, Diego had smiled to himself
upon finding that Don Gabriel had been won round to his view
of Señorita Castro. However, after reading the final lines, his
smile disappeared. He didn't like the idea of Gabriel visiting
a house of ill repute. Who could tell what consequences that
might bring? He looked up at the portrait of Alba and asked
himself what she would have done in this strange situation.
Was his butler a disloyal traitor or a man who had repented
his errors? Did Don Enrique wish evil upon Castamar or was
he just a proud and licentious noble? Was Señorita Castro the
defenceless young victim of a powerful man or an unscrupulous
schemer? These doubts had built within him like a house of
cards, and one bad decision might precipitate disaster. Had she
been there, Alba would have known what to do, although she
too would surely have hesitated as to what he should do with his
other problem: Señorita Belmonte.
   He could not deny that he took pleasure both in giving her
those books and, perhaps even more, in eating the dishes that
she prepared with such skill from the recipes they contained.
But he had to recognize that there was something else, that
he had drawn even more enjoyment from the note she had
sent him following his most recent gift. He did not know

where this might all lead, but he could not deny that he wished it to continue. And so, he picked up his goose quill, postponed his reply to the king, and began to pen a letter to his bookseller.

26 January 1721

In their looks of contempt, Don Gabriel was constantly reminded of the intolerance of the Spanish people, who saw in him not a gentleman but a negro in disguise or a slave who was treated too leniently by his master. This contempt was then followed by surprise and incomprehension at seeing a black man whose mount bore the coat of arms of Castamar. This had been the response upon his arrival in Valladolid and the same was true upon his departure. He had experienced so much hostility throughout his life that he was now inured to it.

After spending two days with his mother and another two on the road, he arrived at Castamar at night-time, as he had promised his brother. Despite going to bed late, he got up early the next morning to walk around the estate with the duke. Notice of Don Melquíades's betrayal and the discovery of the corpses of the four men who had assaulted Señorita Castro by the banks of the Manzanares was enough news for one day. Fortunately, Amelia's situation had improved, although she was still confined to her bedroom. He planned to visit her to see if she could cast any light on matters, but preferred to wait until after mass. He made confession, took communion and said goodbye to the chaplain, Father Antonio Aldecoa, who was one of the few priests whom Gabriel truly respected. Gabriel remembered clearly how, when he was barely ten years old, he had asked the priest why his skin was a different colour. The priest had leaned down and, smiling kindly, had said, 'God loves his creations in all their variety.'

Don Gabriel rode back to the palace, eager to question Señorita Castro about her attackers. One of the grooms was waiting to take his horse's reins, and he dismounted, smoothed out his frock coat, and took a moment to recover his breath before climbing the stairs to the upper floors. Upon reaching her bedroom, he knocked at the door and waited for her reply before entering. He bowed and explained that he had come to check on her condition and to ask if she had received the note he had written her a few days earlier. Amelia made as if to smile but immediately covered her face in shame. Then, looking somewhat sheepish, she said she had received his kind letter and was very grateful for it.

'You don't have to thank me for anything. I just want you to make as swift a recovery as possible.'

'Even so, I am grateful for your care and your support,' she answered haltingly. She paused for a moment to clear her throat. 'The last time you were here, I...'

He knew she wanted to apologize for what had happened when they had been together, how she had pulled her hand away when the servants had entered. Accustomed to such gestures, he had given the matter no importance.

'There is no need to apologize. Your reaction was quite logical.' He changed the topic. 'Señorita Castro, you are an intelligent woman. We both know who caused this scar, but only you know the motive. Perhaps you could clear up those doubts.'

She looked at him in silence. Gabriel noted the hesitation and saw her chin tremble. Her jaw clenched, as if a battle was being fought inside her. Although he had no alternative, he felt bad about upsetting her. It was clear that Diego was even closer to the truth than he had suspected: Señorita Castro, consciously or not, had found herself playing a role for which she was clearly unprepared.

'I was attacked,' she finally said.

Gabriel hesitated for a moment, then despite her discomfort, he insisted. She held the key that would unlock the secret of Don Enrique's plans.

'I understand. But have you no idea who might have given the order? Who might have wanted me to find you and bring you here?'

She closed her eyes and began to weep silently. Then, in her anguish, she asked, 'Do you think it might have been premeditated?'

She wanted to discover what his suspicions were. Although she knew more than she was letting on, she wanted him to show his cards, to reveal what was behind his questions.

'The attackers you described to the watchmen have been silenced. Their bodies were found three days ago on the outskirts of Madrid. And on the night of your attack, I was sent my own card telling me to go to the grove where I was to meet my man, who was keeping an eye on the marquess. I know that the marquess and you have been in close contact these last few months. That is why I deduce that the attack was planned in advance.'

Gabriel could see that she felt trapped. She was struggling to decide whether to reveal the truth and accept the disastrous consequences or to remain silent. She appeared to be weakening, as if her lips were striving to speak the truth and to pronounce the name of Don Enrique de Arcona. Driven more by necessity than by decorum, he pressed her further.

'Señorita Castro, who would have wanted me to find you and bring you to Castamar? Was it the marquess? Did he want to punish you for refusing to marry him? Believe me: your life and your honour are safe here.'

She turned pale and began to shake with terror, as if reliving the attack. Unable to speak, choked by fear, she grasped his hand, then looked away and stammered, 'I don't know.'

Gabriel stayed with her until her nerves calmed, her eyes closed and she fell into a deep sleep. Even then, he did not move, aware that his presence mitigated the panic she felt. He sat there, stroking her hair. And, just as he was about to release her hand, she grasped it tight, raised it to her lips and kissed his fingers.

28 January 1721

El Zurdo thought to himself how life was just a hazardous journey of survival. This whore, Jacinta, was the only person with whom he had any kind of sentimental relationship. He felt a certain fondness for her, albeit mixed with contempt.

As soon as he had finished, he rolled over and ordered her to tell La Zalamera, Sebastián's cook, to prepare some food for him. Women were necessary to satisfy one's needs, but the rest of the time they were little more than an annoyance. At least Jacinta didn't charge too much. And she even put the occasional piece of work his way, like that business with Doña Alba a few years ago. She had overheard a lad asking about the grooms at the stables at Castamar. She already knew that El Zurdo had some dealings with the estate and, suspecting there might be money to be made, had told the lad she might know somebody. The lad had led her to an alleyway. There, a man had questioned her from inside his carriage. Jacinta had not mentioned El Zurdo; she had only said she might know one of the grooms at Castamar.

That night, while he was eating, she had approached and casually let slip, 'Zurdo, the word is you've left the butchery trade.'

'Whose word is that?' he asked, between spoonfuls.

She whispered that people were saying he looked after the horses at Castamar.

He gulped down a mouthful of rough wine and shrugged. 'Life is hard, and everyone does what they can to survive.'

'Is that the only thing that's hard?' she said, slipping her hand between his legs.

He grabbed her wrist and pushed her away. He didn't like being touched without his permission, and certainly not by a whore who had seen as much use as the old razors of a cheap barber.

'I was going to tell you about some work a gentleman mentioned,' she said.

Suddenly, he was all ears. He needed as much money as he could get if he was to have any hope of realizing his dream of setting himself up as a horse breeder. He invited her to sit down.

Somewhat reluctantly, she obeyed and asked him again if he really worked at Castamar. He nodded and she flashed back a smile.

'We could do nicely out of it.'

And so the plans for the death of the Duchess of Castamar had begun to take shape, cooked up between a cheap whore, a stranger in a carriage and El Zurdo. A few nights later, in a lonely Madrid street, in the pouring rain, the final details were agreed. Jacinta had led him there to meet with Doña Sol's man. Nobody told him the name of his client; he had to discover that for himself by following the intermediary to Doña Sol's Madrid townhouse. As far as he could deduce, she had fallen into disgrace as a result of the duchess's actions. Later, when the time had come to collect his debt, he had made it clear that he knew the names of both the go-between and his mistress, and had threatened to reveal their secret.

El Zurdo stretched and his mind came back to the present. Jacinta had gone, leaving the room smelling of sex and sweat, and he got dressed and headed for the saloon, hoping his supper would be ready. There were a few regulars there, in search of a good time. El Zurdo, on seeing that his plate was not on the table, tutted, suspecting that Jacinta had found a customer and had neglected his order. He announced that he'd like something to eat. Sebastián, who knew a good customer when he saw one, gave orders to one of the girls to serve El Zurdo. Eating well was one of the few things El Zurdo spent his money on. Unlike a lot of hired thugs, who squandered their earnings in taverns, he was careful not to waste his cash. He put away what he could for the future and got by on the bare essentials. His only vice was hearty, unpretentious food. He slept in a rented room, close to the Zaguán, a grimy attic in a rundown house where nobody would have thought that, between the beams and the ceiling, he had stashed more than eight thousand reals.

He sat down, and a bowl of beans, a tumbler of wine, and some coarse bread were placed in front of him. As he began eating, he saw Jacinta emerge from one of the bedrooms. She was followed by a fat, dishevelled man.

He looks pleased with himself, he thought. She nodded at him but he ignored her. If he paid her any attention, she would come over and talk, and that was the last thing he felt like doing. Instead, he concentrated on his food. Ever since the kitchen at the Zaguán had been in the hands of La Zalamera, the cooking had improved, and there was no shortage of customers.

He had just taken a sip of wine when Hernaldo de la Marca entered, greeting him with a silent jut of his chin. Since the last time the soldier had visited, El Zurdo had been keeping a close eye on Don Gabriel. Just as Hernaldo had requested, he had found four accomplices, who had taken turns to monitor Gabriel de Castamar's every move.

Just then, the brothel-keeper said to Hernaldo, 'How's your daughter doing? I'm told she's a pretty one.' The whole place fell silent as Hernaldo put his hand to the hilt of his sword and turned. Sebastián took a step back, fearing that the man was going to murder him on the spot.

'Mention my daughter again and I'll run you through, you verminous piece of filth,' Hernaldo spat.

The brothel-keeper raised his hands, hoping to calm the situation. Jacinta, fearing that things were about to turn violent, sidled up to El Zurdo in search of protection. But Hernaldo said nothing more, and simply walked over to El Zurdo and suggested that they speak outside. El Zurdo stood up and told Jacinta to leave.

'Let me come with,' she pleaded, 'I won't be any bother.'

'Why don't you get back to whoring and leave me in peace?' he replied scornfully.

'You never let me take part in anything. Not even when I brought you that business with the lady and the horses at Ca—'

The impact of the slap was so loud it must have made her brain rattle, and the words died on her lips. From across the room, the brothel-keeper shouted that she'd earn less if her face was bruised. El Zurdo raised his hand by way of apology and put sixteen reals down on the table. He turned to find Hernaldo's inquisitive gaze upon him. He shrugged, pretending it was nothing.

'Women!' he muttered. 'Can't keep their mouths shut.'

Hernaldo followed him outside as Jacinta hurled a stream of insults in their wake.

'What job was the whore talking about?' Hernaldo asked.

'Something I did a few years ago for some lady on the Paseo de las Descalzas,' El Zurdo said, carefully. 'She wanted me to train some horses for her.'

'What was the lady's name?' the other man asked.

For a moment, El Zurdo considered stabbing the son of a bitch right there, and fleeing Madrid. But he knew that the marquess would pursue him all the way to the Americas if needs be. He bit his lip as if trying to recall, then shook his head.

'I can't remember, it was a long time ago. I train a lot of horses,' he answered.

Hernaldo looked at him closely. He seemed to be weighing up his options.

'Shall we get down to business?' El Zurdo asked.

Hernaldo nodded and enquired about Don Gabriel's movements, and El Zurdo replied that one of his men had told him that morning that Don Gabriel had arrived from Valladolid two days ago, where he had been visiting his mother, and that he had been making enquiries about the Zaguán. But however much he asked, nobody in the vicinity would give any information to a negro dressed up as a gentleman; they were more likely to try to extract money in exchange for false information than betray the place's whereabouts. The night watchmen would be another matter, though. They were quite capable of providing information if he loosened his purse strings. There was no hint of surprise on Hernaldo de la Marca's face, and El Zurdo deduced that, in some way, the man and his master were already abreast of the situation.

'Look for some men who know how to handle themselves. He'll turn up soon, and we have to be ready for him,' Hernaldo said. 'Your men can charge by the day until he appears.'

'And what should I do when he does?'

'We're going to teach him a lesson.'

PART THREE

16 OCTOBER TO 7 NOVEMBER 1721

28

16 October 1721

A melia was now preparing for her departure, after having spent spring and summer at Castamar. Today was the first day of the annual festivities, but she had decided to set out for El Escorial to visit her mother, prompted by the fact that Don Enrique had just written to politely inform her he would be attending the Castamar dinner that night and hoped to see her there. She was terrified. There was no way of convincing him that she could not meet his demands, that seducing Don Diego was not within her powers. She had now reached the conclusion that if the marquess realized just how far his goal of her marrying Diego was from reality, he might arrange for her and her mother to disappear in one of his accidents.

And so, she had come up with a strategy. She would collect her mother and leave Madrid for Cadiz, fleeing from there to some European country, or even the Americas. If she was successful, she could forget Don Enrique forever. In the meantime, she had to make him believe his objectives could still be achieved.

She even considered asking for Don Gabriel's help but decided against it, since she did not want him to become a target for the marquess. Since he had rescued her, she had abandoned her prejudices towards him. His total dedication to her well-being, the dressings he had personally applied to her face, their walks in the Castamar gardens and their excursions to Villacor, the little notes he'd written her, the poetry he read and the harpsichord music he played had all worked their charms, until one spring day, she had ceased to see the colour of his skin and instead recognized the depths of his spirit. No man was more noble or protective. Don Gabriel was everything a woman could hope to find in a man: handsome, secure, trustworthy and constant. But now her luggage was packed, and she was waiting to bid him a sad farewell. This undefined relationship would only bring misfortune to them both if they let it go any further. She was a single woman, robbed of her virtue and with a scar on her face. His rank only applied within the walls of Castamar; outside he was just another negro.

Don Gabriel knocked at the door and Amelia invited him in. He was dressed impeccably in a morning suit and a sky-blue jacket with silver buttons. She turned to face him, and he removed his cocked hat and greeted her courteously, asking if she still intended to leave Castamar.

'I do not want to cause you more trouble than I already have and, as you see, the belongings you so kindly had transferred from my house in Madrid have already been packed away. I wish to visit my mother.'

He nodded, pursing his lips as he always did when trying not to bring up the topic of the assault. Months ago, she had made it clear that she was not aware of any reason why anyone would attack her. Even if she was, she had added, the most prudent thing would be to keep quiet, since making it public would only bring her disgrace. Those words seemed to be floating in the air between them. A silence settled, as if neither wanted to say goodbye. Then he looked at her with his gleaming, dark eyes and spoke.

'I dearly wish you would stay for dinner tonight.'

She felt a shiver run down her spine at the mere thought of Don Enrique, and she looked down immediately.

'Of course, this invitation also comes from my brother and my mother, who, as you know, are very fond of you,' he added. 'I would be honoured if you would agree to be my companion.'

'I thank you for your kind offer, but being your companion tonight would put me in an uncomfortable situation and I think that you—'

'I understand. Sometimes I forget what I'm asking,' he interrupted gently. 'Don't worry, my invitation was limited to the private dinner, among friends, before the party. Despite my brother's insistence, I never attend the celebration. My skin colour is not adequate for the court, and nor is it for you – I understand that. I fear it would get people talking and I know this would have disastrous conse—'

Amelia came closer and raised her hand.

'You have misunderstood me, Don Gabriel,' she whispered. 'While I can't deny that, at the beginning of my stay at Castamar, I did have some reticence about the colour of your skin, that is now long gone. In any case, I would never do you such a dishonour, especially since you saved my life. You are the best companion I could possibly have at the celebration, and my refusal has nothing to do with your race,' she continued. 'My reason for not attending is my stupid feminine vanity,' she said, stroking the scar, now healed, on her cheek, 'which impedes me from showing myself at such an event.'

Don Gabriel's expression changed immediately.

'Forgive my foolishness,' he said. 'I am so accustomed to the contempt the colour of my skin arouses in most that I thought only of myself, when I should have considered your well-being.'

'Don't blame yourself. I have seen your heart and know its true nature,' Amelia reassured him.

They looked into each other's eyes then looked away.

'Let me protect you,' he said. 'I swear I will not let anyone harm you again.'

He caressed her scar with the tips of his fingers and she, falteringly, stopped his hand for a moment before letting him stroke her face. Just then there was a knock at the door, and they sprang apart. Don Diego appeared in the bedroom, thinking he would find her alone. He halted in consternation, but Don

Gabriel told him not to worry. For a second, Amelia once again felt that strange feeling she had experienced the first few times she had seen the brothers alone with each other. Behind closed doors, there was no rank between them, only a sense of brotherhood that was as strong as steel. Their trust in each other was absolute. This, and a conversation with Don Diego on the topic of slavery, had opened her eyes to the injustice of it all.

'I came to ask Señorita Castro if she would stay for dinner tonight,' Diego said, still a little uncomfortable.

Don Gabriel quickly replied that she had other commitments, but before he could finish his sentence, Amelia stated impulsively that these commitments could wait, and that it would be a pleasure to join them. Don Diego withdrew to tell the servants there would be an extra guest at dinner, and once he had gone, Don Gabriel thanked her for staying.

'It's the least I can do,' she replied.

'Under no circumstances do I wish to inconvenience you. Please know that—'

'It will be my pleasure,' she interrupted.

She had acted according to an internal need, perhaps motivated by the repeated requests, perhaps to feel protected in Don Gabriel's arms, or simply because she refused to be afraid. He left after the duke, and she stayed behind, alone, with terror nestling in her stomach. She sat there looking at her hands and saw that they were shaking uncontrollably. *Be strong, Amelia*, she told herself. *Whatever happens at the dinner, Gabriel will be by your side. If you ever wish to be free, you must confront Don Enrique.*

The private dinner for Don Diego and his friends was going 'marvellously well', in Andrés Moguer's words. The contented silence was broken only by the sighs of pleasure as the diners sampled the meat and the consommés. The maelstrom of the preparation for that event had begun three days earlier, first

with the arrival of Doña Mercedes, the duke's mother, and Don
Enrique de Arcona, her guest, and later with the appearance of
the duke's friends, Don Francisco and Don Alfredo. The annual
event, celebrated since Doña Alba's time, would see almost the
entire Madrid court coming to the estate.

Clara began to plan how the dishes should appear, in what
order, and how they were to be presented at the table. Running
three kitchens and using the same cooks who had delivered
such good results last time, she had been very keen to make
sure everything went according to plan. Unlike the previous
year, this time the French chef, Jean-Pierre de Champfleury,
had happily accepted all her instructions. It seemed he had
heard the praise from circles close to the queen, claiming that
Señorita Belmonte was an extraordinary cook who had much to
teach others. On this occasion, Clara had prepared some small
plates of Italian pasta for His Majesty, seasoned with oregano,
meat, basil and tomato, with a little white wine and a pinch of
sugar to counterbalance the acidity.

The king and queen's personal cooks had also come this
time, on Their Majesties' orders, to supervise and sample the
dishes. That morning both men had given Clara their most
sincere congratulations and some good advice. Since dawn
she had been unable to think about anything but cooking and
giving orders, although from time to time, as she walked from
one stove to another, she let her imagination fly to the shelf in
her bedroom, which now held a collection of fourteen culinary
volumes. Since Doña Ursula's visit on the day of Rosalía's death,
she had preferred to keep them covered with a cloth so that if
the housekeeper came again, she wouldn't be able to see the
books. If Doña Ursula discovered the books, she might find
some way of discrediting Clara in the other servants' eyes.

Clara's relationship with the housekeeper had remained as
cold and distant as ever, and they had argued as recently as
four days ago. Clara, moved to pity by the situation of Don
Melquíades, shut away in his room since January, had decided

to talk to his lordship, hoping to have the head butler pardoned. When Doña Ursula found out, she had come down to the kitchen and publicly ordered her to stop getting involved in matters that had nothing to do with the kitchen. However, it was not this incident that had unsettled Clara, but rather Don Diego's reaction. Her intervention had not gone as she had hoped, and the duke, after listening, had had to contain his anger, snorting and seething before leaving in tense silence. Later, she found out from Elisa that her direct intervention in Don Melquíades's favour was the latest in a long list. The other servants had been campaigning for the duke's forgiveness of Don Melquíades in a more surreptitious way, dropping hints when the duke was nearby, mentioning the forgiveness of sins. In fact, this had become so recurrent that the duke had, some months ago, told Doña Ursula that the case of the head butler was a strictly private matter, and the servants were to stop making such insinuations. Doña Ursula had let everyone know apart from Clara, hoping she would eventually stick her nose in. The duke had preferred to contain his anger rather than shout, but the housekeeper had been quick to appear, triumphant, and tell Clara in front of everyone not to get involved in matters that had nothing to do with her. However much she disliked her, Clara had to admit Doña Ursula had had a point. Defending Don Melquíades was not part of her kitchen duties, but the man had already spent close to nine months living like that, unable to leave Castamar and with his soul in tatters.

It was suspected that some servants had been to the butler's room, but only Simón Casona and Clara had visited him publicly, against the housekeeper's orders, hoping to alleviate his solitude and sorrow. The last time Clara had visited had been just five days ago. He had let his beard and his hair grow long and his room was similarly ill cared for.

'I hope I'm not bothering you,' Clara said.

'I don't see how you could, Señorita Belmonte,' he answered courteously.

Over those months, they had formed a sincere friendship, trusting each other with the difficult details of their lives. Don Melquíades had even revealed to her that in his youth he had fallen in love with a girl of a certain lineage but that the difference in social standing had made the marriage impossible. She had gone north, to Galicia, and he had spent many years completely devastated. On another occasion, some months later, he had confessed to her that when Doña Ursula had begun working at Castamar, he had thought her an attractive woman, of fine character, someone with whom he might have had a lasting friendship. They had both laughed at his naivety.

'We all make mistakes,' Clara said to cheer him up. 'After my father's death, I was a burden to my mother. I couldn't go out or bring money home, and my poor mother spent all her savings on our sustenance and looking after me. My little sister was barely aware of the situation and continued to believe we had money. One day, in my frustration, I mocked her for her naivety. I made it clear we barely had enough to live on, that we'd soon be out on the streets. Just thinking about how I spoke to her fills me with shame.'

As a result of these friendly chats, and without saying a word to the butler, she had made up her mind to intercede for him with Don Diego, and after the duke's reaction, she had spent more than a day feeling completely crestfallen at the thought she might have offended his lordship. In fact, she had been feeling lighter and happier for months now, and often in the morning, she would take one of the books, aiming to please him by cooking a new recipe. If simply looking at the books brought her considerable joy, knowing there was a note hidden in each one brought her even more. Over spring and summer, the frequency of their secret communication had increased. For every note she received from his lordship she would add a copy of her replies, so that she could read them every now and then.

Their correspondence had wrought a change inside her. She felt very close to the duke; his letters allowed her to get to know the man behind the noble title. What was more, she had grown strong enough to confront her terror of open spaces, as she had confessed in one of her little notes.

I hear from Señor Moguer that the leg of lamb was to your taste. Though I must confess a certain fear of not always being able to please you as I do now, I am so happy that you like my cooking so much. Likewise, your acts of generosity towards my person have inspired me so much that I am preparing to overcome my fear of open spaces.

Don Diego had taken no time in responding.

...your attitude befits a strong character and resolved spirit, Señorita Belmonte. Stay on that path and you will doubtless overcome your apprehension before you know it. I fear that my request will not be delivered in time this week, but I hope to bring you the next book before long.

She had had to wait more than eight days before finally receiving the new volume: *Le Nouveau Cuisinier*, a recipe book published in Paris in 1656 by the chef Pierre de Lune. She quickly replied with a few lines recognizing the immense pleasure she felt at being able to serve as his cook at Castamar. More recently, they had begun to correspond even when there were no books to be delivered. On one occasion, when he had left her a note after a meal with his friends in Villacor, she had felt fear and joy in equal measure.

It was certainly a most prudent choice to give you these books, since I am taking great pleasure in each one of the dishes you cook for me. However, I must tell you that this enjoyment pales in comparison with the satisfaction I gain from knowing that they are made with genuine affection. Likewise, whenever I taste your cooking, I feel a genuine affection towards you.

These words had made her heart beat faster. She wondered where this secret they both harboured would lead, whether a duke and a cook sending secret letters to each other was simply an innocent game, or something that would break her heart and end her employment.

29

Same day, 16 October 1721

Gabriel had not let up in his investigation of Don Enrique, suspecting that the marquess's fine manners concealed dubious motives. However, he had not found a single scrap of evidence, other than locating a house of ill repute in Lavapiés, where Don Enrique's lackey regularly met his contacts. He had insisted he should visit the place, but Diego had expressly forbidden him on account that it was too dangerous. And, despite everything, the duke had decided to allow his mother to invite the marquess to Castamar, in part to avoid arguing with her but also because he wanted to keep an eye on the wily fox.

Don Enrique had arrived a few days earlier. The first thing he had done was suggest that it would be better if Señorita Castro did not dine with them, as this would oblige them to look at her disfigured face, which would make her feel uncomfortable. Diego knew that Gabriel had developed a deep affection for her and was on the verge of losing his temper. One glance from Diego had been enough to silence him, however, and the duke had explained to the marquess that Señorita Castro was a guest and that if the marquess could not bear to see her face, then it was he who should not attend the dinner.

At supper, Señorita Castro sat next to Gabriel. As the host, Diego welcomed all the guests: his mother, who, as usual, had managed to lose her hat upon arriving at Castamar, forcing her servant to run down the staircase after it; Don Enrique, whom he had not seen since the previous celebration; Señorita Castro, who avoided meeting the marquess's gaze; Francisco, who was accompanied by their shared friend, Leonor de Bazán, newly arrived from Valencia; and finally, his dear friend Alfredo, who, as always, had not brought a companion. Of last year's guests, the Baroness of Belizón was absent, as was Doña Sol Montijos – and her poor husband, who had died the previous winter in a tragic carriage accident.

As soon as Diego had finished his introductory speech, everyone applauded, and Francisco also stood up to speak.

'Dear friends, I must confess that I am not really at Castamar for the celebrations but rather to enjoy the excellence of the food, which I am sure you all remember. If the cook is as beautiful as she is skilled, the king should give her a title.'

Everyone laughed at Francisco's quip as he sat down.

'And is she beautiful, Diego?' Alfredo asked.

'Very,' he replied, 'although that is just one of her many qualities.'

'How strange to find a woman like that below stairs,' Alfredo noted.

'I seem to recall we spoke of her before: a highly educated spinster, not without physical charm,' Don Enrique commented haughtily.

Diego didn't like the direction the conversation was taking and gave the order for the food to be brought in and the meal to be served.

'Perhaps if we go down to the kitchen, we will discover that I have been lying, and my beautiful cook is actually a fat chef with calloused hands,' Diego joked, and everyone laughed while he looked daggers at the marquess. 'Now, let's eat.'

As if failing to understand that he should change the topic, Don Enrique smiled as the duke's mother explained that, with her background, the girl would make a perfect wife were it not for her dedication to cooking, 'a task more appropriate to those from humble backgrounds'.

Diego shot Francisco a glance, asking him to help change the topic, and he piped up, 'My darling Doña Mercedes, in my opinion – and I know a thing or two about women – under their clothes, they are all the same.'

'You libertine!' the duchess replied, pretending to be shocked. 'Francisco, how dare you utter such indecencies!'

Don Enrique defended the honour of the ladies present, arguing that the beauty of those born into a distinguished family was not something that could be acquired. He irritated Diego yet further by questioning whether the physical charms of Señorita Belmonte could possibly equal those of someone who had been trained for beauty from birth.

'And who will die with it, if God wishes,' he said, with a fleeting glance at Señorita Castro. 'Wouldn't you agree, Don Diego?'

Diego glared at him. The marquess held his gaze, as if to say that he was not afraid, and the duke smiled in reply, suggesting the marquess would be very afraid if he continued in this fashion. However, he refrained from contesting the marquess's remarks and from saying that his cook had no reason to envy the beauty, culture or character of any noblewoman. Instead, as the waiters entered and served the soup, he chose his words carefully.

'I must say I disagree with you, marquess. A title in itself does not confer such qualities.'

'My dear Don Diego,' the marquess replied, taking a sip from his glass, 'if some day you were to express such thoughts at court, people would think you are a revolutionary.'

'I am sorry if my manner of expressing myself upsets you,' the duke said. 'I have a reputation for speaking my mind.'

The marquess laughed as if it were a matter of no importance, and Don Diego thought to himself that the man was a hyena disguised as a peacock.

Alfredo, tired of the marquess's talk, issued a direct challenge.

'Perhaps, Marquess, the best manner to resolve this dispute would be through a bet. If the dinner is excellent, we will call the cook up so that you may contemplate whatever beauty she possesses, and you can also see if she is educated and refined. If she is, you must publicly recognize your absolute ignorance in the matters under discussion.'

Upon hearing his friend, Diego felt a profound desire for the marquess to be held up to ridicule and forced to swallow each and every one of his words. Clara Belmonte was one of the most adorable creatures he had ever laid eyes upon. She was cultured, refined, with an unquestionable gift for cooking, and he was in no doubt as to her talents. Even so, a voice in his head warned him that this was a dangerous game, one that might reveal his feelings for her. He wanted to intervene to put a stop to the foolishness, but Don Enrique gave him no time.

'I'll drink to that,' the marquess said, accepting the challenge. 'And if not, then Don Diego's cook will come into service with me.'

The challenge had suddenly become more serious. But Diego told himself that his cook, with her skill and diligence, would silence the pompous buffoon.

'That seems fair,' he replied.

As the soup was being served – a chicken broth garnished with boiled egg, croutons and small slices of fried liver – he told himself that the marquess would be forced to acknowledge the excellence of Clara Belmonte's cooking, as everyone around the table had fallen silent and the only sound to be heard was the occasional sigh of satisfaction. The next course showed off the cook's decorative skills, with dishes embellished with edible flowers, candied egg yolks, twirls of chocolate and dustings of cinnamon. This was followed by an array of stuffed courgettes, stewed quince and roasted meat. By the time dessert was served, they scarcely had any adjectives left: tarts, rice pudding, honey cakes and blackberries with curd were just some of the dishes Señorita Belmonte had prepared for the guests.

The vote was unanimous: everyone agreed that she should be invited up and congratulated. Diego was bursting with pride. Nobody could make even the slightest criticism without seeming ridiculous.

However, giving groundless opinions, even ones that were indecorous, was so common among the aristocracy that at times he found it almost unbearable. *Foolishness is far from being the exclusive domain of Don Enrique*, he told himself. He had often seen opinions expressed with the sole aim of inflating egos, usually for no constructive purpose. With regard to that evening's supper, for example, both the quality and presentation of which had been impeccable, a couple of contrary opinions and a few waverers would have been enough to establish the notion that Clara Belmonte lacked any special talent in the kitchen. This habit of expressing unfounded opinions, simply in order to gain a little social notoriety, had the effect of destroying the work and indeed the lives of those who put passion into what they did, rendering them victims of the judgements of vanity. His father had always explained that a person's opinions said as much about them as their actions and, like everything in life, should be given sensibly, expressing only what one thought rather than using them as an opportunity to show off.

'Diego, I believe it is only right that we should congratulate the cook in person. Call for her,' Alfredo requested.

'If you will permit, I will fetch her myself,' the duke said, to the astonishment of his mother and the other guests.

He went down to the kitchen but, rather than entering through the main door, took the passage that ran from the cellar and the storeroom. Upon reaching the kitchen door, he waited a moment before going inside. Like some thief in search of stories he peered inside, trying to locate Señorita Belmonte among the throng of bodies. Finally, amid the smoke and the clang of metal, the fire, the oil and the smell of melting lard, he made out her petite, industrious figure. He smiled when he saw her, giving out orders as though she were conducting an orchestra, as if she had some sixth sense that told her when to lift the frying pan, exactly how much spice to add to the beef tenderloin, whether a touch more salt or pepper was needed. Diego felt a thrill at surreptitiously entering Clara Belmonte's world.

Just as when he used to spy on his governess, he now had the privilege of glimpsing the private world of his cook, a reality so far removed from his own that he could never have imagined how much it would fascinate him. He was bewitched by her movements, sylph-like among the tumult of pots and pans, pitchers, basins and tripods. He remembered some of the words he had written to her over the previous months and his mind went back to when they had stood on the threshold of her room, when she had clung to him, distraught at the death of Rosalía. And he had so briefly caressed her lips with his own! She seemed so fragile yet courageous, someone on whom the vicissitudes of life had left an indelible mark. Proof of this was the nervous apprehension she felt when out in the open. He had observed her several times from behind the curtains of the second floor, determinedly confronting her condition and braving the yard. According to Señor Casona, she had made some progress and, with sufficient patience, was now able to take a few steps and sit for a while close to the door. His thoughts were suddenly interrupted when one of the boot boys loudly exclaimed that Castamar would shine again, as it had in the time of Doña Alba. But he did not feel sad, as he was sure that Alba too would wish for Castamar to shine as it had when she was alive. Like Clara, he was smiling when, through the door on the other side of the kitchen, Doña Ursula made her imperious entrance.

'I don't know what everyone is laughing about,' he heard her say to Clara. 'Simply seeing the confusion in here should be enough to make you concerned that everything is not running to order. I remind you that the guests for the ball will be arriving in a matter of minutes.'

'I think that can wait, Señora Berenguer,' the duke interrupted. Everyone stopped and bowed. 'My guests were delighted with tonight's supper and would like to meet you, Señorita Belmonte. Would you be so kind as to accompany me?'

Diego walked ahead of her to avoid giving rise to gossip but held open the door for her. As they walked towards the dining room, he remembered Don Enrique's challenge, but he said nothing of it to her, hoping she would receive the guests' congratulations and then leave as quickly as possible. The moment people saw her, the idiotic marquess would be thoroughly discredited.

He presented her to the guests, she curtseyed, and Francisco stood up and clapped. He was followed by Alfredo, who congratulated her warmly and also applauded. The cook, somewhat abashed, curtseyed again and looked at the floor.

'I am most honoured,' she said, her cheeks burning with embarrassment. 'I don't know what to say... I am very flattered.'

Francisco, with his natural grace, waved his hand.

'Not at all. The honour is ours for the enjoyment of every dish you have prepared.'

Señorita Belmonte looked at him, and Diego couldn't help thinking to himself that her smile was enchanting, as if she were a lady who had just been presented to society. He joined the applause and then took his seat while she thanked everyone again. Then the duke instructed the footman to accompany her to the kitchen. Just as she was taking her leave, the duke sensed the marquess's disconcerting gaze.

'She is certainly an attractive young woman, Don Diego. But before she leaves, I would like to inspect her more closely, to confirm that she is not, as you yourself suggested, a fat chef with calloused hands.'

Señorita Belmonte looked at him quizzically, not understanding what this was all about. Diego, trying to restrain his temper, shot Don Enrique a warning glance. The marquess stood up and strutted over to the cook. Diego tensed and thought to himself that if the marquess humiliated her it would destroy her.

'Her beauty is undeniable, Don Enrique,' Alfredo said. Clara was clearly becoming more uncomfortable by the second, and

Diego realized that accepting the bet had been a terrible mistake, one caused by his stupid desire to show the marquess he was wrong. Out of the corner of his eye, he saw that Señor Moguer was indicating to Señorita Belmonte with a subtle motion of his head that she should leave as quickly as possible. But Clara did not understand the meaning of his instruction.

'I'm afraid you've lost your wager, Marquess,' Leonor pronounced with a smile, raising her glass.

On hearing the word, Clara's expression changed as she realized that she had been brought there not to be congratulated but to settle a bet. Diego felt like a fool. Naively, he had thought she would enter and leave the room without any further consequences, and that the marquess would be made to look ridiculous when everyone confirmed that the cook was as he had described. He had allowed himself to be blinded by Don Enrique's comments about Señorita Belmonte's beauty, her upbringing and her manners. He had been so furious that his only thought had been to inflict a humiliating defeat on the man. He gripped the arms of his chair, cursing himself as he understood Don Enrique's true intentions. The marquess had somehow intuited the duke's feelings towards his cook and had exploited them to upset him.

His brother looked at him, as if to say that this game was not acceptable, particularly as the marquess was inspecting Señorita Belmonte's features, asking her to untie her hair for everyone to see. Don Gabriel understood that Clara must feel like a chattel.

'You see,' the marquess sneered, 'the duke believes that a woman can be virtuous and distinguished regardless of her origin, while I maintain that nobility is an essential component if the feminine virtues are to be elevated to the sublime. What do you think?'

'Take care how you respond, Señorita Belmonte,' Alfredo intervened, delighted at the prospect of the marquess's imminent defeat. 'If you lose the bet, you will enter Don Enrique's service and be obliged to leave Castamar.'

Diego observed his guests and realized that, while his brother and Señorita Castro both looked uncomfortable, this was just another innocent piece of entertainment for the others. The duke felt a sudden urge to challenge Don Enrique on the spot, but he knew that such an intervention would only put his personal interest in Señorita Belmonte beyond any doubt. It would reveal his weakness to Don Enrique and would only help the marquess snare Señorita Belmonte in his web, just as he had trapped Señorita Castro. The duke didn't want to think about what the marquess might be capable of if he discovered just how fond the duke was of his cook.

Catching her eye, he understood that she felt utterly exposed, out of place and judged on both her appearance and her intellect. Then he looked over at his brother, silently pleading with him to do something to bring this farcical situation to an end. Gabriel was just about to say something when Señorita Belmonte suddenly spoke.

'As your excellencies have asked for my opinion on the matter, I will give it gladly.'

Diego looked on as she stood up to Don Enrique, holding his gaze as if she were his equal, and he admired her tenacity in the face of life's vicissitudes.

'I do not believe that nobility makes either man or woman more distinguished,' Señorita Belmonte replied.

Don Enrique walked around her. Diego stirred nervously in his chair while feigning unconcern. He watched in disbelief as he thought he saw the marquess raise his cane so that it was almost touching the cook's buttocks. He could not be sure, but he swore to himself that if the marquess had overstepped the bounds of decency so flagrantly then he would knock him to the floor. Señorita Belmonte said nothing but simply stood there, tense and still. Don Enrique's smile, etched in lines of sarcasm, incensed the duke yet further. Diego tried to stay calm, promising himself that the man would not set foot in Castamar again in his lifetime. He didn't care if his mother decided to stay away as a result.

'And what proof do you have for such a belief?' the marquess asked, haughtily.

'What more proof do you wish than the fact that the majority of the men who have contributed to the progress of science, music and the arts were not of noble birth?'

Her reply silenced the laughter.

'Don't be so insolent,' Doña Mercedes said.

Diego couldn't help savouring the fact that all signs of pleasure had been wiped from Don Enrique's face. It was clear that he felt attacked by Señorita Belmonte's reply and he looked at her with disdain, while the duke's admiration for her only grew.

'You express yourself with great precision and fluency for a simple cook,' the marquess said, clearly intending to offend her.

'And wasn't it the aim of the wager to clarify that matter?'

Don Alfredo applauded and Don Francisco raised his glass. Don Enrique looked at her as if he wished to slap her, but instead he merely smiled and ignored her. He turned and bowed.

'In light of the evidence, I declare myself ignorant in feminine matters,' he declared.

'Then you must withdraw your words,' Diego insisted.

The marquess's smile froze for a moment but he composed himself.

'I do so willingly, your grace.'

Everyone applauded. The marquess and Diego exchanged a look, knowing that in the battle they had just fought both had been wounded. But the duke was aware, by the manner in which Señorita Belmonte took her leave, that the greater part of his loss was perhaps still to come. And so, in order to make amends, he quietly excused himself while the gathering continued, and went in search of her.

He caught up with her in the corridor, where she was hurrying away as if eager to reach the refuge of the kitchens as quickly as possible. He twice called on her to stop before she obeyed.

'Señorita Belmonte, I wish to apologize for what just happened. I didn't—'

'Your grace, never before in my life have I felt so humiliated as I have this evening,' she said, her eyes burning with barely contained fury.

'Señorita Belmonte, it was unforgivably rude on my part, and I am profoundly—'

'Stop!' she said, raising her voice. 'Please, your grace. You may be my master, but you are not my owner. I am not a trophy to be won or lost in a wager. Any decent gentleman would know that.'

He felt deeply wounded by her words. He considered himself, above all, a gentleman – he might have been foolish but he was decent. He told himself that it was her anger and her impotence that were speaking, and he tried to make her see that it had never been his intention to expose her in such a way. But she, upon hearing his words, reacted like a wounded animal, the sense of humiliation still fresh in her mind.

'I will never tolerate you or anyone else treating me like an object to be exchanged in a bet,' she said. 'Any decent gentleman would know not to do such a thing,' she repeated.

'Señorita Belmonte, I think you are going too far,' he said, his jaw clenched. 'I am a gentleman.'

'No!' she interrupted. 'I may only be a humble cook and you may have all the power in the world, but I will never permit—'

'Silence!' he shouted, unable to stand any more.

All of a sudden, he had seen his cook arguing with him as one equal to another, challenging him, stating that he was not a decent gentleman, that his behaviour was intolerable, when it was he who should not allow a servant to judge him, and so unfairly, when he had only wanted to apologize.

'I am your master and the master of Castamar, and I order you to be silent. I am trying to apologize.'

'And this humble cook does not accept your excuses, your

grace. I wish to leave this household,' she said, her cheeks flushed red.

'No! I don't want you to leave,' he said, in a voice that brooked no reply.

'Am I to be held captive at Castamar, then, like Don Melquíades?'

'Of course not!' he roared.

There was silence, and she bowed her head and tried to dry her tears. He smoothed out his frock coat and took two steps forward, not knowing what to do. He had so many conflicting emotions that he was unsure whether to kiss her or to allow her to leave. He wanted to bring the situation under his control, but he could feel it slipping through his fingers like sand. Just then, Alfredo appeared at the door to inform him that the Royal Majesties' carriage had been sighted.

She had turned so that Alfredo would not see that she was crying, and Diego stood between them to keep up the pretence of normality. He waited until Alfredo left and turned to her again. She was trembling like an injured animal. He was about to speak more calmly, when she begged him to allow her to return to the kitchen. He didn't know what more to say. He wanted to hug her, to tell her he had been wrong, that he had been a fool, carried away by his pride, when he heard his mother's voice warning him of the king's imminent arrival.

'You may leave,' he said despondently.

He watched as she retreated down the corridor, reproaching himself for having been such an idiot. He had allowed Don Enrique to control the situation when it was he who was the host. She was right: she had not deserved the humiliation he had inflicted upon her. *You fool*, he reproached himself again. He sighed and told himself that he should give her some time to calm down; then he would try to explain why he had been so foolish as to accept the wager, that his only motive for not intervening had been to protect her.

He turned and walked back towards the main entrance

to receive Their Majesties. As he passed through the dining room, he could still smell the aromas of the banquet, and he stopped for a moment, in the grip of a realization that had suddenly formed clearly and beyond any doubt. He stood there, motionless, knowing that this idea arose from the very depths of his being and that he had no choice but to follow his conscience. He continued on his way, fully aware that he was deeply and irretrievably in love with Señorita Belmonte.

30

Same day, 16 October 1721

Few knew what a curse it was to possess the gifts of Aphrodite as well as Sol did. Since puberty she had watched how her beauty could conspire against her attempts to rise in society. She learned this from being taken to social gatherings by her father, where he would exhibit her as if he were showing a prize cow at a fair. She would become the centre of every man's attention, as if they were caressing her with their eyes. Many women became enslaved to their need for praise and flirtation, frittering away their youths with foolish dalliances until it was too late. Not her. She had understood from early on that men tended to be completely overwhelmed by their desires and would do anything to satisfy them. Knowing this was key to her success, she had made her body into a prize, aware that once her youthful beauty had faded, only her fortune and her social position would matter. *All that matters in life is riches and status – and the good health to enjoy them both,* she had always told herself. *Civilization is simply an extravagant social structure designed to stop men having their way with you at the first opportunity.*

That's why she had made Don Francisco wait, as if she were a fruit ripening on the vine. It was undeniable that some distance had grown between them, and he was pretending to be immune to her charms. But she could read his looks and was sure he still lusted after her.

Since she had rejected him in January, he had become more

elusive, and they had both taken to playing a game of cat and mouse. They had come across one another at different events and gatherings, politely greeting each other and engaging in trivial conversation. Only on one occasion, at a private performance of *The Amazons of Spain*, had the distance between them narrowed briefly. During the performance, held at the Coliseum Theatre, which was housed in the royal palace, they had paid more attention to each other's sideways glances than the opera, which they had both already seen the previous year.

When the duet between Clorilene and Zelauro began, she had noticed that he wasn't in his seat. She began fanning herself in agitation. Chivalry dictated that he at least come and pay his respects after the show. She was lost in these thoughts when one of his men appeared at the door to deliver a note from Francisco inviting her to visit one of the empty boxes on the third floor.

'Let the sender know that I don't understand why he thinks I would be interested in such a thing,' she instructed the man. 'Tell him I do not wish to receive any further notes.'

The lackey nodded and left, while she stayed there waiting to see a humiliated Francisco reappear in his second-floor seat. She was conscious that she had teased him by wetting her lips as she smiled without looking at him, revealing her bare neck and making her bosom heave as she breathed. *How easy it is to tempt men*, she said to herself. But halfway through the act he still hadn't returned to his seat, and she began to suspect that he had left, unable to cope with the shame of rejection.

At the interval, she went to see the Marquess of Sesto, the king's manservant and Queen Isabel's head groom. He nodded politely at her from afar while continuing to speak to his wife. She snaked between the crowds until she reached him. The marquess smiled at her and said that Don Francisco had left with Doña Margarita de Montefriso, and that Don Francisco had said, if Doña Sol felt like it, she could join them for a small gathering afterwards. Sol had asked if the marquess knew where they would be meeting.

'How strange, my dear. He told me he had written you a note.'
She had smiled, pretending to suddenly remember, and
withdrew after a trivial conversation. Shaken, she sat down and
fanned herself, imagining him with the other woman. When
the curtains rose, she shot a sideways glance towards the upper
balconies. She tried to concentrate on the stage, but it was
impossible now. She couldn't stop imagining him caressing other
thighs and kissing a mouth that wasn't her own. Unable to bear
it any longer, she scurried off, excusing herself by saying that she
had to take the air. Dodging servants and ushers, she reached
the third floor. She groped around in complete darkness, telling
herself it was not proper for her to be sneaking about up there.
Just then, she heard a moan, growing in intensity.

She approached the box, saw that the door was open, and
entered to find Francisco and Doña Margarita in flagrante.
Sol wanted to leave but, as if against her will, some obscene
fascination drew her to the couple in the bed. Soon she was
carried away by desire.

She kissed Margarita passionately and whispered in her ear, 'I
will pay you three times more, but you will obey me.'

'I am your most faithful servant,' the woman answered.

It wasn't the first time Sol had enjoyed a woman's body,
although she treated it more as a game aimed at getting what
she wanted from men than as a pleasure in itself. Then Francisco
had joined her, and they both took the young girl like predators
before tossing her aside so that they could devote themselves
exclusively to each other.

Two days later, her lackey had informed her that he had seen
Don Francisco in the company of a certain lady who had come
down from Valencia. This had annoyed her so much that she
had left Francisco's letters unanswered.

Only after the summer had they crossed paths again, in the
corridors of the mansion of the new Duke of Medina Sidonia.
After a polite greeting they both went their separate ways. Then,
in October, she had decided to write him a brief note, with the

aim of finding out if they would be attending the Castamar dinner together. In the meantime, she had learned that the lady from Valencia was the Countess Leonor de Bazán, about whom they had been so merciless at last year's festivities.

After two anxious days, she had received a brief reply. *It will be my pleasure to visit you a few hours before the celebration.* Finally, she could have him to herself for several days at Castamar, without any other lady interfering. The only thing that put her off going was the prospect of encountering Don Enrique, and those letters she had signed that could deprive her of Francisco forever. She told herself she didn't care in the slightest. No man would ever control her heart. She didn't know why Don Enrique wanted to ruin Francisco's reputation – surely it was just another example of the chicanery so widespread at the court. The only thing that mattered now was for her to submit to Don Francisco's desires. This was a personal matter.

When he finally appeared at her house, she kept him waiting before making her entrance and observing that they might be running a little late for the dinner, but would surely make up time along the way. Francisco had replied that there was no rush.

'And why is that? Is the dinner cancelled?' she asked.

Francisco smiled mischievously and took her hand.

'Of course not, my dear. The dinner is still going ahead but I have a companion I agreed to go with some time ago, so I can't take you. I assume you won't want to go alone,' he said, keeping silent as he gauged her reaction. 'That's why I sent you the note: I needed to tell you in person.'

Sol was consumed by jealous thoughts, thoughts which told her she was too old and her beauty was vanishing. She flicked open her fan and hid her feelings behind a frosty smile and a motionless face.

'I thank you for freeing me from the commitment of going to Castamar. I can't pretend I was keen to attend.'

'Certainly,' he joked. 'The dinner would be an inconvenience, I understand perfectly. A party like this one will be attended by all of Madrid high society – King Felipe, Queen Isabel, the grandees... I think even the young dauphin, Luís, will be there. It will doubtless be a tedious affair.'

She had thanked him again and Francisco moved away from her, as if she had been nothing more than an amusement. She had spent a year embroiled in these games and felt utterly defeated. He bade her farewell while she tried as hard as she could to resist the urge to set upon him, slap him and dig her nails into his face.

'So, who is the lucky girl who will be accompanying you?' she asked, unable to resist any longer.

She knew that by doing this she had given him all the cards. He hesitated for a moment before answering, as if wondering whether to press home his advantage. Sol wanted him to show her sufficient respect to allow her a graceful exit, rather than humiliation in defeat. But his smile did not falter.

'Is it your uncontrollable jealousy that makes you ask?'

She laughed, her pride wounded even further, answering that he barely knew her at all if that was what he thought.

'Fear not,' he said. Then, preparing his mortal blow, he whispered sarcastically to her, 'There's no competition: she's your age, also a widow. But she comes from a good family,' he finished, alluding to Sol's plebeian origins.

'She may be my age and have a more noble surname,' she replied, her chin trembling with rage, 'but I am the most distinguished person who could accompany you to the dinner.'

'Don't be so presumptuous,' he replied. 'It's Doña Leonor de Bazán. She's come from Valencia for a few days, and I must go and collect her now.'

He had bowed slightly as he left. As soon as he was out of the room, Sol had to prop herself up on one of the marble dressing tables just to catch her breath. Her overly tight corset and agitated breathing made her break out into a sweat. Her repressed anger erupted out of her throat, and she screamed in a frenzied rage. She tore the hat from her head, picked up a vase and, summoning all her hatred, threw it against the wall. She had looked at her reflection in the mirror and sworn that this affront would not go unpunished.

Francisco had had two dances with Leonor and danced several minuets with some of the most attractive girls in the court. His friend Diego, as always, stayed at the edges, close to the king and queen so that they wanted for nothing. Queen Isabel had grown especially fond of him since her arrival. Diego smiled amiably but Francisco, who knew him well, understood that such gestures were simply part of his armour. His true emotions, the heavy heart he had harboured since winning the bet with Don Enrique, were hidden beneath it. It seemed that the interrogation of the cook had unsettled the duke.

Now Francisco was watching his lady friend dance with their host. He moistened his lips with a sweet sherry and recalled Leonor fifteen years earlier, when he was just a boy. Leonor and he had spent long stretches of summer in the mansion on the Valencian coast that belonged to her and her husband, Roberto de Bazán. However, after the war ended, the years had passed with just a few letters and the odd encounter, something that was largely his fault, as he was the one who had stopped visiting her every summer. That's why he had felt excited about seeing her as soon as she wrote to him. However, despite his pleasure at renewing their acquaintance, it was Sol who spurred his desire like no other woman, Sol he had longed for throughout the past year. He remembered all too well how she had thrown him out of her house, nine months earlier, to make it clear that theirs was a relationship based on power.

After the initial satisfaction of gaining some revenge, he had begun to feel pangs at having humiliated her like that, even if the punishment was well-deserved. She had a long list of spiteful lovers, as well as two dead husbands whose deaths had generated many malicious rumours, and he knew she would be plotting a terrible revenge against him. He remembered her face, frozen with anger, and told himself he would have to tread carefully. Yet he could not deny the animal attraction he felt for her. What was more, a deeper feeling that he did not want to acknowledge whispered to him that he would rather have spent the celebration with her. He longed to return to the phase of their relationship where he had felt happy and at ease. He knew, however, that the only relationship she wished for was one that would have him at her beck and call.

Leonor looked at him from afar. He returned her smile, peacefully imagining himself dancing with Sol. His imagination ran over her curves, her luscious lips, and his strange need to have her there, next to him, without all their stupid games. He couldn't help thinking that this party would be much more boring than last year's.

31

Now that the celebrations were in full flow, Ursula was delighted. It felt as if Doña Alba had come back to life. She observed the full-length portrait of her mistress. And she imagined the duchess gazing at the huge map of the Peninsula that Don Abel de Castamar had commissioned from the renowned cartographer Frederik de Wit, which adorned the wall of the salon.

During the two nights of the annual festivities, Ursula felt more alive than at any other time of the year. She momentarily forgot about her endless struggle to retain control of the servants and instead gave herself over to ensuring that the duke would sense Doña Alba's continuing presence in every corner of the palace. She had relaxed her vigil over the cook and over Don Melquíades, who remained a prisoner in his own room, and her only concern was that Señor Moguer and the rest of the staff would give a good account of themselves. Her private battles were temporarily suspended; all she cared about was Castamar, and Señorita Belmonte was a great help to that end. The ball, the breakfast, lunch and supper, the musical and theatrical performances, the fireworks: everything had been perfect. The king and queen, the grandees and Don Diego himself had praised the banquet, which only enhanced the cook's status.

But life did not stand still. Proof of that was the humiliation Clara Belmonte had suffered at the hands of Don Enrique the previous night. Señor Moguer had witnessed the whole scene in the dining room, when the marquess had taken the liberty of touching the cook's buttocks with the handle of his cane. The next morning, all the servants knew what had happened. According to the sommelier, the cook had reacted with great dignity. Señor Moguer brushed over the details out of a sense of decorum, but he had privately revealed to the housekeeper that the scene had been followed by an argument between the cook and his lordship in the corridor. Unfortunately, the sommelier had only heard the raised voices of both Señorita Belmonte and Don Diego but had not been able to make out the words.

Although she was happy at the prospect of the cook's departure from Castamar, Doña Ursula drew no satisfaction from Clara Belmonte's humiliation. It was enough for her to disappear from the estate and cease to bother them with her exquisite manners. The whole unfortunate episode only went to show that the best thing one could do was keep a safe distance from one's social superiors. *Each to his own and God watching over us all*, she added to her thoughts. Clara Belmonte clearly had ideas above her station. Perhaps the whole embarrassing experience would teach her her true position on the social scale, and she would finally let go of attempting to regain that which she had lost. Even so, the housekeeper took no joy in the situation, and she knew that Doña Alba would have felt the same. Her mistress would never have allowed that pompous ass to take such liberties with a member of her household. Doña Ursula felt an implacable wish to see the man whipped to within an inch of his life, not only for taking liberties, but also, she had to admit, because she admired Señorita Belmonte, just as one admires the courage of an enemy who shows valour in battle. She would never have admitted it, of course, but she was impressed both by the cook's organizational skills and her culinary flair. She respected her determination, her desire to improve, and her honesty. The cook could have undermined Señora Escrivá but had instead maintained a decorous silence, and she had even stood up to the housekeeper when she believed the duke to be injured.

Even so, Ursula could not help hoping that Clara Belmonte would knock on the door of her office and announce that she was leaving. When the knock didn't come, the housekeeper concluded that the cook had swallowed her dignity, forced to recognize that, just like everyone else, she was afraid of starvation should she be out of a job. Ursula tutted, thinking to herself that it would have been all too easy, and returned to her work. Sitting at the butler's desk, having gone through the payments with the registrar and given instructions for money to be withheld from those servants whom she deemed guilty of laziness, she turned her attention to the matter at hand: the dinner for the second night of the festivities and the closing celebrations. She picked up her spectacles and was just about to turn to her plans when she was interrupted by two sharp knocks on the door. She instructed the person to enter, expecting to see the sad, angular face of the sommelier or the square features of the head footman.

Instead, it was Clara Belmonte who appeared in the office, her eyes red from crying. The cook curtseyed in that manner that the housekeeper found so irritating, and Ursula waited for her to speak.

'Doña Ursula, I have come to tell you that I will be leaving Castamar at dawn tomorrow,' she announced. 'Carmen can prepare breakfast. I'll leave everything ready for her.'

The housekeeper removed her spectacles and leaned back in her chair. She tried to guess what might have been said in the argument with the duke to make the young woman, who had already carved out a secure place for herself among the staff, take such a decision. Once again, she had to confess that the girl's resolve surprised her. She had assumed the cook would swallow the marquess's humiliation in order not to forego the position that was earning her a name among the nobility. But she had been wrong. Clara Belmonte had merely waited until her work at Castamar's celebrations was complete, in order to avoid leaving the master and the household without someone to supervise the kitchen during the festivities. Perhaps she had taken her secret correspondence with Don Diego too seriously.

Ursula nodded, commenting that she had heard about what had happened in the dining room. She said nothing more – there was no need for her to express her solidarity publicly.

'I would be grateful if you could deliver this note to his lordship and inform Don Melquíades and Señor Casona that I will write to them soon,' Clara said. 'I don't wish to announce my departure.'

Ursula glanced down at the sealed letter that the cook had placed on her desk before turning back to Clara Belmonte. The housekeeper was suddenly struck by the thought that this slight young woman, with her cinnamon eyes and black hair, was like a fragile porcelain doll, trying to protect itself from shattering – she had taken the decision to leave because of the humiliation she had suffered, and nothing would change her mind. Ursula thought about how hard it must have been to take such a decision, the fear at once again being alone in the world, without references, without a future. Even so, the young woman preferred to leave quietly through the back door, perhaps to avoid the impression that she was resentful or a troublemaker. And this way, she would not have to turn down the entreaties of those who begged her to stay. The housekeeper respected her integrity. Perhaps because, in some ways, it was so similar to the stony resolve which Ursula employed to withstand the trials of life in silence and without a trace of self-pity. *Most people like to portray themselves as martyrs, when in fact they are just revealing their own mediocrity*, she thought. She far preferred Clara Belmonte, even with her airs of refinement, to such weak, pathetic characters. Even so, she could not help but savour her victory, a victory that had been won by her patience over many months as she had waited for an event such as this.

'If that is all, you may leave. You will receive the money you are owed tomorrow. If you wish, Señor Ochando will take you to Madrid in the mule cart,' she said, returning to her notebook. 'You may take food for the journey.'

Clara Belmonte continued to scrutinize her for a few moments, a pensive expression on her face, but the housekeeper did not return her gaze. Finally, the cook turned and headed for the door. Upon seeing that she had paused at the threshold, Ursula raised an eyebrow.

'Doña Ursula, I have never understood the animosity you appear to have felt for me from the first moment you saw me,' Clara said.

The housekeeper did not even deign to look up, though she wondered whether to ignore her or to tell her what she really thought. She waited a few moments, but when Clara sighed and was about to leave, she spoke up.

'As it seems you would like an answer, I will give you one,' she said, placing her spectacles on the desk. 'You do not belong in this world. However hard you work in the kitchen, you will never be one of us; and however well-educated you may be, you will never belong to his lordship's world. And that is why I cannot tolerate your presence in this house, because you represent a new world that is a threat to order. You represent change, and I prefer the world as it is.'

'I thank you for your honesty.'

'There is no need for that,' the housekeeper replied, returning to her work.

The cook was about to say something more, but the housekeeper interrupted her.

'Señorita Belmonte, if you think I am about to enter into a lengthy conversation with you, you are very much mistaken. You may leave.'

The young woman finally left, closing the door behind her, and Ursula felt she was one of the luckiest women in the world. She was the ruler of Castamar, she did not have to answer to any man, and she was now free to hire a new cook, one who would have no influence on the duke. She leaned back in her throne, with not so much as a shadow of opposition, basking in the realization that she had achieved all of her ambitions. Whatever sacrifices she had made in the past had all been for the good.

But she couldn't help sparing a thought for the unfortunate Don Melquíades, her worthy but vanquished opponent, who now had to watch as his kingdom and his legacy fell into her hands. And there was another uncomfortable emotion that disturbed her inner peace. Her joy was marred by a sense of loss. This sentiment, that she could scarcely name but which had been growing over the past months, whispered to her that when Don Melquíades disappeared, her life would be more boring and far more insipid.

It had been difficult to listen to the festivities from his room. Don Melquíades shed a tear as he thought to himself that this was the first time the celebrations had been held without him officiating as head butler of Castamar. He couldn't bear to watch the fireworks through the window and instead lay back on his bed. It was now almost nine months since he had been cloistered away, taking exercise in the mothballed wing of the palace and creeping in and out so as not to encounter the duke. His room had become a cell from which he had observed how his presence at Castamar had gradually become superfluous. And he, in turn, had become little more than a living ghost with an overgrown beard, a phantom who stalked the corridors, spying as the servants continued their routines without his supervision. Nothing had changed at Castamar, save for him and Doña Ursula, who looked down on him from her throne. He was doomed to end his days in isolation or exile. And he deserved nothing more.

The fear he had felt over many years at the consequences of being discovered had been replaced by a sense of acceptance.

He was unworthy, a man who had betrayed the word he had given his masters. *There is nothing worse than a traitor*, he had told himself, time and time again during these months of confinement. Like his father, he owed everything to Castamar, not to a distant king or a land where he no longer lived, however much he might love it. Defending Catalonia had brought him nothing but pain.

His uncle Octavio, who had brought him up like a father for the first twelve years of his life, had taught him the value of the word of the Elquizas, the love for the land where one has been born, and the importance of the sacred bond of family. This defender of the Archduke Carlos and lieutenant colonel of the Habsburg army had asked him to help at the outbreak of the conflict. His uncle had been aware that there was regular correspondence at Castamar on account of the war, and that his nephew was the first person to see the missives. Melquíades enjoyed a privileged position and all he had to do was discreetly ascertain the letters' contents and inform his uncle. At first, he had refused to betray his master's trust, but his belief that the house of Habsburg would protect the interests of the Catalans, and his uncle's argument that abandoning his blood, his family and Catalonia was worse than death, had soon tipped the balance. Don Diego often left his open mail on his desk and sometimes finished composing his despatches while the butler waited. And so, almost since the start of the war, he had kept the Habsburg faction informed of troop movements and the thoughts of members of the Spanish nobility and even of the king. He knew he was responsible for the deaths of many Bourbon soldiers. And, even though he told himself every day that he was doing the right thing, a voice inside his head whispered that Don Diego had always been loyal and true to him and his family. The duke had never lied to them and had always ensured their needs were met. He had procured their best interests in every possible sense. Don Melquíades's problem had not been that the Habsburgs were losing the war but that every fresh betrayal had cut into his soul. After Doña Alba's death, he had written to his uncle to tell him he could not supply any more information. Whoever eventually won the war, it was over for him. His father's brother had not understood his refusal and had replied with a few lines that he would never forget.

You have no idea, nephew, how much good you have done to our cause with all the information you have supplied over the years, and for this, my colonel, my general and I are grateful. However, it is now that we need you most, when our troops are retreating towards Barcelona after the reverses at Brihuega and Villaviciosa. You cannot abandon your blood, your land and your rightful king. Only a vile traitor would betray his own people at a time of such need.

Melquíades never replied. He had simply kept the note in one of his exercise books while he decided what to do with it. If he burned it, he would be severing the ties of blood, while keeping it would preserve the evidence of his own perfidy. But fate would have it that the note was discovered by the housekeeper. Years later, when the war was nearing its end, he had received news that his uncle and his cousins had fallen in the defence of Barcelona. As the last of the Elquizas, he had been informed that they 'died with honour and bravery, like true Catalans', their breasts pierced by Bourbon musketballs.

After the fireworks were over, he fell into a fitful sleep, feeling thoroughly sorry for himself. He was woken up by one of the maids knocking on the door. By the light outside, he judged that he must have overslept and that it was already past midday. She entered with a tray of food, which she placed on the table.

'I didn't know if you were awake,' she said. 'I hope I haven't disturbed you.'

'Not at all,' he replied.

The girl shyly added that she had brought his breakfast that morning but that, after knocking several times and receiving no reply, she had taken it away. Melquíades nodded and the girl added, whispering as if it were a secret, that the duke would come down to speak to him after lunch, while Their Majesties and the other guests were taking their siesta.

He was so surprised by the news that he felt a rush of nausea, but he managed to hide his discomfort until he was alone. He had secretly hoped that the duke would decide his fate directly and bring his calvary to an end. Yet, now that the final verdict was approaching, he felt a sense of unreality. Moreover, he could not understand why Don Diego was putting himself to the inconvenience of visiting him in his own room when it would have been more usual for the butler to be called to attend upon the duke. Perhaps it was born of a wish for discretion, so typical of the duke – the desire to keep the other servants out of the affair.

When he had finished eating, he opened the windows to air the room, made his bed, tidied up his appearance and put on clean clothes to receive his lordship. Then he sat down on the bed and rested his hands on his knees, while the butterflies fluttered in his stomach. A whole hour elapsed before he finally heard footsteps approaching down the corridor. After two sharp knocks, the door opened and Don Diego stood in the doorframe, his eyes blazing and his lips pursed. Don Melquíades got to his feet and bowed his head, just as the duke announced that he wanted to speak to him. The duke's tone seemed gentle given the gravity of the situation, and with shame in his eyes, the butler sat back down on his bed. He felt as if there were a stone trapped in his throat, one that he had to expel as soon as he could. And so, just as his lordship was about to speak, he interrupted, unable to stop the words from flowing from his lips.

'Your grace, before you tell me what you have come to say, I must tell you how ashamed, distraught and repentant I am. I served your father and I served you, and I…' His voice began to falter. 'I defended what I believed in, the king I wanted to follow…'

Don Diego dragged one of the chairs over and sat down next to him. With great tenderness, he placed a hand on the butler's shoulder.

'As we all did,' he said. 'We obeyed our own consciences.'

Overcome by the anxiety of so many months, Melquíades collapsed and begged for forgiveness, repeating that he should never have betrayed the duke and that he would never give his loyalty to another master. Don Diego leaned back and raised his other hand.

'Calm down and listen. It is almost nine months since you had the courage to inform me of your behaviour in times of war, and that is how long it has taken me to digest the information sufficiently to speak to you without bitterness. That day I lost my temper and said things which I regret. I hope you will do me the favour of forgiving me,' he said in a conciliatory tone.

Melquíades shook his head.

'You have nothing to apologize for, your grace, let alone—'

'Listen to what I have to say, Señor Elquiza,' the duke interrupted.

Don Diego took a moment before he continued with his speech, as if he had memorized each word.

'Señor Elquiza, my behaviour was not that of a Castamar, far less that of a duke. If my dear departed wife had seen me, she would have reproached me, and I would not have been admitted to her bedchamber for the same amount of time as you have been confined here.'

'You may be right, your grace.'

'I most certainly am. And that is why I want to tell you that you are the butler of Castamar. You were when I was still a child and I wish you to continue to be so, and I don't want the festivities to conclude without you presiding over them, as you always have. Before tonight's supper you will be restored to your post. Wherever she may be, Doña Alba would be deeply unhappy were I to commit the error of exiling you from the estate, and I could not live with myself either.'

The butler nodded and tried to calm himself. Hoping to show the duke that he still retained some dignity, he had to restrain his desire to throw himself at the man's feet and kiss his hands. He knew that Don Diego was not one for such displays of emotion, and so he simply thanked him for his magnanimity. The duke shook his head.

'No, Señor Elquiza. You are no more guilty than I. We merely argued about a past that no longer exists. Let us forget the whole affair.'

'Yes, your grace,' Melquíades replied, aware that it might take him some time to do so.

'Moreover, I believe that had I not come to this solution, I would have disappointed many of the servants, particularly Señorita Belmonte, who interceded valiantly on your behalf,' he added as he headed for the door. 'And nobody would like to lose such a talented cook.'

Melquíades laughed at the duke's joke, took a deep breath, and struggled to calm his nerves. He suddenly felt himself overcome with gratitude towards that straightforward but educated girl who had stood up for him. He bowed to the duke, who stopped again.

'By the way, Señor Elquiza, I forgot to say. I have ordered hot water to be prepared for your bath, and I will ask my barber to shave you and trim your hair.'

Only after the duke had left did Melquíades fully realize that he had been pardoned and, unable to stop himself, he began to sob.

One hour later, fresh from his bath and shave, Melquíades appeared outside the state room, accompanied by a footman. Don Diego was already waiting for him at the door, his hands behind his back, a smile on his face. The butler greeted the duke with a bow of his head, and the duke nodded and told him that behind the door all the senior servants were gathered. The duke had brought them together to ensure that the butler would once again enjoy the authority that was his due.

The two of them entered with a certain solemnity, the butler a few paces behind his master. Once inside, he looked over at Clara Belmonte, who smiled back at him. For a moment, he sensed that her smile concealed a great sadness. Señor Casona bowed his head slightly by way of a greeting. He was undoubtedly among those who had spoken to the duke on his behalf. The butler also spotted his nephew, who avoided his gaze. He had already been told by Señor Casona that the lad had refused to defend him to the duke. Indeed, he had heard that he had denounced his uncle to the other servants. The butler didn't blame him; he could scarcely forgive himself. He told himself that, when the time was right, he would speak to his nephew in private to embark upon the long path to reconciliation.

'I apologize for distracting you from your duties, in particular on an evening such as this, the second day of the festivities,' the duke said by way of an introduction. 'However, it is important that you all hear what I have to say. Señor Elquiza will continue as head butler and will resume the functions he has always performed. If any of you thought ill of him or were not prepared to defend him...' The duke's eyes settled on the butler's nephew, Roberto, who immediately bowed his head. 'If any of you believed that I was going to punish him for following his conscience during a time of war, then you were wrong. And if any of you continues to doubt the authority of Señor Elquiza for this or any other reason, then you cannot remain at Castamar.'

The servants listened in silence. The butler observed that the duke sought to make eye contact with Clara Belmonte, but that the cook looked at the floor, a reaction which led him to suspect that something disagreeable had happened between the two of them.

'I thank you for your patience. You may now return to your work.'

Melquíades looked up to find himself looking at Doña Ursula, and he could not quite conceal a smile of triumph on seeing her ashen countenance and the defeat in her eyes. His own consternation and repentance had made him quite forget that his return to duty at Castamar signified the housekeeper's failure and the end of her despotic rule over the staff. Now that he was invested with the full authority of the head butler, the woman would be subject to his will. He had always wished that Doña Ursula had behaved differently, that she had acted as a housekeeper, a colleague in whom to place his trust, his affection even. But if, at the start of his service, she had indeed awakened such sentiments in him, she had personally seen to the destruction of any such feelings until they were nothing but a faded memory. Doña Ursula held his gaze, silently declaring that her battalions would continue to be arrayed in every corner of the house, whether in salons thronged with guests or in empty storerooms. For her, Castamar was a battlefield, just as the maps of Europe had been for its royal houses. He didn't care; all he wished to convey was that there was no authority among the servants other than his.

32

Enrique awoke in the guest bedroom at Castamar, in high spirits after two nights of revelry. Though his plans weren't going as well as he had wished, he had managed to spend time with the dauphin, Luís, further strengthening the existing ties between them. And he had enjoyed tormenting Don Diego with his comments, beginning with the incident involving that impertinent cook. But now, after reading the note Hernaldo had sent to him at breakfast, he considered as he rode out to meet his man at their secret spot that there might be less cause for optimism. He told himself he must be patient. Although his original plan with Señorita Castro had failed, it had evolved in a way that remained favourable to his needs. This was the nature of a good intrigue: a well-thought-out plan that could adapt to change.

His original scheme had involved waiting until the duke's mourning period for Alba had ended and then finding a young woman capable of winning the duke's heart again. From what Doña Mercedes had told him, Señorita Castro was the perfect option. With his help, she would seduce him, and once she was engaged to Don Diego, Enrique would reveal his parallel relationship with Señorita Castro to the rest of society, bringing shame upon the whole family. If, by some stroke of luck, he had managed to impregnate her, the shame would be quite unbearable.

Then Enrique would appear the victim, unfairly deceived, just like Don Diego himself, by a crafty fortune-hunter. Whatever Amelia said in her defence would lack credibility. After all, she would have gained riches, the payment of her debts and social standing in exchange for a promise of marriage she had never had any intention of fulfilling. Besides, he would be covered by his unblemished reputation, his personal accounts and the contracts signed with Amelia, along with his many alibis.

Of course, the Castamars would know he was falsely playing the victim and fling vain accusations at him, but there would be no proof to back them up. Don Diego would realize he'd been tricked and feel obliged, as a Spanish grandee, to settle the matter. By this point, the duke would not be able to employ his friends to help him restore his honour, since all of them would be equally disgraced thanks to Enrique's actions; not even his poor brother could assist him, having vanished by then, on a slave ship bound for the Americas.

He had foreseen that Don Diego would try to challenge him – coming to his house or hoping to encounter him at social gatherings – but Enrique would never be there. Instead, he would ensure that they met at the Buen Retiro Palace, with half the court bearing witness. The monarch would intervene of course, since he had prohibited duels, but Don Diego wouldn't care and nor would he, and it would be all the more satisfying to watch the great duke betraying the king's trust. Enrique would accept the duel in front of everyone, and the duke's pride would be so wounded that he wouldn't think twice about betting the Castamar estate. In so doing, having already had Enrique take from him everything that mattered most – his dignity, his honour, his friends, his brother – Don Diego would also become responsible for Enrique taking the place that had been his refuge.

Just before the duel itself, Enrique would request a private talk with the duke, claiming to want to clear up any misunderstandings and forget the whole affair. The duke would be honour-bound to accept, and once they were alone, Enrique would explain to him that Doña Alba's death was Diego's fault and his alone for his stupid decision to swap horses; he would tell him why his friend Alfredo's true identity had gone public, the reason behind Don Francisco's fall from grace, and most importantly of all, he would reveal Don Gabriel's fate. Then Don Diego would be faced with an irresolvable problem – either kill the only man who could tell him where his brother was, the same man he had publicly challenged to a duel, or lose his honour by not accepting the duel and trying to find his brother. Even so, Enrique thought that Don Diego would not be able to resist the opportunity to kill him in a duel.

In that case, other eventualities would work in Enrique's favour. As the one who had been challenged, he would have the right to choose the weapon, which would of course be the pistol rather than the sword – of which Castamar was an unquestioned master. The duke would be so agitated by his thirst for revenge that he would miss his target. Enrique, meanwhile, would not. It wouldn't be the first time he had used such a ruse – when a man was consumed with rage and a desire for vengeance, he could not think clearly, far less keep a cool head. On that fateful day, Don Diego's character would cost him his life, one way or another. Not in vain had Enrique stoked the duke's animosity by provoking him with small barbs, precisely so that, when the moment came, his hatred would cloud his judgement.

But sometimes plans fail, and this one had. He was intelligent enough to know that if Señorita Castro hadn't been able to get into Don Diego's heart by now then she never would. Neither did he believe that Don Gabriel would eventually show up at the Zaguán, where his men had been waiting impatiently for months. Only the part of his plan involving Don Francisco and Don Alfredo seemed to remain on course.

Conscious that he was a long way from fulfilling his objectives, two nights ago Enrique had silently made his way to Señorita Castro's bedroom before dinner. Just as he had expected, the door had been locked and he could not enter. That was when he had heard the voice of the servant who must have been helping her get ready. He waited in the corridor until the maidservant had left, before entering. Poor Señorita Castro, who at that moment was making her way to the door to lock it again, jumped back and threatened to scream, picking up a candelabra. He turned and locked the door with his master key.

'Where did you get that key?' she asked.

He quickly snatched the candelabra from her hand, informing her that he trusted she had not forgotten her promise to him over the past months.

'The attack upon you was most regrettable, but I can assure you, all of the lowlifes responsible are now dead,' he said.

'I know you were behind it. I hate you with all my soul!' Señorita Castro spat, the terror visible in her eyes.

He had to admit he admired her bravery: the more afraid she was, the bolder her resistance.

'But you don't hate your mother, do you? She sends you her best wishes from El Escorial.'

'Get out or I'll scream.'

'Don't get so angry. You don't want to hurt your little scar,' he said, stroking her cheek.

'Don't touch me.'

'That's not what you said in this room last year.'

He grabbed her and kissed her. Señorita Castro tried to wriggle out of his grasp, resisting with all her strength, but Enrique shoved her against the wall. Realizing there was no escape, she surrendered.

'What progress have you made, Señorita Castro?' he asked.

'Please…' she whispered, shaking her head. 'Don't harm my mother. Leave us in peace.'

That was when he had understood that his plan with Señorita Castro had failed, and he had reached a dead end. Later, however, his initial disappointment had turned to jubilation. Although Señorita Castro was no longer any use to him, his strategy could evolve – he would concentrate on the people he could still get something from.

During dinner he had focused on small details and discovered something new: that Señorita Castro had won Don Gabriel's heart and had, in turn, become attached to him. Her displays of courtesy, the manner in which they had both sat down, Don Gabriel's attentiveness towards her. He was her new guardian, and had he discovered Enrique in her bedchambers, there would have been serious trouble. While this was not exactly what he had wished for, it could, he considered, function somewhat in the same way as his original plan. He had changed his strategy. If Señorita Castro could not reach the duke's heart, she might, instead, sleep with Don Gabriel often enough that she would get pregnant.

The mere rumour at court that Don Gabriel had slept with a white woman or, better still, left her pregnant, would cause a scandal which no house could sustain. Everyone at court, even King Felipe, who was so fond of the duke, would turn their back on him. If the aristocracy had proven anything over the years, it was that it overcame any scandal by closing ranks on offenders as if they had never been part of the elite. That was why the nobility would always exist.

With Castamar in disgrace, he would put other wheels in motion to bring about Don Diego's definitive fall, in their long-awaited duel. But even this new strategy may yet need to be reformulated, since Hernaldo's coded message – an empty note with a cross marked on it – meant that it was imperative they meet.

He ascended the track which snaked its way through the hills to their meeting place. Hernaldo greeted him unceremoniously, without dismounting.

'Marquess, I have bad news regarding our interests. Señorita Castro's mother passed away last night,' he said, fidgeting with his hat. 'They called for the priest to administer the last rites. I fear it's public already, and we won't be able to hide it.'

Enrique cursed himself for having left the old woman in the care of such God-fearing servants. He, who saw the Church merely as another manifestation of earthly power, cared little whether the deceased had crossed to the other side with the correct sacraments. He ruminated for a few moments, taking in the fact that not only had his direct method of control over Señorita Castro gone up in smoke, but so had her motive for remaining silent. As soon as the girl arrived at El Escorial, she would hear of her mother's death.

'As soon as she finds out, she'll squeal to Don Diego about you,' Hernaldo said.

'No, she won't say a word to Don Diego. She'll tell Don Gabriel first,' Enrique replied. This fact was unavoidable now, and again, his strategy was in danger of floundering. However, the situation could be controlled in another way. He would have to accelerate his plans for Don Gabriel. 'Prepare your people at the Zaguán. We're going to make him fall into our trap once and for all. Meanwhile, send three experienced men to El Escorial and another group to the house in Madrid, the one in Leganitos. Any communication between Don Gabriel and Castamar must be severed at the root. My dear Hernaldo, it's time to work in the service of love.'

The ex-soldier raised his eyebrows in confusion, since he could not imagine what had passed through the marquess's imagination. Aware of Don Gabriel and Señorita Castro's hidden desires, Enrique guessed that if Señorita Castro's mother was no longer an instrument with which to compel her silence, then Don Gabriel would do in her place. Capturing him had always been part of the plan; now he was simply accelerating the situation.

That very morning, Clara had left Castamar in one of the duke's wagons, with a bandage wrapped around her eyes and terror in the pit of her stomach. The wagon crossed the Puente de Segovia into the capital and delivered her to the central depot. Clara managed to get out of the coach while the coachman found her a safe place inside the building. She had then bought her passage to Alcalá de Henares, a town with several noble houses, more rural and less illustrious than Don Diego's but doubtless more comfortable. There were sure to be vacancies, and obtaining such a position would not be difficult, since Doña Ursula had approached the cook just before leaving and, to Clara's surprise, had handed her a letter containing a glowing reference. When she had asked her the reason behind her recommendation, the housekeeper had quickly cut her off.

'Nothing in this note is false,' she said inscrutably.

Whether it was because Doña Ursula wanted her to find a position in another noble house to ensure she never saw the cook again or simply because she could not tolerate mediocrity, Clara appreciated the gesture, knowing that the letter would sooner or later bring her a job in a decent kitchen. She didn't mind accepting a lower position as the price for being able to leave the Castamar estate as soon as possible. She still remembered how the duke's friend, Don Enrique de Arcona, had humiliated her. It had been obscene and improper, and the worst thing was how Don Diego had just sat there, completely unaffected, unconcerned that she was the victim of his crude bet. *Any decent gentleman would know that*, she had told him sharply. She regretted those harsh words. But saying what she was thinking during heated moments was a defect she could not remedy. So she had had to leave again, her dreams shattered.

She remembered being in the same situation when they were leaving the rented house. On that occasion, her mother, her sister and she were aware that the Belmonte surname, until recently a symbol of medical erudition among aristocrats, had fallen into anonymity. They had become part of a different social stratum, one which had forever distanced them from those times when the only thing that mattered was obtaining a good marriage.

There would be no more gatherings with Madrid high society, no more galas in the Buen Retiro Palace to watch performances by Italian or Spanish theatre companies. While Clara certainly missed it, her mother, who had carved out an entire life in those circles, suffered a wound that would accompany her for the rest of her life. For Clara, that group of privileged people she once belonged to had eventually become nothing more than a 'circle of vanity', where everyone wanted more – to eat more, to drink more, to possess more – forgetting along the way that happiness is not found through gluttonously sating your urges.

Years later, when she and her mother were working in Don Giulio Alberoni's house, they had decided that her sister should continue her music classes, with the idea that she would earn a living as a harpsichord teacher. That was how Elvira had met Ramiro de la Riva, an excellent harpsichord player, who had already given concerts to various nobles in Madrid and Seville. He had courted Elvira for eight months, before he asked for her hand in marriage. After the simple but distinguished wedding, for which Clara cooked almost everything alongside her mother, they had both cried tears of joy as they watched Elvira departing for Vienna. Although it was a modest wedding, it had meant that her sister could leave her problems behind. Clara longed for both her mother and her sister so much that sometimes she couldn't stop imagining seeing them again at some point. However, she had buried this idea beneath the weight of good sense, convincing herself that this would never happen and that hoping for it would only bring her more pain.

The fact that she was leaving Castamar confirmed that she was not protected from setbacks and disappointments. In her sadness, suffering the disappointment in Don Diego and the loss of her position as cook blended into one.

She managed to control her tears before being told that the stagecoach was departing for Alcalá de Henares. She climbed up, followed by an obese washerwoman who was continually sneezing into her apron. Clara instinctively covered her mouth with her hand, and the woman, seeing this, chuckled at her fear of contagion.

'It's just some dust that has got into my nose.'

Even so, Clara backed away from her a little. Then a slight man, who looked like a clerk and was clutching a portfolio as if it were the greatest of treasures, joined them.

She felt somewhat more comfortable upon drawing the curtain and leaned back and tried to sleep, but as soon as she closed her eyes, a tide of images bubbled up in her mind, bathing her in a sea of memories. She was overcome with an immense urge to cry as she recalled the time Don Diego had briefly kissed her and the kind words he had addressed to her in person and in his secret notes. She had gone to an enormous effort to convince herself that all of these memories had not been a mere illusion, one which had been shattered two nights ago when he had bet upon her character as if she were a decorative vase and, worst of all, allowed his friends, specifically the marquess, to humiliate her without moving a single finger in response. Because of this, she had not taken the books he had given her. Even so, she did not wish for him to find out about her departure through others and had left him a few written words by way of a goodbye, so that he would understand the reason behind her leaving and how profoundly sorry she was at having shown a lack of respect towards him by raising her voice.

Despite her need to forget, she couldn't avoid reliving her arrival at Castamar as she left Madrid through the Puerta de Alcalá. *I have left as I came*, she told herself. She turned her face and rested it on the wooden partition wall, trying to sleep so that the other travellers would not notice her tears. She closed her eyes and tried not to think about Don Diego. Perhaps the tiredness was the result of the last few hectic days, or of not being able to sleep at night because of her resentment at having to leave Castamar, but as soon as the image of the duke faded away, her eyelids felt as heavy as stones and she fell into a deep sleep.

She was jolted awake by the sound of thunder and the rain battering against the roof of the coach.

'Don't be afraid, it's just a storm,' the clerk said, still holding his portfolio. 'We've left Torrejón already.'

Clara stretched slightly and noticed the downpour battering against the roof of the coach. The washerwoman had drawn open the curtains, and Clara felt grateful that the evening and the storm had descended so that she couldn't see anything of the world outside the coach.

'Not long now,' the woman added. 'Soon we'll reach Venta de los Viveros.'

She had barely finished talking when the carriage hit a pothole. Clara felt a deep terror at the thought of being exposed to the storm, with no protection of any kind. Outside, the coachman inspected the wheel. She prayed she wouldn't have to abandon the safety provided by the four wooden walls. Just then, the door opened.

'I'm afraid you'll all have to get out. The axle is almost broken and I'll need to return to Madrid to get it repaired,' the coachman said gruffly.

'It's chucking it down,' the washerwoman said.

The coachman, who was already soaked to the skin, simply shrugged again. 'Nothing I can do about that. Venta de los Viveros is just over half a league away,' he told them.

Clara began to shake and she felt her muscles go weak. The washerwoman alighted, and the clerk followed her. The boy was unloading the baggage when the coachman spoke directly to her.

'Come on, get out,' he ordered.

'But sir... I can't. There's too much open space,' she stammered, looking for the bandage for her eyes.

The coachman looked at her uncomprehendingly, like he was dumbstruck or dim-witted.

'Too much what?' he said, frowning.

'I...' she stuttered, her voice cracking as she glimpsed the abyss beyond the coach door. 'I need to stay inside. There's—'

The coachman grabbed her by the wrists.

'Get out, damn it,' he spat, dragging her into the open air.

She stumbled on the steps and, lacking the strength even to stick out her trembling legs, fell face first into the mud. When she opened her eyes, she realized that she had lost her blindfold during the fall. She knelt in terror, hugging the stub of an old elm tree, panic devouring her insides. From behind them the coachman implored the boy to stop helping her and placed himself in front of the mules to pull them by the halter. Keeping her eyes closed, Clara scrabbled for the bandage among the nearby shrubs without any luck, realizing that the strength was quickly escaping her body. Hugging the stump, she used her last ounce of strength to beg for help, her faint voice barely audible in the storm. The washerwoman and the slight man had disappeared along the track, behind the veil of rain and darkness. On the point of fainting, she opened her eyes for a moment and could just make out a grove of trees set back from the path.

She staggered to her feet, resting her face on the ancient, broken bark of the stump. But she had barely taken a few steps when her knees gave way and she fainted. She knew then, before she lost consciousness, that she would probably meet her death that night.

33

Same day, 18 October 1721

As Diego sat down to eat his breakfast, the sommelier informed him that his brother had left for El Escorial. He unfolded his napkin and was suddenly gripped by panic when he tasted the honey and almond rolls. Trying not to show his anxiety, he called Señor Moguer over.

'Please find out who has prepared these rolls. It clearly wasn't my cook,' he said.

He didn't have to wait long until Don Melquíades appeared. It was enough to see the expression on his face to realize that something was amiss. The butler grimaced slightly as he delivered the news.

'I have just heard that Señorita Clara Belmonte left early for Madrid. She left this for you.'

To his lordship, Don Diego de Castamar

Above all, I would like to say that it has been an honour to serve you in the kitchens at Castamar, even if, unfortunately, it has only been for a short period of time. I write to beg your pardon for my lack of etiquette in the presence of your dear mother and of Don Enrique and your friends; please forgive me for the words I uttered so insolently and those which I addressed to you.

Although I suffered a humiliation which was more than my pride could bear, I should not have behaved so discourteously. I know there is a certain injustice in my request, as I am asking

your forgiveness for my actions when I cannot forgive your
own failure to act, particularly when your friend Don Enrique
de Arcona exceeded all the bounds of decency in my regard. I
understand, of course, if you are in turn unable to accept my own
apologies.
  Yours,

                                    Señorita Clara Belmonte

'Why was I not informed of this earlier?' Diego asked, angrily.

Don Melquíades didn't know what to say, having only just found out about it himself. Don Diego strode across the room and the butler followed him like a frightened lamb.

'Tell Don Belisario to saddle my horse immediately,' he ordered. 'Ask the registrar for a bag of reals, and tell the armourer to prepare my sabre, my short sword, two pistols, a cartridge belt, a powder horn and a musket.'

'Should I notify the captain of your personal guard?' the butler asked.

'No. There will be quite enough scandal at my setting off in search of Señorita Belmonte. I don't want people saying I have also mobilized my servants.'

While the preparations were being made, he changed into his travelling clothes and swore that, one way or another, he would have his revenge on Don Enrique. He had dared to touch Clara Belmonte in the duke's presence! *You fool*, he reproached himself, *you should have put an end to the farce and challenged him there and then.* Now he understood Señorita Belmonte's disappointment with him. The tense expression he had observed on her face when the marquess had walked behind her, so concealing Don Enrique's indecorous act. Diego fastened his belt as he remembered how Señorita Belmonte had maintained her dignity, swallowing her shame as the marquess disrespected her. He was engulfed by a sea of emotions: furious with that insidious man, angry with himself for not having defended her, ashamed of how he must have disappointed her, irritated that she had left Castamar against his wishes, and distraught as he imagined her lost and afraid.

Pulling on his riding boots and donning his leather overcoat, he left without informing anyone else, cursing himself for having underestimated Clara's strength of resolve. His friends would soon discover the reason for his absence, and he could only hope the marquess would not learn of it. He was well aware that his setting off in search of a cook would give rise to a scandal at court and that his actions left a flank exposed to potential enemies. But he no longer cared. All he could think was that Señorita Belmonte might be lying by the side of the road or abandoned in some dingy inn.

He had planned to approach her after the festivities were over, to apologize once again and describe the nature of his relationship with Don Enrique, to make it clear that the marquess was in no way a friend and to explain why he had remained silent. He had believed that, once her temper had calmed, she would give him this opportunity. However, Clara Belmonte had displayed a strength of character which any man would find disconcerting.

He was halfway to Madrid when he met Señor Galindo, his coachman, returning with the empty mule cart. From him, he learned that Señorita Belmonte had alighted at the central depot in Madrid with the intention of catching a coach, where to he did not know. The duke cursed his luck and spurred his horse to a gallop. An hour later, a violent storm broke and his conflicting emotions gave way to simple desperation. At the depot, the attendant remembered Señorita Belmonte from the duke's description. He had assumed she was blind. He informed Don Diego that she had left some five hours earlier, headed for Alcalá de Henares. The duke didn't even stop to eat, just gave his horse some water at the trough and set off immediately. He rode on under the downfall, his cocked hat and his leather coat soaked with water, stopping at the staging posts and greasing people's palms with a few reals to loosen their tongues.

When he finally reached Torrejón, the rain was falling in torrents and he could scarcely even make out the drivers and their carts, but a lad approached leading a stubborn old mule. Don Diego asked about the carriage and the lad pointed behind him, saying that the coach had returned a couple of hours ago with a broken axle.

'That's the driver over there,' he added.

Diego made out a tall figure with a scarf around his neck, talking to three other coachmen sitting beneath an overhanging roof. He rode over, hoping that Señorita Belmonte would be safe inside or at a decent inn nearby.

'Do you remember taking a girl towards Toledo? You may have seen her, she had a bandage over her eyes,' he said.

The coachman thought for a moment and Diego prayed that he had left her somewhere safe. The man smiled and nodded.

'Yes, I remember her. She didn't want to leave the coach. The crazy creature said she couldn't get out because there was too much space outside,' he went on. 'I just about had to drag her out feet first.'

The other men laughed but Diego simply frowned. The idea that Señorita Belmonte might be lost beneath the downfall because of some boneheaded idiot of a coach driver tied his stomach in a knot. The coachman added that he had left her about half a league from the inn at Los Viveros. Diego slowly dismounted and walked over to the coachman, while his companions fell silent. The duke, like the seasoned soldier he was, cast an eye over the coachman: his build, his arms, the way he held himself.

The coachman looked up and grunted dismissively, imagining that, having fought with drunks in brothels and inns, he would be able to see off this fop who had never dirtied his hands. But before the coachman had time to react, the duke kicked him in the stomach. The man doubled over with pain and the duke drew his sabre and held it to his throat, pressing just hard enough for the driver to know that his life would be over if he moved.

'Listen carefully, you piece of vermin. I am Don Diego de Castamar,' he said, and the others bowed their heads upon hearing his name. 'You'd better hope I find that girl alive or I'll come back and finish you off.'

Aware that he was wasting precious time, Diego turned, jumped onto his horse and galloped off in the direction of Los Viveros. He was drenched to the bone and the light was failing. Almost without realizing it, he asked himself whether he should pray to that merciless God who had taken Alba from him. Although he wanted to with all his heart, he stopped himself, as if to do so would offend the Almighty after the pain he had caused.

He rode up the hills behind Torrejón, while above his head the sky shook like a gloomy choir, warning the living that they were mere mortals under the power of nature. After some minutes, he had to slow his pace in order not to exhaust his horse, and he regretted not having brought a lantern to light his way. He threw a blanket over his coat to keep warm, but it soon became soaked and heavy with water. When he reached the inn at Los Viveros he became even more downcast. Señorita Belmonte was not there, just some scribe by the name of Casimiro, who told him he hadn't seen her since the carriage had abandoned them.

'It was raining so heavily that I just assumed she was following but when I reached the inn there was no sign of her and I thought she'd returned with the coachman.'

Diego tried to talk to the other passenger, but it seemed she had caught a cold and was running a fever.

He got his hands on an old oil lamp and set out again. Praying that the rain would not extinguish his meagre source of light, he spurred the horse towards the place where Casimiro had told him he had last seen the cook. Apparently, they had alighted from the carriage on a stretch of road flanked by elms, close to a large chestnut tree. The lamp only illuminated what was immediately in front of him and he went slowly, trying to locate the trees the clerk had described. After one league, he decided to dismount and walk by his horse's side, even though the road had turned to mud. Desperate and frustrated at his inability to distinguish chestnut trees from elms, he cried out in anguish and frustration. The only response was a flash of lightning and a crash of thunder. Once again, he felt the urge to pray, to beg God for a clue to follow in the darkness. But he resisted and, instead, called out to Clara, crying out in rage and wishing he had slit the coachman's throat for leaving her in this godforsaken place.

He remembered Clara standing as she received his most recent gift, with that smile that had conquered his soul. He felt again the fear he had experienced when he had lost Alba and told himself he had been a fool not to have stood up and expelled the marquess from Castamar. *If the daughter of Doctor Belmonte had been a guest at Castamar, you would not have permitted it*, he thought. *Fool… you've been a fool. She has always been far more than just an excellent cook.* From time to time, the storm lit up the scene and aided him in his search, allowing him to see more than he could with the lamp alone.

He cried out again, blaming himself, hearing Alba tell him he should never have allowed it, urging himself to carry on searching for her. He walked on, refusing to pray to God, as if the Lord were subjecting him to a test of his pride. For more than two hours, he searched behind every tree until, utterly defeated, his voice hoarse from calling her name and his body exhausted, he fell to his knees in despair.

Just then, the lamp illuminated a piece of maroon cloth. He recognized it immediately as the cloth she used as a blindfold when she was forced to go out into the open. He had observed her sometimes, from the windows of the upper floors, overcoming her affliction to go into the yard or to attend mass. He stood up, raised the lamp and led the horse by its reins. He forced his way through the undergrowth, shouting her name, but there was no reply. Just then, a bolt of lightning lit up a grove of massive chestnut trees emerging from the thicket, as if by a miracle.

Now he knew she must be close by. He kept going, the sky

dark above him, hoping a fresh bolt of lightning would light up the scene. Just then, the faint glow from his lamp revealed a figure a few paces away: the crumpled body of Clara Belmonte. He immediately took one of the dry blankets that was under the horse's saddle. He prayed she was still alive and slapped her gently on the cheeks as soon as he had wrapped her in the blanket. Delirious, she half opened her eyes and asked for her father. Diego touched her forehead and confirmed that she was very cold. He was even more worried when he felt her weak pulse – she desperately needed warmth. She looked at him uncomprehendingly, not understanding who was protecting her from the cold.

'With your permission, I am going to take you in my arms,' he said.

He knew that the girl was not fully aware of what was happening. He fixed the lantern to the saddle of his horse, wrapped a second blanket around Señorita Belmonte and held her in his arms. Her pale face was illuminated by a flash of lightning. Just then, she opened her eyes and looked at him, still in a daze, as if lost in a sea of memories.

'I forgot to tell you,' she said in a faint voice. 'I think—'

'Save your strength, Señorita Belmonte,' he said, trying to warm her with his body. 'Don't speak.'

'I think I've fallen in love with you, your grace.'

He stopped for a moment, stunned by what he had just heard, his heart pounding in his chest and his soul gripped by the fear of losing her. Full of conflicting sentiments, he mounted his horse, still holding her in his arms. He took the reins and prayed that the horse would not be too tired to carry them both, and he whispered words of encouragement to it before they set off towards Los Viveros. As they did so, he considered that, although it seemed that he had saved her life, it was in fact she who had rescued him. It was she who had dispelled the darkness, she who had healed his wounds with her mere presence. And so, he swore to himself, that if she survived that night, he would never allow her to be alone and friendless again, he would never allow anyone to judge or mock her, to disrespect her beauty and her intellect, and he would never allow anyone to insult her for being a mere cook.

19 October 1721

Finally, Señorita Castro was going to tell him what he wanted to know. Gabriel dressed as quickly as he could, keen not to keep Amelia waiting now she had suggested they meet to talk about Don Enrique. It was only yesterday that she had cried in his arms upon receiving the news that her mother had died peacefully after a short illness. Seeing that her mother was at death's door, the servants had called the priest to administer the last rites, and at dawn she had gone to meet her Maker. The priest had stayed with her until the end.

That evening, a mass had been said at the church of San Bernabé, while a fierce storm raged outside. The service was followed by a simple burial. Señorita Castro had stood before her mother's grave, saying a silent farewell beneath the rain. To Gabriel it seemed as if her figure, clad in black, was one of the statues in the cemetery. After a short while, he had offered her some words of consolation and suggested that they seek shelter.

They had decided to spend the night at the guesthouse of the monastery of Los Jerónimos, where they also ate supper. After accompanying her and advising her not to hesitate to wake him if she needed him, Gabriel had retired to his room for the night.

The festivities at Castamar had deepened the mutual regard that had arisen between them during the months of her convalescence, and the more he thought about her situation, the more convinced he was that she was just a victim, not an accomplice.

The day before their departure, and after informing him that the situation with Don Melquíades had been resolved, Diego had changed the subject.

'Can you tell me what is going on between Señorita Castro and you?'

'I'm just concerned for her.'

Diego had laughed.

'Perhaps you can refresh my memory, Gabriel. Who was it who said, "Don't trust her. She's very close to Don Enrique and I'm sure she's up to something"?'

'I don't recall ever saying that,' he had answered, a smile playing on his lips.

'You liar!' Diego exclaimed and tossed a velvet cushion at him.

'Okay, I confess.' He laughed. 'I was wrong about her. I know you're just jealous. You can't bear the fact that Señorita Castro is interested in me.'

'Ha!' Diego replied.

'Nonetheless, the closer I am to Señorita Castro's heart, the greater the chances that she will overcome her fear and tell me what we need to know.'

'I've known you long enough to see that you like her, so I will just remind you of what Father said. Your wife should have the same colour of skin as you – for the sake of your own happiness and that of your children.'

'I am well aware of it, Diego, I assure you.'

A silence had settled upon them until Don Melquíades advised them that supper was ready. They didn't speak of the matter again, but Gabriel couldn't stop thinking about it, conscious that his feelings towards Señorita Castro went deeper than mere affection.

He hadn't objected to their mother inviting Don Enrique to Castamar again because it would allow him to keep the man under observation. The marquess had not exchanged so much as a glance with Señorita Castro in public, beyond a courteous greeting upon his arrival. However, at the start of the private supper, Señorita Castro had approached Don Gabriel and asked him to station a trusted footman at her door, so that she would feel safe. He had done exactly as she asked, but still suspected that something had happened after he had left her in her room.

Whatever the situation, though, he had to recognize that his investigation would be at a standstill until he managed to visit the Zaguán. He had eventually tracked the place down, but his brother had forbidden him to visit it. At the same time, Diego's friends Don Alfredo and Don Francisco had uncovered a certain complicity between Don Enrique and the young dauphin, Luís, who was only fourteen years old. It seemed that Luís had developed a great affection for the marquess, but that was all. Gabriel couldn't help but feel a sense of frustration, as if he was constantly about to grasp the end of a rope, only for it to slip through his fingers once again. And given the lack of information from Señorita Castro, he had – despite her reluctance – insisted on escorting her carriage to El Escorial. He had ridden alongside, while, through the open window, she recounted some of her adventures from when she lived in Cadiz with her father and they had travelled regularly to the capital.

So, he had been surprised when, after a stormy night, she had appeared at the door of his bedchamber looking forlorn.

'Do you remember all those times you asked who might have an interest in my presence at Castamar?' she had said, her face a picture of sorrow.

He had nodded, barely able to contain his curiosity.

'Now that my mother is dead, I am free to tell you what it is you wish to know,' she had gone on. 'For the first time in a long time I am going to be completely honest, although I must warn you that what you are about to hear may well upset you.'

Gabriel thought that his persistence was finally being rewarded. And so, he dressed as quickly as he could, with scarcely enough time to put his things in order. He went down to the courtyard to find her waiting with tears in her eyes. He took her gently by the hand and told her that he would protect her, that she should not worry about whatever it was she was about to say.

She blinked and then told him what he wanted to hear. She had come to Madrid in the hope of making an advantageous match with his brother; she had left Cadiz with her father's debts around her neck and scandal on her heels – not so big a scandal as some claimed but enough to provide material for malicious gossipmongers; deceived by Verónica Salazar, who was under the orders of Don Enrique, she had settled her mother in the house at El Escorial, which was owned by the marquess; he had seduced her, making himself her only creditor and sole benefactor; staring into the abyss of poverty, she had accepted his advances as the only way to free herself of her debts and regain her position in society. The marquess's one obsession was for her to win Don Diego's heart and to marry him and she, fearing for her own life and that of her mother, had submitted to his demands. Finally, the tears flowing freely now, she confessed that, although she had no proof, she was sure Don Enrique, seeing she could no longer visit Castamar, had orchestrated the terrifying assault to which she had been subjected. Indeed, on the first night of the festivities, he had entered her bedchamber and once again threatened her mother's life.

She did not mince her words, expressing both the terror and the torment she had experienced. When she finished, she turned to him for confirmation that she had disappointed him, and he made no attempt to hide his emotions. He let go of her hand.

'You have behaved very badly, Señorita Castro.'

'I am deeply ashamed, and I will understand if you never want to speak to me again, but please, don't judge me,' she said.

'You came to Castamar with the intention of seducing my brother, you accepted money from Don Enrique and had relations with him in exchange… Look what it has all come to.'

'I beg you not to sit in judgement of me,' she repeated. 'I told you everything because I believed it to be my obligation, but I cannot say, with the exception of some specific actions, that I feel any remorse.'

'Well, Señorita Castro, you should,' he reproached her.

'Don Gabriel, it is not fair to judge a woman for desiring a good husband, for wanting to make a good match when she can scarcely support herself. We women are subject to a world ruled by men, where all that matters is an appearance of goodness and our ephemeral beauty. I cannot tolerate your facile judgement when I have only done my best to survive, even if, in so doing, I have committed errors.'

'I cannot condone your collusion with Don Enrique,' Gabriel said. 'You have disappointed me in every possible way. I understand that you found yourself in a difficult situation, but you should never have accepted money for...' There was silence and they looked at each other, he with disappointment in his eyes, she with indignation. 'You became his lover, Señorita Castro. You cannot ask me not to judge you for that. You have plotted against my family and now you ask me simply to accept it.'

'The only thing I have asked is that you do not judge me, Don Gabriel, but you are clearly incapable of doing that!' she exclaimed. 'You are judging me for surviving as best I could,' she continued. 'Was I to be drowned by my father's debts and allow my mother to die? What else was I to do? Perhaps you can tell me!'

Gabriel sensed in her words all the humiliation she had suffered during the past months. For a respectable lady who had fallen into disgrace, the only response had been to strive to maintain a façade of the respectability that she no longer possessed.

'You could marry for love,' he said. 'You are capable of that and many other things.'

She suddenly felt ashamed for losing her temper with him for no reason other than her own suffering, and she apologized. But he had already forgiven her. Amelia had been subjected to terrible pressure and forced to do things that were unworthy of a lady. He looked around to make sure there was nobody to observe them, and kissed her hand.

'I admit I am disappointed,' he said, 'but I also recognize that it must have taken great courage to tell me all of this without sparing me the details.'

'I fear you will not wish to see me again,' she answered, her face a picture of consternation and sadness.

He did not reply. He was still overcome by everything he had heard and, for the moment, preferred not to be in her company. He was deeply hurt – not only had she committed the unforgivable act of plotting against his family at the urging of that contemptible man, but she had also injured his feelings towards her. He knew that her behaviour was the result of desperate circumstances that he could hardly judge, but he found himself unable to forgive her just then.

'If you are in need, come to Castamar and stay as far away from the marquess as possible,' was all he could say.

She told him she was leaving for Cadiz. She wanted to spend some time at the estate, far from her problems, and she trusted the servants there as they had been with her family for many years. The villa was secure and was hers for life, as the marquess had signed a deed renouncing any claim he might have upon it.

'Even so, if you wish to remain in the capital, I can send some men from Castamar for your peace of mind,' he said.

She thanked him but rejected the offer. He bowed farewell and headed for the stables, intending to return to Castamar as quickly as possible.

He gave orders to a stable lad to saddle his horse, offering him an extra maravedí to silence his protests at serving a black man. Over time, he had learned that gold hid his colour better than any blanket. When he turned, he found a boy standing in front of him with a note in his hand.

'Are you Don Gabriel de Castamar?'

'I am. Who is looking for me?'

'I have a message for you, sir,' the boy said, shrugging his shoulders. 'A horseman delivered it for you this morning.'

Gabriel inspected the letter but there was no indication of the sender, just a cheap wax seal that smelled of diluted wine. He broke the seal and read the contents. The handwriting was crude, and the letter appeared to have been written in haste.

I have written proof of the actions of Don Enrique de Arcona and his machinations against Castamar, which I am sure will be of interest to you. If you want to know more, bring money and come alone to the Zaguán on Plaza del Arrabal tomorrow night. There will be no other opportunity, for the following day I leave Madrid and I do not intend to return. When you arrive, wait until you are approached.

Don Gabriel read the letter several times, unsure whether it was the solution to his problems or a trap. After what Señorita Castro had told him, he was sure the marquess was acting against them. He knew neither Don Enrique's motives nor his goals, but if there was indeed written proof then he could not allow the opportunity to pass. If he went first to Castamar, his brother – with his customary caution – would forbid him from attending the meeting or, at the most, would go himself, accompanied by his guards, who would doubtless scare off the mysterious confidant.

Gabriel spurred his horse to a gallop and decided to make for the Zaguán. And yet, a voice inside him whispered that he should be careful. The simple fact that a rider had been sent to El Escorial to bring him the note suggested that whoever was behind it was a person of some means and not the kind of lowlife one would expect to find in a house of ill repute. But he silenced the voice and instead his hand slid from the reins to the épée he had armed himself with upon leaving Castamar. As he did so, he felt reassurance in the knowledge that he was as skilled a swordsman as his brother.

34

Same day, 19 October 1721

Enrique walked noiselessly between the Italian harpsichord and the paintings that decorated the drawing room at Castamar, dimly lit by the waning candles. He felt as if he were in his own home, imagining all of this being his once he had carried out his revenge. He looked outside at the brewing autumn storm then sat down to think, reflecting that he had gone about the Don Diego affair in a rather dim-witted fashion. He had finally understood the nature of the duke's feelings for the cook the previous morning when, upon entering the tearoom, he had come upon a heartbroken Doña Mercedes with tears in her eyes.

'My son went out early this morning to look for the girl,' she had said. 'The lord of Castamar, going after a simple cook.'

It was clear that the duke harboured intense feelings for her, strong enough to make a fool of himself by going out to look for her. The important thing now was to know how deep these feelings went and how far they would lead the duke. *Perhaps the cook could be a new Amelia*, he told himself. It mattered not to him whether Don Diego's heart was in the hands of a cook or Señorita Castro. If one thing other than age and death was common to all men, it was chance, and he would always find a way to make it work for him.

Even so, he contained his initial jubilation, telling himself that while many men lost their heads for servant girls it tended to cause only minor scandals. Doña Mercedes had beseeched him to show absolute discretion to avoid any such outcome. The poor woman could only drink her hot chocolate and sit there, waiting for her son to return. He had assured her that he would stay as long as she needed him. Meanwhile, Don Francisco and Don Alfredo had gone out looking for Don Diego. Don Francisco would return to Madrid to accompany the Countess of Bazán to her home and from there head north. Don Alfredo would head south. As luck would have it, Doña Mercedes did not want to worry Don Gabriel by sending him a note. Had she done so, Enrique's men would have had to intercept it – it was imperative nothing should happen to prevent Don Gabriel showing up at the Zaguán.

In the afternoon, a terrible storm had shaken the earth and heavens, and he had soothed the poor lady's perturbed spirits, assuring her that Don Diego would certainly have sought refuge somewhere. After a while, Doña Mercedes had begun to doze off and he had convinced her to go and rest, promising to let her know as soon as Don Diego appeared. After she had gone, he settled into one of the armchairs to keep watch and entertained himself by musing on Don Diego and the cook, until the sodden, downcast figures of Don Alfredo, Don Francisco and their escorts emerged from under the cloak of rain.

Enrique had risen and stood as he waited, with a glass of anis in his hand. When they had come in, they were worn out and immediately walked over to the fireplace, barely even greeting him properly.

'I understand your search has been fruitless.'

They had both nodded, rubbing their hands to keep warm.

'This whole affair has got out of hand,' Enrique said scornfully. 'She's just a cook.'

Don Alfredo looked at him grimly. 'It's none of your business,' he said.

He put on a pained expression but was laughing inside. Don Alfredo could not have imagined Enrique knew his deepest secret, one which explained why he had never married, why he had no known lovers and why he was so reserved even around his closest friends. Enrique had nothing personal against these two men, so he simply ignored the remark.

'To be honest, Marquess, I don't understand why you're still here,' Don Francisco stated.

Don Enrique had waited a second before answering. 'I'm just supporting my dear friend Doña Mercedes during a difficult time,' he said without looking at him. 'I don't know why that's so hard to understand.'

The young man stood up and approached him threateningly. 'We all know you have other intentions.'

'I have no intentions beyond those stated.'

Don Francisco stood before him, frowning. However, Enrique could see a hidden calmness in his eyes which proved him to be, at the very least, an intelligent, if inexperienced, adversary.

Don Alfredo had cleared his throat from the back of the room. 'It seems that nothing can make you lose your composure.'

'Why would I? Especially over a man who loses his head over a mere cook.'

'You should watch what you say, sir. You are in his house,' Alfredo replied coolly.

'I don't see why I should. I'm just telling the truth,' Enrique countered. 'And if you two are his friends, you should agree with me on this point, just as his mother does and as the entire Madrid court would if they knew.'

'I can tell you one thing that's certain, Don Enrique,' Don Francisco replied. 'I don't like you. I don't like you being here; I don't like looking at you; I don't like listening to what you have to say.'

If he had been hoping to offend Enrique, then he didn't know the marquess in the slightest. Enrique laughed before answering. 'I fear there is nothing I can do to remedy that.'

'You could be quiet,' Don Alfredo suggested.

'What I meant to say,' Enrique quipped, 'is that I fear I have no desire to remedy that.'

Don Francisco had understood that acting like a fighting cock would only lead to defeat, so he had withdrawn to his armchair. Don Alfredo had serenely walked towards the window and looked outside, weighing up the words he was about to say.

'I know your kind all too well, marquess. You covet what you don't have and destroy what others do. Men like you do not know how to love. Indeed, I doubt if you have ever loved,' he said calmly and without looking at him once. He knew how to hurt the marquess.

Don Enrique had waited a moment. He was not unaffected by Don Alfredo's words, since he had loved enough to fill three lifetimes. He took the bottle of rosoli, served himself a glass and raised a silent toast before gulping it down and striking back at the insolent swine.

'I thought you were a wiser man, Don Alfredo,' he said. 'I have loved so much that I never wish to love again. I've descended to the depths of hell for love; I've lived in darkness for love, destroyed my soul for love. The question is whether you have, and if so, to whom exactly such feelings were directed.'

When he spoke these last words, Don Alfredo turned around, looking at him with terror and aversion in his eyes. Even so, he did it slowly, searching for some clue in Enrique's face that would tell him whether that statement was a mere coincidence or if the marquess really knew his secret. Then Enrique gave Don Francisco a sidelong glance. The man appeared stunned by Enrique's declaration, and stood there looking at his friend, waiting for him to reply. *The seed is planted*, Enrique told himself, thinking that soon this conversation would have consequences. It was obvious his question demanded an answer on Don Alfredo's part, even though any answer risked further revealing the man's secret. As someone well acquainted with good manners, Don Alfredo had simply smiled, maintaining his composure, and stated that he was a discreet man.

Then a bitter silence had settled between the three men. Don

Francisco was not old enough to be an equal, and Don Alfredo, despite his age, lacked training. The silence became even deeper, and Enrique spent the following hours pacing around the tearoom, waiting for the duke and praying he would find the cook and not get caught up in the storm. Enrique would personally ensure she was found if she did not appear with the duke by the following morning. He had only just sat down to sleep when dawn broke and Doña Mercedes appeared at the door.

'They're here.'

He had looked out to see the duke dismounting from his horse and walking over to a coach, rented presumably, so that the girl could travel with him. Enrique considered that the duke must certainly be in love to pay for an entire six-mule coach just for her, but as soon as Don Diego took her unconscious body out from the vehicle the marquess understood that love wasn't the sole motive for the coach. The young girl's skin was bruised, and she looked quite ill. He had cursed his luck. If the cook died, his plans were ruined.

They had all gone out to the entrance hall, where the head butler and housekeeper of Castamar were waiting. As soon as Don Diego entered, Francisco held out his arms so that his friend could rest the cook's body in them. The duke seemed exhausted, yet still shone with a determination which Enrique took a few moments to admire. It was music to his ears to hear Don Diego ordering for her to be lodged in his own bedroom. Doña Mercedes had blocked his way, horrified.

'Leave it, Mother,' he responded, attempting to evade her.

'This has gone too far, son. The best thing is for her to be looked after until she has recovered and then for her to depart for another house.'

'No,' he said, flatly.

Still irritated, she had stood in his way and raised her voice.

'I want her to leave.'

'She's staying!'

'She's your cook, not your betrothed. She can't lodge in your quarters!'

Don Diego had stopped and turned towards Doña Mercedes in a rage.

'That's exactly where she'll lodge!' he said.

The duke's last sentence had made Enrique realize just how blind he had been. Everything suddenly came together in his head: the sudden interruptions to go down to the kitchen in person; his rude behaviour during the dinner when she had been bet on like livestock; the fact that he had gone after her during a raging storm, before bringing her home in a coach and lodging her in his own chambers, as if she were his betrothed, in front of the servants and guests. Blessed cook! All this time, the solution to his plan for revenge had been right in front of his eyes, and he hadn't even suspected it until this very moment. How little could he have imagined that the cook would become the duke's Achilles heel. Not wanting to waste the opportunity, he took a step forward and smiled solemnly, knowing that his words would make the duke react again.

'Your grace, I believe that you are too much under the influence of that impertinent cook.'

Don Diego had marched towards him, eyes blazing, and Enrique had retreated instinctively in the face of his advance. Don Alfredo had even tried to put himself between them, but the duke had already been standing a hair's breadth from Enrique's face.

'Marquess, I did not seek your advice or your company,' he said eventually, through gritted teeth. 'Get out of my way or I will move you myself.'

Enrique had let him pass, merely holding his gaze, letting him know that the duke could never scare him and that he was always willing to fight back. Don Diego had disappeared upstairs, giving orders to call for Doctor Evaristo. They must do everything necessary to warm up Señorita Belmonte – that's how he had referred to her, as if she were a lady.

It was obvious that the relationship between Don Diego and the cook had developed naturally over the course of everyday life, and if Enrique knew anything about his enemy's nature it was that he would not allow anyone to meddle with his decision. He wished with all his might that Don Diego's love for the girl would lead him to propose marriage. It would be a guaranteed scandal, even more so if Enrique could ensure she wasn't a virgin. If he took her by force, Don Diego would find out sooner or later. It would matter little what she said on the matter – she was a cook and he was the Marquess of Soto. Don Diego would have no choice but to challenge him to a duel, at which point everything would unfold just as he had predicted. For his plan to work, though, Enrique would have to tame that wild foal. Just thinking about it gave him immense pleasure – not only because it would remove her of those airs and graces, but because it would destroy the thing Don Diego loved most.

Sol loved watching Francisco's tranquil face transform into a feigned smile upon seeing her sitting unexpectedly next to Leonor de Bazán in his own house. She had spent the whole afternoon chatting and drinking hot chocolate with her. When Francisco strode in, she had to admit that he was devastatingly attractive, with the muck from the road and his hair hanging loose, slightly damp and with no wig. He smiled uneasily while Doña Leonor kissed him on the cheek and told him that Doña Sol was a marvellous woman. The poor man was trying to figure out just how, in his absence, Sol had managed to enter his house and end up in a friendly conversation with Doña Leonor.

There was no way he could have guessed that she had instructed her trusted man, Carlos Durán, along with two of his most faithful lackeys, to inform her of Don Francisco and Doña Leonor's movements. However, against all predictions, she had learned that they had appeared at sunset and, to her surprise, Francisco had changed his clothes and, in the middle of the storm, set off again on a new steed. So, knowing that he had not returned and might not arrive until later that afternoon, she had smartened herself up and sent a visiting card announcing her intention to have tea with Don Francisco. Just as she had expected, the Countess of Bazán replied informing her that her friend was not at home. Still, after attending mass, she had showed up at the house with a block of the best chocolate, claiming that the note had not reached her in time. Of course, as soon as she said she would leave, the countess, unaware of the game that was being played, had invited her to stay and have tea with her instead.

After a few polite refusals, Sol had accepted, and in the end, they had spent the entire afternoon together, catching up with court gossip, talking about excursions to shows in Madrid and the king and queen's gatherings. Hours later, the lady had become quite enchanted with Sol. Having achieved this connection, she had only had to wait for Francisco to appear at the door, which he had done just as their conversation was nearing its end.

'Why haven't you told me about the Marchioness of Villamar before, my dear?' Doña Leonor asked him.

'She has a... how shall I put it...?' Francisco answered with an intentional pause as he tried to gauge her intentions. 'A flawless reputation.'

With impeccable decorum, Sol got up and walked towards him.

'My dear, your friend is such a darling. I've already made sure,' she added, popping a grape between her teeth, 'to tell her all about the latest court gossip.'

He remained in limbo, casting surreptitious glances at Sol. She was pleased to see how disoriented he was as he searched for a clue that might reveal her true intentions, but to no avail. She had practised all the known arts of seduction, read everything written on the subject and experimented with every form of pleasure in order to draw up this impenetrable defence. For the first time, she saw him give in to the fear of the unexpected.

'It's getting late, and I'm sure Don Francisco wishes to dine with you alone,' Sol commented with a smile.

He was about to wish her farewell but, as she expected, Doña Leonor's good manners worked against him once more.

'I implore you this minute to invite her to dine and to spend the night here.'

Aware of the game that was being played, he smiled in acceptance.

'Of course, Marchioness, you must stay. Nothing would make us happier,' he said, ending on a slightly sarcastic note.

Once again, in line with the rules of etiquette, Sol refused before eventually giving in. Dinner was rather insubstantial: a chicken consommé and some meat that was poorly spiced and insufficiently seasoned. She focused her attention on the lustful looks her breasts incited in him and the hidden game being played beneath the table.

As he slipped his bare foot beneath her farthingale, she swore that he would have to satisfy himself tonight. Sol wanted to watch his desire consume him. She withheld her next step, waiting for a comment that would give her an opening to continue her strategy. Taking the last piece of cake, she listened attentively as Doña Leonor concluded her last anecdote of the evening: Don Francisco had once fallen face first into the river Jucar while fishing, pushed in by the countess as revenge for her losing at cards a few hours before. This was the moment Doña Sol had been waiting for.

'So, you like fishing?' she asked Don Francisco.

'That depends on the fish,' he answered.

'If you wish, we can visit my estate in Montejo,' she suggested with a devious smile. 'The Jarama flows through it and the fishing is excellent at this time of year.'

Doña Leonor found the idea enchanting, which put him in a difficult situation. He accepted, thinking that it was best to try to control the situation and that he would have a better chance of unveiling her intentions if he kept her close. Then Doña Leonor had retired for the night, and finally, they were left alone.

As soon as the drawing room door was shut, they looked at each other.

'What are you plotting?' he asked her, unable to control his curiosity any longer.

She waited a few moments before replying.

'Not every action has a hidden intention,' she said serenely.

'That's highly unlikely with you.'

'You could have refused my invitation,' she answered, maintaining his gaze. 'Now, if you'll please excuse me, I'm off to bed.'

She turned and walked towards the door but, driven by desire, he made a dash and blocked her way just as she was opening it. Now she had him where she wanted him – just at that delicious moment when he had shown his cards, leaving her perfectly poised to reject and humiliate him.

'What are you doing?' she asked scornfully.

He took his time, scrutinizing her, his breathing heavy and his passions so inflamed that it was as if his very skin was radiating heat. Sol kept her eyes fixed on his, her gaze supremely indifferent, knowing it would hurt him. Yet he did not seem bothered. Suddenly, it was as if the desire she could see in his eyes had been replaced by a deeper feeling, one which made her tremble. It was the first time a man had looked at her as if he were admiring her true character, as if he could observe the darkness of her soul and still find it beautiful.

She felt trapped and uncomfortable, on the verge of giving in, and retreated slowly. His breathing calmer now, he walked towards her until they were face to face. Gently, he brushed a lock of hair away to better contemplate her face. Surprised and slightly lost at this sudden turn of events, she gulped as she realized that Francisco harboured deep feelings towards her, and as he stroked her face it was as if he was the knot that had bound her heart for her entire life. She felt liberated, as if she no longer had to cover up her intentions, as if there were no longer any battles or need for revenge or rules of decorum. She sighed as if an unbearable load had been lifted from her shoulders and, her voice trembling, she asked him again what he was doing. Without moving away from her, he took her with both hands, caressing her cheeks before moving down to her neck.

Though she had sworn not to give in to him, she let herself be carried away. He lifted her onto the table and took her unrelentingly, like a wild animal. Gripping his neck, she sought his mouth, wondering if they could consume all this passion in one go. Francisco fused into her. She almost lost control and confessed that she was hopelessly in love with him, but she bit her lips to stop the words coming out. Instead, seeing him on the brink of collapse, she whispered every kind of obscenity into his ear. As he continued to take her, she realized that she was weeping, and with each new wave of tears, she thought how she had never been loved like this by anyone and that she would never confess how much she loved him. And yet, she was aware that the following day, all of this passion would vanish and be replaced once more by those stupid games of power and vanity. In desolation, she understood this would be a single, terrifying moment in her life, the only one in which she would feel completely free.

35

20 October 1721

Melquíades dipped his quill in the ink pot and continued to record the events of the last two days while he waited for his nephew to arrive. Since he had recovered some of his dignity and started gradually to reacquaint himself with being the head butler of Castamar, many of the serving staff had come forward to congratulate him. Some of these congratulations were sincere; others less so, little more than diplomatic excuses for their failure to visit during the months when he had been under the housekeeper's embargo. It was clear, though, that the majority of the staff were glad to see him back, some out of personal affection and others because it signalled the end of Doña Ursula's despotic regime. A few, though, kept their distance, either because they saw his betrayal of Castamar as unforgivable or because they were unable to bear their own shame at how they had treated him during his exile. And so, after the duke's speech, the butler had publicly asked everyone to forgive him for having failed them and, just as Don Diego had done, made it clear that he would understand if anyone did not wish to work for him. In those instances, he would do everything possible to help them find a position in another household. However, he had explained, he would not tolerate insubordination from those who chose to remain.

As he spoke, his nephew, Roberto, had bowed his head, unable to look at him. Melquíades allowed a couple of days to pass for the lad to reflect on his attitude. In the meantime, along with the weekly consignment of a few reals that he sent to his sister, Angeles, the boy's mother, he had included a short note inviting her to come to Castamar from Buitrago de Lozoya. During this time, his nephew had avoided him, but now that his mother was about to appear, the time had come for them to speak, man to man.

While it was true that his nephew had avoided his gaze during the meeting, there were many others who had not. Moreover, within just a few hours of being restored to his position, Melquíades had received more complaints about the housekeeper from the staff than he had hitherto received in his entire career. *My God, that woman is unbearable,* they told him. *Always looking for trouble and picking quarrels… It must be exhausting to see the whole world as a potential enemy.* But he knew that Doña Ursula would maintain her animosity until the end, and so he told himself he must be careful, despite his newfound power. *Doña Ursula may have antagonized people,* he thought, *but there is no denying that Castamar has run like clockwork under her supervision.*

After the festivities were over, he had summoned her to tell her that things had changed. She appeared in his office, observing him coldly as he wrote in his notebooks. He had kept her waiting for some time, forcing her to clear her throat to make him aware of her presence.

Finally, he looked up. 'Things are going to change at Castamar. To start with, the kitchen and the staff who work there will no longer be part of your domain and will instead be the exclusive responsibility of the head cook.'

'You've lost your mind!' she said, opening her eyes wide in surprise.

He enjoyed contemplating the astonished expression on her face and the nervous twitching of her mouth. Doña Ursula had protested, as was to be expected, but that had merely enhanced his pleasure, as it allowed him to see her desperation at losing the dominion she had held over the servants of Castamar for so many years. Of course, had Doña Alba still been alive, Doña Ursula would have appealed to her, and he knew that, in the duchess's absence, she would no doubt turn to the duke now. If that happened, he would intervene, and have an opportunity to punish her insubordination. *If only she would give it up as a lost cause*, he thought. He viewed her as a spirit who had fed on his misfortune and her own hunger for power. The kind of person who, when they lose their influence, become empty, dried-out and withered. The power and the glory they had acquired turned to pain when taken away, and they are left feeling disoriented and abandoned, lacking both friends and family. But Melquíades also knew that such people would do anything to keep hold of their position, and Doña Ursula would be no exception to this rule.

And indeed, before she left his office, she had taken the opportunity to fire a poisoned dart at him. 'I can tell you, Don Melquíades, that I have no intention of giving up the fight, and that you are mistaken if you believe that Señorita Belmonte is still at Castamar.'

That was how he had learned of Clara's departure. He had stood up while she, her expression unchanging, showed him a note written by Señorita Belmonte and addressed to his lordship.

'And you accepted her resignation?' he asked, his eyes bulging angrily as he snatched the letter from her hand.

'Of course I did. That girl is far too proud to allow anyone else to tell her where to live.'

'Out! I am going to inform his lordship immediately. And you can get back to work.'

The conversation had left them both feeling disappointed. He was annoyed because he could not properly celebrate his victory over the housekeeper, while she was irked by her loss of power. But his concern at the thought of Señorita Belmonte in her weakened state, unable to bear being out in the open, had been enough to fully occupy his attention. He had prayed she was somewhere safe as he hurried off to inform the duke of developments. He had not imagined that Don Diego himself would set off after her, and he knew his master well enough to know that such an action was not the result of a mere impulse. It was clear he had strong feelings for the cook. And suddenly, the butler understood that all the improvements in the duke's demeanour over the last year had been due to the healing influence of Señorita Belmonte.

When Don Melquíades had finally informed the staff of the cook's absence, it was clear they were already aware of the situation. There was a downcast air to the gathering, and many of the servants were casting sideways glances at Doña Ursula, whom they blamed for having allowed Clara to leave. By suppertime, tensions had risen, just like the storm that was raging outside.

It had been Señor Casona who broke the silence.

'Doña Ursula, you should not have permitted Señorita Belmonte to leave the house,' he announced bluntly.

The housekeeper stopped eating and fixed him with a stare. Then she dabbed her lips with her napkin.

'Let me make one thing quite clear. If I was in the same position again, my decision would be unchanged. I would be lying if I professed to feeling any sense of guilt about the matter.'

'No doubt, but I do, for not having foreseen events,' Simón replied. 'Guilt and remorse are what make us human. I don't know what your lack of them makes you.'

A stony silence had followed, everyone concentrating on their food, even though each spoonful of soup – prepared with the best of intentions by Carmen del Castillo – simply highlighted Señorita Belmonte's absence.

And so, Melquíades had passed a wakeful night, awaiting the duke's return, constantly looking out of the high windows that gave onto the flowerbeds, whipped by the wind and the rain. Finally, the duke had arrived, carrying Señorita Belmonte in his arms and ordering she be accommodated in his own rooms, something which disconcerted servants and guests alike. Don Diego had made it clear that her care was to be given absolute priority. Indeed, somewhat later – while he was guarding access to Señorita Belmonte's room and Doctor Evaristo was examining his patient – the butler had overheard a conversation between Don Diego and his friend Don Alfredo regarding his feelings towards her.

'I am responsible for what has happened to her, Alfredo,' the duke had declared.

'Tell me the truth, Diego. Is it just responsibility that you feel? Because I know you. I hope you aren't thinking what I suspect you are.'

'Alfredo, this is hardly the time. You know Alba's death weighs heavily upon me, and I don't want to be responsible for another one, let alone as the result of a stupid wager with that cretin, Don Enrique.'

Just then, Doctor Evaristo had called Melquíades into the room. The doctor informed him that the chambers should be kept warm and that the patient should be given a syrup of garlic and honey, as the cold had clearly taken a hold of her. The butler had nodded and then listened to the rest of the doctor's verdict on Clara's health.

'I cannot pretend that I am anything other than very concerned. Tonight will be critical, and I am afraid we must prepare for the worst. She has been exposed to extremes of temperature, nearly freezing during the night and now running a fever. Worst of all, her pulse is faint.'

The physician's prognosis plunged the room into a gloomy silence.

One glance at Señorita Belmonte's pale face was enough to convince all present that they might well have to bury her in the Castamar cemetery, next to the unfortunate Rosalía. The next day, many of the servants had lit candles at the chapel and said a prayer for the cook. Don Diego had not left her bedside for a single moment, and when Father Aldecoa had appeared to administer the last rites, he had sent him away. The butler, who had been coming and going on errands all day, could not help but be struck by Señorita Belmonte's deathly appearance. Were it not for the light rise and fall of her chest, he might have assumed she had already passed away. And whenever he left the room, he had the sensation that he was leaving behind him not one but two possible corpses. *I can't imagine how the girl's death would affect his already troubled spirit*, he thought to himself. *It might break him completely.* Time had passed with scarcely any improvement to Señorita Belmonte's condition, while he had continued with his duties as head butler. Eventually, he had decided to approach his nephew while the latter was delivering clean blankets to the guests' bedrooms.

'You've been avoiding me,' he said.

'No. I—'

'I know how busy you've been, I'm responsible for overseeing your work, and I know you've been avoiding me,' the butler had interrupted. 'I would like to have a few words with you tonight in my office. Once you are off duty.'

Just as he was about to leave, his nephew had cleared his throat.

'I hope I can find sufficient courage to attend.'

'I hope so too, because your future is at stake,' he answered.

The butler had dedicated the evening to writing in his notebooks, praying for the soul of Señorita Belmonte and awaiting his sister's arrival. She appeared just as he was penning his final lines.

'I would like to wait until your son is here before I explain why I have asked you to come,' he said as she took a seat.

Then he remained silent while poor Angeles fidgeted nervously, imagining the worst. When Roberto entered to find his mother waiting with a worried look on her face, he bowed his head in shame. Melquíades stood up and, before his sister could say anything, asked his nephew to close the door. Then, with all the calm he could muster, he confessed his betrayal of the Duke of Castamar during the war. Angeles opened her eyes wide in astonishment, mingled with panic at the thought that soon she would have nobody to turn to. His sister's reaction was exactly as he had imagined it would be. That was the very reason he had never burdened her with his predicament, as it was he who had betrayed the family's honour and she deserved no share of his suffering.

'Brother, don't worry. Whatever happens, we are family, and we will never abandon you. My son and I—'

'Angeles, don't worry. His lordship already knows all about it and has forgiven me,' he explained, to calm her nerves.

'God be praised! The duke is a saintly man,' she said, crossing herself before hugging her brother.

'I can't tell you how grateful I am for your support. Not because I ever doubted it, but because I wanted Roberto to hear it from your lips.'

Upon hearing this, Angeles looked at her son and asked, in a hesitant voice, what had happened. The butler said that it was best if they spoke alone.

Melquíades had the sense that he had begun to heal the deep wound the whole affair had left. The duke's compassion towards him had tempered the remorse with which he had tortured himself all these years. All he wanted now was for God, in his infinite wisdom, to save Señorita Belmonte's life, as he was sure that this would save the duke's life too. He told himself that if Don Diego had shown himself capable of forgiveness, then perhaps the Almighty would also demonstrate compassion towards Clara Belmonte. And so, after giving instructions for his sister to be made comfortable, he made his way to the chapel to pray for the cook.

It was dark as Gabriel rode towards Lavapiés, a pouch full of reals tied to his saddle. Whores tended to their customers in shady corners while their pimps stood guard a little way off, and before him paraded a motley crew of puffed-up dandies, drunken ruffians and foul-mouthed vagabonds who kept body and soul together by begging for alms and stealing what they could from the market stalls on the Plaza de la Cebada.

The storm had abated but the weather was still as gloomy as his spirits, and during the journey from El Escorial to Madrid, he had been full of doubt about his decision to visit the Zaguán. He was heavily armed and his senses were on the alert, but while he was vigilant to the slightest movement in his vicinity, he could not stop thinking about Señorita Castro.

After saying goodbye, Gabriel had made straight for the Leganitos mansion in Madrid and written Diego a letter telling him he was well and that he would be spending the day in the capital. He then went on to recount what he had learned from Señorita Castro and outlined his intention to visit that house of ill repute, the Zaguán. Then he had sealed the letter and instructed his manservant to send it to the estate that evening. When darkness fell, he had set out for Lavapiés, the letter having been despatched to Castamar.

As usual, he was subjected to the stares and pointing of those who wondered what a negro was doing riding such a steed. He touched the handle of his flintlock pistol and the pommel of his épée and thought that he would do well to spend no longer here than was strictly necessary. He descended Calle de San Pedro el Mayor until he reached the fountain of Lavapiés. From there, he made for the gully which led to the Zaguán, a somewhat ramshackle two-storey building with a rear courtyard. The place exuded the noise of drunken revelry and the smell of unwashed bodies. He felt as if he were Dante descending into hell, and that on the gates he could read *Abandon all hope, ye who enter here.*

He dismounted and tied the reins to the post, under the hostile gaze of the onlookers, who had insults ready on their lips. One man spat on the ground as he passed, but when Gabriel stopped and stared at him, the coward looked away. Gabriel entered the tavern, which was thronged with drunken men, and with women selling their bodies. His presence was enough to cause everyone to fall silent and look at him.

The brothel-keeper came out to meet him, jutting his chin and clicking his fingers.

'Where do you think you're going, negro?' he asked, and pointed at the door. 'Get out. Your type aren't allowed in here.'

'Have you noticed what kind of negro you are talking to?'

'I don't give a damn what kind—'

'My name is Don Gabriel de Castamar!' he shouted. 'And I swear that tomorrow you will have to look for another occupation, because this tavern of yours will be shut down for being nothing more than a vile whorehouse.'

The man stammered, completely taken aback, not knowing whether he should bow to a nobleman or send this insolent negro packing. Blinking, unsure what to do and losing impetus, he said, 'But you... you can't come in here.'

'I certainly can. I am the only black man in Spain who can,' Gabriel replied, to the astonishment of all present, 'because I am a Castamar and the whole kingdom knows what that means.'

The man took a step back, impelled to placate this negro who could quite easily turn his life upside down. He gestured to the whores to get back to work, and conversation gradually resumed, while people stole sidelong glances at him as he prepared a table for Don Gabriel.

'Would you like some wine?' he asked, in an obsequious tone. 'If you would like to entertain yourself with one of the girls, I am sure I can find one who is willing, for a little extra.'

One look from Gabriel was enough to make the brothel-keeper

withdraw. Gabriel sat down, waiting for a silent signal. After half an hour, just as he was beginning to lose hope that anyone would show, a redhead approached carrying a plate of beans. From the way she dressed, her skirt revealing her thigh, Gabriel assumed she was just another whore, although she smelled more of garlic and onion than of cheap perfume.

'I don't mind serving you, whatever colour you are,' she said.

Don Gabriel imagined she had been drawn by his expensive clothes and because she had heard the name of Castamar.

'I'm not hungry, thank you.'

The woman rested her foot on the bench next to him, revealing her thigh.

'You haven't even tasted it,' she said.

'I'm sorry, but I don't want any supper.'

'Go on, give it a try,' she insisted. 'You won't regret it.'

Gabriel stood up and looked her in the eye.

'I'm telling you for the last time, I'm not looking for a woman.'

She leaned in closer. Gabriel placed a hand on his pouch and kept his senses about him. He was aware that half the occupants of the tavern were looking at him.

'Don't be like that, darling... Come with me, La Zalamera will show you things you've never even imagined.'

He narrowed his eyes, trying to work out whether the woman was connected to the person he had arranged to meet. He was just starting to hope that this was not a trap or a complete waste of time when a voice interrupted him.

'I've been asked to tell you that somebody's waiting for you in the back courtyard.'

Gabriel followed the brothel-keeper. As his eyes adjusted to the gloom, he made out a tall figure in the shadows. He started towards the person, but they raised a hand.

'No closer,' a man's voice warned. 'Have you brought the money?'

'If the information and the proof are convincing, there will be plenty of reals for you.'

The man nodded, and just as he was about to speak again, Gabriel heard one of the boards of the porch creaking with the weight of somebody creeping up behind him. Without hesitating, he threw himself to the right, just in time to avoid a nightstick that came crashing down on the ground next to him. That was when he realized there was a hooded man behind him. He drew his sword and slammed the pommel into the face of his assailant, who staggered back and fell onto a pile of sacks. He turned and fired his flintlock. The man who had greeted him with a request for money had asked for his last real. The shot could barely be heard over the shouts, the sighs and the hubbub. Two more figures appeared, and Gabriel was relieved to see they were armed only with truncheons. He immediately concluded that their intention was not to kill him but to take him captive. He needed to finish them off before his hooded attacker had time to recover.

He ran his sword straight through one of them, the man's last breath escaping his throat with a harsh rattle. Sensing that the fourth man had joined the fray, Gabriel tried to take evasive action but a club caught him in the ribs. He felt an excruciating pain and prayed that his hunting jacket had offered some protection against the impact.

Seeing that his attacker was about to hit him again, he jumped backwards to avoid the blow. He slammed the butt of his pistol into the man's face and stabbed him in the crotch with his dagger. The man screamed with pain and sank to his knees. Meanwhile, the hooded man had picked himself up and was brandishing a huge knife. Gabriel retreated but felt the blade slice into his arm and dropped his pistol. He tried to put enough distance between himself and his attacker, but the man was too quick for him. Desperately, he lunged at his enemy, taking care to avoid his blade. He knocked the attacker into the air as if he were a rag doll, then came down on him heavily, trapping his knife-bearing arm. There was a sickening crunch of bones breaking, and his enemy groaned as if he was taking his pleasure in one of the bedrooms on the upper floor. Before the man could react, Gabriel punched him in the face. They were going to regret setting this trap for him, he told himself, as he rammed his fists into the man's face again and again, until his knuckles were covered in blood.

'Who paid you?' he panted. 'Was it Don Enrique de Arcona?'

The man just looked at him, his face bloody and battered, and began to laugh like a madman. Gabriel was about to beat some manners into him when he realized why the man was laughing. He didn't have time to dodge before he felt a blow to the back of his neck, and his eyes misted over. Behind him was a fifth man, who had been waiting for the right moment to act. Gabriel tried to move, but the man kicked him in the stomach, and he curled into a ball in an attempt to protect himself. When he opened his swollen eyes, he made out someone crouching next to the hooded man.

'You've always been as ugly as sin, Zurdo, but now you'd make the devil himself look pretty,' the person said.

Zurdo, Gabriel repeated to himself, and desperately hoped he wouldn't forget the name if he lost consciousness. As they loaded his almost inert body onto a cart, he heard the distorted voices of his captors and glimpsed a figure hiding in the shadows of the stables. Just before he passed out, he saw, between the bales of hay, hidden from his kidnappers, two eyes flicking nervously, witness to his abduction from the security of their hiding place. He recognized the red hair and realized that his fate depended on the courage or cowardice of a whore who went by the name of La Zalamera.

36

Two days later, on Sunday morning, Diego could still feel Señorita Belmonte slipping away from him. Though her fever had subsided and her pulse was more regular, Doctor Evaristo had not shown any signs of optimism. Diego had remained by her side the whole time, dividing his worries between her and his brother.

He had received no news from Gabriel since his brother's departure for El Escorial. At breakfast that morning, Alfredo had offered to go in search of him. Meanwhile, as the days had passed, his mother had begun to show more and more concern for Señorita Belmonte. *She has always been that way*, Diego had thought. *A woman who cannot bear change, but with a heart of gold.*

It had taken a year of arguments with her husband for her to accept Gabriel and, in the end, it was not marital love but Gabriel himself who had won her over, simply by tugging at her skirts and calling her *Mamá*.

Now the same thing was starting to happen with Señorita Belmonte. Alfredo, Francisco and his mother, who had all taken part in the stupid bet with Don Enrique, seemed to feel guilty about what had happened. And his mother had begun asking Simón Casona and Don Melquíades about Clara Belmonte.

Realizing that Clara might die, the duchess had taken the initiative and told Doctor Evaristo he must not leave the estate.

However, that did not mean she looked favourably upon the possibility of her son taking Clara's hand in marriage. In fact, Diego knew perfectly well she would try to stop it if she had the chance, and in fairness, there was no shortage of good reasons. They both knew the Madrid aristocracy would always see her as just a cook.

The ironic thing about that whole affair was that, had he taken Doctor Belmonte's daughter as his wife while that widely respected man had still been alive, the court, despite judging it a highly advantageous match for the Belmonte family, would ultimately have accepted her as a duchess. With time, those familiar with her love of cooking would simply have seen it as an eccentricity. However, because she had already been employed as the cook on the estate, it would be considered less of an advantageous marriage and more of a scandal, one that would spell social death for them all. No noble, far less a grandee, would want to rub shoulders with a duchess who had spent years in service at the stove.

But he knew what it meant to love someone with all your soul, and he could not pass over the chance to be happy again. He had lost his wife a decade ago, and only that year had her ghost started to fade. By going out in the storm in search of Señorita Belmonte, he had finally laid Alba to rest. Since then, he had become fully aware of how in love he was with Clara. Having pondered the question, his next objective became clear: to restore Señorita Belmonte in the eyes of society. His task was to convert her into a noble with royal acceptance before she became Duchess of Castamar. He didn't want her to end up living a life like Gabriel's, imprisoned in a gilded cage. All the good things that had happened at Castamar this last year had arisen due to her presence. He did not wish to leave her for a single moment, and after seeing Alfredo off, he returned to the bedroom to watch her frail, delicate body being consumed by fever.

Her pale skin and sunken eyes left little room for hope. He

wiped the sweat from her brow and made her take regular drinks, just as the doctor had ordered. For the second time in his life, he felt completely paralysed. He had cursed God for revealing the path to salvation only to snatch it away from him once more, but once his rage had abated, he told himself the blame was entirely his.

When the fever rose again, and his mother and the doctor thought it wise to call Father Aldecoa, to give her the last rites, Diego immediately shouted at them to leave. It reminded him of what had happened all those years ago, when Alba's life was hanging by a thread and the priest had entered to administer the sacrament. On that occasion, Father Aldecoa had stood his ground.

'I will not leave, your grace. Strike me, by all means, if it makes you feel better, but Alba needs to go to paradise, and I will give her the last rites. Christ gave her that sacrament and you cannot take it away,' he had said.

This time, the chaplain entered the room sheepishly.

'I will not allow you to give her the last rites yet,' Diego asserted.

'That's not why I'm here,' the priest replied. 'Clara Belmonte is still fighting a fierce battle against death, and I do not believe it is time for her to receive the final sacrament.'

Diego realized that Father Aldecoa was there to speak to him.

'Everyone thinks you are in love with this girl,' the priest said. 'Is it true?'

It felt strange to hear it said out loud, as if he had no right to fall in love again. Diego lowered his head and simply nodded, like he was confessing. The chaplain slowly rested his hand upon his shoulder.

'I am going to pray for Señorita Belmonte in the same way I prayed for Doña Alba ten years ago. You can pray with me if you wish.'

Diego shook his head. 'I've run out of prayers. I used them all up on Alba,' he mumbled. 'If they didn't work back then, they won't now.'

'I can't force you to pray, but just remember, it's for her,' Father Aldecoa said.

Forcing the tears back, Diego looked at him and nodded like a small child. He knelt by the bed and prayed without hope.

Even so, Señorita Belmonte's condition did not improve. The fever kept rising, and only very occasionally did she open her eyes before falling back into long periods of unconsciousness. Again, he spent the night by her side, holding her hand, snatching uncomfortable moments of sleep, waking up with his heart in a flurry to check she was still breathing, as if the fact of his being awake would keep her alive. He forced himself not to think about how much her death would affect him. He had already imprisoned himself behind the walls of Castamar after Alba's death, and he knew that this second blow would be even worse.

The following morning, he woke to the first rays of sun warming his face, opened his eyes and went over to feel her brow... She was no longer burning hot and had more colour in her skin. He let out a sigh of relief. Then he ordered fresh drinking water to be brought and for two girls to change the sheets and to wash her with hot water and a cloth. He waited outside until Doctor Evaristo had finished examining her, on tenterhooks as he awaited the verdict. When he saw the doctor's face, he felt a huge wave of relief.

'Provided the fever doesn't rise again, I believe the worst has now passed.' Doctor Evaristo smiled. 'She must keep drinking and, if awake, eat something. It's a miracle that the girl is alive.'

Diego closed his eyes and thanked the Lord, unable to hold back a smile. He decided to go down to breakfast and see if there had been any sign of his brother or if there was any information from Alfredo, who had gone looking for him the previous day. But when Doña Ursula told him she had had no news, he went from worrying about Señorita Belmonte to worrying about Gabriel. *It seems I shall never have any peace*, he thought. He ate breakfast, hoping to receive news from his brother imminently, and before the housekeeper walked out of the door, he stopped her and asked her to inform his mother and the servants of Señorita Belmonte's improvement.

'And tell Don Enrique too, Señora Berenguer,' he added. 'He must be very concerned.'

Sensing the irony in his tone, she asked him if he wanted anything else.

'Yes, wait a moment,' he replied. 'When Señorita Belmonte has recovered and returned to work, I want you to inform me of any problems she encounters in the kitchen.'

'I don't understand, your grace. What kind of problems might she encounter?'

'None, with you there. And don't accept any further resignations from her, especially not without telling me first.'

She nodded in agreement and told him that it was best he knew that the kitchens were no longer under her jurisdiction, by order of Don Melquíades. Diego was surprised by his butler's decision. Doña Ursula had always managed those affairs in an extremely diligent manner. He frowned and looked at her as she explained.

'Without wanting to venture too far, it's quite possible that, after his incident, Don Melquíades wishes to make it up to your grace with greater effort and efficiency in his work. I certainly let him know that he did not need the extra burden.'

Diego tutted in annoyance. He made it clear to the housekeeper that the kitchens were once again under her command and told her to leave. After finishing his breakfast, he went out for a short ride and returned to watch over the patient, hoping that the fever had not risen again. It hadn't, thank God, and by dinner, he was told that Señorita Belmonte had finally awoken and shown signs of hunger. He nodded and waited to be left alone. Then he allowed the tears he had contained in the chaplain's presence to flow freely and cried in the only way men could: alone.

22 *October 1721*

The note Don Enrique had just received from Hernaldo forced a smile to his lips. With the brief words, *It was quite a challenge, but it's done,* he was informed that Gabriel de Castamar was in his power. The note went on to explain that the next part of the plan was being successfully executed: *It will be public a day after you receive this message. The letters will be circulating in two days.*

However, neither sentence had awoken the pleasure he had expected to feel. On the contrary, he felt empty inside upon thinking that nothing could bring Alba back, however successful he was. This inner emptiness was an old acquaintance, one which had assailed his soul even before he had lost her.

There was a hollow well deep inside him and there had only been two occasions on which he had not felt completely empty. The first was when he had met Alba and the second when she had died and he had remained locked away in his bedroom, drunk and pitying his miserable existence.

Curiously, his salvation had come from Hernaldo's hand. The soldier had come into his room despite orders not to. When the marquess saw him, he had ordered him to leave, but Hernaldo had remained there, fearless. Don Enrique had got up and pointed his sword at the man's neck.

'I'll kill you if you don't get out this instant!' he had shouted.

'Do it, then, because I'm not going anywhere.'

He had wanted to make that wretch pay for all his sorrows, and then, to have the emptiness engulf him completely. And yet, the bravery he had seen in those eyes as they looked into his own, putting his life into Enrique's hands despite his master's drunken state, had provoked only admiration. Nobody in his service had ever contradicted him like that. He had begun laughing when he understood that Hernaldo had been the first and would certainly be the last.

'I have realized that I cannot kill you, Hernaldo,' he had said drunkenly, throwing the blade to the other side of the room. 'It's pathetic but you're the only friend I have.'

Upon saying those words, he knew that Hernaldo had become his one loyal companion, something he could never have suspected when he rescued him from that prison in Seville, seeking only a reliable assassin. The soldier had led him to bed, asking him how long he had gone without sleep. He had shrugged and sworn that he would destroy Don Diego de Castamar even if it cost him his life, and the soldier had nodded mechanically as he shook the sheets.

Enrique grabbed him by the shirt.

'You're not listening to me!' he had shouted. 'He's taken everything from me: victory in war, the woman I loved, the title of grandee! I will not cease until he's lost everything he owns, even if I lose my own life in the process.'

Hernaldo had just sighed and looked at him impassively.

'You'll never achieve any kind of revenge without resting first.'

The marquess had collapsed, but soon realized that, if the soldier left that room, his inner void would simply expand. He had begged him not to leave, and Hernaldo had remained throughout those hellish days and nights – Enrique collapsed in a heap and the hired assassin sitting on a chair by the wall.

The years had passed that way – some days better, others where he felt like quitting this life for good – until something had changed inside him, and one morning he had emerged from the gloom, his mind made up to seek vengeance.

Since then, he had believed that, as his strategy played out, his happiness would increase until it was complete. Now, finally, the fate of Don Gabriel was in his hands and Don Enrique had ordered that he be lashed after capture, so he would never forget his true place in the world. Then they would transport him to Portugal and sell him under a different name as a slave, so that he would be shipped off to the Americas.

Other plans were progressing too. *The letters will be in circulation in two days' time*, he reminded himself. Little could Don Alfredo and Don Francisco imagine how life was going to change for them when they became the objects of utmost scorn in the eyes of the Madrid court. The first – an unimpeachable man, very knowledgeable on politics, loved and respected by the whole court and Their Majesties – would fall into the deepest ignominy for being a sodomite. The second because, beyond his celebrated reputation as a libertine, he was also a degenerate. As proof of this, Enrique had in his possession the correspondence which Doña Sol, Marchioness of Villamar, had kept up with him. In her latest letter to Don Enrique, she had told him in consternation that a friend, in a drunken slip of the tongue, had informed her of Francisco's orgies with Don Alfredo de Carrión.

It little mattered that this was false, since the part about Don Alfredo was certainly true, and the inevitable contagion would make any defence impossible: the entire court knew that the two men were always together. The evidence against both would circulate throughout Madrid, and from there, it was only a question of sitting down and waiting for people's morbid nature to do the rest of the work.

At the same time, the other part of his plan was gathering pace, and to this end, he was going to meet an anguished Doña Mercedes. Just then, his thoughts were interrupted by a manservant, who informed him that Doña Mercedes was waiting for him, already mounted on her steed for a ride around the estate. He nodded and said he would be there in a moment. He burned the letter he had just received from Hernaldo and headed for the stables.

He rode with Doña Mercedes to the limits of the estate, the duchess keeping a restless silence, which Enrique tried to break by exchanging a few glances with her, until at last she mentioned the disappearance of her adoptive son. He pretended to be concerned, hoping the conversation would end soon so they could turn their attention to the relationship between the duke and the cook. He scrutinized her for a few moments and saw that, beyond her exaggerated manners, her elegant hat and the ornate mask of her face, the old woman was greatly upset. *The poor thing*, he thought. *Such a shame for a woman like her to suffer so much for a worthless negro.*

'From your expression, I'm guessing you've had no news from Don Alfredo.'

Doña Mercedes shook her head.

'You mustn't worry. I'm sure it will all end well,' he continued.

'You are a loyal friend,' Doña Mercedes said in response to his consolation. 'You've always been there for me in difficult times.'

'And I always shall be,' he answered. 'I'm sure your son is safe and well.'

'I remember when my Abel first brought him home,' she said. 'So small, so quiet, so dark... I thought my husband had taken leave of his senses.'

Enrique only had to glimpse the heavy expression on Doña Mercedes's face to know that her heart would split in two if she knew her adoptive son was being lashed as they spoke.

'Your husband should not have let it happen.' He took her hand to comfort her. 'Adopting a coloured son leads to no end of problems. None of us will ever accept him as an equal. It's absurd.'

'It is,' Doña Mercedes agreed. 'And yet now, Don Enrique, strange as it sounds, Gabriel is my son.'

She let a few minutes go by in silence.

'If you wish, I can go out and look for him in person. I can't bear to see you like this.'

She thanked him and kissed him on the brow. That took him so by surprise that he froze on the spot. His parents had never displayed affection towards him: his mother had been dedicated to her lovers and his father to power. He was paralysed for a moment, assailed by a strange urge to free the African and ease this old woman's suffering.

But he regained his composure before speaking.

'True loyalty can only be proven at the direst moments,' he replied.

They rode on and he waited to recover from the terror which that display of affection had provoked in him. He was struck by the thought that, had Doña Mercedes been his mother, perhaps he would have had a different nature, less cruel and more honest. He took a deep breath as he forced himself to suppress such thoughts.

'At least the cook's condition has improved,' he observed. 'That's some cause for joy.'

He wasn't lying. Without Señorita Belmonte, his plan would have to operate through Señorita Castro, a lost cause. Doña Mercedes sighed, and Enrique read her thoughts.

'You're in a difficult situation, my dear friend.'

She nodded, holding the horse's reins and fidgeting nervously in the saddle.

'I know. It's not natural for Diego to end up with his own cook, after so much time without any kind of woman at all,' she confessed suddenly.

Enrique was relieved to hear those words, which helped his new strategy along.

'Perhaps Don Diego is confused.'

'My son has never been confused. That's what really concerns me.'

He saw the opening and gave her a concerned look as he replied, 'That insolent girl is the real problem. The sooner she leaves Castamar, the sooner your son will feel better.'

For Enrique, it was already obvious that Diego was smitten with her. It was clear from the fact that he had not left her bedside for a moment.

'That may be so, but Diego will not let Señorita Belmonte leave,' the duchess explained. 'I think he may be considering marrying her. And that would be a disaster. The Castamar name passing through the womb of a cook! And that's assuming she can conceive, since she's no longer so young, and according to my maid, her mother only had girls.'

'I can't bear to see you suffer like this,' he said solicitously.

'I can't even think about it without feeling dizzy.'

'If I may suggest a solution...'

'Whatever it is, tell me,' she said, anxious to hear.

He pretended to hesitate.

'In God's name, Enrique, speak your mind,' she begged.

'The best you could do is get someone to talk to her, make her see the ill effect she is having on Don Diego by staying here. Make her understand the scandal it would mean for Castamar if the court heard that the duke had ridden off in the rain to find her and then hosted her in his own bedchambers. If, in addition, it were to spread that he may be intending to marry her, that would surely be fatal. If the girl chooses to leave of her own volition, your son will escape her influence.'

Doña Mercedes's face lit up.

'Perhaps we just need to get her a position at another house. That's all commoners care about deep down,' he added. 'The important thing is to find the right person for such a delicate mission.'

'Perhaps you could try?'

Now he would have the consent of Doña Mercedes, and therefore that of the servants, which would give him the opportunity to get close to the girl. He looked at her with all the affection he could display and declared that he would be delighted to help. Of course he would try, and he would be sure to fail utterly! *Poor old dear. She'll die of a heart attack when she finds out her son is the object of so much criticism.*

He fully intended to promote the scandal when the opportunity arose. Once the rumour had spread, it would be impossible to prove that he had been behind the rumours. The duke had made his feelings towards the cook so clear that any of the servants at Castamar could be the one responsible. All he needed to know now was whether Don Diego really intended to propose marriage. If the impertinent young girl rejected the duke, it would only spur him on, and if she accepted, it would mean a relationship that would never be accepted by high society. Even so, Enrique would not lift a finger until he was certain of the proposal, or at least of the duke's intention, since a rumour could turn against you as quickly as the wind could change the course of a fire. To this end, he needed to talk to the girl alone and uninterrupted, to get it straight from her mouth. If the duke did indeed harbour such intentions, his plan to drag her honour through the mud until he was challenged to a duel could once again become a reality.

'Now, now, my dear friend, I'm sure everything will turn out fine. Just tell me when, and I'll do what I can to convince the cook that she must leave.'

37

*I**ntrigues silently accumulate until it is too late to avoid their consequences*, Alfredo thought. He had spent too long at court not to realize that the skies were darkening over Castamar. It was less than a day since Diego, worried that there had been neither sight nor sound of his brother, had asked Alfredo to go to El Escorial in search of him, while he looked after Señorita Belmonte.

'I'm sure there's nothing to worry about. He's probably decided to stay and keep Señorita Castro company,' Alfredo had told him.

'If that's the case, then Gabriel must be more taken with her than he has let on.'

The duke's response had taken him by surprise. He could not imagine a relationship between a negro and a respectable lady. Although who was he to judge others? They had said nothing more, and Alfredo set off for El Escorial, hoping to find Don Gabriel in the monastery gardens with Señorita Castro. But when he arrived, a lad had told him that Don Gabriel had left for Madrid on Sunday morning, after receiving a private letter, and Señorita Castro, her mother now buried, had left for Cadiz.

Alfredo had ridden to the Castamar mansion on Calle Leganitos but the servants informed him that Don Gabriel had left on Monday evening, leaving instructions for a letter to be despatched to Castamar that same night. This heightened

Alfredo's concerns. He had been at Castamar until Tuesday, and no letter had arrived that Monday night or the following day.

He had changed his mount, borrowing a steed, and galloped along the Illescas road in search of Señorita Castro. He had stopped at every post from Getafe to Villaseca de la Sagra and finally caught up with her at an inn in Toledo. He apologized for interrupting her supper and explained the reason for his presence. She had not disguised her concern upon hearing of Don Gabriel's disappearance, saying that, after he had taken his leave of her at El Escorial, she had heard nothing more from him.

Alfredo spent the night at the inn and set out for Madrid the next day. It was clear that Don Enrique was at the centre of everything: the wager on Señorita Belmonte, the attack on Señorita Castro, the murder of Don Gabriel's ally, Daniel Forrado, and, finally, the disappearance of Diego's brother. He suspected that some misfortune had befallen Don Gabriel, and worried that he too was one of the marquess's targets. He recalled the words the marquess had addressed to him at Castamar. *I've descended to the depths of hell for love; I've lived in darkness for love, destroyed my soul for love. The question is whether you have, and if so, to whom exactly such feelings were directed.* He shivered at the thought that the man might know his secret.

He went up to the drawing room, where his butler, the most loyal man he knew, was waiting for him with a downcast air. With a forced smile, the butler stopped him at the door.

'I must tell you that Don Ignacio del Monte is waiting inside,' he informed him.

One look was enough to tell Alfredo that his servant, the only man who knew his secret, thought he should have the visitor thrown out unceremoniously. Alfredo ignored him as one might ignore the advice of an elderly parent and entered the drawing room, where the man who for so long had been his lover was awaiting him.

As soon as their eyes met, he felt desire rising within him

again. Don Ignacio was unchanged: the blue eyes, the powerful chin, the fair hair. There were just a few lines chiselled into his beautiful countenance.

His old lover, with his eternal smile, came closer.

'Aren't you pleased to see me?' the man asked.

Alfredo recalled the last time he had seen him, beside himself with rage, insulting him as only a wounded lover can. His butler had discovered that Ignacio had been stealing large sums of money from him, before losing them at the gaming tables. Gambling had taken such a hold of Ignacio that he had then fallen prey to moneylenders, one of whom had threatened to cut off his nose and ears if he did not repay what he owed. Alfredo, hoping to catch him red-handed, had pretended to be asleep one night after they had made love, waiting until Ignacio got up and went to his office to pilfer his funds. Alfredo had surprised him in the act but the whole experience had been deeply painful. When he refused to give Ignacio the money, his lover had exploded and said the most hurtful things. In the end, Alfredo had given him some money to spare the man's life, while expelling him from his own. But he had always suspected that, sooner or later, he would be back to ask for more.

'I'm not here for what you think. I came because I owe you an apology,' Ignacio said, leaning closer.

He's lying, Alfredo told himself. *Like always*. He pulled away. He had allowed himself to be deceived in the past, but he would never let it happen again. He went over to the cabinet and poured two glasses of brandy.

'You've taken a long time to regret the words you said that night,' he observed.

Ignacio made a dismissive gesture.

'If you carry on lying to me, I'll have you thrown out,' Alfredo continued. 'How much have you lost this time?'

With no possible escape, Ignacio bowed his head.

'They'll kill me if I don't pay.'

'Leave!' Alfredo ordered.

The love he had once felt for this man could not coexist with Ignacio's addiction. Ignacio approached, his chin trembling.

'Listen to me—'

'I said leave.'

'Didn't you hear what I said? They're going to kill me.'

'I don't care.'

A look of panic came over Ignacio's face, and he transformed into a grotesque creature as he threw his arms out and begged for compassion. He searched in vain for Alfredo's lips, declaring his unconditional and undying love, told him he had never forgotten him, that he had always been devoted to him. Just when Alfredo was about to push him away and order his servants to throw him out, Ignacio told him the truth.

'When they see me coming out of here, they'll kill me. They want me to spend the night with you!'

Alfredo's nerves were suddenly on edge. Ignacio's pursuers knew where he was, and they were after more than money. He had always assumed that Ignacio, for his own preservation, would not speak of their relationship. Society and the law condemned men like them, and he could not imagine anyone willingly incriminating himself. But his old lover had sold their secret to the moneylenders. He suddenly understood that Don Enrique de Arcona's words to him a few days ago had had nothing whatsoever to do with romance. He was caught in the spider's web the marquess had woven for Castamar, and he suspected that the same thing had happened to Francisco. In his own case, he could end up being permanently exiled. He was already imagining pamphlets circulating at court, pasted to walls around Madrid, illustrated with satirical drawings.

Alfredo struck Ignacio hard, sending him sprawling to the floor. He was disgusted. He, who was discretion personified, who had borne his condition in silence without sharing it with anyone, who was careful to avoid public scandal, would now be exposed to the censure of the court, to the ignominy that would attach to his name and the dishonouring of his reputation. He clenched his teeth in fury. His father, Don Bernardo de Carrión, who had marked his body with a riding crop to teach him discipline, would be spinning in his grave. *Get married and produce an heir*, had been his unchanging advice. But Alfredo had ignored those paternal instructions. He had never married and nor had he ever had any intention of doing so. His parents' marriage had shown him how unjust it can be for a woman to marry someone who will never love her, and he did not wish to be responsible for the unhappiness of a wife who would be condemned to a barren and hostile partnership.

'I gave them our letters,' Ignacio confessed. 'By tomorrow, all Madrid will know about it.'

On hearing this, Alfredo raised his fist in anger, but he suddenly had a vision of when his own father used to beat him. He brought his fist down against his own leg, staying true to his oath that he would never be like his father. Ignacio threw himself at Alfredo's feet, begging forgiveness, swearing that he was only a weakling who loved him.

'Who are they?' Alfredo asked. 'Is Don Enrique de Arcona behind all this?'

'Don Enrique? He's a loyal friend...' Ignacio babbled in terror. 'I don't know why you're asking.'

Alfredo could tell he was not lying, but the very fact that Ignacio spoke of the marquess as a friend confirmed his suspicions.

'Speak!' he shouted. 'Or I'll throw you out of here and let them deal with you.'

'I don't know, I swear! Their faces were covered. I don't know who they are. I owe money to lots of people!'

Alfredo shook Ignacio off and stormed out. He changed his clothes and called the butler to ask if Ignacio was still there.

'He's still lying on the drawing room floor, whimpering.'

'Prepare a room for him,' he ordered.

'Sir, will he be staying long?'

'Don't look at me like that,' he said. 'Get rid of him tomorrow and don't give him any money. I'm afraid that if I kick him out just now, he won't live to see another day. I'm going back to Leganitos to see if there's any sign of Don Gabriel, but I fear the worst. Then I'm off to Castamar. Tomorrow promises to be a difficult day, and I want to talk to Diego before he hears the news from other sources.'

He crossed Madrid to the Castamar mansion at Leganitos, but when he arrived, he was told there was no news of Don Gabriel. As he was preparing to leave, the butler opened the front door to a disreputable-looking redhead. The butler shooed her away.

'Out of here!' he said. 'We don't deal with your kind in this house.'

'A curse on you!' she shouted back, from down the street.

'Who is that woman?' Alfredo asked.

'I don't know, sir. She's been four times, looking for Don Diego, claiming she has some important news for him,' he answered. 'She's a prostitute, not to be trusted. They're always up to no good.'

Alfredo rode after her and called on her to stop, but she quickened her pace and made for Plaza de Santo Domingo. He spurred his horse until he was at her side and tossed a pouch of coins at her.

'They're yours if you talk to me.'

The woman stopped and warily picked up the pouch. Alfredo dismounted, explaining that he was Alfredo de Carrión, Baron of Aguasdulces, and a personal friend of Don Diego. She nodded, but her eyes were full of suspicion.

'I don't know where the negro is,' she blurted out, 'but I know who's taken him.'

His heart skipped a beat, and he moved closer and asked her to explain. She recoiled, afraid. Her face, contorted by a mixture of fear and greed, made him suspect that she was an opportunist rather than somebody who was part of a plot.

'This bag's a bit light,' she said, shaking it so that the coins clinked.

'Are you trying to extort money from me?' he asked.

'I don't know what you mean, sir,' she said, 'but if you give me a few more coins, I'll give you more than just news.'

He needed to know what information she had, and having her clapped in irons would just waste precious time.

'Okay, I don't have any more money here,' he said, 'but if you'll accompany me.'

The woman shook her head and recoiled again, like an alley cat.

'I'm not going nowhere. Meet me in two hours in Plaza de la Cebada, with another bag the same as this, and I'll tell you everything.'

He grabbed her by the arm.

'You'd better be there, because if not, I'll track you down and you'll spend the rest of your life behind bars.'

The whore nodded and, as soon as he released her, she scuttled off into the shadows. Alfredo hurried back to his house and, feeling he had no other option, wrote letters to both Diego and Francisco explaining his predicament and his shame at the fact that they would learn about his secret in this manner. Then he chose two of his most trusted servants to carry the letters, warning them of the possible dangers to which they could be exposed.

He collected the extra money and set out again, attentive to any sign that he was being followed. As he approached the Plaza de la Cebada, he thought to himself that everyone has secrets, even those who hide them from themselves: like Diego, who harboured feelings for his cook, or Don Gabriel, who was in love with a white woman. The question was how to deal with the consequences when such secrets were revealed. He would accept them with his head held high, even if it came to the loss of his friends.

He spotted the whore and she signalled to him to follow. She turned the corner into Calle de la Sierpe, and as he lost sight of her, the idea that the whole thing could be a trap crossed his mind. But it made no sense. All she wanted was money – in fact, if he'd had enough with him when they first met, she would already have spoken to him. And anyway, why go to the effort of arranging his social death if they planned to kill him?

Calle de la Sierpe was a narrow, gloomy street, which dog-legged in the middle. He looked up to see that the woman had stopped at the corner. He glanced either way, nervously, then he saw her face suddenly contract in a grotesque grimace. The tip of a blade poked through her chest, followed by a spurt of blood which splashed the wall. She fell forward, revealing a cloaked figure standing behind her.

The assassin withdrew his sword from the body, which lay prone on the ground, like a puppet whose strings had been cut. Alfredo drew his own sword and charged but the other man stood his ground and parried Alfredo's blow. Alfredo thrust his sword at the man's neck and stomach, but the man had clearly learned his trade on the streets rather than from a master, and crudely but effectively blocked him and launched an attack of his own. Alfredo responded with a quick cut to the man's head. His enemy parried him again and, protecting himself from Alfredo's blade, he thrust at Alfredo's abdomen. Alfredo turned quickly, trying to dodge the steel, but felt it pierce his flesh. He groaned with pain and, without hesitating, struck the man in the chest with the hilt of his sword. But rather than retreating, his attacker charged at him, pushing him back. Alfredo lost his footing on the stony ground and fell backwards. Then, instead of pressing home his advantage, his assailant disappeared into the darkness of the alleyway.

Alfredo got up and touched his side, feeling a deep wound. Then he heard a gurgling sound: the whore was trying to tell him something with her last breath. He brought his ear close to her mouth and, just before she expired, she said, 'El Zurdo, El Zurdo.'

* * *

It was now clear that Don Alfredo didn't carry his sword just for show, so much so that Hernaldo had been forced to wound him in order to save his own skin, despite Don Enrique's express orders not to harm the man. The marquess planned for Alfredo to be exposed as a degenerate, not for him to die in a street brawl. It was only a day since Hernaldo's men had informed him that Don Alfredo had shown up at the Leganitos house asking about the negro's whereabouts. He no doubt already knew that Gabriel had sent a letter to Castamar reporting his findings but that the missive had never arrived. Perhaps Señorita Castro had already told him what she had told Don Gabriel at El Escorial, but whatever the truth of the matter, time was running out. Their only concern had been La Zalamera. If Hernaldo had arrived any later, the whore would have blabbed to the baron and told him everything that had happened at the Zaguán. This time he had El Zurdo – and luck – to thank.

Hernaldo smiled at the memory of El Zurdo's face, his nose flattened and his left cheekbone broken. Since then, the one thought on El Zurdo's mind had been to pay the negro back in person. He had taken a room at the Zaguán where he could be looked after by Jacinta and make the quickest possible recovery. Hernaldo had met with him very early the day before, when the place was still closed to customers. He had wanted to warn El Zurdo that the men he had hired to deal with Don Gabriel needed to keep quiet about it, as Don Alfredo de Carrión was asking awkward questions all over town.

Hernaldo had left but, as he later learned, El Zurdo had then heard some noise from the kitchen. He had waited silently until La Zalamera appeared. When he asked her what she was doing there so early, she had answered that it was her turn to open up that morning. El Zurdo had said nothing and hid his suspicions, but from that point on he didn't take his eyes off her. And so, the next morning he had followed her and observed her visiting

Don Diego's mansion. El Zurdo had tried to get urgent word to Hernaldo to tell him what had happened but had been unable to find him because Hernaldo had been busy spreading leaflets around Madrid printed with the caricature of Don Alfredo and his friend Don Francisco. But this had allowed chance to smile on Hernaldo.

He remembered how El Zurdo had unceremoniously silenced Jacinta when she was about to say something about a job he had done for a rich woman. The reaction had not gone unnoticed at the time, and nor had the scant explanation the thug had offered him. Perhaps it was time to dig deeper. When he had arrived at the Zaguán, the whores told him that El Zurdo was out looking for him, so when he saw Jacinta, he had invited her to follow him upstairs. She had been expecting to do some business, but when she started to remove her corset he had raised his finger to stop her.

'Tell me about that piece of work you were just about to mention when El Zurdo slapped you across the face,' he ordered. She had feigned incomprehension, as if she had no recollection of the conversation. Hernaldo had grabbed her by the throat and slammed her up against the wall.

'Listen carefully,' he said. 'If you don't tell me everything you know, I'll cut you open like a pig.'

Jacinta had nodded in terror and, as soon as he released her, she began to tell a story about something that had happened years ago, about a job El Zurdo had done at Castamar with some horses. She had never met the woman who hired him, but she had spoken to the man who acted as her intermediary. As she described a skinny man with spectacles, Hernaldo realized that El Zurdo had done the dirty on him in some way. He interrupted Jacinta's account to ask her what the man was called. When she struggled to remember, Hernaldo had threatened her again.

'I swear I don't remember!' she cried. 'I don't know. Durán or something like that.'

Terrified, she had told him how she had introduced the clerk to El Zurdo but how the latter had sent her away to avoid cutting her in on the business.

'The son of a bitch,' she said indignantly. 'I found him the job – he could at least have given me something.'

Just then the door had opened and El Zurdo's battered face appeared, asking what the two of them were doing. The two men had stared at each other, their hands on their swords. Hernaldo had considered slitting the man's stomach open there and then, but decided against it. He tossed a few coins onto the bed, declaring that he'd decided to sample Jacinta's wares, and El Zurdo fell silent until the whore, a better liar than him, had shouted at El Zurdo to leave, to stop ruining her business, and to make sure he knocked the next time. That seemed to convince El Zurdo, who had relaxed his stance and told Hernaldo he had some problems with La Zalamera and that, given his condition, it wasn't something he could take care of on his own.

'It was all I could do to get out to look for you,' he panted. 'She's going to mess everything up for a few escudos. She hasn't been here all day because she's been hanging around Don Diego's house.'

Hernaldo had run off in search of her and spied her on the way back. He imagined she had already talked, but cautious as he was, he had decided to make sure. If she'd received her money, she would leave Madrid that night; if not, she still had to meet her paymaster. He followed her from a distance until she disappeared down Calle de la Sierpe. He had gone around the other way and had been in time to see Alfredo approaching from the far end of the alley. And he had rudely interrupted La Zalamera before she had the chance to say so much as a single word to Alfredo.

Just as Alfredo had been unable to save her, so he would be unable to prevent the scandal that was going to break the next day. Don Enrique had come across the man's lover two years ago, almost by chance, during an evening of cards. Don Ignacio, somewhat drunk, had asked for credit, giving his word as a gentleman, and had lost a huge sum. Needless to say, many of those present, including the marquess, had demanded payment. The unfortunate gambler had declared that he could satisfy all his debts, as his benefactor was Don Alfredo de Carrión. That was when the marquess had intervened, buying up the other gamblers' debts and taking Don Ignacio into his confidence.

For a few months, Don Alfredo's lover had found a friend in Don Enrique, who subsidized his gambling and his other vices. The marquess had made it clear that his friendship was above any prejudices and that, while he himself was not that way inclined, he understood that a man must satisfy his desires.

Finally, one night, his tongue loosened by drink, Ignacio had confessed that Don Alfredo had been his lover and that he had letters to prove it. The rest had been quick. Don Enrique had stopped covering Ignacio's gambling expenses so that he was soon deep in debt again. It was no surprise when four ruffians showed up and put the fear of death into him. He had handed over the documents. Then, sometime later, they had snatched him from a brothel one evening and taken him to Don Alfredo's house, where they instructed him to spend the night. It was the best way of ensuring there was a reliable witness. And if he refused, they would kill him, on the orders of their master. That was how scandals worked, like a house of cards: if you didn't keep your mouth closed, or if you put a foot wrong, everything came tumbling down. That was why, after Hernaldo had spoken to Jacinta, he had suspected that the death of Doña Alba had not been the result of her accidentally choosing the wrong horse but, rather, completely intentional. A rich lady, a clerk looking for El Zurdo... Before upsetting Don Enrique, he needed to get the bottom of the affair.

He got home to find that his daughter had already lit the oil lamps and he entered the kitchen just as she was setting out a supper of stewed artichokes, carrots and black bread. When she looked at him, the smile froze on her lips.

'Have you just killed somebody?' she blurted out. He realized that his jerkin, his gloves and his trousers were stained with La Zalamera's blood, and he cursed himself silently.

'Yes,' he replied, bluntly.

She said nothing and served him his supper. He sat and began to eat silently while Adela drew the curtain that divided the room, lay down on the bed and began to sob. It broke his heart to hear her cry and to see that his daughter could not bear this life of his, as a hired killer, slitting some poor unfortunate's · throat one day, doing away with some whore the next, killing an innocent beggar whose only mistake was to be in the wrong place at the wrong time. He went over and sat by her side. But she ignored him.

'I can't change my ways now, my dear. But you have your whole future ahead of you. Maybe it's time for you to stop looking after your father.'

She turned, her jaw clenched, and slapped him as hard as she could. Then she turned away again. He didn't react and simply took her hand, squeezed it for a moment, and returned to the table.

'I'll never leave you,' Adela said from the other side of the curtain. 'And if you tell me to leave again, I'll turn whore, just to punish you.'

That night, Hernaldo could scarcely sleep as the faces of all those he had killed paraded before him. Lying in the darkness, he looked into their sunken eyes and told himself that, sooner or later, he would join them in the fires of hell. Then, thinking about what he would do to El Zurdo if the man confirmed his suspicions, he fell asleep, hoping that by the morning his dark mood would have lifted.

38

Same day, 23 October 1721

Gusts of wind shook the glass in the windowpanes and the inclement weather seemed to be trying to force its way in through the cracks and the chimneys. Clara had regained consciousness the previous day, waking up to find Don Diego by her side, his beard unkempt and clearly worried about her.

According to Elisa, she had been delirious, her pulse low and her temperature through the roof ever since her rescue. She could barely remember what had happened after exiting the coach and fainting. The only image she had was of the open countryside beneath an unabating storm, her wits unravelling with every lightning strike. Her last memory was of Don Diego appearing. After that there persisted only the nonsensical, fractured visions that had continued to visit her during her convalescence: angels of death with the deformed faces of her late father, her mother, her sister, Doña Ursula and even Señora Moncada from the hospital. But the image of Don Diego had risen above them all, anchoring her body to life like Atlas bearing the world upon his shoulders. He had mopped her brow, held her hand and even knelt in prayer at her feet, though it was well known that his lordship had not prayed since his beloved wife's death. Don Diego had shown immeasurable concern for her, treating her as if she was the daughter of Doctor Belmonte and not his cook.

This fact struck her even more when, after dining on chicken consommé with egg and rice prepared by Carmen del

Castillo, she had realized that she was resting in the duke's private chambers. The first thought she had was of the servants. Without doubt, the rumours would already be flying. It was not until the next morning that Elisa, carrying a silver tray with hot chocolate, some boiled eggs and some freshly baked rolls, had given her the full story.

The moment he had learned of her departure, the duke had left in search of her, and when he arrived the following day, carrying her in his arms, he had given express orders to accommodate her in his own bedroom, which had caused great commotion.

'They say he's in love with you,' her friend said with a half-smile. 'Everyone is up in arms about it.'

Clara did not reply, as she battled with conflicting emotions. She had sworn she would forget Don Diego forever and did not know what to make of the fact that he had gone out to look for her, rescued her and nursed her in his bedroom. On the one hand, she told herself, the duke had behaved entirely like a gentleman, going above and beyond what was demanded by good manners. On the other hand, he had also previously allowed her to be tarnished without lifting a finger in her defence. If he had previously disappointed her by allowing Don Enrique to publicly disrespect her, he had now definitively shown his feelings for her, even if these went beyond those which her social position permitted him to feel.

With Elisa's help, she had washed and put on a clean nightgown, and returned to a fresh bed with clean sheets. Outside, the last rays of sunlight had afforded a view of the tops of the poplars swaying in the wind, and she felt just like them, moving back and forth between her feelings and her reason. Her desire to see Don Diego, to thank him for saving her life and for his dedication and care, made the promise she had made herself, to forget him, even harder to keep. She knew exactly where this desire came from. It was a place she didn't even want to look, a place Don Diego had infiltrated without her realizing, a dangerous place where no one had been allowed to enter since her father's death and she feared she would be left exposed, both as a woman and as his servant. And yet, every time someone knocked at the door, she anxiously hoped it was the duke, despite denying to herself that she wanted to see him. Night had fallen as slowly as the day had passed and she dined in a silence that was broken only by the crackling of the logs in the fireplace. When the servants had withdrawn, she had taken refuge under the sheets, overcome by exhaustion.

At nearly eleven o'clock, she had heard two knocks at the door. Don Diego had appeared, freshly shaved and smelling of lavender.

'If you will allow me,' he said, taking her hand. 'Before anything else, I wish to apologize for not having visited you this morning, but I had to leave for El Escorial. My brother has been missing for days, and so has Don Alfredo, who went out looking for him, and I felt compelled to see if someone might give me any information. Unfortunately, I haven't found much.'

'Don't apologize, your grace,' she said. 'Your brother and your dear friend must come first. You've already done so much by looking after me with such care and attention. You don't know how grateful I am.'

'Señorita Belmonte, I am the one who is grateful that you are once again among us, and it is I who must apologize for the shameful treatment to which you were subjected as a result of my foolish pride.'

She was about to reply when he interrupted her.

'I wish to speak first, and I would be very appreciative if you would be so kind as to listen all the way through,' he said in a conciliatory tone. 'I don't expect you to forgive the lack of courtesy I showed towards you, but at the very least I hope you will let me repair the damage I have caused. In my admittedly feeble defence, I should say that nothing would have given me more pleasure than to defend you before Don Enrique, but there were two reasons for my not doing so. The first is that he is not my friend, quite the opposite. In fact, it was my pride which led me to take part in his stupid bet, without foreseeing the consequences it would have for you.'

She frowned to hear him speak so categorically. She had taken it for granted that Enrique was his friend and that he had taken part in that pantomime because, as a noble, he was blind to the suffering of the less fortunate classes.

'Don Enrique was invited here at my mother's express wishes, for she has been taken in by his good manners, but I have reason to believe he seeks to harm me, to harm Castamar and possibly those close to me as well. It's quite likely that he is behind my brother's disappearance. My intention in not defending you publicly was to avoid displaying the deep feelings I harbour for you. My indifference was intended only to protect you from any malicious intentions Don Enrique might harbour towards me.

'The second reason,' he continued, 'is that I did not find out about Don Enrique's shameless behaviour towards you until I read your note. Had I known, you can be sure that I would not have let that act go unpunished, nor would I have hesitated to show my feelings in public. Be that as it may, there is no possible excuse for my unforgivable crime of not defending you, and especially of exposing you to that stupid bet. As you put it so eloquently, any decent gentleman would know that. I must tell you that all those present, especially Don Alfredo, who was the one who suggested the bet, have told me how much they regret what happened, and have asked me to seek your forgiveness on their part.'

She nodded without taking her eyes off him, and a silence settled between them. Her voice cracked and her nerves took hold of her stomach.

'Your grace, in the first place, I must thank you for saving my life, and at the same time, once again, I ask your forgiveness for my show of disrespect that night, when I raised my voice. I was stupid not to let you explain yourself. I'm sure that, if I had, none of this would have happened,' she said. 'So, there is no need for me to forgive you. No servant in my position could have a better master.'

'You are not just a servant,' he said. 'At least not to me.'

They sat there like statues, their hands joined, enveloped in a dense cloud of delicious discomfort and stillness. Don Diego's tranquil face transported her back to those days when she used to dance minuets in the ballrooms of high society, to the polite manners of the court and the lack of concern for tomorrow she had once felt, a tranquillity long forgotten owing to her need for survival. However, she had to remain cautious, since although he had said he harboured deep feelings towards her, once she opened her heart, she would not be able to close it.

She was conscious that they had not taken their eyes off each other during the whole of that silent interlude.

'You have the most intense gaze I have ever seen in a man, your grace,' she declared, unable to control her thoughts.

'I am only returning yours,' he replied, smiling.

She was overcome by fear, aware that if she continued down this road it would condemn her to social ostracism. She was about to look away when he took her chin gently in his fingers and forced her to keep looking at him.

'I'm not afraid of anything,' he said. 'If you so permit it, I will never leave you.'

Then he very slowly moved closer and she closed her eyes, allowing herself to be carried away by her most profound desires. But, just as his lips were brushing against hers, there were two sharp knocks at the door.

Doña Ursula appeared at the door.

'I'm sorry to bother you, your grace, but a letter has arrived from Don Alfredo and I thought you would want to see it immediately.'

The housekeeper then turned her gaze towards Clara.

'I'm very happy your health has improved,' she said to Clara, who returned her gaze and thanked her with a gesture. 'We all want you to recover fully and be back in the kitchen soon,' she added.

Clara did not answer. Don Diego said the housekeeper could go and leave the letter in his office. He would follow immediately after. The housekeeper curtseyed and left.

Clara waited a few seconds to make sure Doña Ursula was not listening in on their conversation and looked at Don Diego, whose face had changed since he had heard the news of Don Alfredo's message. She gulped before telling him that, in her opinion, it was best she move to her own quarters tomorrow. He nodded, understanding the delicate situation she found herself in.

'I do not expect good news from this letter, and I fear I shall have to depart imminently,' he revealed. 'But when I return, by which point I hope you will be much recovered, I would like to have a private conversation with you.'

Clara could only agree, repressing a burning impulse to ask him to kiss her again.

Don Diego got up and bade farewell.

Then Clara remained alone, scarcely able to believe that he might soon ask for her hand in marriage. She got carried away with this thought, imagining a life that was not hers among the immense corridors of Castamar, with gatherings at the Buen Retiro Palace and visits to the Alcázar. She saw herself, as if in a dream, dancing with the duke. *Not in his wildest dreams could my father have hoped for such a marriage*, she thought, *and with no dowry whatsoever*.

A smile was settling on her face when she heard raised voices. She swore she could hear two people having a heated argument on the lower floors. Her smile disappeared completely and the weight of reality flattened her against the sheets. On the one hand, she felt scared and confused, completely overwhelmed by the thought of the conversation she was going to have with the duke upon his return. On the other hand, she was striving to contain a sense of excitement she had not felt in years. If she was the subject of that argument, it meant that the duke did not care one bit about her social status, nor the fact that she was his servant; it meant that Don Diego was so courageous, he was willing to put his lineage under scrutiny. She prayed that only she, and not all of the servants, had heard those shouts. Suddenly, she felt the dam inside her break, and she could no longer hold back her feelings. She began to weep, fully aware, at last, that she was hopelessly in love with him.

39

Same day, 23 October 1721

Ursula paced the corridors, thinking to herself that if Doña Alba could see how the duke had allowed himself to be bewitched by the good manners of a cook, she would disown him. Ursula might have understood such weakness in another man, but not in Don Diego, whom she had always looked up to. She had been a fool, an innocent unable to read the feelings of those around her. She, who prided herself on ruling over others, had been defeated by her own blindness. Clara Belmonte had clearly won the duke's heart. If she had suspected as much when his lordship had set off after her like a dog pursuing a bitch on heat, without a thought for the memory of his deceased wife, it was now beyond any doubt.

When she had gone up to Don Diego's chambers with news of the letter, she had seen and heard more than she would have wished. She had been about to knock on the door but it was already ajar and she had witnessed the encounter between Clara Belmonte and his lordship, heard him declare that he would never leave her and seen him move closer to kiss her. The thought that the cook might become the mistress of Castamar had been enough to impel her to interrupt. But that was not the worst of it.

After she had taken her leave of the duke and Señorita Belmonte, she had closed the door and pretended to depart, taking only a few steps down the corridor before returning on tiptoe and pressing her ear to the door to hear the duke promise to talk to the cook about the matter again within a few days. She knew Don Diego sufficiently well to know that, if he gave his word that he would marry Clara Belmonte, nothing on earth would stop him, and this would herald disaster for Castamar. Furthermore, judging from the cook's response when he had been about to kiss her, Clara Belmonte did not harbour any intention of rejecting him. If Ursula didn't take action, it would not be long before the Belmontes were parading around as if they owned the place. A cook would be responsible for perpetuating the Castamar name!

And so, she hurried along, a feeling of nausea rising within her. When she reached her room, she locked the door, pulled out the clean basin from beneath the bed and threw up her supper. Then she lay down and tried to calm her breathing. She was furious with herself for having concentrated on her struggle with Don Melquíades and for having been unaware of what the cook was up to. Recovering her jurisdiction over the kitchen would be of little comfort if Clara Belmonte were to become the mistress of the whole house. She had to find allies who also understood the danger that threatened Castamar. Since she herself had no power to prevent the marriage, she needed to find someone who did.

But then she suddenly remembered that there was indeed someone who might understand the misfortune that threatened Castamar's good name, someone who wielded influence over the duke: Doña Mercedes. She had to go about it carefully. She couldn't just go to her and tell her she had been eavesdropping on her son's private conversation. She had to make it look more spontaneous, so that she would not be accused of indiscretion. She sighed and set off in search of the duchess. She was sure she would find her playing pontoon with Don Enrique. She climbed the stairs to the second floor. On her way, she came across a few servants finishing off their duties. She barely paid them any attention, although she could not help noticing that some of them scuttled away from her, perhaps fearing she would assign them some fresh task. She finally reached the oriental salon, which was so called because it was decorated with objects and furniture from China.

She knocked and Doña Mercedes invited her to enter. The housekeeper greeted her courteously and asked if the duchess required anything before Ursula retired for the evening. Doña Mercedes, squinting at her cards by the light of the oil lamp, waved her hand to indicate that the housekeeper was free to go. Ursula thanked her and then, as planned, informed her that the duke had received a letter from Don Alfredo and that it might bring good news about Don Gabriel. Both of the card players looked up, Doña Mercedes with a worried look and the marquess with an impassive expression that she could not interpret.

'When did this letter arrive?' Don Enrique asked.

'Just a few minutes ago. I had to interrupt the' – she paused briefly, as if searching for the right word – 'conversation his lordship was having with Señorita Belmonte when I informed him in his chambers.'

Doña Mercedes stood up to go and look for him, ignoring the housekeeper's brief silence. Ursula thought her ploy had failed, but just then the marquess's voice brought Doña Mercedes to an abrupt halt.

'What kind of conversation did you interrupt, exactly?'

Ursula remained silent, as the man was not her master and she owed him no obedience in the presence of Doña Mercedes. The duchess's expression changed completely as she understood that the scene the housekeeper had witnessed had not been a mere courtesy visit to a convalescent.

'You may answer, Señora Berenguer,' she said.

Ursula pretended that she did not wish to be indiscreet. 'It is a private matter and is not for me to judge,' she replied.

'Not for you perhaps, but for the duchess it certainly is,' Don Enrique said. 'Speak up now.'

Again, she remained silent, aware that the longer she withheld the information, the more power her words would have when she finally spoke. Just as she had hoped, Doña Mercedes, fearing what her silence concealed, ordered her to recount everything she had heard or seen, as the future of Castamar itself could be at stake.

'Señora Berenguer,' she said, her chin trembling, 'nobody will question your discretion as you are obeying my direct order and I was the duchess here long before my son became duke.'

Pretending to give in, Ursula told everything: the unconditional declaration, the approach to kiss, the veiled hint at marriage. Doña Mercedes had to sit down at the news, and when she had finished, the housekeeper repeated that she had heard everything by chance, as the door was ajar. To her astonishment, the marquess then gave her two silver reals and thanked her for her services.

'I imagine this will be satisfactory recompense,' he said.

She took a step back, barely able to contain her indignation as the colour left her lips. Then, to the nobleman's surprise, she fixed him with an icy stare.

'I am afraid I cannot accept, even if by so doing I risk offending you. My interest was none other than to protect his lordship,' she declared.

The marquess laughed in surprise and took back the money.

'For heaven's sake, Enrique! Señora Berenguer is not that kind of servant,' Doña Mercedes said. 'Don't worry, my dear, you have acted in the interests of Castamar this evening.'

Then Doña Mercedes began to sob uncontrollably, as if the disappearance of her son Gabriel, combined with what she had just heard, would be enough to finish her off. Ursula understood that the duchess imagined herself the victim of whispered gossip and withering stares due to the duke's impulsiveness. Don Enrique consoled her.

'Your son must be very troubled if he is losing his head over a cook,' he said.

Doña Mercedes stood up and threw the cards to the floor.

'I don't care how troubled he is. It's time for you to act, Don Enrique,' she declared as she made for the door. 'Señora Berenguer. As soon as she recovers you must secure a private audience for the marquess with the cook. We can only trust that, if I am unable to convince my son of his madness, Don Enrique can make the young woman understand the disgrace she would bring to Castamar. You will do it for me, for all your years of loyalty, for Castamar and, of course, for Doña Alba, who will always be irreplaceable.'

All doubt was now dispelled. Mention of Doña Alba had been enough to make Ursula's heart swell with pride at doing the right thing. *One must assist their lordships in so far as one can, even if that means helping them to rectify their own mistakes*, she told herself.

Doña Mercedes left in search of her son, and Ursula followed behind at a discreet distance, knowing that mother and son were about to have a showdown and that both her own fate and that of Castamar hung on the outcome. She suspected that the marquess and the duchess had already spoken about what to do in such a situation and deduced that she had simply prompted them into action. Doña Mercedes asked where her son was and was told that he was in the armoury. She went straight there, aware that Ursula was following close behind. She descended the stairs in a fury and flung the doors open. Don Diego appeared to be preparing to leave, even though night had long since fallen. Ursula stopped outside and pressed herself up against the wall.

'You've lost your mind!' Doña Mercedes shouted at the duke.

'Please, Mother. Not now. I have to leave for Madrid.'

'Do you think it makes me proud to see my son running after a cook?'

'Mother, that's enough,' he replied.

'No! Do you expect me to remain silent while you make a fool of yourself?' she said, standing in his way.

Don Diego, shaking his head, again told her to drop the subject.

'Do you think I'm saying it because of that poor thing who was on the verge of death? I'm saying it for you. If they find out at court—'

'Enough!' he said, banging the table. 'I have to go to Madrid! It's vital that—'

He was interrupted by a slap from the duchess. Peering from her vantage point, the housekeeper saw Don Diego clench his jaw in fury.

'Don't you shout at me, Diego de Castamar!' the duchess cried. 'I am your mother, and you owe me respect.'

The duke clenched his fists and shook his head. But the duchess continued.

'You're going to listen to every last word I have to say,' Doña Mercedes hissed. 'You endangered the name of your father and of this house when you decided not to remarry, you endangered it when you ran after the cook, and you will be endangering it again if you insist on your foolishness. She isn't even young! She might not even be able to bear children. Or perhaps she'll only give you daughters, like her mother! Have you thought about that? If you marry her, what will become of the Castamar name?'

'Well, you'd better pray that she can bear children, because she represents the only chance of our line being continued!' he thundered.

'Not like this, Diego. You weren't bequeathed the legacy of generations for this!'

'Enough! I am the Duke of Castamar!' he shouted. 'I will decide the future of our name, like my father before me, and I swear to God that if she accepts me, Clara Belmonte will be my wife and I won't let anyone stand in my way, not even you!'

A frosty silence descended. The only sound was the duke's agitated breathing as he continued to make his preparations. Ursula realized it would not be good if Don Diego found her there, and so she took refuge in a nearby cupboard. Following the conversation between the duke and his mother, her only hope lay in the possibility that the Marquess de Soto would make Clara Belmonte see reason and understand that such a marriage would only bring destruction to Castamar.

'Mother, I must leave for Madrid,' Don Diego said, breaking the silence. 'From the note I have just received, I fear that everything that is happening is the product of Don Enrique's sick mind.'

'Don Enrique is a loyal friend who—'

'Don't defend him,' he interrupted. 'It's clear he planned the attack on Señorita Castro, the disappearance of Gabriel, and Don Alfredo's impending fall from grace. And I'm not alone in that view. Gabriel thought so too, as did others,' he concluded, holding out Don Alfredo's letter. 'Don't blame yourself too much, Mother. I permitted the marquess to continue to visit us because I wanted to keep him close. I don't have any proof and nor, apparently, does anyone else. However, I no longer need it.' And with that he swept out of the armoury.

Ursula waited until he had left before emerging from her hiding place, and inside the armoury, she saw Doña Mercedes leaning against the wall, clutching the letter from Don Alfredo de Carrión in her shaking hands. Ursula, feeling terribly sorry for her, knocked on the door to offer consolation.

'The best you can do, mistress, is go to bed and rest,' she suggested.

Doña Mercedes drew herself up to her full height. Ursula sensed that what mattered to her most was leaving that room with her dignity intact.

'You may retire when you wish, Señora Berenguer,' she said, 'you have done enough work for one day.'

Ursula waited until the duchess left and then tidied the room, which had been disordered by the duke's display of rage. She didn't want the armourer to be alarmed the next day and think the place had been ransacked by thieves. That was when she noticed Don Alfredo's letter lying on the floor. She picked it up and looked nervously around her. She read the first page, in which the nobleman described his visit to El Escorial, the disappearance of Gabriel, his suspicions regarding Don Enrique de Arcona, the conversation with Amelia and the meeting with a whore who had promised to give him information, of which he hoped to write later. The next page outlined a rather different question.

What I am now about to write is the most difficult thing I have ever written in my life. Despite my shame and embarrassment, the time has now come for me to be candid with you and with Francisco, to whom I have sent a similar letter. Tomorrow at dawn all Madrid, including the king, the queen and the entire court, will be made aware of some letters which I once sent to the only person I have ever loved in my life, and to whom I will always regret having given my affections. To my discredit before God, this person was a man, Don Ignacio del Monte. This secret is one that has accompanied me throughout my life, and in a sense, now that it is to be published, I feel relieved to be able to share it with you. I will not deny it and nor will I hide. I have done that for too long, although I have never been a coward. However, I will understand if you do not wish to see or speak to me, as I would understand the same reaction from your mother, whom I know will suffer at this news, for the affection which she holds for me.

I must alert you to the fact that, only two days ago, while you were out searching for Señorita Belmonte, Don Enrique and I held a tense conversation in which I accused him of not knowing love. His reply made me suspect that he knew my secret. It is very likely that it is he who has circulated the letters. I know this is not conclusive evidence, but it certainly points in that direction. If this is the case, I fear that Francisco may also be subject to some kind of machination, although I do not know what motive might push that man to conspire against you and against us.

Your true and loyal friend,

Don Alfredo de Carrión, Baron of Aguasdulces

Postscriptum: Do not forget to communicate to Señorita Belmonte my most sincere apologies for the rudeness to which she was exposed on my account. We humans are fickle creatures, condemned to say one thing and do another. As soon as I obtain the information from the harlot, I will send you a second letter.

Ursula shuddered when she finished reading. Now she could better interpret the look Don Enrique had given her when she had reported the arrival of a letter from Don Alfredo. That cold stare, the look of a merciless predator, might have indicated his concern that his plans had gone awry. Perhaps Don Alfredo's letter might even endanger him. If the marquess desired the downfall of the house of Castamar and its allies, then he had severely underestimated Doña Ursula. She might be a simple housekeeper, but she would do anything to protect the legacy of Doña Alba and Don Diego.

She folded the letter and extinguished the lamps. Then she closed the door and turned to find Don Enrique standing right in front of her. Ursula had the sense that, if she had eavesdropped on the conversation between Don Diego and his mother, then the marquess must have spied on them all from some other vantage point. She curtseyed and was about to leave when he stopped her.

'Give me that letter,' he said, holding out his hand.

'I'm afraid it is not addressed to you, sir,' she answered, jutting her chin defiantly.

'I know it is not for me,' he said, 'but give it to me regardless.'

The marquess looked at her as if she was an insignificant bug that he could crush, and she glared back defiantly. She waited for a moment, then stepped closer so that their faces were only inches apart.

'No,' she answered, resolutely.

Don Enrique gave a twisted smile as he considered that he could have her snuffed out with a mere click of his fingers.

With the image of Doña Alba in her head, she wordlessly

declared that she would not cede to his demands, and she certainly would not allow herself to be intimidated. The marquess raised his stick threateningly. She looked at him with disdain.

'You can hit me if you want. It won't be the first time a man has done so, but the last time a nobleman touched one of his lordship's servants, he was beaten to within an inch of his life,' she said icily.

He laughed dismissively and turned to set off upstairs. Anyone would have thought he was victorious, as if the interest he had shown in that letter were of no importance.

'If I had been better acquainted with you sooner, Señora Berenguer,' he said, over his shoulder, 'I would have done anything to have you in my service. You are quite formidable!'

His laughter receded down the corridor and the housekeeper had to stop to regain her breath before continuing on her way. She realized that the marquess was not just an illustrious nobleman dedicated to a life of leisure. And she had a familiar, bitter sensation, born from her fear that the plots of Don Enrique and the love that Don Diego felt for Señorita Belmonte could bring an end to the life she knew at Castamar. She tried to shoo the sensation away, but the more she tried to do so, the tighter its hold on her became.

Upon reaching her bedroom, she undressed quickly. She checked that the door was locked, as if in doing so she could rid herself of the sense that the ghost of her husband had been following her, like a silent fox, along the corridors of Castamar. She got into bed and pulled the blankets tight around her. Curled up in the dim light of an oil lamp, she lay there haunted by the idea that her husband was calling to her from the past, warning her that the life of fear she had known with him could return at any moment.

24 October 1721

That Monday night, after Francisco's arrival at the Montejo estate, Sol had eagerly received him in her bedroom, and that encounter was followed by others: the next day at midday, during the afternoon siesta, and at night. He was more solicitous than ever, showering her with attention when they were out walking, at the dining table, or fishing. But that idyll had come to a sudden end with the arrival of Don Alfredo's letter. In it, he wrote that his sexual preferences had been revealed and that the whole court knew of Don Alfredo's inclinations. He also reported his suspicion that Don Enrique might be intriguing against Francisco.

'That bastard Don Enrique is behind all of this,' he had said out loud.

'You don't know that, my darling,' she responded. 'You can't accuse a marquess without proof.'

'It was him. He's been conspiring against Castamar for some time, and also, it appears, against the rest of us.'

Francisco's outburst had left her profoundly worried. She was caught between seeking a solution that would salvage their relationship, and concern at the thought that Francisco might come to harm if he confronted the most dangerous man she had ever met.

'I don't know what to do,' Francisco said. 'I don't wish to see Alfredo again, but I also feel I should go to Madrid immediately in case Diego needs my help.'

'I'm sure Don Diego would write to you if that was the case,' she said, kissing him on the lips. 'Wait for things to calm down and for your nerves to settle before you go back. You can't think clearly in the heat of the moment.'

Sol knew only too well that, if he travelled to Madrid, he would discover that it was she who had helped to sully his reputation.

'Whatever happens in Madrid, I won't abandon you. I will always be by your side,' she said.

'Thank you,' he replied. 'Thank you for not using this as a weapon in our silly power games.'

'I would never do such a thing,' she responded. 'Not with something so serious. Let's stay here. Madrid will be waiting for you once the storm has passed. Don Alfredo hasn't done you any favours by hiding his vice.'

Finally, she had found a man whom she could trust, and now he was about to slip from her grasp. She understood that the marquess's strategy would completely destroy Francisco. The deep friendship that bound him to Don Alfredo would prevent him from defending the words she herself had written to Don Enrique. It was not some trifling blackmail in which there were competing versions of the same event, as she had naively thought, imagining she would be able to make her excuses to Francisco, claiming she had only written that defamatory letter under duress, threatened by Don Enrique and his sinister lackey. Now she realized he would never believe her. He knew her well enough to know that nobody could have forced her in such a fashion, that she had been willingly involved in the plot in some way. It would be of no avail to explain to Francisco that she knew nothing of his friend's inclinations or of the implications for him. He wouldn't listen to her. And yet, she was desperate to hold him close, to keep him away from Madrid for as long as possible, clinging to that which she had already lost.

Damn the marquess, she thought to herself. *I hope he dies a slow and painful death.* She suspected that Don Enrique's plans for Castamar were wider and more ambitious than he had let on, and involved ruining all the duke's friends into the bargain. However, the duke had the favour of the Crown and belonged to one of the most powerful and influential families in Spain.

She lay back and, giving in to a sense of defeat, went over the day's events in her mind.

Francisco scarcely spoke for the rest of the day and, as the hours passed, his countenance became sadder and sadder.

She had hoped he would awaken from his siesta in better spirits. But her own sense of guilt made it impossible for her to cheer him up. They barely spoke; he just lay there, his head in her lap, while she stroked his hair. Unable to contain her sadness any longer, she began to weep silently. And she knew that her tears were the result not just of her having betrayed and manipulated the only man she had ever loved but also of her grief for what she had become. Her soul was empty, deformed by her own greed, vengefulness and resentment. She couldn't bear to look into his eyes. She knew that in his countenance she would see her own reflection, looking back at her, telling her she was a murderess, someone who brought nothing but destruction to those around her.

40

Same day, 24 October 1721

Diego removed his leather coat and enquired after his friend. Alfredo's butler looked evasive but said nothing, leading the duke to fear that Alfredo might have had an accident.

'Tell me!' Diego said.

'He's been wounded, but… your grace, he has made it clear he does not wish to see anyone,' he answered.

Diego looked at the servant and, pushing him aside with his stick, advanced down the corridor.

'Alfredo,' he thundered while the butler followed behind, trying to dissuade him. 'Alfredo!'

'Your grace, he gave me this note outlining his investigations for you,' the servant was saying from behind.

Diego ignored him and continued to stride down the corridor, with a determined look in his eyes. He would not leave without seeing his friend, especially when he had been wounded due to his involvement in an affair relating to Castamar. After the argument with his mother and his departure from Castamar, he had reached the Madrid mansion with a broken heart. Discovering his friend's weakness had made such a deep impression on him that he had had to stop his horse halfway through the journey to take a breath. The worst would come tomorrow, when all of Madrid would point the finger at Alfredo for having illicit relations with another man. For his part, he could not help but have conflicted feelings. On the one hand, it went against the laws of society, God and all reason, and forced the affected man to live a secret double life. He couldn't even imagine what it was to feel desire for another man's body. On the other hand, he loved Alfredo like a brother, and nothing would ever change that. And so, he headed down the corridor towards his friend's room, calling out his name. He turned the handle despite the butler's hesitance and marched in.

'Why can't you respect anything I ask of you? Don't you understand the shame I feel, Diego? I can barely look you in the eye,' Alfredo said. 'I've hidden this secret about my nature, which only makes me hate myself, which has made me live in perpetual fear and...'

Alfredo could not continue, his words remaining stuck in his throat. Diego walked over and embraced him.

'Though I do not understand your inclination, I will never abandon you,' Diego declared. 'I won't stop being your friend because of this.'

Alfredo nodded without looking at him.

'Thank you, Diego,' he said, utterly embarrassed. 'I know it's hard to understand. Even for me sometimes. My unnatural inclination is... a desire similar to what you would feel towards a woman.'

'I only ask that, if you have ever felt attracted to me, or if such a thing were to happen in the future, then you must never even speak of it,' Diego said, stammering for the first time in his life, his face bright red.

'Diego, that has never happened, and it never will. I think of you as a brother,' Alfredo reassured him. 'You should stay away from me,' he went on. 'I'm a social outcast, and if you stick with me, your reputation—'

'Quiet, now,' Diego replied. 'I'm about to propose to my cook, it can't get much worse than that.'

Alfredo shook his head and said his friend was mad as he rested on the divan, his wound clearly troubling him. Diego just smiled and told him he would find a way for the marriage offer not to harm his family's reputation too much.

'I am going to re-establish the prestige of the Belmonte family,' he declared. 'I want her to be given a title first.'

'Good God, Diego, a title? She's a cook!' his friend exclaimed softly. 'May I know how you are going to achieve such a thing?'

'I don't know yet, Alfredo. But I do know that she wasn't always a cook,' Diego replied.

'I fear that, with my reputation being dragged through the streets of Madrid, I will be of little help to you.'

'Thank you, my friend, but you've already been a great help,' he said, looking over at the wound to Alfredo's ribs.

'It's nothing, a scratch,' Alfredo lied.

Diego pretended to believe him.

'What did you find out?'

Alfredo stirred on the divan and asked for something to eat. Then he narrated in full detail his encounter on Calle de la Sierpe and his duel with the prostitute's murderer. During her last moments, La Zalamera had mentioned a person called El Zurdo. That name meant nothing to him, although he was sure he would be found at the Zaguán. He was convinced that the letter Gabriel had received at El Escorial had caused him to fall into a trap laid at the brothel. According to the late Daniel Forrado, one of the marquess's men – called Hernaldo – always met local assassins there. It was clear that this den of iniquity held secrets which he needed to access.

Diego felt that both he and Alfredo should rest, so he went to one of his friend's bedrooms. He gave instructions that he be woken early, since he wished to visit the Zaguán and track down El Zurdo.

He woke up feeling nervous and out of sorts, having barely rested. His dreams faded quickly in contrast to the waking visions of his lost brother's face and the memory of his own frustrated kiss with Clara Belmonte. This last image had remained with him, and he had been reaching his hand over the bedcovers and whispering Clara's name when he had realized that a servant was knocking at the door. He judged from the light filtering in through the curtains that they had woken him a little earlier than he had requested. He told the servant to come in, and was informed that there was a young lady in the drawing room who wished to see him. To begin with, she had asked for Don Alfredo, but when she discovered Don Diego was there she had preferred to speak to him directly. Intrigued, Diego put on one of his friend's robes and went down to see who it was. To his surprise, it was Señorita Castro, who curtseyed in greeting.

'I apologize for visiting you at such an ungodly hour.'

'Not at all,' Diego replied as he returned her greeting.

'My concern for Don Gabriel's safety and the things I know have impelled me to return to Madrid rather than conclude my journey to Cadiz,' she said.

He offered her a seat and expressed his condolences for her mother's recent death. Settling on one of the sofas, she thanked him with a sad smile, through which he could glimpse a soul tormented by guilt and sorrow. Her eyelashes fluttered again just as they had when they were both at Villacor and she had almost come clean with him. Something in Amelia had changed, and Diego felt that the scar on her face had become a doorway to her soul. Seeing that she was not quite ready to talk, Diego offered her some breakfast.

'I thank you, but I don't have much of an appetite, your grace,' she said.

Diego waited a few moments to allow Señorita Castro to find sufficient courage to tell her story. Finally, she was able to tell the truth: her plan to marry him, the nature of her relationship with Don Enrique and the way that man had bribed and coerced her to seduce Don Diego at all costs. Diego admired her courage for revealing the facts without trying to present herself as a victim.

'To start with, I was only looking for a husband in order to survive, but once I had become reacquainted with you, I would never have been able to deceive you had it not been for the fact that Don Enrique was threatening to kill my mother and me. That was why I was forced to keep quiet. I'm certain Don Enrique was behind my assault, in the hope that it would ensure my return to Castamar, and I fear that your brother's disappearance is also his handiwork,' she said, trembling with fear. 'Your grace is surely aware that Don Alfredo came to visit me, and I preferred not to tell him, foolishly thinking that to do so would result in Gabriel being murdered. If that did happen...' She fell silent for a moment, trying not to be overcome by tears. 'I couldn't bear Gabriel dying. I'm sorry.'

Diego, who had not said a word for the duration of her speech, stood up slowly, observing her still-trembling figure on the sofa. He took her hands and gently made her get up so that he could look her in the eye.

'Señorita Castro, I am deeply grateful for your honesty. It can't have been easy, and I want you to know that I am proud to count you as a friend,' he declared.

He embraced her, and at that point she let the tears flow as she repeated that she would never have forgiven herself if something bad had happened to him because of her silence.

'As far as I know, Don Enrique is still at Castamar, but you must stay away from him. For your peace of mind, I will send an armed guard to your house,' Diego said.

She remained in his arms for a while, her breathing unsteady, wanting to feel protected. Finally, she stepped back, looked at him and kissed him on the cheek as she implored him to find Don Gabriel, for there was no better man in all the world. In the gaps between her words, he could see that Señorita Castro had deep feelings for his brother, feelings she doubtless had not revealed to herself. *When we are in love, we are blind to our own feelings*, he thought to himself. *We will deny it until it's obvious that we are making fools of ourselves by hiding it.*

Although Señorita Castro had revealed a great deal regarding the marquess's intentions to cause harm to Castamar, he still knew nothing about Don Enrique's motives. It didn't matter

– that foolish popinjay had crossed a line and would pay with his life.

After saying goodbye to Señorita Castro, he breakfasted with Alfredo and told him of his plans to go to the brothel in search of El Zurdo. As if propelled by a spring, Alfredo looked up from his boiled egg and wiped his lips with a napkin.

'I won't let you go alone,' he declared.

Diego did not respond immediately, but simply looked at him as he sipped his coffee.

'You cannot come, but don't worry, I shall not go alone,' he said. 'I intend to go to the barracks at the Puerta de Conde Duque. I'm going to gather some of my most faithful men and shut down that stinking pit,' he concluded.

Hearing this, Alfredo understood that his friend would not make a false step and relaxed a little. After finishing off his coffee, Diego asked his friend to write to Francisco immediately. The last he had heard from him was that he had left Doña Sol's villa with their mutual friend Leonor. Although Francisco had insisted Diego send a letter if Gabriel was not found, Diego had not done so, thinking it would be of little help now that he was less than one day's journey from the capital. Even so, Francisco had already to some extent been informed, for in the letter revealing his predilections and the scandal, Alfredo had also expressed his initial suspicions.

'I will write to him again,' Alfredo said, a look of resignation on his face. Diego suspected he was suffering because of the lack of news from his friend. 'I don't know if you have read the letter I sent you three days ago, but Don Enrique is a very real danger, and I will not stop until everyone knows it.'

Diego said goodbye to his friend with a heartfelt hug and mounted his horse.

As he rode, he considered his next movements, aware that, if he did not put a stop to Don Enrique's plotting, he and all those he cherished would be ruined. He told himself that, whatever happened, he would go that night to the Zaguán and find answers regarding Gabriel, even if it meant laying waste to half of Lavapiés.

El Zurdo was waiting for someone else to finish with Jacinta. He had spent all day looking for her, finally locating her in the yard behind the Zaguán.

After the beating he had received from Don Gabriel, he had taken one of the bedrooms at the Zaguán so that Jacinta could look after him. *That whore must be good for something beyond fornicating*, he had thought. During his convalescence he had caught La Zalamera listening in on things that weren't her business. By noon that day, as he was returning to Madrid after enjoying acting out his revenge on the negro, news was already spreading that La Zalamera had been found dead and disembowelled on Calle de la Sierpe. It was only what she deserved. *That's whores for you*, Zurdo thought. *Treacherous rats*.

He hoped that Jacinta would be different, that she hadn't run her mouth off, because if she had, he'd slash her to pieces. He wanted her to explain what she had been doing with Hernaldo de la Marca when he had told her not to go near him; he couldn't get it out of his head. The only thing that calmed him was telling himself that if the soldier knew he had betrayed them all for money with the business of the horses at Castamar, the man would have shown up immediately.

When he had been unable to locate the harlot earlier, he had chosen to act out his revenge upon Don Gabriel instead. Early that morning, he had made his way to a solitary villa set back from the Toledo road, property of the marquess, where the negro had been left, shackled to a rack. By the time he'd finished with him, Don Gabriel's back was a mess of raw flesh. He had ordered the men to put him in a cramped wooden cage. When the mercenaries told him the negro had been packed up, he had ordered them to send him to Lisbon, where he would be sold at the port. Then he had returned to Lavapiés, trying to figure out if he could leave Madrid and take one step closer towards his dream of the stud farm.

Upon reaching the city, still uneasy about the Hernaldo affair, he had decided to go and look for Jacinta, who was not to be found at the brothel. All day he had gone around asking thugs and lowlifes about her, and it had been night by the time he found out she had been seen with someone in one of the back alleys. Like a hound on the scent of his prey, he had found her in the shed behind the Zaguán.

Once the client had finished, he pulled up his trousers and left without a word. El Zurdo waited for him to disappear into the darkness before entering, closing the door behind him.

'I've been looking for you,' he said.

Jacinta jumped, twitching nervously, leading him to suspect she had indeed run her mouth off to Hernaldo. He approached her, putting on his best smile, a knife hidden behind his back.

'I haven't stopped thinking about you,' he said.

Unable to hide her fear, she attempted to untangle herself from his clutches. Again, he did not let her, enjoying this moment when she still felt she had a chance. She let him kiss her breasts to hide her nerves and told him he could enjoy her any way he liked tomorrow. He took her forcefully by the waist and fixed his murderous gaze upon her.

'Open your mouth,' he ordered menacingly.

She remained silent and gulped in terror. She said nothing further, fell to her knees and unbuttoned his trousers. El Zurdo ordered her to do her work gently and she went about her task with the skill expected from someone of her experience. Then, while Jacinta put all her effort into pleasuring him, he slid his hand round to his back to take out the weapon. At that moment, he was suddenly seized by an unimaginable pain. Summoning all her strength, Jacinta had squeezed his testicles while at the same time savagely biting his member. He tried to reach for his knife to slit her throat, but he was in such torturous pain that all he could do was try to shake himself free of his tormentor, shrieking the whole time. Like a feral cat, she sank her teeth into his manhood so fiercely that he truly believed that she was going to tear it off completely. On the verge of passing out, he struck her on the head several times, which only made her squeeze her jaw tighter. He shrieked like a lunatic and drew his knife. Jacinta withdrew rapidly, but even so, she couldn't avoid the blade slashing her face.

She tried to stand while he fell forward onto his knees. Gripped by pain, he held out his arms and grabbed her hair. Barely having had the chance to get up, she found herself on her knees once more, and before she could rise again, he pulled her towards him, plunging the blade into her guts. He heard her let out a low death rattle as he continued to plunge the blade in over and over again, overcome with hatred and rage.

Expelling her last few breaths, she fell to the floor, from where she smiled up at him, as if something had amused her during her final moments. Covering his torn member with his shirttails, he had moved closer to finish the job, when Jacinta spoke.

'You son of a bitch. Hernaldo knows everything,' she whispered.

Then he noted a presence behind him. He had been about to turn when he felt his backbone splitting in two and his guts coming out of his body along with the blade. He fell forward and saw Hernaldo de la Marca from the corner of his eye. With the meagre strength that remained, he dragged himself over to the wall and propped himself up. He looked up and saw that Jacinta's soul had already left her body. Meanwhile, Hernaldo walked over and smiled as he squatted down to look at him.

'You're going to die like the son of a bitch you always were,' he said. 'Poor and ugly.'

'Finish me off once and for all and leave me in peace,' El Zurdo begged.

But Hernaldo got up and walked off in silence, and Zurdo

realized he was going to leave him there to die in agony, like a dog. He thought how foolish he had been not to kill Hernaldo when he had first seen him in the room with Jacinta. He railed against death, as if that could change his fate. He felt hatred for everyone: that stuck-up fool Don Enrique, that bastard Hernaldo and that disgusting pig Doña Sol Montijos. His only regrets in life were not having slit all their throats and having tortured those two beautiful steeds ten years ago, the most beautiful specimens he had ever seen. He wept as he recalled them, feeling the ineradicable mark that incident had left on him. The torture he had inflicted on those beautiful animals had not been worth it. He lay there, thinking about the horses, the stud farm he would never have, and the eight thousand reals he had hidden away in his house and which would soon belong to someone else.

41

Same day, 24 October 1721

The Marquess of Moya was delighted to receive Diego at the Puerta de Conde Duque barracks and asked no questions when the latter requested thirty armed men. He told him he would assign his most loyal soldiers to the task, and that he would sign whatever orders were required.

That night, after sending some guards to the house of Señorita Castro for her protection, Diego and his trusted friend Manuel Villacañas, Baron of Salinasmellado, divided their forces into three groups. The first entered by the Puerta de Lavapiés, the second along Calle Ave María and the third by Nuestra Señora del Pilar. Before anyone at the Zaguán could react, the place was completely surrounded.

Diego strode into the brothel, accompanied by ten men. The place fell deadly silent.

'I am Don Diego de Castamar!' he announced.

Everyone present scrambled to their feet to show their respect and stared at him slack-jawed, their eyes open wide in astonishment.

'Who is the owner of this pigsty?' he asked.

A man shuffled forward, his head bowed, and said that his name was Sebastián and that he was the proprietor. Diego brought his face to within an inch of the brothel-keeper's and looked straight into his eyes, forcing the man to look away.

'I'm going to reduce this place to ashes,' he said. 'Where is El Zurdo?'

Wiping the cold sweat from his face, the man told him that El Zurdo had gone out to the shed in the yard to find one of the whores, Jacinta.

'And Hernaldo de la Marca?' he asked.

'I don't know… He comes and goes.'

'Do you know where he lives?'

The man nodded and told him the house was close by.

'He lives with his daughter. Adela, I think she's called. Hernaldo loves her more than anything in this world. One wrong word about her and he'd kill you.'

Aware that time was short, Diego made for the yard, hoping to find El Zurdo in the shed. He gestured as he went for Manuel Villacañas to follow with his men.

When he opened the door of the shed, he found a dying El Zurdo lying on the floor, his guts sliced open and his manhood horribly mutilated; next to him lay the body of a poor harlot who had been brutally murdered.

El Zurdo recognized Don Diego immediately, while the duke had a feeling that this was not the first time he had seen this man. Contorted by pain and aware he did not have long to live, El Zurdo grimaced.

'I'll do a deal with you,' he whispered.

'I don't do deals with scum,' the duke replied. 'Tell me where my brother is, or I'll make your final moments on this earth unbearable.'

'You can't kill me without knowing what happened to the negro.'

'I wasn't thinking of killing you,' Diego answered.

'I'm not afraid of your threats,' El Zurdo groaned.

'Where's my brother?' Diego yelled. 'Where is he?'

'Like I said, if you want to know, you'll have to do a deal.'

Diego kicked El Zurdo in the stomach and he screamed

in pain. But then he laughed again and told Diego that every second he allowed his pride to prevent him from striking a deal just brought him closer to losing his brother forever. Diego knelt down and grabbed the man by the throat.

'What do you want?' he asked.

'I want to die knowing that they're going to pay for it... Don Enrique and that son of a bitch Hernaldo de la Marca,' El Zurdo replied.

'Done,' the duke said, making no effort to conceal his disgust. 'Tell me everything you know, and I swear on my honour that they'll be punished.'

El Zurdo grinned ghoulishly, aware that the duke would never forget what he was about to hear.

'I killed your wife.'

Diego stood up and staggered backwards.

'What? What did you say?'

'I killed your wife. I trained her horse so it would crush her at the sound of my whistle, and if I had had more time to train yours, it would have crushed you too. Now you have to decide whether to kill me or to wait for me to tell you where your wretched brother is.'

Diego, trembling with rage, clenched his fists, containing his anger to prevent himself from killing the only person who could reveal Gabriel's whereabouts. He paced up and down like a caged animal, beat his fists against the walls and cried out with impotent fury, desperate to contain the murderous desire to do away with the piece of human detritus that lay before him. Just then, El Zurdo began to talk, revealing the events of the past, one after another. Don Enrique's plan to murder Don Diego, crushed to death by his own horse on the inaudible signal of a whistle; Doña Sol's commission, under which he had secretly betrayed the marquess's plans, leading inexorably to Alba's death; the murder of the negro who served Don Diego's brother; the attack on Señorita Castro; the death of La Zalamera and the kidnapping of Don Gabriel. It was all Don Enrique's doing.

What was more, nobody knew the marquess's true motive for plotting the destruction of Castamar. Unable to contain himself any longer, Diego threw himself on El Zurdo. He rained down punches on him until the man's face was a bloody mess. Had Manuel Villacañas and his men not restrained the duke, he would have lost the chance to find Gabriel.

El Zurdo groaned and spat blood.

'Tell me!' Diego shouted. 'Tell me where my brother is, and I swear before God they will all be punished.'

'He's on the way to Portugal... to be sold as a slave. Escorted by four men. He's in a cage... concealed inside a wooden crate. And there's one more thing,' El Zurdo added. 'I marked your brother's back with my whip. Now he's a proper—'

Before he was able to finish, Diego blew the top of his head off with a flintlock pistol.

26 October 1721

That Sunday's sermon had touched Don Melquíades deeply. Father Aldecoa had spoken of the power of forgiveness, and the butler thought about how moved he had been by the duke's generosity towards him, how this had in turn prompted him to repair his relationship with his nephew, and how he should also resolve his differences with Doña Ursula. He had spent too long at war with the housekeeper and was tired of maintaining such a belligerent attitude. He had to bring the situation to an end. He couldn't help but recognize that Doña Ursula had many fine qualities. She had shown herself quite capable of filling the role of butler in his absence. She was diligent, hard-working, serious; she had always kept things under tight control, and in all her years of service, he had never known her to be imprudent or negligent.

The problem had always been her difficult personality, which meant that everybody kept their distance from her. He hoped the conversation he would have with her might soften her attitude. But he was also braced for the possibility of failure, as he had tried to improve their relationship before. The difference this time was that he had recovered his power and was finally free of the yoke that she had hung around his neck.

However, the housekeeper had managed to retain control of the kitchens after a conversation with his lordship, and the butler had not yet been able to speak with Don Diego in this regard. The duke had left suddenly three days ago, after arguing with his mother. The duchess had been left distraught, locked in her room or pacing the corridors with Don Enrique as her only company. Speaking personally, Don Melquíades had never liked the man, without ever knowing exactly why. As a result, he had instructed Señor Moguer to ensure that a footman was always in close attendance to Doña Mercedes. He understood the duchess's travails, as they were shared by the whole household: the disappearance of Don Gabriel, and the possibility that Don Diego might propose marriage to Señorita Belmonte.

In a private conversation with Señor Casona, he had confessed his fears that the duke, by marrying the cook, would bring disgrace upon Castamar. Simón, older and wiser than him, had remarked that it might also bring happiness to Don Diego. Melquíades had his doubts. However one looked at it – and regardless of her education, her manners and the fact that she was the daughter of Doctor Belmonte – Señorita Belmonte was the head cook. Perhaps it was seeing Doña Mercedes in such distress or the lack of news concerning the duke or his brother, but the butler's concern had only grown. However, at least he was able to celebrate the fact that Señorita Belmonte's health had improved to the point where she had asked the housekeeper for permission to be restored to her duties this week.

There were two sharp knocks on the door, which he recognized to be those of Doña Ursula. He stood up, pulled out a chair for her, and sat down again. She asked how she could be of assistance, and he stroked his moustache before announcing that he was going to be frank with her.

'This situation between the two of us…' He paused, searching for the best words to signal his good intentions. 'I am tired of it, worn out. I am not a resentful man and I appreciate that you are a highly talented housekeeper.'

There was a silence and Doña Ursula raised an eyebrow, as if to thank him for the compliment even if she did not know where the conversation was headed. He awaited further response, but she remained imperturbable. Melquíades went on to explain to the housekeeper that she was, unfortunately, feared by many among the staff. Ursula raised her eyebrow further.

'I don't care what the servants think so long as they perform their duties well,' she replied.

He paused for a moment and rubbed his forehead, thinking to himself how difficult it was to soften the spirit of Doña Ursula, particularly after so many years of strife. He took a deep breath and sighed.

'I would like to propose a permanent peace between us, as it is clear that his lordship holds a very high opinion of you and that nobody wishes to be without your services.'

There was another silence, and this time he waited for her to speak. Doña Ursula pursed her lips, with that sceptical expression that drove him to distraction, scarcely even blinking.

'Is that everything, Don Melquíades?' she asked.

'Well, I mean… I am making an offer of peace and understanding.'

'I know you are, Don Melquíades.'

'And what is your reply?'

She gave him a superior look, as if her response was not going to please him.

'Don Melquíades, you were once an excellent butler, but I am afraid that now you are no more than a mediocre one at best. The years have drained you of your spirit, your strength and your talent, and you have become accommodated to the slow passing of your life,' she said with absolute indifference. 'I cannot stand the idea that someone with so little talent as you should believe you deserve your position at Castamar, let alone see yourself as my superior. I am convinced that your peace offer is nothing but an attempt to hide this reality.'

He could scarcely believe what he was hearing. He stood up and banged the desk.

'You stole the letter from the pages of my notebook with the sole aim of subjecting me to your will, and not for any altruistic concern for the fate of Castamar!' he shouted. 'You have played your hand and failed, and if I have any motive to dismiss you, I won't hesitate to do so. If you want war, then so be it.'

She stood up defiantly.

'To tell the truth, the only thing I want is for you to disappear from Castamar as soon as possible. I don't care how it happens.'

'You are incorrigible!' he shouted. 'You are insufferable, pitiless, inhumane, cruel and unreasonable!'

'Please stop shouting at me, Don Melquíades, it is quite unnecessary,' she replied, sounding upset in her turn.

Driven by resentment, he told her not to hold back from saying what she thought; after all, he had put up with her indifference for many years when all he had ever wanted was to win her admiration and her respect. If he had somehow offended her then he was glad for it, as her presence at Castamar had only elicited the very same hatred, discord and disillusionment from which she had supposedly been fleeing, as nobody loved her and nobody ever would.

'It's all just about power for you!' he added. 'You never loved Doña Alba; you were just desperate to gain power over the other servants!'

Doña Ursula's eyes prickled with tears. The butler didn't care if what he had said was true or not. Seeing her weakness, he pressed home his advantage.

'Nobody saw you shed a single tear for the duchess!' he

shouted. 'Nobody! And do you know why? Because you don't know how to love! You never loved Doña Alba or Don Diego or the unborn child that died with its mother!'

Her whole body trembling, Doña Ursula slapped him across the face. But nothing could silence him now. Ten years of pain and fury came spilling out. He kicked the chair, sending it flying across the room, and carried on shouting.

'All you know how to do is crush people!' he yelled, beside himself with rage. 'All you know is how to humiliate your fellow human beings so that you can rule over them!'

'Men have to be crushed before they crush you!' she shot back. 'It's not my fault if you don't understand what is really going on in this house. The danger that Señorita Belmonte poses to the reputation of Castamar! The danger that stalks this family with the presence of Don Enrique!'

'Out!' he said, pointing at the door.

'You can't give me orders!' she answered angrily.

'I certainly can!' he shouted, drawing closer to her so that their faces were only a few inches apart. 'I will find a way to have you expelled from the estate,' he hissed.

'I'm not afraid of you or your empty threats.'

'Get out!' he ordered. 'With a character like yours, I don't know how I've managed to love you in silence for so many years!'

The housekeeper's expression suddenly changed at this unexpected declaration, and she took a step back. He held his breath, as surprised by his own words as she was. With a certain dignity he smoothed out his frock coat. Doña Ursula looked at him in shock. For the first time in her life, she didn't know what to say. Her chin was trembling, as if she was searching for the words to calm her spirit. In stunned silence, she took a few small steps backwards.

'What did you say?' she said at last, after a huge effort.

'You heard me, Doña Ursula,' he replied, calmer now.

She gulped, a look of shock on her face, and made for the door. He followed her with his gaze, still struggling to contain himself, and Doña Ursula stopped for a moment on the threshold. She turned, as if unable to understand or accept what he had just said.

'You have lost your mind, Don Melquíades,' she said, in a voice that was barely a whisper.

He didn't answer. As he watched her leave, he knew that their argument would already be the talk of the servants. His peace plan had failed disastrously and had only made a bad situation worse. He slumped into his chair, which creaked under his weight, as if complaining that it was too old to support him. After ten years of blackmail, humiliation and contempt, his secret had burst forth from the bottom of his soul in a single, passionate sentence that left him with a strange sense of relief. He had expressed his thoughts so spontaneously that even he did not understand why he had spoken. No doubt because he had never wanted to admit it to himself. That was why he felt relieved, freed from the chains of his own conscience and of Doña Ursula's power over him.

But, despite his own dismay, and the knowledge that he had gifted his enemy a powerful weapon with which to inflict even more damage on his spirit, he had to admit that he had enjoyed seeing her look so surprised and lost for words. *It's understandable*, he thought to himself. *I was lost for words myself.* Then, as he mentally reviewed the argument, he realized that not only had he hidden his true feelings all these years, he had also suppressed them so thoroughly he had not even set them down in writing in his notebooks.

42

27 October 1721

Gabriel opened his eyes, feeling that he had recovered a small fraction of his strength. The sunlight filtered through the cracks in the cage in which he had been imprisoned for the last few days.

After being captured, he had awoken naked, with a black cloth bag over his head and completely bound to a wooden rack. When he had reached what, judging from the damp, cold air, he assumed to be a basement or cellar, he had cursed wildly while he attempted to wriggle himself loose, soon realizing it was futile. After the first few days, all he could do was bemoan his fate. He had used the twice-daily lashings with the leather whip to mark the passing of the days.

No one had said a word to him the whole time, just lashed him over and over again until his will was completely broken. Eventually, he had started wetting himself with terror whenever he heard the heavy door creak, praying that it was not his torturers entering but his brother coming to rescue him. But as soon as heard the cracking of the whip, he knew his prayers had not been heard. After each session, he had been given enough water to ensure he remained conscious, and some bread and a vegetable stew so bitter it seemed as if it had been made with rotten cabbages. He had concluded that those men wanted to keep him alive – for now at least.

As his captivity had continued, his captors had begun leaving him alone more and more often, as if they had forgotten about him. In the end, he had grown so weak he completely lost track of time. The cold, dank basement had soon become a pit of his own filth, since no one ever came to clear up his urine, excrement or dried blood, and the stench was unbearable. An army of flies were his constant companions, and his torturers let out cries of disgust whenever they entered. As he weakened further, he began to drift in and out of consciousness.

In his delirium he had been visited by his father and mother, and even thought he saw his brother, come to free him from his imprisonment. He was visited by demons, corrupt and deformed beings who traded in human souls and tried to pull him into the abyss. Beset with fever, no longer knowing where he was, he had survived through pure determination. His wrists drained of blood, his body exhausted and his spirit about to admit defeat, he had focused his thoughts upon a single idea, one which kept away the demons and their *danse macabre*.

There, in his dungeon, he had invoked the figure of Señorita Castro, Amelia. She had appeared, taking him by the hand and making him open his eyes beneath his hood. She stroked his face and kissed his lips, as if her lips contained a purifying nectar. He opened his mouth and drank from her until he was sated. He thanked her for coming and explained how stupid he had been to judge her, how much he loved her and how much he regretted his harsh words during their last conversation. *I've been the most senseless man to ever set foot on this earth*, he had told her in his hallucination. *I'm in love with you and I was a fool to let you leave for Cadiz...* She did not reply, but simply stared at him with her green eyes and kissed him again. He confessed how sorry he was for the hurt he had caused her, for he really did understand how much she had suffered, how much she had sacrificed to survive in a world made for white men. Little by little, the image of Amelia would begin to fade, returning him to the harsh reality of his situation: chained with iron shackles to a torture rack. He understood that he had grown ever weaker and that the delirium would soon come back to finish him off. He had considered that the hallucinations could be the product of the asphyxiating hood, which barely allowed him to breathe, or something in the food. Whatever it was, he had thought, he had to do something, so he had begun to gnaw at the lining of the hood with his mouth to let some fresh air in. This had taken several hours until at last he was able to separate the fibres with his tongue, and the air around his head felt lighter. That was when he had noticed that someone had entered the cell, retching as they took in the stench.

As they walked, he had asked them who they were. He had thought they were about to leave but then he had heard the whip crack. Knowing what was coming, he had begun to cry. Without emitting a sound, this person whipped him like a beast, thrashing his back red raw, until the pain was so overwhelming his senses had grown dull. That monster had panted away, not even pausing to take a breath as he had whipped him over and over again, until he lost consciousness.

After that, he had no idea how much time had passed. When Gabriel had come to, he'd tried to stand up, but his body had felt like a limp mass of flesh. Suddenly, he had heard the door creaking and thought he was going to be lashed again, only for two men to remove the shackles from his hands and feet. He had moaned with the temporary relief of seeing his wrists and ankles freed and the pain of feeling his maimed back making contact with the cold ground. Silently, they had carried him and placed him in a cage that was barely waist-high. Hunched up inside that restricted space, he had finally been able to remove his hood. Above him, all he could see was a wooden roof, suggesting the cage was completely sealed. Even so, he had sighed with relief as he realized that, at least, his torture on the rack was over.

Outside that miniature dungeon, he had heard voices and the soft cracks of a whip, which made his hair stand on end. He had just enough strength to shift along so that his back would have as little contact as possible with the bars. That way he was able to sleep for several hours. From the way the cage was rattling, he assumed he must be being transported in some kind of carriage. From the lack of street noise, he guessed they were already outside of Madrid. He summoned the strength to speak to his captors, but only one of them answered.

'Shut up! Don't make us put you in a worse state than you're already in.'

He said nothing more and fell into unconsciousness once more, until he had been woken by daylight.

A boy of thirteen or so was looking down at him with curiosity, covering his mouth because of the smell. He had lifted off the roof of the cage and given him a bowl of cheese, olives and cold meat, along with a mug of water. Gabriel had devoured it all and thanked him. The boy, whose eyes were full of compassion, had looked to either side and covertly dropped a big bit of sausage into the cage as he gathered the bowl and mug.

'Water, more water,' Gabriel had begged the boy. He could barely get the words out of his throat.

Having weighed up the risks, the boy had disappeared, before returning with the refilled mug.

They had rattled along those roads for two nights and three days, a period of time he was once again able to count, perhaps because of the strength he had recovered thanks to the extra food which the lad and his younger brother had been giving him. Besides that, they had been kind enough to cover the cage with blankets so that he could better bear the cool temperatures of the mountains.

During this period, with his wits more about him, he had managed to identify four different men, as well as the coachman, who was the father of the two boys. From what he could deduce, the coachman had accepted the task of taking the cargo to somewhere in Portugal, Lisbon maybe, without knowing there was a man inside. Of course, to them he was only a slave, but the boys' father couldn't have been very pleased with the deal since he had complained on several occasions that he was no slave trader and that this was not what they had agreed. During the coachman's most recent protest, the leader of the soldiers of fortune had told him to stop whining like an old biddy unless he wanted his children growing up without a father. The driver had not complained again, though Gabriel believed he was encouraging his children to give Gabriel food and drink without the four thugs knowing.

He slept a little better that night, despite his discomfort and the foul smell. They stopped for lunch, and through the gaps in the wood, he could see they were in some remote oak grove. He knew they were away from the road because he could hear a stream flowing. The lid to the cage opened and he stretched out his limp, numb arms. When he looked up, he saw the younger boy holding his finger to his lips, imploring him to stay silent. The boy threw him a little bread and cheese and gave him something to drink. Gabriel smiled and the boy returned the smile, nodding as if it were a game. He was about to ask the boy's name when suddenly a huge hand knocked the poor lad to one side. The soldier kicked the boy in the stomach, and he began to cry.

'This bloody kid's been giving the negro extra food,' he shouted, sinking his foot into the boy's stomach again.

Gabriel cursed him from inside the cage, gripping onto the bars and using his meagre strength to lift himself up. The soldier went to hit him with the butt of his musket but stopped suddenly when he heard the voice of the coachman, coming from the other side of the encampment.

'Hey, you son of a bitch!'

Gabriel could just make out the boy's father striding across the encampment wielding an enormous knife. Without blinking, the coachman climbed into the wagon and stood before the lowlife.

'Touch my son again and I'll cut your balls off,' he threatened.

The solider faced him and lowered his hand towards his rapier as he considered slitting the coach driver's throat there and then.

'Easy, damn it. Let's get going; it'll be dark soon,' the head thug said from the other side of the encampment.

The coachman grabbed his son by the scruff of the neck and got down from the wagon, shielding the boy with his body while the soldier watched him, clearly suppressing an urge to cut him open and watch his guts spill out. Suddenly, as if remembering Gabriel's attempt to intervene in the boy's favour, he peered into the cage at him. Then, poking the butt of his gun through the bars, he began to ram it at Gabriel's head. Gabriel tried to raise his arms to defend himself but was unable to do it fast enough and felt his head crunch with the impact of one of the blows. He felt incredibly dizzy, and his vision went cloudy. He raised his chin a little and received another brutal blow close to the temple, which left him dazed and drooling uncontrollably. He felt his muscles giving way and everything around him growing dark.

Usually, Clara could only stand for a few minutes without feeling faint in open spaces, but this time, she felt different and managed to remain standing, not feeling the usual vertigo. She advanced further, towards the centre of the courtyard, leaving the safety of the building behind her. She noticed a slight surge of nausea but didn't let it bother her. She felt stronger than on other occasions; something inside her had changed. She guessed that confronting her affliction over the last year, along with the exposure to the open countryside which had nearly cost her life, had toughened her up. Her sickness seemed to be waning. In the end, trying to calm her breathing, she decided to go back, not wishing to push her luck. She had regained much of her strength after the weekend and did not wish to lose it again. Besides, she had suggested returning to work in the kitchens that very morning and did not want to relapse under any circumstances.

She adjusted her headgear, thinking, as always, of Don Diego. Having said goodbye four days ago, she longed only for his return, somewhat regretful at not having been more forceful in expressing her feelings towards him during their conversation. She would have told him how much gratitude and devotion she felt towards him. The first two days had been broken up by friendly visits from Señor Casona and Don Melquíades, until, feeling much recovered, she had decided the sensible thing to do was to abandon Don Diego's bedroom and return to her own.

She entered the kitchen and greeted all the staff – including Beatriz Ulloa who had approached her and told her she had realized her mistake and wished to learn everything she could from her.

Clara was happy for the girl. Then the rest of the servants began appearing, all showing great concern for her health. She was moved at discovering how cherished she was, despite never having spoken to some of them. She spent the morning working, until a beaming, carefree Elisa entered the kitchen.

'They've all shown great interest, and I am very grateful for it but… I don't understand.'

'Come on, woman. They've ceased to see you as the cook of Castamar. Some believe the duke has already asked for your hand,' she answered. 'It's rumoured that he and Doña Mercedes had a fierce row over it.'

Clara blushed to hear these words. It seemed many of the servants had already calculated that she could become the next duchess. That seemed unreal to her, and she felt so dizzy, just thinking about it, that she had to rest against the wall. Although no one except her really knew Don Diego's true intentions, they all took it as a given that the duke had proposed to her.

'If not, why was he arguing with his mother?' Elisa suggested. 'Come on then, confess. Did he propose to you?'

'No, no, no!' she shouted. She could face most things in life, but when it came to love, she felt lost and scared. 'Listen, Elisa,' she said cautiously, 'Don Diego hasn't said anything of the kind. That rumour is false!'

'Well, after lodging you in his own room and staying by your side all that time, I'm sure he will,' she said. 'I wouldn't expect anything less.'

'Good God! What are you saying!' Clara exclaimed nervously. 'His lordship has no obligation to do anything, Elisa.'

'Fine, fine,' Elisa replied. 'Don't shoot the messenger.'

Clara brought her hand to her face, trying to take it all in, reflecting on the weak position in which she now found herself. All the servants saw it as a given that Don Diego would make the proposal, which, Clara had to admit, was a feasible possibility based on their last conversation. But what if the brief brushing of their lips did not indicate this... or if, perhaps, he now regretted what he had said. Then the rumours would turn to mockery: *How could she have really thought that? The poor girl thought she was going to be duchess, but she's only good for the stoves. Fancy, a cook who thought she would be lady of all Castamar!* With all that expectation around her, she was in a very dangerous position. If the duke did not end up making a move, Clara realized that all that talk would inevitably lead to her having to leave Castamar. But how could she categorically deny the rumours when it was possible that Don Diego *would* propose marriage to her upon his return? She looked into Elisa's eyes and took her by the hand.

'Forgive my temper, Elisa,' she said. 'I only hope this goes no further than the walls of Castamar.'

Elisa smiled again and clasped Clara's hand tight. 'Don't worry about that,' she answered. 'Don Melquíades has ordered everyone to keep their mouths shut or risk being dismissed. I suppose they don't want it to end up circulating in the Madrid rumour mills.'

Clara thought how naive she had been to think that the gossip would stop when she returned to her post.

'Do you know if Doña Ursula has commented on the affair?'

Elisa shook her head.

'All I know about is the shouting match she had with Don Melquíades,' Elisa told her. 'It seems she had him under her thumb all that time because she had proof he was a traitor.'

'Señorita Belmonte,' a cold voice said. 'I understand you are not completely recovered, but I won't tolerate you distracting the other servants. Back to work, Elisa.'

Doña Ursula had burst into the kitchen, stopping all the activity. Clara looked up and noticed that there was a boy next to her, an apprentice quartermaster of some fifteen years of age, who followed her with his head lowered.

'I'm sorry, Doña Ursula,' she said.

Elisa vanished as quickly as possible. The housekeeper walked over and stopped in front of Clara. She looked her up and down as if she could see into her soul, wondering what on earth Don Diego saw in her. They both stared at each other, in the tensest silence either had ever experienced.

'Follow me,' Ursula ordered. 'Somebody wishes to speak with you.'

Clara walked alongside the apprentice, in short steps behind Doña Ursula's striking heels, which made the wooden stairs resound as she climbed them to the second floor. Once there, they headed down the corridors to the forgotten wing of Castamar, which was only ever opened to accommodate guests during the annual celebration. They made their way over to the grand drawing rooms and the small, adjoined colosseum, where Doña Alba used to enjoy private theatre performances. They advanced down the corridors until they reached one of the old duchess's private rooms.

The housekeeper made them both stop in front of a door decorated with gold leaf panels and signalled at Clara to go in. Clara nodded and, just as she was about to touch the handle, Doña Ursula took her gently by the arm and stopped her for a moment, weighing up what she was about to say. Clara waited while the housekeeper scrutinized her. She sensed a genuine unease in Doña Ursula, something which made her actually seem human.

'It's no secret, Señorita Belmonte, that we both possess contrarian, ungovernable spirits,' she said finally. 'But I do not, under any circumstances, wish for you to enter the room blind, since Don Enrique is waiting for you in there, and we both know he is a dangerous man.'

Clara took a deep breath now that she understood the reason behind the housekeeper's nerves. She remembered that noble's attractive face, that dangerous smile. The idea of having to see him alone made her stomach turn.

'I want you to know I will be waiting right outside until you come out,' Doña Ursula concluded.

Clara understood that the housekeeper must have received orders to bring her here, possibly from Doña Mercedes, since Don Diego was not at home. She thanked her sincerely, for it was obvious Doña Ursula was no opportunist seeking to earn Clara's favour because of her potential marriage to the duke. She had behaved in the same gruff manner as always, and she was not one to change the way she did things simply because Clara might become the Duchess of Castamar. Despite being absolutely certain that Doña Ursula did not want that marriage to go ahead, the housekeeper had also made it clear that under no circumstances did she want to be complicit in what might happen in that room, or for Clara to come to any harm at the marquess's hands. It was obvious she felt that way towards Clara because they were both women and because she felt in some way responsible for all the staff at Castamar. Clara nodded to Doña Ursula by way of goodbye and sighed before entering the room.

There, looking out at the fields through the window, was Don Enrique. The marquess barely turned his head as she opened the door.

'Close the door and come here,' he ordered. 'Take a seat.'

She curtseyed.

'I prefer to stand, your grace,' she said, keeping her head lowered.

He turned around, resting his predatory eyes on her and gesturing at her to approach. Clara walked unsteadily, aware that this man could eat her whole. Don Enrique looked her up and down in silence, as if he were contemplating an object and not a person.

'How blind I have been with you, cook,' he said.

'I don't understand what you mean,' Clara answered cautiously.

The marquess moved closer, stopping in front of her, seeming to enjoy her unease. Clara avoided showing her agitation and kept her head lowered, waiting for him to speak. He said nothing, clearly intending to make her uncomfortable, and began circling her, as if preparing to pounce at any moment.

'Are you aware of the harm you are doing to Don Diego? You will cast disgrace on Castamar when it becomes public that the duke ran after you like a dog pursuing a bitch on heat. Even more so if he has decided to propose marriage... has he?' he asked.

Clara preferred to say nothing. Then he placed the head of his stick beneath her buttocks, just as he had done at the dinner. Unable to bear it, she moved away. The marquess stopped right behind her.

'I insist you tell me if Don Diego has proposed, and under what terms,' he whispered.

She resisted, her body tense and her eyes burning, challenging him with her silence again. Don Enrique forced her to turn around, pushing her head up with the handle of his stick. She looked at him at last, aware that the marquess was now blocking her access to the exit. He brought his face closer to hers until they were almost touching.

'Don Diego has treated you like a lady, but you're nothing more than a servant.'

She took a step back, wondering if Doña Ursula really was still outside in the corridor, as she had promised. Perhaps the housekeeper had just been covering her back should Don Diego hear of their conversation. Suddenly feeling defenceless, Clara continued to retreat in the face of his advance.

'I just want you to answer one simple question, cook. Has he proposed or declared his love?' he demanded.

'Your grace, you can't expect me to answer that question, for I would not, even if the King of Spain himself were asking, far less a guest in this house who is not even my own master,' she answered, concealing the fear which this man provoked in her. 'Ask him yourself, if you want to know so badly.'

'I don't need to ask him. He loves you. You only have to see the way he looks at you.'

'If that were the case, it wouldn't be your place to tell me, your grace,' she said, without avoiding his gaze.

He smiled and halted his advance by one of the sofas, gently placing down his stick and laying his jacket on it. That was when Clara knew he intended to do something more than simply intimidate her, and she tried to create some distance between them. Don Enrique didn't care.

'Believe me when I tell you that I will not stop your marriage, quite the contrary, in fact – I'm delighted about it, and I've even thought about the wedding present I'm going to give you. Don't say I'm not generous, cook,' he said mockingly. 'Don't you want to know what it is?'

She stopped when she felt the wall behind her and gulped again.

'Answer me,' the marquess demanded. 'Don't you want to know?'

Clara frowned and told herself that she had to get out of there. She noticed that her silence was only spurring Don Enrique on. He stopped, looked at her and prepared to pounce. Knowing conflict was inevitable, she tried to get past him. She couldn't. The marquess's hand closed around her neck like an iron shackle while he used the other one to tug at her hair. A blow to the throat left her breathless and gurgling.

Don Enrique rammed her against the wall. She tried again to call for help from Doña Ursula, but she could barely let out a squeak with the marquess's fingers closed around her neck. She felt another blow, this time to the stomach, which made her keel over. She broke out in a cold sweat, and felt she was on the cusp of losing consciousness. Don Enrique made her sit up straight and slapped her on the cheeks to stop her from fainting. Her vision blurry now, she prayed silently for Doña Ursula to come in and interrupt the scene.

'Sssh, don't be rude, answer the question,' he said icily, as if he had already composed the scene in his head. 'Don't you want to know what present I'm planning to give to you and the duke?'

Gasping for air, she tried to spit at him, but the phlegm only dribbled down her chin. He laughed and told her to nod or he'd slit her throat. She resisted but gave in when she realized his hands were getting tighter.

'That's it. See how easy it was, cook?' He smiled as she tried to wrest herself free from his grip so she could take a breath.

Clara understood that the more time passed, the less strength she would have to resist. The tears were ready to fall, but she told herself that crying would only give him more satisfaction.

'The present I am going to give you is very special indeed, for it consists of three parts,' the marquess continued. 'The first is for you, since I intend to deflower you, so that you know what a real man is and long for me on your wedding night.'

She trembled as she heard the marquess utter these words. Removing a hand from her neck he hit her again in her stomach to stop her from struggling. A sharp pain spread throughout her chest.

'Let me finish,' he continued serenely. 'The second part is for Don Diego since, once I have had my way with you, I want him to challenge me to a duel.'

She tried to bend over but he pinned her against the wall.

'I have saved the best for last, cook – this part is for both of you. Today, I intend to leave my seed inside you, and nine months from now, you could be celebrating the birth of a new life. By then, Don Diego will no longer be among the living, but you and I shall always have something by which to remember this unforgettable day.'

At this moment, Clara became far more conscious of why Don Diego had not leaped to her defence that night. It was clear Don Enrique did not wish to kill her but rather wanted to provoke a duel and make her the motive for such a challenge, one in which the duke could easily die. She cursed herself for having trusted Doña Ursula's promise to keep watch. She had been so stupid for making Don Diego go out looking for her, thus provoking his own ruin, and stupid for not having declared her unconditional love to him. Now all she could see was her attacker's grinning face, as if promising the scene he had just played out was simply a preamble to something far worse.

Don Enrique freed one of his hands and removed the glove with his teeth. Clara tried to wrestle free, weaker with each attempt, as she felt his claws between her legs. The marquess smiled as he lifted her skirts.

Less restricted now, since he was only gripping her throat with one hand, she turned her head and managed to take a fuller breath. She let out a few gurgles and felt her temples pounding and her body growing still weaker.

She tried to shout again, but she couldn't get free of the shackle of Don Enrique's hand. She felt his hand stroking her underneath her skirt, a grotesque grin frozen on his face. Feeling his touch, she closed her legs as much as she could, noticing that the more she resisted the more pleasure it gave him. She felt disgust and terror as Don Enrique used his thigh to lever open her legs. He rubbed himself against her sex, thrusting twice in a way which repelled her. She knew then that it was inevitable he would take her by force and deflower her.

This thought made her struggle with all the energy she had left. He pushed her neck harder against the wall. She glared at him with a contempt which overpowered even her fear.

Suddenly, he stopped, and Clara fell to the ground, coughing and gulping down mouthfuls of air, looking up to see Doña Ursula, standing as firm as a lighthouse in a storm, holding a sharpened letter opener against the marquess's neck.

'Let go of her, you bastard, or I swear I'll slit your throat,' Doña Ursula said. 'Get behind me, girl.'

The marquess clenched his jaw, as if unable to believe that a simple housekeeper could have ruined his plans. Clara dragged herself away from Don Enrique and positioned herself behind the housekeeper, who was still holding the knife to the marquess's neck, alert to any movements he might make. Clara staggered to her feet. Doña Ursula shot a quick look at her to check if she was injured.

'Go,' she ordered.

Don Enrique tried to turn round, and the housekeeper, conscious of the threat he posed to them, pushed the blade further so that he knew she would not hesitate to slit his throat, even if she ended up on the gallows.

'Get out of here, Señorita Belmonte,' she repeated. 'The boy who was with me has gone to raise the alarm.'

'I won't leave without you, Doña Ursula,' she answered.

'I said go!' she ordered.

'You can't make me,' Clara replied.

That was when the marquess jumped out of the way, trying to dodge the blade, and went to grab the stick he'd left on the sofa. Sensing him move, Doña Ursula attacked without hesitation. The blade sliced along Don Enrique's cheek, causing him to let out a howl of surprise. Clara took the housekeeper's arm and pulled her towards the door. The marquess ran to block their way. Still holding Doña Ursula's hand, Clara rushed towards the door handle. She could sense the troubled breathing of the housekeeper and, further away, that of the marquess.

She ran, hearing Doña Ursula crying for help behind her, before suddenly her legs gave way and she fell towards the doorway. Before she could place her hands on the door, it opened and Don Melquíades, alongside several of the estate's armed guards, stood before them, holding a pistol. She stumbled into the arms of a lieutenant. Looking back, she could see Don Melquíades pointing his pistol at the marquess and Doña Ursula sheltering behind him.

'I fear your time in this house has come to an end, Marquess,' the butler said. 'These men will escort you to the gates.'

Grimacing, Don Enrique unleashed his fury by smashing some of the nearby vases. Then he carefully put his jacket back on and adjusted his cuffs. He walked over to Don Melquíades, looking him in the eye.

'Send a message to the duke. I assume he will wish to restore his honour.'

Don Melquíades lowered his pistol.

'Have no doubt, there is nowhere in this world where you will be able to hide from my master.'

Don Enrique was about to head for the exit when Don Melquíades stepped in front of him.

'And have no doubt, your grace, that if you had done any irreparable damage to either of these two women, I would have put a bullet in your head myself,' he said. 'Even though I am not your equal and I would have hanged for it.'

Don Melquíades's direct manner made Doña Ursula look at him in a way which Clara had never seen before, a mixture of surprise and astonishment. Don Enrique looked at the butler as if weighing up whether or not to kill him for his boldness then tried to force him to move aside. He did not budge.

'Pray to the Almighty that your master is still alive, because I will remember your words if he is not,' the marquess whispered, before finally making his way through the door.

Clara stood up, supporting herself in the lieutenant's arms, and looked over at Doña Ursula.

'Thank you for intervening, Don Melquíades,' she said.

The butler nodded without taking his eyes off the marquess as he grew smaller down the long corridor. Just as Don Enrique was about to leave the corridor, he stopped, turned and pointed at Clara menacingly. Clara looked up, holding her head high, despite how intimidated she felt, and stood firm until he was out of sight. She breathed unsteadily, still feeling the marquess's hand between her legs. A fit of profound disgust took root in the pit of her stomach, and she felt like vomiting. Overcome, she ran off without taking leave of those present. She asked for a large basin of warm water to be brought to her room and, the moment it arrived, plunged straight into it without even removing her skirt.

43

From his vantage point, Diego could see the cart. On it was the wooden case which hid the barred cell in which his brother lay prisoner. He advanced silently with his men, preparing to fall upon the mercenaries who were guarding it.

He's alive, he told himself again, trying to keep his hopes up. He had ridden at full speed, his cuffs still smelling of gunpowder, to the house of Don Luís de Mirabal, one of his father's best friends and the chairman of the Council of Castile, the highest legal authority in the land after the king himself.

Upon seeing him, escorted by the royal guard, Don Luís had been shocked. 'You look like you've seen a ghost,' he said.

Without pausing for breath, Diego launched into an account of everything he had been told by El Zurdo. By the time he had finished, it was Don Luís who looked as if he'd seen a ghost. Manuel Villacañas confirmed Diego's account and Don Luís assured him he would take care of the matter. Then, just as Don Diego was about to leave, Don Luís warned him there was sufficient evidence to take action against his friend Don Alfredo Carrión for gross moral indecency.

'In such circumstances, we are all men of honour,' Diego had replied, 'and Alfredo will accept whatever punishment may be imposed. I hope that you are wise enough to recognize what kind of man the Baron of Aguasdulces is, beyond any malady from which he may suffer.'

Don Luís had simply nodded and assured him that the Holy Inquisition would have no role in the affair.

'If you don't mind, I would like to write Alfredo a letter explaining everything that has happened. I would be very grateful if you could make sure it reaches him.'

'Of course. There's no need to worry about that.'

Then Diego had added, 'By the way, I am investigating the death of Doctor Armando Belmonte during the war. Did you know him?'

'Don Armando Belmonte, you say? I never had the pleasure of meeting him.'

Diego thanked him for his help and, after dashing off a note for Alfredo, he left. Meanwhile, Don Luís wrote a letter to the *regidor* instructing him to arrest Doña Sol, Marchioness of Villamar, for the murder of Alba de Montepardo, but to do it without creating a scandal. The aim was to capture her without alerting the marquess or his henchman Hernaldo before Diego had rescued his brother. Fortunately, this aim was assisted by the marquess's plan to be at Castamar, close to Don Diego's mother and far from the scene of any crime in which he might be implicated. And this was exactly what Diego needed – Don Enrique kept in the dark so that he believed his sinister plan had been successful just when everything was actually unravelling. Hence, Diego had ordered one of his men to notify him if the marquess left the estate. Once the marquess's strategy had been thwarted, then it would be time to deal with him – just at the moment he thought he was about to taste victory, he would be defeated.

At the break of dawn, Diego had set out for Portugal with a group of armed men that included the company's surgeon. He knew that, if his brother crossed the border and was sold as a slave, it would be much more difficult to find him. Along the way, he sought solace in prayer. Now that he knew Alba's death had not been an accident, he could hardly continue to blame the Almighty. He finally understood his chaplain's affirmation that

God's will was mysterious and that we could not blame Him without knowing His motives. For so long, Diego had believed that Alba's death had been a divine event, and when he realized he had been wrong, he had felt ashamed, just as he would if he had blamed a loved one for an injustice they had not committed. As he recalled this, he had prayed fervently to the Lord that his brother might still be alive.

They had ridden as fast as their horses would carry them, and late in the afternoon of the fourth day they had spotted the wagon escorted by four mercenaries. Instead of attacking them immediately, they had waited until the kidnappers halted for the night. As the mercenaries settled around the campfire, Diego decided that the time had come.

The coachman and his lads were feeding the mules, who seemed tired after pulling the cart for days on end, and the guards were talking among themselves.

Diego kept hearing El Zurdo's words. *I killed your wife. I trained her horse so it would crush her at the sound of my whistle, and if I had had more time to train yours, it would have crushed you too.* If he allowed himself to be carried away by rage and his desire for revenge, he would kill every last one of them. But the two lads were barely old enough to grow a beard and the mercenaries had only been hired to protect the cargo from bandits. He was quite sure that, unless one of them was Hernaldo de la Marca, none of them could even have imagined they were transporting a free man, far less the brother of a Spanish grandee.

He turned and told Manuel Villacañas and his lieutenant to get ready. Not wanting to cause any unnecessary deaths, he decided to take the camp by surprise before the mercenaries had time to resist. They approached slowly, taking care to stay downwind so that the sound of their footsteps would be carried away from their targets. Diego waited until all of his men were in position and then gave the signal. He raced into the clearing. Before the first man had time to react, Diego slammed his musket into the mercenary's face and threatened to fill the second man's chest with musketballs if he dared to move. Seeing the third man pick up a blunderbuss, Manuel fired his musket and blew two of the man's fingers off. The fourth mercenary, who was a little way off and seemed to be in charge, made a grab for his pistol, but the lieutenant kicked him in the face. The two lads, upon seeing two dozen men come rushing out of the woods armed to the teeth, threw themselves to the ground, and the coachman, who must have been their father, protected them with his own body.

'Don't shoot!' he cried.

The situation now under control, Diego seized a lantern and jumped up onto the cart, shouting Gabriel's name. When he opened the cage, he was knocked back by the nauseating stench. Inside lay the inert body of his brother, lying in his own filth.

After a pleasant night back in his own bed, Enrique had to confess that so much time spent on the duke's estate had bored him. Enrique had summoned Hernaldo the moment he arrived back from Castamar. He had just been informed that the man was there to see him.

'I will receive him in the upstairs salon,' he informed his butler, instructing him to bring a glass of wine and some cheese and olives.

While he waited for his lackey to appear, he thought about how his latest actions would unleash the final part of the storm. He had always had a talent for guiding life's troubles down the desired channels. And he couldn't help feeling a certain disappointment at having been expelled from Castamar without having deflowered the cook. Even so, he was sure that, sooner or later, the duke would challenge him to a duel. By now, Don Gabriel would already be in Portugal or perhaps dead, and even if Don Diego was on his brother's tracks, he would never find him. Don Alfredo had been accused of gross indecency, and exile – or worse – awaited him. Don Francisco's reputation was ruined, and he would, in all probability, be expelled from the court. Doña Sol's last letter had been magnificent! He calmly awaited Hernaldo's appearance as he sipped his wine and snacked on the cheese and olives.

Of this whole murky affair, the things he would miss most were his conversations with Doña Mercedes. After she had been informed of his behaviour towards the cook, she had written him a tearful letter, saying that she had trusted him like a son and that he had behaved like a scoundrel. He was upset, but ultimately, he could not allow himself to be carried away by sentimentality, particularly when the lady in question was not his mother.

If she had been, of course, he would have killed for her. While Doña Mercedes was a venerable lady who maintained her noble bearing at all times, the marquess's own mother had been a sad woman who had made an unfortunate marriage. The marquess had once found her gasping in her lover's arms as she cuckolded her husband. Later, at supper, he had mischievously alluded to the scene in front of his father, who had leaped to his feet and beaten his wife with his belt while the young Enrique looked on as if he were attending a theatre performance. It was, after all, a show he had orchestrated, and it was only right that he should enjoy it.

His father was a man whose ambitions outstripped his abilities, who had been reduced to representing the interests of others. The only things Enrique had learned from him were how not to behave, and the importance of wielding power for oneself. *One must be the master of one's own vices and the lord of others' actions*, he had told himself as he had watched his father lie dying. Before expiring, his progenitor had begged him to secure the title of Grandee of Spain for the Arcona name. And Don Enrique had promised that he would.

He had been brought up by his nursemaid and had driven her half crazy, tormenting her from an early age by forcing her to repeat the same task again and again. If she dressed him, he undressed and called her to do it again; he deliberately spilled food on himself so that she would have to find new clothes for him to wear. She never complained about his behaviour. Even though he was a small child and she was an old woman, he used to sit on her back as if she was a horse, forcing her to gallop. The poor thing had silently passed away one night from exhaustion, and the next morning, when young Enrique awoke, he had been exasperated that his nursemaid failed to answer his call. But his anger had turned to tears when he found her dead, and he had wept unconsolably – something he did not do for either of his parents.

Poor Dolores, he thought to himself, *she never understood my character.* They said that children possessed a special form of malice that, if not corrected, only worsened. Perhaps his upbringing, lacking in all discipline, had turned him into the pitiless adult he had become. The only thing he had ever desired in his life was Alba de Montepardo because she represented a path to salvation, even if, in reality, the marriage would have been a disaster from the moment she discovered his true nature.

Her death only propelled your destructive nature into action, he thought. But as soon as he met Alba, he had sensed that she had the power to dispel the darkness of his spirit, and he believed that his adoration of her would have transformed him to the point where he forgot his political ambitions and the intrigues he had inherited from his father.

But he would never know, due to the mere coincidence of Don Diego swapping horses with her. If the duke had not been his political enemy, if he had not thwarted his plans to place the Archduke Carlos on the throne, if he had not thus prevented the marquess from becoming a Grandee of Spain, if he had not deprived him of Alba when everything had been going so smoothly... he might have accepted that the change of horses had been a matter of chance. Instead, he blamed the duke for it, just as he blamed him for everything else. Don Diego had to pay for that – by losing his friends, his reputation and, of course, Castamar. One of the first things the marquess would do upon becoming lord of Castamar would be to order the painful death of the horse that had crushed his beloved Alba. He had loathed seeing it standing beside his own steed, chewing contentedly on its fodder in the stables, while the groom brushed its coat. *The beast should have been butchered and turned into horsemeat*, he thought.

His thoughts were interrupted when the usher came in to advise him that Hernaldo was waiting outside the door. He put his wine glass down. Hernaldo entered and, cautious as ever, didn't speak until the door had closed behind him. One look was enough to tell Don Enrique that all was not well.

'The horses weren't swapped,' Hernaldo blurted out. The marquess raised an eyebrow and looked him up and down. The soldier stood trembling slightly. The marquess calmly drained his glass. Then he stood up.

'I'm sorry, Hernaldo. Could you say that again?' he asked, softly.

'The horses weren't swapped,' he repeated. 'El Zurdo trained Doña Alba's horse.'

The marquess closed his eyes, recalling the only time he had kissed her and how she had responded. He kept his eyes closed, trying to contain his mixed feelings of anger, pain and remorse. When he opened his eyes, he fixed Hernaldo with a stare.

'And why did he decide to do that?' he asked.

'For money, sir,' Hernaldo replied, immediately. 'He was paid by Doña Sol Montijos. My suspicions were aroused when a whore called—'

'I don't care!' Don Enrique interrupted.

'El Zurdo—'

'I don't care!' Don Enrique roared. He sat down again, summoning all his strength to resist being carried away by the emotions that were bubbling up inside him. He looked at

Hernaldo again, who remained standing silently before him, his head bowed.

'Listen to what I am about to tell you,' he said. 'I want you to go to Doña Sol's house, making sure you are not seen, tear her heart from her chest, and bring it to me.'

Hernaldo looked at him doubtfully. Don Enrique understood his reservations; ending the marchioness's life in such a fashion would attract the notice of the authorities. Doing away with a troublesome whore or an inconvenient thug was quite different from cutting out a noblewoman's heart. They would search every inch of Madrid for the culprit. He had once made clear his prohibition on directly assassinating Don Diego and the same principle surely applied here. But he was so furious that only the thought of that bitch Doña Sol choking on her own blood offered some prospect of recompense. He no longer cared about anything.

'Sir,' Hernaldo insisted, as he fidgeted with his cocked hat, 'with all due respect, I think that will expose us to—'

'Cut her heart out!' Don Enrique yelled, even louder than before.

Enrique sat motionless, trying to remind himself that anger was not the best counsellor, that succumbing to the temptation for revenge would only lead to defeat just when he was on the verge of victory. He told Hernaldo to wait and not to do anything until he instructed him to do so.

'If you weren't my closest confidant, I would tear your skin off in strips for your incompetence,' he said, trying to find an avenue to vent his fury. 'Now go.'

He was left with suffering and rage as his only companions, just as they had been throughout his life. He walked over to the window and, looking out at the green hills beyond, began to cry. He suddenly felt small and grotesque, and was gripped by the urge to bring his own existence to an end. Don Diego had stolen his dreams of greatness and his love for Alba, but he had not been responsible, even indirectly, for her death. That was the doing of Doña Sol Montijos. His hatred for Don Diego had not diminished but rather was accompanied by an equal loathing directed at himself for having been such a fool, and he sank slowly to the floor.

He tried to gather up sufficient strength to finish what he had started, so that Don Diego would pay for what he had done – and Doña Sol would pay even more. While he could not bear the existence of the former, it was the latter who had achieved something that the duke had not: she had caused Don Enrique to hate himself. He suddenly came to a simple conclusion that he had been avoiding. He was the principal cause of Alba's death. All this time he had behaved like a coward, taking refuge from his guilt in his hatred of his enemy.

And so he lay there, his cold tears falling on the rug. He was gripped by a sense of loneliness, demons stalked his soul, and at the very epicentre of his pain was a powerful longing, one that drove him to seek refuge in those two kisses that had both terrified him and filled his spirit with happiness: the kiss that Doña Mercedes had offered him as a mother, and the one he had procured from Alba as the loving wife of Enrique de Arcona that she had never become.

44

Same day, 29 October 1721

Francisco awoke in Sol's arms. He turned to stroke her breasts and kiss her on the brow, as if doing that could rid him of all his worries. He had concluded that her power games were just a form of entertainment. In his hour of need she had shown true concern, not leaving his side for a single day. The devotion she had shown made him realize that Sol had made a bigger imprint on his heart than any other woman in his life. The superficial power games had given way to something far deeper.

They had reached Madrid the previous night, despite Sol begging for them to stay at her farm. She had wanted to remain there until the Alfredo problem was fully resolved, possibly through Alfredo's exile. But Francisco couldn't stay hidden away any longer without knowing what was happening at Castamar. Just after he arrived, Alfredo had appeared at his door, hoping to talk to him. The porters had blocked his way and expelled him from the house. After ordering any mail from Alfredo to be returned unopened, Francisco had sent him a note.

Don't try to see me anymore, Alfredo. I don't wish to see you – it will only cause us both more harm.

Francisco rose, taking care not to wake Sol. She moaned as he untangled himself but did not open her eyes. He went over to his bureau and saw that he had no mail. He was surprised not to have received any mail at Sol's farm, from Diego or for that matter from Alfredo. Not having received any visiting cards in Madrid was even more unusual. He assumed then that things must have settled at Castamar and that maybe Don Enrique was not behind all the trouble. At the end of the day, Alfredo's predilections were his own doing, and his having hidden it for so long had nothing to do with the marquess.

Francisco put on a gown and slippers and made his way to the room next to his bedroom where he usually breakfasted before getting ready. His butler received him with an odd smile that he could not decipher. He waited patiently until the servants appeared, carrying several trays. They too seemed oddly on edge. He could not understand their complicit, fleeting glances.

'Is there something I should know about, Señor Torres?' he asked his butler.

The man's expression turned to stone, as if he had seen an apparition from the beyond, and he shook his head nervously.

'Speak, man… Clearly, something is happening.'

'I… wouldn't know how to tell you, sir. There's nothing…'

Francisco, even more confused by his butler's reaction, felt too tired to argue. All he wanted was to be alone. He had enough on his mind already to worry about domestic problems.

'Alright, let me eat my breakfast in peace.'

His servants left the room, as if they had somewhere urgent to get to, and he began to eat.

It wasn't until a while later that he heard his bedroom door opening. Assuming Sol must have woken up, he continued to savour his boiled eggs. He waited a few minutes for her to appear. *She must be getting ready*, he thought. He had got up to go and surprise her when he heard voices behind his bedroom door. Surprised, he approached it slowly.

'We must be very quick, my lady,' he heard a male voice say.

He peered through the crack in the door and saw Sol getting dressed as quickly as possible, helped by her notary, Carlos Durán.

'I have everything prepared, my lady,' he was saying, 'including the box with all your jewellery.'

He was shocked. It was clear that Sol had to leave quickly along with most of her fortune. He was about to interrupt the scene when the notary's words stopped him.

'They showed up at the house with a warrant for your arrest,' he said. 'It won't take long for them to find you here.'

Francisco understood immediately that Sol must have committed a serious crime. He prayed she had nothing to do with the spreading of Alfredo's secret and that the love she had shown him over those days had not been a lie. Hiding behind the door, he saw her walk around the bed and head over to the window to see if someone was waiting for her on the street. While her servant was gathering her jewels from the dressing table, Francisco opened the door and burst in.

'What are they going to arrest you for?' he asked.

Sol jumped and the notary took a step back. She mumbled something, looking at her man in terror. He had to ask again. Durán, who had broken out in a sweat, had begun to reach behind his back, making Francisco guess he may be carrying a loaded weapon.

'I have to go, right now,' Sol said, and headed for the door.

The notary was about to follow her when Francisco closed the door, blocking their exit. A heavy silence settled as the three shot darting glances at each other. Francisco took a step towards the notary, in case he attempted to take out the hidden weapon.

'You will not leave until you tell me what crime you are accused of, Sol,' he said, blocking her way.

She looked at him.

'Get out of the way and let me go. Now's not the time for talking.'

'On the contrary, it's the best possible time,' he said. 'What crime are you accused of?'

Sol approached Francisco with her chin raised high.

'It's a gambling debt.'

He chuckled at her obvious lie, and she slapped him impotently.

'Let me out now, Francisco,' she demanded.

'No,' he answered serenely, looking at the notary from the corner of his eye. 'Tell me why they want to take you to prison, or I'll take you there myself.'

Seeing that the other man had finally got his hand inside his coat, he threw himself at the notary before he could get the weapon out. The untrained notary had only just produced his pistol when Francisco punched him in the face and the weapon flew onto the bed. Before the notary could react, Francisco kicked him in the stomach, causing him to keel over onto the floor. The little man looked up at him, raising his hands to defend himself.

'Stop immediately,' Sol ordered him.

Francisco turned towards her to ask again about the crime she had committed but fell silent when he saw her pointing the loaded weapon at him.

'Get out of my way, Francisco,' she said. 'I won't let them arrest me.'

He realized the offence must be very serious for her to threaten him in this way. He looked her up and down and asked again about the crime.

'Move aside or I'll pull the trigger.'

He tried to calculate whether or not she would actually do it. Sol moved closer and pointed the gun at his head.

'Move!' she screamed desperately. 'I don't want to kill you!'

Seeing her reddened eyes welling up with tears, Francisco shook his head, maintaining eye contact, while the notary stood up, still gasping for air. Francisco moved close to Sol and held out his hand to stroke her face.

'Good God, Sol. What have you done?'

Trembling, she kept the weapon held high, the end of his life one pull of the trigger away. She was overcome by his soft touch and the moments they would never share now. As her resolve crumbled, she looked for a way to articulate the words that would justify her crime. Finally, she felt impelled to verbalize the impossible. She screamed with rage before gritting her teeth. Francisco waited as she finally answered him in one simple, devastating sentence.

'I ordered the death of Doña Alba de Montepardo.'

Suddenly, she discharged the gun into his arm. Francisco was overcome by a sharp pain running up his spine, and by the time he opened his eyes she had thrown the weapon away and left with her notary. An icy chill extended down his left arm. He tried to gather his wits and follow her, but barely took two steps before losing his balance.

He covered the wound on his arm to avoid losing more blood, trying to calculate the extent of the damage. He realized that the bullet had gone all the way through the fleshy part of his shoulder. From the volume of blood seeping out and its dark red colour he believed that no main artery had been damaged, but it was sufficiently serious that he could die without urgent medical attention. He shouted to his servants to come and help him, but it wasn't until the third cry that his butler came in to find him there.

He ordered the manservants to come in and place him on the bed, applying pressure to the wound while others went out in search of a doctor and a skilled surgeon. His servant started searching the room for the lead bullet. He found it lodged in one of the legs of the dressing tables, mumbling that his master had been lucky.

Time passed slowly.

His manservants took turns to apply pressure to the wound and staunch the flow of blood, but as he bit the sheets to manage the pain, he knew that he would bleed to death if help did not come soon.

It didn't seem fair that he would depart this life with so much trouble and tribulation still on his mind: Alfredo's letter, his loss of prestige, the bullet wound burning in his shoulder, and most of all, Sol's atrocious confession that she had ordered Doña Alba's death.

The doctor and the surgeon appeared three quarters of an hour later. They administered opium, and straightaway he felt so relaxed that he fell into a heavy sleep. He didn't know if he was dying or if the surgeon had managed to contain the bleeding in time; he didn't know if he'd stopped breathing or if he was simply asleep. He felt himself floating into a delirium; he called out to Alfredo and told him he was terribly afraid of dying. Alfredo, sitting next to him, took his hand and soothed him, whispering words of consolation. Before completely losing consciousness, he saw Leonor, crying by his side and telling him how much she loved him. As he slipped into nothingness, he remembered the most important moments in his life. He relived his childhood on the Valencian coast; his life in Paris at the Collège de Louis-le-Grande; his dying father, Rodrigo Marlango, begging him to live a sensible life, with a wife and heirs; his long nights out roving with Alfredo and Diego; and his tireless need to seduce older women.

Between dizzy spells, he suddenly recalled himself at an evening event at Castamar, with Diego and the splendid Alba, with Alfredo and that night's conquest, the widowed Doña Cristina de Madrigales. He was overcome with an extreme melancholy as he tried to pin down that moment as one of the sweetest of his entire existence. He felt the beauty of that moment dissolving in time, and drunk on nostalgia, he told himself that, as in one of Shakespeare's tragedies, he was going to die both for and from love. Then his eyes clouded over, and he felt nothing more.

1 November 1721

Despite his brother's dire condition, the man's sheer physical strength had kept him alive. After removing him from that disgusting cage, Diego ordered Gabriel to be washed with warm water. The company surgeon, Martín Ojeda, dressed the welts on his back. Poor Gabriel barely complained and could only summon a faint smile when he opened his eyes. Diego consoled him and kissed his brow. Then they took the road back to Madrid, where they arrived four days later, heading straight for the Leganitos house to rest from the journey. After bathing his brother and calling for Doctor Evaristo, he decided to attend to the mail he had received while away.

The first of the letters was from his captain, informing him that the marquess had left the estate some days ago. Then he read another from Don Luís de Mirabal, the president of the Council of Castile, with news that the Marchioness of Villamar, Doña Sol Montijos, had escaped and that her whereabouts was unknown. At the end of the missive, he had added a brief postscript: *My dear boy, I have done some research into the name of Don Armando Belmonte. It seems that Don José de Grimaldo has some information regarding him and has assured me he will write to you soon. I hope he can help you with your investigations.*

Diego smiled. There was, indeed, a letter from the secretary of state, Don José de Grimaldo, among his missives. There were many anonymous heroes in the war who had died at the hands of the Habsburgs. He knew that all too well, having seen them perish on the battlefields, torn to pieces by the bombardments. However, he intuited that Doctor Belmonte's case had been different, since he had not been a military doctor but a civil one who had been asked to help. He should have been safe in the rearguard, among the blood and guts of the wounded, and Diego did not understand how he could have died in that way. Somewhat apprehensively, he opened and unfolded the letter.

Dear Don Diego,

I am very pleased to hear news of you from Don Luís. I hope I can answer your questions regarding Don Armando Belmonte, his family and how he died, bravely giving his life for His Majesty. He was a man of unblemished reputation and a most accomplished doctor.

Regarding your questions as to how he died, he did so heroically, before a detachment of Habsburgs who assaulted the hospital encampment which I myself had asked him to run. He left a widow and two daughters. After his death, the king wanted to grant him a posthumous title, but with the war raging, it was not possible to do so. However, once it was over, and when I realized his widow had sent me some letters asking for help, I took care of the matter in a letter to their private residence.

In it, I confirmed to them that, after a conversation with His Majesty, he personally wanted to honour his wish to give them a title. To my surprise, I received a reply from Don Armando's brother, Don Julián Belmonte, who sent me a letter stating that both his sister-in-law and nieces were in a foreign country and would not be returning, but that he was ready to accept said prerogatives in the family's name.

His Majesty made it clear to me that he would only grant the title to the widow and her daughters, and not under any circumstances to the doctor's brother. So I wrote to him saying this was not possible, but that, if he told me in which foreign country they could be found or could give me an address, then I would personally get in touch with them. By return post, Don Julián Belmonte informed me that they had departed for France and from there to some other European nation, but lamentably he had no further news from them. I investigated for a few months in Paris, but my search was in vain.

I trust that this information is of use to you, and as always, I hope you make more appearances at the court, knowing the high esteem in which Their Majesties and I hold you.

With nothing more to report, please receive my congratulations
for the most recent celebrations at Castamar.
    Yours,

                    Don José de Grimaldo, Secretary of State

Diego took a deep breath. Don José could not imagine what a favour he had done him by writing those lines. He would have married Clara, come what may; nevertheless, he wanted her to be happy, and now there was the possibility that taking her as his wife would not have to result in the loss of his prestige or be the cause of any scandal at court. The finer details were not yet clear to him, but that letter allowed him to come up with a plan which would involve presenting Don Armando's case to the king and queen. He had to make sure the title was given, even though he knew that alone would not guarantee the family's acceptance at court.

The only thing about the affair which didn't quite square was the involvement of this Julián Belmonte. From what he knew, only Don Armando's widow had left the country. He knew nothing of the younger daughter, but it was obvious from her credentials that Clara had never left the Kingdom of Spain. He suspected that there was something awry and swore to himself that it would be Don Armando himself who would restore the prestige of the Belmonte family from the grave, with Diego's help.

Without any further ado, he sat at his desk and wrote a letter to his mother, informing her that his brother and he were well and would arrive the following day. Then he sent another to Clara, and a further two thanking Don Luís de Mirabal and Don José de Grimaldo. Finally, he wrote to Señorita Castro.

Dear Señorita Castro,
    I write to inform you that my brother, for whom you harbour noble sentiments, is safe in our house in Leganitos, having arrived

there only a few hours ago, and from where I write this note. I know that this will alleviate the anguish in your spirit, and I hope in mine as well. My brother has been cruelly tortured and lashed and will recover slowly, under the care of the doctors. If it suits you, I would be most grateful if you should come to my house as a guest once more. I know that Gabriel, though unconscious with the pain he is enduring, will be deeply grateful for your presence and all the care you will give him. Besides, I will rest easy knowing you are with him, since I must attend to urgent matters in Madrid and I can think of no one better to watch over my brother.

You know the relief that a friendly face brings in moments of suffering, and I hope you do not resist coming because of past events. I must reveal to you that my brother desires your company more than mine. I am certain of this because, in the delirium provoked by the opium and the pain of his wounds, he keeps pronouncing your name, and takes my hand in his as if he were holding yours. Of course, I hope you will keep this as a little secret between us until my brother is recovered. According to the doctors, his recovery will not be quick, although he is already out of danger.

I await your prompt response,
Yours,

Don Diego de Castamar

He felt calmer now, with his brother recuperating, Señorita Castro safe and sound and on her way, and his plan concerning Clara in motion. He began to go over the plan he had devised to deal with the marquess. He would not be tried or transported to Valencia or Cadiz to be shackled by the leg for life and nor would he be condemned to spend the rest of his days on a galley ship. No, Diego would not give up the satisfaction of seeing Don Enrique defeated with his plan still in its early days. He would not give up seeing him humiliated by the understanding that Diego was the author of his end, and above all, under no circumstances would he miss out on looking him in the eye as he took the marquess's life with his rapier.

45

2 November 1721

As dawn broke over Castamar, the dewy fields glistened in the first rays of the winter sun. Clara was curled up in a chair, wrapped in blankets and silently looking out over the tree-lined avenue, as she eagerly awaited the return of Don Diego. She had struggled to calm her nerves and her unease during his absence, and every now and then she glanced out expectantly over the flowerbeds. If nothing else, it helped to distract her from the unpleasant memory of the incident with the marquess. Since then, she had been unable to avoid feeling a certain repulsion towards her own body and had been bathing compulsively. Even so, she had still had the sense that Don Enrique's peach fragrance continued to cling to her skin.

It took her some time to realize that there was no smell and that it was just the effect of her imagination. After a few days, the marquess's nauseating scent had disappeared, only returning when she found herself recalling what had happened. Otherwise, she tried to feign normality by preparing meals for Doña Mercedes, who had fallen into a depression upon learning of what Don Enrique had tried to do to Clara.

Clara had tried to lift the duchess's spirits by preparing her favourite dishes: partridge fricassee, stewed with cinnamon, pepper and cloves; pork shoulder in white wine; and a hearty stew with beans, black pudding and chicken. For dessert, which was what the duchess most enjoyed, Clara had made a tart with egg yolks and sugar and some almond nougat and custard.

But Doña Mercedes's spirits remained downcast as the days failed to bring news of either of her sons. And it was not long before her despair spread to the servants. The only good effect of it all was that it stifled the idle chatter about Clara's possible marriage to Don Diego. Even so, a melancholy air hung over the household. Simón Casona seemed tired and sad, Don Melquíades issued half-hearted instructions, and even Doña Ursula was less strict than usual.

The relationship between the cook and the housekeeper had shifted from antagonism to one of cold cordiality. During the first few days, neither of them mentioned what had happened but, bearing in mind that Doña Ursula had saved her from losing her honour, Clara felt she should at least thank her, as she had already done with Don Melquíades. When she had thanked him, he had taken her hands and told her that he would not have permitted anything bad to befall her, even if he had not been the butler of Castamar. By contrast, Doña Ursula had looked her up and down from her vantage point behind her desk and, before Clara could continue, had interrupted her icily, stating that there was no need for her to say anything of the matter and that she would have done the same for any other member of the serving staff. Clara was not an exception. To the housekeeper's surprise, Clara had clutched her hand.

'Even so, I would like to thank you,' she said.

'Well, now you have. You may leave,' the housekeeper replied.

From that moment on, Doña Ursula had entered into a strange trancelike state, as if she was unable to understand the changes taking place at Castamar. Perhaps it was the rigidity of her character or the belief that, if she softened in response to the kindness of others, it would only make her more vulnerable. *Perhaps we are all a little like that*, Clara thought. *After all, who is not afraid of love?* If there was a sentiment that could terrify anyone it was that, and Doña Ursula, who appeared never to have experienced it herself, who had only received punishment and hostility from the world, was disarmed by displays of affection. Perhaps this was why she snatched fleeting glances at Don Melquíades at mealtimes, glances the butler was well aware of, though he sought to keep up pretences in front of the other staff.

Clara could have sworn that the war between them had ended in some manner that she did not understand or, at least, that a truce had been established. The two spoke in a more relaxed tone. One day, in the pantry, Clara came upon the housekeeper stroking her lips with the tips of her fingers while she gazed out of the window at the gardens beyond. Upon being discovered, the housekeeper started and briefly pretended to be carrying out an inspection before she made her excuses and left. When she had gone, Clara went over to the window. Outside was Don Melquíades, directing the porters who were delivering supplies from Madrid.

As the days passed with no news of Don Diego, Clara's unease had grown. Elisa told her that every morning she found the duchess standing at the window, awaiting the return of Don Diego and Don Gabriel. Clara had barely been able to sleep herself, and she could only imagine how a mother would feel at the prospect of losing both her sons, particularly given how she had been an innocent accomplice in Don Enrique's plans. Clara's own concern had led her to imitate Doña Mercedes, spending her time looking out over the avenue, hoping to spy some distant movement that might indicate the return of Don Diego or the delivery of a letter. That morning was no exception and, as she combed her wet hair, the sun was already breaking through the clouds.

'Doña Ursula told me I might find you here,' a voice said, catching her by surprise.

She started and let out a little sigh. In the corner of the room, a silhouette gradually took the form of Doña Mercedes. Clara didn't know how the housekeeper was aware of her morning routine, but nor was she surprised. *There's nothing she doesn't know,* she thought. Clara acknowledged the duchess with a slight bow of her head. She couldn't help noticing that the duchess's usual slightly peremptory tone had given way to something more respectful. Doña Mercedes stopped in front of her, her figure bathed in the pale autumn sunlight.

The duchess looked as if she hadn't slept properly for days. And yet, she also seemed more at ease than she had, as if she had somehow been relieved of the pain of her eternal wait. The duchess took a deep breath before she spoke.

'My son appears to be quite taken with you.'

Clara blushed.

'And it is clear that you are also taken with him.'

Clara's eyes prickled and she felt slightly uncomfortable. Even so, she held the duchess's gaze as the older woman stroked Clara's cheek, as if she were able to see into her soul.

'Your angelic face speaks of your good heart,' she said, 'and I can tell from your eyes that you are strong-willed.'

Clara acknowledged the compliment with a bow of her head and sighed lightly.

'I came to look for you because I've just received a letter from my son,' Doña Mercedes added.

Clara's heart began to pound at the news that he was still alive and that perhaps all would be well.

'At noon you will see him ride down this avenue that we have both been keeping a constant vigil over. Thankfully, he will be accompanied by Don Gabriel, whom he rescued before he reached Portugal to be sold into slavery.'

'Thank the Lord!' Clara said, unable to contain her relief. The duchess's eyes filled with tears, and Clara sensed that she was feeling a mixture of joy at the successful conclusion of events and guilt and remorse for her part in what had happened.

'My son, my Gabriel...' she stammered, 'has been brutally whipped and beaten. That was why Diego stopped in Madrid, to seek urgent help.'

Clara raised her hand to cover her mouth in shock.

'My son would despise me as a mother if, in addition to unwittingly contributing to such pain, anything happened to you,' she went on, and suddenly hugged Clara. 'I didn't want to believe what my sons had told me, or the words of their friend Don Alfredo. All because I trusted in someone who was not of my blood.'

Clara returned the duchess's embrace, seeking to console her.

'You should not blame yourself for the actions of that heartless devil. The marquess played upon your good heart.'

'I must beg your forgiveness,' the duchess finally said, 'because it was me who exposed you to unnecessary danger by asking Don Enrique to convince you to leave Castamar for the good of the family name.'

Clara was at a loss as to how to react and simply bowed her head. She understood that it was inevitable that a woman of the duchess's social standing would have such concerns.

'No apology is necessary, your grace. It was you who were deceived as to Don Enrique's intentions,' she replied. 'It is not for me to grant or withhold forgiveness when your behaviour was motivated solely by your love for your son.'

The two women looked at each other, and Clara thought she detected a certain unease in the duchess.

'Señorita Belmonte, I hope that you understand the scale of the danger to which my son will be exposed if he decides to ask for your hand in marriage,' the duchess said.

Clara knew that she was being tested, and a silence followed. It was the duchess's way of forcing her to decide whether she would assume responsibility for tarnishing the Castamar name, or whether, on the contrary, she would reject the duke's proposal. Clara took a deep breath before responding.

'Allow me, with the greatest of respect that I have towards you, to reserve my answer for Don Diego, as it is to him alone that I must give such a response should the question be posed,' she said. 'However, I will say that any sensible woman would accept such a proposal from him, even if he were but a poor man with no title whatsoever.'

'Now I see how much you admire him,' Doña Mercedes replied. 'I am quite old enough to understand what it means to see you standing vigil here every morning awaiting his arrival. I only want you to know that I will not stand in the way of my son's happiness… or of your own, even if it means the destruction of our name.'

Clara, who all this time had thought that they would never have the duchess's blessing, was about to thank her, but Doña Mercedes placed her fingers to her lips to signify that it was not necessary. The duchess looked her in the eye, then took her face between her hands, as if performing a scene from a play in which she was unable to contain her emotions.

'If only you had never come to Castamar, never cooked for us, never met my son. Would it be that love arose only between equals, Señorita Belmonte,' she said, her voice breaking with emotion. 'Everything would be perfect, simpler, easier, less complicated. But God does not wish for such a dull world,' she concluded, and kissed Clara on the cheek as if she were her daughter.

Clara understood that Doña Mercedes had renounced any intention of fighting her son and his disastrous marriage plans. Perhaps she knew she lacked the strength to change Don Diego's mind, especially when she had seen him suffer so after Doña Alba's death. Her son's calvary had lasted ten years but finally he had found happiness in a commoner.

Just as she was about to leave the room, Doña Mercedes turned and placed a small, sealed envelope on the table.

'The letter I received this morning contained this note for you.'

Without another word, she swept out of the room, and one of the ushers closed the door behind her. Clara opened the note with nervous fingers and began to read.

Dear Señorita Belmonte,

Given my delay in returning, I find myself bound by decorum to dedicate these lines to you explaining my absence. As you will no doubt have realized, I have been kept away from the estate for reasons of great importance, as the life of my beloved brother, Don Gabriel de Castamar, was at stake. That having been said, I wish to let you know that I am still resolved to have that conversation, which we left pending, upon my return.

Do not believe that distance has undermined the deep affection I feel for you or the decision I wish to communicate to you. I am a temperamental man with strong beliefs, but am not given to exaggeration or to futile gestures. I hope that you have not, in the meantime, harboured any doubts as to my intentions. As I informed you before my departure, I will never leave you. I should arrive at Castamar, in the company of Señorita Castro and my brother, who is making a good recovery, this very day.

Moreover, and quite apart from any private conversation between us, it is imperative that I speak to you regarding certain past events of which I have become aware, events directly related to the death of your father.

Yours,

Don Diego de Castamar

Both pieces of news left her shaken. The first because she understood that Don Diego intended to ask for her hand in marriage. The second because she could not imagine what the duke could have discovered about the death of her father, who had sacrificed his life valiantly defending the hospital camp. She had to read the letter several times. Just looking outside brought her out in a cold sweat.

As she returned to her bedroom, she wondered how she would react when she saw him, how they would both behave – if he would come to see her as soon as he arrived or if he would wait a little to avoid arousing too much curiosity. And try as she might, she could not sleep. An hour later, she was in the kitchen to ensure that the Sunday staff were performing their duties. Then, along with most of the other servants, she went to midday mass. Her ability to tolerate open spaces had grown over the recent days and she decided she could do without her blindfold inside the carriage. Throughout Father Antonio Aldecoa's sermon, she couldn't stop looking at the entrance in case Don Diego should appear. As they returned to the house, the only thought on her mind was whether Don Diego would have arrived before them.

It was Don Melquíades, sitting next to her, who said that the master must have returned, since there was a carriage, a wagon and several horsemen at the house. She calmed her nerves, aware that everyone would be observing her reaction. She was relieved that Doña Ursula, who was sitting opposite her, appeared to be more interested in Don Melquíades. When they arrived, she placed the blindfold over her eyes and, guided by the butler's arm, crossed the same courtyard she had traversed more than a year ago. She thanked Don Melquíades for his kindness and was heading for the kitchen when the under butler informed her that the duke was waiting for her in one of the upstairs rooms.

Her hands clammy and her breathing coming fast, she left the kitchen and the inquisitive glances behind, ascended the stairs and walked along the gallery towards the small library where Don Diego often played the harpsichord. She told herself there was no reason to be nervous. Hanging on the walls were portraits of the duke's ancestors and she felt as if they were watching her. She stopped before the final painting, the one of Don Diego and Doña Alba. She admired the duchess's distinguished appearance and felt a pang of fear that she would never be capable of satisfying the expectations of the highest echelons of the Spanish aristocracy. Just then, the notes of the harpsichord floated down the corridor. She waited until the piece had finished before continuing to the library, where two ushers stood guarding the door. One of the ushers knocked and the duke invited her to enter.

Don Diego asked the servant to close the door behind him and to ensure they were not interrupted by anyone and that nobody would be in a position to overhear them. When Clara looked up, Don Diego was standing silhouetted against the window, calmly contemplating her.

He seemed not to care what the servants might make of the fact that he had called her without delay. Indeed, the only thing he seemed to care about was talking to her, as if there were no time but the present and the separation had been a torture for him. He strode over, with that self-confidence that accompanied all his actions, and which sometimes overawed her. She was so nervous that she forgot to curtsy, instead drawn to him as if by some magnetic force.

She stopped, her heart pounding in her chest, and waited for him to reach her and take her by the hand. With exquisite decorum, Don Diego kissed her hands and she wordlessly allowed herself to be enveloped by his fragrance. They looked at each other in a silence that was heavy with unspoken words.

'Señorita Belmonte,' he said, fixing her with his gaze. 'I don't think I can contain my desire to kiss you any longer, and so I am here with the sole purpose of asking you to do me the honour of becoming my wife. I cannot stand the idea that you do not know that I love you intensely, more than any other person on this earth, and if you accept me, I will be your most devoted husband. I will look after you, I will protect you, and I will never abandon you.'

Clara, barely able to contain herself, did not even answer. Instead, she simply drew closer, nodded, and stroked his face. He sought out her lips with his own and she felt secure in his embrace. Their mouths met, as if they were drinking from each other. A torrent of emotions rose up within her as the devotion that she felt for this man whom she loved against all expectations was finally released. For the first time since the death of her father, she felt safe and protected.

The painful memories of the past blurred, as if the pain of

that dark phase of her life was now fading. The titanic burden she had carried for all those years – her father's death, the fall into poverty and misfortune, the break-up of her family – all those things went up in smoke.

Then she gently nibbled his earlobe and clung to him as she whispered, 'I am yours, your grace. I have been for a long time.'

3 November 1721

Since finding Gabriel at the Leganitos mansion surrounded by Doctor Evaristo and the other doctors, Amelia had not left his side. He was lying face down, his back a mass of wounds. She felt a mixture of pity and shame on seeing him in that state. She sat down by his side and gently took his hand. She stayed there, caring for his wounds, which appeared to be healing well, attentive to any change in his condition.

That same evening, Don Gabriel awoke to find her sleeping in her chair. He squeezed her hand, and when she sat up, he asked her what she was doing there when she was meant to be in Cadiz. Leaning over, she explained that she was there at his brother's request, and that she had been unable to continue with her journey when she learned he had been taken captive by Don Enrique.

'Your brother is taking care of the culprits, I am told,' she concluded. 'I will understand if you would prefer me to leave—'

Don Gabriel raised two fingers and, turning his face towards her, asked her to come closer. He took her by the hand.

'I don't wish you to leave, despite the deplorable condition in which you find me,' he said. 'I must confess, Señorita Castro, that during my captivity it was your image that gave me the strength to endure my suffering.'

She was about to reply when Doctor Evaristo knocked on the

door. Don Gabriel tried to release her hand, but she gripped his yet more tightly and told the doctor to enter. After examining his patient, the doctor said it was clear that Don Gabriel was in excellent hands, and that he would have supper sent up in half an hour. When the door had closed, Señorita Castro spoke.

'I must confess that I have not ceased thinking about you and the unhappy manner in which we said goodbye, not for a single moment.'

He closed his eyes and nodded, giving her to understand that he had experienced the same emotions.

'I should not have judged you,' he said. 'I spoke in bitterness, and I ask your forgiveness, Señorita Castro.'

Tears welled up in her eyes and she shook her head.

'I was the fool,' she said. 'I can never regret enough having remained silent the day your brother questioned me at Villacor. You have every right to despise me for—'

Just then, he drew her hand towards him and kissed her fingertips. She immediately fell silent and knelt before him. Don Gabriel looked at her, her face pressed against the mattress, her lips trembling, and said two simple words.

'Kiss me.'

She had felt herself drowning in his dark eyes, and very gently, she drew close and placed her lips on his. They kissed for what seemed an eternity, as if they would never part.

After breakfast the next day, they had left Madrid, arriving at Castamar some two hours later. Doña Mercedes fainted when she saw Gabriel's condition and had to be revived with smelling salts. The duchess was soon well enough to declare her delight at having Señorita Castro at Castamar again, explaining that the loneliness of the huge rooms was unbearable. Amelia's only wish was to remain by Don Gabriel's side, but she humoured the old lady, who gradually began to talk of less weighty matters as it became clear that her son was out of danger. Amelia took every opportunity to visit Don Gabriel, who put on a brave face despite being in terrible pain. At times, she felt as if her soul was divided. On the one hand, she felt completely at one with him, and the colour of his skin – which had once been such a barrier – now seemed beautiful. But on the other hand, she worried that any relationship would be doomed to failure and suffering.

After hearing that Don Diego had asked his cook, Señorita Belmonte, for her hand in marriage, both she and Gabriel had congratulated him. Even Don Diego's mother had given her blessing. Only once, when they were taking tea in the drawing room, had the duchess let slip her belief that there should be a law forbidding children to marry without the consent of their parents. The duchess was sure that some day a wise king would introduce such a measure to prevent unequal alliances.

Before setting out for Madrid at dawn, Don Diego begged them not to share the news with anyone until his plan to restore the good name of Belmonte had borne fruit. Amelia could hardly imagine that the Spanish court would tolerate the ennoblement of a mere cook. However, Don Diego was one of the most powerful and influential men in the entire kingdom, and it was also true that Señorita Belmonte came from an unblemished family and that her father had been very well respected.

Amelia could not help thinking of her own situation. Scandal followed her wherever she went, from Cadiz to Madrid, and Don Gabriel would never be able to change his skin. Sometimes she was surprised to realize how comfortable she felt kissing him or holding his hands; black and white were separated by an abyss but their love seemed to soar above it. She herself had once believed Africans to belong to an inferior race, incapable of higher thought, born to be nothing more than slaves. In Cadiz, some merchants left letters of manumission in their wills as an expression of the affection they had acquired towards their former possessions, feelings that were often compared to the fondness one might feel for a dog or a horse. However, what Amelia felt for Don Gabriel went far beyond the affection one might have for an animal. She loved him just as she might have loved a white man, and this love had changed her previous views.

And she was sure that he loved her, even though he had not said so. They would both face the same problem. If they didn't marry, either she would be seen as a negro's concubine or he would have to pass as a white woman's slave. Either way, they would be forced to live a lie. And if they did marry (and Father Aldecoa might be willing to perform the rites, as there was nothing in canon law to prevent it) then it would further tarnish the name of Castamar, the more so as she herself was not a virgin.

She knew, though, that Don Gabriel's state precluded any conversation about their future for the time being. He had avoided the topic and she had not forced it. However, he had made it clear that he was not afraid. And this confidence of his gave her strength, told her that he was the man of her life and that she would not find another to equal him. In contrast with his brother, Gabriel did not hide his emotions, and in this they were alike. He would never lose his calm and he would always adore her, and she knew it. *Any woman would want to be adored like that*, she told herself.

That night, he sent a message to her to come and visit him. He smiled when she entered his room and invited her to sit down beside him.

'Señorita Castro, Amelia,' he said, taking her hand. 'I wanted to wait until I had made a full recovery, but I am afraid I cannot delay any longer. I would like you to be my wife and for us to leave Castamar together.'

Diego took a deep breath and leaned back in the seat of his carriage. Behind him were the Alcázar and his audience with the king and queen. There in one of the apartments that still held memories of the times of the Habsburgs, he had had a private meeting with Their Majesties and Don José de Grimaldo. Don Diego had explained that the doctor was a war hero, a civilian who had saved many lives and sacrificed his own in the struggle for Spain, and whose death had brought misfortune on his wife and his daughters. The king had been so moved that he had ordered the duke to bring Señorita Belmonte to the Alcázar.

'We must meet her in person and recompense her for her father's sacrifice,' Felipe said. 'What do you think would be appropriate, cousin?'

'A title, Your Majesty,' he replied. 'It would demonstrate your generosity.'

'What do you think, Don José?'

'Well, you had already considered it,' Don José de Grimaldo remarked.

'In that case, if my beloved wife is in agreement,' Felipe said.

Isabel looked at him and smiled mischievously.

'Diego knows I never oppose anything he asks of me,' she answered.

After spending the rest of the morning with them, he was able to talk to Don José alone. The latter told him to leave the matter of the title in his hands.

'As soon as I can, I will organize a meeting and call you.'

'You don't know how grateful I am, Don José,' the duke replied. He was sure the king would keep his word. It had been important to emphasize the qualities of Doctor Belmonte so that any favour would be seen as a well-deserved reward for his family. He was fortunate that doctors enjoyed a good reputation among the aristocracy. They were, for example, exempt from the taxes that other commoners had to pay to the king. And now, with the king and queen on their side, all the aristocracy of Madrid would share his compassion for Clara Belmonte, seeing her as a symbol of the suffering of war.

As the carriage rattled over the rough surface of the city streets, the duke stroked his chin and reflected that the most difficult part of his plan was yet to come. The title in itself would not give Clara access to the court – securing the social acceptance of a commoner was going to be the real challenge. For that reason, he must move carefully and ensure that Their Majesties accepted a simple request once the title had been granted: that Clara Belmonte be accepted as one of the ladies-in-waiting of the royal children. This would certainly be a difficult obstacle to overcome, as the ladies-in-waiting of the queen and her children were normally drawn only from the highest born. And so, before he even submitted this request to the king and queen, before he moved so much as a finger in that direction, he needed to find allies for his cause, other nobles whose support he could rely upon, otherwise his plan would be doomed to failure. And so, he was going to meet the Countess of Altamira, Doña Ángela Foch de Aragón, the queen's first lady-in-waiting. In the duke's favour was the fact that each year he had personally spoken to her at the Alcázar to invite her to attend the festivities at Castamar with her son. She had, moreover, been one of Alba's closest friends and had mourned her death greatly.

If Don Diego secured her support, then it would be easier to obtain Clara's entrance into the royal court. Only then would he tell Their Majesties how deeply in love he was with Clara Belmonte, the eldest daughter of Don Armando, and how important it was to his spiritual well-being that he be able to marry her. He knew that the king, who had always encouraged him to remarry, just as he himself had done, and who confided his melancholic states to the duke by letter, would do whatever was within his power to make Don Diego a more frequent visitor to the court. He suspected that Queen Isabel would take a different tack and would wish to make the girl's acquaintance before granting her consent. If Their Majesties gave their approval, then nobody would oppose the match.

As he descended from the carriage, Doña Ángela came to greet him with open arms.

'My dear Don Diego, I was so pleased to receive your visiting card.'

'Doña Ángela,' he said, taking her hand. 'I hoped to see you at the Alcázar.'

'I had to leave, with the queen's permission, to resolve some family matters.'

'I know I gave my word that I would visit you after the festivities but believe me I have my excuses.'

'You are always excused, Don Diego,' she smiled. 'No explanations are necessary.'

'Even so, allow me to explain the reasons for my delay.'

46

5 November 1721

Ursula now found herself in a terrifying, unknown land. Never in all her life had she felt as much panic as during the hours she spent watching her office door, waiting for Don Melquíades. She had been completely defeated in the war between them, with only one ephemeral victory in many months. Her goal of expelling the cook had also ended in unconditional surrender.

Two days ago, Don Diego had addressed the servants, informing them that Señorita Belmonte had recovered her lost social rank and would now be a guest in the house, one with access to the kitchens. All the staff knew that the duke had asked for her hand in strict secret, officially making her his betrothed. Many applauded this, but to Ursula the situation was intolerable, and she had to flee whenever she encountered Señorita Belmonte. Nothing made sense. Thirteen months ago, this girl had been a simple kitchen hand, and now she was going to be the mistress of Castamar. It made her stomach turn; she saw the young woman as an intruder, a grotesque being born into this new era in which different classes mixed. *Good God*, she thought. *Where will this all end?*

Yet, she also had to acknowledge that her admiration for Clara Belmonte had hugely increased, especially since those words of hers that had become engraved on Ursula's soul: 'I won't leave without you, Doña Ursula.' She had said this in full knowledge that the vile Don Enrique wanted to rape her. Anyone else would have run off in terror, especially when Doña Ursula had given her an excuse by ordering her to leave. Ursula knew that fear all too well. She had experienced it with her father for many years and then at the hands of her husband. She knew the terror that took hold of you, warning you to keep your head down to avoid being hit with the strap of the belt or, worse still, the buckle. Upon seeing fear and determination distilled at once in Clara Belmonte's eyes, Ursula's admiration for her had become a kind of affection.

She kept telling herself that it was only natural for her to be disoriented by seeing Señorita Belmonte as the mistress of the house. Perhaps the best thing to do was to leave Castamar before she burst from consternation. Even so, Señorita Belmonte, now living in one of the guest rooms, continued working in the kitchens as if it were quite normal. To make matters worse, Don Diego was seeking to ennoble the Belmonte name. Knowing the duke's determination, unless God stopped him, there was nothing Ursula could do to change the fact that she would have to put up with seeing Señorita Belmonte become Duchess Clara of Castamar.

Both Doña Mercedes and Señorita Belmonte had tried to persuade Don Diego to leave Don Enrique in the hands of the king's justice. Don Diego had shown great calm as he listened to their petitions, as if he had everything under control. Then he told them that this man had insulted him in every way possible, had tried to destroy everything he loved and had caused the destruction of his first marriage, and for that, he must die by Don Diego's hand. Seeing that no one could convince him, on the morning of the previous day, Ursula had had a second meeting with Doña Mercedes, Don Melquíades and Señorita Belmonte, in which they had decided to tell him what had happened.

'Whose idea was it for you to see him alone?' he asked, furious.

'That doesn't matter,' Señorita Belmonte replied.

'I demand to know, damn it!' the duke said, his knuckles white with fury.

His betrothed looked at him and took a calm, steady breath.

'I'm not going to tell you because it's not important,' she said.

'Good God, the women in this house!' he complained. 'They're simply ungovernable!'

Ursula, following her own maxim that servants must be faithful even when it might result in harm, stepped forward and said it had been her idea, that the responsibility lay solely with her, since she had accepted the marquess's request. But before Don Diego could say anything, Doña Mercedes's voice burst forth from the back of the room.

'It was me,' she said. 'I won't let you take the blame for something you didn't do, Señora Berenguer.'

The duke, frozen with rage, clutched his glass so tightly the housekeeper worried it would shatter.

'I will understand if you wish me to leave Castamar,' Doña Mercedes said.

Don Diego had stormed out in a rage, his lips sealed so that he wouldn't say anything he would regret. He spent the whole day alone, not even wishing to see Clara. Finally, Don Diego had left suddenly, without saying goodbye. Thanks to Doña Mercedes, Ursula discovered that his lordship had received a letter a few days ago from his friend Alfredo informing him that Francisco had been wounded by Doña Sol, who was nowhere to be found.

Everyone hoped the duke would not get himself killed by walking into a trap, but Ursula was not worried about that. Don Diego was a hot-blooded man, but once his rage had subsided, he had the tactician's cool temperament. Even so, all the events of the last few days felt strange to her, as if she were living in a world she did not recognize, and if Señorita Belmonte's social ascent and behaviour felt strange to her, then the feelings which Don Melquíades had revealed to her at the height of their pitched battle were even more so.

That man is completely loopy, she'd thought several times. She did not understand how he could have loved her in silence after all the pain she had caused him. She had been so overwhelmed by his confession that she had run off immediately. But her bewilderment had only grown when Don Melquíades had entered with a gun to rescue her from that odious nobleman. Ursula, who always spurned any male contact, had sought refuge in his arms and let him take her by the waist. Though she didn't know how things had come to this, she couldn't help constantly remembering the comforting warmth she had felt as she sheltered behind his body. Not only had he saved her from the predatory Don Enrique, he had also said something to the marquess that had penetrated deep into her soul: 'And have no doubt, your grace, that if you had done any irreparable damage to either of these two women, I would have put a bullet in your head myself. Even though I am not your equal and I would have hanged for it.' He had not only defended Señorita Belmonte's honour but hers too.

It seemed that declaring his love at such a heated moment had renewed his weary spirit. In fact, she had been amazed by how efficiently he had been running Castamar recently. It was like the early days, when Don Melquíades had seemed to have the gift of being everywhere at once. Her view of him had changed radically, no matter how much it pained her to accept it. Now she could no longer make out her enemy beneath that strong countenance, but rather a man who looked at her with a sincere desire, a tenderness that tore her apart. In his presence, a voice whispered dangerous words into her ears, stating that another kind of life was possible: one in which she would not be on a constant war footing, one in which she might experience relationships not based on victory or defeat. But this change made her so afraid of becoming a lifeless puppet again that she repeatedly told herself it was all a trick.

The days had passed in this way, their exchanges limited only to work matters, until he took the initiative and called her to have a private conversation.

'We can't continue this way, Doña Ursula, I beg you to respond to my declaration in some way,' he said.

'I don't have to make any comment on the topic,' she answered drily. 'My silence says it all, Don Melquíades.'

From the way he had looked at her, it was as if she had just caused him more damage than all that accumulated over the previous years. At that moment, Ursula had not known what to say or do. He had got up and placed himself right in front of her. Without taking his eyes off her, he had nodded, and the housekeeper believed that his stupid declaration of love would die in that office.

'But you must understand that I deserve to hear your answer from your own lips.'

She had been paralysed, completely bewildered by this combination of strength and vulnerability.

'If you insist,' she said, her voice trembling more than she would have liked. 'I don't love you, and I never will. In fact, I could not love you even if you were the last man on earth. I despise you.'

Don Melquíades had looked at her with an unusual air of fortitude, enduring her harsh words. She had backed away when he took a step forward. She had wanted her words to be sufficiently forceful that he would never insinuate anything again. *This fool just won't give up*, she told herself. Then Don Melquíades, having apologized and told her he would never mention the matter again, had turned around and said he had spoken to Don Diego about the management of the kitchen and that they had decided that she would remain in charge of the kitchens after all. Once he had left, she had felt hugely relieved, as if everything were returning to normal. However, as time had gone by, something had begun to stir inside her and she felt a sense of discomfort, as if Don Melquíades's acceptance of his defeat had left her utterly alone.

By the following morning, the feeling of loss had been so great that she had deliberately bumped into him on several occasions. She constantly scolded herself for these feelings, but the more time passed, the stronger she felt she could no longer tolerate the unhappiness she had always felt and that she did not want to miss out on the opportunity of having another kind of life. However, these thoughts were soon followed by others denying any kind of attraction towards him. She insulted him under her breath and told herself she was simply shaken by his unexpected declaration. Finally, after Don Diego's sudden departure, she had been unable to avoid stealing sidelong glances at Don Melquíades during the servants' meal.

The daylight now fading, she felt compelled to know what he was doing, and slipped away to spy on him while he took care of business with the registrar. There, behind the safety of the doors, she had watched him, seeing him in a different light, becoming so absorbed that Don Melquíades and the registrar almost discovered her when they left the room. She couldn't be sure they hadn't seen her before she had run off around the corner like a little girl. Two hours later, Don Melquíades had paid a seemingly routine visit to her office to ask her to check if his lordship's silver was clean. Then Don Melquíades had suddenly come closer and whispered to her.

'I know what you're going through. And tonight, once the working day is over, I will come and talk to you again.'

'I don't know what you're referring to, Don Melquíades,' she answered, gripped by a terror which made her clasp the chair tight. 'I believe I've told you everything you need to hear.'

He left without a word, and she had to sit down and try to regain her calm. *What does this man want from me?* she asked herself. But she could not deny that a deep wish for peace had become rooted in her, along with the need to feel the protection and tenderness that pleased her so. *Entering that world means accepting defeat*, she told herself. *What am I thinking? That man is an irresponsible lunatic, a fool, an insufferable oaf!* And yet she recognized that Don Melquíades had never sought war. In reality, Ursula knew the battle had been one-sided – she alone had tried to subjugate and humiliate him. *It's only what he deserves*, she had convinced herself. But these words lacked their former power and sense. *I am not remotely interested in what that scruffy mediocrity of a man has to say to me*, she resolved as she left the office. *I will not even dignify him with a response.*

Now that sunset was approaching, she felt a strong sense of trepidation as she waited for Don Melquíades to call for her. *What have I got to say to a fool like that?* she repeated to herself. Deciding that the best thing she could do was go to bed early, she asked one of the maids to inform the head butler that she was retiring to her bedroom until tomorrow. A timely retreat was no different from a victory. Don Melquíades could not visit her in her room without causing a scandal. She walked down the corridor, feeling a sense of relief when she closed the door behind her. She began to relax as she realized that the day was over and Melquíades had not shown up. She undressed and got into bed, imagining what would have happened if their conversation had taken place, what he would have said and how she would have reacted. She tried to drift off to sleep, telling herself again that he was an insufferable man. She had just leaned over to put out the lantern on the bedside table when she heard a knock at the door.

It's him, she thought. *That man has truly lost the plot. Coming to my room in the middle of the night!*

When she opened the door, she saw Don Melquíades grinning serenely and stroking his moustache.

'What do you want?' she whispered. 'Go away and leave me in peace.'

'Allow me to enter,' he said loudly.

'Have you lost whatever wits you still possess? Who do you think you are, coming here in the middle of the night?' she whispered indignantly. 'Out, fool!'

Don Melquíades put his foot in the way, pushed until the door was open and entered the room. Astonished, she told him she had nothing to say to him.

'When Don Diego finds out you forced your way into this bedroom, you will be expelled from Castamar,' she whispered as he made his way inexorably forward and she retreated. 'You might as well quit now, Don Melquíades – tomorrow will be your last day. Get out!'

He remained silent, waiting for her to calm down a little, before stopping his advance and taking a breath as he looked at her tenderly.

'I love you,' he said.

On hearing this, her eyes nearly popped out of their sockets. She was about to answer when he came even closer. Ursula just stood there like an idiot, waiting for him to stop looking at her like that, as if he could see her wounded spirit, her broken soul. He advanced a step further, and she stepped back. Ursula repeated that she wanted him to leave immediately, though far less emphatically this time. When he reached out his hands to brush her lips, she bit the tips of his fingers. He moaned a little but did not put up any resistance. He simply looked at her, enduring the pain.

'Ursula,' he said. 'Look at me.'

She looked up and understood that she did not need to fight any longer.

'You should not love me,' she whispered. 'I hate you.'

'Then make sure I am dismissed tomorrow,' he said quietly.

'You're a dullard, an idiot, an unbearable mediocrity,' she said, 'and I hate you with all my soul.'

He kissed her gently. Ursula moved away and slapped him. Don Melquíades kissed her again and she slapped him again. Don Melquíades looked at her and once more placed his lips on her cheek.

'Why are you doing this?' she asked.

'Because I love you. I always have and I always will.'

She slapped him again and he grabbed her by the waist and kissed her passionately. Ursula felt the hairs standing up on the back of her neck, and for the first time in her life she did not feel disgusted by a man's kiss. She understood that deep down in her heart she harboured a desire for love, that contemptible sentiment which she had always hated, and which made her as scandalously human as everyone else.

47

6–7 November 1721

As he rode down Calle Leganitos, forging a path through the crowds, Hernaldo thought to himself that at least his daughter was safe. He had spent the last few days in Don Enrique's house while the marquess decided what to do about Doña Sol, and had it not been for the message he had received from Don Diego, he would have continued to waste his time in that mansion, which was as sad and gloomy as the marquess himself. Don Enrique remained locked in silence, afflicted by a melancholy that, if it continued, would surely carry him to the grave without any need for Don Diego to put a bullet in his head. And now there was another problem. Hernaldo found himself forced to choose between Don Enrique and his daughter, and in this contest, there could be only one winner.

To Hernaldo de la Marca,
On this day, two of my personal guards presented themselves at your dwelling to deliver a letter written by my hand to your daughter, Adela. The letter explained that she would be escorted to my house in Leganitos, whence I write these lines.
Before causing more pain and injury than you have already provoked, I beg you to think of your daughter's future, as it would be unfortunate were she to have to live with the contempt of those around her if they knew her to be the daughter of a murderer. To give you an idea of your true situation, I will only say that I am

already cognizant of criminal actions towards my wife, my friends
and myself. We know that you murdered Daniel Forrado and a
prostitute by the name of La Zalamera, among others, on the orders
of your master, and that you orchestrated the assault on Señorita
Castro and the abduction of my brother, Don Gabriel de Castamar.

It is my hope that you will not choose the path of perdition
by advising Don Enrique of this communication, and that you
will instead present yourself at my house on Calle Leganitos to
surrender to the forces of justice. If you do so, I give my word that
your daughter's future will not be compromised.

Yours,

Don Diego de Castamar

Hernaldo's blood had frozen in his veins and his guts had
been gripped by fear. He had begun to shake and sweat, and he
had to sit down. The serenity he displayed when depriving his
unfortunate victims of their lives had abandoned him. The mere
thought of his daughter's misfortune made his knees tremble.
Something had gone wrong, some loose end he had left untied.

The negro was surely on his way to the Americas, and La
Zalamera, Jacinta and El Zurdo were dead. The only possibility
was that the latter had arranged for some proof to come into
Don Diego's possession in the event of his death. But El Zurdo
was not so cunning, he had nobody to trust, and he barely knew
how to write. When Hernaldo had despatched him in the yard
and left him to die, he had not had the impression that the man
had something up his sleeve. Had that been the case, the dying
man would surely have boasted of it. Only Doña Sol could have
revealed the details of the mission the marquess had assigned
to him and the events surrounding the death of the duke's wife.
However, the duke had made no mention of her in his note. El
Zurdo was the only one who knew the full story. *It must have*
been him, he thought. *He was the only one with nothing to lose.*
Even so, it was inexplicable. He had left El Zurdo at death's
door. Whatever the truth of the matter, it was no longer of much

importance: Don Diego knew about the conspiracy. The only surprise was that Don Diego had not appeared at the marquess's estate at the head of an army of watchmen, guards and bailiffs to arrest them. There was no question that the duke had enough power and influence to make the machinery of justice turn against them. But he had preferred to show the most absolute discretion in untangling the web they had woven. Indeed, as Hernaldo reread the lines about the capture of Don Gabriel, he had the sense that the negro had already been rescued.

Now treachery was his only option. He would not consent to his daughter becoming a pariah, and he knew that if Don Diego so wished he could ruin Adela's reputation throughout Spain and indeed the Americas with just one click of his fingers. Once her father was whipped and hanged in the public square, she would be stigmatized wherever she went; she would be the daughter of a traitor and a villain, nobody would employ her, nobody would marry her, and she would be forced to sell her body to survive. His own death would destroy his life's only dream: to see his daughter prosper. *I won't allow Adela to pay for my crimes*, he told himself. He and no other was responsible for his vile actions.

There was no point informing the marquess now. And so, without giving any explanation, he had taken one of Don Enrique's horses and set off without delay for Calle Leganitos.

He entered the capital as the sun was setting and galloped down San Juan Bautista towards the fountain of Leganitos. A group of guards was stationed outside Don Diego's mansion, waiting to take his horse, disarm him and escort him into the duke's presence. He was led into a large courtyard, which gave onto the house itself, the servants' quarters, the gardens and the stables. Don Diego was waiting for him, sitting by an ornate fountain, holding a small knife in his hand with which he was peeling an apple. Hernaldo walked slowly towards him, well aware that the guards were elite soldiers who would easily overpower him at the slightest false move. He could tell that

Don Diego was sizing him up, noting his age and his physical strength, like an expert soldier. Hernaldo expected nothing less.

Afraid that Don Diego might have harmed his daughter, he immediately asked where Adela was. Don Diego didn't reply and instead gestured to Hernaldo to be silent. As the two men held each other's gaze, as if in a silent duel, Hernaldo understood that this man, whom Don Enrique had sought to destroy, had a fierce, indomitable spirit and that he would sooner die than surrender to his adversaries.

'Listen to me, murderer,' Don Diego said calmly. 'Don't ever confuse your methods with mine.'

Hernaldo knew that his question had offended the duke, and that nobody there would touch a hair on Adela's head. He also knew, from Don Diego's self-assured movements, that the duke felt completely sure of his victory, and that Hernaldo was there for one reason only: to allow the duke to obtain justice.

'I don't need your daughter to force you to do my bidding,' he continued. 'Unlike you and that master of yours, I have brought her here for her own safety. Had Don Enrique heard that you had come to see me, he would have been quite capable of ordering her abduction to ensure your silence. Your daughter is a guest in this house, something you will never be.'

'I beg your forgiveness, your grace,' Hernaldo said, 'and I thank you for your consideration towards Adela. If there is anything I can do for you before I am taken away, please say so.'

Don Diego nodded and told him there were two ways in which he could leave this world.

'In the first, the whole world will know you are a murderer, capable of killing and mutilating men and even women. That public knowledge will become an unbearable burden for your daughter. In the second, you will embark upon your journey to hell with discretion, without a public execution. In that event, Adela will not suffer the consequences of your actions and I will ensure that, if she does not marry, she will find employment in a noble house.'

Hernaldo did not need to consider his options.

'Then you may go in and take your leave of your daughter,' Don Diego said. 'We will conclude our conversation later.'

Hernaldo sighed as he realized that his days were coming to an end, and his only regret was that he would not be there to see his darling married. Don Diego made for one of the courtyard gates but suddenly stopped.

'Tell me, what was Don Enrique's motive for organizing my downfall in this manner?'

'You stole victory from the Habsburg party of which the marquess was a secret supporter, and with that you robbed him of the chance of becoming a Grandee of Spain,' he replied. 'But he might perhaps have forgiven you that and accepted his defeat had you not also deprived him of the person he loved most.'

Don Diego frowned, unable to make sense of what he had just heard. The duke's confusion confirmed Hernaldo's suspicion that he had never known of the depth of the friendship between his wife and Don Enrique, nor of the latter's ambitions in her regard. It was clear the duchess had remained silent on the subject.

'Doña Alba, your grace,' he said, to the duke's continuing perplexity. 'The marquess had been about to propose to her when your own betrothal to her was announced. Your wife's death plunged the marquess into such despair that he was on the verge of committing suicide and, unless I am much mistaken, he may do so now.'

Don Diego was silent as he tried to absorb this information.

Hernaldo was shown through a small wooden door that gave onto a gallery. He climbed the stairs to the floor above and the lieutenant led him into a drawing room. There, his daughter was waiting for him, her eyes red and swollen from crying, aware that these would be their final moments together.

'Have they told you everything?' Hernaldo asked. Adela nodded and, distraught, embraced him and wept, soaking his dirty shirt with her tears. He told her she was the best thing that had ever happened in his life, that any happiness he had experienced on this earth had been provided by her. Adela just hugged him more tightly – as she used to do when she was a little girl and woke up in the middle of the night – trying to dispel the rising sense of panic.

'It's time for you to fly free, my bird. I have done all I can to ensure that, when I am no longer here, you can fend for yourself.'

Hernaldo encircled her with his arms, as if wanting to protect her for eternity.

'I am a vile and miserable man, but I have been lucky enough to have you in my life.'

Trembling, she clung to him more tightly still, her whole body gripped by anguish.

'Father,' she said, 'Father…'

Hernaldo fixed the embrace in his memory, so that he could relive it when he was on the scaffold and fend off the fear of being reunited with the ghosts awaiting him on the other side. He calmed himself, kissed her on the forehead and told her to take the money and, after his execution, travel to the coast to see the sea, as she had always wanted. She clung to him, trying to stop him from leaving.

'You have to let me go, my little bird,' he said. 'It's time for me to stop killing and to cease being a burden to you.'

Adela slowly loosened her embrace. He stopped on the threshold and looked back, and he exchanged a final glance with his daughter – she silently telling him that she loved him, and he replying that not even death could destroy his feelings for her. Then the door closed and Adela let out a cry.

He was led away to find out what Don Diego wanted of him.

In the drawing room, the duke awaited him, warming himself at the fire that was burning in the hearth. The duke instructed him to sit, and Hernaldo thanked him again for his treatment of Adela. Don Diego scrutinized Hernaldo's weather-beaten face for a moment before he spoke.

'I thought you were just another murderer like El Zurdo,'

Don Diego said, 'another man with no morals who doesn't know the meaning of love.'

'That may be the only difference between El Zurdo and me, your grace,' Hernaldo replied. 'I don't doubt that you will keep your word with respect to my daughter, and I swear that I will do whatever I must.'

'You will spend the night here, and at dawn you will return to your master's house,' the duke said smoothly, 'and you will persuade him to come to the oak wood on the edge of his estate that same morning. Can you do that?'

Hernaldo nodded. It would be sufficient to tell the marquess that he and his man had captured Doña Sol Montijos, for whom Don Enrique harboured an intense hatred, he explained. Don Diego seemed to be in agreement, although Hernaldo saw him wince at mention of the marquess's name.

He guessed that Don Diego had decided not to involve the forces of the law in the case of Don Enrique. His intention, rather, was to challenge him to a duel and put him to death. Unfortunately for the marquess, this duel would not be fought with flintlocks, as he would have preferred, but with swords. Hernaldo stood up and saluted the duke, as if he were his military superior rather than a nobleman, and thought to himself that his betrayal of his master would be his final act of villainy. He stopped for a moment and, his curiosity getting the better of him, asked if the duke would clear up a doubt he had. The duke nodded.

'How did you find out about everything?' he asked. 'It was El Zurdo, wasn't it?'

'You don't deserve to know,' the duke replied curtly, closing the matter. 'You are a man who has misplaced his loyalties.'

The duke's refusal notwithstanding, Hernaldo thanked him for his reply and was escorted away, thinking that maybe Don Diego was right. All his life he had served the interests of others, who had only caused death and suffering. Perhaps he would have lived a better life serving somebody like the duke;

he would have led a quieter existence guarding Don Diego's estate and protecting his horses from thieves. The only thing that would have calmed his addiction to blood and death would have been his daughter. And so long as he was with her, he would have happily spent his years wandering the grounds of Castamar, by the side of a master who would never have ordered him to perform ignoble acts. *I was never a good or a just man*, he told himself. *The only person I have known how to love was my little bird. Caring for her is the only good thing I have done with my life.*

He was led to a small room and given some supper and a clean mattress to sleep on. They locked the door and left him there, his only company the moonlight that filtered in through a small window in the ceiling. He lay down, aware that his life's journey was coming to its end. *Dying is just one more tedious errand*, he thought. He closed his eyes and was soon fast asleep.

When he opened his eyes again, it was still dark outside but they were already hammering on the door to rouse him. He was to be escorted on his final mission. One more act of villainy, this time perpetuated against the only man who had ever treated him with decency.

The journey back to Soto de Navamedina would take a couple of hours, and Hernaldo left Madrid resolved to meet his death, in the knowledge that in this way he would not bring further misfortune on his daughter. Under escort, he rode out through the Puerta de San Joaquín, leaving the Molino Quemado path on his left, and riding up the Manzanares valley. As the sun appeared on the horizon, he imagined Don Enrique's face when he understood that his most loyal servant had led him into a trap. He felt dirty at the thought of committing the only crime he had not yet committed: breaking his word.

However, now that he was about to leave this world for the burning fires of hell, he cared little for the pain this would inflict on the marquess, even if he had been a good master, caring for him and his daughter, maintaining him and ensuring he never endured hunger, never asking him to do anything beyond that which they had agreed.

The lieutenant pointed out an oak wood, not far beyond the bounds of Don Enrique's estate, as the place to which he should lead the marquess. The perfect setting for a duel, well away from roads and passers-by, with a stream close at hand should they need to wash their wounds afterwards. Hernaldo told the lieutenant he was familiar with the spot. He crossed the boundary to the Soto de Navamedina estate and rode up the avenue to the manor house. He left the marquess's horse in the stables and calmly set out to commit his act of treachery. He asked one of the footmen where the marquess was, and was informed that Don Enrique had risen early and had gone out to practise his marksmanship. He made his way towards the sound of the pistol shots and, on finding the marquess practising for a duel that he would never fight, he felt a burning in his entrails, a pain that told him there was nothing left of him now – no honour, no loyalty, just betrayal and death.

Enrique was taking aim at the trunk of a chestnut tree when he was informed of his man's arrival. He smiled, as if by so doing, he could erase his feelings of frustration, sadness and bitterness. Even though he had washed and shaved that morning, his impeccable appearance was nothing but a mask which concealed the truth about Alba's death. And so, he had decided to take out his pistols, hoping that imagining he was blowing Doña Sol's head off would help him to relax.

Enrique stole a sideways glance at Hernaldo, who had stopped a few yards off, waiting until the marquess signalled to him to approach.

'I didn't see you last night,' Enrique told him.

'One of my men sent word that they had the opportunity of capturing Doña Sol alive.'

The marquess's eyes lit up.

'Do you have her?' he asked, and Hernaldo nodded, without breaking eye contact. 'Where is she?'

'My men have her in a clearing near the estate, in the wood by the Valdeurraca stream. I told them to keep her there so she wouldn't be linked to you,' he said. 'I wanted to be sure Don Diego's spies wouldn't see us bringing her to the mansion.'

Enrique felt a macabre excitement. Doña Sol couldn't imagine the pain she would have to endure before he finally ended her life. He knew that the satisfaction of seeing her suffer would only deepen the bottomless pit of his soul, but he didn't care. He ordered his butler to prepare his horse and gestured to Hernaldo to follow him.

'You have perhaps been cautious in excess, as the roads have been kept clear upon my orders, but if you have her captive, then we will keep her there until nightfall before we bring her here,' he said.

They both galloped off as if there were no time to lose. They left the estate and rode across country. Then, following the course of the stream, they headed for the wood. When they came to the clearing and dismounted, Enrique sensed that something was wrong. There was no sign of any men, of a cart or of Doña Sol. He frowned and looked to Hernaldo for an explanation, while his intuition told him that the only man he trusted had betrayed him.

'I'm sorry, Don Enrique,' Hernaldo confirmed. 'I know you don't deserve it.'

Enrique said nothing, and simply stood there as the guards appeared from among the trees and surrounded him. He fixed his henchman with a sad smile. A shadow came over his face and his lips blanched when he saw Don Diego de Castamar appear. His frock coat was open, revealing his épée. Hernaldo tried to speak but Enrique held up a hand and stopped him.

'It doesn't matter, Hernaldo,' he said. 'It's time to bring this tragedy to an end. I imagine they already know everything and that we, unfortunately, will once again find ourselves on the losing side. I hope Adela is well.'

Hernaldo nodded.

Enrique faced Don Diego. The duke threw a sword at his feet.

'You may choose whether to take up the challenge or be taken to the jail so that you may be judged and hanged in the public square, while you soil yourself before all present.'

Enrique stared at him rigidly. The duke was well aware that no noble wanted to die before the mob, and so, he bent down to pick up the sword. Then he drew it from its scabbard.

'I want to say something before we fight,' Diego said.

'Speak,' Enrique replied, with a forced smile on his lips. 'Nobody is stopping you.'

'My brother is safe, Señorita Castro and my wife to be, Señorita Belmonte, are also safe, and your man has betrayed you,' he said, slowly.

'Then I can only congratulate you upon your victory, your grace,' Enrique replied sarcastically.

'And the only thing that remains to you is to have sufficient valour to accept an ineluctable truth,' Don Diego continued, as if he had not heard the marquess's response.

'That I loathe you with every fibre in my body.'

'That is where you are wrong,' Don Diego answered, his eyes flashing with fury, approaching until he was just inches away. 'Accept, once and for all, that the hatred you feel for me is just a reflection of that which you feel for yourself, as the man with sole responsibility for the death of my wife, my darling Alba.'

Enrique's expression suddenly darkened, his smile vanished, and he took a step back. Those words had inflicted a mortal wound, cutting deeper than any steel. He had deceived himself for all these years in a desperate attempt to survive, filling his empty soul with the hatred of others in order not to direct it at himself. He had covered his guilt for the death of Alba with vengeance, intrigue and deceit. But now there were no alleyways down which to flee nor plots in which to seek refuge. Don Diego's words confronted him with a truth from which he had been running for ten years.

'I can't-deny the truth, your grace. As always. She loved you more, she married you, and she died because of me.' And saying this, driven by bitterness, he threw himself at Don Diego.

Without hesitating, the duke drove his sword into the marquess's chest, and he watched the life drain from his eyes.

'But you won't escape this duel uninjured,' Don Enrique said, with a twisted smile. 'Alba and I were kindred spirits, and I drank from her lips when she was already your wife.'

He laughed as he fell on his knees before his enemy, who looked at him with contempt. Then he emitted a final groan of pain as Don Diego placed his boot on his chest and withdrew his sword. Don Enrique's vision clouded over, and in the mist, he searched only for Alba, calling her name. He allowed himself to be carried away on a string of beautiful but fleeting memories: his maid, Dolores, playing at hoops; drinking with Hernaldo at a simple supper. Then, suddenly, Alba appeared, eternal, on horseback, riding by the Jarama; sitting beneath a sunshade on a summer evening, drinking tea; lying there while the war raged in the world beyond, their fingers intertwined as they watched the stars come out; observing as the warm breeze caressed the hairs on the back of her neck during one of their trips to the coast. Alba, Alba, and more Alba. He saw himself observing her silken lips and her bright eyes, listening to her soothing voice. As his life drained away, he travelled from one scene to the next until he finally came to rest, on that sunny spring day in the Alcázar, she in her white dress, with that face that could rule an empire. He had gone to fetch some almond milk and had turned to catch her observing him, spellbound, from a short distance away. She looked away and hid behind her fan, and he smiled and gave her the glass.

'I caught you looking at me,' he said.

She nodded, blushed delightfully, and took him by the arm.

'Of course, my dear marquess, there is not a single lady at this gathering who would not be eager to marry you.'

PART FOUR

23 FEBRUARY TO 26 NOVEMBER

1722

48

Alfredo gazed out at the open sea. For someone as unaccustomed to sailing as he was, the first days on board had been sheer hell. Overcome with seasickness, he had vomited repeatedly. After the first week, however, he was able to go out on deck and walk among the crew. Now, after almost two months' journey, he could admire the way the ship sailed gracefully into the setting sun.

Almost four months after his private life had been exposed, he no longer lamented his exile or the scandal; he was instead overcome with sadness at not having seen Francisco before his death. His friend had decided to keep him away until the end, and after his passing, his notary had delivered Alfredo a dictated letter. Terrified at the possibility that Francisco's last words would be ones of reproach or contempt, he had been unable to summon the courage to even open it.

That's why he was now toying with his friend's missive, trying to decide whether to read it or to throw it into the sea unread. Just thinking of Francisco had the power to dispirit him further and make him feel even guiltier. The simple act of attending his burial had made Alfredo cry bitter tears for days on end.

There had been little difference between the funeral of Don Enrique, buried with no witnesses in his family pantheon, and that of Francisco, which had drawn only a small crowd. This hurt, since in life, few people had had more friends than

Francisco. It weighed heavy on Alfredo to think that his own choices had harmed his friend. Alfredo had chosen to keep a prudent distance, since his sentence of exile had been made public and he did not wish for his loss of prestige to affect the Marlango family. Ever since his predilections had become public knowledge, none of the aristocracy had come near him, except for Diego. He was a social pariah.

After Francisco's funeral, Alfredo had left Madrid; only Señorita Castro, Doña Mercedes, Diego and Señorita Belmonte had received him at Castamar before his departure. Clara's cooking had awoken a desire for conversation, though Francisco's memory was present throughout the meal despite some recent good news.

They had learned that the king wished to ennoble the Belmontes as a reward for Don Armando's heroic death. Señorita Belmonte's misfortunes had become a common topic of conversation among the nobility. The king and queen and members of the court were very impressed by her. Queen Isabel, so fascinated by the Italian dishes Señorita Belmonte had cooked, had requested that they walk together so that she could get to know her personally. Diego had arranged for Clara's mother, sister and brother-in-law to travel to the estate from their different locations in Europe. A month later, they had learned that His Majesty had given the Belmontes the title of Baronesses of Pleamar. At last, Don Diego's plan had begun to come to fruition.

With Alfredo's exile from Spain set in stone by then, that evening at Castamar had been a farewell dinner. Everyone knew he could not attend the wedding and so, when he had said goodbye, he gave his most sincere congratulations. Diego, visibly upset at his departure, had hugged him and told him he would do everything he could to ensure his return to Spain as soon as possible.

'Leave it be, Diego,' Alfredo had replied. 'First, I have to find a way to forgive myself for destroying Francisco's honour and deceiving you all for so long. Besides, returning here would mean having to make a series of sacrifices, such as getting married, and what would be the value in coming back only to be an outcast in my own land?'

Diego told him it would be painful to have him so far away, especially after Francisco's death, which had left him with these same feelings of loss and abandonment. Besides, whenever Diego and he mentioned Francisco's name, both perceived in each other the dangerous rancour they held towards themselves for not having got there in time, for not having been more involved, for allowing Doña Sol to escape to God knows where. Sometime after the funeral, Alfredo had discovered that Francisco had never read beyond the first letter he sent him: the others had been discovered in Doña Sol's bureau at her estate in Montijos.

When Diego had arrived at Francisco's house, he was told that his friend had been drifting in and out of consciousness throughout his ordeal. While awake, Francisco had found out about being ostracized and that Doña Sol was responsible for defaming him. Francisco's butler had told Diego that upon discovering this he had simply closed his eyes and smiled faintly. Then he had only enough strength left to dictate the letter to Alfredo before losing consciousness for good. Having watched him die, Diego had left with his heart broken, his only aim now to defeat Don Enrique in a duel and find Doña Sol.

After dispensing with the marquess, Diego had spent a great deal of time and money trying to find Doña Sol and bring her back to Spain. Alfredo considered it a lost cause, since the well-resourced Doña Sol would likely have settled in Denmark, Vienna or perhaps London, and it would be impossible to force her to return. She would have made powerful friends, enemies of Spain who would protect her.

'I know that what I'm going to say will be difficult for you to hear,' Alfredo had told Diego, 'but if you don't find Doña

Sol soon, forget about her. You are going to marry a wonderful woman, and if you insist on obsessively seeking justice it will only bring misfortune. You will neglect your new wife for a compensation that will only leave you empty.'

Diego had thanked him for his honesty, as if he understood the value Alberto's words held. And so, Alfredo had left Castamar with a broken heart, aware that he might never see his friend again.

He gulped, continuing to finger the seal of Francisco's letter with his fingertips. Impulsively, he opened it in the hope that the words written by a dying Francisco would save him.

Dear Alfredo,

I am going to die because of the vice of accepting dangerous widows into my bed. You did warn me that I might be biting off more than I could chew with Doña Sol.

Now that I barely have the strength to dictate these words, and find myself wavering between life and death, I must dedicate these lines to you, in a tribute to our long-lasting friendship. I will not deny that I felt deeply disappointed on finding out about your predilection, especially the fact that you have deceived me for so long. Despite this sense of disappointment, I must tell you that the friendship, affection and admiration I have felt for you all my life, even more so in my last moments, have not reduced one iota. Because of this, I wish you to know that all that remains in my heart is our sincere love and friendship, for when a man is close to death, all that matters to him is the life he has lived, and you, Alfredo, have always been an older brother to me.

Now that I am at the gates of death, and my entire life has come into view, all that remains is to offer you some last pieces of advice, born from my deep affection towards you, my friend: try as much as you can to accept who and what you are, since there is no greater calamity than hating oneself.

When your hour comes, you will understand, as I understand now, that all that aversion and self-loathing with which you have punished yourself has been a waste of time. This comes from a man who, as you know all too well, has lived in the most licentious way possible, seeking the pleasures of the flesh without worrying about tomorrow. As my end draws near, I also understand that my burning desire for immediate gratification has stopped me from finding true love. My only wish now is to depart this world in peace.

Expressing all the love I have for you, I hope to watch over you from heaven, where the Lord will keep me as I await your arrival.

Your friend always,

Francisco

Alfredo looked away from the paper, gazed out at the frothing waves and stood up straight. Then he reread the last lines and had to hold back his tears as he did so.

Men, his friend had written, only gain a clear perspective on life when death draws near, and perhaps because of this, Francisco's advice was a valuable thing, a lesson he must learn. It would not be easy to accept his nature. He had fought so much against it and had gained only pain and remorse in return. Yet Francisco's words did not exhort him to wage eternal war with his demons but rather to accept them. That forced him to detach himself from his Christian education, accept he might be going to hell for it and there was no redemption possible save to plough on through the waves, sail through the waters and accept that was the only way to stay afloat. He had to swim until his reason was an amalgam of the nature that God, or perhaps the devil, had given him.

He glanced at the letter one last time before opening his fingers slowly, letting his friend's note fall into the sea. He felt relieved as he did it, as if in letting it fly away, he was celebrating his own burial, the burial of his past life. He watched the sheet of paper rest on the surface of the sea before it was engulfed by the waves. Then he turned and headed towards his cabin, and as he did so, something inside him said that this thorny path opening up before him was his only chance at finding peace with himself.

18 September 1722

Sol walked over to the balcony and looked out, expecting to see her notary's carriage approaching. Señor Durán's letter stated that he would reach the house two days after she received it. So now, having had breakfast, she was anxiously awaiting his arrival. In the note, Señor Durán had told her he had collected a letter from Don Francisco and had news concerning him.

Sol had managed to escape to England via La Coruña and had not stopped thinking about Francisco for the entire journey, praying to the Almighty that he was still alive.

She had settled in a rented mansion near Hatfield, where she mingled with the local aristocracy, whose wives had rushed to visit her as soon as they learned there was a Spanish lady of noble birth living nearby. A marchioness, no less, who had decided to swap the warm air of Spain for the cold climate of England. She had explained to them that the doctors had advised her to escape the heat of the Peninsula. They were favourably impressed by her exquisite manners, and it was only much later, at a gathering that she hosted, that certain unexpected problems had begun to arise.

That night she had met a certain Thomas Hereby. He had come from London, along with a mutual acquaintance, having been sent by the first Lord of the Treasury, Sir Robert Walpole, to find out if she was a Spanish spy implicated in a plot to dethrone the Hanoverians. She had known nothing of any conspiracy but feared this unfortunate coincidence would condemn her to the fate she had managed to avoid in Madrid. However, after telling her story – in which she had portrayed herself as an innocent victim who had been seduced by Don Enrique – Hereby had understood it would be useful to keep her alive, since it was impossible for her to return to Spain.

By early May, five months after her arrival, she had consolidated her position in England, and Mr Hereby would often show up at her house to gather information concerning King Felipe and the court. A few weeks later, Sol had already set her sights on Sir Nicholas Hubbington, a wealthy rural widower whose only interests were hunting and social gatherings.

Finally, her notary, Carlos Durán – to whom she owed her life for having prepared the boxes containing her riches and the carriage which had allowed her to escape – had returned to Spain in secret to gather the rest of her fortune. Once there, he would use a trusted contact to act as a front, selling her properties and goods without raising suspicion. To do this, he was to arrange secret auctions to which a fixed number of wealthy families would be invited.

As the months had passed, she gradually felt more and more helpless, and often surprised herself by talking to her new friends about Spain. She was overcome with melancholy when she touched on the void left by Francisco. Naively, she told herself that time would pardon her for causing Doña Alba's death, although at heart, she knew this was a vain fantasy designed to soothe the fear inside her.

As she awaited her servant's arrival, she felt that this country was not for her, with its endless wind and rain, and that damp which got into your bones no matter how much you wrapped up. It was a climate that encouraged melancholy and the constant memory of Francisco, whose image she could not escape in the corridors of her rented mansion. She felt lost, abandoned to a life that was not hers and invaded by the ghosts she had left along the way.

She had just walked over to the window again when she heard the carriage containing her notary drawing close. She was shocked to see not Carlos Durán descending from inside the carriage but a small man with a birdlike face. Something told her things had not gone well in Madrid. Her heart pounding, she waited, hoping to discover something about Francisco's condition, praying that Carlos Durán had not been captured and revealed her whereabouts to Don Diego.

The man greeted her and walked over, holding a letter bearing her own seal. She asked the birdlike man where her notary was, and he answered that he did not know who she was talking about; he was tasked only with delivering the letter. Frowning, she took it, opened the seal and read it hurriedly.

> *To Doña Sol Montijos, Marchioness of Villamar,*
>
> *I know that the arrival of this letter will come as a shock to you, especially when you only recently received a letter informing you of my imminent arrival, but I must, after all my years of service to you, at least offer an explanation for my absence. My motive for convincing you to allow me to travel to Madrid was just as I said, to collect your fortune and sell your property for the maximum profit, but I was not at all honest when I neglected to mention that I would be the sole beneficiary of this auction…*

She stopped reading immediately and felt herself turning pale. She had to sit down, her eyes glued to the paper, unable to believe what she had just read. Then, gripped with the fear that her notary had pocketed her entire fortune before leaving, she ran straight to her bedroom. There were only two bags of coins left in the box, all that remained of her life in Spain. Weeping, she grabbed the letter opener in a rage and slashed the mattress as if it were Carlos Durán himself.

> *Likewise, I feel obliged to inform you that there was an auction of all your property and belongings, which were acquired by various families. Although I will enjoy their proceeds, the sales will sooner or later lead Don Diego's investigators to you. I hope the friends you have made during these months in England will*

help you keep one step ahead; nevertheless, I left some savings so that you may live a dignified life for a few months while you find a protector.

I am aware that you will feel disappointed by my actions, and I understand the anger you may feel towards me, but as you once told me, life is too short for scruples. Understand that if I am unlucky enough to be captured before leaving the Peninsula, I will have to reveal your whereabouts.

Finally, I should tell you that Don Enrique de Arcona met his end in a duel with Castamar, and the rest of his collaborators ended their lives on the gallows. As for you, my lady, in addition to the death of Alba de Montepardo, you are also wanted for the murder of Don Francisco Marlango. It seems the blood poisoning caused by the wound took him to the grave a few days after we left.

Sincerely yours,

Don Carlos Durán

He's dead, she said to herself. *He's dead.* She sank to the floor and curled into a ball, unable to see anything other than the image of Francisco gently caressing her. She felt lost, with no one to run to for help, and she sobbed, unable to bear any more pain.

At dawn, she rose and walked to the mirror. Her hair was unkempt, she had bags under her eyes, and it was as if she had aged ten years in a single night. No longer crying, she sat down, aware that she was now nothing more than a piece of empty flesh that would pass through life like a ghost in a cemetery. Parsimoniously, she began tidying her hair and putting on her make-up, until eventually she had restored the mask which had allowed her to survive all these years. She washed and sought out her best outfit. She was not minded to run from kingdom to kingdom until Don Diego's men finally caught her and dragged her back to Spain. Rather than spend her days in prison or die on the gallows, she preferred to walk into the stormy sea at Brighton and drown in its cold waters.

With Francisco's image still in her mind's eye, she looked herself up and down once more before going out. She looked tired, older. *Age isn't the worst punishment God has invented, even though there is no way of escaping it other than an early death*, she thought. *Love, without a shadow of a doubt, is the worst calamity in this world, because it is the only sentiment not conquered by death, and therefore the torture and suffering also accompany you into the beyond.*

Then, without looking back, aware there was not much time, she ordered her butler to prepare the carriage. Adjusting a small pair of eyeglasses on her face and putting on her best smile, she sat down in the coach with implacable determination.

'To Sir Nicholas Hubbington's house,' she ordered the driver.

Hiding her misfortunes behind her fan, she told herself that she should never again think about Francisco Marlango, for to do so would lead her to perdition; the only thing she would show from now on was the living corpse she had become.

49

25 October 1722

Gabriel was sitting and waiting, enjoying the fresh breeze that rustled the fallen leaves while the boot boys loaded up the last of his belongings. He gazed into the distance, thinking about how strange the last few months had been. Castamar had come back to life, and with it, his brother. After Clara had spent another three months at court, Don Diego could no longer hide his feelings. He had declared that he was head over heels in love with Señorita Belmonte and asked the king and queen for their permission to marry her. They had given their consent, assigning an honorific dowry to the barony as a reward for Doctor Belmonte's heroic service.

As far as Diego was concerned, the money was of no concern; his sole motive had been to secure the acceptance of his future wife at court. The marriage had been celebrated at Castamar in September and was one of the social events of the year. There had been five days of celebration, with all manner of entertainment. The event had passed in a breathless whirl of plays, riding displays, concerts, readings, fireworks, balls and other games. And the Belmonte family had added a special touch, with mother and daughter concocting a range of delightful dishes for Their Majesties and the other guests. The duke's wedding had been so grand that nobody missed the celebration of Alba's birthday, and it was established that from now on the annual festivities at Castamar would always be held on 28 September.

The threats of Don Enrique and Hernaldo de la Marca were now a thing of the past. Even Diego had gradually lost his interest in Doña Sol, despite having tracked her down to the south of England, where she had married a rural aristocrat with contacts at court and in the army. After that, Diego had given up on his plans for bringing Doña Sol back and resigned himself to accepting that the murderer of his wife and of his friend Francisco would remain at liberty.

'Alfredo told me not to become obsessed with revenge, as it would eat me up and make me ignore the happiness that was right in front of me,' he had told Gabriel.

Meanwhile, Gabriel's life had become an endless search for opportunities to be alone with Señorita Castro. While Castamar seemed to be rising from the ashes and regaining the splendour it had enjoyed during Doña Alba's time, he had stoically awaited Señorita Castro's decision as to whether to accept his marriage proposal and leave with him. He didn't blame her for having doubts, for fearing that her future would be a thorny path which, bit by bit, would tear their love to shreds and leave them both miserable. In her view, it was a delusion to think that leaving Spain and travelling somewhere far away would allow him to escape the problems that derived from the colour of his skin, while he had continuously tried to convince her of the contrary.

Amelia, who was caught in a tangle of doubt, had appeared in his bedroom two nights ago, her hair down and wearing only a fine linen nightgown.

'We must be married before we lie together,' he had said.

She had placed her candlestick on the dressing table, wrapped her arms around him, and whispered in his ear, 'Make me yours without thinking about tomorrow.'

He had understood that her unexpected appearance in his bedroom presaged that she would not marry him, far less travel with him into uncertainty. And so, he gave in to his passion, aware that he would never be able to do so again, and that the next day their love would be eternally kept in a box, pure and untroubled by the tribulations that come from cohabitation. He had caressed her skin with his lips, breathing in her fragrance, committing every moment to memory as if each one was the greatest of treasures.

'Can you imagine being able to share a bed every night?' Gabriel said.

Amelia had looked at him sadly, as if overwhelmed by love, and kissed him on the lips as she curled up in his arms. They had taken their leave of each other before the rest of the household was awake, neither of them having slept. When he was alone, he had naively dared to hope that perhaps she might finally say yes to him. The next day they had agreed to see each other, once Gabriel had made the final preparations for his departure.

Gabriel sighed as he looked up and saw Amelia approaching. Upon reaching him, she greeted him courteously while he bowed and offered her his arm so that they might walk together. Gabriel said nothing, simply waiting for her to speak. Amelia gripped his arm tightly.

'I can't follow you where you are going,' Amelia said in a faint voice.

He continued walking but made no reply.

'Please, Gabriel. Say something,' Amelia urged him.

'I don't have anything to say, other than to let you know I respect your decision,' he replied. 'I know that, if my skin were a different colour, you would not turn me down.'

'If you were white, you wouldn't have to leave or to hide during your brother's festivities or avoid anyone seeing us together,' she said, 'but you know that's not what makes me refuse. It is my love for you that I wish to preserve, and if I give in to temptation now, then soon, nothing will be left of it or of us. Wherever we go, I will be a white woman and you will be a freed African whose back has been marked for life.'

Gabriel fell silent again at these words, aware that she was right, that society would always see them as an aberration, a pernicious and irrational mixture that would bring destruction to all around them. But he could no longer live in the gilded cage that was Castamar. He had to leave, travel to distant realms where the colour of his skin was not a curse that would condemn him to the lash.

Without Amelia, he would travel to the distant borders of Asia, the far reaches of Africa or the islands of the Orient. He would explore and open new frontiers to close the circle that his father, Abel de Castamar, had begun. 'Perhaps I should be the bravest negro in Flanders,' he had told his brother, in reference to the play he had read at Villacor in what seemed like another lifetime, just two years ago.

Amelia stood before him and tenderly stroked his face. Gabriel suddenly felt lost at the prospect of being without her, and struggled with all his might to find an argument that could change her mind, one that would make her understand that they would be miserable if they were not together. He was about to lay bare his soul and declare his feelings when she pulled him towards the shade of a large chestnut tree and kissed him softly on the lips. Then she dried her tears and entwined her fingers with his.

'I came to Castamar in search of a husband,' she said, 'and yet I am rejecting the very best of men... You should marry someone of your own race. And, however painful it may be, I want you to know that I will do the same.'

'You won't make me hate you,' he replied. 'You will only make me jealous of the man who gets to share your life.'

He hugged her close again, knowing that this kiss would be the last. He took her by the waist and felt her respond, as if their separation was impossible. Then he felt his soul shatter as Amelia abruptly moved away and declared, sobbing, that the best he could do was to forget her, before she turned and ran away. All he could do was whisper her name weakly, instinctively, like someone uttering a lament that they will repeat time and time again throughout eternity.

He stood there stiffly, his cheek wet with Amelia's tears and his spirit desolate. He swallowed, took a deep breath, and sat down on one of the granite benches around the fountain with its sculpture of Jason and the Argonauts displaying the golden fleece. As he looked at the sculpture, he felt like one of those heroes, on the verge of tragedy, facing the harshest of challenges and dying in the attempt. That was how he would have told his own story. He had won Amelia's heart only to find that his enjoyment of it would be but a fleeting moment.

She left that evening without delay, finally resuming the journey to Cadiz that she had started almost a year ago, and Gabriel departed Castamar three days later, with a hamper of food prepared by his sister-in-law, the inconsolable sadness of his mother, and the boundless love of his brother in the memory of his final embrace. He had promised to write, wherever he was, and Diego had promised to answer as soon as his letter was delivered. He set out on horseback, armed and provisioned and with sufficient money, and travelled for Valencia with no notion of his destination other than to travel east.

One week later, he was on his way to the Kingdom of Naples, with the intention of reaching Cairo, which was ruled by the Ottomans, where he would buy some local attire so that he would stand out less. The colour of his skin would help conceal his religion. All he wanted was to be able to control his own life. He might find employment, learn the language of the desert or even search for his African roots, anything that could remove Amelia and the moments they had shared from his thoughts. He needed to find relief, but he was tormented by memories of the single, joyful night they had spent together. He only hoped time would temper them until they had healed and scarred like his back.

2 November 1722

Ursula gathered up her hair and, after inspecting herself in the mirror, left her bedroom. During the past year, she had allowed her former enemy to become something more than a lover. She had of course said no to Don Melquíades's repeated proposals of marriage. He had explained that the duke would allow them to marry and that they could live in one of the houses on the estate. She, however, felt herself far too old for such complications. Firstly, because, as far as she knew, her husband, Elías, was still alive; and secondly, because she had obtained her independence as a housekeeper and was not prepared to lose it in exchange for a husband.

'Don't go making assumptions, Don Melquíades,' she had said. 'I still haven't told you I love you, so I'm hardly going to marry you.'

'But Doña Ursula, don't you see that otherwise we will be living in sin?' he had argued. 'If the duke finds out.'

'The duke won't do anything,' she said. 'I'm sure the whole staff already know, given the way you've been strutting about. And now, let me get on with my work.'

He had shaken his head, in search of an argument that might convince her. It was clear the servants knew their relationship went beyond what was required by their duties, and he strongly suspected that the duke was also aware. But nobody would say a word. Their closeness, as if they were already an old married couple, was something so familiar at Castamar that over the years the notion that they maintained carnal relations in secret had become quite established. Indeed, the rumours may have stretched all the way back to the war.

During that last year, over the course of which her bellicose spirit had softened, her feelings towards the butler had intensified, although she would never recognize this in public. At the beginning, he had revealed his passion slowly, and she, for fear of being exposed, had rebuffed him harshly. The poor man bore it with great patience. 'You're a fool if you think I'm ever going to love you.' 'I enjoy your company but it's no more than a game.' 'Don't talk nonsense, don't be ridiculous, why on earth would I love you?'

Even so, Don Melquíades had persisted, and he still dreamed that one day she would sleep in his bed as his wife, blessed in holy matrimony by the Father, the Son and the Holy Ghost. She found it almost moving to see that this big, awkward man loved her so much he wanted to sleep with her every night. And she had to recognize that Don Melquíades was all a woman could desire. He was protective, hard-working, he had a heart of gold, and he was constantly concerned with her comfort. He admired and adored her in equal parts. He taught her that living with a man could be a source of joy.

All her experiences with men prior to Don Melquíades had only caused her pain and disgust. Her husband had mounted her like an animal, using her for his own pleasure. Don Melquíades, by contrast, surrendered passionately to her, investigating her body to discover what gave her greatest satisfaction. Even so, during the first few months, she would occasionally slam the door in his face, saying she wanted nothing to do with him and advising him to find a way of relieving himself alone, as they were both too old for such nonsense. However, as the weeks passed, she had realized that not only did she appreciate his qualities as a lover, she was also becoming besotted with him as a person.

She had been forced to recognize the truth of the situation one night, after waking from a nightmare. He was there, calming her as he wrapped her in his strong arms, enveloping her so that nobody could harm her, whispering comforting words in her ear. That was when she knew he would never leave her. As the year progressed, she had begun to care less about her power within the household, and even the sight of the duke – so happy, so bewitched by his wife, Doña Clara – gave her a feeling of well-being.

That change had come about thanks to the goodness of Don Melquíades, the way he treated her, the whispered words of affection. He was no fool and he noticed the change, and when their paths crossed during the day, he brushed his hand against hers as if by accident, as if he were living a second youth. It seemed that many of the staff were better disposed towards her; even Señor Casona, upon hearing that the housekeeper was teaching Beatriz Ulloa to read and write, remarked during a servants' mealtime that it was as if she had undergone a conversion. Doña Ursula had turned her icy stare on him.

'I don't understand your reasoning. It is perfectly normal that I, the housekeeper, should teach one of the serving girls,' she replied.

Everyone had fallen silent, and when the meal was over, the head gardener had whispered in her ear, 'Of course it's normal, but that doesn't mean it isn't surprising, Doña Ursula. Who would have thought you had a heart of gold, after all?'

'That's enough nonsense,' she had replied in a severe tone that was undermined by a slight smile. 'I have work to do and I'm sure you do, too.'

Ursula had continued to suppress her smile as she left the kitchen, telling the new cook, Federica Martín, that she would go over the notes from the pantry later. However, she had overheard Señor Casona opine that, despite her good actions, nothing could change her difficult character. She didn't care; the truth was that she wished neither to change her character nor to be mistaken for some lovesick fool. Whatever happened, she was determined to maintain her reputation to ensure that Castamar continued to function as it should. Now, every time she remembered the silent war she had fought against that calm and gentle soul, Don Melquíades, she thought to herself that she had been taking out on him all the suffering and misfortune the world had heaped upon her. Although the struggle had now abated, she couldn't help noticing that, whenever she saw the new Duchess of Castamar walking arm in arm with Don

Diego or talking to his mother, she felt a little stab of pain. The memory of Doña Alba arose, and she could not stand to see Doña Clara take her place. At the same time, she knew that her beloved mistress would never return, and that this young woman was the guarantee of Don Diego's happiness. However much she might wish to look down on him for falling in love with a cook, she knew that it was a lost cause. And so, she had forgiven her master, telling herself that, if she had been gifted a second chance at happiness with Don Melquíades, then at the very least, she could allow the same for a man who had looked after her for all these years.

In addition to the idyll with Don Melquíades, this was one of the main reasons behind her decision to remain at Castamar. Another, almost as important, was the conversation she had had with Doña Clara. The new duchess continued to insist on visiting the kitchens from time to time, despite Federica Martín's appointment, and had called the housekeeper to her chambers some months after the wedding. Despite her many years of service, Doña Ursula feared that perhaps she was about to be dismissed. That was when she understood how lost she would feel if she were told to depart. She had not considered the possibility of having to leave Castamar at someone else's behest, and had already berated herself as an idiot and a fool for not foreseeing that the duchess would dismiss her, despite the fact that Doña Ursula had saved her from being raped. *How did you ever allow this to happen?* she reproached herself. And so, she had gone in expecting the worst.

'I entered this house two years ago,' Doña Clara said, her back to Ursula as she looked out on the gardens. 'During all this time, I had always thought that the resentment you felt towards life was directed at me because, as you yourself said, I did not belong either to the world of the servants or to the world of his lordship.'

'I have not changed my views in that regard, your grace,' she had replied, bluntly. 'Nobody can deny that you are now the

Duchess of Castamar, and nor can they deny that you are a doctor's daughter.'

'You are right on both counts, Doña Ursula. However, at least let me have the conversation that you would not permit the day I left Castamar,' Doña Clara had said.

'Seeing as you are the Duchess of Castamar, I have no alternative.'

'You do. If you don't want to listen to what I am about to say, you may leave—'

'Your grace,' the housekeeper had interrupted, 'if you wish to order me to leave this house, I understand and will not object. Indeed, I will beg both Don Diego and Don Melquíades not to intercede on my behalf. I will only ask that I be given the best possible references to help me find a position in another noble household.'

Then she had fallen silent, fully expecting the duchess to agree to this request, and to thank her for accepting her defeat. Instead, a look of surprise had come over Doña Clara's face.

'You are very mistaken if you think that I wish to dispense with your services,' she had said, taking Doña Ursula's hand. 'If you will allow me to finish, Doña Ursula, the only thing I want to say to you is that, despite our differences, I have never ceased to admire and respect you.'

On hearing this, Ursula had dropped her guard, unable to repress a slight trembling in her chin.

'I have learned many lessons from you: never to give up, never to abandon a cause as lost, and that one may achieve whatever one sets one's mind upon. You oversaw Castamar single-handedly for nine months with impeccable diligence, something that no other woman in Spain can say.'

'I thank you for your kind words, your grace,' the housekeeper had replied, trying to conceal her emotion.

'Of course, I hope that any troubles I may have caused you when I was the cook in this household will be forgotten,' the duchess had continued, 'as I am going to need all your help.'

The housekeeper had been astonished, trying to make sense of the impression that Doña Clara was facing some adverse circumstance that had paralysed her and left her unable to act.

'I am with child,' she had said, suddenly, 'and I don't know what to do. I'm terrified. I haven't told a soul, not even my mother. I didn't know who to turn to.'

Just then, Ursula had remembered that fateful morning when Doña Alba told her she was carrying Don Diego's offspring in her womb. She was gripped by a terrible fear, feeling that if she failed to react favourably to this confession then the tragedy that had shaken Castamar might repeat itself. A shiver had run down her spine and she tried to hide her apprehension. She had told herself that she could not permit the heir of Castamar come to any harm, and she took on the role she knew was hers: looking after Don Diego, his new wife and his unborn child. Although Clara would never match up to her predecessor, it was the least she could do for Doña Alba.

She had not had children herself, but she perfectly understood the fear a woman must feel when facing childbirth, in which any complications could be fatal. She had sighed, aware that the long campaign she had fought with the girl was finally over. She would have to tolerate her intrusions in the kitchen, however much it disturbed her to see the mistress of the house at the stoves. She had neither the authority nor the stomach to prevent her, particularly now that Doña Clara was carrying the heir to Castamar. And so, Ursula had smiled and taken Doña Clara by the hand.

'There is nothing you can do other than to allow nature to run its course,' she had reassured her. 'Don't worry about the rest of it, your grace. You can be sure that your housekeeper will take care of everything.'

Three days later, Don Diego was beside himself with joy, Ursula's forebodings were all forgotten, and Doña Clara and her mother – who cooked like an angel – had prepared a small banquet for all the servants.

Now, as she patrolled the corridors checking that the maids had performed their work correctly, rattling the keys that were the symbol of her authority at Castamar, she became aware of a sense of calm. It was as if she had been granted a forbidden and dangerous gift that might disappear in a whisper or the blink of an eye, something in whose existence she had never believed out of fear that it would bring her nothing but misfortune. Love. And so, as she observed the plump, well-built figure of Don Melquíades giving orders at the far end of the corridor, she could not repress a smile, aware that this gift was hers for the first time in her life, and that she was, quite simply, happy.

50

26 November 1722

Despite having separate bedrooms, Clara and Diego had slept together every night since their wedding. She loved waking up next to him and placing her ear on his chest until she could feel his heart beating. Sometimes, in the mornings, she would wake him up by dangling her locks of hair over his face, until they tickled him and made him sneeze.

'I love you so much,' Diego would say. 'You have given me life, my dear Clara.'

'The first time I saw you I thought you were such an oaf,' she told him, laughing at the change in his expression her unexpected frankness had caused. 'One of those proud, arrogant noblemen who behave rudely in front of women.'

He smiled mischievously, remembering the day he had discovered her behind the door. He grabbed her by the waist.

'You were the rude one for spying on other people's conversations.'

They remained silent, caressing each other in silence, their fingers interlaced, looking at each other like two young lovers who had just met, completely losing track of time.

'Shall we go out for a ride?' Diego asked.

'Let's take the opportunity while we can,' she said, kissing him on the lips. 'Because my mother is visiting us this afternoon and we're preparing something special for you.'

He nodded enthusiastically, since this was part of the silent pact they had signed upon getting married. Clara knew that any husband, not to mention a nobleman, would have tried to stop her from spending time among the odours of onion and garlic, of frying and roasting, but she would not have agreed to any marriage without making it clear that her husband must accept this need of hers. With Diego, she didn't even have to say it out loud: it was taken as given from the outset. He would never force her to abandon the kitchen, not only because his stomach would be rewarded for it, but because all he desired was her complete happiness. This was not the only privilege Clara enjoyed: she also had the pleasure of visiting Castamar's huge library, attending theatrical performances, having her own musical ensemble, not having to worry about money when she bought all kinds of books from Señor Bernabé, being invited by Their Majesties to see the works that were being carried out in San Ildefonso, and many more things besides.

Of course, not everything had been so agreeable. Ever since Their Majesties had decided to give the Barony of Pleamar to the Belmontes, she had found herself becoming part of a different world, one more concerned with social relations and proximity to the king. She was forced to feign an interest in the frivolous thoughts that concerned the noble ladies of the court – which imported French dress to wear or how many servants they should have. It was an alien world to her, dealing with matters she found trivial, especially when royal subjects were living in squalor in the cities and villages of the kingdom. She understood, then, that the best one could do at court was to keep one's distance and play a discreet and defined role.

Diego had suggested that Clara's mother live at Castamar for as long as she wished, to make up for the long years they had spent apart. Doña Mercedes had also stayed, introducing her counterpart to life at the court, frightening away opportunists who saw her as a rich widow, and introducing her to honourable gentlemen and ladies.

Diego had decided to personally invite Julián Belmonte to

the wedding, and Clara's uncle was as shamelessly opportunistic as was to be expected, telling everyone he was a close relative of the future duchess. Not only did he manage to deceive Don Melquíades with his two-faced good manners, he had also accosted Don Diego to publicly express his concern for the well-being of the family. Diego, who had been expecting this, had ordered his notary to investigate the estate which the Belmonte ladies had lost after Clara's father's death. It wasn't long before Señor Graneros appeared with some news. Careless Uncle Julián could not have imagined that his visit would end in such disaster.

One day, he and Diego rode out to the furthest edges of Castamar.

'I intend to help you raise your social status so that you are level with the rest of the family,' Diego told him.

'Sincerely, your grace,' Julián replied, 'I am not worthy of such an honour.'

'Yes, you are. Besides, I know how much of a worry it must have been not to have had any news of your family for so long.'

'Truly, it has been one of the worst periods of my life. I thought I would never see them again,' Clara's uncle said.

'In that case, dear relative,' Diego had replied with a smile, 'you will find it befitting to return the estate you inherited upon your brother's death to your niece Clara, since, as she is now the Baroness of Pleamar, it is rightfully hers.'

'I'm sorry, I don't understand, your grace?' Julián said, suddenly turning as pale as a ghost.

'Weren't you aware of that clause in the will? It declares that all the properties included in the inheritance will pass as a matter of priority into the hands of the closest male relative... unless the first direct descendent, even though she be a woman, is ennobled.'

Uncle Julián, who had already pictured himself among the highest aristocracy, understood there and then that he would lose the estate.

'I was not aware of such a clause,' he said, terrified and attempting in vain to find a way out. 'I shall have to reread the will again to make sure.'

Diego stopped his horse and frowned at him.

'Do you doubt my word?' he asked.

Julián began to stammer, struggling to find a response, and Diego moved menacingly closer.

'Listen carefully, Uncle,' he said. 'I will personally be supervising your transfer of this generous gift to your niece, and I hope I don't have to resort to other means. Believe me, if that does become necessary, you will struggle to make any kind of living in the Kingdom of Spain ever again.'

Soon after, the estate had been transferred to Clara, who could finally return to the house she loved. Little more was heard of Uncle Julián, except that no one wanted to hire him as a jurist anymore, and that he ended his days in poverty and exile in France.

In autumn, Clara's mother had departed for the house in which she had lived most of her life. Doña Mercedes also left discreetly and only occasionally returned to Castamar, and always at her son's request.

After her ride under a pale sun and clear sky, Clara walked a while longer in the fields, humming a little ditty as she went. Señor Casona stopped to greet her. After exchanging a few friendly words, she let him continue with his work.

Finally, she reached a small pond. She sat down and placed her hand on her belly, thinking about the life forming inside her. She looked up towards the palace and smiled as she once again pictured herself in the past, on the day she arrived at Castamar, hiding beneath the hay bales of a loaded carriage and sheltering from the incessant rain. She closed her eyes and that dreary vision of herself, alone and beaten down by the harshness of the world, began to vanish, making way for another, more pleasant one: herself as an old woman, with her children all grown up and Diego slightly stooped over with age, stroking her face and whispering words of love unchanged from those he used with her now. She knew that idyllic vision of the future was just an illusion – if, in the space of just two years, she had gone from being a kitchen hand to becoming Don Diego's wife and the Duchess of Castamar, then anything could happen. If she had learned anything over the course of her ordeal, it was that life is unpredictable.

As she reflected on the events of those two years, she stood and picked up a dry leaf and threw it into the pond. She remained standing for a moment, then before she could see if the leaf sank or floated, she turned around and headed back to the house. With every step she took, her fear of the unpredictability of existence gave way to a calm acceptance of the inevitable, as if she knew her life to come belonged more in the kingdom of the imaginary than in the real world.

When she reached the library on the first floor, she found her husband ensconced in his armchair, his legs crossed, a letter lying open on the side table.

'Alfredo has reached Florida,' he said, 'and finds himself in perfect health.'

She nodded and smiled before kneeling down and resting her head in Diego's lap, feeling his hand stroking her hair. She allowed herself to simply enjoy the complete happiness that instant offered her and wished with all her soul that such a feeling would never end. She saw herself reflected in the leaf she had thrown into the pond, its journey to the water dictated by so much chance. Then, at last, she understood that life impels each soul to steer the rudder of its own ship, before eventually discovering that, in the stormy sea of existence, it can do nothing but drift.

ABOUT THE AUTHOR

FERNANDO J. MÚÑEZ was born in Madrid in 1972 and developed a taste for writing from a very young age. He started work on his first novel at the age of fourteen and his first film scripts at eighteen. After graduating with a degree in Philosophy, he started his career as an advertising producer whilst directing his first short films and completed his training in cinematography in the United States. Since then he has published more than fifty books for children and young adults. In 2012 he directed the film 'Las Nornas' ('The Norns') which was shown at the Alicante festival and the Seminci de Valladolid. The Netflix adaptation of *The Cook of Castamar* was released in 2021.

ABOUT THE TRANSLATORS

TIM GUTTERIDGE is a creative translator based in Edinburgh, Scotland. He translates literary fiction and non-fiction, theatre, and texts for the Spanish audiovisual and publishing sectors. His recent translations include *The Hand That Feeds You* (Bitter Lemon Press) and *The Island* (Cervantes Theatre, London).

RAHUL BERY translates from Portuguese and Spanish to English, and is based in Cardiff, Wales. His published translations from Spanish include *Rolling Fields* by David Trueba and *Centroeuropa* by Vicente Luis Mora.